A NORTON CRITICAL EDITION

Edith Wharton
THE HOUSE OF MIRTH

AUTHORITATIVE TEXT
BACKGROUNDS AND CONTEXTS
CRITICISM

Edited by

ELIZABETH AMMONS

TUFTS UNIVERSITY

W · W · NORTON & COMPANY · *New York* · *London*

Printed in the United States of America.

The text of this book is composed in Electra, with display type set in Bernhard
Modern. Composition by Vail Ballou. Manufacturing by The Maple Vail Book Group.
Book design by Antonina Krass.

Library of Congress Cataloging in Publication Data
ISBN 0-393-95901-5

W. W. Norton & Company, Inc., 500 Fifth Avenue, New York, N.Y. 10110
W. W. Norton & Company Ltd., 10 Coptic Street, London WC1A 1PU

9 0

Contents

Preface   vii
Acknowledgment   ix
A Note on the Text   ix
The Text of *The House of Mirth*   5
Backgrounds and Contexts   257

    Edith Wharton • Selected Letters   259
    Thorstein Veblen • [Conspicuous Leisure and Conspicuous   264
    Consumption]
    Mrs. Burton Kingsland • [The Duties of a House-Guest]   271
    C. Lothrop Higgins • [Vocations for the Trained Woman: 274
    Millinery]
    Mrs. John Van Vorst and Marie Van Vorst • [The Experi-   276
    ence of a Lady as a Factory Girl]
    Mary Cadwalader Jones • [Working Girls' Clubs]   278
    Charles Dana Gibson • [Marrying for Money]   284
    Charlotte Perkins Gilman • [Women and Economics]   288
    Olive Schreiner • [Sex-Parasitism]   293
    Lorine Pruette, Ph.D. • [The Waste of Women in America]   295
    John Higham • Ideological Anti-Semitism in the Gilded Age   296
    Tableau Vivant of "The Dying Gladiator"   304

Criticism   305

    Contemporary Reviews   307
      The Independent • Mrs. Wharton's Latest Novel   307
      E. E. Hale, Jr. • Mrs. Wharton's "The House of Mirth" 309
      Mary Moss • [Review of *The House of Mirth*]   309
      Mary K. Ford • [Excerpt from "Two Studies in Luxury"] 311
      The Nation • [Review of *The House of Mirth*]   311
      The Saturday Review • [Review of *The House of Mirth*] 313

Modern Critical Views   314

Millicent Bell • [Wharton as Businesswoman: Publishing *The*   314
House of Mirth]

Louis Auchincloss • [*The House of Mirth* and Old and New   316
New York]

Cynthia Griffin Wolff • Lily Bart and the Beautiful Death   320

R. W. B. Lewis • [*The House of Mirth* Biographically]   339

Elizabeth Ammons • [Edith Wharton's Hard-Working Lily: 345
The House of Mirth and the Marriage Market]

Elaine Showalter • The Death of the Lady (Novelist):   357
Wharton's *House of Mirth*

Edith Wharton: A Chronology   373

Selected Bibliography   374

Preface

The House of Mirth made Edith Wharton famous. Published in 1905, the novel became a national bestseller and launched her career as America's foremost novelist in the two decades that opened the twentieth century.

Wharton was born in 1862. Christened Edith Newbold Jones, she was the only daughter of leisure-class parents who descended from aristocratic Old New York families; her parents, like others of their class, lived off accumulated wealth rather than having to labor for an income. Because her two brothers were teenagers when she was born, Edith grew up, in effect, as an only child. Typical of her time and class, she and her family traveled a great deal, dividing their time annually among New York, Europe, and Newport, Rhode Island; she was privately tutored; and she made her debut at the age of seventeen. So when she married Edward ("Teddy") Wharton in 1885, her future seemed clear. She appeared conventionally headed for leisure-class life as a hostess, wife, and mother. That she would become instead one of America's most accomplished and prolific novelists was hardly foreseeable. Not only did her class and gender combine to mitigate against a literary career, but her individual family environment did as well. According to Wharton, her parents distrusted emotion and had little interest in art or the life of the mind. She spent many hours as a child reading and making up stories in her father's dark, seldom-used library; but the activity, at least as the adult author recalled it, was undertaken in spite of, not because of, family tastes and values.

Sharing very few interests, Edith Wharton and her husband grew apart the longer they were married. Edith suffered bouts of acute depression during the 1890s that were alleviated only by medical treatment and by her establishing an independent intellectual and creative life for herself as a writer. In 1913, against the Wharton family's wishes, she secured a divorce, an action that deepened the chronic depression into which Teddy Wharton had progressively sunk the healthier his wife became. During some of these years (from about 1907 to 1910), Edith Wharton had an affair with a slightly younger man, Morton Fullerton, which was successfully kept secret while she was alive and for many years after her death. Wharton had no children and, following her divorce, made her permanent home in France. By the time she died in 1937, she had published eighteen novels and novellas, eleven volumes of short stories, a handful of poems, numerous essays, a memoir, and several books of argument and analysis. During her lifetime she was widely honored. She was made a Chevalier of the French Legion of Honor for her war work on behalf of refugees during the First World War; and for her accomplishments as a writer she received, among other distinctions, a Pulitzer Prize in 1921 and an honorary doctorate from Yale University in 1923.

Wharton's critical reception during the twentieth century has followed the major shifts in mainstream American critical attitudes toward women writers. During the first two decades of the twentieth century, her reputation, like that of many other white women writers at the time, such as Ellen Glasgow or Mary Austin or Willa Cather, swelled. Enthusiasm about the ambitions and achievements of such women, while not without its detractors, ran very high at the turn of the century, with the work of Edith Wharton and *The House of Mirth* in particular routinely singled out for praise. Then the widespread, deep-seated reaction against work by women that set in during the 1920s and continued through the mid 1960s, especially among scholars and critics in colleges and universities, effectively reversed that early high assessment. Although there are important exceptions, most critics and teachers from the 1920s to the 1970s, when they thought of Wharton at all, which was seldom, dismissed her either as a novelist of manners, a lesser genre in American literature according to the prevailing mid-twentieth-century academic preference for male psychological dramas and escape fantasies, or as an imitator and inferior version of Henry James. With the revival of serious attention to women writers that occurred as a result of the women's movement of the late 1960s and early 1970s, which in turn grew out of the civil rights movement of the 1960s, interest in Edith Wharton dramatically revived. No longer considered simply or even primarily the heir of Henry James, and certainly not dismissed as a "mere" novelist of manners, a form that itself is enjoying reassessment, she is today once again widely read and written about as a major American fiction writer. Most frequently, as the critical essays in this volume illustate, she is read as a writer especially, although not exclusively, interested in writing about women.

Beginning in a very narrow, rarefied world of upper-class leisure and privilege but ending in a far different place, *The House of Mirth* raises a number of questions about American capitalism and class structure, gender relations in the worlds Wharton focuses on, connections and animosities among women within and across particular economic and social boundaries, white family structure in the United States, and the dynamic of ethnic assimilation and bias. Wharton, like many writers, was both the unthinking product of her time, place, class, and culture and a sharp critic and questioner. Although she by no means escaped many of the prejudices and privileges of her world, she brought to her investigation of American life, particularly at the top, a cool, penetrating gaze, and she did not invent issues as much as she reflected them. As the historical selections and excerpts following the novel in this volume suggest, when she wrote critically about conspicuous consumption in the leisure class, the economics of marriage for white middle- and upper-class women, or the physical rigors and deprivations of working-class life for many Americans, she was reflecting in fiction issues and arguments broadly current in the culture.

In her own day Wharton's appeal was wide and various. In her letters at the turn of the century to Fanny Quincy Howe, published in 1977 as *The Maimie Papers*, the former prostitute Maimie Pinzer named *The House of Mirth* as one of her favorite books. Upon its publication the novel attracted warm praise from fellow writers such as Hamlin Garland and Owen Wister. In her advice to young black Americans who aspired to be writers, the Harlem Renaissance author Jessie Redmon Fauset in 1923 identified Wharton as one of six authors (only two of them American, the other being W. E. B. Du Bois) who should be taught and emulated. Although *The House of Mirth* examines only a small section of American life, its artistry—Wharton's elegance and control as a stylist—and insight have made it a book, in its own time and now, of broad and major importance.

Acknowledgment

For helpful preliminary research assistance, I am grateful to Blythe Forcey. For excellent and substantial aid, especially in preparing the notes, I am indebted to Katherine Kleitz. Also I wish to thank Paz Mendoza of the Tufts University Library interlibrary loan office for her assistance.

A Note on the Text

This edition of *The House of Mirth* is reprinted from the original 1905 edition published by Charles Scribner's Sons. The illustrations by A. B. Wenzell appeared in that original edition as well as in the prior serialization of the novel in *Scribner's Magazine* from January 1905 through November 1905. No editorial changes have been made in the text.

The Text of
THE HOUSE OF MIRTH

She lingered on the broad stairway, looking down into the hall below.

THE HOUSE OF MIRTH

BY

EDITH WHARTON

WITH ILLUSTRATIONS BY A. B. WENZELL

NEW YORK

CHARLES SCRIBNER'S SONS
MDCCCCV

The House of Mirth

I

Selden paused in surprise. In the afternoon rush of the Grand Central Station[1] his eyes had been refreshed by the sight of Miss Lily Bart.

It was a Monday in early September, and he was returning to his work from a hurried dip into the country; but what was Miss Bart doing in town at that season? If she had appeared to be catching a train, he might have inferred that he had come on her in the act of transition between one and another of the country-houses which disputed her presence after the close of the Newport season;[2] but her desultory air perplexed him. She stood apart from the crowd, letting it drift by her to the platform or the street, and wearing an air of irresolution which might, as he surmised, be the mask of a very definite purpose. It struck him at once that she was waiting for some one, but he hardly knew why the idea arrested him. There was nothing new about Lily Bart, yet he could never see her without a faint movement of interest: it was characteristic of her that she always roused speculation, that her simplest acts seemed the result of far-reaching intentions.

An impulse of curiosity made him turn out of his direct line to the door, and stroll past her. He knew that if she did not wish to be seen she would contrive to elude him; and it amused him to think of putting her skill to the test.

"Mr. Selden—what good luck!"

She came forward smiling, eager almost, in her resolve to intercept him. One or two persons, in brushing past them, lingered to look; for Miss Bart was a figure to arrest even the suburban traveller rushing to his last train.

Selden had never seen her more radiant. Her vivid head, relieved against the dull tints of the crowd, made her more conspicuous than in a ball-room, and under her dark hat and veil she regained the girlish smoothness, the purity of tint, that she was beginning to lose after eleven

---

1. One of two enormous railroad terminals in downtown Manhattan, begun in 1903 and completed in 1913. A remarkable engineering and architectural feat, it was important as a symbol of modernity and as a center of activity for the whole United States.

2. Very wealthy people at the turn of the century often summered in Newport, Rhode Island, a fashionable ocean resort, where many members of New York high society had summer houses and mansions, sometimes referred to as "cottages," in which they entertained lavishly.

years of late hours and indefatigable dancing. Was it really eleven years, Selden found himself wondering, and had she indeed reached the nine-and-twentieth birthday with which her rivals credited her?

"What luck!" she repeated. "How nice of you to come to my rescue!"

He responded joyfully that to do so was his mission in life, and asked what form the rescue was to take.

"Oh, almost any—even to sitting on a bench and talking to me. One sits out a cotillion—why not sit out a train? It isn't a bit hotter here than in Mrs. Van Osburgh's conservatory—and some of the women are not a bit uglier."

She broke off, laughing, to explain that she had come up to town from Tuxedo, on her way to the Gus Trenors' at Bellomont, and had missed the three-fifteen train to Rhinebeck.

"And there isn't another till half-past five." She consulted the little jewelled watch among her laces. "Just two hours to wait. And I don't know what to do with myself. My maid came up this morning to do some shopping for me, and was to go on to Bellomont at one o'clock, and my aunt's house is closed, and I don't know a soul in town." She glanced plaintively about the station. "It *is* hotter than Mrs. Van Osburgh's, after all. If you can spare the time, do take me somewhere for a breath of air."

He declared himself entirely at her disposal: the adventure struck him as diverting. As a spectator, he had always enjoyed Lily Bart; and his course lay so far out of her orbit that it amused him to be drawn for a moment into the sudden intimacy which her proposal implied.

"Shall we go over to Sherry's[3] for a cup of tea?"

She smiled assentingly, and then made a slight grimace.

"So many people come up to town on a Monday—one is sure to meet a lot of bores. I'm as old as the hills, of course, and it ought not to make any difference; but if I'm old enough, you're not," she objected gaily. "I'm dying for tea—but isn't there a quieter place?"

He answered her smile, which rested on him vividly. Her discretions interested him almost as much as her imprudences: he was so sure that both were part of the same carefully-elaborated plan. In judging Miss Bart, he had always made use of the "argument from design."

"The resources of New York are rather meagre," he said; "but I'll find a hansom first, and then we'll invent something."

He led her through the throng of returning holiday makers, past sallow-faced girls in preposterous hats, and flat-chested women struggling with paper bundles and palm-leaf fans. Was it possible that she belonged to the same race? The dinginess, the crudity of this average section of womanhood made him feel how highly specialized she was.

A rapid shower had cooled the air, and clouds still hung refreshingly over the moist street.

---

3. A stylish New York restaurant located at Fifth Avenue and Forty-fourth Street.

"How delicious! Let us walk a little," she said as they emerged from the station.

They turned into Madison Avenue and began to stroll northward. As she moved beside him, with her long light step, Selden was conscious of taking a luxurious pleasure in her nearness: in the modelling of her little ear, the crisp upward wave of her hair—was it ever so slightly brightened by art?—and the thick planting of her straight black lashes. Everything about her was at once vigorous and exquisite, at once strong and fine. He had a confused sense that she must have cost a great deal to make, that a great many dull and ugly people must, in some mysterious way, have been sacrificed to produce her. He was aware that the qualities distinguishing her from the herd of her sex were chiefly external: as though a fine glaze of beauty and fastidiousness had been applied to vulgar clay. Yet the analogy left him unsatisfied, for a coarse texture will not take a high finish; and was it not possible that the material was fine, but that circumstance had fashioned it into a futile shape?

As he reached this point in his speculations the sun came out, and her lifted parasol cut off his enjoyment. A moment or two later she paused with a sigh.

"Oh, dear, I'm so hot and thirsty—and what a hideous place New York is!" She looked despairingly up and down the dreary thoroughfare. "Other cities put on their best clothes in summer, but New York seems to sit in its shirt-sleeves." Her eyes wandered down one of the side-streets. "Some one has had the humanity to plant a few trees over there. Let us go into the shade."

"I am glad my street meets with your approval," said Selden as they turned the corner.

"Your street? Do you live here?"

She glanced with interest along the new brick and limestone house-fronts, fantastically varied in obedience to the American craving for novelty, but fresh and inviting with their awnings and flower-boxes.

"Ah, yes—to be sure: *The Benedick*. What a nice-looking building! I don't think I've ever seen it before." She looked across at the flat-house with its marble porch and pseudo-Georgian façade. "Which are your windows? Those with the awnings down?"

"On the top floor—yes."

"And that nice little balcony is yours? How cool it looks up there!"

He paused a moment. "Come up and see," he suggested. "I can give you a cup of tea in no time—and you won't meet any bores."

Her colour deepened—she still had the art of blushing at the right time—but she took the suggestion as lightly as it was made.

"Why not? It's too tempting—I'll take the risk," she declared.

"Oh, I'm not dangerous," he said in the same key. In truth, he had never liked her as well as at that moment. He knew she had accepted without afterthought: he could never be a factor in her calculations, and there was a surprise, a refreshment almost, in the spontaneity of her consent.

On the threshold he paused a moment, feeling for his latch-key.

"There's no one here; but I have a servant who is supposed to come in the mornings, and it's just possible he may have put out the tea-things and provided some cake."

He ushered her into a slip of a hall hung with old prints. She noticed the letters and notes heaped on the table among his gloves and sticks; then she found herself in a small library, dark but cheerful, with its walls of books, a pleasantly faded Turkey rug, a littered desk, and, as he had foretold, a tea-tray on a low table near the window. A breeze had sprung up, swaying inward the muslin curtains, and bringing a fresh scent of mignonette and petunias from the flower-box on the balcony.

Lily sank with a sigh into one of the shabby leather chairs.

"How delicious to have a place like this all to one's self! What a miserable thing it is to be a woman." She leaned back in a luxury of discontent.

Selden was rummaging in a cupboard for the cake.

"Even women," he said, "have been known to enjoy the privileges of a flat."

"Oh, governesses—or widows. But not girls—not poor, miserable, marriageable girls!"

"I even know a girl who lives in a flat."

She sat up in surprise. "You do?"

"I do," he assured her, emerging from the cupboard with the sought-for cake.

"Oh, I know—you mean Gerty Farish." She smiled a little unkindly. "But I said *marriageable*— and besides, she has a horrid little place, and no maid, and such queer things to eat. Her cook does the washing and the food tastes of soap. I should hate that, you know."

"You shouldn't dine with her on wash-days," said Selden, cutting the cake.

They both laughed, and he knelt by the table to light the lamp under the kettle, while she measured out the tea into a little tea-pot of green glaze. As he watched her hand, polished as a bit of old ivory, with its slender pink nails, and the sapphire bracelet slipping over her wrist, he was struck with the irony of suggesting to her such a life as his cousin Gertrude Farish had chosen. She was so evidently the victim of the civilization which had produced her, that the links of her bracelet seemed like manacles chaining her to her fate.

She seemed to read his thought. "It was horrid of me to say that of Gerty," she said with charming compunction. "I forgot she was your cousin. But we're so different, you know: she likes being good, and I like being happy. And besides, she is free and I am not. If I were, I daresay I could manage to be happy even in her flat. It must be pure bliss to arrange the furniture just as one likes, and give all the horrors to the ash-man. If I could only do over my aunt's drawing-room I know I should be a better woman."

"Is it so very bad?" he asked sympathetically.

She smiled at him across the tea-pot which she was holding up to be filled.

"That shows how seldom you come there. Why don't you come oftener?"

"When I do come, it's not to look at Mrs. Peniston's furniture."

"Nonsense," she said. "You don't come at all—and yet we get on so well when we meet."

"Perhaps that's the reason," he answered promptly. "I'm afraid I haven't any cream, you know—shall you mind a slice of lemon instead?"

"I shall like it better." She waited while he cut the lemon and dropped a thin disk into her cup. "But that is not the reason," she insisted.

"The reason for what?"

"For your never coming." She leaned forward with a shade of perplexity in her charming eyes. "I wish I knew—I wish I could make you out. Of course I know there are men who don't like me—one can tell that at a glance. And there are others who are afraid of me: they think I want to marry them." She smiled up at him frankly. "But I don't think you dislike me—and you can't possibly think I want to marry you."

"No—I absolve you of that," he agreed.

"Well, then——?"

He had carried his cup to the fireplace, and stood leaning against the chimney-piece and looking down on her with an air of indolent amusement. The provocation in her eyes increased his amusement—he had not supposed she would waste her powder on such small game; but perhaps she was only keeping her hand in; or perhaps a girl of her type had no conversation but of the personal kind. At any rate, she was amazingly pretty, and he had asked her to tea and must live up to his obligations.

"Well, then," he said with a plunge, "perhaps *that's* the reason."

"What?"

"The fact that you don't want to marry me. Perhaps I don't regard it as such a strong inducement to go and see you." He felt a slight shiver down his spine as he ventured this, but her laugh reassured him.

"Dear Mr. Selden, that wasn't worthy of you. It's stupid of you to make love to me, and it isn't like you to be stupid." She leaned back, sipping her tea with an air so enchantingly judicial that, if they had been in her aunt's drawing-room, he might almost have tried to disprove her deduction.

"Don't you see," she continued, "that there are men enough to say pleasant things to me, and that what I want is a friend who won't be afraid to say disagreeable ones when I need them? Sometimes I have fancied you might be that friend—I don't know why, except that you are neither a prig nor a bounder, and that I shouldn't have to pretend with you or be on my guard against you." Her voice had dropped to a note of seriousness, and she sat gazing up at him with the troubled gravity of a child.

"You don't know how much I need such a friend," she said. "My aunt is full of copy-book axioms, but they were all meant to apply to conduct in the early fifties. I always feel that to live up to them would include wearing book-muslin with gigot sleeves.[4] And the other women— my best friends—well, they use me or abuse me; but they don't care a straw what happens to me. I've been about too long—people are getting tired of me; they are beginning to say I ought to marry."

There was a moment's pause, during which Selden meditated one or two replies calculated to add a momentary zest to the situation; but he rejected them in favour of the simple question: "Well, why don't you?"

She coloured and laughed. "Ah, I see you *are* a friend after all, and that is one of the disagreeable things I was asking for."

"It wasn't meant to be disagreeable," he returned amicably. "Isn't marriage your vocation? Isn't it what you're all brought up for?"

She sighed. "I suppose so. What else is there?"

"Exactly. And so why not take the plunge and have it over?"

She shrugged her shoulders. "You speak as if I ought to marry the first man who came along."

"I didn't mean to imply that you are as hard put to it as that. But there must be some one with the requisite qualifications."

She shook her head wearily. "I threw away one or two good chances when I first came out—I suppose every girl does; and you know I am horribly poor—and very expensive. I must have a great deal of money."

Selden had turned to reach for a cigarette-box on the mantelpiece. "What's become of Dillworth?" he asked.

"Oh, his mother was frightened—she was afraid I should have all the family jewels reset. And she wanted me to promise that I wouldn't do over the drawing-room."

"The very thing you are marrying for!"

"Exactly. So she packed him off to India."

"Hard luck—but you can do better than Dillworth."

He offered the box, and she took out three or four cigarettes, putting one between her lips and slipping the others into a little gold case attached to her long pearl chain.

"Have I time? Just a whiff, then." She leaned forward, holding the tip of her cigarette to his. As she did so, he noted, with a purely impersonal enjoyment, how evenly the black lashes were set in her smooth white lids, and how the purplish shade beneath them melted into the pure pallour of the cheek.

She began to saunter about the room, examining the book-shelves between the puffs of her cigarette-smoke. Some of the volumes had the ripe tints of good tooling and old morocco, and her eyes lingered on them caressingly, not with the appreciation of the expert, but with the pleasure in agreeable tones and textures that was one of her inmost susceptibilities. Suddenly her expression changed from desultory enjoyment to active conjecture, and she turned to Selden with a question.

---

4. Popular in the 1890s, this fabric was a thin white cotton formerly used for covering books and here shaped into sleeves, otherwise known as leg-of- mutton sleeves; they were very large and puffy on the upper arm but close-fitting on the forearm.

"You collect, don't you—you know about first editions and things?"

"As much as a man may who has no money to spend. Now and then I pick up something in the rubbish heap; and I go and look on at the big sales."

She had again addressed herself to the shelves, but her eyes now swept them inattentively, and he saw that she was preoccupied with a new idea.

"And Americana—do you collect Americana?"

Selden stared and laughed.

"No, that's rather out of my line. I'm not really a collector, you see; I simply like to have good editions of the books I am fond of."

She made a slight grimace. "And Americana are horribly dull, I suppose?"

"I should fancy so—except to the historian. But your real collector values a thing for its rarity. I don't suppose the buyers of Americana sit up reading them all night—old Jefferson Gryce certainly didn't."

She was listening with keen attention. "And yet they fetch fabulous prices, don't they? It seems so odd to want to pay a lot for an ugly badly-printed book that one is never going to read! And I suppose most of the owners of Americana are not historians either?"

"No; very few of the historians can afford to buy them. They have to use those in the public libraries or in private collections. It seems to be the mere rarity that attracts the average collector."

He had seated himself on an arm of the chair near which she was standing, and she continued to question him, asking which were the rarest volumes, whether the Jefferson Gryce collection was really considered the finest in the world, and what was the largest price ever fetched by a single volume.

It was so pleasant to sit there looking up at her, as she lifted now one book and then another from the shelves, fluttering the pages between her fingers, while her drooping profile was outlined against the warm background of old bindings, that he talked on without pausing to wonder at her sudden interest in so unsuggestive a subject. But he could never be long with her without trying to find a reason for what she was doing, and as she replaced his first edition of La Bruyère[5] and turned away from the bookcases, he began to ask himself what she had been driving at. Her next question was not of a nature to enlighten him. She paused before him with a smile which seemed at once designed to admit him to her familiarity, and to remind him of the restrictions it imposed.

"Don't you ever mind," she asked suddenly, "not being rich enough to buy all the books you want?"

He followed her glance about the room, with its worn furniture and shabby walls.

"Don't I just? Do you take me for a saint on a pillar?"

5. Jean de la Bruyère (1645–96) was a French writer best known for *Characters of Theophrastus*, partly a translation of the Greek philosopher, partly la Bruyère's own ironic comments on the personalities and morals of his own time.

"And having to work—do you mind that?"

"Oh, the work itself is not so bad—I'm rather fond of the law."

"No; but the being tied down: the routine—don't you ever want to get away, to see new places and people?"

"Horribly—especially when I see all my friends rushing to the steamer."

She drew a sympathetic breath. "But do you mind enough—to marry to get out of it?"

Selden broke into a laugh. "God forbid!" he declared.

She rose with a sigh, tossing her cigarette into the grate.

"Ah, there's the difference—a girl must, a man may if he chooses." She surveyed him critically. "Your coat's a little shabby—but who cares? It doesn't keep people from asking you to dine. If I were shabby no one would have me: a woman is asked out as much for her clothes as for herself. The clothes are the background, the frame, if you like: they don't make success, but they are a part of it. Who wants a dingy woman? We are expected to be pretty and well-dressed till we drop—and if we can't keep it up alone, we have to go into partnership."

Selden glanced at her with amusement: it was impossible, even with her lovely eyes imploring him, to take a sentimental view of her case.

"Ah, well, there must be plenty of capital on the lookout for such an investment. Perhaps you'll meet your fate to-night at the Trenors'."

She returned his look interrogatively.

"I thought you might be going there—oh, not in that capacity! But there are to be a lot of your set—Gwen Van Osburgh, the Wetheralls, Lady Cressida Raith—and the George Dorsets."

She paused a moment before the last name, and shot a query through her lashes; but he remained imperturbable.

"Mrs. Trenor asked me; but I can't get away till the end of the week; and those big parties bore me."

"Ah, so they do me," she exclaimed.

"Then why go?"

"It's part of the business—you forget! And besides, if I didn't, I should be playing bézique with my aunt at Richfield Springs."

"That's almost as bad as marrying Dillworth," he agreed, and they both laughed for pure pleasure in their sudden intimacy.

She glanced at the clock.

"Dear me! I must be off. It's after five."

She paused before the mantelpiece, studying herself in the mirror while she adjusted her veil. The attitude revealed the long slope of her slender sides, which gave a kind of wild-wood grace to her outline—as though she were a captured dryad subdued to the conventions of the drawing-room; and Selden reflected that it was the same streak of sylvan freedom in her nature that lent such savour to her artificiality.

He followed her across the room to the entrance-hall; but on the threshold she held out her hand with a gesture of leave-taking.

"It's been delightful; and now you will have to return my visit."

"But don't you want me to see you to the station?"

"No; good bye here, please."

She let her hand lie in his a moment, smiling up at him adorably.

"Good bye, then—and good luck at Bellomont!" he said, opening the door for her.

On the landing she paused to look about her. There were a thousand chances to one against her meeting anybody, but one could never tell, and she always paid for her rare indiscretions by a violent reaction of prudence. There was no one in sight, however, but a char-woman who was scrubbing the stairs. Her own stout person and its surrounding implements took up so much room that Lily, to pass her, had to gather up her skirts and brush against the wall. As she did so, the woman paused in her work and looked up curiously, resting her clenched red fists on the wet cloth she had just drawn from her pail. She had a broad sallow face, slightly pitted with small-pox, and thin straw-coloured hair through which her scalp shone unpleasantly.

"I beg your pardon," said Lily, intending by her politeness to convey a criticism of the other's manner.

The woman, without answering, pushed her pail aside, and continued to stare as Miss Bart swept by with a murmur of silken linings. Lily felt herself flushing under the look. What did the creature suppose? Could one never do the simplest, the most harmless thing, without subjecting one's self to some odious conjecture? Half way down the next flight, she smiled to think that a char-woman's stare should so perturb her. The poor thing was probably dazzled by such an unwonted apparition. But *were* such apparitions unwonted on Selden's stairs? Miss Bart was not familiar with the moral code of bachelors' flat-houses, and her colour rose again as it occurred to her that the woman's persistent gaze implied a groping among past associations. But she put aside the thought with a smile at her own fears, and hastened downward, wondering if she should find a cab short of Fifth Avenue.

Under the Georgian porch she paused again, scanning the street for a hansom. None was in sight, but as she reached the sidewalk she ran against a small glossy-looking man with a gardenia in his coat, who raised his hat with a surprised exclamation.

"Miss Bart? Well—of all people! This *is* luck," he declared; and she caught a twinkle of amused curiosity between his screwed-up lids.

"Oh, Mr. Rosedale—how are you?" she said, perceiving that the irrepressible annoyance on her face was reflected in the sudden intimacy of his smile.

Mr. Rosedale stood scanning her with interest and approval. He was a plump rosy man of the blond Jewish type, with smart London clothes fitting him like upholstery, and small sidelong eyes which gave him the air of appraising people as if they were bric-a-brac. He glanced up interrogatively at the porch of the Benedick.

"Been up to town for a little shopping, I suppose?" he said, in a tone which had the familiarity of a touch.

The woman continued to stare as Miss Bart swept by.

Miss Bart shrank from it slightly, and then flung herself into precipitate explanations.

"Yes—I came up to see my dress-maker. I am just on my way to catch the train to the Trenors'."

"Ah—your dress-maker; just so," he said blandly. "I didn't know there were any dress-makers in the Benedick."

"The Benedick?" She looked gently puzzled. "Is that the name of this building?"

"Yes, that's the name: I believe it's an old word for bachelor, isn't it? I happen to own the building—that's the way I know." His smile deepened as he added with increasing assurance: "But you must let me take you to the station. The Trenors are at Bellomont, of course? You've barely time to catch the five-forty. The dress-maker kept you waiting, I suppose."

Lily stiffened under the pleasantry.

"Oh, thanks," she stammered; and at that moment her eye caught a hansom drifting down Madison Avenue, and she hailed it with a desperate gesture.

"You're very kind; but I couldn't think of troubling you," she said, extending her hand to Mr. Rosedale; and heedless of his protestations, she sprang into the rescuing vehicle, and called out a breathless order to the driver.

II

In the hansom she leaned back with a sigh.

Why must a girl pay so dearly for her least escape from routine? Why could one never do a natural thing without having to screen it behind a structure of artifice? She had yielded to a passing impulse in going to Lawrence Selden's rooms, and it was so seldom that she could allow herself the luxury of an impulse! This one, at any rate, was going to cost her rather more than she could afford. She was vexed to see that, in spite of so many years of vigilance, she had blundered twice within five minutes. That stupid story about her dress-maker was bad enough—it would have been so simple to tell Rosedale that she had been taking tea with Selden! The mere statement of the fact would have rendered it innocuous. But, after having let herself be surprised in a falsehood, it was doubly stupid to snub the witness of her discomfiture. If she had had the presence of mind to let Rosedale drive her to the station, the concession might have purchased his silence. He had his race's accuracy in the appraisal of values, and to be seen walking down the platform at the crowded afternoon hour in the company of Miss Lily Bart would have been money in his pocket, as he might himself have phrased it. He knew, of course, that there would be a large house-party at Bellomont, and the possibility of being taken for one of Mrs. Trenor's guests was doubtless included in his calculations. Mr. Rosedale was still at a stage in his social ascent when it was of importance to produce such impressions.

The provoking part was that Lily knew all this—knew how easy it would have been to silence him on the spot, and how difficult it might be to do so afterward. Mr. Simon Rosedale was a man who made it his business to know everything about every one, whose idea of showing himself to be at home in society was to display an inconvenient familiarity with the habits of those with whom he wished to be thought intimate. Lily was sure that within twenty-four hours the story of her visiting her dress-maker at the Benedick would be in active circulation among Mr. Rosedale's acquaintances. The worst of it was that she had always snubbed and ignored him. On his first appearance—when her improvident cousin, Jack Stepney, had obtained for him (in return for favours too easily guessed) a card to one of the vast impersonal Van Osburgh "crushes"—Rosedale, with that mixture of artistic sensibility and business astuteness which characterizes his race, had instantly gravitated toward Miss Bart. She understood his motives, for her own course was guided by as nice calculations. Training and experience had taught her to be hospitable to newcomers, since the most unpromising might be useful later on, and there were plenty of available *oubliettes* to swallow them if they were not. But some intuitive repugnance, getting the better of years of social discipline, had made her push Mr. Rosedale into his *oubliette* without a trial. He had left behind only the ripple of amusement which his speedy despatch had caused among her friends; and though later (to shift the metaphor) he reappeared lower down the stream, it was only in fleeting glimpses, with long submergences between.

Hitherto Lily had been undisturbed by scruples. In her little set Mr. Rosedale had been pronounced "impossible," and Jack Stepney roundly snubbed for his attempt to pay his debts in dinner invitations. Even Mrs. Trenor, whose taste for variety had led her into some hazardous experiments, resisted Jack's attempts to disguise Mr. Rosedale as a novelty, and declared that he was the same little Jew who had been served up and rejected at the social board a dozen times within her memory; and while Judy Trenor was obdurate there was small chance of Mr. Rosedale's penetrating beyond the outer limbo of the Van Osburgh crushes. Jack gave up the contest with a laughing "You'll see," and, sticking manfully to his guns, showed himself with Rosedale at the fashionable restaurants, in company with the personally vivid if socially obscure ladies who are available for such purposes. But the attempt had hitherto been vain, and as Rosedale undoubtedly paid for the dinners, the laugh remained with his debtor.

Mr. Rosedale, it will be seen, was thus far not a factor to be feared—unless one put one's self in his power. And this was precisely what Miss Bart had done. Her clumsy fib had let him see that she had something to conceal; and she was sure he had a score to settle with her. Something in his smile told her he had not forgotten. She turned from the thought with a little shiver, but it hung on her all the way to the station, and dogged her down the platform with the persistency of Mr. Rosedale himself.

She had just time to take her seat before the train started; but having arranged herself in her corner with the instinctive feeling for effect which never forsook her, she glanced about in the hope of seeing some other member of the Trenors' party. She wanted to get away from herself, and conversation was the only means of escape that she knew.

Her search was rewarded by the discovery of a very blond young man with a soft reddish beard, who, at the other end of the carriage, appeared to be dissembling himself behind an unfolded newspaper. Lily's eye brightened, and a faint smile relaxed the drawn lines of her mouth. She had known that Mr. Percy Gryce was to be at Bellomont, but she had not counted on the luck of having him to herself in the train; and the fact banished all perturbing thoughts of Mr. Rosedale. Perhaps, after all, the day was to end more favourably than it had begun.

She began to cut the pages of a novel,[1] tranquilly studying her prey through downcast lashes while she organized a method of attack. Something in his attitude of conscious absorption told her that he was aware of her presence: no one had ever been quite so engrossed in an evening paper! She guessed that he was too shy to come up to her, and that she would have to devise some means of approach which should not appear to be an advance on her part. It amused her to think that any one as rich as Mr. Percy Gryce should be shy; but she was gifted with treasures of indulgence for such idiosyncrasies, and besides, his timidity might serve her purpose better than too much assurance. She had the art of giving self-confidence to the embarrassed, but she was not equally sure of being able to embarrass the self-confident.

She waited till the train had emerged from the tunnel and was racing between the ragged edges of the northern suburbs. Then, as it lowered its speed near Yonkers, she rose from her seat and drifted slowly down the carriage. As she passed Mr. Gryce, the train gave a lurch, and he was aware of a slender hand gripping the back of his chair. He rose with a start, his ingenuous face looking as though it had been dipped in crimson: even the reddish tint in his beard seemed to deepen.

The train swayed again, almost flinging Miss Bart into his arms. She steadied herself with a laugh and drew back; but he was enveloped in the scent of her dress, and his shoulder had felt her fugitive touch.

"Oh, Mr. Gryce, is it you? I'm so sorry—I was trying to find the porter and get some tea."

She held out her hand as the train resumed its level rush, and they stood exchanging a few words in the aisle. Yes—he was going to Bellomont. He had heard she was to be of the party—he blushed again as he admitted it. And was he to be there for a whole week? How delightful!

But at this point one or two belated passengers from the last station

---

1. At the turn of the century in the United States, books, particularly novels, were printed on large sheets of paper that were then folded and sewn together so that the reader needed to cut the folds apart in order to create the pages.

forced their way into the carriage, and Lily had to retreat to her seat.

"The chair next to mine is empty—do take it," she said over her shoulder; and Mr. Gryce, with considerable embarrassment, succeeded in effecting an exchange which enabled him to transport himself and his bags to her side.

"Ah—and here is the porter, and perhaps we can have some tea."

She signalled to that official, and in a moment, with the ease that seemed to attend the fulfilment of all her wishes, a little table had been set up between the seats, and she had helped Mr. Gryce to bestow his encumbering properties beneath it.

When the tea came he watched her in silent fascination while her hands flitted above the tray, looking miraculously fine and slender in contrast to the coarse china and lumpy bread. It seemed wonderful to him that any one should perform with such careless ease the difficult task of making tea in public in a lurching train. He would never have dared to order it for himself, lest he should attract the notice of his fellow-passengers; but, secure in the shelter of her conspicuousness, he sipped the inky draught with a delicious sense of exhilaration.

Lily, with the flavour of Selden's caravan tea on her lips, had no great fancy to drown it in the railway brew which seemed such nectar to her companion; but, rightly judging that one of the charms of tea is the fact of drinking it together, she proceeded to give the last touch to Mr. Gryce's enjoyment by smiling at him across her lifted cup.

"Is it quite right—I haven't made it too strong?" she asked solicitously; and he replied with conviction that he had never tasted better tea.

"I daresay it is true," she reflected; and her imagination was fired by the thought that Mr. Gryce, who might have sounded the depths of the most complex self-indulgence, was perhaps actually taking his first journey alone with a pretty woman.

It struck her as providential that she should be the instrument of his initiation. Some girls would not have known how to manage him. They would have over-emphasized the novelty of the adventure, trying to make him feel in it the zest of an escapade. But Lily's methods were more delicate. She remembered that her cousin Jack Stepney had once defined Mr. Gryce as the young man who had promised his mother never to go out in the rain without his overshoes; and acting on this hint, she resolved to impart a gently domestic air to the scene, in the hope that her companion, instead of feeling that he was doing something reckless or unusual, would merely be led to dwell on the advantage of always having a companion to make one's tea in the train.

But in spite of her efforts, conversation flagged after the tray had been removed, and she was driven to take a fresh measurement of Mr. Gryce's limitations. It was not, after all, opportunity but imagination that he lacked: he had a mental palate which would never learn to distinguish between railway tea and nectar. There was, however, one topic she could rely on: one spring that she had only to touch to set his simple machinery in motion. She had refrained from touching it because it was a last resource, and she had relied on other arts to stimulate other sensations; but as a settled look of dulness began to creep over his candid features, she saw that extreme measures were necessary.

"And how," she said, leaning forward, "are you getting on with your Americana?"

His eye became a degree less opaque: it was as though an incipient film had been removed from it, and she felt the pride of a skilful operator.

"I've got a few new things," he said, suffused with pleasure, but lowering his voice as though he feared his fellow-passengers might be in league to despoil him.

She returned a sympathetic enquiry, and gradually he was drawn on to talk of his latest purchases. It was the one subject which enabled him to forget himself, or allowed him, rather, to remember himself without constraint, because he was at home in it, and could assert a superiority that there were few to dispute. Hardly any of his acquaintances cared for Americana, or knew anything about them; and the consciousness of this ignorance threw Mr. Gryce's knowledge into agreeable relief. The only difficulty was to introduce the topic and to keep it to the front; most people showed no desire to have their ignorance dispelled, and Mr. Gryce was like a merchant whose warehouses are crammed with an unmarketable commodity.

But Miss Bart, it appeared, really did want to know about Americana; and moreover, she was already sufficiently informed to make the task of farther instruction as easy as it was agreeable. She questioned him intelligently, she heard him submissively; and, prepared for the look of lassitude which usually crept over his listeners' faces, he grew eloquent under her receptive gaze. The "points" she had had the presence of mind to glean from Selden, in anticipation of this very contingency, were serving her to such good purpose that she began to think her visit to him had been the luckiest incident of the day. She had once more shown her talent for profiting by the unexpected, and dangerous theories as to the advisability of yielding to impulse were germinating under the surface of smiling attention which she continued to present to her companion.

Mr. Gryce's sensations, if less definite, were equally agreeable. He felt the confused titillation with which the lower organisms welcome the gratification of their needs, and all his senses floundered in a vague well-being, through which Miss Bart's personality was dimly but pleasantly perceptible.

Mr. Gryce's interest in Americana had not originated with himself: it was impossible to think of him as evolving any taste of his own. An uncle had left him a collection already noted among bibliophiles; the existence of the collection was the only fact that had ever shed glory on the name of Gryce, and the nephew took as much pride in his inheritance as though it had been his own work. Indeed, he gradually came to regard it as such, and to feel a sense of personal complacency when he chanced on any reference to the Gryce Americana. Anxious as he was to avoid personal notice, he took, in the printed mention of his name, a pleasure so exquisite and excessive that it seemed a compensation for his shrinking from publicity.

To enjoy the sensation as often as possible, he subscribed to all the reviews dealing with book-collecting in general, and American history in particular, and as allusions to his library abounded in the pages of these journals, which formed his only reading, he came to regard himself as figuring prominently in the public eye, and to enjoy the thought of the interest which would be excited if the persons he met in the street, or sat among in travelling, were suddenly to be told that he was the possessor of the Gryce Americana.

Most timidities have such secret compensations, and Miss Bart was discerning enough to know that the inner vanity is generally in proportion to the outer self-deprecation. With a more confident person she would not have dared to dwell so long on one topic, or to show such exaggerated interest in it; but she had rightly guessed that Mr. Gryce's egoism was a thirsty soil, requiring constant nurture from without. Miss Bart had the gift of following an undercurrent of thought while she appeared to be sailing on the surface of conversation; and in this case her mental excursion took the form of a rapid survey of Mr. Percy Gryce's future as combined with her own. The Gryces were from Albany, and but lately introduced to the metropolis, where the mother and son had come, after old Jefferson Gryce's death, to take possession of his house in Madison Avenue—an appalling house, all brown stone without and black walnut within, with the Gryce library in a fire-proof annex that looked like a mausoleum. Lily, however, knew all about them: young Mr. Gryce's arrival had fluttered the maternal breasts of New York, and when a girl has no mother to palpitate for her she must needs be on the alert for herself. Lily, therefore, had not only contrived to put herself in the young man's way, but had made the acquaintance of Mrs. Gryce, a monumental woman with the voice of a pulpit orator and a mind preoccupied with the iniquities of her servants, who came sometimes to sit with Mrs. Peniston and learn from that lady how she managed to prevent the kitchen-maid's smuggling groceries out of the house. Mrs. Gryce had a kind of impersonal benevolence: cases of individual need she regarded with suspicion, but she subscribed to Institutions when their annual reports showed an impressive surplus. Her domestic duties were manifold, for they extended from furtive inspections of the servants' bedrooms to unannounced descents to the cellar; but she had never allowed herself many pleasures. Once, however, she had had a special edition of the Sarum Rule[2] printed in rubric and presented to every clergyman in the diocese; and the gilt album in which their letters of thanks were pasted formed the chief ornament of her drawing-room table.

Percy had been brought up in the principles which so excellent a

---

2. The classic form of Christian liturgy in Latin used in England before the protestant Reformation and remaining the source of the modern Anglican or Episcopal liturgy.

woman was sure to inculcate. Every form of prudence and suspicion
had been grafted on a nature originally reluctant and cautious, with the
result that it would have seemed hardly needful for Mrs. Gryce to extract
his promise about the overshoes, so little likely was he to hazard himself
abroad in the rain. After attaining his majority, and coming into the
fortune which the late Mr. Gryce had made out of a patent device for
excluding fresh air from hotels, the young man continued to live with
his mother in Albany; but on Jefferson Gryce's death, when another
large property passed into her son's hands, Mrs. Gryce thought that what
she called his "interests" demanded his presence in New York. She
accordingly installed herself in the Madison Avenue house, and Percy,
whose sense of duty was not inferior to his mother's, spent all his week
days in the handsome Broad Street office where a batch of pale men on
small salaries had grown grey in the management of the Gryce estate,
and where he was initiated with becoming reverence into every detail of
the art of accumulation.

As far as Lily could learn, this had hitherto been Mr. Gryce's only
occupation, and she might have been pardoned for thinking it not too
hard a task to interest a young man who had been kept on such low diet.
At any rate, she felt herself so completely in command of the situation
that she yielded to a sense of security in which all fear of Mr. Rosedale,
and of the difficulties on which that fear was contingent, vanished beyond
the edge of thought.

The stopping of the train at Garrisons would not have distracted her
from these thoughts, had she not caught a sudden look of distress in her
companion's eye. His seat faced toward the door, and she guessed that
he had been perturbed by the approach of an acquaintance; a fact confirmed by the turning of heads and general sense of commotion which
her own entrance into a railway-carriage was apt to produce.

She knew the symptoms at once, and was not surprised to be hailed
by the high notes of a pretty woman, who entered the train accompanied
by a maid, a bull-terrier, and a footman staggering under a load of bags
and dressing-cases.

"Oh, Lily—are you going to Bellomont? Then you can't let me have
your seat, I suppose? But I *must* have a seat in this carriage—porter, you
must find me a place at once. Can't some one be put somewhere else? I
want to be with my friends. Oh, how do you do, Mr. Gryce? Do please
make him understand that I must have a seat next to you and Lily."

Mrs. George Dorset, regardless of the mild efforts of a traveller with a
carpet-bag, who was doing his best to make room for her by getting out
of the train, stood in the middle of the aisle, diffusing about her that
general sense of exasperation which a pretty woman on her travels not
infrequently creates.

She was smaller and thinner than Lily Bart, with a restless pliability
of pose, as if she could have been crumpled up and run through a ring,
like the sinuous draperies she affected. Her small pale face seemed the
mere setting of a pair of dark exaggerated eyes, of which the visionary

gaze contrasted curiously with her self-assertive tone and gestures; so that, as one of her friends observed, she was like a disembodied spirit who took up a great deal of room.

Having finally discovered that the seat adjoining Miss Bart's was at her disposal, she possessed herself of it with a farther displacement of her surroundings, explaining meanwhile that she had come across from Mount Kisco in her motor-car that morning, and had been kicking her heels for an hour at Garrisons, without even the alleviation of a cigarette, her brute of a husband having neglected to replenish her case before they parted that morning.

"And at this hour of the day I don't suppose you've a single one left, have you, Lily?" she plaintively concluded.

Miss Bart caught the startled glance of Mr. Percy Gryce, whose own lips were never defiled by tobacco.

"What an absurd question, Bertha!" she exclaimed, blushing at the thought of the store she had laid in at Lawrence Selden's.

"Why, don't you smoke? Since when have you given it up? What—you never——And you don't either, Mr. Gryce? Ah, of course—how stupid of me—I understand."

And Mrs. Dorset leaned back against her travelling cushions with a smile which made Lily wish there had been no vacant seat beside her own.

III

Bridge at Bellomont usually lasted till the small hours; and when Lily went to bed that night she had played too long for her own good.

Feeling no desire for the self-communion which awaited her in her room, she lingered on the broad stairway, looking down into the hall below, where the last card-players were grouped about the tray of tall glasses and silver-collared decanters which the butler had just placed on a low table near the fire.

The hall was arcaded, with a gallery supported on columns of pale yellow marble. Tall clumps of flowering plants were grouped against a background of dark foliage in the angles of the walls. On the crimson carpet a deerhound and two or three spaniels dozed luxuriously before the fire, and the light from the great central lantern overhead shed a brightness on the women's hair and struck sparks from their jewels as they moved.

There were moments when such scenes delighted Lily, when they gratified her sense of beauty and her craving for the external finish of life; there were others when they gave a sharper edge to the meagreness of her own opportunities. This was one of the moments when the sense of contrast was uppermost, and she turned away impatiently as Mrs. George Dorset, glittering in serpentine spangles, drew Percy Gryce in her wake to a confidential nook beneath the gallery.

It was not that Miss Bart was afraid of losing her newly-acquired hold over Mr. Gryce. Mrs. Dorset might startle or dazzle him, but she had neither the skill nor the patience to effect his capture. She was too self-engrossed to penetrate the recesses of his shyness, and besides, why should she care to give herself the trouble? At most it might amuse her to make sport of his simplicity for an evening—after that he would be merely a burden to her, and knowing this, she was far too experienced to encourage him. But the mere thought of that other woman, who could take a man up and toss him aside as she willed, without having to regard him as a possible factor in her plans, filled Lily Bart with envy. She had been bored all the afternoon by Percy Gryce—the mere thought seemed to waken an echo of his droning voice—but she could not ignore him on the morrow, she must follow up her success, must submit to more boredom, must be ready with fresh compliances and adaptabilities, and all on the bare chance that he might ultimately decide to do her the honour of boring her for life.

It was a hateful fate—but how escape from it? What choice had she? To be herself, or a Gerty Farish. As she entered her bedroom, with its softly-shaded lights, her lace dressing-gown lying across the silken bed-spread, her little embroidered slippers before the fire, a vase of carnations filling the air with perfume, and the last novels and magazines lying uncut on a table beside the reading-lamp, she had a vision of Miss Farish's cramped flat, with its cheap conveniences and hideous wall-papers. No; she was not made for mean and shabby surroundings, for the squalid compromises of poverty. Her whole being dilated in an atmosphere of luxury; it was the background she required, the only climate she could breathe in. But the luxury of others was not what she wanted. A few years ago it had sufficed her: she had taken her daily meed of pleasure without caring who provided it. Now she was beginning to chafe at the obligations it imposed, to feel herself a mere pensioner on the splendour which had once seemed to belong to her. There were even moments when she was conscious of having to pay her way.

For a long time she had refused to play bridge. She knew she could not afford it, and she was afraid of acquiring so expensive a taste. She had seen the danger exemplified in more than one of her associates—in young Ned Silverton, for instance, the charming fair boy now seated in abject rapture at the elbow of Mrs. Fisher, a striking divorcée with eyes and gowns as emphatic as the head-lines of her "case." Lily could remember when young Silverton had stumbled into their circle, with the air of a strayed Arcadian who has published charming sonnets in his college journal. Since then he had developed a taste for Mrs. Fisher and bridge, and the latter at least had involved him in expenses from which he had been more than once rescued by harassed maiden sisters, who treasured the sonnets, and went without sugar in their tea to keep their darling afloat. Ned's case was familiar to Lily: she had seen his charming eyes—which had a good deal more poetry in them than the sonnets—

change from surprise to amusement, and from amusement to anxiety, as he passed under the spell of the terrible god of chance; and she was afraid of discovering the same symptoms in her own case.

For in the last year she had found that her hostesses expected her to take a place at the card-table. It was one of the taxes she had to pay for their prolonged hospitality, and for the dresses and trinkets which occasionally replenished her insufficient wardrobe. And since she had played regularly the passion had grown on her. Once or twice of late she had won a large sum, and instead of keeping it against future losses, had spent it in dress or jewelry; and the desire to atone for this imprudence, combined with the increasing exhilaration of the game, drove her to risk higher stakes at each fresh venture. She tried to excuse herself on the plea that, in the Trenor set, if one played at all one must either play high or be set down as priggish or stingy; but she knew that the gambling passion was upon her, and that in her present surroundings there was small hope of resisting it.

Tonight the luck had been persistently bad, and the little gold purse which hung among her trinkets was almost empty when she returned to her room. She unlocked the wardrobe, and taking out her jewel-case, looked under the tray for the roll of bills from which she had replenished the purse before going down to dinner. Only twenty dollars were left: the discovery was so startling that for a moment she fancied she must have been robbed. Then she took paper and pencil, and seating herself at the writing-table, tried to reckon up what she had spent during the day. Her head was throbbing with fatigue, and she had to go over the figures again and again; but at last it became clear to her that she had lost three hundred dollars at cards. She took out her cheque-book to see if her balance was larger than she remembered, but found she had erred in the other direction. Then she returned to her calculations; but figure as she would, she could not conjure back the vanished three hundred dollars. It was the sum she had set aside to pacify her dressmaker—unless she should decide to use it as a sop to the jeweller. At any rate, she had so many uses for it that its very insufficiency had caused her to play high in the hope of doubling it. But of course she had lost—she who needed every penny, while Bertha Dorset, whose husband showered money on her, must have pocketed at least five hundred, and Judy Trenor, who could have afforded to lose a thousand a night, had left the table clutching such a heap of bills that she had been unable to shake hands with her guests when they bade her good night.

A world in which such things could be seemed a miserable place to Lily Bart; but then she had never been able to understand the laws of a universe which was so ready to leave her out of its calculations.

She began to undress without ringing for her maid, whom she had sent to bed. She had been long enough in bondage to other people's pleasure to be considerate of those who depended on hers, and in her bitter moods it sometimes struck her that she and her maid were in the same position, except that the latter received her wages more regularly.

As she sat before the mirror brushing her hair, her face looked hollow and pale, and she was frightened by two little lines near her mouth, faint flaws in the smooth curve of the cheek.

"Oh, I must stop worrying!" she exclaimed. "Unless it's the electric light——" she reflected, springing up from her seat and lighting the candles on the dressing-table.

She turned out the wall-lights, and peered at herself between the candle-flames. The white oval of her face swam out waveringly from a background of shadows, the uncertain light blurring it like a haze; but the two lines about the mouth remained.

Lily rose and undressed in haste.

"It is only because I am tired and have such odious things to think about," she kept repeating; and it seemed an added injustice that petty cares should leave a trace on the beauty which was her only defence against them.

But the odious things were there, and remained with her. She returned wearily to the thought of Percy Gryce, as a wayfarer picks up a heavy load and toils on after a brief rest. She was almost sure she had "landed" him: a few days' work and she would win her reward. But the reward itself seemed unpalatable just then: she could get no zest from the thought of victory. It would be a rest from worry, no more—and how little that would have seemed to her a few years earlier! Her ambitions had shrunk gradually in the desiccating air of failure. But why had she failed? Was it her own fault or that of destiny?

She remembered how her mother, after they had lost their money, used to say to her with a kind of fierce vindictiveness: "But you'll get it all back—you'll get it all back, with your face." . . . The remembrance roused a whole train of association, and she lay in the darkness reconstructing the past out of which her present had grown.

A house in which no one ever dined at home unless there was "company"; a door-bell perpetually ringing; a hall-table showered with square envelopes which were opened in haste, and oblong envelopes[1] which were allowed to gather dust in the depths of a bronze jar; a series of French and English maids giving warning amid a chaos of hurriedly-ransacked wardrobes and dress-closets; an equally changing dynasty of nurses and footmen; quarrels in the pantry, the kitchen and the drawing-room; precipitate trips to Europe, and returns with gorged trunks and days of interminable unpacking; semi-annual discussions as to where the summer should be spent, grey interludes of economy and brilliant reactions of expense—such was the setting of Lily Bart's first memories.

Ruling the turbulent element called home was the vigorous and determined figure of a mother still young enough to dance her ball-dresses to rags, while the hazy outline of a neutral-tinted father filled an intermediate space between the butler and the man who came to wind the clocks. Even to the eyes of infancy, Mrs. Hudson Bart had appeared young; but

---

1. At the turn of the century, oblong envelopes usually contained bills while square ones had in them invitations and personal cards or notes.

Lily could not recall the time when her father had not been bald and slightly stooping, with streaks of grey in his hair, and a tired walk. It was a shock to her to learn afterward that he was but two years older than her mother.

Lily seldom saw her father by daylight. All day he was "down town"; and in winter it was long after nightfall when she heard his fagged step on the stairs and his hand on the school-room door. He would kiss her in silence, and ask one or two questions of the nurse or the governess; then Mrs. Bart's maid would come to remind him that he was dining out, and he would hurry away with a nod to Lily. In summer, when he joined them for a Sunday at Newport or Southampton, he was even more effaced and silent than in winter. It seemed to tire him to rest, and he would sit for hours staring at the sea-line from a quiet corner of the verandah, while the clatter of his wife's existence went on unheeded a few feet off. Generally, however, Mrs. Bart and Lily went to Europe for the summer, and before the steamer was half way over Mr. Bart had dipped below the horizon. Sometimes his daughter heard him denounced for having neglected to forward Mrs. Bart's remittances; but for the most part he was never mentioned or thought of till his patient stooping figure presented itself on the New York dock as a buffer between the magnitude of his wife's luggage and the restrictions of the American custom-house.

In this desultory yet agitated fashion life went on through Lily's teens: a zig-zag broken course down which the family craft glided on a rapid current of amusement, tugged at by the underflow of a perpetual need— the need of more money. Lily could not recall the time when there had been money enough, and in some vague way her father seemed always to blame for the deficiency. It could certainly not be the fault of Mrs. Bart, who was spoken of by her friends as a "wonderful manager." Mrs. Bart was famous for the unlimited effect she produced on limited means; and to the lady and her acquaintances there was something heroic in living as though one were much richer than one's bank-book denoted.

Lily was naturally proud of her mother's aptitude in this line: she had been brought up in the faith that, whatever it cost, one must have a good cook, and be what Mrs. Bart called "decently dressed." Mrs. Bart's worst reproach to her husband was to ask him if he expected her to "live like a pig"; and his replying in the negative was always regarded as a justification for cabling to Paris for an extra dress or two, and telephoning to the jeweller that he might, after all, send home the turquoise bracelet which Mrs. Bart had looked at that morning.

Lily knew people who "lived like pigs," and their appearance and surroundings justified her mother's repugnance to that form of existence. They were mostly cousins, who inhabited dingy houses with engravings from Cole's Voyage of Life[2] on the drawing-room walls, and

---

2. A set of inexpensive engravings depicting "Childhood," "Youth," "Manhood," and "Age" by the American artist Thomas Cole (1801–48), one of the founders of the Hudson River School of semi-mystical American landscape painting. Enormously popular by the end of the nineteenth century, the series grew to be synonymous with genteel middle-class culture.

slatternly parlour-maids who said "I'll go and see" to visitors calling at
an hour when all right-minded persons are conventionally if not actually
out. The disgusting part of it was that many of these cousins were rich,
so that Lily imbibed the idea that if people lived like pigs it was from
choice, and through the lack of any proper standard of conduct. This
gave her a sense of reflected superiority, and she did not need Mrs. Bart's
comments on the family frumps and misers to foster her naturally lively
taste for splendour.

Lily was nineteen when circumstances caused her to revise her view
of the universe.

The previous year she had made a dazzling début fringed by a heavy
thunder-cloud of bills. The light of the début still lingered on the horizon, but the cloud had thickened; and suddenly it broke. The suddenness added to the horror; and there were still times when Lily relived
with painful vividness every detail of the day on which the blow fell.
She and her mother had been seated at the luncheon-table, over the
chaufroix and cold salmon of the previous night's dinner: it was one of
Mrs. Bart's few economies to consume in private the expensive remnants
of her hospitality. Lily was feeling the pleasant languor which is youth's
penalty for dancing till dawn; but her mother, in spite of a few lines
about the mouth, and under the yellow waves on her temples, was as
alert, determined and high in colour as if she had risen from an untrou-
bled sleep.

In the centre of the table, between the melting *marrons glacés* and
candied cherries, a pyramid of American Beauties lifted their vigorous
stems; they held their heads as high as Mrs. Bart, but their rose-colour
had turned to a dissipated purple, and Lily's sense of fitness was disturbed by their reappearance on the luncheon-table.

"I really think, mother," she said reproachfully, "we might afford a
few fresh flowers for luncheon. Just some jonquils or lilies-of-the-valley——"

Mrs. Bart stared. Her own fastidiousness had its eye fixed on the world
and she did not care how the luncheon-table looked when there was no
one present at it but the family. But she smiled at her daughter's innocence.

"Lilies-of-the-valley," she said calmly, "cost two dollars a dozen at
this season."

Lily was not impressed. She knew very little of the value of money.

"It would not take more than six dozen to fill that bowl," she argued.

"Six dozen what?" asked her father's voice in the doorway.

The two women looked up in surprise; though it was a Saturday, the
sight of Mr. Bart at luncheon was an unwonted one. But neither his
wife nor his daughter was sufficiently interested to ask an explanation.

Mr. Bart dropped into a chair, and sat gazing absently at the fragment
of jellied salmon which the butler had placed before him.

"I was only saying," Lily began, "that I hate to see faded flowers at
luncheon; and mother says a bunch of lilies-of-the-valley would not cost

more than twelve dollars. Mayn't I tell the florist to send a few every day?"

She leaned confidently toward her father: he seldom refused her anything, and Mrs. Bart had taught her to plead with him when her own entreaties failed.

Mr. Bart sat motionless, his gaze still fixed on the salmon, and his lower jaw dropped; he looked even paler than usual, and his thin hair lay in untidy streaks on his forehead. Suddenly he looked at his daughter and laughed. The laugh was so strange that Lily coloured under it: she disliked being ridiculed, and her father seemed to see something ridiculous in the request. Perhaps he thought it foolish that she should trouble him about such a trifle.

"Twelve dollars—twelve dollars a day for flowers? Oh, certainly, my dear—give him an order for twelve hundred." He continued to laugh.

Mrs. Bart gave him a quick glance.

"You needn't wait, Poleworth—I will ring for you," she said to the butler.

The butler withdrew with an air of silent disapproval, leaving the remains of the *chaufroix* on the sideboard.

"What is the matter, Hudson? Are you ill?" said Mrs. Bart severely.

She had no tolerance for scenes which were not of her own making, and it was odious to her that her husband should make a show of himself before the servants.

"Are you ill?" she repeated.

"Ill?——No, I'm ruined," he said.

Lily made a frightened sound, and Mrs. Bart rose to her feet.

"Ruined——?" she cried; but controlling herself instantly, she turned a calm face to Lily.

"Shut the pantry door," she said.

Lily obeyed, and when she turned back into the room her father was sitting with both elbows on the table, the plate of salmon between them, and his head bowed on his hands.

Mrs. Bart stood over him with a white face which made her hair unnaturally yellow. She looked at Lily as the latter approached: her look was terrible, but her voice was modulated to a ghastly cheerfulness.

"Your father is not well—he doesn't know what he is saying. It is nothing—but you had better go upstairs; and don't talk to the servants," she added.

Lily obeyed; she always obeyed when her mother spoke in that voice. She had not been deceived by Mrs. Bart's words: she knew at once that they were ruined. In the dark hours which followed, that awful fact overshadowed even her father's slow and difficult dying. To his wife he no longer counted: he had become extinct when he ceased to fulfil his purpose, and she sat at his side with the provisional air of a traveller who waits for a belated train to start. Lily's feelings were softer: she pitied him in a frightened ineffectual way. But the fact that he was for the most part unconscious, and that his attention, when she stole into the room, drifted away from her after a moment, made him even more of a stranger than in the nursery days when he had never come home till after dark. She seemed always to have seen him through a blur—first of sleepiness, then of distance and indifference—and now the fog had thickened till he was almost indistinguishable. If she could have performed any little services for him, or have exchanged with him a few of those affecting words which an extensive perusal of fiction had led her to connect with such occasions, the filial instinct might have stirred in her; but her pity, finding no active expression, remained in a state of spectatorship, overshadowed by her mother's grim unflagging resentment. Every look and act of Mrs. Bart's seemed to say: "You are sorry for him now—but you will feel differently when you see what he has done to us."

It was a relief to Lily when her father died.

Then a long winter set in. There was a little money left, but to Mrs. Bart it seemed worse than nothing—the mere mockery of what she was entitled to. What was the use of living if one had to live like a pig? She sank into a kind of furious apathy, a state of inert anger against fate. Her faculty for "managing" deserted her, or she no longer took sufficient pride in it to exert it. It was well enough to "manage" when by so doing one could keep one's own carriage; but when one's best contrivance did not conceal the fact that one had to go on foot, the effort was no longer worth making.

Lily and her mother wandered from place to place, now paying long visits to relations whose house-keeping Mrs. Bart criticized, and who deplored the fact that she let Lily breakfast in bed when the girl had no prospects before her, and now vegetating in cheap continental refuges, where Mrs. Bart held herself fiercely aloof from the frugal tea-tables of her companions in misfortune. She was especially careful to avoid her old friends and the scenes of her former successes. To be poor seemed to her such a confession of failure that it amounted to disgrace; and she detected a note of condescension in the friendliest advances.

Only one thought consoled her, and that was the contemplation of Lily's beauty. She studied it with a kind of passion, as though it were some weapon she had slowly fashioned for her vengeance. It was the last asset in their fortunes, the nucleus around which their life was to be rebuilt. She watched it jealously, as though it were her own property and Lily its mere custodian; and she tried to instil into the latter a sense of the responsibility that such a charge involved. She followed in imagination the career of other beauties, pointing out to her daughter what might be achieved through such a gift, and dwelling on the awful warning of those who, in spite of it, had failed to get what they wanted: to Mrs. Bart, only stupidity could explain the lamentable dénouement of some of her examples. She was not above the inconsistency of charging fate, rather than herself, with her own misfortunes; but she inveighed so acrimoniously against love-matches that Lily would have fancied her own marriage had been of that nature, had not Mrs. Bart frequently assured her that she had been "talked into it"—by whom, she never made clear.

Lily was duly impressed by the magnitude of her opportunities. The dinginess of her present life threw into enchanting relief the existence to which she felt herself entitled. To a less illuminated intelligence Mrs. Bart's counsels might have been dangerous; but Lily understood that beauty is only the raw material of conquest, and that to convert it into success other arts are required. She knew that to betray any sense of superiority was a subtler form of the stupidity her mother denounced, and it did not take her long to learn that a beauty needs more tact than the possessor of an average set of features.

Her ambitions were not as crude as Mrs. Bart's. It had been among that lady's grievances that her husband—in the early days, before he was too tired—had wasted his evenings in what she vaguely described as "reading poetry"; and among the effects packed off to auction after his death were a score or two of dingy volumes which had struggled for existence among the boots and medicine bottles of his dressing-room shelves. There was in Lily a vein of sentiment, perhaps transmitted from this source, which gave an idealizing touch to her most prosaic purposes. She liked to think of her beauty as a power for good, as giving her the opportunity to attain a position where she should make her influence felt in the vague diffusion of refinement and good taste. She was fond of pictures and flowers, and of sentimental fiction, and she could not help thinking that the possession of such tastes ennobled her desire for worldly advantages. She would not indeed have cared to marry a man who was merely rich: she was secretly ashamed of her mother's crude passion for money. Lily's preference would have been for an English nobleman with political ambitions and vast estates; or, for second choice, an Italian prince with a castle in the Apennines and an hereditary office in the Vatican. Lost causes had a romantic charm for her, and she liked to picture herself as standing aloof from the vulgar press of the Quirinal,[3] and sacrificing her pleasure to the claims of an immemorial tradition. . . .

How long ago and how far off it all seemed! Those ambitions were hardly more futile and childish than the earlier ones which had centered about the possession of a French jointed doll with real hair. Was it only ten years since she had wavered in imagination between the English earl and the Italian prince? Relentlessly her mind travelled on over the dreary interval. . . .

After two years of hungry roaming Mrs. Bart had died—died of a deep disgust. She had hated dinginess, and it was her fate to be dingy. Her visions of a brilliant marriage for Lily had faded after the first year.

"People can't marry you if they don't see you—and how can they see

---

3. Built in the Renaissance as a summer home in Rome for the popes, the Palazzo del Quirinale after 1870 became the heavily guarded seat of secular government and is now the official residence of the president of the republic of Italy.

you in these holes where we're stuck?" That was the burden of her lament;
and her last adjuration to her daughter was to escape from dinginess if
she could.

"Don't let it creep up on you and drag you down. Fight your way out
of it somehow—you're young and can do it," she insisted.

She had died during one of their brief visits to New York, and there
Lily at once became the centre of a family council composed of the
wealthy relatives whom she had been taught to despise for living like
pigs. It may be that they had an inkling of the sentiments in which she
had been brought up, for none of them manifested a very lively desire
for her company; indeed, the question threatened to remain unsolved
till Mrs. Peniston with a sigh announced: "I'll try her for a year."

Every one was surprised, but one and all concealed their surprise, lest
Mrs. Peniston should be alarmed by it into reconsidering her decision.

Mrs. Peniston was Mr. Bart's widowed sister, and if she was by no
means the richest of the family group, its other members nevertheless
abounded in reasons why she was clearly destined by Providence to assume
the charge of Lily. In the first place she was alone, and it would be
charming for her to have a young companion. Then she sometimes
travelled, and Lily's familiarity with foreign customs—deplored as a misfortune by her more conservative relatives—would at least enable her to
act as a kind of courier. But as a matter of fact Mrs. Peniston had not
been affected by these considerations. She had taken the girl simply
because no one else would have her, and because she had the kind of
moral *mauvaise honte*[4] which makes the public display of selfishness
difficult, though it does not interfere with its private indulgence. It would
have been impossible for Mrs. Peniston to be heroic on a desert island,
but with the eyes of her little world upon her she took a certain pleasure
in her act.

She reaped the reward to which disinterestedness is entitled, and found
an agreeable companion in her niece. She had expected to find Lily
headstrong, critical and "foreign"—for even Mrs. Peniston, though she
occasionally went abroad, had the family dread of foreignness—but the
girl showed a pliancy, which, to a more penetrating mind than her aunt's,
might have been less reassuring than the open selfishness of youth. Misfortune had made Lily supple instead of hardening her, and a pliable
substance is less easy to break than a stiff one.

Mrs. Peniston, however, did not suffer from her niece's adaptability.
Lily had no intention of taking advantage of her aunt's good nature. She
was in truth grateful for the refuge offered her: Mrs. Peniston's opulent
interior was at least not externally dingy. But dinginess is a quality which
assumes all manner of disguises; and Lily soon found that it was as latent
in the expensive routine of her aunt's life as in the makeshift existence
of a continental pension.

Mrs. Peniston was one of the episodical persons who form the padding

---

4. False shame; a desire for things to appear a certain way solely to avoid embarrassment or censure,
rather than because one cares about the underlying reality.

of life. It was impossible to believe that she had herself ever been a focus of activities. The most vivid thing about her was the fact that her grand-mother had been a Van Alstyne. This connection with the well-fed and industrious stock of early New York revealed itself in the glacial neatness of Mrs. Peniston's drawing-room and in the excellence of her cuisine. She belonged to the class of old New Yorkers who have always lived well, dressed expensively, and done little else; and to these inherited obligations Mrs. Peniston faithfully conformed. She had always been a looker-on at life, and her mind resembled one of those little mirrors which her Dutch ancestors were accustomed to affix to their upper win-dows, so that from the depths of an impenetrable domesticity they might see what was happening in the street.

Mrs. Peniston was the owner of a country-place in New Jersey, but she had never lived there since her husband's death—a remote event, which appeared to dwell in her memory chiefly as a dividing point in the personal reminiscences that formed the staple of her conversation. She was a woman who remembered dates with intensity, and could tell at a moment's notice whether the drawing-room curtains had been renewed before or after Mr. Peniston's last illness.

Mrs. Peniston thought the country lonely and trees damp, and cher-ished a vague fear of meeting a bull. To guard against such contingen-cies she frequented the more populous watering-places, where she installed herself impersonally in a hired house and looked on at life through the matting screen of her verandah. In the care of such a guardian, it soon became clear to Lily that she was to enjoy only the material advantages of good food and expensive clothing; and, though far from underrating these, she would gladly have exchanged them for what Mrs. Bart had taught her to regard as opportunities. She sighed to think what her moth-er's fierce energies would have accomplished, had they been coupled with Mrs. Peniston's resources. Lily had abundant energy of her own, but it was restricted by the necessity of adapting herself to her aunt's habits. She saw that at all costs she must keep Mrs. Peniston's favour till, as Mrs. Bart would have phrased it, she could stand on her own legs. Lily had no mind for the vagabond life of the poor relation, and to adapt herself to Mrs. Peniston she had, to some degree, to assume that lady's passive attitude. She had fancied at first that it would be easy to draw her aunt into the whirl of her own activities, but there was a static force in Mrs. Peniston against which her niece's efforts spent themselves in vain. To attempt to bring her into active relation with life was like tugging at a piece of furniture which has been screwed to the floor. She did not, indeed, expect Lily to remain equally immovable: she had all the American guardian's indulgence for the volatility of youth. She had indulgence also for certain other habits of her niece's. It seemed to her natural that Lily should spend all her money on dress, and she supple-mented the girl's scanty income by occasional "handsome presents" meant to be applied to the same purpose. Lily, who was intensely practical, would have preferred a fixed allowance; but Mrs. Peniston liked the periodical recurrence of gratitude evoked by unexpected cheques, and was perhaps shrewd enough to perceive that such a method of giving kept alive in her niece a salutary sense of dependence.

Beyond this, Mrs. Peniston had not felt called upon to do anything for her charge: she had simply stood aside and let her take the field. Lily had taken it, at first with the confidence of assured possessorship, then with gradually narrowing demands, till now she found herself actually struggling for a foothold on the broad space which had once seemed her own for the asking. How it happened she did not yet know. Sometimes she thought it was because Mrs. Peniston had been too passive, and again she feared it was because she herself had not been passive enough. Had she shown an undue eagerness for victory? Had she lacked patience, pliancy and dissimulation? Whether she charged herself with these faults or absolved herself from them, made no difference in the sum-total of her failure. Younger and plainer girls had been married off by dozens; and she was nine-and-twenty, and still Miss Bart.

She was beginning to have fits of angry rebellion against fate, when she longed to drop out of the race and make an independent life for herself. But what manner of life would it be? She had barely enough money to pay her dress-makers' bills and her gambling debts; and none of the desultory interests which she dignified with the name of tastes was pronounced enough to enable her to live contentedly in obscurity. Ah, no—she was too intelligent not to be honest with herself. She knew that she hated dinginess as much as her mother had hated it, and to her last breath she meant to fight against it, dragging herself up again and again above its flood till she gained the bright pinnacles of success which presented such a slippery surface to her clutch.

IV

The next morning, on her breakfast tray, Miss Bart found a note from her hostess.

"Dearest Lily," it ran, "if it is not too much of a bore to be down by ten, will you come to my sitting-room to help me with some tiresome things?"

Lily tossed aside the note and subsided on her pillows with a sigh. It *was* a bore to be down by ten—an hour regarded at Bellomont as vaguely synchronous with sunrise—and she knew too well the nature of the tiresome things in question. Miss Pragg, the secretary, had been called away, and there would be notes and dinner-cards to write, lost addresses to hunt up, and other social drudgery to perform. It was understood that Miss Bart should fill the gap in such emergencies, and she usually recognized the obligation without a murmur.

Today, however, it renewed the sense of servitude which the previous night's review of her cheque-book had produced. Everything in her surroundings ministered to feelings of ease and amenity. The windows stood open to the sparkling freshness of the September morning, and between

the yellow boughs she caught a perspective of hedges and parterres leading by degrees of lessening formality to the free undulations of the park.
Her maid had kindled a little fire on the hearth, and it contended cheerfully with the sunlight which slanted across the moss-green carpet and
caressed the curved sides of an old marquetry desk. Near the bed stood
a table holding her breakfast tray, with its harmonious porcelain and
silver, a handful of violets in a slender glass, and the morning paper
folded beneath her letters. There was nothing new to Lily in these tokens
of a studied luxury; but, though they formed a part of her atmosphere,
she never lost her sensitiveness to their charm. Mere display left her with
a sense of superior distinction; but she felt an affinity to all the subtler
manifestations of wealth.

Mrs. Trenor's summons, however, suddenly recalled her state of
dependence, and she rose and dressed in a mood of irritability that she
was usually too prudent to indulge. She knew that such emotions leave
lines on the face as well as in the character, and she had meant to take
warning by the little creases which her midnight survey had revealed.

The matter-of-course tone of Mrs. Trenor's greeting deepened her
irritation. If one did drag one's self out of bed at such an hour, and come
down fresh and radiant to the monotony of note-writing, some special
recognition of the sacrifice seemed fitting. But Mrs. Trenor's tone showed
no consciousness of the fact.

"Oh, Lily, that's nice of you," she merely sighed across the chaos of
letters, bills and other domestic documents which gave an incon-
gruously commercial touch to the slender elegance of her writing-table.

"There are such lots of horrors this morning," she added, clearing a
space in the centre of the confusion and rising to yield her seat to Miss
Bart.

Mrs. Trenor was a tall fair woman, whose height just saved her from
redundancy. Her rosy blondness had survived some forty years of futile
activity without showing much trace of ill-usage except in a diminished
play of feature. It was difficult to define her beyond saying that she seemed
to exist only as a hostess, not so much from any exaggerated instinct of
hospitality as because she could not sustain life except in a crowd. The
collective nature of her interests exempted her from the ordinary rivalries
of her sex, and she knew no more personal emotion than that of hatred
for the woman who presumed to give bigger dinners or have more amusing house-parties than herself. As her social talents, backed by Mr. Trenor's
bank-account, almost always assured her ultimate triumph in such com-
petitions, success had developed in her an unscrupulous good nature
toward the rest of her sex, and in Miss Bart's utilitarian classification of
her friends, Mrs. Trenor ranked as the woman who was least likely to
"go back" on her.

"It was simply inhuman of Pragg to go off now," Mrs. Trenor declared,
as her friend seated herself at the desk. "She says her sister is going to
have a baby—as if that were anything to having a house-party! I'm sure
I shall get most horribly mixed up and there will be some awful rows.

When I was down at Tuxedo I asked a lot of people for next week, and I've mislaid the list and can't remember who is coming. And this week is going to be a horrid failure too—and Gwen Van Osburgh will go back and tell her mother how bored people were. I didn't mean to ask the Wetheralls—that was a blunder of Gus's. They disapprove of Carry Fisher, you know. As if one could help having Carry Fisher! It *was* foolish of her to get the second divorce—Carry always overdoes things—but she said the only way to get a penny out of Fisher was to divorce him and make him pay alimony. And poor Carry has to consider every dollar. It's really absurd of Alice Wetherall to make such a fuss about meeting her, when one thinks of what society is coming to. Some one said the other day that there was a divorce and a case of appendicitis in every family one knows. Besides, Carry is the only person who can keep Gus in a good humour when we have bores in the house. Have you noticed that *all* the husbands like her? All, I mean, except her own. It's rather clever of her to have made a specialty of devoting herself to dull people—the field is such a large one, and she has it practically to herself. She finds compensations, no doubt—I know she borrows money of Gus—but then I'd *pay* her to keep him in good humour, so I can't complain, after all."

Mrs. Trenor paused to enjoy the spectacle of Miss Bart's efforts to unravel her tangled correspondence.

"But it isn't only the Wetheralls and Carry," she resumed, with a fresh note of lament. "The truth is, I'm awfully disappointed in Lady Cressida Raith."

"Disappointed? Hadn't you known her before?"

"Mercy, no—never saw her till yesterday. Lady Skiddaw sent her over with letters to the Van Osburghs, and I heard that Maria Van Osburgh was asking a big party to meet her this week, so I thought it would be fun to get her away, and Jack Stepney, who knew her in India, managed it for me. Maria was furious, and actually had the impudence to make Gwen invite herself here, so that they shouldn't be *quite* out of it—if I'd known what Lady Cressida was like, they could have had her and welcome! But I thought any friend of the Skiddaws' was sure to be amusing. You remember what fun Lady Skiddaw was? There were times when I simply had to send the girls out of the room. Besides, Lady Cressida is the Duchess of Beltshire's sister, and I naturally supposed she was the same sort; but you never can tell in those English families. They are so big that there's room for all kinds, and it turns out that Lady Cressida is the moral one—married a clergyman and does missionary work in the East End.[1] Think of my taking such a lot of trouble about a clergyman's wife, who wears Indian jewelry and botanizes! She made Gus take her all through the glasshouses yesterday, and bothered him to death by asking him the names of the plants. Fancy treating Gus as if he were the gardener!"

---

1. An area of London containing infamous slums.

Mrs. Trenor brought this out in a *crescendo* of indignation.

"Oh, well, perhaps Lady Cressida will reconcile the Wetheralls to meeting Carry Fisher," said Miss Bart pacifically.

"I'm sure I hope so! But she is boring all the men horribly, and if she takes to distributing tracts, as I hear she does, it will be too depressing. The worst of it is that she would have been so useful at the right time. You know we have to have the Bishop once a year, and she would have given just the right tone to things. I always have horrid luck about the Bishop's visits," added Mrs. Trenor, whose present misery was being fed by a rapidly rising tide of reminiscence; "last year, when he came, Gus forgot all about his being here, and brought home the Ned Wintons and the Farleys—five divorces and six sets of children between them!"

"When is Lady Cressida going?" Lily enquired.

Mrs. Trenor cast up her eyes in despair. "My dear, if one only knew! I was in such a hurry to get her away from Maria that I actually forgot to name a date, and Gus says she told some one she meant to stop here all winter."

"To stop here? In this house?"

"Don't be silly—in America. But if no one else asks her—you know they *never* go to hotels."

"Perhaps Gus only said it to frighten you."

"No—I heard her tell Bertha Dorset that she had six months to put in while her husband was taking the cure in the Engadine.[2] You should have seen Bertha look vacant! But it's no joke, you know—if she stays here all the autumn she'll spoil everything, and Maria Van Osburgh will simply exult."

At this affecting vision Mrs. Trenor's voice trembled with self-pity.

"Oh, Judy—as if any one were ever bored at Bellomont!" Miss Bart tactfully protested. "You know perfectly well that, if Mrs. Van Osburgh were to get all the right people and leave you with all the wrong ones, you'd manage to make things go off, and she wouldn't."

Such an assurance would usually have restored Mrs. Trenor's complacency; but on this occasion it did not chase the cloud from her brow.

"It isn't only Lady Cressida, " she lamented. "Everything has gone wrong this week. I can see that Bertha Dorset is furious with me."

"Furious with you? Why?"

"Because I told her that Lawrence Selden was coming; but he wouldn't, after all, and she's quite unreasonable enough to think it's my fault."

Miss Bart put down her pen and sat absently gazing at the note she had begun.

"I thought that was all over," she said.

"So it is, on his side. And of course Bertha hasn't been idle since. But I fancy she's out of a job just at present—and some one gave me a hint that I had better ask Lawrence. Well, I *did* ask him—but I couldn't make

2. A valley in Switzerland through which the river En fiows, lined with picturesque resort villages.

him come; and now I suppose she'll take it out of me by being perfectly nasty to every one else."

"Oh, she may take it out of *him* by being perfectly charming—to some one else."

Mrs. Trenor shook her head dolefully. "She knows he wouldn't mind. And who else is there? Alice Wetherall won't let Lucius out of her sight. Ned Silverton can't take his eyes off Carry Fisher—poor boy! Gus is bored by Bertha, Jack Stepney knows her too well—and—well, to be sure, there's Percy Gryce!"

She sat up smiling at the thought.

Miss Bart's countenance did not reflect the smile.

"Oh, she and Mr. Gryce would not be likely to hit it off."

"You mean that she'd shock him and he'd bore her? Well, that's not such a bad beginning, you know. But I hope she won't take it into her head to be nice to him, for I asked him here on purpose for you."

Lily laughed. "*Merci du compliment!* I should certainly have no show against Bertha."

"Do you think I am uncomplimentary? I'm not really, you know. Every one knows you're a thousand times handsomer and cleverer than Bertha; but then you're not nasty. And for always getting what she wants in the long run, commend me to a nasty woman."

Miss Bart stared in affected reproval. "I thought you were so fond of Bertha."

"Oh, I am—it's much safer to be fond of dangerous people. But she *is* dangerous—and if I ever saw her up to mischief it's now. I can tell by poor George's manner. That man is a perfect barometer—he always knows when Bertha is going to——"

"To fall?" Miss Bart suggested.

"Don't be shocking! You know he believes in her still. And of course I don't say there's any real harm in Bertha. Only she delights in making people miserable, and especially poor George."

"Well, he seems cut out for the part—I don't wonder she likes more cheerful companionship."

"Oh, George is not as dismal as you think. If Bertha didn't worry him he would be quite different. Or if she'd leave him alone, and let him arrange his life as he pleases. But she doesn't dare lose her hold of him on account of the money, and so when *he* isn't jealous she pretends to be."

Miss Bart went on writing in silence, and her hostess sat following her train of thought with frowning intensity.

"Do you know," she exclaimed after a long pause, "I believe I'll call up Lawrence on the telephone and tell him he simply *must* come?"

"Oh, don't," said Lily, with a quick suffusion of colour. The blush surprised her almost as much as it did her hostess, who, though not commonly observant of facial changes, sat staring at her with puzzled eyes.

"Good gracious, Lily, how handsome you are!——Why? Do you dislike him so much?"

"Not at all; I like him. But if you are actuated by the benevolent intention of protecting me from Bertha—I don't think I need your protection."

Mrs. Trenor sat up with an exclamation. "Lily!——Percy? Do you mean to say you've actually done it?"

Miss Bart smiled. "I only mean to say that Mr. Gryce and I are getting to be very good friends."

"H'm—I see." Mrs. Trenor fixed a rapt eye upon her. "You know they say he has eight hundred thousand a year—and spends nothing, except on some rubbishy old books. And his mother has heart-disease and will leave him a lot more. *Oh, Lily, do go slowly,*" her friend adjured her.

Miss Bart continued to smile without annoyance. "I shouldn't, for instance," she remarked, "be in any haste to tell him that he had a lot of rubbishy old books."

"No, of course not; I know you're wonderful about getting up people's subjects. But he's horribly shy, and easily shocked, and —and——"

"Why don't you say it, Judy? I have the reputation of being on the hunt for a rich husband?"

"Oh, I don't mean that; he wouldn't believe it of you—at first," said Mrs. Trenor, with candid shrewdness. "But you know things are rather lively here at times—I must give Jack and Gus a hint—and if he thought you were what his mother would call fast—oh, well, you know what I mean. Don't wear your scarlet *crêpe-de-chine* for dinner, and don't smoke if you can help it, Lily dear!"

Lily pushed aside her finished work with a dry smile. "You're very kind, Judy: I'll lock up my cigarettes and wear that last year's dress you sent me this morning. And if you are really interested in my career, perhaps you'll be kind enough not to ask me to play bridge again this evening."

"Bridge? Does he mind bridge, too? Oh, Lily, what an awful life you'll lead! But of course I won't—why didn't you give me a hint last night? There's nothing I wouldn't do, you poor duck, to see you happy!"

And Mrs. Trenor, glowing with her sex's eagerness to smooth the course of true love, enveloped Lily in a long embrace.

"You're quite sure," she added solicitously, as the latter extricated herself, "that you wouldn't like me to telephone for Lawrence Selden?"

"Quite sure," said Lily.

The next three days demonstrated to her own complete satisfaction Miss Bart's ability to manage her affairs without extraneous aid.

As she sat, on the Saturday afternoon, on the terrace at Bellomont, she smiled at Mrs. Trenor's fear that she might go too fast. If such a warning had ever been needful, the years had taught her a salutary lesson, and she flattered herself that she now knew how to adapt her pace

to the object of pursuit. In the case of Mr. Gryce she had found it well
to flutter ahead, losing herself elusively and luring him on from depth
to depth of unconscious intimacy. The surrounding atmosphere was
propitious to this scheme of courtship. Mrs. Trenor, true to her word,
had shown no signs of expecting Lily at the bridge-table, and had even
hinted to the other card-players that they were to betray no surprise at
her unwonted defection. In consequence of this hint, Lily found herself
the centre of that feminine solicitude which envelops a young woman
in the mating season. A solitude was tacitly created for her in the crowded
existence of Bellomont, and her friends could not have shown a greater
readiness for self-effacement had her wooing been adorned with all the
attributes of romance. In Lily's set this conduct implied a sympathetic
comprehension of her motives, and Mr. Gryce rose in her esteem as she
saw the consideration he inspired.

The terrace at Bellomont on a September afternoon was a spot propitious to sentimental musings, and as Miss Bart stood leaning against
the balustrade above the sunken garden, at a little distance from the
animated group about the tea-table, she might have been lost in the
mazes of an inarticulate happiness. In reality, her thoughts were finding
definite utterance in the tranquil recapitulation of the blessings in store
for her. From where she stood she could see them embodied in the form
of Mr. Gryce, who, in a light overcoat and muffler, sat somewhat nervously on the edge of his chair, while Carry Fisher, with all the energy
of eye and gesture with which nature and art had combined to endow
her, pressed on him the duty of taking part in the task of municipal
reform.

Mrs. Fisher's latest hobby was municipal reform. It had been preceded by an equal zeal for socialism, which had in turn replaced an
energetic advocacy of Christian Science. Mrs. Fisher was small, fiery
and dramatic; and her hands and eyes were admirable instruments in
the service of whatever cause she happened to espouse. She had, however, the fault common to enthusiasts of ignoring any slackness of response
on the part of her hearers, and Lily was amused by her unconsciousness
of the resistance displayed in every angle of Mr. Gryce's attitude. Lily
herself knew that his mind was divided between the dread of catching
cold if he remained out of doors too long at that hour, and the fear that,
if he retreated to the house, Mrs. Fisher might follow him up with a
paper to be signed. Mr. Gryce had a constitutional dislike to what he
called "committing himself," and tenderly as he cherished his health,
he evidently concluded that it was safer to stay out of reach of pen and
ink till chance released him from Mrs. Fisher's toils. Meanwhile he cast
agonized glances in the direction of Miss Bart, whose only response was
to sink into an attitude of more graceful abstraction. She had learned
the value of contrast in throwing her charms into relief, and was fully
aware of the extent to which Mrs. Fisher's volubility was enhancing her
own repose.

She was roused from her musings by the approach of her cousin Jack

Stepney who, at Gwen Van Osburgh's side, was returning across the garden from the tennis court.

The couple in question were engaged in the same kind of romance in which Lily figured, and the latter felt a certain annoyance in contemplating what seemed to her a caricature of her own situation. Miss Van Osburgh was a large girl with flat surfaces and no high lights: Jack Stepney had once said of her that she was as reliable as roast mutton. His own taste was in the line of less solid and more highly-seasoned diet; but hunger makes any fare palatable, and there had been times when Mr. Stepney had been reduced to a crust.

Lily considered with interest the expression of their faces: the girl's turned toward her companion's like an empty plate held up to be filled, while the man lounging at her side already betrayed the encroaching boredom which would presently crack the thin veneer of his smile.

"How impatient men are!" Lily reflected. "All Jack has to do to get everything he wants is to keep quiet and let that girl marry him; whereas I have to calculate and contrive, and retreat and advance, as if I were going through an intricate dance, where one misstep would throw me hopelessly out of time."

As they drew nearer she was whimsically struck by a kind of family likeness between Miss Van Osburgh and Percy Gryce. There was no resemblance of feature. Gryce was handsome in a didactic way—he looked like a clever pupil's drawing from a plaster-cast—while Gwen's countenance had no more modelling than a face painted on a toy balloon. But the deeper affinity was unmistakable: the two had the same prejudices and ideals, and the same quality of making other standards non-existent by ignoring them. This attribute was common to most of Lily's set: they had a force of negation which eliminated everything beyond their own range of perception. Gryce and Miss Van Osburgh were, in short, made for each other by every law of moral and physical correspondence——

"Yet they wouldn't look at each other," Lily mused, "they never do. Each of them wants a creature of a different race, of Jack's race and mine, with all sorts of intuitions, sensations and perceptions that they don't even guess the existence of. And they always get what they want."

She stood talking with her cousin and Miss Van Osburgh, till a slight cloud on the latter's brow advised her that even cousinly amenities were subject to suspicion, and Miss Bart, mindful of the necessity of not exciting enmities at this crucial point of her career, dropped aside while the happy couple proceeded toward the tea-table.

Seating herself on the upper step of the terrace, Lily leaned her head against the honeysuckles wreathing the balustrade. The fragrance of the late blossoms seemed an emanation of the tranquil scene, a landscape tutored to the last degree of rural elegance. In the foreground glowed the warm tints of the gardens. Beyond the lawn, with its pyramidal pale-gold maples and velvety firs, sloped pastures dotted with cattle; and through a long glade the river widened like a lake under the silver light of September. Lily did not want to join the circle about the tea-table. They represented the future she had chosen, and she was content with it, but in no haste to anticipate its joys. The certainty that she could marry Percy Gryce when she pleased had lifted a heavy load from her mind, and her money troubles were too recent for their removal not to leave a sense of relief which a less discerning intelligence might have taken for happiness. Her vulgar cares were at an end. She would be able to arrange her life as she pleased, to soar into that empyrean of security where creditors cannot penetrate. She would have smarter gowns than Judy Trenor, and far, far more jewels than Bertha Dorset. She would be free forever from the shifts, the expedients, the humiliations of the relatively poor. Instead of having to flatter, she would be flattered; instead of being grateful, she would receive thanks. There were old scores she could pay off as well as old benefits she could return. And she had no doubts as to the extent of her power. She knew that Mr. Gryce was of the small chary type most inaccessible to impulses and emotions. He had the kind of character in which prudence is a vice, and good advice the most dangerous nourishment. But Lily had known the species before: she was aware that such a guarded nature must find one huge outlet of egoism, and she determined to be to him what his Americana had hitherto been: the one possession in which he took sufficient pride to spend money on it. She knew that this generosity to self is one of the forms of meanness, and she resolved so to identify herself with her husband's vanity that to gratify her wishes would be to him the most exquisite form of self-indulgence. The system might at first necessitate a resort to some of the very shifts and expedients from which she intended it should free her; but she felt sure that in a short time she would be able to play the game in her own way. How should she have distrusted her powers? Her beauty itself was not the mere ephemeral possession it might have been in the hands of inexperience: her skill in enhancing it, the care she took of it, the use she made of it, seemed to give it a kind of permanence. She felt she could trust it to carry her through to the end.

And the end, on the whole, was worth while. Life was not the mockery she had thought it three days ago. There was room for her, after all, in this crowded selfish world of pleasure whence, so short a time since, her poverty had seemed to exclude her. These people whom she had ridiculed and yet envied were glad to make a place for her in the charmed circle about which all her desires revolved. They were not as brutal and self-engrossed as she had fancied—or rather, since it would no longer be necessary to flatter and humour them, that side of their nature became less conspicuous. Society is a revolving body which is apt to be judged according to its place in each man's heaven; and at present it was turning its illuminated face to Lily.

In the rosy glow it diffused her companions seemed full of amiable qualities. She liked their elegance, their lightness, their lack of emphasis: even the self-assurance which at times was so like obtuseness now seemed the natural sign of social ascendency. They were lords of the only world she cared for, and they were ready to admit her to their ranks and let her lord it with them. Already she felt within her a stealing allegiance to their standards, an acceptance of their limitations, a disbelief in the things they did not believe in, a contemptuous pity for the people who were not able to live as they lived.

The early sunset was slanting across the park. Through the boughs of the long avenue beyond the gardens she caught the flash of wheels, and divined that more visitors were approaching. There was a movement behind her, a scattering of steps and voices: it was evident that the party about the tea-table was breaking up. Presently she heard a tread behind her on the terrace. She supposed that Mr. Gryce had at last found means to escape from his predicament, and she smiled at the significance of his coming to join her instead of beating an instant retreat to the fire-side.

She turned to give him the welcome which such gallantry deserved; but her greeting wavered into a blush of wonder, for the man who had approached her was Lawrence Selden.

"You see I came after all," he said; but before she had time to answer, Mrs. Dorset, breaking away from a lifeless colloquy with her host, had stepped between them with a little gesture of appropriation.

V

The observance of Sunday at Bellomont was chiefly marked by the punctual appearance of the smart omnibus destined to convey the household to the little church at the gates. Whether any one got into the omnibus or not was a matter of secondary importance, since by standing there it not only bore witness to the orthodox intentions of the family, but made Mrs. Trenor feel, when she finally heard it drive away, that she had somehow vicariously made use of it.

It was Mrs. Trenor's theory that her daughters actually did go to church every Sunday; but their French governess's convictions calling her to the rival fane, and the fatigues of the week keeping their mother in her room till luncheon, there was seldom any one present to verify the fact. Now and then, in a spasmodic burst of virtue—when the house had been too uproarious over night—Gus Trenor forced his genial bulk into a tight frock-coat and routed his daughters from their slumbers; but habitually, as Lily explained to Mr. Gryce, this parental duty was forgotten till the church bells were ringing across the park, and the omnibus had driven away empty.

Lily had hinted to Mr. Gryce that this neglect of religious observances was repugnant to her early traditions, and that during her visits to Bellomont she regularly accompanied Murial and Hilda to church. This tallied with the assurance, also confidentially imparted, that, never having played bridge before, she had been "dragged into it" on the night of her arrival, and had lost an appalling amount of money in consequence of her ignorance of the game and of the rules of betting. Mr. Gryce was undoubtedly enjoying Bellomont. He liked the ease and glitter of the life, and the lustre conferred on him by being a member of this group of rich and conspicuous people. But he thought it a very materialistic society; there were times when he was frightened by the talk of the men and the looks of the ladies, and he was glad to find that Miss Bart, for all her ease and self-possession, was not at home in so ambiguous an atmosphere. For this reason he had been especially pleased to learn that she would, as usual, attend the young Trenors to church on Sunday morning; and as he paced the gravel sweep before the door, his light overcoat on his arm and his prayer-book in one carefully-gloved hand, he reflected agreeably on the strength of character which kept her true to her early training in surroundings so subversive to religious principles.

For a long time Mr. Gryce and the omnibus had the gravel sweep to themselves; but, far from regretting this deplorable indifference on the part of the other guests, he found himself nourishing the hope that Miss Bart might be unaccompanied. The precious minutes were flying, however; the big chestnuts pawed the ground and flecked their impatient sides with foam; the coachman seemed to be slowly petrifying on the box, and the groom on the doorstep; and still the lady did not come. Suddenly, however, there was a sound of voices and a rustle of skirts in the doorway, and Mr. Gryce, restoring his watch to his pocket, turned with a nervous start; but it was only to find himself handing Mrs. Wetherall into the carriage.

The Wetheralls always went to church. They belonged to the vast group of human automata who go through life without neglecting to perform a single one of the gestures executed by the surrounding puppets. It is true that the Bellomont puppets did not go to church; but others equally important did—and Mr. and Mrs. Wetherall's circle was so large that God was included in their visiting-list. They appeared, therefore, punctual and resigned, with the air of people bound for a dull "At Home," and after them Hilda and Muriel straggled, yawning and pinning each other's veils and ribbons as they came. They had promised Lily to go to church with her, they declared, and Lily was such a dear old duck that they did n't mind doing it to please her, though they could n't fancy what had put the idea in her head, and though for their own part they would much rather have played lawn tennis with Jack and Gwen, if she had n't told them she was coming. The Misses Trenor were followed by Lady Cressida Raith, a weather-beaten person in Liberty silk and ethnological trinkets, who, on seeing the omnibus, expressed her surprise that they were not to walk across the park; but at Mrs. Wetherall's horrified protest that the church was a mile away, her ladyship, after a glance at the height of the other's heels, acquiesced in the necessity of driving, and poor Mr. Gryce found himself rolling off between four ladies for whose spiritual welfare he felt not the least concern.

It might have afforded him some consolation could he have known that Miss Bart had really meant to go to church. She had even risen earlier than usual in the execution of her purpose. She had an idea that the sight of her in a grey gown of devotional cut, with her famous lashes drooped above a prayer-book, would put the finishing touch to Mr. Gryce's subjugation, and render inevitable a certain incident which she had resolved should form a part of the walk they were to take together after luncheon. Her intentions in short had never been more definite; but poor Lily, for all the hard glaze of her exterior, was inwardly as malleable as wax. Her faculty for adapting herself, for entering into other people's feelings, if it served her now and then in small contingencies, hampered her in the decisive moments of life. She was like a waterplant in the flux of the tides, and today the whole current of her mood was carrying her toward Lawrence Selden. Why had he come? Was it to see herself or Bertha Dorset? It was the last question which, at that moment, should have engaged her. She might better have contented herself with thinking that he had simply responded to the despairing summons of his hostess, anxious to interpose him between herself and the ill-humour of Mrs. Dorset. But Lily had not rested till she learned from Mrs. Trenor that Selden had come of his own accord.

"He did n't even wire me—he just happened to find the trap at the station. Perhaps it's not over with Bertha after all," Mrs. Trenor musingly concluded; and went away to arrange her dinner-cards accordingly.

Perhaps it was not, Lily reflected; but it should be soon, unless she had lost her cunning. If Selden had come at Mrs. Dorset's call, it was at her own that he would stay. So much the previous evening had told her. Mrs. Trenor, true to her simple principle of making her married friends happy, had placed Selden and Mrs. Dorset next to each other at dinner; but, in obedience to the time-honoured traditions of the match-maker, she had separated Lily and Mr. Gryce, sending in the former with George Dorset, while Mr. Gryce was coupled with Gwen Van Osburgh.

George Dorset's talk did not interfere with the range of his neighbour's thoughts. He was a mournful dyspeptic, intent on finding out the deleterious ingredients of every dish and diverted from this care only by the sound of his wife's voice. On this occasion, however, Mrs. Dorset took no part in the general conversation. She sat talking in low murmurs with Selden, and turning a contemptuous and denuded shoulder toward her host, who, far from resenting his exclusion, plunged into the excesses of the *menu* with the joyous irresponsibility of a free man. To Mr. Dorset, however, his wife's attitude was a subject of such evident concern that, when he was not scraping the sauce from his fish, or scooping the moist bread-crumbs from the interior of his roll, he sat straining his thin neck for a glimpse of her between the lights.

Mrs. Trenor, as it chanced, had placed the husband and wife on opposite sides of the table, and Lily was therefore able to observe Mrs. Dorset also, and by carrying her glance a few feet farther, to set up a rapid comparison between Lawrence Selden and Mr. Gryce. It was that comparison which was her undoing. Why else had she suddenly grown interested in Selden? She had known him for eight years or more: ever since her return to America he had formed a part of her background. She had always been glad to sit next to him at dinner, had found him more agreeable than most men, and had vaguely wished that he pos-

sessed the other qualities needful to fix her attention; but till now she
had been too busy with her own affairs to regard him as more than one
of the pleasant accessories of life. Miss Bart was a keen reader of her own
heart, and she saw that her sudden preoccupation with Selden was due
to the fact that his presence shed a new light on her surroundings. Not
that he was notably brilliant or exceptional; in his own profession he was
surpassed by more than one man who had bored Lily through many a
weary dinner. It was rather that he had preserved a certain social detachment, a happy air of viewing the show objectively, of having points of
contact outside the great gilt cage in which they were all huddled for the
mob to gape at. How alluring the world outside the cage appeared to
Lily, as she heard its door clang on her! In reality, as she knew, the door
never clanged: it stood always open; but most of the captives were like
flies in a bottle, and having once flown in, could never regain their
freedom. It was Selden's distinction that he had never forgotten the way
out.

That was the secret of his way of readjusting her vision. Lily, turning
her eyes from him, found herself scanning her little world through his
retina: it was as though the pink lamps had been shut off and the dusty
daylight let in. She looked down the long table, studying its occupants
one by one, from Gus Trenor, with his heavy carnivorous head sunk
between his shoulders, as he preyed on a jellied plover, to his wife, at
the opposite end of the long bank of orchids, suggestive, with her glaring
good-looks, of a jeweller's window lit by electricity. And between the
two, what a long stretch of vacuity! How dreary and trivial these people
were! Lily reviewed them with a scornful impatience: Carry Fisher, with
her shoulders, her eyes, her divorces, her general air of embodying a
"spicy paragraph"; young Silverton, who had meant to live on proof-
reading and write an epic, and who now lived on his friends and had
become critical of truffles; Alice Wetherall, an animated visiting-list,
whose most fervid convictions turned on the wording of invitations and
the engraving of dinnercards; Wetherall, with his perpetual nervous nod
of acquiescence, his air of agreeing with people before he knew what
they were saying; Jack Stepney, with his confident smile and anxious
eyes, half way between the sheriff and an heiress; Gwen Van Osburgh,
with all the guileless confidence of a young girl who has always been
told that there is no one richer than her father.

Lily smiled at her classification of her friends. How different they had
seemed to her a few hours ago! Then they had symbolized what she was
gaining, now they stood for what she was giving up. That very afternoon
they had seemed full of brilliant qualities; now she saw that they were
merely dull in a loud way. Under the glitter of their opportunities she
saw the poverty of their achievement. It was not that she wanted them
to be more disinterested; but she would have liked them to be more
picturesque. And she had a shamed recollection of the way in which, a
few hours since, she had felt the centripetal force of their standards. She
closed her eyes an instant, and the vacuous routine of the life she had

chosen stretched before her like a long white road without dip or turning: it was true she was to roll over it in a carriage instead of trudging it on foot, but sometimes the pedestrian enjoys the diversion of a short cut which is denied to those on wheels.

She was roused by a chuckle which Mr. Dorset seemed to eject from the depths of his lean throat.

"I say, do look at her," he exclaimed, turning to Miss Bart with lugubrious merriment—"I beg your pardon, but do just look at my wife making a fool of that poor devil over there! One would really suppose she was gone on him—and it's all the other way round, I assure you."

Thus adjured, Lily turned her eyes on the spectacle which was affording Mr. Dorset such legitimate mirth. It certainly appeared, as he said, that Mrs. Dorset was the more active participant in the scene: her neighbour seemed to receive her advances with a temperate zest which did not distract him from his dinner. The sight restored Lily's good humour, and knowing the peculiar disguise which Mr. Dorset's marital fears assumed, she asked gaily: "Are n't you horribly jealous of her?"

Dorset greeted the sally with delight. "Oh, abominably—you've just hit it—keeps me awake at night. The doctors tell me that's what has knocked my digestion out—being so infernally jealous of her.— I can't eat a mouthful of this stuff, you know," he added suddenly, pushing back his plate with a clouded countenance; and Lily, unfailingly adaptable, accorded her radiant attention to his prolonged denunciation of other people's cooks, with a supplementary tirade on the toxic qualities of melted butter.

It was not often that he found so ready an ear; and, being a man as well as a dyspeptic, it may be that as he poured his grievances into it he was not insensible to its rosy symmetry. At any rate he engaged Lily so long that the sweets were being handed when she caught a phrase on her other side, where Miss Corby, the comic woman of the company, was bantering Jack Stepney on his approaching engagement. Miss Corby's rôle was jocularity: she always entered the conversation with a handspring.

"And of course you'll have Sim Rosedale as best man!" Lily heard her fling out as the climax of her prognostications; and Stepney responded, as if struck: "Jove, that's an idea. What a thumping present I'd get out of him!"

Sim Rosedale! The name, made more odious by its diminutive, obtruded itself on Lily's thoughts like a leer. It stood for one of the many hated possibilities hovering on the edge of life. If she did not marry Percy Gryce, the day might come when she would have to be civil to such men as Rosedale. *If she did not marry him?* But she meant to marry him—she was sure of him and sure of herself. She drew back with a shiver from the pleasant paths in which her thoughts had been straying, and set her feet once more in the middle of the long white road. . . .

When she went upstairs that night she found that the late post had brought her a fresh batch of bills. Mrs. Peniston, who was a conscientious woman, had forwarded them all to Bellomont.

Miss Bart, accordingly, rose the next morning with the most earnest conviction that it was her duty to go to church. She tore herself betimes from the lingering enjoyment of her breakfast-tray, rang to have her grey gown laid out, and despatched her maid to borrow a prayer-book from Mrs. Trenor.

But her course was too purely reasonable not to contain the germs of rebellion. No sooner were her preparations made than they roused a smothered sense of resistance. A small spark was enough to kindle Lily's imagination, and the sight of the grey dress and the borrowed prayer-book flashed a long light down the years. She would have to go to church with Percy Gryce every Sunday. They would have a front pew in the most expensive church in New York, and his name would figure handsomely in the list of parish charities. In a few years, when he grew stouter, he would be made a warden. Once in the winter the rector would come to dine, and her husband would beg her to go over the list and see that no *divorcées* were included, except those who had showed signs of penitence by being re-married to the very wealthy. There was nothing especially arduous in this round of religious obligations; but it stood for a fraction of that great bulk of boredom which loomed across her path. And who could consent to be bored on such a morning? Lily had slept well, and her bath had filled her with a pleasant glow, which was becomingly reflected in the clear curve of her cheek. No lines were visible this morning, or else the glass was at a happier angle.

And the day was the accomplice of her mood: it was a day for impulse and truancy. The light air seemed full of powdered gold; below the dewy bloom of the lawns the woodlands blushed and smouldered, and the hills across the river swam in molten blue. Every drop of blood in Lily's veins invited her to happiness.

The sound of wheels roused her from these musings, and leaning behind her shutters she saw the omnibus take up its freight. She was too late, then—but the fact did not alarm her. A glimpse of Mr. Gryce's crestfallen face even suggested that she had done wisely in absenting herself, since the disappointment he so candidly betrayed would surely whet his appetite for the afternoon walk. That walk she did not mean to miss; one glance at the bills on her writing-table was enough to recall its necessity. But meanwhile she had the morning to herself, and could muse pleasantly on the disposal of its hours. She was familiar enough with the habits of Bellomont to know that she was likely to have a free field till luncheon. She had seen the Wetheralls, the Trenor girls and Lady Cressida packed safely into the omnibus; Judy Trenor was sure to be having her hair shampooed; Carry Fisher had doubtless carried off her host for a drive, Ned Silverton was probably smoking the cigarette of young despair in his bedroom; and Kate Corby was certain to be playing tennis with Jack Stepney and Miss Van Osburgh. Of the ladies, this left only Mrs. Dorset unaccounted for, and Mrs. Dorset never came down till luncheon: her doctors, she averred, had forbidden her to expose herself to the crude air of the morning.

To the remaining members of the party Lily gave no special thought; wherever they were, they were not likely to interfere with her plans. These, for the moment, took the shape of assuming a dress somewhat more rustic and summerlike in style than the garment she had first selected, and rustling downstairs, sunshade in hand, with the disengaged air of a lady in quest of exercise. The great hall was empty but for the knot of dogs by the fire, who, taking in at a glance the out-door aspect of Miss Bart, were upon her at once with lavish offers of companionship. She put aside the ramping paws which conveyed these offers, and assuring the joyous volunteers that she might presently have a use for their company, sauntered on through the empty drawing-room to the library at the end of the house. The library was almost the only surviving portion of the old manor-house of Bellomont: a long spacious room, revealing the traditions of the mother-country in its classically-cased doors, the Dutch tiles of the chimney, and the elaborate hobgrate with its shining brass urns. A few family portraits of lantern-jawed gentlemen in tie-wigs, and ladies with large head-dresses and small bodies, hung between the shelves lined with pleasantly-shabby books: books mostly contemporaneous with the ancestors in question, and to which the subsequent Trenors had made no perceptible additions. The library at Bellomont was in fact never used for reading, though it had a certain popularity as a smoking-room or a quiet retreat for flirtation. It had occurred to Lily, however, that it might on this occasion have been resorted to by the only member of the party in the least likely to put it to its original use. She advanced noiselessly over the dense old rug scattered with easy-chairs, and before she reached the middle of the room she saw that she had not been mistaken. Lawrence Selden was in fact seated at its farther end; but though a book lay on his knee, his attention was not engaged with it, but directed to a lady whose lace-clad figure, as she leaned back in an adjoining chair, detached itself with exaggerated slimness against the dusky leather of the upholstery.

Lily paused as she caught sight of the group; for a moment she seemed about to withdraw, but thinking better of this, she announced her approach by a slight shake of her skirts which made the couple raise their heads, Mrs. Dorset with a look of frank displeasure, and Selden with his usual quiet smile. The sight of his composure had a disturbing effect on Lily; but to be disturbed was in her case to make a more brilliant effort at self-possession.

"Dear me, am I late?" she asked, putting a hand in his as he advanced to greet her.

"Late for what?" enquired Mrs. Dorset tartly. "Not for luncheon, certainly—but perhaps you had an earlier engagement?"

"Yes, I had," said Lily confidingly.

"Really? Perhaps I am in the way, then? But Mr. Selden is entirely at your disposal." Mrs. Dorset was pale with temper, and her antagonist felt a certain pleasure in prolonging her distress.

"Oh, dear, no—do stay," she said good-humouredly. "I don't in the least want to drive you away."

"You're awfully good, dear, but I never interfere with Mr. Selden's engagements."

The remark was uttered with a little air of proprietorship not lost on its object, who concealed a faint blush of annoyance by stooping to pick up the book he had dropped at Lily's approach. The latter's eyes widened charmingly and she broke into a light laugh.

"But I have no engagement with Mr. Selden! My engagement was to go to church; and I'm afraid the omnibus has started without me. Has it started, do you know?"

She turned to Selden, who replied that he had heard it drive away some time since.

"Ah, then I shall have to walk; I promised Hilda and Muriel to go to church with them. It's too late to walk there, you say? Well, I shall have the credit of trying, at any rate—and the advantage of escaping part of the service. I'm not so sorry for myself, after all!"

And with a bright nod to the couple on whom she had intruded, Miss Bart strolled through the glass doors and carried her rustling grace down the long perspective of the garden walk.

She was taking her way churchward, but at no very quick pace; a fact not lost on one of her observers, who stood in the doorway looking after her with an air of puzzled amusement. The truth is that she was conscious of a somewhat keen shock of disappointment. All her plans for the day had been built on the assumption that it was to see her that Selden had come to Bellomont. She had expected, when she came downstairs, to find him on the watch for her; and she had found him, instead, in a situation which might well denote that he had been on the watch for another lady. Was it possible, after all, that he had come for Bertha Dorset? The latter had acted on the assumption to the extent of appearing at an hour when she never showed herself to ordinary mortals, and Lily, for the moment, saw no way of putting her in the wrong. It did not occur to her that Selden might have been actuated merely by the desire to spend a Sunday out of town: women never learn to dispense with the sentimental motive in their judgments of men. But Lily was not easily disconcerted; competition put her on her mettle, and she reflected that Selden's coming, if it did not declare him to be still in Mrs. Dorset's toils, showed him to be so completely free from them that he was not afraid of her proximity.

These thoughts so engaged her that she fell into a gait hardly likely to carry her to church before the sermon, and at length, having passed from the gardens to the wood-path beyond, so far forgot her intention as to sink into a rustic seat at a bend of the walk. The spot was charming, and Lily was not insensible to the charm, or to the fact that her presence enhanced it; but she was not accustomed to taste the joys of solitude except in company, and the combination of a handsome girl and a romantic scene struck her as too good to be wasted. No one, however, appeared to profit by the opportunity; and after a half hour of fruitless waiting she rose and wandered on. She felt a stealing sense of fatigue as she walked; the sparkle had died out of her, and the taste of life was stale on her lips. She hardly knew what she had been seeking, or why the failure to find it had so blotted the light from her sky: she was only aware of a vague sense of failure, of an inner isolation deeper than the loneliness about her.

Her footsteps flagged, and she stood gazing listlessly ahead, digging the ferny edge of the path with the tip of her sun-shade. As she did so a step sounded behind her, and she saw Selden at her side.

"How fast you walk!" he remarked. "I thought I should never catch up with you."

She answered gaily: "You must be quite breathless! I've been sitting under that tree for an hour."

"Waiting for me, I hope?" he rejoined; and she said with a vague laugh:

"Well—waiting to see if you would come."

"I seize the distinction, but I don't mind it, since doing the one involved doing the other. But were n't you sure that I should come?"

"If I waited long enough—but you see I had only a limited time to give to the experiment."

"Why limited? Limited by luncheon?"

"No; by my other engagement."

"Your engagement to go to church with Muriel and Hilda?"

"No; but to come home from church with another person."

"Ah, I see; I might have known you were fully provided with alternatives. And is the other person coming home this way?"

Lily laughed again. "That's just what I don't know; and to find out, it is my business to get to church before the service is over."

"Exactly; and it is my business to prevent your doing so; in which case the other person, piqued by your absence, will form the desperate resolve of driving back in the omnibus."

Lily received this with fresh appreciation; his nonsense was like the bubbling of her inner mood. "Is that what you would do in such an emergency?" she enquired.

Selden looked at her with solemnity. "I am here to prove to you," he cried, "what I am capable of doing in an emergency!"

"Walking a mile in an hour—you must own that the omnibus would be quicker!"

"Ah—but will he find you in the end? That's the only test of success."

They looked at each other with the same luxury of enjoyment that they had felt in exchanging absurdities over his tea-table; but suddenly Lily's face changed, and she said: "Well, if it is, he has succeeded."

Selden, following her glance, perceived a party of people advancing toward them from the farther bend of the path. Lady Cressida had evidently insisted on walking home, and the rest of the church-goers had thought it their duty to accompany her. Lily's companion looked rapidly from one to the other of the two men of the party; Wetherall walking respectfully at Lady Cressida's side with his little sidelong look of nervous attention, and Percy Gryce bringing up the rear with Mrs. Wetherall and the Trenors.

"Ah—now I see why you were getting up your Americana!" Selden exclaimed with a note of the freest admiration; but the blush with which the sally was received checked whatever amplifications he had meant to give it.

That Lily Bart should object to being bantered about her suitors, or even about her means of attracting them, was so new to Selden that he had a momentary flash of surprise, which lit up a number of possibilities; but she rose gallantly to the defence of her confusion, by saying, as its object approached: "That was why I was waiting for you—to thank you for having given me so many points!"

"Ah, you can hardly do justice to the subject in such a short time," said Selden, as the Trenor girls caught sight of Miss Bart; and while she signalled a response to their boisterous greeting, he added quickly: "Won't you devote your afternoon to it? You know I must be off tomorrow morning. We'll take a walk, and you can thank me at your leisure."

VI

The afternoon was perfect. A deeper stillness possessed the air, and the glitter of the American autumn was tempered by a haze which diffused the brightness without dulling it.

In the woody hollows of the park there was already a faint chill; but as the ground rose the air grew lighter, and ascending the long slopes beyond the high-road, Lily and her companion reached a zone of lingering summer. The path wound across a meadow with scattered trees; then it dipped into a lane plumed with asters and purpling sprays of bramble, whence, through the light quiver of ash-leaves, the country unrolled itself in pastoral distances.

Higher up, the lane showed thickening tufts of fern and of the creeping glossy verdure of shaded slopes; trees began to overhang it, and the shade deepened to the checkered dusk of a beech-grove. The boles of the trees stood well apart, with only a light feathering of undergrowth; the path wound along the edge of the wood, now and then looking out on a sunlit pasture or on an orchard spangled with fruit.

Lily had no real intimacy with nature, but she had a passion for the appropriate and could be keenly sensitive to a scene which was the fitting background of her own sensations. The landscape outspread below her seemed an enlargement of her present mood, and she found something of herself in its calmness, its breadth, its long free reaches. On the nearer slopes the sugar-maples wavered like pyres of light; lower down was a massing of grey orchards, and here and there the lingering green of an oak-grove. Two or three red farm-houses dozed under the apple-trees, and the white wooden spire of a village church showed beyond the shoulder of the hill; while far below, in a haze of dust, the high-road ran between the fields.

"Let us sit here," Selden suggested, as they reached an open ledge of rock above which the beeches rose steeply between mossy boulders.

Lily dropped down on the rock, glowing with her long climb. She sat quiet, her lips parted by the stress of the ascent, her eyes wandering peacefully over the broken ranges of the landscape. Selden stretched himself on the grass at her feet, tilting his hat against the level sun-rays, and clasping his hands behind his head, which rested against the side of the rock. He had no wish to make her talk; her quick-breathing silence seemed a part of the general hush and harmony of things. In his own mind there was only a lazy sense of pleasure, veiling the sharp edges of sensation as the September haze veiled the scene at their feet. But Lily, though her attitude was as calm as his, was throbbing inwardly with a rush of thoughts. There were in her at the moment two beings, one drawing deep breaths of freedom and exhilaration, the other gasping for air in a little black prison-house of fears. But gradually the captive's gasps grew fainter, or the other paid less heed to them: the horizon expanded, the air grew stronger, and the free spirit quivered for flight.

She could not herself have explained the sense of buoyancy which seemed to lift and swing her above the sun-suffused world at her feet. Was it love, she wondered, or a mere fortuitous combination of happy thoughts and sensations? How much of it was owing to the spell of the perfect afternoon, the scent of the fading woods, the thought of the dulness she had fled from? Lily had no definite experience by which to test the quality of her feelings. She had several times been in love with fortunes or careers, but only once with a man. That was years ago, when she first came out, and had been smitten with a romantic passion for a young gentleman named Herbert Melson, who had blue eyes and a little wave in his hair. Mr. Melson, who was possessed of no other negotiable securities, had hastened to employ these in capturing the eldest Miss Van Osburgh: since then he had grown stout and wheezy, and was given to telling anecdotes about his children. If Lily recalled this early emotion it was not to compare it with that which now possessed her; the only point of comparison was the sense of lightness, of emancipation, which she remembered feeling, in the whirl of a waltz or the seclusion of a conservatory, during the brief course of her youthful romance. She had not known again till today that lightness, that glow of freedom; but now it was something more than a blind groping of the blood. The peculiar charm of her feeling for Selden was that she understood it; she could put her finger on every link of the chain that was drawing them together. Though his popularity was of the quiet kind, felt rather than actively expressed among his friends, she had never mistaken his inconspicuousness for obscurity. His reputed cultivation was generally regarded as a slight obstacle to easy intercourse, but Lily, who prided herself on her broad-minded recognition of literature, and always carried an Omar Khayyam[1] in her travelling-bag, was attracted by this attribute, which she felt would have had its distinction in an older society. It was, moreover, one of his gifts to look his part; to have a height which lifted his head above the crowd, and the keenly-modelled dark features which, in a land of amorphous types, gave him the air of belonging to a more specialized race, of carrying the impress of a concentrated past. Expansive persons found him a little dry, and very young girls thought him sarcastic; but this air of friendly aloofness, as far removed as possible from any assertion of personal advantage, was the quality which piqued Lily's interest. Everything about him accorded with the fastidious element in her taste, even to the light irony with which he surveyed what seemed to her most sacred. She admired him most of all, perhaps, for being able to convey as distinct a sense of superiority as the richest man she had ever met.

It was the unconscious prolongation of this thought which led her to say presently, with a laugh: "I have broken two engagements for you today. How many have you broken for me?"

"None," said Selden calmly. "My only engagement at Bellomont was with you."

She glanced down at him, faintly smiling.

"Did you really come to Bellomont to see me?"

"Of course I did."

Her look deepened meditatively. "Why?" she murmured, with an accent which took all tinge of coquetry from the question.

"Because you're such a wonderful spectacle: I always like to see what you are doing."

"How do you know what I should be doing if you were not here?"

Selden smiled. "I don't flatter myself that my coming has deflected your course of action by a hair's breadth."

"That's absurd—since, if you were not here, I could obviously not be taking a walk with you."

"No; but your taking a walk with me is only another way of making use of your material. You are an artist and I happen to be the bit of colour you are using today. It's a part of your cleverness to be able to produce premeditated effects extemporaneously."

Lily smiled also: his words were too acute not to strike her sense of humour. It was true that she meant to use the accident of his presence as part of a very definite effect; or that, at least, was the secret pretext she had found for breaking her promise to walk with Mr. Gryce. She had sometimes been accused of being too eager—even Judy Trenor had warned her to go slowly. Well, she would not be too eager in this case; she would

---

1. A fifteenth-century Persian poet whose work, *The Rubaiyat*, was made popular in a translation by Edward FitzGerald in 1859. Khayyám's quatrains were famous for their melancholy emphasis on sensual pleasure and on living for the moment; FitzGerald's version set the tone for much fin de siècle poetry in English.

give her suitor a longer taste of suspense. Where duty and inclination jumped together, it was not in Lily's nature to hold them asunder. She had excused herself from the walk on the plea of a headache: the horrid headache which, in the morning, had prevented her venturing to church. Her appearance at luncheon justified the excuse. She looked languid, full of a suffering sweetness; she carried a scent-bottle in her hand. Mr. Gryce was new to such manifestations; he wondered rather nervously if she were delicate, having far-reaching fears about the future of his progeny. But sympathy won the day, and he besought her not to expose herself: he always connected the outer air with ideas of exposure.

Lily had received his sympathy with languid gratitude, urging him, since she should be such poor company, to join the rest of the party who, after luncheon, were starting in automobiles on a visit to the Van Osburghs at Peekskill. Mr. Gryce was touched by her disinterestedness, and, to escape from the threatened vacuity of the afternoon, had taken her advice and departed mournfully, in a dust-hood and goggles: as the motor-car plunged down the avenue she smiled at his resemblance to a baffled beetle.

Selden had watched her manœuvres with lazy amusement. She had made no reply to his suggestion that they should spend the afternoon together, but as her plan unfolded itself he felt fairly confident of being included in it. The house was empty when at length he heard her step on the stair and strolled out of the billiard-room to join her. She had on a hat and walking-dress, and the dogs were bounding at her feet.

"I thought, after all, the air might do me good," she explained; and he agreed that so simple a remedy was worth trying.

The excursionists would be gone at least four hours; Lily and Selden had the whole afternoon before them, and the sense of leisure and safety gave the last touch of lightness to her spirit. With so much time to talk, and no definite object to be led up to, she could taste the rare joys of mental vagrancy.

She felt so free from ulterior motives that she took up his charge with a touch of resentment.

"I don't know," she said, "why you are always accusing me of premeditation."

"I thought you confessed to it: you told me the other day that you had to follow a certain line—and if one does a thing at all it is a merit to do it thoroughly."

"If you mean that a girl who has no one to think for her is obliged to think for herself, I am quite willing to accept the imputation. But you must find me a dismal kind of person if you suppose that I never yield to an impulse."

"Ah, but I don't suppose that: have n't I told you that your genius lies in converting impulses into intentions?"

"My genius?" she echoed with a sudden note of weariness. "Is there any final test of genius but success? And I certainly have n't succeeded."

Selden pushed his hat back and took a side-glance at her. "Success—
what is success? I shall be interested to have your definition."

"Success?" She hesitated. "Why, to get as much as one can out of
life, I suppose. It's a relative quality, after all. Is n't that your idea of it?"

"My idea of it? God forbid!" He sat up with sudden energy, resting
his elbows on his knees and staring out upon the mellow fields. "My
idea of success," he said, "is personal freedom."

"Freedom? Freedom from worries?"

"From everything—from money, from poverty, from ease and anxiety, from all the material accidents. To keep a kind of republic of the
spirit—that's what I call success."

She leaned forward with a responsive flash. "I know—I know—it's
strange; but that's just what I've been feeling today."

He met her eyes with the latent sweetness of his. "Is the feeling so
rare with you?" he said.

She blushed a little under his gaze. "You think me horribly sordid,
don't you? But perhaps it's rather that I never had any choice. There
was no one, I mean, to tell me about the republic of the spirit."

"There never is—it's a country one has to find the way to one's self."

"But I should never have found my way there if you had n't told me."

"Ah, there are sign-posts—but one has to know how to read them."

"Well, I have known, I have known!" she cried with a glow of eagerness. "Whenever I see you, I find myself spelling out a letter of the
sign—and yesterday—last evening at dinner—I suddenly saw a little way
into your republic."

Selden was still looking at her, but with a changed eye. Hitherto he
had found, in her presence and her talk, the aesthetic amusement which
a reflective man is apt to seek in desultory intercourse with pretty women.
His attitude had been one of admiring spectatorship, and he would have
been almost sorry to detect in her any emotional weakness which should
interfere with the fulfilment of her aims. But now the hint of this weakness had become the most interesting thing about her. He had come on
her that morning in a moment of disarray; her face had been pale and
altered, and the diminution of her beauty had lent her a poignant charm.
That is how she looks when she is alone! had been his first thought; and
the second was to note in her the change which his coming produced.
It was the danger-point of their intercourse that he could not doubt the
spontaneity of her liking. From whatever angle he viewed their dawning
intimacy, he could not see it as part of her scheme of life; and to be the
unforeseen element in a career so accurately planned was stimulating
even to a man who had renounced sentimental experiments.

"Well," he said, "did it make you want to see more? Are you going to
become one of us?"

He had drawn out his cigarettes as he spoke, and she reached her hand
toward the case.

"Oh, do give me one—I have n't smoked for days!"

"Why such unnatural abstinence? Everybody smokes at Bellomont."

"Yes—but it is not considered becoming in a *jeune fille à marier*; and at the present moment I am a *jeune fille à marier*."[2]

"Ah, then I'm afraid we can't let you into the republic."

"Why not? Is it a celibate order?"

"Not in the least, though I'm bound to say there are not many married people in it. But you will marry some one very rich, and it's as hard for rich people to get into as the kingdom of heaven."

"That's unjust, I think, because, as I understand it, one of the conditions of citizenship is not to think too much about money, and the only way not to think about money is to have a great deal of it."

"You might as well say that the only way not to think about air is to have enough to breathe. That is true enough in a sense; but your lungs are thinking about the air, if you are not. And so it is with your rich people—they may not be thinking of money, but they're breathing it all the while; take them into another element and see how they squirm and gasp!"

Lily sat gazing absently through the blue rings of her cigarette-smoke.

"It seems to me," she said at length, "that you spend a good deal of your time in the element you disapprove of."

Selden received this thrust without discomposure. "Yes; but I have tried to remain amphibious: it's all right as long as one's lungs can work in another air. The real alchemy consists in being able to turn gold back again into something else; and that's the secret that most of your friends have lost."

Lily mused. "Don't you think," she rejoined after a moment, "that the people who find fault with society are too apt to regard it as an end and not a means, just as the people who despise money speak as if its only use were to be kept in bags and gloated over? Isn't it fairer to look at them both as opportunities, which may be used either stupidly or intelligently, according to the capacity of the user?"

"That is certainly the sane view; but the queer thing about society is that the people who regard it as an end are those who are in it, and not the critics on the fence. It's just the other way with most shows—the audience may be under the illusion, but the actors know that real life is on the other side of the footlights. The people who take society as an escape from work are putting it to its proper use; but when it becomes the thing worked for it distorts all the relations of life." Selden raised himself on his elbow. "Good heavens!" he went on, "I don't underrate the decorative side of life. It seems to me the sense of splendour has justified itself by what it has produced. The worst of it is that so much human nature is used up in the process. If we're all the raw stuff of the cosmic effects, one would rather be the fire that tempers a sword than the fish that dyes a purple cloak. And a society like ours wastes such good material in producing its little patch of purple! Look at a boy like

2. A marriageable young woman.

Ned Silverton—he's really too good to be used to refurbish anybody's social shabbiness. There's a lad just setting out to discover the universe. Is n't it a pity he should end by finding it in Mrs. Fisher's drawing-room?"

"Ned is a dear boy, and I hope he will keep his illusions long enough to write some nice poetry about them; but do you think it is only in society that he is likely to lose them?"

Selden answered her with a shrug. "Why do we call all our generous ideas illusions, and the mean ones truths? Is n't it a sufficient condemnation of society to find one's self accepting such phraseology? I very nearly acquired the jargon at Silverton's age, and I know how names can alter the colour of beliefs."

She had never heard him speak with such energy of affirmation. His habitual touch was that of the eclectic, who lightly turns over and compares; and she was moved by this sudden glimpse into the laboratory where his faiths were formed.

"Ah, you are as bad as the other sectarians," she exclaimed; "why do you call your republic a republic? It is a close corporation, and you create arbitrary objections in order to keep people out."

"It is not *my* republic; if it were, I should have a *coup d'état* and seat you on the throne."

"Whereas, in reality, you think I can never even get my foot across the threshold? Oh, I understand what you mean. You despise my ambitions—you think them unworthy of me!"

Selden smiled, but not ironically. "Well, is n't that a tribute? I think them quite worthy of most of the people who live by them."

She had turned to gaze on him gravely. "But is n't it possible that, if I had the opportunities of these people, I might make a better use of them? Money stands for all kinds of things—its purchasing quality is n't limited to diamonds and motor-cars."

"Not in the least: you might expiate your enjoyment of them by founding a hospital."

"But if you think they are what I should really enjoy, you must think my ambitions are good enough for me."

Selden met this appeal with a laugh. "Ah, my dear Miss Bart, I am not divine Providence, to guarantee your enjoying the things you are trying to get!"

"Then the best you can say for me is, that after struggling to get them I probably shan't like them?" She drew a deep breath. "What a miserable future you foresee for me!"

"Well—have you never foreseen it for yourself?"

The slow colour rose to her cheek, not a blush of excitement but drawn from the deep wells of feeling; it was as if the effort of her spirit had produced it.

"Often and often," she said. "But it looks so much darker when you show it to me!"

He made no answer to this exclamation, and for a while they sat silent, while something throbbed between them in the wide quiet of the air. But suddenly she turned on him with a kind of vehemence.

"Why do you do this to me?" she cried. "Why do you make the things I have chosen seem hateful to me, if you have nothing to give me instead?"

The words roused Selden from the musing fit into which he had fallen. He himself did not know why he had led their talk along such lines; it was the last use he would have imagined himself making of an afternoon's solitude with Miss Bart. But it was one of those moments when neither seemed to speak deliberately, when an indwelling voice in each called to the other across unsounded depths of feeling.

"No, I have nothing to give you instead," he said, sitting up and turning so that he faced her. "If I had, it should be yours, you know."

She received this abrupt declaration in a way even stranger than the manner of its making: she dropped her face on her hands and he saw that for a moment she wept.

It was for a moment only, however; for when he leaned nearer and drew down her hands with a gesture less passionate than grave, she turned on him a face softened but not disfigured by emotion, and he said to himself, somewhat cruelly, that even her weeping was an art.

The reflection steadied his voice as he asked, between pity and irony: "Is n't it natural that I should try to belittle all the things I can't offer you?"

Her face brightened at this, but she drew her hand away, not with a gesture of coquetry, but as though renouncing something to which she had no claim.

"But you belittle *me*, don't you," she returned gently, "in being so sure they are the only things I care for?"

Selden felt an inner start; but it was only the last quiver of his egoism. Almost at once he answered quite simply: "But you do care for them, don't you? And no wishing of mine can alter that."

He had so completely ceased to consider how far this might carry him, that he had a distinct sense of disappointment when she turned on him a face sparkling with derision.

"Ah," she cried, "for all your fine phrases you're really as great a coward as I am, for you would n't have made one of them if you had n't been so sure of my answer."

The shock of this retort had the effect of crystallizing Selden's wavering intentions.

"I am not so sure of your answer," he said quietly. "And I do you the justice to believe that you are not either."

It was her turn to look at him with surprise; and after a moment— "Do you want to marry me?" she asked.

He broke into a laugh. "No, I don't want to—but perhaps I should if you did!"

"That's what I told you—you're so sure of me that you can amuse yourself with experiments." She drew back the hand he had regained, and sat looking down on him sadly.

"I am not making experiments," he returned. "Or if I am, it is not on you but on myself. I don't know what effect they are going to have on me—but if marrying you is one of them, I will take the risk."

She smiled faintly. "It would be a great risk, certainly—I have never concealed from you how great."

"Ah, it's you who are the coward!" he exclaimed.

She had risen, and he stood facing her with his eyes on hers. The soft isolation of the falling day enveloped them: they seemed lifted into a finer air. All the exquisite influences of the hour trembled in their veins, and drew them to each other as the loosened leaves were drawn to the earth.

"It's you who are the coward," he repeated, catching her hands in his.

She leaned on him for a moment, as if with a drop of tired wings: he felt as though her heart were beating rather with the stress of a long flight than the thrill of new distances. Then, drawing back with a little smile of warning—"I shall look hideous in dowdy clothes; but I can trim my own hats," she declared.

They stood silent for a while after this, smiling at each other like adventurous children who have climbed to a forbidden height from which they discover a new world. The actual world at their feet was veiling itself in dimness, and across the valley a clear moon rose in the denser blue.

Suddenly they heard a remote sound, like the hum of a giant insect, and following the high-road, which wound whiter through the surrounding twilight, a black object rushed across their vision.

Lily started from her attitude of absorption; her smile faded and she began to move toward the lane.

"I had no idea it was so late! We shall not be back till after dark," she said, almost impatiently.

Selden was looking at her with surprise: it took him a moment to regain his usual view of her; then he said, with an uncontrollable note of dryness: "That was not one of our party; the motor was going the other way."

"I know—I know——" She paused, and he saw her redden through the twilight. "But I told them I was not well—that I should not go out. Let us go down!" she murmured.

Selden continued to look at her; then he drew his cigarette-case from his pocket and slowly lit a cigarette. It seemed to him necessary, at that moment, to proclaim, by some habitual gesture of this sort, his recovered hold on the actual: he had an almost puerile wish to let his companion see that, their flight over, he had landed on his feet.

She waited while the spark flickered under his curved palm; then he held out the cigarettes to her.

She took one with an unsteady hand, and putting it to her lips, leaned forward to draw her light from his. In the indistinctness the little red gleam lit up the lower part of her face, and he saw her mouth tremble into a smile.

"Were you serious?" she asked, with an odd thrill of gaiety which she might have caught up, in haste, from a heap of stock inflections, without having time to select the just note.

Selden's voice was under better control. "Why not?" he returned. "You see I took no risks in being so." And as she continued to stand before him, a little pale under the retort, he added quickly: "Let us go down."

VII

It spoke much for the depth of Mrs. Trenor's friendship that her voice, in admonishing Miss Bart, took the same note of personal despair as if she had been lamenting the collapse of a house-party.

"All I can say is, Lily, that I can't make you out!" She leaned back, sighing, in the morning abandon of lace and muslin, turning an indifferent shoulder to the heaped-up importunities of her desk, while she considered, with the eye of a physician who has given up the case, the erect exterior of the patient confronting her.

"If you had n't told me you were going in for him seriously—but I'm sure you made that plain enough from the beginning! Why else did you ask me to let you off bridge, and to keep away Carry and Kate Corby? I don't suppose you did it because he amused you; we could none of us imagine you putting up with him for a moment unless you meant to marry him. And I'm sure everybody played fair! They all wanted to help it along. Even Bertha kept her hands off—I will say that—till Lawrence came down and you dragged him away from her. After that she had a right to retaliate—why on earth did you interfere with her? You've known Lawrence Selden for years—why did you behave as if you had just discovered him? If you had a grudge against Bertha it was a stupid time to show it—you could have paid her back just as well after you were married! I told you Bertha was dangerous. She was in an odious mood when she came here, but Lawrence's turning up put her in a good humour, and if you'd only let her think he came for *her* it would have never occurred to her to play you this trick. Oh, Lily, you'll never do anything if you're not serious!"

Miss Bart accepted this exhortation in a spirit of the purest impartiality. Why should she have been angry? It was the voice of her own conscience which spoke to her through Mrs. Trenor's reproachful accents. But even to her own conscience she must trump up a semblance of defence.

"I only took a day off—I thought he meant to stay on all this week, and I knew Mr. Selden was leaving this morning."

Mrs. Trenor brushed aside the plea with a gesture which laid bare its weakness.

"He did mean to stay—that's the worst of it. It shows that he's run away from you; that Bertha's done her work and poisoned him thoroughly."

Lily gave a slight laugh. "Oh, if he's running I'll overtake him!"

Her friend threw out an arresting hand. "Whatever you do, Lily, do nothing!"

Miss Bart received the warning with a smile. "I don't mean, literally, to take the next train. There are ways——" But she did not go on to specify them.

Mrs. Trenor sharply corrected the tense. "There *were* ways—plenty of them! I did n't suppose you needed to have them pointed out. But don't deceive yourself—he's thoroughly frightened. He has run straight home to his mother, and she'll protect him!"

"Oh, to the death," Lily agreed, dimpling at the vision.

"How you can *laugh*——" her friend rebuked her; and she dropped back to a soberer perception of things with the question: "What was it Bertha really told him?"

"Don't ask me—horrors! She seemed to have raked up everything. Oh, you know what I mean—of course there is n't anything, *really*; but I suppose she brought in Prince Varigliano—and Lord Hubert—and there was some story of your having borrowed money of old Ned Van Alstyne: did you ever?"

"He is my father's cousin," Miss Bart interposed.

"Well, of course she left *that* out. It seems Ned told Carry Fisher; and she told Bertha, naturally. They're all alike, you know: they hold their tongues for years, and you think you're safe, but when their opportunity comes they remember everything."

Lily had grown pale: her voice had a harsh note in it. "It was some money I lost at bridge at the Van Osburghs'. I repaid it, of course."

"Ah, well, they would n't remember that; besides, it was the idea of the gambling debt that frightened Percy. Oh, Bertha knew her man— she knew just what to tell him!"

In this strain Mrs. Trenor continued for nearly an hour to admonish her friend. Miss Bart listened with admirable equanimity. Her naturally good temper had been disciplined by years of enforced compliance, since she had almost always had to attain her ends by the circuitous path of other people's; and, being naturally inclined to face unpleasant facts as soon as they presented themselves, she was not sorry to hear an impartial statement of what her folly was likely to cost, the more so as her own thoughts were still insisting on the other side of the case. Presented in the light of Mrs. Trenor's vigorous comments, the reckoning was certainly a formidable one, and Lily, as she listened, found herself gradually reverting to her friend's view of the situation. Mrs. Trenor's words were moreover emphasized for her hearer by anxieties which she herself could scarcely guess. Affluence, unless stimulated by a keen imagination, forms but the vaguest notion of the practical strain of poverty. Judy knew it must be "horrid" for poor Lily to have to stop to consider whether she could afford real lace on her petticoats, and not to have a motor-car and a steam-yacht at her orders; but the daily friction of unpaid bills, the daily nibble of small temptations to expenditure, were trials as far out of her experience as the domestic problems of the char-woman. Mrs. Trenor's unconsciousness of the real stress of the situation had the effect of making it more galling to Lily. While her friend reproached her for missing the opportunity to eclipse her rivals, she was once more battling in imagination with the mounting tide of indebtedness from which she had so nearly escaped. What wind of folly had driven her out again on those dark seas?

If anything was needed to put the last touch to her self-abasement it was the sense of the way her old life was opening its ruts again to receive her. Yesterday her fancy had fluttered free pinions above a choice of occupations; now she had to drop to the level of the familiar routine, in which moments of seeming brilliancy and freedom alternated with long hours of subjection.

She laid a deprecating hand on her friend's. "Dear Judy! I'm sorry to have been such a bore, and you are very good to me. But you must have some letters for me to answer—let me at least be useful."

She settled herself at the desk, and Mrs. Trenor accepted her resumption of the morning's task with a sigh which implied that, after all, she had proved herself unfit for higher uses.

The luncheon table showed a depleted circle. All the men but Jack Stepney and Dorset had returned to town (it seemed to Lily a last touch of irony that Selden and Percy Gryce should have gone in the same train), and Lady Cressida and the attendant Wetheralls had been despatched by motor to lunch at a distant country-house. At such moments of diminished interest it was usual for Mrs. Dorset to keep her room till the afternoon; but on this occasion she drifted in when luncheon was half over, hollowed-eyed and drooping, but with an edge of malice under her indifference.

She raised her eyebrows as she looked about the table. "How few of us are left! I do so enjoy the quiet—don't you, Lily? I wish the men would always stop away—it's really much nicer without them. Oh, you don't count, George: one does n't have to talk to one's husband. But I thought Mr. Gryce was to stay for the rest of the week?" she added enquiringly. "Did n't he intend to, Judy? He's such a nice boy—I wonder what drove him away? He is rather shy, and I'm afraid we may have shocked him: he has been brought up in such an old-fashioned way. Do you know, Lily, he told me he had never seen a girl play cards for money till he saw you doing it the other night? And he lives on the interest of his income, and always has a lot left over to invest!"

Mrs. Fisher leaned forward eagerly. "I do believe it is some one's duty to educate that young man. It is shocking that he has never been made to realize his duties as a citizen. Every wealthy man should be compelled to study the laws of his country."

Mrs. Dorset glanced at her quietly. "I think he *has* studied the divorce laws. He told me he had promised the Bishop to sign some kind of a petition against divorce."

Mrs. Fisher reddened under her powder, and Stepney said with a laughing glance at Miss Bart: "I suppose he is thinking of marriage, and wants to tinker up the old ship before he goes aboard."

His betrothed looked shocked at the metaphor, and George Dorset exclaimed with a sardonic growl: "Poor devil! It is n't the ship that will do for him, it's the crew."

"Or the stowaways," said Miss Corby brightly. "If I contemplated a voyage with him I should try to start with a friend in the hold."

Miss Van Osburgh's vague feeling of pique was struggling for appropriate expression. "I'm sure I don't see why you laugh at him; I think he's very nice," she exclaimed; "and, at any rate, a girl who married him would always have enough to be comfortable."

She looked puzzled at the redoubled laughter which hailed her words, but it might have consoled her to know how deeply they had sunk into the breast of one of her hearers.

Comfortable! At that moment the word was more eloquent to Lily Bart than any other in the language. She could not even pause to smile over the heiress's view of a colossal fortune as a mere shelter against want: her mind was filled with the vision of what that shelter might have been to her. Mrs. Dorset's pin-pricks did not smart, for her own irony cut deeper: no one could hurt her as much as she was hurting herself, for no one else—not even Judy Trenor—knew the full magnitude of her folly.

She was roused from these unprofitable considerations by a whispered request from her hostess, who drew her apart as they left the luncheon-table.

"Lily, dear, if you've nothing special to do, may I tell Carry Fisher that you intend to drive to the station and fetch Gus? He will be back at four, and I know she has it in her mind to meet him. Of course I'm very glad to have him amused, but I happen to know that she has bled him rather severely since she's been here, and she is so keen about going to fetch him that I fancy she must have got a lot more bills this morning. It seems to me," Mrs. Trenor feelingly concluded, "that most of her alimony is paid by other women's husbands!"

Miss Bart, on her way to the station, had leisure to muse over her friend's words, and their peculiar application to herself. Why should she have to suffer for having once, for a few hours, borrowed money of an elderly cousin, when a woman like Carry Fisher could make a living unrebuked from the good-nature of her men friends and the tolerance of their wives? It all turned on the tiresome distinction between what a married woman might, and a girl might not, do. Of course it was shocking for a married woman to borrow money—and Lily was expertly aware of the implication involved—but still, it was the mere *malum prohibitum* [1] which the world decries but condones, and which, though it may be punished by private vengeance, does not provoke the collective disapprobation of society. To Miss Bart, in short, no such opportunities were

1. Something considered wrong not for itself but because it is forbidden.

possible. She could of course borrow from her women friends—a hundred here or there, at the utmost—but they were more ready to give a gown or a trinket, and looked a little askance when she hinted her preference for a cheque. Women are not generous lenders, and those among whom her lot was cast were either in the same case as herself, or else too far removed from it to understand its necessities. The result of her meditations was the decision to join her aunt at Richfield. She could not remain at Bellomont without playing bridge, and being involved in other expenses; and to continue her usual series of autumn visits would merely prolong the same difficulties. She had reached a point where abrupt retrenchment was necessary, and the only cheap life was a dull life. She would start the next morning for Richfield.

At the station she thought Gus Trenor seemed surprised, and not wholly unrelieved, to see her. She yielded up the reins of the light runabout in which she had driven over, and as he climbed heavily to her side, crushing her into a scant third of the seat, he said: "Halloo! It isn't often you honour me. You must have been uncommonly hard up for something to do."

The afternoon was warm, and propinquity made her more than usually conscious that he was red and massive, and that beads of moisture had caused the dust of the train to adhere unpleasantly to the broad expanse of cheek and neck which he turned to her; but she was aware also, from the look in his small dull eyes, that the contact with her freshness and slenderness was as agreeable to him as the sight of a cooling beverage.

The perception of this fact helped her to answer gaily: "It's not often I have the chance. There are too many ladies to dispute the privilege with me."

"The privilege of driving me home? Well, I'm glad you won the race, anyhow. But I know what really happened—my wife sent you. Now didn't she?"

He had the dull man's unexpected flashes of astuteness, and Lily could not help joining in the laugh with which he had pounced on the truth.

"You see, Judy thinks I'm the safest person for you to be with; and she's quite right," she rejoined.

"Oh, is she, though? If she is, it's because you wouldn't waste your time on an old hulk like me. We married men have to put up with what we can get: all the prizes are for the clever chaps who've kept a free foot. Let me light a cigar, will you? I've had a beastly day of it."

He drew up in the shade of the village street, and passed the reins to her while he held a match to his cigar. The little flame under his hand cast a deeper crimson on his puffing face, and Lily averted her eyes with a momentary feeling of repugnance. And yet some women thought him handsome!

As she handed back the reins, she said sympathetically: "Did you have such a lot of tiresome things to do?"

"I should say so—rather!" Trenor, who was seldom listened to, either by his wife or her friends, settled down into the rare enjoyment of a confidential talk. "You don't know how a fellow has to hustle to keep this kind of thing going." He waved his whip in the direction of the Bellomont acres, which lay outspread before them in opulent undulations. "Judy has no idea of what she spends—not that there is n't plenty to keep the thing going," he interrupted himself, "but a man has got to keep his eyes open and pick up all the tips he can. My father and mother used to live like fighting-cocks on their income, and put by a good bit of it too—luckily for me—but at the pace we go now, I don't know where I should be if it were n't for taking a flyer now and then. The women all think—I mean Judy thinks—I've nothing to do but to go down town once a month and cut off coupons,[2] but the truth is it takes a devilish lot of hard work to keep the machinery running. Not that I ought to complain to-day, though," he went on after a moment, "for I did a very neat stroke of business, thanks to Stepney's friend Rosedale: by the way, Miss Lily, I wish you'd try to persuade Judy to be decently civil to that chap. He's going to be rich enough to buy us all out one of these days, and if she'd only ask him to dine now and then I could get almost anything out of him. The man is mad to know the people who don't want to know him, and when a fellow's in that state there is nothing he won't do for the first woman who takes him up."

Lily hesitated a moment. The first part of her companion's discourse had started an interesting train of thought, which was rudely interrupted by the mention of Mr. Rosedale's name. She uttered a faint protest.

"But you know Jack did try to take him about, and he was impossible."

"Oh, hang it—because he's fat and shiny, and has a shoppy manner! Well, all I can say is that the people who are clever enough to be civil to him now will make a mighty good thing of it. A few years from now he'll be in it whether we want him or not, and then he won't be giving away a half-a-million tip for a dinner."

Lily's mind had reverted from the intrusive personality of Mr. Rosedale to the train of thought set in motion by Trenor's first words. This vast mysterious Wall Street world of "tips" and "deals"—might she not find in it the means of escape from her dreary predicament? She had often heard of women making money in this way through their friends: she had no more notion than most of her sex of the exact nature of the transaction, and its vagueness seemed to diminish its indelicacy. She could not, indeed, imagine herself, in any extremity, stooping to extract a "tip" from Mr. Rosedale; but at her side was a man in possession of that precious commodity, and who, as the husband of her dearest friend, stood to her in a relation of almost fraternal intimacy.

In her inmost heart Lily knew it was not by appealing to the fraternal instinct that she was likely to move Gus Trenor; but this way of explaining the situation helped to drape its crudity, and she was always scru-

---

2. Clip off a detachable printed statement on a bond to redeem for cash.

pulous about keeping up appearances to herself. Her personal fastidiousness had a moral equivalent, and when she made a tour of inspection in her own mind there were certain closed doors she did not open.

As they reached the gates of Bellomont she turned to Trenor with a smile.

"The afternoon is so perfect—don't you want to drive me a little farther? I've been rather out of spirits all day, and it's so restful to be away from people, with some one who won't mind if I'm a little dull."

She looked so plaintively lovely as she proffered the request, so trustfully sure of his sympathy and understanding, that Trenor felt himself wishing that his wife could see how other women treated him—not battered wire-pullers like Mrs. Fisher, but a girl that most men would have given their boots to get such a look from.

"Out of spirits? Why on earth should you ever be out of spirits? Is your last box of Doucet dresses[3] a failure, or did Judy rook you out of everything at bridge last night?"

Lily shook her head with a sigh. "I have had to give up Doucet; and bridge too—I can't afford it. In fact I can't afford any of the things my friends do, and I am afraid Judy often thinks me a bore because I don't play cards any longer, and because I am not as smartly dressed as the other women. But you will think me a bore too if I talk to you about my worries, and I only mention them because I want you to do me a favour— the very greatest of favours."

Her eyes sought his once more, and she smiled inwardly at the tinge of apprehension that she read in them.

"Why, of course—if it's anything I can manage——" He broke off, and she guessed that his enjoyment was disturbed by the remembrance of Mrs. Fisher's methods.

"The greatest of favours," she rejoined gently. "The fact is, Judy is angry with me, and I want you to make my peace."

"Angry with you? Oh, come, nonsense——" his relief broke through in a laugh. "Why, you know she's devoted to you."

"She is the best friend I have, and that is why I mind having to vex her. But I daresay you know what she has wanted me to do. She has set her heart—poor dear—on my marrying—marrying a great deal of money."

She paused with a slight falter of embarrassment, and Trenor, turning abruptly, fixed on her a look of growing intelligence.

"A great deal of money? Oh, by Jove—you don't mean Gryce? What— you do? Oh, no, of course I won't mention it—you can trust me to keep my mouth shut—but Gryce—good Lord, *Gryce!* Did Judy really think you could bring yourself to marry that portentous little ass? But you could n't, eh? And so you gave him the sack, and that's the reason why he lit out by the first train this morning?" He leaned back, spreading himself farther across the seat, as if dilated by the joyful sense of his own discernment, "How on earth could Judy think you would do such a

---

3. Gowns designed by Jacques Doucet, a famous French couturier.

thing? *I* could have told her you'd never put up with such a little milk-sop!"

Lily signed more deeply. "I sometimes think," she murmured, "that men understand a woman's motives better than other women do."

"Some men—I'm certain of it! I could have *told* Judy," he repeated, exulting in the implied superiority over his wife.

"I thought you would understand; that's why I wanted to speak to you," Miss Bart rejoined. "I *can't* make that kind of marriage; it's impossible. But neither can I go on living as all the women in my set do. I am almost entirely dependent on my aunt, and though she is very kind to me she makes me no regular allowance, and lately I've lost money at cards, and I don't dare tell her about it. I have paid my card debts, of course, but there is hardly anything left for my other expenses, and if I go on with my present life I shall be in horrible difficulties. I have a tiny income of my own, but I'm afraid it's badly invested, for it seems to bring in less every year, and I am so ignorant of money matters that I don't know if my aunt's agent, who looks after it, is a good adviser." She paused a moment, and added in a lighter tone: "I did n't mean to bore you with all this, but I want your help in making Judy understand that I can't, at present, go on living as one must live among you all. I am going away tomorrow to join my aunt at Richfield, and I shall stay there for the rest of the autumn, and dismiss my maid and learn how to mend my own clothes."

At this picture of loveliness in distress, the pathos of which was heightened by the light touch with which it was drawn, a murmur of indignant sympathy broke from Trenor. Twenty-four hours earlier, if his wife had consulted him on the subject of Miss Bart's future, he would have said that a girl with extravagant tastes and no money had better marry the first rich man she could get; but with the subject of discussion at his side, turning to him for sympathy, making him feel that he understood her better than her dearest friends, and confirming the assurance by the appeal of her exquisite nearness, he was ready to swear that such a marriage was a desecration, and that, as a man of honour, he was bound to do all he could to protect her from the results of her disinterestedness. This impulse was reinforced by the reflection that if she had married Gryce she would have been surrounded by flattery and approval, whereas, having refused to sacrifice herself to expediency, she was left to bear the whole cost of her resistance. Hang it, if he could find a way out of such difficulties for a professional sponge like Carry Fisher, who was simply a mental habit corresponding to the physical titillations of the cigarette or the cock-tail, he could surely do as much for a girl who appealed to his highest sympathies, and who brought her troubles to him with the trustfulness of a child.

Trenor and Miss Bart prolonged their drive till long after sunset; and before it was over he had tried, with some show of success, to prove to her that, if she would only trust him, he could make a handsome sum of money for her without endangering the small amount she possessed.

She was too genuinely ignorant of the manipulations of the stock-market to understand his technical explanations, or even perhaps to perceive that certain points in them were slurred; the haziness enveloping the transaction served as a veil for her embarrassment, and through the general blur her hopes dilated like lamps in a fog. She understood only that her modest investments were to be mysteriously multiplied without risk to herself; and the assurance that this miracle would take place within a short time, that there would be no tedious interval for suspense and reaction, relieved her of her lingering scruples.

Again she felt the lightening of her load, and with it the release of repressed activities. Her immediate worries conjured, it was easy to resolve that she would never again find herself in such straits, and as the need of economy and self-denial receded from her foreground she felt herself ready to meet any other demand which life might make. Even the immediate one of letting Trenor, as they drove homeward, lean a little nearer and rest his hand reassuringly on hers, cost her only a momentary shiver of reluctance. It was part of the game to make him feel that her appeal had been an uncalculated impulse, provoked by the liking he inspired; and the renewed sense of power in handling men, while it consoled her wounded vanity, helped also to obscure the thought of the claim at which his manner hinted. He was a coarse dull man who, under all his show of authority, was a mere supernumerary in the costly show for which his money paid: surely, to a clever girl, it would be easy to hold him by his vanity, and so keep the obligation on his side.

VIII

The first thousand dollar[1] cheque which Lily received with a blotted scrawl from Gus Trenor strengthened her self-confidence in the exact degree to which it effaced her debts.

The transaction had justified itself by its results: she saw now how absurd it would have been to let any primitive scruple deprive her of this easy means of appeasing her creditors. Lily felt really virtuous as she dispensed the sum in sops to her tradesmen, and the fact that a fresh order accompanied each payment did not lessen her sense of disinterestedness. How many women, in her place, would have given the orders without making the payment!

She had found it reassuringly easy to keep Trenor in a good humour. To listen to his stories, to receive his confidences and laugh at his jokes, seemed for the moment all that was required of her, and the complacency with which her hostess regarded these attentions freed them of the least hint of ambiguity. Mrs. Trenor evidently assumed that Lily's growing intimacy with her husband was simply an indirect way of returning her own kindness.

"I'm so glad you and Gus have become such good friends," she said

---

1. This amount of money in 1905 was roughly equivalent to twelve thousand dollars in the late 1980s.

approvingly. "It's too delightful of you to be so nice to him, and put up with all his tiresome stories. I know what they are, because I had to listen to them when we were engaged—I'm sure he is telling the same ones still. And now I shan't always have to be asking Carry Fisher here to keep him in a good-humour. She's a perfect vulture, you know; and she has n't the least moral sense. She is always getting Gus to speculate for her, and I'm sure she never pays when she loses."

Miss Bart could shudder at this state of things without the embarrassment of a personal application. Her own position was surely quite different. There could be no question of her not paying when she lost, since Tremor had assured her that she was certain not to lose. In sending her the cheque he had explained that he had made five thousand for her out of Rosedale's "tip," and had put four thousand back in the same venture, as there was the promise of another "big rise"; she understood therefore that he was now speculating with her own money, and that she consequently owed him no more than the gratitude which such a trifling service demanded. She vaguely supposed that, to raise the first sum, he had borrowed on her securities; but this was a point over which her curiosity did not linger. It was concentrated, for the moment, on the probable date of the next "big rise."

The news of this event was received by her some weeks later, on the occasion of Jack Stepney's marriage to Miss Van Osburgh. As a cousin of the bridegroom, Miss Bart had been asked to act as bridesmaid; but she had declined on the plea that, since she was much taller than the other attendant virgins, her presence might mar the symmetry of the group. The truth was, she had attended too many brides to the altar: when next seen there she meant to be the chief figure in the ceremony. She knew the pleasantries made at the expense of young girls who have been too long before the public, and she was resolved to avoid such assumptions of youthfulness as might lead people to think her older than she really was.

The Van Osburgh marriage was celebrated in the village church near the paternal estate on the Hudson. It was the "simple country wedding" to which guests are convoyed in special trains, and from which the hordes of the uninvited have to be fended off by the intervention of the police. While these sylvan rites were taking place, in a church packed with fashion and festooned with orchids, the representatives of the press were threading their way, note-book in hand, through the labyrinth of wedding presents, and the agent of a cinematograph syndicate was setting up his apparatus at the church door. It was the kind of scene in which Lily had often pictured herself as taking the principal part, and on this occasion the fact that she was once more merely a casual spectator, instead of the mystically veiled figure occupying the centre of attention, strengthened her resolve to assume the latter part before the year was over. The fact that her immediate anxieties were relieved did not blind her to a possibility of their recurrence; it merely gave her enough buoyancy to rise once more above her doubts and feel a renewed faith in her beauty, her power, and her general fitness to attract a brilliant destiny. It could not be that one conscious of such aptitudes for mastery and enjoyment was doomed to a perpetuity of failure; and her mistakes looked easily reparable in the light of her restored self-confidence.

A special appositeness was given to these reflections by the discovery, in a neighbouring pew, of the serious profile and neatly-trimmed beard of Mr. Percy Gryce. There was something almost bridal in his own aspect: his large white gardenia had a symbolic air that struck Lily as a good omen. After all, seen in an assemblage of his kind he was not ridiculous-looking: a friendly critic might have called his heaviness weighty, and he was at his best in the attitude of vacant passivity which brings out the oddities of the restless. She fancied he was the kind of man whose sentimental associations would be stirred by the conventional imagery of a wedding, and she pictured herself, in the seclusion of the Van Osburgh conservatories, playing skilfully upon sensibilities thus prepared for her touch. In fact, when she looked at the other women about her, and recalled the image she had brought away from her own glass, it did not seem as though any special skill would be needed to repair her blunder and bring him once more to her feet.

The sight of Selden's dark head, in a pew almost facing her, disturbed for a moment the balance of her complacency. The rise of her blood as their eyes met was succeeded by a contrary motion, a wave of resistance and withdrawal. She did not wish to see him again, not because she feared his influence, but because his presence always had the effect of cheapening her aspirations, of throwing her whole world out of focus. Besides, he was a living reminder of the worst mistake in her career, and the fact that he had been its cause did not soften her feelings toward him. She could still imagine an ideal state of existence in which, all else being superadded, intercourse with Selden might be the last touch of luxury; but in the world as it was, such a privilege was likely to cost more than it was worth.

"Lily, dear, I never saw you look so lovely! You look as if something delightful had just happened to you!"

The young lady who thus formulated her admiration of her brilliant friend did not, in her own person, suggest such happy possibilities. Miss Gertrude Farish, in fact, typified the mediocre and the ineffectual. If there were compensating qualities in her wide frank glance and the freshness of her smile, these were qualities which only the sympathetic observer would perceive before noticing that her eyes were of a workaday grey and her lips without haunting curves. Lily's own view of her wavered between pity for her limitations and impatience at her cheerful acceptance of them. To Miss Bart, as to her mother, acquiescence in dinginess was evidence of stupidity; and there were moments when, in the consciousness of her own power to look and to be so exactly what the occasion required, she almost felt that other girls were plain and inferior from choice. Certainly no one need have confessed such acquiescence in her lot as was revealed in the "useful" colour of Gerty Farish's gown and the subdued lines of her hat: it is almost as stupid to let your clothes betray that you know you are ugly as to have them proclaim that you think you are beautiful.

Of course, being fatally poor and dingy, it was wise of Gerty to have taken up philanthropy and symphony concerts; but there was something irritating in her assumption that existence yielded no higher pleasures, and that one might get as much interest and excitement out of life in a cramped flat as in the splendours of the Van Osburgh establishment. Today, however, her chirping enthusiasms did not irritate Lily. They seemed only to throw her own exceptionalness into becoming relief, and give a soaring vastness to her scheme of life.

"Do let us go and take a peep at the presents before every one else leaves the dining-room!" suggested Miss Farish, linking her arm in her friend's. It was characteristic of her to take a sentimental and unenvious interest in all the details of a wedding: she was the kind of person who always kept her handkerchief out during the service, and departed clutching a box of wedding-cake.

"Is n't everything beautifully done?" she pursued, as they entered the distant drawing-room assigned to the display of Miss Van Osburgh's bridal spoils. "I always say no one does things better than cousin Grace! Did you ever taste anything more delicious than that *mousse* of lobster with champagne sauce? I made up my mind weeks ago that I would n't miss this wedding, and just fancy how delightfully it all came about. When Lawrence Selden heard I was coming, he insisted on fetching me himself and driving me to the station, and when we go back this evening I am to dine with him at Sherry's. I really feel as excited as if I were getting married myself!"

Lily smiled: she knew that Selden had always been kind to his dull cousin, and she had sometimes wondered why he wasted so much time in such an unremunerative manner; but now the thought gave her a vague pleasure.

"Do you see him often?" she asked.

"Yes; he is very good about dropping in on Sundays. And now and then we do a play together; but lately I have n't seen much of him. He does n't look well, and he seems nervous and unsettled. The dear fellow! I do wish he would marry some nice girl. I told him so today, but he said he did n't care for the really nice ones, and the other kind did n't care for him—but that was just his joke, of course. He could never marry a girl who *was n't* nice. Oh, my dear, did you ever see such pearls?"

They had paused before the table on which the bride's jewels were displayed, and Lily's heart gave an envious throb as she caught the refraction of light from their surfaces—the milky gleam of perfectly matched pearls, the flash of rubies relieved against contrasting velvet, the intense blue rays of sapphires kindled into light by surrounding diamonds: all these precious tints enhanced and deepened by the varied art of their setting. The glow of the stones warmed Lily's veins like wine.

More completely than any other expression of wealth they symbolized the life she longed to lead, the life of fastidious aloofness and refinement in which every detail should have the finish of a jewel, and the whole form a harmonious setting to her own jewel-like rareness.

"Oh, Lily, do look at this diamond pendant—it's as big as a dinner-plate! Who can have given it!" Miss Farish bent short-sightedly over the accompanying card. "*Mr. Simon Rosedale.* What, that horrid man? Oh, yes—I remember he's a friend of Jack's, and I suppose cousin Grace had to ask him here today; but she must rather hate having to let Gwen accept such a present from him."

Lily smiled. She doubted Mrs. Van Osburgh's reluctance, but was aware of Miss Farish's habit of ascribing her own delicacies of feeling to the persons least likely to be encumbered by them.

"Well, if Gwen does n't care to be seen wearing it she can always exchange it for something else," she remarked.

"Ah, here is something so much prettier," Miss Farish continued. "Do look at this exquisite white sapphire. I'm sure the person who chose it must have taken particular pains. What is the name? Percy Gryce? Ah, then I'm not surprised!" She smiled significantly as she replaced the card. "Of course you've heard that he's perfectly devoted to Evie Van Osburgh? Cousin Grace is so pleased about it—it's quite a romance! He met her first at the George Dorsets', only about six weeks ago, and it's just the nicest possible marriage for dear Evie. Oh, I don't mean the money—of course she has plenty of her own—but she's such a quiet stay-at-home kind of girl, and it seems he has just the same tastes; so they are exactly suited to each other."

Lily stood staring vacantly at the white sapphire on its velvet bed. Evie Van Osburgh and Percy Gryce? The names rang derisively through her brain. *Evie Van Osburgh?* The youngest, dumpiest, dullest of the four dull and dumpy daughters whom Mrs. Van Osburgh, with unsurpassed astuteness, had "placed" one by one in enviable niches of existence! Ah, lucky girls who grow up in the shelter of a mother's love—a mother who knows how to contrive opportunities without conceding favours, how to take advantage of propinquity without allowing appetite to be dulled by habit! The cleverest girl may miscalculate where her own interests are concerned, may yield too much at one moment and withdraw too far at the next: it takes a mother's unerring vigilance and forsight to land her daughters safely in the arms of wealth and suitability.

Lily's passing light-heartedness sank beneath a renewed sense of failure. Life was too stupid, too blundering! Why should Percy Gryce's millions be joined to another great fortune, why should this clumsy girl be put in possession of powers she would never know how to use?

She was roused from these speculations by a familiar touch on her arm, and turning saw Gus Trenor beside her. She felt a thrill of vexation: what right had he to touch her? Luckily Gerty Farish had wandered off to the next table, and they were alone.

Trenor, looking stouter than ever in his tight frockcoat, and unbecomingly flushed by the bridal libations, gazed at her with undisguised approval.

"By Jove, Lily, you do look a stunner!" He had slipped insensibly into the use of her Christian name, and she had never found the right moment to correct him. Besides, in her set all the men and women called each other by their Christian names; it was only on Trenor's lips that the familiar address had an unpleasant significance.

"Well," he continued, still jovially impervious to her annoyance, "have you made up your mind which of these little trinkets you mean to duplicate at Tiffany's tomorrow? I've got a cheque for you in my pocket that will go a long way in that line!"

Lily gave him a startled look: his voice was louder than usual, and the room was beginning to fill with people. But as her glance assured her that they were still beyond ear-shot a sense of pleasure replaced her apprehension.

"Another dividend?" she asked, smiling and drawing near him in the desire not to be overheard.

"Well, not exactly: I sold out on the rise and I've pulled off four thou' for you. Not so bad for a beginner, eh? I suppose you'll begin to think you're a pretty knowing speculator. And perhaps you won't think poor old Gus such an awful ass as some people do."

"I think you the kindest of friends; but I can't thank you properly now."

She let her eyes shine into his with a look that made up for the hand-clasp he would have claimed if they had been alone—and how glad she was that they were not! The news filled her with the glow produced by a sudden cessation of physical pain. The world was not so stupid and blundering after all: now and then a stroke of luck came to the unluckiest. At the thought her spirits began to rise: it was characteristic of her that one trifling piece of good fortune should give wings to all her hopes. Instantly came the reflection that Percy Gryce was not irretrievably lost; and she smiled to think of the excitement of recapturing him from Evie Van Osburgh. What chance could such a simpleton have against her if she chose to exert herself? She glanced about, hoping to catch a glimpse of Gryce; but her eyes lit instead on the glossy countenance of Mr. Rosedale, who was slipping through the crowd with an air half obsequious, half obtrusive, as though, the moment his presence was recognized, it would swell to the dimensions of the room.

Not wishing to be the means of effecting this enlargement, Lily quickly transferred her glance to Trenor, to whom the expression of her gratitude seemed not to have brought the complete gratification she had meant it to give.

"Hang thanking me—I don't want to be thanked, but I *should* like the chance to say two words to you now and then," he grumbled. "I thought you were going to spend the whole autumn with us, and I've hardly laid eyes on you for the last month. Why can't you come back to Bellomont this evening? We're all alone, and Judy is as cross as two sticks. Do come and cheer a fellow up. If you say yes I'll run you over in the motor, and you can telephone your maid to bring your traps from town by the next train."

Lily shook her head with a charming semblance of regret. "I wish I could—but it's quite impossible. My aunt has come back to town, and I must be with her for the next few days."

"Well, I've seen a good deal less of you since we've got to be such pals than I used to when you were Judy's friend," he continued with unconscious penetration.

"When I was Judy's friend? Am I not her friend still? Really, you say the most absurd things! If I were always at Bellomont you would tire of me much sooner than Judy—but come and see me at my aunt's the next afternoon you are in town; then we can have a nice quiet talk, and you can tell me how I had better invest my fortune."

It was true that, during the last three or four weeks, she had absented herself from Bellomont on the pretext of having other visits to pay; but she now began to feel that the reckoning she had thus contrived to evade had rolled up interest in the interval.

The prospect of the nice quiet talk did not appear as all-sufficing to Trenor as she had hoped, and his brows continued to lower as he said: "Oh, I don't know that I can promise you a fresh tip every day. But there's one thing you might do for me; and that is, just to be a little civil to Rosedale. Judy has promised to ask him to dine when we get to town, but I can't induce her to have him at Bellomont, and if you would let me bring him up now it would make a lot of difference. I don't believe two women have spoken to him this afternoon, and I can tell you he's a chap it pays to be decent to."

Miss Bart made an impatient movement, but suppressed the words which seemed about to accompany it. After all, this was an unexpectedly easy way of acquitting her debt; and had she not reasons of her own for wishing to be civil to Mr. Rosedale?

"Oh, bring him by all means," she said smiling; "perhaps I can get a tip out of him on my own account."

Trenor paused abruptly, and his eyes fixed themselves on hers with a look which made her change colour.

"I say, you know—you'll please remember he's a blooming bounder," he said; and with a slight laugh she turned toward the open window near which they had been standing.

The throng in the room had increased, and she felt a desire for space and fresh air. Both of these she found on the terrace, where only a few men were lingering over cigarettes and liqueur, while scattered couples strolled across the lawn to the autumn-tinted borders of the flower-garden.

As she emerged, a man moved toward her from the knot of smokers, and she found herself face to face with Selden. The stir of the pulses which his nearness always caused was increased by a slight sense of constraint. They had not met since their Sunday afternoon walk at Bello-

mont, and that episode was still so vivid to her that she could hardly
believe him to be less conscious of it. But his greeting expressed no more
than the satisfaction which every pretty woman expects to see reflected
in masculine eyes; and the discovery, if distasteful to her vanity, was
reassuring to her nerves. Between the relief of her escape from Trenor,
and the vague apprehension of her meeting with Rosedale, it was pleasant to rest a moment on the sense of complete understanding which
Lawrence Selden's manner always conveyed.

"This is luck," he said smiling. "I was wondering if I should be able
to have a word with you before the special snatches us away. I came with
Gerty Farish, and promised not to let her miss the train, but I am sure
she is still extracting sentimental solace from the wedding presents. She
appears to regard their number and value as evidence of the disinterested
affection of the contracting parties."

There was not the least trace of embarrassment in his voice, and as
he spoke, leaning slightly against the jamb of the window, and letting
his eyes rest on her in the frank enjoyment of her grace, she felt with a
faint chill of regret that he had gone back without an effort to the footing
on which they had stood before their last talk together. Her vanity was
stung by the sight of his unscathed smile. She longed to be to him something more than a piece of sentient prettiness, a passing diversion to his
eyes and brain; and the longing betrayed itself in her reply.

"Ah," she said, "I envy Gerty that power she has of dressing up with
romance all our ugly and prosaic arrangements! I have never recovered
my self-respect since you showed me how poor and unimportant my
ambitions were."

The words were hardly spoken when she realized their infelicity. It
seemed to be her fate to appear at her worst to Selden.

"I thought, on the contrary," he returned lightly, "that I had been the
means of proving they were more important to you than anything else."

It was as if the eager current of her being had been checked by a
sudden obstacle which drove it back upon itself. She looked at him helplessly, like a hurt or frightened child: this real self of hers, which he had
the faculty of drawing out of the depths, was so little accustomed to go
alone!

The appeal of her helplessness touched in him, as it always did, a
latent chord of inclination. It would have meant nothing to him to discover that his nearness made her more brilliant, but this glimpse of a
twilight mood to which he alone had the clue seemed once more to set
him in a world apart with her.

"At least you can't think worse things of me than you say!" she exclaimed
with a trembling laugh; but before he could answer, the flow of comprehension between them was abruptly stayed by the reappearance of Gus
Trenor, who advanced with Mr. Rosedale in his wake.

"Hang it, Lily, I thought you'd given me the slip: Rosedale and I have
been hunting all over for you!"

His voice had a note of conjugal familiarity: Miss Bart fancied she detected in Rosedale's eye a twinkling perception of the fact, and the idea turned her dislike of him to repugnance.

She returned his profound bow with a slight nod, made more disdainful by the sense of Selden's surprise that she should number Rosedale among her acquaintances. Trenor had turned away, and his companion continued to stand before Miss Bart, alert and expectant, his lips parted in a smile at whatever she might be about to say, and his very back conscious of the privilege of being seen with her.

It was the moment for tact; for the quick bridging over of gaps; but Selden still leaned against the window, a detached observer of the scene, and under the spell of his observation Lily felt herself powerless to exert her usual arts. The dread of Selden's suspecting that there was any need for her to propitiate such a man as Rosedale checked the trivial phrases of politeness. Rosedale still stood before her in an expectant attitude, and she continued to face him in silence, her glance just level with his polished baldness. The look put the finishing touch to what her silence implied.

He reddened slowly, shifting from one foot to the other, fingered the plump black pearl in his tie, and gave a nervous twist to his moustache; then, running his eye over her, he drew back, and said, with a side-glance at Selden: "Upon my soul, I never saw a more ripping get-up. Is that the last creation of the dress-maker you go to see at the Benedick? If so, I wonder all the other women don't go to her too!"

The words were projected sharply against Lily's silence, and she saw in a flash that her own act had given them their emphasis. In ordinary talk they might have passed unheeded; but following on her prolonged pause they acquired a special meaning. She felt, without looking, that Selden had immediately seized it, and would inevitably connect the allusion with her visit to himself. The consciousness increased her irritation against Rosedale, but also her feeling that now, if ever, was the moment to propitiate him, hateful as it was to do so in Selden's presence.

"How do you know the other women don't go to my dress-maker?" she returned. "You see I'm not afraid to give her address to my friends!"

Her glance and accent so plainly included Rosedale in this privileged circle that his small eyes puckered with gratification, and a knowing smile drew up his moustache.

"By Jove, you need n't be!" he declared. "You could give 'em the whole outfit and win at a canter!"

"Ah, that's nice of you; and it would be nicer still if you would carry me off to a quiet corner, and get me a glass of lemonade or some innocent drink before we all have to rush for the train."

She turned away as she spoke, letting him strut at her side through the gathering groups on the terrace, while every nerve in her throbbed with the consciousness of what Selden must have thought of the scene.

But under her angry sense of the perverseness of things, and the light surface of her talk with Rosedale, a third idea persisted: she did not mean to leave without an attempt to discover the truth about Percy Gryce. Chance, or perhaps his own resolve, had kept them apart since his hasty withdrawal from Bellomont; but Miss Bart was an expert in making the most of the unexpected, and the distasteful incidents of the last few minutes—the revelation to Selden of precisely that part of her life which she most wished him to ignore—increased her longing for shelter, for escape from such humiliating contingencies. Any definite situation would be more tolerable than this buffeting of chances, which kept her in an attitude of uneasy alertness toward every possibility of life.

Indoors there was a general sense of dispersal in the air, as of an audience gathering itself up for departure after the principal actors had left the stage; but among the remaining groups, Lily could discover neither Gryce nor the youngest Miss Van Osburgh. That both should be missing struck her with foreboding; and she charmed Mr. Rosedale by proposing that they should make their way to the conservatories at the farther end of the house. There were just enough people left in the long suite of rooms to make their progress conspicuous, and Lily was aware of being followed by looks of amusement and interrogation, which glanced off as harmlessly from her indifference as from her companion's self-satisfaction. She cared very little at that moment about being seen with Rosedale: all her thoughts were centred on the object of her search. The latter, however, was not discoverable in the conservatories, and Lily, oppressed by a sudden conviction of failure, was casting about for a way to rid herself of her now superfluous companion, when they came upon Mrs. Van Osburgh, flushed and exhausted, but beaming with the consciousness of duty performed.

She glanced at them a moment with the benign but vacant eye of the tired hostess, to whom her guests have become mere whirling spots in a kaleidoscope of fatigue; then her attention became suddenly fixed, and she seized on Miss Bart with a confidential gesture.

"My dear Lily, I have n't had time for a word with you, and now I suppose you are just off. Have you seen Evie? She's been looking everywhere for you: she wanted to tell you her little secret; but I daresay you have guessed it already. The engagement is not to be announced till next week—but you are such a friend of Mr. Gryce's that they both wished you to be the first to know of their happiness."

IX

In Mrs. Peniston's youth, fashion had returned to town in October; therefore on the tenth day of the month the blinds of her Fifth Avenue residence were drawn up, and the eyes of the Dying Gladiator in bronze [1] who occupied the drawing-room window resumed their survey of that deserted thoroughfare.

1. A copy of a famous statue in the Capitoline Museum in Rome depicting a wounded Gaul; reproductions such as this one were very popular in the United States in the nineteenth century. See p. 304.

The first two weeks after her return represented to Mrs. Peniston the domestic equivalent of a religious retreat. She "went through" the linen and blankets in the precise spirit of the penitent exploring the inner folds of conscience; she sought for moths as the stricken soul seeks for lurking infirmities. The topmost shelf of every closet was made to yield up its secret, cellar and coal-bin were probed to their darkest depths and, as a final stage in the lustral rites, the entire house was swathed in penitential white and deluged with expiatory soapsuds.

It was on this phase of the proceedings that Miss Bart entered on the afternoon of her return from the Van Osburgh wedding. The journey back to town had not been calculated to soothe her nerves. Though Evie Van Osburgh's engagement was still officially a secret, it was one of which the innumerable intimate friends of the family were already possessed; and the trainful of returning guests buzzed with allusions and anticipations. Lily was acutely aware of her own part in this drama of innuendo: she knew the exact quality of the amusement the situation evoked. The crude forms in which her friends took their pleasure included a loud enjoyment of such complications: the zest of surprising destiny in the act of playing a practical joke. Lily knew well enough how to bear herself in difficult situations. She had, to a shade, the exact manner between victory and defeat: every insinuation was shed without an effort by the bright indifference of her manner. But she was beginning to feel the strain of the attitude; the reaction was more rapid, and she lapsed to a deeper self-disgust.

As was always the case with her, this moral repulsion found a physical outlet in a quickened distaste for her surroundings. She revolted from the complacent ugliness of Mrs. Peniston's black walnut, from the slippery gloss of the vestibule tiles, and the mingled odour of sapolio and furniture-polish that met her at the door.

The stairs were still carpetless, and on the way up to her room she was arrested on the landing by an encroaching tide of soapsuds. Gathering up her skirts, she drew aside with an impatient gesture; and as she did so she had the odd sensation of having already found herself in the same situation but in different surroundings. It seemed to her that she was again descending the staircase from Selden's rooms; and looking down to remonstrate with the dispenser of the soapy flood, she found herself met by a lifted stare which had once before confronted her under similar circumstances. It was the char-woman of the Benedick who, resting on crimson elbows, examined her with the same unflinching curiosity, the same apparent reluctance to let her pass. On this occasion, however, Miss Bart was on her own ground.

"Don't you see that I wish to go by? Please move your pail," she said sharply.

The woman at first seemed not to hear; then, without a word of excuse, she pushed back her pail and dragged a wet floor-cloth across the landing, keeping her eyes fixed on Lily while the latter swept by. It was insufferable that Mrs. Peniston should have such creatures about the house; and Lily entered her room resolved that the woman should be dismissed that evening.

Mrs. Peniston, however, was at the moment inaccessible to remonstrance: since early morning she had been shut up with her maid, going over her furs, a process which formed the culminating episode in the drama of household renovation. In the evening also Lily found herself alone, for her aunt, who rarely dined out, had responded to the summons of a Van Alstyne cousin who was passing through town. The house, in its state of unnatural immaculateness and order, was as dreary as a tomb, and as Lily, turning from her brief repast between shrouded sideboards, wandered into the newly-uncovered glare of the drawing-room she felt as though she were buried alive in the stifling limits of Mrs. Peniston's existence.

She usually contrived to avoid being at home during the season of domestic renewal. On the present occasion, however, a variety of reasons had combined to bring her to town; and foremost among them was the fact that she had fewer invitations than usual for the autumn. She had so long been accustomed to pass from one country-house to another, till the close of the holidays brought her friends to town, that the unfilled gaps of time confronting her produced a sharp sense of waning popularity. It was as she had said to Selden—people were tired of her. They would welcome her in a new character, but as Miss Bart they knew her by heart. She knew herself by heart too, and was sick of the old story. There were moments when she longed blindly for anything different, anything strange, remote and untried; but the utmost reach of her imagination did not go beyond picturing her usual life in a new setting. She could not figure herself as anywhere but in a drawing-room, diffusing elegance as a flower sheds perfume.

Meanwhile, as October advanced she had to face the alternative of returning to the Trenors or joining her aunt in town. Even the desolating dulness of New York in October, and the soapy discomforts of Mrs. Peniston's interior, seemed preferable to what might await her at Bellomont; and with an air of heroic devotion she announced her intention of remaining with her aunt till the holidays.

Sacrifices of this nature are sometimes received with feelings as mixed as those which actuate them; and Mrs. Peniston remarked to her confidential maid that, if any of the family were to be with her at such a crisis (though for forty years she had been thought competent to see to the hanging of her own curtains), she would certainly have preferred Miss Grace to Miss Lily. Grace Stepney was an obscure cousin, of adaptable manners and vicarious interests, who "ran in" to sit with Mrs. Peniston when Lily dined out too continuously; who played bézique, picked up dropped stitches, read out the deaths from the Times, and sincerely admired the purple satin drawing-room curtains, the Dying Gladiator in the window, and the seven-by-five painting of Niagara which represented the one artistic excess of Mr. Peniston's temperate career.

Mrs. Peniston, under ordinary circumstances, was as much bored by her excellent cousin as the recipient of such services usually is by the person who performs them. She greatly preferred the brilliant and unreliable Lily, who did not know one end of a crochet-needle from the other, and had frequently wounded her susceptibilities by suggesting that the drawing-room should be "done over." But when it came to hunting for missing napkins, or helping to decide whether the backstairs needed recarpeting, Grace's judgment was certainly sounder than Lily's: not to mention the fact that the latter resented the smell of beeswax and brown soap, and behaved as though she thought a house ought to keep clean of itself, without extraneous assistance.

Seated under the cheerless blaze of the drawing-room chandelier—Mrs. Peniston never lit the lamps unless there was "company"—Lily seemed to watch her own figure retreating down vistas of neutral-tinted dulness to a middle age like Grace Stepney's. When she ceased to amuse Judy Trenor and her friends she would have to fall back on amusing Mrs. Peniston; whichever way she looked she saw only a future of servitude to the whims of others, never the possibility of asserting her own eager individuality.

A ring at the door-bell, sounding emphatically through the empty house, roused her suddenly to the extent of her boredom. It was as though all the weariness of the past months had culminated in the vacuity of that interminable evening. If only the ring meant a summons from the outer world—a token that she was still remembered and wanted!

After some delay a parlour-maid presented herself with the announcement that there was a person outside who was asking to see Miss Bart; and on Lily's pressing for a more specific description, she added:

"It's Mrs. Haffen, Miss; she won't say what she wants."

Lily, to whom the name conveyed nothing, opened the door upon a woman in a battered bonnet, who stood firmly planted under the hall-light. The glare of the unshaded gas shone familiarly on her pock-marked face and the reddish baldness visible through thin strands of straw-coloured hair. Lily looked at the char-woman in surprise.

"Do you wish to see me?" she asked.

"I should like to say a word to you, Miss." The tone was neither aggressive nor conciliatory: it revealed nothing of the speaker's errand. Nevertheless, some precautionary instinct warned Lily to withdraw beyond earshot of the hovering parlour-maid.

She signed to Mrs. Haffen to follow her into the drawing-room, and closed the door when they had entered.

"What is it that you wish?" she enquired.

The char-woman, after the manner of her kind, stood with her arms folded in her shawl. Unwinding the latter, she produced a small parcel wrapped in dirty newspaper.

"I have something here that you might like to see, Miss Bart." She spoke the name with an unpleasant emphasis, as though her knowing it made a part of her reason for being there. To Lily the intonation sounded like a threat.

"You have found something belonging to me?" she asked, extending her hand.

Mrs. Haffen drew back. "Well, if it comes to that, I guess it's mine as much as anybody's," she returned.

Lily looked at her perplexedly. She was sure, now, that her visitor's manner conveyed a threat; but, expert as she was in certain directions, there was nothing in her experience to prepare her for the exact significance of the present scene. She felt, however, that it must be ended as promptly as possible.

"I don't understand; if this parcel is not mine, why have you asked for me?"

The woman was unabashed by the question. She was evidently prepared to answer it, but like all her class she had to go a long way back to make a beginning, and it was only after a pause that she replied: "My husband was janitor to the Benedick till the first of the month; since then he can't get nothing to do."

Lily remained silent and she continued: "It wasn't no fault of our own, neither: the agent had another man he wanted the place for, and we was put out, bag and baggage, just to suit his fancy. I had a long sickness last winter, and an operation that ate up all we'd put by; and it's hard for me and the children, Haffen being so long out of a job."

After all, then, she had come only to ask Miss Bart to find a place for her husband; or, more probably, to seek the young lady's intervention with Mrs. Peniston. Lily had such an air of always getting what she wanted that she was used to being appealed to as an intermediary, and, relieved of her vague apprehension, she took refuge in the conventional formula.

"I am sorry you have been in trouble," she said.

"Oh, that we have, Miss, and it's on'y just beginning. If on'y we'd 'a got another situation—but the agent, he's dead against us. It ain't no fault of ours, neither, but——"

At this point Lily's impatience overcame her. "If you have anything to say to me——" she interposed.

The woman's resentment of the rebuff seemed to spur her lagging ideas.

"Yes, Miss; I'm coming to that," she said. She paused again, with her eyes on Lily, and then continued, in a tone of diffuse narrative: "When we was at the Benedick I had charge of some of the gentlemen's rooms; leastways, I swep' 'em out on Saturdays. Some of the gentlemen got the greatest sight of letters: I never saw the like of it. Their waste-paper baskets 'd be fairly brimming, and papers falling over on the floor. Maybe havin' so many is how they get so careless. Some of 'em is worse than others. Mr. Selden, Mr. Lawrence Selden, he was always one of the carefullest: burnt his letters in winter, and tore 'em in little bits in summer. But sometimes he'd have so many he'd just bunch 'em together, the way the others did, and tear the lot through once—like this."

While she spoke she had loosened the string from the parcel in her hand, and now she drew forth a letter which she laid on the table between Miss Bart and herself. As she had said, the letter was torn in two; but with a rapid gesture she laid the torn edges together and smoothed out the page.

A wave of indignation swept over Lily. She felt herself in the presence of something vile, as yet but dimly conjectured—the kind of vileness of which people whispered, but which she had never thought of as touching her own life. She drew back with a motion of disgust, but her withdrawal was checked by a sudden discovery: under the glare of Mrs. Peniston's chandelier she had recognized the hand-writing of the letter. It was a large disjointed hand, with a flourish of masculinity which but slightly disguised its rambling weakness, and the words, scrawled in heavy ink on pale-tinted note-paper, smote on Lily's ear as though she had heard them spoken.

At first she did not grasp the full import of the situation. She understood only that before her lay a letter written by Bertha Dorset, and addressed, presumably, to Lawrence Selden. There was no date, but the blackness of the ink proved the writing to be comparatively recent. The packet in Mrs. Haffen's hand doubtless contained more letters of the same kind—a dozen, Lily conjectured from its thickness. The letter before her was short, but its few words, which had leapt into her brain before she was conscious of reading them, told a long history—a history over which, for the last four years, the friends of the writer had smiled and shrugged, viewing it merely as one among the countless "good situations" of the mundane comedy. Now the other side presented itself to Lily, the volcanic nether side of the surface over which conjecture and innuendo glide so lightly till the first fissure turns their whisper to a shriek. Lily knew that there is nothing society resents so much as having given its protection to those who have not known how to profit by it: it is for having betrayed its connivance that the body social punishes the offender who is found out. And in this case there was no doubt of the issue. The code of Lily's world decreed that a woman's husband should be the only judge of her conduct: she was technically above suspicion while she had the shelter of his approval, or even of his indifference. But with a man of George Dorset's temper there could be no thought of condonation—the possessor of his wife's letters could overthrow with a touch the whole structure of her existence. And into what hands Bertha Dorset's secret had been delivered! For a moment the irony of the coincidence tinged Lily's disgust with a confused sense of triumph. But the disgust prevailed—all her instinctive resistances, of taste, of training, of blind inherited scruples, rose against the other feeling. Her strongest sense was one of personal contamination.

She moved away, as though to put as much distance as possible between herself and her visitor. "I know nothing of these letters," she said; "I have no idea why you have brought them here."

Mrs. Haffen faced her steadily. "I'll tell you why, Miss. I brought 'em to you to sell, because I ain't got no other way of raising money, and if we don't pay our rent by tomorrow night we'll be put out. I never done anythin' of the kind before, and if you'd speak to Mr. Selden or to Mr. Rosedale about getting Haffen taken on again at the Benedick—I seen you talking to Mr. Rosedale on the steps that day you come out of Mr. Selden's rooms——"

The blood rushed to Lily's forehead. She understood now—Mrs. Haffen supposed her to be the writer of the letters. In the first leap of her anger she was about to ring and order the woman out; but an obscure impulse restrained her. The mention of Selden's name had started a new train of thought. Bertha Dorset's letters were nothing to her—they might go where the current of chance carried them! But Selden was inextricably involved in their fate. Men do not, at worst, suffer much from such exposure; and in this instance the flash of divination which had carried the meaning of the letters to Lily's brain had revealed also that they were appeals—repeated and therefore probably unanswered—for the renewal of a tie which time had evidently relaxed. Nevertheless, the fact that the correspondence had been allowed to fall into strange hands would convict Selden of negligence in a matter where the world holds it least pardonable; and there were graver risks to consider where a man of Dorset's ticklish balance was concerned.

If she weighed all these things it was unconsciously: she was aware only of feeling that Selden would wish the letters rescued, and that therefore she must obtain possession of them. Beyond that her mind did not travel. She had, indeed, a quick vision of returning the packet to Bertha Dorset, and of the opportunities the restitution offered; but this thought lit up abysses from which she shrank back ashamed.

Meanwhile Mrs. Haffen, prompt to perceive her hesitation, had already opened the packet and ranged its contents on the table. All the letters had been pieced together with strips of thin paper. Some were in small fragments, the others merely torn in half. Though there were not many, thus spread out they nearly covered the table. Lily's glance fell on a word here and there—then she said in a low voice: "What do you wish me to pay you?"

Mrs. Haffen's face reddened with satisfaction. It was clear that the young lady was badly frightened, and Mrs. Haffen was the woman to make the most of such fears. Anticipating an easier victory than she had foreseen, she named an exorbitant sum.

But Miss Bart showed herself a less ready prey than might have been expected from her imprudent opening. She refused to pay the price named, and after a moment's hesitation, met it by a counter-offer of half the amount.

Mrs. Haffen immediately stiffened. Her hand travelled toward the outspread letters, and folding them slowly, she made as though to restore them to their wrapping.

"I guess they're worth more to you than to me, Miss, but the poor has got to live as well as the rich," she observed sententiously.

Lily was throbbing with fear, but the insinuation fortified her resistance.

"You are mistaken," she said indifferently. "I have offered all I am willing to give for the letters; but there may be other ways of getting them."

Mrs. Haffen raised a suspicious glance: she was too experienced not to know that the traffic she was engaged in had perils as great as its rewards, and she had a vision of the elaborate machinery of revenge which a word of this commanding young lady's might set in motion. She applied the corner of her shawl to her eyes, and murmured through it that no good came of bearing too hard on the poor, but that for her part she had never been mixed up in such business before, and that on her honour as a Christian all she and Haffen had thought of was that the letters mustn't go any farther.

Lily stood motionless, keeping between herself and the char-woman the greatest distance compatible with the need of speaking in low tones. The idea of bargaining for the letters was intolerable to her, but she knew that, if she appeared to weaken, Mrs. Haffen would at once increase her original demand.

She could never afterward recall how long the duel lasted, or what was the decisive stroke which finally, after a lapse of time recorded in minutes by the clock, in hours by the precipitate beat of her pulses, put her in possession of the letters; she knew only that the door had finally closed, and that she stood alone with the packet in her hand.

She had no idea of reading the letters; even to unfold Mrs. Haffen's dirty newspaper would have seemed degrading. But what did she intend to do with its contents? The recipient of the letters had meant to destroy them, and it was her duty to carry out his intention. She had no right to keep them—to do so was to lessen whatever merit lay in having secured their possession. But how destroy them so effectually that there should be no second risk of their falling in such hands? Mrs. Peniston's icy drawing-room grate shone with a forbidding lustre: the fire, like the lamps, was never lit except when there was company.

Miss Bart was turning to carry the letters upstairs when she heard the opening of the outer door, and her aunt entered the drawing-room. Mrs. Peniston was a small plump woman, with a colourless skin lined with trivial wrinkles. Her grey hair was arranged with precision, and her clothes looked excessively new and yet slightly old-fashioned. They were always black and tightly fitting, with an expensive glitter: she was the kind of woman who wore jet at breakfast. Lily had never seen her when she was not cuirassed in shining black, with small tight boots, and an air of being packed and ready to start; yet she never started.

She looked about the drawing-room with an expression of minute scrutiny. "I saw a streak of light under one of the blinds as I drove up: it's extraordinary that I can never teach that woman to draw them down evenly."

Having corrected the irregularity, she seated herself on one of the glossy purple arm-chairs; Mrs. Peniston always sat on a chair, never in it. Then she turned her glance to Miss Bart.

"My dear, you look tired; I suppose it's the excitement of the wedding. Cornelia Van Alstyne was full of it: Molly was there, and Gerty Farish ran in for a minute to tell us about it. I think it was odd, their serving melons before the *consummé*: a wedding breakfast should always begin with *consummé*. Molly didn't care for the bridesmaids' dresses. She had it straight from Julia Melson that they cost three hundred dollars apiece at Céleste's, but she says they didn't look it. I'm glad you decided not to be a bridesmaid; that shade of salmon-pink wouldn't have suited you."

Mrs. Peniston delighted in discussing the minutest details of festivities in which she had not taken part. Nothing would have induced her to undergo the exertion and fatigue of attending the Van Osburgh wedding, but so great was her interest in the event that, having heard two versions of it, she now prepared to extract a third from her niece. Lily, however, had been deplorably careless in noting the particulars of the entertainment. She had failed to observe the colour of Mrs. Van Osburgh's gown, and could not even say whether the old Van Osburgh Sévres had been used at the bride's table: Mrs. Peniston, in short, found that she was of more service as a listener than as a narrator.

"Really, Lily, I don't see why you took the trouble to go to the wedding, if you don't remember what happened or whom you saw there. When I was a girl I used to keep the *menu* of every dinner I went to, and write the names of the people on the back; and I never threw away my cotillion favours till after your uncle's death, when it seemed unsuitable to have so many coloured things about the house. I had a whole closet-full, I remember; and I can tell to this day what balls I got them at. Molly Van Alstyne reminds me of what I was at that age; it's wonderful how she notices. She was able to tell her mother exactly how the wedding-dress was cut, and we knew at once, from the fold in the back, that it must have come from Paquin."[2]

Mrs. Peniston rose abruptly, and, advancing to the ormulu clock surmounted by a helmeted Minerva, which throned on the chimney-piece between two malachite vases, passed her lace handkerchief between the helmet and its visor.

"I knew it—the parlour-maid never dusts there!" she exclaimed, triumphantly displaying a minute spot on the handkerchief; then, reseating herself, she went on: "Molly thought Mrs. Dorset the best-dressed woman at the wedding. I've no doubt her dress *did* cost more than any one else's, but I can't quite like the idea—a combination of sable and *point de Milan*.[3] It seems she goes to a new man in Paris, who won't take an order till his client has spent a day with him at his villa at Neuilly. He says he must study his subject's home life—a most peculiar arrangement, I should say! But Mrs. Dorset told Molly about it herself: she said

2. A French turn-of-the-century couturiere, Madame Paquin was the most famous woman designer of her time.

3. Fine handmade lace originating in Milan, Italy.

the villa was full of the most exquisite things and she was really sorry to leave. Molly said she never saw her looking better; she was in tremendous spirits, and said she had made a match between Evie Van Osburgh and Percy Gryce. She really seems to have a very good influence on young men. I hear she is interesting herself now in that silly Silverton boy, who has had his head turned by Carry Fisher, and has been gambling so dreadfully. Well, as I was saying, Evie is really engaged: Mrs. Dorset had her to stay with Percy Gryce, and managed it all, and Grace Van Osburgh is in the seventh heaven—she had almost despaired of marrying Evie."

Mrs. Peniston again paused, but this time her scrutiny addressed itself, not to the furniture, but to her niece.

"Cornelia Van Alstyne was so surprised: she had heard that you were to marry young Gryce. She saw the Wetheralls just after they had stopped with you at Bellomont, and Alice Wetherall was quite sure there was an engagement. She said that when Mr. Gryce left unexpectedly one morning, they all thought he had rushed to town for the ring."

Lily rose and moved toward the door.

"I believe I *am* tired: I think I will go to bed," she said; and Mrs. Peniston, suddenly distracted by the discovery that the easel sustaining the late Mr. Peniston's crayon-portrait was not exactly in line with the sofa in front if it, presented an absent-minded brow to her kiss.

In her own room Lily turned up the gas-jet and glanced toward the grate. It was as brilliantly polished as the one below, but here at least she could burn a few papers with less risk of incurring her aunt's disapproval. She made no immediate motion to do so, however, but dropping into a chair looked wearily about her. Her room was large and comfortably-furnished—it was the envy and admiration of poor Grace Stepney, who boarded; but, contrasted with the light tints and luxurious appointments of the guest-rooms where so many weeks of Lily's existence were spent, it seemed as dreary as a prison. The monumental wardrobe and bedstead of black walnut had migrated from Mr. Peniston's bedroom, and the magenta "flock" wall-paper, of a pattern dear to the early 'sixties, was hung with large steel engravings of an anecdotic character. Lily had tried to mitigate this charmless background by a few frivolous touches, in the shape of a lace-decked toilet table and a little painted desk surmounted by photographs; but the futility of the attempt struck her as she looked about the room. What a contrast to the subtle elegance of the setting she had pictured for herself—an apartment which should surpass the complicated luxury of her friends' surroundings by the whole extent of that artistic sensibility which made her feel herself their superior; in which every tint and line should combine to enhance her beauty and give distinction to her leisure! Once more the haunting sense of physical ugliness was intensified by her mental depression, so that each piece of the offending furniture seemed to thrust forth its most aggressive angle.

Her aunt's words had told her nothing new; but they had revived the vision of Bertha Dorset, smiling, flattered, victorious, holding her up to ridicule by insinuations intelligible to every member of their little group. The thought of the ridicule struck deeper than any other sensation: Lily knew every turn of the allusive jargon which could flay its victims without the shedding of blood. Her cheek burned at the recollection, and she rose and caught up the letters. She no longer meant to destroy them: that intention had been effaced by the quick corrosion of Mrs. Peniston's words.

Instead, she approached her desk, and lighting a taper, tied and sealed the packet; then she opened the wardrobe, drew out a despatch-box, and deposited the letters within it. As she did so, it struck her with a flash of irony that she was indebted to Gus Trenor for the means of buying them.

X

The autumn dragged on monotonously. Miss Bart had received one or two notes from Judy Trenor, reproaching her for not returning to Bellomont; but she replied evasively, alleging the obligation to remain with her aunt. In truth, however, she was fast wearying of her solitary existence with Mrs. Peniston, and only the excitement of spending her newly-acquired money lightened the dulness of the days.

All her life Lily had seen money go out as quickly as it came in, and whatever theories she cultivated as to the prudence of setting aside a part of her gains, she had unhappily no saving vision of the risks of the opposite course. It was a keen satisfaction to feel that, for a few months at least, she would be independent of her friends' bounty, that she could show herself abroad without wondering whether some penetrating eye would detect in her dress the traces of Judy Trenor's refurbished splendour. The fact that the money freed her temporarily from all minor obligations obscured her sense of the greater one it represented, and having never before known what it was to command so large a sum, she lingered delectably over the amusement of spending it.

It was on one of these occasions that, leaving a shop where she had spent an hour of deliberation over a dressing-case of the most complicated elegance, she ran across Miss Farish, who had entered the same establishment with the modest object of having her watch repaired. Lily was feeling unusually virtuous. She had decided to defer the purchase of the dressing-case till she should receive the bill for her new opera-cloak, and the resolve made her feel much richer than when she had entered the shop. In this mood of self-approval she had a sympathetic eye for others, and she was struck by her friend's air of dejection.

Miss Farish, it appeared, had just left the committee-meeting of a struggling charity in which she was interested. The object of the association was to provide comfortable lodgings, with a reading-room and other modest distractions, where young women of the class employed in down town offices might find a home when out of work, or in need of rest, and the first year's financial report showed so deplorably small a balance that Miss Farish, who was convinced of the urgency of the work, felt proportionately discouraged by the small amount of interest it aroused. The other-regarding sentiments had not been cultivated in Lily, and she was often bored by the relation of her friend's philanthropic efforts, but today her quick dramatizing fancy seized on the contrast between her own situation and that represented by some of Gerty's "cases." These were young girls, like herself; some perhaps pretty, some not without a trace of her finer sensibilities. She pictured herself leading such a life as theirs—a life in which achievement seemed as squalid as failure—and the vision made her shudder sympathetically. The price of the dressing-case was still in her pocket; and drawing out her little gold purse she slipped a liberal fraction of the amount into Miss Farish's hand.

The satisfaction derived from this act was all that the most ardent moralist could have desired. Lily felt a new interest in herself as a person of charitable instincts: she had never before thought of doing good with the wealth she had so often dreamed of possessing, but now her horizon was enlarged by the vision of a prodigal philanthropy. Moreover, by some obscure process of logic, she felt that her momentary burst of generosity had justified all previous extravagances, and excused any in which she might subsequently indulge. Miss Farish's surprise and gratitude confirmed this feeling, and Lily parted from her with a sense of self-esteem which she naturally mistook for the fruits of altruism.

About this time she was farther cheered by an invitation to spend the Thanksgiving week at a camp in the Adirondacks. The invitation was one which, a year earlier, would have provoked a less ready response, for the party, though organized by Mrs. Fisher, was ostensibly given by a lady of obscure origin and indomitable social ambitions, whose acquaintance Lily had hitherto avoided. Now, however, she was disposed to coincide with Mrs. Fisher's view, that it didn't matter who gave the party, as long as things were well done; and doing things well (under competent direction) was Mrs. Wellington Bry's strong point. The lady (whose consort was known as "Welly" Bry on the Stock Exchange and in sporting circles) had already sacrificed one husband, and sundry minor considerations, to her determination to get on; and, having obtained a hold on Carry Fisher, she was astute enough to perceive the wisdom of committing herself entirely to that lady's guidance. Everything, accordingly, was well done, for there was no limit to Mrs. Fisher's prodigality when she was not spending her own money, and as she remarked to her pupil, a good cook was the best introduction to society. If the company was not as select as the *cuisine*, the Welly Brys at least had the satisfaction of figuring for the first time in the society columns in company with one or two noticeable names; and foremost among these was of course Miss Bart's. The young lady was treated by her hosts with corresponding deference; and she was in the mood when such attentions are acceptable, whatever their source. Mrs. Bry's admiration was a mirror in which Lily's self-complacency recovered its lost outline. No insect hangs its nest on threads as frail as those which will sustain the weight of human vanity; and the sense of being of importance among the insignificant was enough to restore to Miss Bart the gratifying consciousness of power If these people paid court to her it proved that she was still conspicuous in the world to which they aspired; and she was not above a certain enjoyment in dazzling them by her fineness, in developing their puzzled perception of her superiorities.

Perhaps, however, her enjoyment proceeded more than she was aware from the physical stimulus of the excursion, the challenge of crisp cold and hard exercise, the responsive thrill of her body to the influences of the winter woods. She returned to town in a glow of rejuvenation, conscious of a clearer colour in her cheeks, a fresh elasticity in her muscles. The future seemed full of a vague promise, and all her apprehensions were swept out of sight on the buoyant current of her mood.

A few days after her return to town she had the unpleasant surprise of a visit from Mr. Rosedale. He came late, at the confidential hour when the tea-table still lingers by the fire in friendly expectancy; and his manner showed a readiness to adapt itself to the intimacy of the occasion.

Lily, who had a vague sense of his being somehow connected with her lucky speculations, tried to give him the welcome he expected; but there was something in the quality of his geniality which chilled her own, and she was conscious of marking each step in their acquaintance by a fresh blunder.

Mr. Rosedale—making himself promptly at home in an adjoining easy-chair, and sipping his tea critically, with the comment: "You ought to go to my man for something really good"—appeared totally unconscious of the repugnance which kept her in frozen erectness behind the urn. It was perhaps her very manner of holding herself aloof that appealed to his collector's passion for the rare and unattainable. He gave, at any rate, no sign of resenting it and seemed prepared to supply in his own manner all the ease that was lacking in hers.

His object in calling was to ask her to go to the opera in his box on the opening night, and seeing her hesitate he said persuasively: "Mrs. Fisher is coming, and I've secured a tremendous admirer of yours, who'll never forgive me if you don't accept."

As Lily's silence left him with this allusion on his hands, he added with a confidential smile: "Gus Trenor has promised to come to town on purpose. I fancy he'd go a good deal farther for the pleasure of seeing you."

Miss Bart felt an inward motion of annoyance: it was distasteful enough to hear her name coupled with Trenor's, and on Rosedale's lips the allusion was peculiarly unpleasant.

"The Trenors are my best friends—I think we should all go a long way to see each other," she said, absorbing herself in the preparation of fresh tea.

Her visitor's smile grew increasingly intimate. "Well, I wasn't thinking of Mrs. Trenor at the moment—they say Gus doesn't always, you know." Then, dimly conscious that he had not struck the right note, he added, with a well-meant effort at diversion: "How's your luck been going in Wall Street, by the way? I hear Gus pulled off a nice little pile for you last month."

Lily put down the tea-caddy with an abrupt gesture. She felt that her hands were trembling, and clasped them on her knee to steady them; but her lip trembled too, and for a moment she was afraid the tremor might communicate itself to her voice. When she spoke, however, it was in a tone of perfect lightness.

"Ah, yes—I had a little bit of money to invest, and Mr. Trenor, who helps me about such matters, advised my putting it in stocks instead of a mortgage, as my aunt's agent wanted me to do; and as it happened, I made a lucky 'turn'—is that what you call it? For you make a great many yourself, I believe."

She was smiling back at him now, relaxing the tension of her attitude, and admitting him, by imperceptible gradations of glance and manner, a step farther toward intimacy. The protective instinct always nerved her to successful dissimulation, and it was not the first time she had used her beauty to divert attention from an inconvenient topic.

When Mr. Rosedale took leave, he carried with him, not only her acceptance of his invitation, but a general sense of having comported himself in a way calculated to advance his cause. He had always believed he had a light touch and a knowing way with women, and the prompt manner in which Miss Bart (as he would have phrased it) had "come into line," confirmed his confidence in his powers of handling the skittish sex. Her way of glossing over the transaction with Trenor he regarded at once as a tribute to his own acuteness, and a confirmation of his suspicions. The girl was evidently nervous, and Mr. Rosedale, if he saw no other means of advancing his acquaintance with her, was not above taking advantage of her nervousness.

He left Lily to a passion of disgust and fear. It seemed incredible that Gus Trenor should have spoken of her to Rosedale. With all his faults, Trenor had the safeguard of his traditions, and was the less likely to overstep them because they were so purely instinctive. But Lily recalled with a pang that there were convivial moments when, as Judy had confided to her, Gus "talked foolishly": in one of these, no doubt, the fatal word had slipped from him. As for Rosedale, she did not, after the first shock, greatly care what conclusions he had drawn. Though usually adroit enough where her own interests were concerned, she made the mistake, not uncommon to persons in whom the social habits are instinctive, of supposing that the inability to acquire them quickly implies a general dulness. Because a blue-bottle bangs irrationally against a window-pane, the drawing-room naturalist may forget that under less artificial conditions it is capable of measuring distances and drawing conclusions with all the accuracy needful to its welfare; and the fact that Mr. Rosedale's drawing-room manner lacked perspective made Lily class him with Trenor and the other dull men she knew, and assume that a little flattery, and the occasional acceptance of his hospitality, would suffice to render him innocuous. However, there could be no doubt of the expediency of showing herself in his box on the opening night of the opera; and after all, since Judy Trenor had promised to take him up that winter, it was as well to reap the advantage of being first in the field.

For a day or two after Rosedale's visit, Lily's thoughts were dogged by the consciousness of Trenor's shadowy claim, and she wished she had a clearer notion of the exact nature of the transaction which seemed to have put her in his power; but her mind shrank from any unusual application, and she was always helplessly puzzled by figures. Moreover she had not seen Trenor since the day of the Van Osburgh wedding, and in his continued absence the trace of Rosedale's words was soon effaced by other impressions.

When the opening night of the opera came, her apprehensions had so completely vanished that the sight of Trenor's ruddy countenance in the back of Mr. Rosedale's box filled her with a sense of pleasant reassurance. Lily had not quite reconciled herself to the necessity of appearing as Rosedale's guest on so conspicuous an occasion, and it was a relief to find herself supported by any one of her own set—for Mrs. Fisher's social habits were too promiscuous for her presence to justify Miss Bart's.

To Lily, always inspirited by the prospect of showing her beauty in public, and conscious tonight of all the added enhancements of dress, the insistency of Trenor's gaze merged itself in the general stream of admiring looks of which she felt herself the centre. Ah, it was good to be young, to be radiant, to glow with the sense of slenderness, strength and elasticity, of well-poised lines and happy tints, to feel one's self lifted to a height apart by that incommunicable grace which is the bodily counterpart of genius!

All means seemed justifiable to attain such an end, or rather, by a happy shifting of lights with which practice had familiarized Miss Bart, the cause shrank to a pinpoint in the general brightness of the effect. But brilliant young ladies, a little blinded by their own effulgence, are apt to forget that the modest satellite drowned in their light is still performing its own revolutions and generating heat at its own rate. If Lily's poetic enjoyment of the moment was undisturbed by the base thought that her gown and opera cloak had been indirectly paid for by Gus Trenor, the latter had not sufficient poetry in his composition to lose sight of these prosaic facts. He knew only that he had never seen Lily look smarter in her life, that there wasn't a woman in the house who showed off good clothes as she did, and that hitherto he, to whom she owed the opportunity of making this display, had reaped no return beyond that of gazing at her in company with several hundred other pairs of eyes.

It came to Lily therefore as a disagreeable surprise when, in the back of the box, where they found themselves alone between two acts, Trenor said, without preamble, and in a tone of sulky authority: "Look here, Lily, how is a fellow ever to see anything of you? I'm in town three or four days in the week, and you know a line to the club will always find me, but you don't seem to remember my existence nowadays unless you want to get a tip out of me."

The fact that the remark was in distinctly bad taste did not make it any easier to answer, for Lily was vividly aware that it was not the moment for that drawing up of her slim figure and surprised lifting of the brows by which she usually quelled incipient signs of familiarity.

"I'm very much flattered by your wanting to see me," she returned, essaying lightness instead, "but, unless you have mislaid my address, it would have been easy to find me any afternoon at my aunt's—in fact, I rather expected you to look me up there."

If she hoped to mollify him by this last concession the attempt was a failure, for he only replied, with the familiar lowering of the brows that made him look his dullest when he was angry: "Hang going to your aunt's, and wasting the afternoon listening to a lot of other chaps talking to you! You know I'm not the kind to sit in a crowd and jaw—I'd always rather clear out when that sort of circus is going on. But why can't we go off somewhere on a little lark together—a nice quiet little expedition like that drive at Bellomont, the day you met me at the station?"

He leaned unpleasantly close in order to convey this suggestion, and she fancied she caught a significant aroma which explained the dark flush on his face and the glistening dampness of his forehead.

The idea that any rash answer might provoke an unpleasant outburst tempered her disgust with caution, and she answered with a laugh: "I don't see how one can very well take country drives in town, but I am not always surrounded by an admiring throng, and if you will let me know what afternoon you are coming I will arrange things so that we can have a nice quiet talk."

"Hang talking! That's what you always say," returned Trenor, whose expletives lacked variety. "You put me off with that at the Van Osburgh wedding—but the plain English of it is that, now you've got what you wanted out of me, you'd rather have any other fellow about."

His voice had risen sharply with the last words, and Lily flushed with annoyance, but she kept command of the situation and laid a persuasive hand on his arm.

"Don't be foolish, Gus; I can't let you talk to me in that ridiculous way. If you really want to see me, why shouldn't we take a walk in the Park some afternoon? I agree with you that it's amusing to be rustic in town, and if you like I'll meet you there, and we'll go and feed the squirrels, and you shall take me out on the lake in the steam-gondola."

She smiled as she spoke, letting her eyes rest on his in a way that took the edge from her banter and made him suddenly malleable to her will.

"All right, then: that's a go. Will you come tomorrow? Tomorrow at three o'clock, at the end of the Mall? I'll be there sharp, remember; you won't go back on me, Lily?"

But to Miss Bart's relief the repetition of her promise was cut short by the opening of the box door to admit George Dorset.

"You don't seem to remember my existence nowadays."

Trenor sulkily yielded his place, and Lily turned a brilliant smile on the newcomer. She had not talked with Dorset since their visit at Bellomont, but something in his look and manner told her that he recalled the friendly footing on which they had last met. He was not a man to whom the expression of admiration came easily: his long sallow face and distrustful eyes seemed always barricaded against the expansive emotions. But, where her own influence was concerned, Lily's intuitions sent out thread-like feelers, and as she made room for him on the narrow sofa she was sure he found a dumb pleasure in being near her. Few women took the trouble to make themselves agreeable to Dorset, and Lily had been kind to him at Bellomont, and was now smiling on him with a divine renewal of kindness.

"Well, here we are, in for another six months of caterwauling," he began complainingly. "Not a shade of difference between this year and last, except that the women have got new clothes and the singers haven't got new voices. My wife's musical, you know—puts me through a course of this every winter. It isn't so bad on Italian nights—then she comes late, and there's time to digest. But when they give Wagner[1] we have to rush dinner, and I pay up for it. And the draughts are damnable—asphyxia in front and pleurisy in the back. There's Trenor leaving the box without drawing the curtain! With a hide like that draughts don't make any difference. Did you ever watch Trenor eat? If you did, you'd wonder why he's alive; I suppose he's leather inside too.—But I came to say that my wife wants you to come down to our place next Sunday. Do for heaven's sake say yes. She's got a lot of bores coming—intellectual ones, I mean; that's her new line, you know, and I'm not sure it ain't worse than the music. Some of 'em have long hair, and they start an argument with the soup, and don't notice when things are handed to them. The consequence is the dinner gets cold, and I have dyspepsia. That silly ass Silverton brings them to the house—he writes poetry, you know, and Bertha and he are getting tremendously thick. She could write better than any of 'em if she chose, and I don't blame her for wanting clever fellows about; all I say is: 'Don't let me see 'em eat!' "

The gist of this strange communication gave Lily a distinct thrill of pleasure. Under ordinary circumstances, there would have been nothing surprising in an invitation from Bertha Dorset; but since the Bellomont episode an unavowed hostility had kept the two women apart. Now, with a start of inner wonder, Lily felt that her thirst for retaliation had died out. *If you would forgive your enemy*, says the Malay proverb, *first inflict a hurt on him*; and Lily was experiencing the truth of the apothegm. If she had destroyed Mrs. Dorset's letters, she might have continued to hate her; but the fact that they remained in her possession had fed her resentment to satiety.

1. Opera in New York at the turn of the century divided clearly into the Italian and the German schools with works by the Italian composers Giuseppe Verdi, Gioacchino Antonio Rossini, and Giacomo Puccini lasting about three hours and being more melodious and brilliant than operas by Richard Wagner, the prime German composer, whose music was convoluted and whose operas lasted five or six hours.

She uttered a smiling acceptance, hailing in the renewal of the tie an escape from Trenor's importunities.

XI

Meanwhile the holidays had gone by and the season was beginning. Fifth Avenue had become a nightly torrent of carriages surging upward to the fashionable quarters about the park, where illuminated windows and outspread awnings betokened the usual routine of hospitality. Other tributary currents crossed the main stream, bearing their freight to the theatres, restaurants or opera; and Mrs. Peniston, from the secluded watch-tower of her upper window, could tell to a nicety just when the chronic volume of sound was increased by the sudden influx setting toward a Van Osburgh ball, or when the multiplication of wheels meant merely that the opera was over, or that there was a big supper at Sherry's.

Mrs. Peniston followed the rise and culmination of the season as keenly as the most active sharer in its gaieties; and, as a looker-on, she enjoyed opportunities of comparison and generalization such as those who take part must proverbially forego. No one could have kept a more accurate record of social fluctuations, or have put a more unerring finger on the distinguishing features of each season: its dulness, its extravagance, its lack of balls or excess of divorces. She had a special memory for the vicissitudes of the "new people" who rose to the surface with each recurring tide, and were either submerged beneath its rush or landed triumphantly beyond the reach of envious breakers; and she was apt to display a remarkable retrospective insight into their ultimate fate, so that, when they had fulfilled their destiny, she was almost always able to say to Grace Stepney—the recipient of her prophecies—that she had known exactly what would happen.

This particular season Mrs. Peniston would have characterized as that in which everybody "felt poor" except the Welly Brys and Mr. Simon Rosedale. It had been a bad autumn in Wall Street, where prices fell in accordance with that peculiar law which proves railway stocks and bales of cotton to be more sensitive to the allotment of executive power than many estimable citizens trained to all the advantages of self-government. Even fortunes supposed to be independent of the market either betrayed a secret dependence on it, or suffered from a sympathetic affection: fashion sulked in its country-houses, or came to town incognito, general entertainments were discountenanced, and informality and short dinners became the fashion.

But society, amused for a while at playing Cinderella, soon wearied of the hearthside rôle, and welcomed the Fairy God-mother in the shape of any magician powerful enough to turn the shrunken pumpkin back again into the golden coach. The mere fact of growing richer at a time when most people's investments are shrinking, is calculated to attract envious attention; and according to Wall Street rumours, Welly Bry and Rosedale had found the secret of performing this miracle.

Rosedale, in particular, was said to have doubled his fortune, and there was talk of his buying the newly-finished house of one of the victims of the crash, who, in the space of twelve short months, had made the same number of millions, built a house in Fifth Avenue, filled a picture-gallery with old masters, entertained all New York in it, and been smuggled out of the country between a trained nurse and a doctor, while his creditors mounted guard over the old masters, and his guests explained to each other that they had dined with him only because they wanted to see the pictures. Mr. Rosedale meant to have a less meteoric career. He knew he should have to go slowly, and the instincts of his race fitted him to suffer rebuffs and put up with delays. But he was prompt to perceive that the general dulness of the season afforded him an unusual opportunity to shine, and he set about with patient industry to form a background for his growing glory. Mrs. Fisher was of immense service to him at this period. She had set off so many newcomers on the social stage that she was like one of those pieces of stock scenery which tell the experienced spectator exactly what is going to take place. But Mr. Rosedale wanted, in the long run, a more individual environment. He was sensitive to shades of difference which Miss Bart would never have credited him with perceiving, because he had no corresponding variations of manner; and it was becoming more and more clear to him that Miss Bart herself possessed precisely the complementary qualities needed to round off his social personality.

Such details did not fall within the range of Mrs. Peniston's vision. Like many minds of panoramic sweep, hers was apt to overlook the *minutiæ* of the foreground, and she was much more likely to know where Carry Fisher had found the Welly Brys' *chef* for them, than what was happening to her own niece. She was not, however, without purveyors of information ready to supplement her deficiencies. Grace Stepney's mind was like a kind of moral fly-paper, to which the buzzing items of gossip were drawn by a fatal attraction, and where they hung fast in the toils of an inexorable memory. Lily would have been surprised to know how many trivial facts concerning herself were lodged in Miss Stepney's head. She was quite aware that she was of interest to dingy people, but she assumed that there is only one form of dinginess, and that admiration for brilliancy is the natural expression of its inferior state. She knew that Gerty Farish admired her blindly, and therefore supposed that she inspired the same sentiments in Grace Stepney, whom she classified as a Gerty Farish without the saving traits of youth and enthusiasm.

In reality, the two differed from each other as much as they differed from the object of their mutual contemplation. Miss Farish's heart was a fountain of tender illusions, Miss Stepney's a precise register of facts as manifested in their relation to herself. She had sensibilities which, to Lily, would have seemed comic in a person with a freckled nose and red eye-lids, who lived in a boarding-house and admired Mrs. Peniston's drawing-room; but poor Grace's limitations gave them a more concentrated inner life, as poor soil starves certain plants into intenser efflores- cence. She had in truth no abstract propensity to malice: she did not dislike Lily because the latter was brilliant and predominant, but because she thought that Lily disliked her. It is less mortifying to believe one's self unpopular than insignificant, and vanity prefers to assume that indif- ference is a latent form of unfriendliness. Even such scant civilities as Lily accorded to Mr. Rosedale would have made Miss Stepney her friend for life; but how could she foresee that such a friend was worth cultivat- ing? How, moreover, can a young woman who has never been ignored measure the pang which this injury inflicts? And, lastly, how could Lily, accustomed to choose between a pressure of engagements, guess that she had mortally offended Miss Stepney by causing her to be excluded from one of Mrs. Peniston's infrequent dinner-parties?

Mrs. Peniston disliked giving dinners, but she had a high sense of family obligation, and on the Jack Stepneys' return from their honey- moon she felt it incumbent upon her to light the drawing-room lamps and extract her best silver from the Safe Deposit vaults. Mrs. Peniston's rare entertainments were preceded by days of heart-rending vacillation as to every detail of the feast, from the seating of the guests to the pattern of the table-cloth, and in the course of one of these preliminary discus- sions she had imprudently suggested to her cousin Grace that, as the dinner was a family affair, she might be included in it. For a week the prospect had lighted up Miss Stepney's colourless existence; then she had been given to understand that it would be more convenient to have her another day. Miss Stepney knew exactly what had happened. Lily, to whom family reunions were occasions of unalloyed dulness, had per- suaded her aunt that a dinner of "smart" people would be much more to the taste of the young couple, and Mrs. Peniston, who leaned help- lessly on her niece in social matters, had been prevailed upon to pro- nounce Grace's exile. After all, Grace could come any other day; why should she mind being put off?

It was precisely because Miss Stepney could come any other day— and because she knew her relations were in the secret of her unoccupied evenings—that this incident loomed gigantically on her horizon. She was aware that she had Lily to thank for it; and dull resentment was turned to active animosity.

Mrs. Peniston, on whom she had looked in a day or two after the dinner, laid down her crochet-work and turned abruptly from her oblique survey of Fifth Avenue.

"Gus Trenor?—Lily and Gus Trenor?" she said, growing so suddenly pale that her visitor was almost alarmed.

"Oh, cousin Julia . . . of course I don't mean . . ."

"I don't know what you *do* mean," said Mrs. Peniston, with a fright- ened quiver in her small fretful voice. "Such things were never heard of in my day. And my own niece! I'm not sure I understand you. Do people say he's in love with her?"

Mrs. Peniston's horror was genuine. Though she boasted an

unequalled familiarity with the secret chronicles of society, she had the innocence of the school-girl who regards wickedness as a part of "history," and to whom it never occurs that the scandals she reads of in lesson-hours may be repeating themselves in the next street. Mrs. Peniston had kept her imagination shrouded, like the drawing-room furniture. She knew, of course, that society was "very much changed," and that many women her mother would have thought "peculiar" were now in a position to be critical about their visiting-lists; she had discussed the perils of divorce with her rector, and had felt thankful at times that Lily was still unmarried; but the idea that any scandal could attach to a young girl's name, above all that it could be lightly coupled with that of a married man, was so new to her that she was as much aghast as if she had been accused of leaving her carpets down all summer, or of violating any of the other cardinal laws of house-keeping.

Miss Stepney, when her first fright had subsided, began to feel the superiority that greater breadth of mind confers. It was really pitiable to be as ignorant of the world as Mrs. Peniston!

She smiled at the latter's question. "People always say unpleasant things—and certainly they're a great deal together. A friend of mine met them the other afternoon in the Park—quite late, after the lamps were lit. It's a pity Lily makes herself so conspicuous."

"*Conspicuous!*" gasped Mrs. Peniston. She bent forward, lowering her voice to mitigate the horror. "What sort of things do they say? That he means to get a divorce and marry her?"

Grace Stepney laughed outright. "Dear me, no! He would hardly do that. It—it's a flirtation—nothing more."

"A flirtation? Between my niece and a married man? Do you mean to tell me that, with Lily's looks and advantages, she could find no better use for her time than to waste it on a fat stupid man almost old enough to be her father?" This argument had such a convincing ring that it gave Mrs. Peniston sufficient reassurance to pick up her work, while she waited for Grace Stepney to rally her scattered forces.

But Miss Stepney was on the spot in an instant. "That's the worst of it—people say she isn't wasting her time! Every one knows, as you say, that Lily is too handsome and—and charming—to devote herself to a man like Gus Trenor unless——"

"Unless?" echoed Mrs. Peniston.

Her visitor drew breath nervously. It was agreeable to shock Mrs. Peniston, but not to shock her to the verge of anger. Miss Stepney was not sufficiently familiar with the classic drama to have recalled in advance how bearers of bad tidings are proverbially received, but she now had a rapid vision of forfeited dinners and a reduced wardrobe as the possible consequence of her disinterestedness. To the honour of her sex, however, hatred of Lily prevailed over more personal considerations. Mrs. Peniston had chosen the wrong moment to boast of her niece's charms.

"Unless," said Grace, leaning forward to speak with low-toned emphasis, "unless there are material advantages to be gained by making herself agreeable to him."

She felt that the moment was tremendous, and remembered suddenly that Mrs. Peniston's black brocade, with the cut jet fringe, would have been hers at the end of the season.

Mrs. Peniston put down her work again. Another aspect of the same idea had presented itself to her, and she felt that it was beneath her dignity to have her nerves racked by a dependent relative who wore her old clothes.

"If you take pleasure in annoying me by mysterious insinuations," she said coldly, "you might at least have chosen a more suitable time than just as I am recovering from the strain of giving a large dinner."

The mention of the dinner dispelled Miss Stepney's last scruples. "I don't know why I should be accused of taking pleasure in telling you about Lily. I was sure I shouldn't get any thanks for it," she returned with a flare of temper. "But I have some family feeling left, and as you are the only person who has any authority over Lily, I thought you ought to know what is being said of her."

"Well," said Mrs. Peniston, "what I complain of is that you haven't told me yet what *is* being said."

"I didn't suppose I should have to put it so plainly. People say that Gus Trenor pays her bills."

"Pays her bills—her bills?" Mrs. Peniston broke into a laugh. "I can't imagine where you can have picked up such rubbish. Lily has her own income—and I provide for her very handsomely——"

"Oh, we all know that," interposed Miss Stepney drily. "But Lily wears a great many smart gowns——"

"I like her to be well-dressed—it's only suitable!"

"Certainly; but then there are her gambling debts besides."

Miss Stepney, in the beginning, had not meant to bring up this point; but Mrs. Peniston had only her own incredulity to blame. She was like the stiff-necked unbelievers of Scripture, who must be annihilated to be convinced.

"Gambling debts? Lily?" Mrs. Peniston's voice shook with anger and bewilderment. She wondered whether Grace Stepney had gone out of her mind. "What do you mean by her gambling debts?"

"Simply that if one plays bridge for money in Lily's set one is liable to lose a great deal—and I don't suppose Lily always wins."

"Who told you that my niece played cards for money?"

"Mercy, cousin Julia, don't look at me as if I were trying to turn you against Lily! Everybody knows she is crazy about bridge. Mrs. Gryce told me herself that it was her gambling that frightened Percy Gryce—it seems he was really taken with her at first. But, of course, among Lily's friends it's quite the custom for girls to play for money. In fact, people are inclined to excuse her on that account——"

"To excuse her for what?"

"For being hard up—and accepting attentions from men like Gus Trenor—and George Dorset——"

Mrs. Peniston gave another cry. "George Dorset? Is there any one else? I should like to know the worst, if you please."

"Don't put it in that way, cousin Julia. Lately Lily has been a good deal with the Dorsets, and he seems to admire her—but of course that's only natural. And I'm sure there is no truth in the horrid things people say; but she *has* been spending a great deal of money this winter. Evie Van Osburgh was at Céleste's ordering her trousseau the other day—yes, the marriage takes place next month—and she told me that Céleste showed her the most exquisite things she was just sending home to Lily. And people say that Judy Trenor has quarrelled with her on account of Gus; but I'm sure I'm sorry I spoke, though I only meant it as a kindness."

Mrs. Peniston's genuine incredulity enabled her to dismiss Miss Stepney with a disdain which boded ill for that lady's prospect of succeeding to the black brocade; but minds impenetrable to reason have generally some crack through which suspicion filters, and her visitor's insinuations did not glide off as easily as she had expected. Mrs. Peniston disliked scenes, and her determination to avoid them had always led her to hold herself aloof from the details of Lily's life. In her youth, girls had not been supposed to require close supervision. They were generally assumed to be taken up with the legitimate business of courtship and marriage, and interference in such affairs on the part of their natural guardians was considered as unwarrantable as a spectator's suddenly joining in a game. There had of course been "fast" girls even in Mrs. Peniston's early experience; but their fastness, at worst, was understood to be a mere excess of animal spirits, against which there could be no graver charge than that of being "unladylike." The modern fastness appeared synonymous with immorality, and the mere idea of immorality was as offensive to Mrs. Peniston as a smell of cooking in the drawing-room: it was one of the conceptions her mind refused to admit.

She had no immediate intention of repeating to Lily what she had heard, or even of trying to ascertain its truth by means of discreet interrogation. To do so might be to provoke a scene; and a scene, in the shaken state of Mrs. Peniston's nerves, with the effects of her dinner not worn off, and her mind still tremulous with new impressions, was a risk she deemed it her duty to avoid. But there remained in her thoughts a settled deposit of resentment against her niece, all the denser because it was not to be cleared by explanation or discussion. It was horrible of a young girl to let herself be talked about; however unfounded the charges against her, she must be to blame for their having been made. Mrs. Peniston felt as if there had been a contagious illness in the house, and she was doomed to sit shivering among her contaminated furniture.

XII

Miss Bart had in fact been treading a devious way, and none of her critics could have been more alive to the fact than herself; but she had a fatalistic sense of being drawn from one wrong turning to another, without ever perceiving the right road till it was too late to take it.

Lily, who considered herself above narrow prejudices, had not imagined that the fact of letting Gus Trenor make a little money for her would ever disturb her self-complacency. And the fact in itself still seemed harmless enough; only it was a fertile source of harmful complications. As she exhausted the amusement of spending the money these complications became more pressing, and Lily, whose mind could be severely logical in tracing the causes of her ill-luck to others, justified herself by the thought that she owed all her troubles to the enmity of Bertha Dorset. This enmity, however, had apparently expired in a renewal of friendliness between the two women. Lily's visit to the Dorsets had resulted, for both, in the discovery that they could be of use to each other; and the civilized instinct finds a subtler pleasure in making use of its antagonist than in confounding him. Mrs. Dorset was, in fact, engaged in a new sentimental experiment, of which Mrs. Fisher's late property, Ned Silverton, was the rosy victim; and at such moments, as Judy Trenor had once remarked, she felt a peculiar need of distracting her husband's attention. Dorset was as difficult to amuse as a savage; but even his self-engrossment was not proof against Lily's arts, or rather these were especially adapted to soothe an uneasy egoism. Her experience with Percy Gryce stood her in good stead in ministering to Dorset's humours, and if the incentive to please was less urgent, the difficulties of her situation were teaching her to make much of minor opportunities.

Intimacy with the Dorsets was not likely to lessen such difficulties on the material side. Mrs. Dorset had none of Judy Trenor's lavish impulses, and Dorset's admiration was not likely to express itself in financial "tips," even had Lily cared to renew her experiences in that line. What she required, for the moment, of the Dorsets' friendship, was simply its social sanction. She knew that people were beginning to talk of her; but this fact did not alarm her as it had alarmed Mrs. Peniston. In her set such gossip was not unusual, and a handsome girl who flirted with a married man was merely assumed to be pressing to the limit of her opportunities. It was Trenor himself who frightened her. Their walk in the Park had not been a success. Trenor had married young, and since his marriage his intercourse with women had not taken the form of the sentimental small-talk which doubles upon itself like the paths in a maze. He was first puzzled and then irritated to find himself always led back to the same starting-point, and Lily felt that she was gradually losing control of the situation. Trenor was in truth in an unmanageable mood. In spite of his understanding with Rosedale he had been somewhat heavily "touched" by the fall in stocks; his household expenses weighed on him, and he seemed to be meeting, on all sides, a sullen opposition to his wishes, instead of the easy good luck he had hitherto encountered.

Mrs. Trenor was still at Bellomont, keeping the townhouse open, and descending on it now and then for a taste of the world, but preferring the recurrent excitement of week-end parties to the restrictions of a dull season. Since the holidays she had not urged Lily to return to Bellomont, and the first time they met in town Lily fancied there was a shade of coldness in her manner. Was it merely the expression of her displeasure at Miss Bart's neglect, or had disquieting rumours reached her? The latter contingency seemed improbable, yet Lily was not without a sense of uneasiness. If her roaming sympathies had struck root anywhere, it was in her friendship with Judy Trenor. She believed in the sincerity of her friend's affection, though it sometimes showed itself in self-interested ways, and she shrank with peculiar reluctance from any risk of estranging it. But, aside from this, she was keenly conscious of the way in which such an estrangement would react on herself. The fact that Gus Trenor was Judy's husband was at times Lily's strongest reason for disliking him, and for resenting the obligation under which he had placed her.

To set her doubts at rest, Miss Bart, soon after the New Year, "proposed" herself for a week-end at Bellomont. She had learned in advance that the presence of a large party would protect her from too great assiduity on Trenor's part, and his wife's telegraphic "come by all means" seemed to assure her of her usual welcome.

Judy received her amicably. The cares of a large party always prevailed over personal feelings, and Lily saw no change in her hostess's manner. Nevertheless, she was soon aware that the experiment of coming to Bellomont was destined not to be successful. The party was made up of what Mrs. Trenor called "poky people"—her generic name for persons who did not play bridge—and, it being her habit to group all such obstructionists in one class, she usually invited them together, regardless of their other characteristics. The result was apt to be an irreducible combination of persons having no other quality in common than their abstinence from bridge, and the antagonisms developed in a group lacking the one taste which might have amalgamated them, were in this case aggravated by bad weather, and by the ill-concealed boredom of their host and hostess. In such emergencies, Judy would usually have turned to Lily to fuse the discordant elements; and Miss Bart, assuming that such a service was expected of her, threw herself into it with her accustomed zeal. But at the outset she perceived a subtle resistance to her efforts. If Mrs. Trenor's manner toward her was unchanged, there was certainly a faint coldness in that of the other ladies. An occasional caustic allusion to "your friends the Wellington Brys," or to "the little Jew who has bought the Greiner house—some one told us you knew him, Miss Bart,"—showed Lily that she was in disfavour with that portion of society which, while contributing least to its amusement, has assumed the right to decide what forms that amusement shall take. The indication was a slight one, and a year ago Lily would have smiled at it, trusting to the charm of her personality to dispel any prejudice against her. But now she had grown more sensitive to criticism and less confident in her power of disarming it. She knew, moreover, that if the ladies at Bellomont permitted themselves to criticize her friends openly, it was a proof that they were not afraid of subjecting her to the same treatment behind her back. The nervous dread lest anything in Trenor's manner should seem to justify their disapproval made her seek every pretext for avoiding him, and she left Bellomont conscious of having failed in every purpose which had taken her there.

In town she returned to preoccupations which, for the moment, had the happy effect of banishing troublesome thoughts. The Welly Brys, after much debate, and anxious counsel with their newly acquired friends, had decided on the bold move of giving a general entertainment. To attack society collectively, when one's means of approach are limited to a few acquaintances, is like advancing into a strange country with an insufficient number of scouts; but such rash tactics have sometimes led to brilliant victories, and the Brys had determined to put their fate to the touch. Mrs. Fisher, to whom they had entrusted the conduct of the affair, had decided that *tableaux vivants*[1] and expensive music were the two baits most likely to attract the desired prey, and after prolonged negotiations, and the kind of wirepulling in which she was known to excel, she had induced a dozen fashionable women to exhibit themselves in a series of pictures which, by a farther miracle of persuasion, the distinguished portrait painter, Paul Morpeth, had been prevailed upon to organize.

Lily was in her element on such occasions. Under Morpeth's guidance her vivid plastic sense, hitherto nurtured on no higher food than dress-making and upholstery, found eager expression in the disposal of draperies, the study of attitudes, the shifting of lights and shadows. Her dramatic instinct was roused by the choice of subjects, and the gorgeous reproductions of historic dress stirred an imagination which only visual impressions could reach. But keenest of all was the exhilaration of displaying her own beauty under a new aspect: of showing that her loveliness was no mere fixed quality, but an element shaping all emotions to fresh forms of grace.

Mrs. Fisher's measures had been well-taken, and society, surprised in a dull moment, succumbed to the temptation of Mrs. Bry's hospitality. The protesting minority were forgotten in the throng which abjured and came; and the audience was almost as brilliant as the show.

Lawrence Selden was among those who had yielded to the proffered inducements. If he did not often act on the accepted social axiom that a man may go where he pleases, it was because he had long since learned that his pleasures were mainly to be found in a small group of the like-minded. But he enjoyed spectacular effects, and was not insensible to

---

1. Literally "living pictures," these entertainments were silent, motionless reproductions by live performers of famous canvases, sculptures, or historical scenes. See p. 304.

the part money plays in their production: all he asked was that the very rich should live up to their calling as stage-managers, and not spend their money in a dull way. This the Brys could certainly not be charged with doing. Their recently built house, whatever it might lack as a frame for domesticity, was almost as well-designed for the display of a festal assemblage as one of those airy pleasure-halls which the Italian architects improvised to set off the hospitality of princes. The air of improvisation was in fact strikingly present: so recent, so rapidly-evoked was the whole *mise-en-scène* that one had to touch the marble columns to learn they were not of cardboard, to seat one's self in one of the damask-and-gold arm-chairs to be sure it was not painted against the wall.

Selden, who had put one of these seats to the test, found himself, from an angle of the ball-room, surveying the scene with frank enjoyment. The company, in obedience to the decorative instinct which calls for fine clothes in fine surroundings, had dressed rather with an eye to Mrs. Bry's background than to herself. The seated throng, filling the immense room without undue crowding, presented a surface of rich tissues and jewelled shoulders in harmony with the festooned and gilded walls, and the flushed splendours of the Venetian ceiling. At the farther end of the room a stage had been constructed behind a proscenium arch curtained with folds of old damask; but in the pause before the parting of the folds there was little thought of what they might reveal, for every woman who had accepted Mrs. Bry's invitation was engaged in trying to find out how many of her friends had done the same.

Gerty Farish, seated next to Selden, was lost in that indiscriminate and uncritical enjoyment so irritating to Miss Bart's finer perceptions. It may be that Selden's nearness had something to do with the quality of his cousin's pleasure; but Miss Farish was so little accustomed to refer her enjoyment of such scenes to her own share in them, that she was merely conscious of a deeper sense of contentment.

"Wasn't it dear of Lily to get me an invitation? Of course it would never have occurred to Carry Fisher to put me on the list, and I should have been so sorry to miss seeing it all—and especially Lily herself. Some one told me the ceiling was by Veronese[2]—you would know, of course, Lawrence. I suppose it's very beautiful, but his women are so dreadfully fat. Goddesses? Well, I can only say that if they'd been mortals and had to wear corsets, it would have been better for them. I think our women are much handsomer. And this room is wonderfully becoming—every one looks so well! Did you ever see such jewels? Do look at Mrs. George Dorset's pearls—I suppose the smallest of them would pay the rent of our Girls' Club[3] for a year. Not that I ought to complain

---

2. Paolo Veronese (c. 1528–88), famous for painting the ceiling of the doge's palace in Venice, was known for the sensuality of his style and the secularism of his approach even when painting supposedly religious scenes. E.g., the Veronese "supper" mentioned on p. 106 probably refers to his notorious painting of the *Last Supper of Christ*, which the Catholic Church caused to be retitled *Feast in the House of Levi* because of the decadence of the scene.

3. An organization or facility to provide independent young women workers with opportunities for wholesome recreation and self-improvement; usually the clubs were financed and administered by philanthropic women of the upper-middle and upper classes. See pp. 278–283 in this volume.

about the club; every one has been so wonderfully kind. Did I tell you that Lily had given us three hundred dollars? Wasn't it splendid of her? And then she collected a lot of money from her friends—Mrs. Bry gave us five hundred, and Mr. Rosedale a thousand. I wish Lily were not so nice to Mr. Rosedale, but she says it's no use being rude to him, because he doesn't see the difference. She really can't bear to hurt people's feelings—it makes me so angry when I hear her called cold and conceited! The girls at the club don't call her that. Do you know she has been there with me twice?—yes, Lily! And you should have seen their eyes! One of them said it was as good as a day in the country just to look at her. And she sat there, and laughed and talked with them—not a bit as if she were being *charitable*, you know, but as if she liked it as much as they did. They've been asking ever since when she's coming back; and she's promised me——oh!"

Miss Farish's confidences were cut short by the parting of the curtain on the first *tableau*—a group of nymphs dancing across flower-strewn sward in the rhythmic postures of Botticelli's Spring.[4] *Tableaux vivants* depend for their effect not only on the happy disposal of lights and the delusive interposition of layers of gauze, but on a corresponding adjustment of the mental vision. To unfurnished minds they remain, in spite of every enhancement of art, only a superior kind of wax-works; but to the responsive fancy they may give magic glimpses of the boundary world between fact and imagination. Selden's mind was of this order: he could yield to vision-making influences as completely as a child to the spell of a fairy-tale. Mrs. Bry's *tableaux* wanted none of the qualities which go to the producing of such illusions, and under Morpeth's organizing hand the pictures succeeded each other with the rhythmic march of some splendid frieze, in which the fugitive curves of living flesh and the wandering light of young eyes have been subdued to plastic harmony without losing the charm of life.

The scenes were taken from old pictures, and the participators had been cleverly fitted with characters suited to their types. No one, for instance, could have made a more typical Goya than Carry Fisher, with her short dark-skinned face, the exaggerated glow of her eyes, the provocation of her frankly-painted smile. A brilliant Miss Smedden from Brooklyn showed to perfection the sumptuous curves of Titian's Daughter, lifting her gold salver laden with grapes above the harmonizing gold of rippled hair and rich brocade, and a young Mrs. Van Alstyne, who showed the frailer Dutch type, with high blue-veined forehead and pale eyes and lashes, made a characteristic Vandyck, in black satin, against a curtained archway. Then there were Kauffmann[5] nymphs garlanding

4. A work by the Florentine painter Sandro Botticelli (c. 1445–1510), it depicts, among other figures, the Three Graces very lightly clad and dancing in a circle with Spring herself entering in gauzy robes and strewing flowers about her.

5. The four painters referred to in this paragraph had distinctly different styles. Francesco de Goya y Lucientes (1746–1828), for most of his life the

official painter of the Spanish court, portrayed the nobility in exaggerated and generally unflattering poses that often displayed their prosperity, arrogance, and casual brutality. Tiziano Vecelli (c. 1487–1576), called Titian and known as the most famous painter of the sensuous Venetian School, is noted for depicting a certain shade of reddish-gold hair, which appears in the painting referred the altar of Love; a Veronese supper, all sheeny textures, pearl-woven heads and marble architecture; and a Watteau group of lute-playing comedians, lounging by a fountain in a sunlit glade.

Each evanescent picture touched the vision-building faculty in Selden, leading him so far down the vistas of fancy that even Gerty Farish's running commentary—"Oh, how lovely Lulu Melson looks!" or: "That must be Kate Croby, to the right there, in purple"—did not break the spell of the illusion. Indeed, so skilfully had the personality of the actors been subdued to the scenes they figured in that even the least imaginative of the audience must have felt a thrill of contrast when the curtain suddenly parted on a picture which was simply and undisguisedly the portrait of Miss Bart.

Here there could be no mistaking the predominance of personality—the unanimous "Oh!" of the spectators was a tribute, not to the brushwork of Reynolds's "Mrs. Lloyd"[6] but to the flesh and blood loveliness of Lily Bart. She had shown her artistic intelligence in selecting a type so like her own that she could embody the person represented without ceasing to be herself. It was as though she had stepped, not out of, but into, Reynolds's canvas, banishing the phantom of his dead beauty by the beams of her living grace. The impulse to show herself in a splendid setting—she had thought for a moment of representing Tiepolo's Cleopatra[7]—had yielded to the truer instinct of trusting to her unassisted beauty, and she had purposely chosen a picture without distracting accessories of dress or surroundings. Her pale draperies, and the background of foliage against which she stood, served only to relieve the long dryad-like curves that swept upward from her poised foot to her lifted arm. The noble buoyancy of her attitude, its suggestion of soaring grace, revealed the touch of poetry in her beauty that Selden always felt in her presence, yet lost the sense of when he was not with her. Its expression was now so vivid that for the first time he seemed to see before him the real Lily Bart, divested of the trivialities of her little world, and catching for a moment a note of that eternal harmony of which her beauty was a part.

"Deuced bold thing to show herself in that get-up; but, gad, there isn't a break in the lines anywhere, and I suppose she wanted us to know it!"

These words, uttered by that experienced connoisseur, Mr. Ned Van Alstyne, whose scented white moustache had brushed Selden's shoulder

---

to here, although it is no longer considered to be of Titian's daughter and is known simply as *Girl with Dish of Fruit*. Sir Anthony van Dyck (1599–1641), a Belgian who ended his life as court painter under Charles I of England, is known for his portraits tinged with melancholy. Angelica Kauffmann (1741–1807), a very popular Swiss painter, spent fifteen years in London under the auspices of the painter Joshua Reynolds and her name became synonymous with a certain style of decorative painting.

6. A painting by Sir Joshua Reynolds (1723–92), easily the most influential figure in eighteenth- and nineteenth-century British art. The canvas, now in a private collection, shows a full-length view of the voluptuous, diaphanously clad Mrs. Lloyd carving her husband's name in a tree.

7. An image from a series of scenes relating the story of Antony and Cleopatra for the Palazzo Labia in Venice by the rococo painter Giovanni Battista Tiepolo (1696–1770).

whenever the parting of the curtains presented any exceptional opportunity for the study of the female outline, affected their hearer in an
unexpected way. It was not the first time that Selden had heard Lily's
beauty lightly remarked on, and hitherto the tone of the comments had
imperceptibly coloured his view of her. But now it woke only a motion
of indignant contempt. This was the world she lived in, these were the
standards by which she was fated to be measured! Does one go to Caliban for a judgment on Miranda?[8]

In the long moment before the curtain fell, he had time to feel the
whole tragedy of her life. It was as though her beauty, thus detached
from all that cheapened and vulgarized it, had held out suppliant hands
to him from the world in which he and she had once met for a moment,
and where he felt an overmastering longing to be with her again.

He was roused by the pressure of ecstatic fingers. "Wasn't she too
beautiful, Lawrence? Don't you like her best in that simple dress? It
makes her look like the real Lily—the Lily I know."

He met Gerty Farish's brimming gaze. "The Lily we know," he corrected; and his cousin, beaming at the implied understanding, exclaimed
joyfully: "I'll tell her that! She always says you dislike her."

The performance over, Selden's first impulse was to seek Miss Bart.
During the interlude of music which succeeded the *tableaux*, the actors
had seated themselves here and there in the audience, diversifying its
conventional appearance by the varied picturesqueness of their dress.
Lily, however, was not among them, and her absence served to protract
the effect she had produced on Selden: it would have broken the spell to
see her too soon in the surroundings from which accident had so happily
detached her. They had not met since the day of the Van Osburgh
wedding, and on his side the avoidance had been intentional. Tonight,
however, he knew that, sooner or later, he should find himself at her
side; and though he let the dispersing crowd drift him whither it would,
without making an immediate effort to reach her, his procrastination
was not due to any lingering resistance, but to the desire to luxuriate a
moment in the sense of complete surrender.

Lily had not an instant's doubt as to the meaning of the murmur
greeting her appearance. No other *talbeau* had been received with that
precise note of approval: it had obviously been called forth by herself,
and not by the picture she impersonated. She had feared at the last
moment that she was risking too much in dispensing with the advantages
of a more sumptuous setting, and the completeness of her triumph gave
her an intoxicating sense of recovered power. Not caring to diminish the
impression she had produced, she held herself aloof from the audience
till the movement of dispersal before supper, and thus had a second
opportunity of showing herself to advantage, as the throng poured slowly
into the empty drawing-room where she was standing.

8. In Shakespeare's play *The Tempest*, Caliban is a subhuman bestial creature while Miranda is the
beautiful daughter of the island's ruler, Prospero.

She was soon the centre of a group which increased and renewed itself as the circulation became general, and the individual comments on her success were a delightful prolongation of the collective applause. At such moments she lost something of her natural fastidiousness, and cared less for the quality of the admiration received than for its quantity. Differences of personality were merged in a warm atmosphere of praise, in which her beauty expanded like a flower in sunlight; and if Selden had approached a moment or two sooner he would have seen her turning on Ned Van Alstyne and George Dorset the look he had dreamed of capturing for himself.

Fortune willed, however, that the hurried approach of Mrs. Fisher, as whose aide-de-camp Van Alstyne was acting, should break up the group before Selden reached the threshold of the room. One or two of the men wandered off in search of their partners for supper, and the others, noticing Selden's approach, gave way to him in accordance with the tacit free-masonry of the ball-room. Lily was therefore standing alone when he reached her; and finding the expected look in her eye, he had the satisfaction of supposing he had kindled it. The look did indeed deepen as it rested on him, for even in that moment of self-intoxication Lily felt the quicker beat of life that his nearness always produced. She read, too, in his answering gaze the delicious confirmation of her triumph, and for the moment it seemed to her that it was for him only she cared to be beautiful.

Selden had given her his arm without speaking. She took it in silence, and they moved away, not toward the supper-room, but against the tide which was setting thither. The faces about her flowed by like the streaming images of sleep: she hardly noticed where Selden was leading her, till they passed through a glass doorway at the end of the long suite of rooms and stood suddenly in the fragrant hush of a garden. Gravel grated beneath their feet, and about them was the transparent dimness of a midsummer night. Hanging lights made emerald caverns in the depths of foliage, and whitened the spray of a fountain falling among lilies. The magic place was deserted: there was no sound but the plash of the water on the lily-pads, and a distant drift of music that might have been blown across a sleeping lake.

Selden and Lily stood still, accepting the unreality of the scene as a part of their own dream-like sensations. It would not have surprised them to feel a summer breeze on their faces, or to see the lights among the boughs reduplicated in the arch of a starry sky. The strange solitude about them was no stranger than the sweetness of being alone in it together.

At length Lily withdrew her hand, and moved away a step, so that her white-robed slimness was outlined against the dusk of the branches. Selden followed her, and still without speaking they seated themselves on a bench beside the fountain.

Suddenly she raised her eyes with the beseeching earnestness of a child. "You never speak to me—you think hard things of me," she murmured.

"I think of you at any rate, God knows!" he said.

"Then why do we never see each other? Why can't we be friends? You promised once to help me," she continued in the same tone, as though the words were drawn from her unwillingly.

"The only way I can help you is by loving you," Selden said in a low voice.

She made no reply, but her face turned to him with the soft motion of a flower. His own met it slowly, and their lips touched.

She drew back and rose from her seat. Selden rose too, and they stood facing each other. Suddenly she caught his hand and pressed it a moment against her cheek.

"Ah, love me, love me—but don't tell me so!" she sighed with her eyes in his; and before he could speak she had turned and slipped through the arch of boughs, disappearing in the brightness of the room beyond.

Selden stood where she had left him. He knew too well the transiency of exquisite moments to attempt to follow her; but presently he reëntered the house and made his way through the deserted rooms to the door. A few sumptuously-cloaked ladies were already gathered in the marble vestibule, and in the coat-room he found Van Alstyne and Gus Trenor.

The former, at Selden's approach, paused in the careful selection of a cigar from one of the silver boxes invitingly set out near the door.

"Hallo, Selden, going too? You're an Epicurean like myself, I see: you don't want to see all those goddesses gobbling terrapin. Gad, what a show of good-looking women; but not one of 'em could touch that little cousin of mine. Talk of jewels—what's a woman want with jewels when she's got herself to show? The trouble is that all these fal-bals they wear cover up their figures when they've got 'em. I never knew till tonight what an outline Lily has."

"It's not her fault if everybody don't know it now," growled Trenor, flushed with the struggle of getting into his fur-lined coat. "Damned bad taste, I call it—no, no cigar for me. You can't tell what you're smoking in one of these new houses—likely as not the *chef* buys the cigars. Stay for supper? Not if I know it! When people crowd their rooms so that you can't get near any one you want to speak to, I'd as soon sup in the elevated at the rush hour. My wife was dead right to stay away: she says life's too short to spend it in breaking in new people."

XIII

Lily woke from happy dreams to find two notes at her bed-side.

One was from Mrs. Trenor, who announced that she was coming to town that afternoon for a flying visit, and hoped Miss Bart would be able to dine with her. The other was from Selden. He wrote briefly that an important case called him to Albany, whence he would be unable to return till the evening, and asked Lily to let him know at what hour on the following day she would see him.

Lily, leaning back among her pillows, gazed musingly at his letter.

The scene in the Brys' conservatory had been like a part of her dreams; she had not expected to wake to such evidence of its reality. Her first movement was one of annoyance: this unforeseen act of Selden's added another complication to life. It was so unlike him to yield to such an irrational impulse! Did he really mean to ask her to marry him? She had once shown him the impossibility of such a hope, and his subsequent behaviour seemed to prove that he had accepted the situation with a reasonableness somewhat mortifying to her vanity. It was all the more agreeable to find that this reasonableness was maintained only at the cost of not seeing her; but, though nothing in life was as sweet as the sense of her power over him, she saw the danger of allowing the episode of the previous night to have a sequel. Since she could not marry him, it would be kinder to him, as well as easier for herself, to write a line amicably evading his request to see her: he was not the man to mistake such a hint, and when next they met it would be on their usual friendly footing.

Lily sprang out of bed, and went straight to her desk. She wanted to write at once, while she could trust to the strength of her resolve. She was still languid from her brief sleep and the exhilaration of the evening, and the sight of Selden's writing brought back the culminating moment of her triumph: the moment when she had read in his eyes that no philosophy was proof against her power. It would be pleasant to have that sensation again . . . no one else could give it to her in its fulness; and she could not bear to mar her mood of luxurious retrospection by an act of definite refusal. She took up her pen and wrote hastily: "*Tomorrow at four;*" murmuring to herself, as she slipped the sheet into its envelope: "I can easily put him off when tomorrow comes."

Judy Trenor's summons was very welcome to Lily. It was the first time she had received a direct communication from Bellomont since the close of her last visit there, and she was still visited by the dread of having incurred Judy's displeasure. But this characteristic command seemed to reëstablish their former relations; and Lily smiled at the thought that her friend had probably summoned her in order to hear about the Brys' entertainment. Mrs. Trenor had absented herself from the feast, perhaps for the reason so frankly enunciated by her husband, perhaps because, as Mrs. Fisher somewhat differently put it, she "couldn't bear new people when she hadn't discovered them herself." At any rate, though she remained haughtily at Bellomont, Lily suspected in her a devouring eagerness to hear of what she had missed, and to learn exactly in what measure Mrs. Wellington Bry had surpassed all previous competitors for social recognition. Lily was quite ready to gratify this curiosity, but it happened that she was dining out. She determined, however, to see Mrs. Trenor for a few moments, and ringing for her maid she despatched a telegram to say that she would be with her friend that evening at ten.

She was dining with Mrs. Fisher, who had gathered at an informal feast a few of the performers of the previous evening. There was to be plantation music in the studio after dinner—for Mrs. Fisher, despairing of the republic, had taken up modelling, and annexed to her small crowded house a spacious apartment, which, whatever its uses in her hours of plastic inspiration, served at other times for the exercise of an indefatigable hospitality. Lily was reluctant to leave, for the dinner was amusing, and she would have liked to lounge over a cigarette and hear a few songs; but she could not break her engagement with Judy, and shortly after ten she asked her hostess to ring for a hansom, and drove up Fifth Avenue to the Trenors'.

She waited long enough on the doorstep to wonder that Judy's presence in town was not signalized by a greater promptness in admitting her; and her surprise was increased, when, instead of the expected footman, pushing his shoulders into a tardy coat, a shabby caretaking person in calico let her into the shrouded hall. Trenor, however, appeared at once on the threshold of the drawing-room, welcoming her with unusual volubility while he relieved her of her cloak and drew her into the room.

"Come along to the den; it's the only comfortable place in the house. Doesn't this room look as if it was waiting for the body to be brought down? Can't see why Judy keeps the house wrapped up in this awful slippery white stuff—it's enough to give a fellow pneumonia to walk through these rooms on a cold day. You look a little pinched yourself, by the way: it's rather a sharp night out. I noticed it walking up from the club. Come along, and I'll give you a nip of brandy, and you can toast yourself over the fire and try some of my new Egyptians—that little Turkish chap at the Embassy put me on to a brand that I want you to try, and if you like 'em I'll get out a lot for you: they don't have 'em here yet, but I'll cable."

He led her through the house to the large room at the back, where Mrs. Trenor usually sat, and where, even in her absence, there was an air of occupancy. Here, as usual, were flowers, newspapers, a littered writing-table, and a general aspect of lamp-lit familiarity, so that it was a surprise not to see Judy's energetic figure start up from the arm-chair near the fire.

It was apparently Trenor himself who had been occupying the seat in question, for it was overhung by a cloud of cigar smoke, and near it stood one of those intricate folding tables which British ingenuity has devised to facilitate the circulation of tobacco and spirits. The sight of such appliances in a drawing-room was not unusual in Lily's set, where smoking and drinking were unrestricted by considerations of time and place, and her first movement was to help herself to one of the cigarettes recommended by Trenor, while she checked his loquacity by asking, with a surprised glance: "Where's Judy?"

Trenor, a little heated by his unusual flow of words, and perhaps by prolonged propinquity with the decanters, was bending over the latter to decipher their silver labels.

"Here, now, Lily, just a drop of cognac in a little fizzy water—you do look pinched, you know: I swear the end of your nose is red. I'll take another glass to keep you company—Judy?—Why, you see, Judy's got a devil of a headache—quite knocked out with it, poor thing—she asked me to explain—make it all right, you know—Do come up to the fire, though; you look deadbeat, really. Now do let me make you comfortable, there's a good girl."

He had taken her hand, half-banteringly, and was drawing her toward a low seat by the hearth; but she stopped and freed herself quietly.

"Do you mean to say that Judy's not well enough to see me? Doesn't she want me to go upstairs?"

Trenor drained the glass he had filled for himself, and paused to set it down before he answered.

"Why, no—the fact is, she's not up to seeing anybody. It came on suddenly, you know, and she asked me to tell you how awfully sorry she was—if she'd known where you were dining she'd have sent you word."

"She did know where I was dining; I mentioned it in my telegram. But it doesn't matter, of course. I suppose if she's so poorly she won't go back to Bellomont in the morning, and I can come and see her then."

"Yes: exactly—that's capital. I'll tell her you'll pop in tomorrow morning. And now do sit down a minute, there's a dear, and let's have a nice quiet jaw together. You won't take a drop, just for sociability? Tell me what you think of that cigarette. Why, don't you like it? What are you chucking it away for?"

"I am chucking it away because I must go, if you'll have the goodness to call a cab for me," Lily returned with a smile.

She did not like Trenor's unusual excitability, with its too evident explanation, and the thought of being alone with him, with her friend out of reach upstairs, at the other end of the great empty house, did not conduce to a desire to prolong their *tête-à-tête*.

But Trenor, with a promptness which did not escape her, had moved between herself and the door.

"Why must you go, I should like to know? If Judy'd been here you'd have sat gossiping till all hours—and you can't even give me five minutes! It's always the same story. Last night I couldn't get near you—I went to that damned vulgar party just to see you, and there was everybody talking about you, and asking me if I'd ever seen anything so stunning, and when I tried to come up and say a word, you never took any notice, but just went on laughing and joking with a lot of asses who only wanted to be able to swagger about afterward, and look knowing when you were mentioned."

He paused, flushed by his diatribe, and fixing on her a look in which resentment was the ingredient she least disliked. But she had regained her presence of mind, and stood composedly in the middle of the room, while her slight smile seemed to put an ever increasing distance between herself and Trenor.

Across it she said: "Don't be absurd, Gus. It's past eleven, and I must really ask you to ring for a cab."

He remained immovable, with the lowering forehead she had grown to detest.

"And supposing I won't ring for one—what'll you do then?"

"I shall go upstairs to Judy if you force me to disturb her."

Trenor drew a step nearer and laid his hand on her arm. "Look here, Lily: won't you give me five minutes of your own accord?"

"Not tonight, Gus: you——"

"Very good, then: I'll take 'em. And as many more as I want." He had squared himself on the threshold, his hands thrust deep in his pockets. He nodded toward the chair on the hearth.

"Go and sit down there, please: I've got a word to say to you."

Lily's quick temper was getting the better of her fears. She drew herself up and moved toward the door.

"If you have anything to say to me, you must say it another time. I shall go up to Judy unless you call a cab for me at once."

He burst into a laugh. "Go upstairs and welcome, my dear; but you won't find Judy. She ain't there."

Lily cast a startled look upon him. "Do you mean that Judy is not in the house—not in town?" she exclaimed.

"That's just what I do mean," returned Trenor, his bluster sinking to sullenness under her look.

"Nonsense—I don't believe you. I am going upstairs," she said impatiently.

He drew unexpectedly aside, letting her reach the threshold unimpeded.

"Go up and welcome; but my wife is at Bellomont."

But Lily had a flash of reassurance. "If she hadn't come she would have sent me word——"

"She did; she telephoned me this afternoon to let you know."

"I received no message."

"I didn't send any."

The two measured each other for a moment, but Lily still saw her opponent through a blur of scorn that made all other considerations indistinct.

"I can't imagine your object in playing such a stupid trick on me; but if you have fully gratified your peculiar sense of humour I must again ask you to send for a cab."

It was the wrong note, and she knew it as she spoke. To be stung by irony it is not necessary to understand it, and the angry streaks on Trenor's face might have been raised by an actual lash.

"Look here, Lily, don't take that high and mighty tone with me." He had again moved toward the door, and in her instinctive shrinking from him she let him regain command of the threshold. "I *did* play a trick on you; I own up to it; but if you think I'm ashamed you're mistaken. Lord knows I've been patient enough—I've hung round and looked like an ass. And all the while you were letting a lot of other fellows make up to you . . . letting 'em make fun of me, I daresay . . . I'm not sharp, and can't dress my friends up to look funny, as you do . . . but I can tell when it's being done to me . . . I can tell fast enough when I'm made a fool of . . ."

"Ah, I shouldn't have thought that!" flashed from Lily; but her laugh dropped to silence under his look.

"No; you wouldn't have thought it; but you'll know better now. That's what you're here for tonight. I've been waiting for a quiet time to talk things over, and now I've got it I mean to make you hear me out."

His first rush of inarticulate resentment had been followed by a steadiness and concentration of tone more disconcerting to Lily than the excitement preceding it. For a moment her presence of mind forsook her. She had more than once been in situations where a quick sword-play of wit had been needful to cover her retreat; but her frightened heart-throbs told her that here such skill would not avail.

To gain time she repeated: "I don't understand what you want."

Trenor had pushed a chair between herself and the door. He threw himself in it, and leaned back, looking up at her.

"I'll tell you what I want: I want to know just where you and I stand. Hang it, the man who pays for the dinner is generally allowed to have a seat at table."

She flamed with anger and abasement, and the sickening need of having to conciliate where she longed to humble.

"I don't know what you mean—but you must see, Gus, that I can't stay here talking to you at this hour——"

"Gad, you go to men's houses fast enough in broad daylight—strikes me you're not always so deuced careful of appearances."

The brutality of the thrust gave her the sense of dizziness that follows on a physical blow. Rosedale had spoken then—this was the way men talked of her—She felt suddenly weak and defenceless: there was a throb of self-pity in her throat. But all the while another self was sharpening her to vigilance, whispering the terrified warning that every word and gesture must be measured.

"If you have brought me her to say insulting things——" she began.

Trenor laughed. "Don't talk stage-rot. I don't want to insult you. But a man's got his feelings—and you've played with mine too long. I didn't begin this business—kept out of the way, and left the track clear for the other chaps, till you rummaged me out and set to work to make an ass of me—and an easy job you had of it, too. That's the trouble—it was too easy for you—you got reckless—thought you could turn me inside out, and chuck me in the gutter like an empty purse. But, by gad, that ain't playing fair: that's dodging the rules of the game. Of course I know now what you wanted—it wasn't my beautiful eyes you were after—but I tell you what, Miss Lily, you've got to pay up for making me think so——"

He rose, squaring his shoulders aggressively, and stepped toward her with a reddening brow; but she held her footing, though every nerve tore at her to retreat as he advanced.

"I mean to make you hear me out."

"Pay up?" she faltered. "Do you mean that I owe you money?"

He laughed again. "Oh, I'm not asking for payment in kind. But there's such a thing as fair play—and interest on one's money—and hang me if I've had as much as a look from you——"

"Your money? What have I to do with your money? You advised me how to invest mine . . . you must have seen I knew nothing of business . . . you told me it was all right——"

"It *was* all right—it is, Lily: you're welcome to all of it, and ten times more. I'm only asking for a word of thanks from you." He was closer still, with a hand that grew formidable; and the frightened self in her was dragging the other down.

"I *have* thanked you; I've shown I was grateful. What more have you done than any friend might do, or any one accept from a friend?"

Trenor caught her up with a sneer. "I don't doubt you've accepted as much before—and chucked the other chaps as you'd like to chuck me. I don't care how you settled your score with them—if you fooled 'em I'm that much to the good. Don't stare at me like that—I know I'm not talking the way a man is supposed to talk to a girl—but, hang it, if you don't like it you can stop me quick enough—you know I'm mad about you—damn the money, there's plenty more of it—if *that* bothers you . . . I was a brute, Lily—Lily!—just look at me——"

Over and over her the sea of humiliation broke—wave crashing on wave so close that the moral shame was one with the physical dread. It seemed to her that self-esteem would have made her invulnerable—that it was her own dishonour which put a fearful solitude about her.

His touch was a shock to her drowning consciousness. She drew back from him with a desperate assumption of scorn.

"I've told you I don't understand—but if I owe you money you shall be paid——"

Trenor's face darkened to rage: her recoil of abhorrence had called out the primitive man.

"Ah—you'll borrow from Selden or Rosedale—and take your chances of fooling them as you've fooled me! Unless—unless you've settled your other scores already—and I'm the only one left out in the cold!"

She stood silent, frozen to her place. The words—the words were worse than the touch! Her heart was beating all over her body—in her throat, her limbs, her helpless useless hands. Her eyes travelled despairingly about the room—they lit on the bell, and she remembered that help was in call. Yes, but scandal with it—a hideous mustering of tongues. No, she must fight her way out alone. It was enough that the servants knew her to be in the house with Trenor—there must be nothing to excite conjecture in her way of leaving it.

She raised her head, and achieved a last clear look at him.

"I am here alone with you," she said. "What more have you to say?"

To her surprise, Trenor answered the look with a speechless stare. With his last gust of words the flame had died out, leaving him chill and humbled. It was as though a cold air had dispersed the fumes of his libations, and the situation loomed before him black and naked as the ruins of a fire. Old habits, old restraints, the hand of inherited order, plucked back the bewildered mind which passion had jolted from its ruts. Trenor's eye had the haggard look of the sleep-walker waked on a deathly ledge.

"Go home! Go away from here"——he stammered, and turning his back on her walked toward the hearth.

The sharp release from her fears restored Lily to immediate lucidity. The collapse of Trenor's will left her in control, and she heard herself, in a voice that was her own yet outside herself, bidding him ring for the servant, bidding him give the order for a hansom, directing him to put her in it when it came. Whence the strength came to her she knew not; but an insistent voice warned her that she must leave the house openly, and nerved her, in the hall before the hovering care-taker, to exchange light words with Trenor, and charge him with the usual messages for Judy, while all the while she shook with inward loathing. On the door-step, with the street before her, she felt a mad throb of liberation, intoxicating as the prisoner's first draught of free air; but the clearness of brain continued, and she noted the mute aspect of Fifth Avenue, guessed at the lateness of the hour, and even observed a man's figure—was there something half-familiar in its outline?—which, as she entered the hansom, turned from the opposite corner and vanished in the obscurity of the side street.

But with the turn of the wheels reaction came, and shuddering darkness closed on her. "I can't think—I can't think," she moaned, and leaned her head against the rattling side of the cab. She seemed a stranger to herself, or rather there were two selves in her, the one she had always known, and a new abhorrent being to which it found itself chained. She had once picked up, in a house where she was staying, a translation of the *Eumenides*,[1] and her imagination had been seized by the high terror of the scene where Orestes, in the cave of the oracle, finds his implacable huntresses asleep, and snatches an hour's repose. Yes, the Furies might sometimes sleep, but they were there, always there in the dark corners, and now they were awake and the iron clang of their wings was in her brain . . . She opened her eyes and saw the streets passing—the familiar alien streets. All she looked on was the same and yet changed. There was a great gulf fixed between today and yesterday. Everything in the past seemed simple, natural, full of daylight—and she was alone in a place of darkness and pollution—Alone! It was the loneliness that frightened her. Her eyes fell on an illuminated clock at a street corner, and she saw that the hands marked the half hour after eleven. Only half-past eleven—there were hours and hours left of the night! And she must spend them alone, shuddering sleepless on her bed. Her soft nature recoiled from this ordeal, which had none of the stimulus of conflict to

1. A play by the Greek playwright Aeschylus (525– 456 B.C.) telling of the harassment of Prince Orestes by the Furies, mythological snaky-haired women who drive guilty people to madness. The play opens with the scene Wharton describes.

goad her through it. Oh, the slow cold drip of the minutes on her head! She had a vision of herself lying on the black walnut bed—and the darkness would frighten her, and if she left the light burning the dreary details of the room would brand themselves forever on her brain. She had always hated her room at Mrs. Peniston's—its ugliness, its impersonality, the fact that nothing in it was really hers. To a torn heart uncomforted by human nearness a room may open almost human arms, and the being to whom no four walls mean more than any others, is, at such hours, expatriate everywhere.

Lily had no heart to lean on. Her relation with her aunt was as superficial as that of chance lodgers who pass on the stairs. But even had the two been in closer contact, it was impossible to think of Mrs. Peniston's mind as offering shelter or comprehension to such misery as Lily's. As the pain that can be told is but half a pain, so the pity that questions has little healing in its touch. What Lily craved was the darkness made by enfolding arms, the silence which is not solitude, but compassion holding its breath.

She started up and looked forth on the passing streets. Gerty!—they were nearing Gerty's corner. If only she could reach there before this labouring anguish burst from her breast to her lips—if only she could feel the hold of Gerty's arms while she shook in the ague-fit of fear that was coming upon her! She pushed up the door in the roof and called the address to the driver. It was not so late—Gerty might still be waking. And even if she were not, the sound of the bell would penetrate every recess of her tiny apartment, and rouse her to answer her friend's call.

XIV

Gerty Farish, the morning after the Wellington Brys' entertainment, woke from dreams as happy as Lily's. If they were less vivid in hue, more subdued to the half-tints of her personality and her experience, they were for that very reason better suited to her mental vision. Such flashes of joy as Lily moved in would have blinded Miss Farish, who was accustomed, in the way of happiness, to such scant light as shone through the cracks of other people's lives.

Now she was the centre of a little illumination of her own: a mild but unmistakable beam, compounded of Lawrence Selden's growing kindness to herself and the discovery that he extended his liking to Lily Bart. If these two factors seem incompatible to the student of feminine psychology, it must be remembered that Gerty had always been a parasite in the moral order, living on the crumbs of other tables, and content to look through the window at the banquet spread for her friends. Now that she was enjoying a little private feast of her own, it would have seemed incredibly selfish not to lay a plate for a friend; and there was no one with whom she would rather have shared her enjoyment than Miss Bart.

As to the nature of Selden's growing kindness, Gerty would no more have dared to define it than she would have tried to learn a butterfly's colours by knocking the dust from its wings. To seize on the wonder would be to brush off its bloom, and perhaps see it fade and stiffen in her hand: better the sense of beauty palpitating out of reach, while she held her breath and watched where it would alight. Yet Selden's manner at the Brys' had brought the flutter of wings so close that they seemed to be beating in her own heart. She had never seen him so alert, so responsive, so attentive to what she had to say. His habitual manner had an absent-minded kindliness which she accepted, and was grateful for, as the liveliest sentiment her presence was likely to inspire; but she was quick to feel in him a change implying that for once she could give pleasure as well as receive it.

And it was so delightful that this higher degree of sympathy should be reached through their interest in Lily Bart! Gerty's affection for her friend—a sentiment that had learned to keep itself alive on the scantiest diet—had grown to active adoration since Lily's restless curiosity had drawn her into the circle of Miss Farish's work. Lily's taste of beneficence had wakened in her a momentary appetite for well-doing. Her visit to the Girls' Club had first brought her in contact with the dramatic contrasts of life. She had always accepted with philosophic calm the fact that such existences as hers were pedestalled on foundations of obscure humanity. The dreary limbo of dinginess lay all around and beneath that little illuminated circle in which life reached its finest efflorescence, as the mud and sleet of a winter night enclose a hot-house filled with tropical flowers. All this was in the natural order of things, and the orchid basking in its artificially created atmosphere could round the delicate curves of its petals undisturbed by the ice on the panes.

But it is one thing to live comfortably with the abstract conception of poverty, another to be brought in contact with its human embodiments. Lily had never conceived of these victims of fate otherwise than in the mass. That the mass was composed of individual lives, innumerable separate centres of sensation, with her own eager reachings for pleasure, her own fierce revulsions from pain—that some of these bundles of feeling were clothed in shapes not so unlike her own, with eyes meant to look on gladness, and young lips shaped for love—this discovery gave Lily one of those sudden shocks of pity that sometimes decentralize a life. Lily's nature was incapable of such renewal: she could feel other demands only through her own, and no pain was long vivid which did not press on an answering nerve. But for the moment she was drawn out of herself by the interest of her direct relation with a world so unlike her own. She had supplemented her first gift by personal assistance to one or two of Miss Farish's most appealing subjects, and the admiration and interest her presence excited among the tired workers at the club ministered in a new form to her insatiable desire to please.

Gerty Farish was not a close enough reader of character to disentangle the mixed threads of which Lily's philanthropy was woven. She supposed her beautiful friend to be actuated by the same motive as herself—that sharpening of the moral vision which makes all human suffering so near and insistent that the other aspects of life fade into remoteness. Gerty lived by such simple formulas that she did not hesitate to class her friend's state with the emotional "change of heart" to which her dealings with the poor had accustomed her; and she rejoiced in the thought that she had been the humble instrument of this renewal. Now she had an answer to all criticisms of Lily's conduct: as she had said, she knew "the real Lily," and the discovery that Selden shared her knowledge raised her placid acceptance of life to a dazzled sense of its possibilities—a sense farther enlarged, in the course of the afternoon, by the receipt of a telegram from Selden asking if he might dine with her that evening.

While Gerty was lost in the happy bustle which this announcement produced in her small household, Selden was at one with her in thinking with intensity of Lily Bart. The case which had called him to Albany was not complicated enough to absorb all his attention, and he had the professional faculty of keeping a part of his mind free when its services were not needed. This part—which at the moment seemed dangerously like the whole—was filled to the brim with the sensations of the previous evening. Selden understood the symptoms: he recognized the fact that he was paying up, as there had always been a chance of his having to pay up, for the voluntary exclusions of his past. He had meant to keep free from permanent ties, not from any poverty of feeling, but because, in a different way, he was, as much as Lily, the victim of his environment. There had been a germ of truth in his declaration to Gerty Farish that he had never wanted to marry a "nice" girl: the adjective connoting, in his cousin's vocabulary, certain utilitarian qualities which are apt to preclude the luxury of charm. Now it had been Selden's fate to have a charming mother: her graceful portrait, all smiles and Cashmere, still emitted a faded scent of the undefinable quality. His father was the kind of man who delights in a charming woman: who quotes her, stimulates her, and keeps her perennially charming. Neither one of the couple cared for money, but their disdain of it took the form of always spending a little more than was prudent. If their house was shabby, it was exquisitely kept; if there were good books on the shelves there were also good dishes on the table. Selden senior had an eye for a picture, his wife an understanding of old lace; and both were so conscious of restraint and discrimination in buying that they never quite knew how it was that the bills mounted up.

Though many of Selden's friends would have called his parents poor, he had grown up in an atmosphere where restricted means were felt only as a check on aimless profusion: where the few possessions were so good that their rarity gave them a merited relief, and abstinence was combined with elegance in a way exemplified by Mrs. Selden's knack of wearing her old velvet as if it were new. A man has the advantage of being delivered early from the home point of view, and before Selden left college he had learned that there are as many different ways of going without money as of spending it. Unfortunately, he found no way as agreeable as that practised at home; and his views of womankind in especial were tinged by the remembrance of the one woman who had given him his sense of "values." It was from her that he inherited his detachment from the sumptuary side of life: the stoic's carelessness of material things, combined with the Epicurean's pleasure in them. Life shorn of either feeling appeared to him a diminished thing; and nowhere was the blending of the two ingredients so essential as in the character of a pretty woman.

It had always seemed to Selden that experience offered a great deal besides the sentimental adventure, yet he could vividly conceive of a love which should broaden and deepen till it became the central fact of life. What he could not accept, in his own case, was the makeshift alternative of a relation that should be less than this: that should leave some portions of his nature unsatisfied, while it put an undue strain on others. He would not, in other words, yield to the growth of an affection which might appeal to pity yet leave the understanding untouched: sympathy should no more delude him than a trick of the eyes, the grace of helplessness than a curve of the cheek.

But now—that little *but* passed like a sponge over all his vows. His reasoned-out resistances seemed for the moment so much less important than the question as to when Lily would receive his note! He yielded himself to the charm of trivial preoccupations, wondering at what hour her reply would be sent, with what words it would begin. As to its import he had no doubt—he was as sure of her surrender as of his own. And so he had leisure to muse on all its exquisite details, as a hard worker, on a holiday morning, might lie still and watch the beam of light travel gradually across his room. But if the new light dazzled, it did not blind him. He could still discern the outline of facts, though his own relation to them had changed. He was no less conscious than before of what was said of Lily Bart, but he could separate the woman he knew from the vulgar estimate of her. His mind turned to Gerty Farish's words, and the wisdom of the world seemed a groping thing beside the insight of innocence. *Blessed are the pure in heart, for they shall see God*[1]—even the hidden god in their neighbour's breast! Selden was in the state of impassioned self-absorption that the first surrender to love produces. His craving was for the companionship of one whose point of view should justify his own, who should confirm, by deliberate observation, the truth to which his intuitions had leaped. He could not wait for the midday recess, but seized a moment's leisure in court to scribble his telegram to Gerty Farish.

Reaching town, he was driven direct to his club, where he hoped a note from Miss Bart might await him. But his box contained only a line of rapturous assent from Gerty, and he was turning away disappointed when he was hailed by a voice from the smoking room.

"Hallo, Lawrence! Dining here? Take a bite with me—I've ordered a canvas-back."

---

1. Matthew 5.8; one of the Beatitudes.

He discovered Trenor, in his day clothes, sitting, with a tall glass at his elbow, behind the folds of a sporting journal.

Selden thanked him, but pleaded an engagement.

"Hang it, I believe every man in town has an engagement tonight. I shall have the club to myself. You know how I'm living this winter, rattling round in that empty house. My wife meant to come to town today, but she's put it off again, and how is a fellow to dine alone in a room with the looking-glasses covered, and nothing but a bottle of Harvey sauce on the side-board? I say, Lawrence, chuck your engagement and take pity on me—it gives me the blue devils to dine alone, and there's nobody but that canting ass Wetherall in the club."

"Sorry, Gus—I can't do it."

As Selden turned away, he noticed the dark flush on Trenor's face, the unpleasant moisture of his intensely white forehead, the way his jewelled rings were wedged in the creases of his fat red fingers. Certainly the beast was predominating—the beast at the bottom of the glass. And he had heard this man's name coupled with Lily's! Bah—the thought sickened him; all the way back to his rooms he was haunted by the sight of Trenor's fat creased hands——

On his table lay the note: Lily had sent it to his rooms. He knew what was in it before he broke the seal—a grey seal with *Beyond!* beneath a flying ship. Ah, he would take her beyond—beyond the ugliness, the pettiness, the attrition and corrosion of the soul——

Gerty's little sitting-room sparkled with welcome when Selden entered it. Its modest "effects," compact of enamel paint and ingenuity, spoke to him in the language just then sweetest to his ear. It is surprising how little narrow walls and a low ceiling matter, when the roof of the soul has suddenly been raised. Gerty sparkled too; or at least shone with a tempered radiance. He had never before noticed that she had "points"—really, some good fellow might do worse . . . Over the little dinner (and here, again, the effects were wonderful) he told her she ought to marry—he was in a mood to pair off the whole world. She had made the caramel custard with her own hands? It was sinful to keep such gifts to herself. He reflected with a throb of pride that Lily could trim her own hats—she had told him so the day of their walk at Bellomont.

He did not speak of Lily till after dinner. During the little repast he kept the talk on his hostess, who, fluttered at being the centre of observation, shone as rosy as the candle-shades she had manufactured for the occasion. Selden evinced an extraordinary interest in her household arrangements: complimented her on the ingenuity with which she had utilized every inch of her small quarters, asked how her servant managed about afternoons out, learned that one may improvise delicious dinners in a chafing-dish, and uttered thoughtful generalizations on the burden of a large establishment.

When they were in the sitting-room again, where they fitted as snugly as bits in a puzzle, and she had brewed the coffee, and poured it into her grandmother's egg-shell cups, his eye, as he leaned back, basking in the warm fragrance, lighted on a recent photograph of Miss Bart, and the desired transition was effected without an effort. The photograph was well enough—but to catch her as she had looked last night! Gerty agreed with him—never had she been so radiant. But could photography capture that light? There had been a new look in her face—something different; yes, Selden agreed there had been something different. The coffee was so exquisite that he asked for a second cup: such a contrast to the watery stuff at the club! Ah, your poor bachelor with his impersonal club fare, alternating with the equally impersonal *cuisine* of the dinner-party! A man who lived in lodgings missed the best part of life—he pictured the flavourless solitude of Trenor's repast, and felt a moment's compassion for the man . . . But to return to Lily—and again and again he returned, questioning, conjecturing, leading Gerty on, draining her inmost thoughts of their stored tenderness for her friend.

At first she poured herself out unstintingly, happy in this perfect communion of their sympathies. His understanding of Lily helped to confirm her own belief in her friend. They dwelt together on the fact that Lily had had no chance. Gerty instanced her generous impulses—her restlessness and discontent. The fact that her life had never satisfied her proved that she was made for better things. She might have married more than once—the conventional rich marriage which she had been taught to consider the sole end of existence—but when the opportunity came she had always shrunk from it. Percy Gryce, for instance, had been in love with her—every one at Bellomont had supposed them to be engaged, and her dismissal of him was thought inexplicable. This view of the Gryce incident chimed too well with Selden's mood not to be instantly adopted by him, with a flash of retrospective contempt for what had once seemed the obvious solution. If rejection there had been—and he wondered now that he had ever doubted it!—then he held the key to the secret, and the hillsides of Bellomont were lit up, not with sunset, but with dawn. It was he who had wavered and disowned the face of opportunity—and the joy now warming his breast might have been a familiar inmate if he had captured it in its first flight.

It was at this point, perhaps, that a joy just trying its wings in Gerty's heart dropped to earth and lay still. She sat facing Selden, repeating mechanically: "No, she has never been understood——" and all the while she herself seemed to be sitting in the centre of a great glare of comprehension. The little confidential room, where a moment ago their thoughts had touched elbows like their chairs, grew to unfriendly vastness, separating her from Selden by all the length of her new vision of the future—and that future stretched out interminably, with her lonely figure toiling down it, a mere speck on the solitude.

"She is herself with a few people only; and you are one of them," she heard Selden saying. And again: "Be good to her, Gerty, won't you?" and: "She has it in her to become whatever she is believed to be—you'll help her by believing the best of her?"

The words beat on Gerty's brain like the sound of a language which has seemed familiar at a distance, but on approaching is found to be unintelligible. He had come to talk to her of Lily—that was all! There had been a third at the feast she had spread for him, and that third had taken her own place. She tried to follow what he was saying, to cling to her own part in the talk—but it was all as meaningless as the boom of waves in a drowning head, and she felt, as the drowning may feel, that to sink would be nothing beside the pain of struggling to keep up.

Selden rose, and she drew a deep breath, feeling that soon she could yield to the blessed waves.

"Mrs. Fisher's? You say she was dining there? There's music afterward; I believe I had a card from her." He glanced at the foolish pink-faced clock that was drumming out this hideous hour. "A quarter past ten? I might look in there now; the Fisher evenings are amusing. I haven't kept you up too late, Gerty? You look tired—I've rambled on and bored you." And in the unwonted overflow of his feelings, he left a cousinly kiss upon her cheek.

At Mrs. Fisher's, through the cigar-smoke of the studio, a dozen voices greeted Selden. A song was pending as he entered, and he dropped into a seat near his hostess, his eyes roaming in search of Miss Bart. But she was not there, and the discovery gave him a pang out of all proportion to its seriousness; since the note in his breast-pocket assured him that at four the next day they would meet. To his impatience it seemed immeasurably long to wait, and half-ashamed of the impulse, he leaned to Mrs. Fisher to ask, as the music ceased, if Miss Bart had not dined with her.

"Lily? She's just gone. She had to run off, I forget where. Wasn't she wonderful last night?"

"Who's that? Lily?" asked Jack Stepney, from the depths of a neighbouring arm-chair. "Really, you know, I'm no prude, but when it comes to a girl standing there as if she was up at auction—I thought seriously of speaking to cousin Julia."

"You didn't know Jack had become our social censor?" Mrs. Fisher said to Selden with a laugh; and Stepney spluttered, amid the general derision: "But she's a cousin, hang it, and when a man's married—*Town Talk* was full of her this morning."

"Yes: lively reading that was," said Mr. Ned Van Alstyne, stroking his moustache to hide the smile behind it. "Buy the dirty sheet? No, of course not; some fellow showed it to me—but I'd heard the stories before. When a girl's as good-looking as that she'd better marry; then no questions are asked. In our imperfectly organized society there is no provision as yet for the young woman who claims the privileges of marriage without assuming its obligations."

"Well, I understand Lily is about to assume them in the shape of Mr. Rosedale," Mrs. Fisher said with a laugh.

"Rosedale—good heavens!" exclaimed Van Alstyne, dropping his eye-glass. "Stepney, that's your fault for foisting the brute on us."

"Oh, confound it, you know, we don't *marry* Rosedale in our family," Stepney languidly protested; but his wife, who sat in oppressive bridal finery at the other side of the room, quelled him with the judicial reflection: "In Lily's circumstances it's a mistake to have too high a standard."

"I hear even Rosedale has been scared by the talk lately," Mrs. Fisher rejoined; "but the sight of her last night sent him off his head. What do you think he said to me after her *tableau?* 'My God, Mrs. Fisher, if I could get Paul Morpeth to paint her like that, the picture'd appreciate a hundred per cent in ten years.' "

"By Jove,—but isn't she about somewhere?" exclaimed Van Alstyne, restoring his glass with an uneasy glance.

"No; she ran off while you were all mixing the punch down stairs. Where was she going, by the way? What's on tonight? I hadn't heard of anything."

"Oh, not a party, I think," said an inexperienced young Farish who had arrived late. "I put her in her cab as I was coming in, and she gave the driver the Trenors' address."

"The Trenors'?" exclaimed Mrs. Jack Stepney. "Why, the house is closed—Judy telephoned me from Bellomont this evening."

"Did she? That's queer. I'm sure I'm not mistaken. Well, come now, Trenor's there, anyhow—I—oh, well—the fact is, I've no head for numbers," he broke off, admonished by the nudge of an adjoining foot, and the smile that circled the room.

In its unpleasant light Selden had risen and was shaking hands with his hostess. The air of the place stifled him, and he wondered why he had stayed in it so long.

On the doorstep he stood still, remembering a phrase of Lily's: "It seems to me you spend a good deal of time in the element you disapprove of."

Well—what had brought him there but the quest of her? It was her element, not his. But he would lift her out of it, take her beyond! That *Beyond!* on her letter was like a cry for rescue. He knew that Perseus's task is not done when he has loosed Andromeda's chains,[2] for her limbs are numb with bondage, and she cannot rise and walk, but clings to him with dragging arms as he beats back to land with his burden. Well, he had strength for both—it was her weakness which had put the strength in him. It was not, alas, a clean rush of waves they had to win through, but a clogging morass of old associations and habits, and for the moment its vapours were in his throat. But he would see clearer, breathe freer in her presence: she was at once the dead weight at his breast and the spar

2. In Greek mythology, the hero Perseus on his winged horse Pegasus rescues Andromeda, who is chained naked to a sacrificial rock in the sea. Perseus swoops down and beheads the monster whose prey she is and, after cutting her chains, snatches her up as she falls fainting into the waves. Perseus then carries Andromeda off to be his bride, his payment for her rescue.

which should float them to safety. He smiled at the whirl of metaphor with which he was trying to build up a defence against the influences of the last hour. It was pitiable that he, who knew the mixed motives on which social judgments depend, should still feel himself so swayed by them. How could he lift Lily to a freer vision of life, if his own view of her was to be coloured by any mind in which he saw her reflected?

The moral oppression had produced a physical craving for air, and he strode on, opening his lungs to the reverberating coldness of the night. At the corner of Fifth Avenue Van Alstyne hailed him with an offer of company.

"Walking? A good thing to blow the smoke out of one's head. Now that women have taken to tobacco we live in a bath of nicotine. It would be a curious thing to study the effect of cigarettes on the relation of the sexes. Smoke is almost as great a solvent as divorce: both tend to obscure the moral issue."

Nothing could have been less consonant with Selden's mood than Van Alstyne's after-dinner aphorisms, but as long as the latter confined himself to generalities his listener's nerves were in control. Happily Van Alstyne prided himself on his summing up of social aspects, and with Selden for audience was eager to show the sureness of his touch. Mrs. Fisher lived in an East side street near the Park, and as the two men walked down Fifth Avenue the new architectural developments of that versatile thorough-fare invited Van Alstyne's comment.

"That Greiner house, now—a typical rung in the social ladder! The man who built it came from a *milieu* where all the dishes are put on the table at once. His façade is a complete architectural meal; if he had omitted a style his friends might have thought the money had given out. Not a bad purchase for Rosedale, though: attracts attention, and awes the Western sight-seer. By and bye he'll get out of that phase, and want something that the crowd will pass and the few pause before. Especially if he marries my clever cousin——"

Selden dashed in with the query: "And the Wellington Brys'? Rather clever of its kind, don't you think?"

They were just beneath the wide white façade, with its rich restraint of line, which suggested the clever corseting of a redundant figure.

"That's the next stage; the desire to imply that one has been to Europe, and has a standard. I'm sure Mrs. Bry thinks her house a copy of the *Trianon*;[3] in America every marble house with gilt furniture is thought to be a copy of the *Trianon*. What a clever chap that architect is, though— how he takes his client's measure! He has put the whole of Mrs. Bry in his use of the composite order. Now for the Trenors, you remember, he chose the Corinthian: exuberant, but based on the best precedent. The Trenor house is one of his best things—doesn't look like a banqueting-

---

3. An ornate French chateau famous for its pink marble and gilt, located on the grounds of Louis XIV's Chateau de Versailles and inhabited most notably by his mistress, Madame de Maintenon, and later by Napoleon's second empress, Marie-Louise. It became a guest house for dignitaries and royalty such as Queen Victoria in the nineteenth century.

hall turned inside out. I hear Mrs. Trenor wants to build out a new ball-room, and that divergence from Gus on that point keeps her at Bellomont. The dimensions of the Brys' ball-room must rankle: you may be sure she knows 'em as well as if she'd been there last night with a yard-measure. Who said she was in town, by the way? That Farish boy? She isn't, I know; Mrs. Stepney was right; the house is dark, you see: I suppose Gus lives in the back."

He had halted opposite the Trenors' corner, and Selden perforce stayed his steps also. The house loomed obscure and uninhabited; only an oblong gleam above the door spoke of provisional occupancy.

"They've bought the house at the back: it gives them a hundred and fifty feet in the side street. There's where the ball-room's to be, with a gallery connecting it: billiard-room and so on above. I suggested changing the entrance, and carrying the drawing-room across the whole Fifth Avenue front: you see the front door corresponds with the windows——"

The walking-stick which Van Alstyne swung in demonstration dropped to a startled "Hallo!" as the door opened and two figures were seen silhouetted against the hall-light. At the same moment a hansom halted at the curb-stone, and one of the figures floated down to it in a haze of evening draperies; while the other, black and bulky remained persistently projected against the light.

For an immeasurable second the two spectators of the incident were silent; then the house-door closed, the hansom rolled off, and the whole scene slipped by as if with the turn of a stereopticon.

Van Alstyne dropped his eye-glass with a low whistle.

"A—hem—nothing of this, eh, Selden? As one of the family, I know I may count on you—appearances are deceptive—and Fifth Avenue is so imperfectly lighted——"

"Goodnight," said Selden, turning sharply down the side street without seeing the other's extended hand.

Alone with her cousin's kiss, Gerty stared upon her thoughts. He had kissed her before—but not with another woman on his lips. If he had spared her that she could have drowned quietly, welcoming the dark flood as it submerged her. But now the flood was shot through with glory, and it was harder to drown at sunrise than in darkness. Gerty hid her face from the light, but it pierced to the crannies of her soul. She had been so contented, life had seemed so simple and sufficient—why had he come to trouble her with new hopes? And Lily—Lily, her best friend! Woman-like, she accused the woman. Perhaps, had it not been for Lily, her fond imagining might have become truth. Selden had always liked her—had understood and sympathized with the modest independence of her life. He, who had the reputation of weighing all things in the nice balance of fastidious perceptions, had been uncritical and simple in his view of her: his cleverness had never overawed her because she had felt at home in his heart. And now she was thrust out, and the door barred against her by Lily's hand! Lily, for whose admission there she herself had pleaded! The situation was lighted up by a dreary flash of irony. She knew Selden—she saw how the force of her faith in Lily must have helped to dispel his hesitations. She remembered, too, how Lily had talked of him—she saw herself bringing the two together, making them known to each other. On Selden's part, no doubt, the wound inflicted was inconscient; he had never guessed her foolish secret; but Lily—Lily must have known! When, in such matters, are a woman's perceptions at fault? And if she knew, then she had deliberately despoiled her friend, and in mere wantonness of power, since, even to Gerty's suddenly flaming jealousy, it seemed incredible that Lily should wish to be Selden's wife. Lily might be incapable of marrying for money, but she was equally incapable of living without it, and Selden's eager investigations into the small economies of house-keeping made him appear to Gerty as tragically duped as herself.

She remained long in her sitting-room, where the embers were crumbling to cold grey, and the lamp paled under its gay shade. Just beneath it stood the photograph of Lily Bart, looking out imperially on the cheap gim-cracks, the cramped furniture of the little room. Could Selden picture her in such an interior? Gerty felt the poverty, the insignificance of her surroundings: she beheld her life as it must appear to Lily. And the cruelty of Lily's judgments smote upon her memory. She saw that she had dressed her idol with attributes of her own making. When had Lily ever really felt, or pitied, or understood? All she wanted was the taste of new experiences: she seemed like some cruel creature experimenting in a laboratory.

The pink-faced clock drummed out another hour, and Gerty rose with a start. She had an appointment early the next morning with a district visitor on the East side.[4] She put out her lamp, covered the fire, and went into her bedroom to undress. In the little glass above her dressing-table she saw her face reflected against the shadows of the room, and tears blotted the reflection. What right had she to dream the dreams of loveliness? A dull face invited a dull fate. She cried quietly as she undressed, laying aside her clothes with her habitual precision, setting everything in order for the next day, when the old life must be taken up as though there had been no break in its routine. Her servant did not come till eight o'clock, and she prepared her own tea-tray and placed it beside the bed. Then she locked the door of the flat, extinguished her light and lay down. But on her bed sleep would not come, and she lay face to face with the fact that she hated Lily Bart. It closed with her in the darkness like some formless evil to be blindly grappled with. Reason, judgment, renunciation, all the sane daylight forces, were beaten back in the sharp struggle for self-preservation. She wanted happiness—wanted it as fiercely and unscrupulously as Lily did, but without Lily's power of

4. A social worker assigned to the Lower East Side of Manhattan, which at the turn of the century was a ghetto crowded with newly arrived immigrants, primarily Italian and Jewish.

obtaining it. And in her conscious impotence she lay shivering, and hated her friend——

A ring at the door-bell caught her to her feet. She struck a light and stood startled, listening. For a moment her heart beat incoherently, then she felt the sobering touch of fact, and remembered that such calls were not unknown in her charitable work. She flung on her dressing-gown to answer the summons, and unlocking her door, confronted the shining vision of Lily Bart.

Gerty's first movement was one of revulsion. She shrank back as though Lily's presence flashed too sudden a light upon her misery. Then she heard her name in a cry, had a glimpse of her friend's face, and felt herself caught and clung to.

"Lily—what is it?" she exclaimed.

Miss Bart released her, and stood breathing brokenly, like one who has gained shelter after a long flight.

"I was so cold—I couldn't go home. Have you a fire?"

Gerty's compassionate instincts, responding to the swift call of habit, swept aside all her reluctances. Lily was simply some one who needed help—for what reason, there was no time to pause and conjecture: disciplined sympathy checked the wonder on Gerty's lips, and made her draw her friend silently into the sitting-room and seat her by the darkened hearth.

"There is kindling wood here: the fire will burn in a minute."

She knelt down, and the flame leapt under her rapid hands. It flashed strangely through the tears which still blurred her eyes, and smote on the white ruin of Lily's face. The girls looked at each other in silence; then Lily repeated: "I couldn't go home."

"No—no—you came here, dear! You're cold and tired—sit quiet, and I'll make you some tea."

Gerty had unconsciously adopted the soothing note of her trade: all personal feeling was merged in the sense of ministry, and experience had taught her that the bleeding must be stayed before the wound is probed.

Lily sat quiet, leaning to the fire: the clatter of cups behind her soothed her as familiar noises hush a child whom silence has kept wakeful. But when Gerty stood at her side with the tea she pushed it away, and turned an estranged eye on the familiar room.

"I came here because I couldn't bear to be alone," she said.

Gerty set down the cup and knelt beside her.

"Lily! Something has happened—can't you tell me?"

"I couldn't bear to lie awake in my room till morning. I hate my room at Aunt Julia's—so I came here——"

She stirred suddenly, broke from her apathy, and clung to Gerty in a fresh burst of fear.

"Oh, Gerty, the furies . . . you know the noise of their wings—

"Oh, Gerty, the furies . . . you know the noise of their wings?"

alone, at night, in the dark? But you don't know—there is nothing to make the dark dreadful to you——"

The words, flashing back on Gerty's last hours, struck from her a faint derisive murmur; but Lily, in the blaze of her own misery, was blinded to everything outside it.

"You'll let me stay? I shan't mind when daylight comes—Is it late? Is the night nearly over? It must be awful to be sleepless—everything stands by the bed and stares——"

Miss Farish caught her straying hands. "Lily, look at me! Something has happened—an accident? You have been frightened—what has frightened you? Tell me if you can—a word or two—so that I can help you."

Lily shook her head.

"I am not frightened: that's not the word. Can you imagine looking into your glass some morning and seeing a disfigurement—some hideous change that has come to you while you slept? Well, I seem to myself like that—I can't bear to see myself in my own thoughts—I hate ugliness, you know—I've always turned from it—but I can't explain to you—you wouldn't understand."

She lifted her head and her eyes fell on the clock.

"How long the night is! And I know I shan't sleep tomorrow. Some one told me my father used to lie sleepless and think of horrors. And he was not wicked, only unfortunate—and I see now how he must have suffered, lying alone with his thoughts! But I am bad—a bad girl—all my thoughts are bad—I have always had bad people about me. Is that any excuse? I thought I could manage my own life—I was proud—proud! but now I'm on their level——"

Sobs shook her, and she bowed to them like a tree in a dry storm.

Gerty knelt beside her, waiting, with the patience born of experience, till this gust of misery should loosen fresh speech. She had first imagined some physical shock, some peril of the crowded streets, since Lily was presumably on her way home from Carry Fisher's; but she now saw that other nerve-centres were smitten, and her mind trembled back from conjecture.

Lily's sobs ceased, and she lifted her head.

"There are bad girls in your slums. Tell me—do they ever pick themselves up? Ever forget, and feel as they did before?"

"Lily! you mustn't speak so—you're dreaming."

"Don't they always go from bad to worse? There's no turning back—your old self rejects you, and shuts you out."

She rose, stretching her arms as if in utter physical weariness. "Go to bed, dear! You work hard and get up early. I'll watch here by the fire, and you'll leave the light, and your door open. All I want is to feel that you are near me." She laid both hands on Gerty's shoulders, with a smile that was like sunrise on a sea strewn with wreckage.

"I can't leave you, Lily. Come and lie on my bed. Your hands are frozen—you must undress and be made warm." Gerty paused with sudden compunction. "But Mrs. Peniston—it's past midnight! What will she think?"

"She goes to bed. I have a latch-key. It doesn't matter—I can't go back there."

"There's no need to: you shall stay here. But you must tell me where you have been. Listen, Lily—it will help you to speak!" She regained Miss Bart's hands, and pressed them against her. "Try to tell me—it will clear your poor head. Listen—you were dining at Carry Fisher's." Gerty paused and added with a flash of heroism: "Lawrence Selden went from here to find you."

At the word, Lily's face melted from locked anguish to the open misery of a child. Her lips trembled and her gaze widened with tears.

"He went to find me? And I missed him! Oh, Gerty, he tried to help me. He told me—he warned me long ago—he foresaw that I should grow hateful to myself!"

The name, as Gerty saw with a clutch at the heart, had loosened the springs of self-pity in her friend's dry breast, and tear by tear Lily poured out the measure of her anguish. She had dropped sideways in Gerty's big arm-chair, her head buried where lately Selden's had leaned, in a beauty of abandonment that drove home to Gerty's aching senses the inevitableness of her own defeat. Ah, it needed no deliberate purpose on Lily's part to rob her of her dream! To look on that prone loveliness was to see in it a natural force, to recognize that love and power belong to such as Lily, as renunciation and service are the lot of those they despoil. But if Selden's infatuation seemed a fatal necessity, the effect that his name produced shook Gerty's steadfastness with a last pang. Men pass through such superhuman loves and outlive them: they are the probation subduing the heart to human joys. How gladly Gerty would have welcomed the ministry of healing: how willingly have soothed the sufferer back to tolerance of life! But Lily's self-betrayal took this last hope from her. The mortal maid on the shore is helpless against the siren who loves her prey: such victims are floated back dead from their adventure.

Lily sprang up and caught her with strong hands. "Gerty, you know him—you understand him—tell me; if I went to him, if I told him everything—if I said: 'I am bad through and through—I want admiration, I want excitement, I want money—' yes, *money!* That's my shame, Gerty—and it's known, it's said of me—it's what men think of me—If I said it all to him—told him the whole story—said plainly: 'I've sunk lower than the lowest, for I've taken what they take, and not paid as they pay'—oh, Gerty, you know him, you can speak for him: if I told him everything would he loathe me? Or would he pity me, and understand me, and save me from loathing myself?"

Gerty stood cold and passive. She knew the hour of her probation had come, and her poor heart beat wildly against its destiny. As a dark river sweeps by under a lightning flash, she saw her chance of happiness surge past under a flash of temptation. What prevented her from saying: "He is like other men"? She was not so sure of him, after all! But to do so would have been like blaspheming her love. She could not put him before herself in any light but the noblest: she must trust him to the height of her own passion.

"Yes: I know him; he will help you," she said; and in a moment Lily's passion was weeping itself out against her breast.

There was but one bed in the little flat, and the two girls lay down on it side by side when Gerty had unlaced Lily's dress and persuaded her to put her lips to the warm tea. The light extinguished, they lay still in the darkness, Gerty shrinking to the outer edge of the narrow couch to avoid contact with her bed-fellow. Knowing that Lily disliked to be caressed, she had long ago learned to check her demonstrative impulses toward her friend. But tonight every fibre in her body shrank from Lily's nearness: it was torture to listen to her breathing, and feel the sheet stir with it. As Lily turned, and settled to completer rest, a strand of her hair swept Gerty's cheek with its fragrance. Everything about her was warm and soft and scented: even the stains of her grief became her as rain-drops do the beaten rose. But as Gerty lay with arms drawn down her side, in the motionless narrowness of an effigy, she felt a stir of sobs from the breathing warmth beside her, and Lily flung out her hand, groped for her friend's, and held it fast.

"Hold me, Gerty, hold me, or I shall think of things," she moaned; and Gerty silently slipped an arm under her, pillowing her head in its hollow as a mother makes a nest for a tossing child. In the warm hollow Lily lay still and her breathing grew low and regular. Her hand still clung to Gerty's as if to ward off evil dreams, but the hold of her fingers relaxed, her head sank deeper into its shelter, and Gerty felt that she slept.

XV

When Lily woke she had the bed to herself, and the winter light was in the room.

She sat up, bewildered by the strangeness of her surroundings; then memory returned, and she looked about her with a shiver. In the cold slant of light reflected from the back wall of a neighbouring building, she saw her evening dress and opera cloak lying in a tawdry heap on a chair. Finery laid off is as unappetizing as the remains of a feast, and it occurred to Lily that, at home, her maid's vigilance had always spared her the sight of such incongruities. Her body ached with fatigue, and with the constriction of her attitude in Gerty's bed. All through her troubled sleep she had been conscious of having no space to toss in, and the long effort to remain motionless made her feel as if she had spent her night in a train.

This sense of physical discomfort was the first to assert itself; then she perceived, beneath it, a corresponding mental prostration, a languor of horror more insufferable than the first rush of her disgust. The thought of having to wake every morning with this weight on her breast roused her tired mind to fresh effort. She must find some way out of the slough into which she had stumbled: it was not so much compunction as the dread of her morning thoughts that pressed on her the need of action. But she was unutterably tired; it was weariness to think connectedly. She lay back, looking about the poor slit of a room with a renewal of physical distaste. The outer air, penned between high buildings, brought no freshness through the window; steam-heat was beginning to sing in a coil of dingy pipes, and a smell of cooking penetrated the crack of the door.

The door opened, and Gerty, dressed and hatted, entered with a cup of tea. Her face looked sallow and swollen in the dreary light, and her dull hair shaded imperceptibly into the tones of her skin.

She glanced shyly at Lily, asking in an embarrassed tone how she felt; Lily answered with the same constraint, and raised herself up to drink the tea.

"I must have been over-tired last night; I think I had a nervous attack in the carriage," she said, as the drink brought clearness to her sluggish thoughts.

"You were not well; I am so glad you came here," Gerty returned.

"But how am I go get home? And Aunt Julia——?"

"She knows; I telephoned early, and your maid has brought your things. But won't you eat something? I scrambled the eggs myself."

Lily could not eat; but the tea strengthened her to rise and dress under her maid's searching gaze. It was a relief to her that Gerty was obliged to hasten away: the two kissed silently, but without a trace of the previous night's emotion.

Lily found Mrs. Peniston in a state of agitation. She had sent for Grace Stepney and was taking digitalis. Lily breasted the storm of enquiries as best she could, explaining that she had had an attack of faintness on her way back from Carry Fisher's; that, fearing she would not have strength to reach home, she had gone to Miss Farish's instead; but that a quiet night had restored her, and that she had no need of a doctor.

This was a relief to Mrs. Peniston, who could give herself up to her own symptoms, and Lily was advised to go and lie down, her aunt's panacea for all physical and moral disorders. In the solitude of her own room she was brought back to a sharp contemplation of facts. Her daylight view of them necessarily differed from the cloudy vision of the night. The winged furies were not prowling gossips who dropped in on each other for tea. But her fears seemed the uglier, thus shorn of their vagueness; and besides, she had to act, not rave. For the first time she forced herself to reckon up the exact amount of her debt to Trenor; and the result of this hateful computation was the discovery that she had, in all, received nine thousand dollars from him. The flimsy pretext on which it had been given and received shrivelled up in the blaze of her shame: she knew that not a penny of it was her own, and that to restore her self-respect she must at once repay the whole amount. The inability thus to solace her outraged feelings gave her a paralyzing sense of insignificance. She was realizing for the first time that a woman's dignity may cost more to keep up than her carriage; and that the maintenance of a moral attribute should be dependent on dollars and cents, made the world appear a more sordid place than she had conceived it.

After luncheon, when Grace Stepney's prying eyes had been removed, Lily asked for a word with her aunt. The two ladies went upstairs to the sitting-room, where Mrs. Peniston seated herself in her black satin arm-chair tufted with yellow buttons, beside a bead-work table bearing a bronze box with a miniature of Beatrice Cenci[1] in the lid. Lily felt for these objects the same distaste which the prisoner may entertain for the fittings of the court-room. It was here that her aunt received her rare confidences, and the pink-eyed smirk of the turbaned Beatrice was associated in her mind with the gradual fading of the smile from Mrs. Peniston's lips. That lady's dread of a scene gave her an inexorableness which the greatest strength of character could not have produced, since it was inde-pendent of all considerations of right or wrong; and knowing this, Lily seldom ventured to assail it. She had never felt less like making the attempt than on the present occasion; but she had sought in vain for any other means of escape from an intolerable situation.

Mrs. Peniston examined her critically. "You're a bad colour, Lily: this incessant rushing about is beginning to tell on you," she said.

Miss Bart saw an opening. "I don't think it's that, Aunt Julia; I've had worries," she replied.

"Ah," said Mrs. Peniston, shutting her lips with the snap of a purse closing against a beggar.

"I'm sorry to bother you with them," Lily continued, "but I really believe my faintness last night was brought on partly by anxious thoughts——"

"I should have said Carry Fisher's cook was enough to account for it. She has a woman who was with Maria Melson in 1891—the spring of the year we went to Aix—and I remember dining there two days before we sailed, and feeling *sure* the coppers hadn't been scoured."

"I don't think I ate much; I can't eat or sleep." Lily paused, and then said abruptly: "The fact is, Aunt Julia, I owe some money.'

Mrs. Peniston's face clouded perceptibly, but did not express the astonishment her niece had expected. She was silent, and Lily was forced to continue: "I have been foolish——"

"No doubt you have: extremely foolish," Mrs. Peniston interposed. "I fail to see how any one with your income, and no expenses—not to mention the handsome presents I've always given you——"

"Oh, you've been most generous, Aunt Julia; I shall never forget your kindness. But perhaps you don't quite realize the expense a girl is put to nowadays——"

---

1. Beatrice Cenci (1577–99) was an Italian accused of conspiring to murder her father, who had forced her into incestuous relations. She was regarded as a great tragic heroine in the nineteenth century, largely because of an affecting portrait of her sup- posedly by Guido Reni, to which Wharton is referring here. This painting was one of the most famous and most reproduced artworks of the cen- tury, inspiring, e.g., Shelley's play *The Cenci*.

"I don't realize that *you* are put to any expense except for your clothes and your railway fares. I expect you to be handsomely dressed; but I paid Céleste's bill for you last October."

Lily hesitated: her aunt's implacable memory had never been more inconvenient. "You were as kind as possible; but I have had to get a few things since——"

"What kind of things? Clothes? How much have you spent? Let me see the bill—I daresay the woman is swindling you."

"Oh, no, I think not: clothes have grown so frightfully expensive; and one needs so many different kinds, with country visits, and golf and skating, and Aiken and Tuxedo——"[2]

"Let me see the bill," Mrs. Peniston repeated.

Lily hesitated again. In the first place, Mme. Céleste had not yet sent in her account, and secondly, the amount it represented was only a fraction of the sum that Lily needed.

"She hasn't sent in the bill for my winter things, but I *know* it's large; and there are one or two other things; I've been careless and imprudent—I'm frightened to think of what I owe——"

She raised the troubled loveliness of her face to Mrs. Peniston, vainly hoping that a sight so moving to the other sex might not be without effect upon her own. But the effect produced was that of making Mrs. Peniston shrink back apprehensively.

"Really, Lily, you are old enough to manage your own affairs, and after frightening me to death by your performance of last night you might at least choose a better time to worry me with such matters." Mrs. Peniston glanced at the clock, and swallowed a tablet of digitalis. "If you owe Céleste another thousand, she may send me her account," she added, as though to end the discussion at any cost.

"I am very sorry, Aunt Julia; I hate to trouble you at such a time; but I have really no choice—I ought to have spoken sooner—I owe a great deal more than a thousand dollars."

"A great deal more? Do you owe two? She must have robbed you!"

"I told you it was not only Céleste. I—there are other bills—more pressing—that must be settled."

"What on earth have you been buying? Jewelry? You must have gone off your head," said Mrs. Peniston with asperity. "But if you have run into debt, you must suffer the consequences, and put aside your monthly income till your bills are paid. If you stay quietly here until next spring, instead of racing about all over the country, you will have no expenses at all, and surely in four or five months you can settle the rest of your bills if I pay the dress-maker now."

Lily was again silent. She knew she could not hope to extract even a thousand dollars from Mrs. Peniston on the mere plea of paying Céleste's bill: Mrs. Peniston would expect to go over the dress-maker's account,

2. Aiken, South Carolina, and Tuxedo, New York, were fancy country resorts of the very wealthy where fashionable clothing was expected. Tuxedo, e.g., gave its name to the man's formal dinner jacket we know today.

and would make out the cheque to her and not to Lily. And yet the money must be obtained before the day was over!

"The debts I speak of are—different—not like tradesmen's bills," she began confusedly; but Mrs. Peniston's look made her almost afraid to continue. Could it be that her aunt suspected anything? The idea precipitated Lily's avowal.

"The fact is, I've played cards a good deal—bridge; the women all do it; girls too—it's expected. Sometimes I've won—won a good deal—but lately I've been unlucky—and of course such debts can't be paid off gradually——"

She paused: Mrs. Peniston's face seemed to be petrifying as she listened.

"Cards—you've played cards for money? It's true, then: when I was told so I wouldn't believe it. I won't ask if the other horrors I was told were true too; I've heard enough for the state of my nerves. When I think of the example you've had in this house! But I suppose it's your foreign bringing-up—no one knew where your mother picked up her friends. And her Sundays were a scandal—that I know." Mrs. Peniston wheeled round suddenly. "You play cards on Sunday?"

Lily flushed with the recollection of certain rainy Sundays at Bellomont and with the Dorsets.

"You're hard on me, Aunt Julia: I have never really cared for cards, but a girl hates to be thought priggish and superior, and one drifts into doing what the others do. I've had a dreadful lesson, and if you'll help me out this time I promise you——"

Mrs. Peniston raised her hand warningly. "You needn't make any promises: it's unnecessary. When I offered you a home I didn't undertake to pay your gambling debts."

"Aunt Julia! You don't mean that you won't help me?"

"I shall certainly not do anything to give the impression that I countenance your behaviour. If you really owe your dress-maker, I will settle with her—beyond that I recognize no obligation to assume your debts."

Lily had risen, and stood pale and quivering before her aunt. Pride stormed in her, but humiliation forced the cry from her lips: "Aunt Julia, I shall be disgraced—I——" But she could go no farther. If her aunt turned such a stony ear to the fiction of the gambling debts, in what spirit would she receive the terrible avowal of the truth?

"I consider that you *are* disgraced, Lily: disgraced by your conduct far more than by its results. You say your friends have persuaded you to play cards with them; well, they may as well learn a lesson too. They can probably afford to lose a little money—and at any rate, I am not going to waste any of mine in paying them. And now I must ask you to leave me—this scene has been extremely painful, and I have my own health to consider. Draw down the blinds, please; and tell Jennings I will see no one this afternoon but Grace Stepney."

Lily went up to her own room and bolted the door. She was trembling with fear and anger—the rush of the furies' wings was in her ears. She walked up and down the room with blind irregular steps. The last door of escape was closed—she felt herself shut in with her dishonour——

Suddenly her wild pacing brought her before the clock on the chimney-piece. Its hands stood at half-past three, and she remembered that Selden was to come to her at four. She had meant to put him off with a word—but now her heart leaped at the thought of seeing him. Was there not a promise of rescue in his love? As she had lain at Gerty's side the night before, she had thought of his coming, and of the sweetness of weeping out her pain upon his breast. Of course she had meant to clear herself of its consequences before she met him—she had never really doubted that Mrs. Peniston would come to her aid. And she had felt, even in the full storm of her misery, that Selden's love could not be her ultimate refuge; only it would be so sweet to take a moment's shelter there, while she gathered fresh strength to go on.

But now his love was her only hope, and as she sat alone with her wretchedness the thought of confiding in him became as seductive as the river's flow to the suicide. The first plunge would be terrible—but afterward, what blessedness might come! She remembered Gerty's words: "I know him—he will help you"; and her mind clung to them as a sick person might cling to a healing relic. Oh, if he really understood—if he would help her to gather up her broken life, and put it together in some new semblance in which no trace of the past should remain! He had always made her feel that she was worthy of better things, and she had never been in greater need of such solace. Once and again she shrank at the thought of imperilling his love by her confession: for love was what she needed—it would take the glow of passion to weld together the shattered fragments of her self-esteem. But she recurred to Gerty's words and held fast to them. She was sure that Gerty knew Selden's feelings for her, and it had never dawned upon her blindness that Gerty's own judgment of him was coloured by emotions far more ardent than her own.

Four o'clock found her in the drawing-room: she was sure that Selden would be punctual. But the hour came and passed—it moved on feverishly, measured by her impatient heart-beats. She had time to take a fresh survey of her wretchedness, and to fluctuate anew between the impulse to confide in Selden and the dread of destroying his illusions. But as the minutes passed the need of throwing herself on his comprehension became more urgent: she could not bear the weight of her misery alone. There would be a perilous moment, perhaps: but could she not trust to her beauty to bridge it over, to land her safe in the shelter of his devotion?

But the hour sped on and Selden did not come. Doubtless he had been detained, or had misread her hurriedly scrawled note, taking the four for a five. The ringing of the door-bell a few minutes after five confirmed this supposition, and made Lily hastily resolve to write more legibly in future. The sound of steps in the hall, and of the butler's voice preceding them, poured fresh energy into her veins. She felt herself once more the alert and competent moulder of emergencies, and the remem-

brance of her power over Selden flushed her with sudden confidence.
But when the drawing-room door opened it was Rosedale who came in.

The reaction caused her a sharp pang, but after a passing movement
of irritation at the clumsiness of fate, and at her own carelessness in not
denying the door to all but Selden, she controlled herself and greeted
Rosedale amicably. It was annoying that Selden, when he came, should
find that particular visitor in possession, but Lily was mistress of the art
of ridding herself of superfluous company, and to her present mood
Rosedale seemed distinctly negligible.

His own view of the situation forced itself upon her after a few moments'
conversation. She had caught at the Brys' entertainment as an easy
impersonal subject, likely to tide them over the interval till Selden
appeared, but Mr. Rosedale, tenaciously planted beside the tea-table,
his hands in his pockets, his legs a little too freely extended, at once gave
the topic a personal turn.

"Pretty well done—well, yes, I suppose it was: Welly Bry's got his back
up and don't mean to let go till he's got the hang of the thing. Of course,
there were things here and there—things Mrs. Fisher couldn't be expected
to see to—the champagne wasn't cold, and the coats got mixed in the
coat-room. I would have spent more money on the music. But that's my
character: if I want a thing I'm willing to pay: I don't go up to the counter,
and then wonder if the article's worth the price. I wouldn't be satisfied
to entertain like the Welly Brys; I'd want something that would look
more easy and natural, more as if I took it in my stride. And it takes
just two things to do that, Miss Bart: money, and the right woman to
spend it."

He paused, and examined her attentively while she affected to rear-
range the tea-cups.

"I've got the money," he continued, clearing his throat, "and what I
want is the woman—and I mean to have her too."

He leaned forward a little, resting his hands on the head of his walking-stick. He had seen men of Ned Van Alstyne's type bring their hats
and sticks into a drawing-room, and he thought it added a touch of
elegant familiarity to their appearance.

Lily was silent, smiling faintly, with her eyes absently resting on his
face. She was in reality reflecting that a declaration would take some
time to make, and that Selden must surely appear before the moment of
refusal had been reached. Her brooding look, as of a mind withdrawn
yet not averted, seemed to Mr. Rosedale full of a subtle encouragement.
He would not have liked any evidence of eagerness.

"I mean to have her too," he repeated, with a laugh intended to
strengthen his self-assurance. "I generally *have* got what I wanted in life,
Miss Bart. I wanted money, and I've got more than I know how to invest;
and now the money doesn't seem to be of any account unless I can spend
it on the right woman. That's what I want to do with it: I want my wife
to make all the other women feel small. I'd never grudge a dollar that
was spent on that. But it isn't every woman can do it, no matter how

much you spend on her. There was a girl in some history book who wanted gold shields, or something, and the fellows threw 'em at her, and she was crushed under 'em: they killed her. Well, that's true enough: some women looked buried under their jewelry. What I want is a woman who'll hold her head higher the more diamonds I put on it. And when I looked at you the other night at the Brys', in that plain white dress, looking as if you had a crown on, I said to myself: 'By gad, if she had one she'd wear it as if it grew on her.' "

Still Lily did not speak, and he continued, warming with his theme: "Tell you what it is, though, that kind of woman costs more than all the rest of 'em put together. If a woman's going to ignore her pearls, they want to be better than anybody else's—and so it is with everything else. You know what I mean—you know it's only the showy things that are cheap. Well, I should want my wife to be able to take the earth for granted if she wanted to. I know there's one thing vulgar about money, and that's the thinking about it; and my wife would never have to demean herself in that way." He paused, and then added, with an unfortunate lapse to an earlier manner: "I guess you know the lady I've got in view, Miss Bart."

Lily raised her head, brightening a little under the challenge. Even through the dark tumult of her thoughts, the clink of Mr. Rosedale's millions had a faintly seductive note. Oh, for enough of them to cancel her one miserable debt! But the man behind them grew increasingly repugnant in the light of Selden's expected coming. The contrast was too grotesque: she could scarcely suppress the smile it provoked. She decided that directness would be best.

"If you mean me, Mr. Rosedale, I am very grateful—very much flattered; but I don't know what I have ever done to make you think——"

"Oh, if you mean you're not dead in love with me, I've got sense enough left to see that. And I ain't talking to you as if you were—I presume I know the kind of talk that's expected under those circumstances. I'm confoundedly gone on you—that's about the size of it—and I'm just giving you a plain business statement of the consequences. You're not very fond of me—yet—but you're fond of luxury, and style, and amusement, and of not having to worry about cash. You like to have a good time, and not to have to settle for it; and what I propose to do is to provide for the good time and do the settling."

He paused, and she returned with a chilling smile: "You are mistaken in one point, Mr. Rosedale: whatever I enjoy I am prepared to settle for."

She spoke with the intention of making him see that, if his words implied a tentative allusion to her private affairs, she was prepared to meet and repudiate it. But if he recognized her meaning it failed to abash him, and he went on in the same tone: "I didn't mean to give offence; excuse me if I've spoken too plainly. But why ain't you straight with me—why do you put up that kind of bluff? You know there've been times when you were bothered—damned bothered—and as a girl gets older, and things keep moving along, why, before she knows it, the things she wants are liable to move past her and not come back. I don't say it's anywhere near that with you yet; but you've had a taste of bothers that a girl like yourself ought never to have known about, and what I'm offering you is the chance to turn your back on them once for all "

The colour burned in Lily's face as he ended; there was no mistaking the point he meant to make, and to permit it to pass unheeded was a fatal confession of weakness, while to resent it too openly was to risk offending him at a perilous moment. Indignation quivered on her lip; but it was quelled by the secret voice which warned her that she must not quarrel with him. He knew too much about her, and even at the moment when it was essential that he should show himself at his best, he did not scruple to let her see how much he knew. How then would he use his power when her expression of contempt had dispelled his one motive for restraint? Her whole future might hinge on her way of answering him: she had to stop and consider that, in the stress of her other anxieties, as a breathless fugitive may have to pause at the cross-roads and try to decide coolly which turn to take.

"You are quite right, Mr. Rosedale. I *have* had bothers; and I am grateful to you for wanting to relieve me of them. It is not always easy to be quite independent and self-respecting when one is poor and lives among rich people; I have been careless about money, and have worried about my bills. But I should be selfish and ungrateful if I made that a reason for accepting all you offer, with no better return to make than the desire to be free from my anxieties. You must give me time—time to think of your kindness—and of what I could give you in return for it——"

She held out her hand with a charming gesture in which dismissal was shorn of its rigour. Its hint of future leniency made Rosedale rise in obedience to it, a little flushed with his unhoped-for success, and disciplined by the tradition of his blood to accept what was conceded, without undue haste to press for more. Something in his prompt acquiescence frightened her; she felt behind it the stored force of a patience that might subdue the strongest will. But at least they had parted amicably, and he was out of the house without meeting Selden—Selden, whose continued absence now smote her with a new alarm. Rosedale had remained over an hour, and she understood that it was not too late to hope for Selden. He would write explaining his absence, of course; there would be a note from him by the late post. But her confession would have to be postponed; and the chill of the delay settled heavily on her fagged spirit.

It lay heavier when the postman's last ring brought no note for her, and she had to go upstairs to a lonely night—a night as grim and sleepless as her tortured fancy had pictured it to Gerty. She had never learned to live with her own thoughts, and to be confronted with them through such hours of lucid misery made the confused wretchedness of her previous vigil seem easily bearable.

Daylight disbanded the phantom crew, and made it clear to her that she would hear from Selden before noon; but the day passed without his writing or coming. Lily remained at home, lunching and dining alone with her aunt, who complained of flutterings of the heart, and talked icily on general topics. Mrs. Peniston went to bed early, and when she had gone Lily sat down and wrote a note to Selden. She was about to ring for a messenger to despatch it when her eye fell on a paragraph in the evening paper which lay at her elbow: "Mr. Lawrence Selden was among the passengers sailing this afternoon for Havana and the West Indies on the Windward Liner Antilles."

She laid down the paper and sat motionless, staring at her note. She understood now that he was never coming—that he had gone away because he was afraid that he might come. She rose, and walking across the floor stood gazing at herself for a long time in the brightly-lit mirror about the mantelpiece. The lines in her face came out terribly—she looked old; and when a girl looks old to herself, how does she look to other people? She moved away, and began to wander aimlessly about the room, fitting her steps with mechanical precision between the monstrous roses of Mrs. Peniston's Axminster.[3] Suddenly she noticed that the pen with which she had written to Selden still rested against the uncovered ink-stand. She seated herself again, and taking out an envelope, addressed it rapidly to Rosedale. Then she laid out a sheet of paper, and sat over it with suspended pen. It had been easy enough to write the date, and "Dear Mr. Rosedale"—but after that her inspiration flagged. She meant to tell him to come to her, but the words refused to shape themselves. At length she began: "I have been thinking——" then she laid the pen down, and sat with her elbows on the table and her face hidden in her hands.

Suddenly she started up at the sound of the door-bell. It was not late—barely ten o'clock—and there might still be a note from Selden, or a message—or he might be there himself, on the other side of the door! The announcement of his sailing might have been a mistake—it might be another Lawrence Selden who had gone to Havana—all these possibilities had time to flash through her mind, and build up the conviction that she was after all to see or hear from him, before the drawing-room door opened to admit a servant carrying a telegram.

Lily tore it open with shaking hands, and read Bertha Dorset's name below the message: "Sailing unexpectedly tomorrow. Will you join us on a cruise in Mediterranean?"

3. A machine-loomed rug from Axminster, England. In the nineteenth century, mass-produced rugs such as this became available to many middle-class Americans who previously could not afford woven rugs; it is another indication of Mrs. Peniston's conventional taste.

Book II

It came vividly to Selden on the Casino steps that Monte Carlo had, more than any other place he knew, the fit of accommodating itself to each man's humour.

His own, at the moment, lent it a festive readiness of welcome that might well, in a disenchanted eye, have turned to paint and facility. So frank an appeal for participation—so outspoken a recognition of the holiday vein in human nature—struck refreshingly on a mind jaded by prolonged hard work in surroundings made for the discipline of the senses. As he surveyed the white square set in an exotic coquetry of architecture, the studied tropicality of the gardens, the groups loitering in the foreground against mauve mountains which suggested a sublime stage-setting forgotten in a hurried shifting of scenes—as he took in the whole outspread effect of light and leisure, he felt a movement of revulsion from the last few months of his life.

The New York winter had presented an interminable perspective of snow-burdened days, reaching toward a spring of raw sunshine and furious air, when the ugliness of things rasped the eye as the gritty wind ground into the skin. Selden, immersed in his work, had told himself that external conditions did not matter to a man in his state, and that cold and ugliness were a good tonic for relaxed sensibilities. When an urgent case summoned him abroad to confer with a client in Paris, he broke reluctantly with the routine of the office; and it was only now that, having despatched his business, and slipped away for a week in the south, he began to feel the renewed zest of spectatorship that is the solace of those who take an objective interest in life.

The multiplicity of its appeals—the perpetual surprise of its contrasts and resemblances! All these tricks and turns of the show were upon him with a spring as he descended the Casino steps and paused on the pavement at its doors. He had not been abroad for seven years—and what changes the renewed contact produced! If the central depths were untouched, hardly a pin-point of surface remained the same. And this was the very place to bring out the completeness of the renewal. The sublimities, the perpetuities, might have left him as he was but this tent pitched for a day's revelry spread a roof of oblivion between himself and his fixed sky.

It was mid-April, and one felt that the revelry had reached its climax and that the desultory groups in the square and gardens would soon dissolve and re-form in other scenes. Meanwhile the last moments of the performance seemed to gain an added brightness from the hovering threat of the curtain. The quality of the air, the exuberance of the flowers, the blue intensity of sea and sky, produced the effect of a closing *tableau*, when all the lights are turned on at once. This impression was presently heightened by the way in which a consciously conspicuous group of people advanced to the middle front, and stood before Selden with the air of the chief performers gathered together by the exigencies of the final effect. Their appearance confirmed the impression that the show had been staged regardless of expense, and emphasized its resemblance to one of those "costume-plays" in which the protagonists walk through the passions without displacing a drapery. The ladies stood in unrelated attitudes calculated to isolate their effects, and the men hung about them as irrelevantly as stage heroes whose tailors are named in the programme. It was Selden himself who unwittingly fused the group by arresting the attention of one of its members.

"Why, Mr. Selden!" Mrs. Fisher exclaimed in surprise; and with a gesture toward Mrs. Jack Stepney and Mrs. Wellington Bry, she added plaintively: "We're starving to death because we can't decide where to lunch."

Welcomed into their group, and made the confidant of their difficulty, Selden learned with amusement that there were several places where one might miss something by not lunching, or forfeit something by lunching; so that eating actually became a minor consideration on the very spot consecrated to its rites.

"Of course one gets the best things at the *Terrasse*—but that looks as if one hadn't any other reason for being there: the Americans who don't know any one always rush for the best food. And the Duchess of Belt-shire has taken up Bécassin's lately," Mrs. Bry earnestly summed up.

Mrs. Bry, to Mrs. Fisher's despair, had not progressed beyond the point of weighing her social alternatives in public. She could not acquire the air of doing things because she wanted to, and making her choice the final seal of their fitness.

Mr. Bry, a short pale man, with a business face and leisure clothes, met the dilemma hilariously.

"I guess the Duchess goes where it's cheapest, unless she can get her meal paid for. If you offered to blow her off at the *Terrasse* she'd turn up fast enough."

But Mrs. Jack Stepney interposed. "The Grand Dukes go to that little place at the Condamine. Lord Hubert says it's the only restaurant in Europe where they can cook peas."

Lord Hubert Dacey, a slender shabby-looking man, with a charming worn smile, and the air of having spent his best years in piloting the wealthy to the right restaurant, assented with gentle emphasis: "It's quite that."

"*Peas?*" said Mr. Bry contemptuously. "Can they cook terrapin? It

just shows," he continued, "what these European markets are, when a
fellow can make a reputation cooking peas!"

Jack Stepney intervened with authority. "I don't know that I quite
agree with Dacey: there's a little hole in Paris, off the Quai Voltaire—
but in any case, I can't advise the Condamine *gargote;*[1] at least not with
ladies."

Stepney, since his marriage, had thickened and grown prudish, as the
Van Osburgh husbands were apt to do; but his wife, to his surprise and
discomfiture, had developed an earth-shaking fastness of gait which left
him trailing breathlessly in her wake.

"That's where we'll go then!" she declared, with a heavy toss of her
plumage. "I'm so tired of the *Terrasse:* it's as dull as one of mother's
dinners. And Lord Hubert has promised to tell us who all the awful
people are at the other place—hasn't he, Carry? Now, Jack, don't look
so solemn!"

"Well," said Mrs. Bry, "all I want to know is who their dress-makers are."

"No doubt Dacey can tell you that too," remarked Stepney, with an
ironic intention which the other received with the light murmur, "I can
at least *find out,* my dear fellow"; and Mrs. Bry having declared that she
couldn't walk another step, the party hailed two or three of the light
phaetons which hover attentively on the confines of the gardens, and
rattled off in procession toward the Condamine.

Their destination was one of the little restaurants overhanging the
boulevard which dips steeply down from Monte Carlo to the low intermediate quarter along the quay. From the window in which they presently found themselves installed, they overlooked the intense blue curve
of the harbour, set between the verdure of twin promontories: to the
right, the cliff of Monaco, topped by the mediæval silhouette of its church
and castle, to the left the terraces and pinnacles of the gambling-
house. Between the two, the waters of the bay were furrowed by a light
coming and going of pleasure-craft, through which, just at the culminating moment of luncheon, the majestic advance of a great steam-
yacht drew the company's attention from the peas.

"By, Jove, I believe that's the Dorsets back!" Stepney exclaimed; and
Lord Hubert, dropping his single eye-glass, corroborated: "It's the
Sabrina[2]—yes."

"So soon? They were to spend a month in Sicily," Mrs. Fisher observed.

"I guess they feel as if they had: there's only one up-to-date hotel in
the whole place," said Mr. Bry disparagingly.

"It was Ned Silverton's idea—but poor Dorset and Lily Bart must have
been horribly bored." Mrs. Fisher added in an undertone to Selden: "I
do hope there hasn't been a row."

---

1. A *gargote* is a cheap eating-house; here Stepney
uses the term to describe with contempt the restaurant of the Hotel Condamine.
2. The Dorsets' yacht *Sabrina* is named after a

nymph who drowned in the Severn River of England; also Sabrina appears as a character in Mil-
ton's *Comus.*

"It's most awfully jolly having Miss Bart back," said Lord Hubert, in his mild deliberate voice; and Mrs. Bry added ingenuously: "I daresay the Duchess will dine with us, now that Lily's here."

"The Duchess admires her immensely: I'm sure she'd be charmed to have it arranged," Lord Hubert agreed, with the professional promptness of the man accustomed to draw his profit from facilitating social contacts: Selden was struck by the businesslike change in his manner.

"Lily has been a tremendous success here," Mrs. Fisher continued, still addressing herself confidentially to Selden. "She looks ten years younger—I never saw her so handsome. Lady Skiddaw took her everywhere in Cannes, and the Crown Princess of Macedonia had her to stop for a week at Cimiez. People say that was one reason why Bertha whisked the yacht off to Sicily: the Crown Princess didn't take much notice of her, and she couldn't bear to look on at Lily's triumph."

Selden made no reply. He was vaguely aware that Miss Bart was cruising in the Mediterranean with the Dorsets, but it had not occurred to him that there was any chance of running across her on the Riviera, where the season was virtually at an end. As he leaned back, silently contemplating his filigree cup of Turkish coffee, he was trying to put some order in his thoughts, to tell himself how the news of her nearness was really affecting him. He had a personal detachment enabling him, even in moments of emotional high-pressure, to get a fairly clear view of his feelings, and he was sincerely surprised by the disturbance which the sight of the Sabrina had produced in him. He had reason to think that his three months of engrossing professional work, following on the sharp shock of his disillusionment, had cleared his mind of its sentimental vapours. The feeling he had nourished and given prominence to was one of thankfulness for his escape: he was like a traveller so grateful for rescue from a dangerous accident that at first he is hardly conscious of his bruises. Now he suddenly felt the latent ache, and realized that after all he had not come off unhurt.

An hour later, at Mrs. Fisher's side in the Casino gardens, he was trying to find fresh reasons for forgetting the injury received in the contemplation of the peril avoided. The party had dispersed with the loitering indecision characteristic of social movements at Monte Carlo, where the whole place, and the long gilded hours of the day, seem to offer an infinity of ways of being idle. Lord Hubert Dacey had finally gone off in quest of the Duchess of Beltshire, charged by Mrs. Bry with the delicate negotiation of securing that lady's presence at dinner, the Stepneys had left for Nice in their motor-car, and Mr. Bry had departed to take his place in the pigeon-shooting match which was at the moment engaging his highest faculties.

Mrs. Bry, who had a tendency to grow red and stertorous after luncheon, had been judiciously prevailed upon by Carry Fisher to withdraw to her hotel for an hour's repose; and Selden and his companion were thus left to a stroll propitious to confidences. The stroll soon resolved itself into a tranquil session on a bench overhung with laurel and Bank-

sian roses, from which they caught a dazzle of blue sea between marble
balusters, and the fiery shafts of cactus-blossoms shooting meteor-like
from the rock. The soft shade of their niche, and the adjacent glitter of
the air, were conducive to an easy lounging mood, and to the smoking
of many cigarettes; and Selden, yielding to these influences, suffered
Mrs. Fisher to unfold to him the history of her recent experiences. She
had come abroad with the Welly Brys at the moment when fashion flees
the inclemency of the New York spring. The Brys, intoxicated by their
first success, already thirsted for new kingdoms, and Mrs. Fisher, viewing the Riviera as an easy introduction to London society, had guided
their course thither. She had affiliations of her own in every capital, and
a facility for picking them up again after long absences; and the carefully
disseminated rumour of the Brys' wealth had at once gathered about
them a group of cosmopolitan pleasure-seekers.

"But things are not going as well as I expected," Mrs. Fisher frankly
admitted. "It's all very well to say that everybody with money can get
into society; but it would be truer to say that *nearly* everybody can. And
the London market is so glutted with new Americans that, to succeed
there now, they must be either very clever or awfully queer. The Brys
are neither. *He* would get on well enough if she'd let him alone; they
like his slang and his brag and his blunders. But Louisa spoils it all by
trying to repress him and put herself forward. If she'd be natural herself—fat and vulgar and bouncing—it would be all right; but as soon as
she meets anybody smart she tries to be slender and queenly. She tried
it with the Duchess of Beltshire and Lady Skiddaw, and they fled. I've
done my best to make her see her mistake—I've said to her again and
again: 'Just let yourself go, Louisa'; but she keeps up the humbug even
with me—I believe she keeps on being queenly in her own room, with
the door shut.

"The worst of it is," Mrs. Fisher went on, "that she thinks it's all *my*
fault. When the Dorsets turned up here six weeks ago, and everybody
began to make a fuss about Lily Bart, I could see Louisa thought that if
she'd had Lily in tow instead of me she would have been hobnobbing
with all the royalties by this time. She doesn't realize that it's Lily's
beauty that does it: Lord Hubert tells me Lily is thought even handsomer
than when he knew her at Aix ten years ago. It seems she was tremendously admired there. An Italian Prince, rich and the real thing, wanted
to marry her; but just at the critical moment a good-looking step-son
turned up, and Lily was silly enough to flirt with him while her mar-
riage-settlements with the step-father were being drawn up. Some people
said the young man did it on purpose. You can fancy the scandal: there
was an awful row between the men, and people began to look at Lily so
queerly that Mrs. Peniston had to pack up and finish her cure elsewhere.
Not that *she* ever understood: to this day she thinks that Aix didn't suit
her, and mentions her having been sent there as proof of the incompe-
tence of French doctors. That's Lily all over, you know: she works like
a slave preparing the ground and sowing her seed; but the day she ought

to be reaping the harvest she over-sleeps herself or goes off on a picnic."

Mrs. Fisher paused and looked reflectively at the deep shimmer of sea between the cactus-flowers. "Sometimes," she added, "I think it's just flightiness—and sometimes I think it's because, at heart, she despises the things she's trying for. And it's the difficulty of deciding that makes her such an interesting study." She glanced tentatively at Selden's motionless profile, and resumed with a slight sigh: "Well, all I can say is, I wish she'd give *me* some of her discarded opportunities. I wish we could change places now, for instance. She could make a very good thing out of the Brys if she managed them properly, and I should know just how to look after George Dorset while Bertha is reading Verlaine[3] with Neddy Silverton."

She met Selden's sound of protest with a sharp derisive glance. "Well, what's the use of mincing matters? We all know that's what Bertha brought her abroad for. When Bertha wants to have a good time she has to provide occupation for George. At first I thought Lily was going to play her cards well *this* time, but there are rumours that Bertha is jealous of her success here and at Cannes, and I shouldn't be surprised if there were a break any day. Lily's only safeguard is that Bertha needs her badly—oh, very badly. The Silverton affair is in the acute stage: it's necessary that George's attention should be pretty continuously distracted. And I'm bound to say Lily *does* distract it: I believe he'd marry her tomorrow if he found out there was anything wrong with Bertha. But you know him—he's as blind as he's jealous; and of course Lily's present business is to keep him blind. A clever woman might know just the right moment to tear off the bandage: but Lily isn't clever in that way, and when George does open his eyes she'll probably contrive not to be in his line of vision."

Selden tossed away his cigarette. "By Jove—it's time for my train," he exclaimed, with a glance at his watch; adding, in reply to Mrs. Fisher's surprised comment—"Why, I thought of course you were at Monte!"— a murmured word to the effect that he was making Nice his head-quarters.

"The worst of it is, she snubs the Brys now," he heard irrelevantly flung after him.

Ten minutes later, in the high-perched bedroom of an hotel overlooking the Casino, he was tossing his effects into a couple of gaping portmanteaux, while the porter waited outside to transport them to the cab at the door. It took but a brief plunge down the steep white road to the station to land him safely in the afternoon express for Nice; and not till he was installed in the corner of an empty carriage, did he exclaim to himself, with a reaction of self-contempt: "What the deuce am I running away from?"

The pertinence of the question checked Selden's fugitive impulse before

3. The French Symbolist writer Paul Verlaine (1844–96) was known for the delicate beauty of his poetry and for the disorder of his love life, which began with the abandonment of his young wife, included a prison sentence for wounding his lover with a pistol, and ended in drunken debauchery.

the train had started. It was ridiculous to be flying like an emotional coward from an infatuation his reason had conquered. He had instructed his bankers to forward some important business letters to Nice, and at Nice he would quietly await them. He was already annoyed with himself for having left Monte Carlo, where he had intended to pass the week which remained to him before sailing; but it would now be difficult to return on his steps without an appearance of inconsistency from which his pride recoiled. In his inmost heart he was not sorry to put himself beyond the probability of meeting Miss Bart. Completely as he had detached himself from her, he could not yet regard her merely as a social instance; and viewed in a more personal way she was not likely to be a reassuring object of study. Chance encounters, or even the repeated mention of her name, would send his thoughts back into grooves from which he had resolutely detached them; whereas, if she could be entirely excluded from his life, the pressure of new and varied impressions, with which no thought of her was connected, would soon complete the work of separation. Mrs. Fisher's conversation had, indeed, operated to that end; but the treatment was too painful to be voluntarily chosen while milder remedies were untried; and Selden thought he could trust himself to return gradually to a reasonable view of Miss Bart, if only he did not see her.

Having reached the station early, he had arrived at this point in his reflections before the increasing throng on the platform warned him that he could not hope to preserve his privacy; the next moment there was a hand on the door, and he turned to confront the very face he was fleeing.

Miss Bart, glowing with the haste of a precipitate descent upon the train, headed a group composed of the Dorsets, young Silverton and Lord Hubert Dacey, who had barely time to spring into the carriage, and envelop Selden in ejaculations of surprise and welcome, before the whistle of departure sounded. The party, it appeared, were hastening to Nice in response to a sudden summons to dine with the Duchess of Beltshire and to see the water-fête in the bay; a plan evidently improvised—in spite of Lord Hubert's protesting "Oh, I say, you know,"—for the express purpose of defeating Mrs. Bry's endeavour to capture the Duchess.

During the laughing relation of this manœuvre, Selden had time for a rapid impression of Miss Bart, who had seated herself opposite to him in the golden afternoon light. Scarcely three months had elapsed since he had parted from her on the threshold of the Brys' conservatory; but a subtle change had passed over the quality of her beauty. Then it had had a transparency through which the fluctuations of the spirit were sometimes tragically visible; now its impenetrable surface suggested a process of crystallization which had fused her whole being into one hard brilliant substance. The change had struck Mrs. Fisher as a rejuvenation: to Selden it seemed like that moment of pause and arrest when the warm fluidity of youth is chilled into its final shape.

He felt it in the way she smiled on him, and in the readiness and competence with which, flung unexpectedly into his presence, she took up the thread of their intercourse as though that thread had not been snapped with a violence from which he still reeled. Such facility sickened him—but he told himself that it was with the pang which precedes recovery. Now he would really get well—would eject the last drop of poison from his blood. Already he felt himself calmer in her presence than he had learned to be in the thought of her. Her assumptions and elisions, her short-cuts and long *détours*, the skill with which she contrived to meet him at a point from which no inconvenient glimpses of the past were visible, suggested what opportunities she had had for practising such arts since their last meeting. He felt that she had at last arrived at an understanding with herself: had made a pact with her rebellious impulses, and achieved a uniform system of self-government, under which all vagrant tendencies were either held captive or forced into the service of the state.

And he saw other things too in her manner: saw how it had adjusted itself to the hidden intricacies of a situation in which, even after Mrs. Fisher's elucidating flashes, he still felt himself agrope. Surely Mrs. Fisher could no longer charge Miss Bart with neglecting her opportunities! To Selden's exasperated observation she was only too completely alive to them. She was "perfect" to every one: subservient to Bertha's anxious predominance, good-naturedly watchful of Dorset's moods, brightly companionable to Silverton and Dacey, the latter of whom met her on an evident footing of old admiration, while young Silverton, portentously self-absorbed, seemed conscious of her only as of something vaguely obstructive. And suddenly, as Selden noted the fine shades of manner by which she harmonized herself with her surroundings, it flashed on him that, to need such adroit handling, the situation must indeed be desperate. She was on the edge of something—that was the impression left with him. He seemed to see her poised on the brink of a chasm, with one graceful foot advanced to assert her unconsciousness that the ground was failing her.

On the Promenade des Anglais, where Ned Silverton hung on him for the half hour before dinner, he received a deeper impression of the general insecurity. Silverton was in a mood of Titanic pessimism. How any one could come to such a damned hole as the Riviera—any one with a grain of imagination—with the whole Mediterranean to choose from: but then, if one's estimate of a place depended on the way they broiled a spring chicken! Gad! what a study might be made of the tyranny of the stomach—the way a sluggish liver or insufficient gastric juices might affect the whole course of the universe, over-shadow everything in reach—chronic dyspepsia ought to be among the "statutory causes"; a woman's life might be ruined by a man's inability to digest fresh bread. Grotesque? Yes—and tragic—like most absurdities. There's nothing grimmer than the tragedy that wears a comic mask. . . . Where was he? Oh—the reason they chucked Sicily and rushed back? Well—partly, no doubt, Miss Bart's desire to get back to bridge and smartness.

Dead as a stone to art and poetry—the light never *was* on sea or land for
her! And of course she persuaded Dorset that the Italian food was bad
for him. Oh, she could make him believe anything—*anything! Mrs.*
Dorset was aware of it—oh, perfectly: nothing *she* didn't see! But she
could hold her tongue—she'd had to, often enough. Miss Bart was an
intimate friend—she wouldn't hear a word against her. Only it hurts a
woman's pride—there are some things one doesn't get used to . . . . All
this in confidence, of course? Ah—and there were the ladies signalling
from the balcony of the hotel. . . . He plunged across the Promenade,
leaving Selden to a meditative cigar.

The conclusions it led him to were fortified, later in the evening, by
some of those faint corroborative hints that generate a light of their own
in the dusk of a doubting mind. Selden, stumbling on a chance acquaintance, had dined with him, and adjourned, still in his company, to the
brightly lit Promenade, where a line of crowded stands commanded the
glittering darkness of the waters. The night was soft and persuasive.
Overhead hung a summer sky furrowed with the rush of rockets; and
from the east a late moon, pushing up beyond the lofty bend of the
coast, sent across the bay a shaft of brightness which paled to ashes in
the red glitter of the illuminated boats. Down the lantern-hung Promenade, snatches of band-music floated above the hum of the crowd and
the soft tossing of boughs in dusky gardens; and between these gardens
and the backs of the stands there flowed a stream of people in whom the
vociferous carnival mood seemed tempered by the growing languor of
the season.

Selden and his companion, unable to get seats on one of the stands
facing the bay, had wandered for a while with the throng, and then
found a point of vantage on a high garden-parapet above the Promenade. Thence they caught but a triangular glimpse of the water, and of
the flashing play of boats across its surface; but the crowd in the street
was under their immediate view, and seemed to Selden, on the whole,
of more interest than the show itself. After a while, however, he wearied
of his perch and, dropping alone to the pavement, pushed his way to
the first corner and turned into the moonlit silence of a side street. Long
garden-walls overhung by trees made a dark boundary to the pavement;
an empty cab trailed along the deserted thoroughfare, and presently Selden saw two persons emerge from the opposite shadows, signal to the
cab, and drive off in it toward the centre of the town. The moonlight
touched them as they paused to enter the carriage, and he recognized
Mrs. Dorset and young Silverton.

Beneath the nearest lamp-post he glanced at his watch and saw that
the time was close on eleven. He took another cross street, and without
breasting the throng on the Promenade, made his way to the fashionable
club which overlooks that thoroughfare. Here, amid the blaze of crowded
baccarat tables, he caught sight of Lord Hubert Dacey, seated with his
habitual worn smile behind a rapidly dwindling heap of gold. The heap
being in due course wiped out, Lord Hubert rose with a shrug, and

joining Selden, adjourned with him to the deserted terrace of the club. It was now past midnight, and the throng on the stands was dispersing, while the long trails of red-lit boats scattered and faded beneath a sky repossessed by the tranquil splendour of the moon.

Lord Hubert looked at his watch. "By Jove, I promised to join the Duchess for supper at the *London House*; but it's past twelve, and I suppose they've all scattered. The fact is, I lost them in the crowd soon after dinner, and took refuge here, for my sins. They had seats on one of the stands, but of course they couldn't stop quiet: the Duchess never can. She and Miss Bart went off in quest of what they call adventures— gad, it ain't their fault if they don't have some queer ones!" He added tentatively, after pausing to grope for a cigarette; "Miss Bart's an old friend of yours, I believe? So she told me.—Ah, thanks—I don't seem to have one left." He lit Selden's proffered cigarette, and continued, in his high-pitched drawling tone: "None of my business, of course, but I didn't introduce her to the Duchess. Charming woman, the Duchess, you understand; and a very good friend of mine; but *rather* a liberal education."

Selden received this in silence, and after a few puffs Lord Hubert broke out again: "Sort of thing one can't communicate to the young lady—though young ladies nowadays are so competent to judge for themselves; but in this case—I'm an old friend too, you know . . . and there seemed no one else to speak to. The whole situation's a little mixed, as I see it—but there used to be an aunt somewhere, a diffuse and innocent person, who was great at bridging over chasms she didn't see . . . Ah, in New York, is she? Pity New York's such a long way off!"

II

Miss Bart, emerging late the next morning from her cabin, found herself alone on the deck of the Sabrina.

The cushioned chairs, disposed expectantly under the wide awning, showed no signs of recent occupancy, and she presently learned from a steward that Mrs. Dorset had not yet appeared, and that the gentlemen—separately—had gone ashore as soon as they had breakfasted. Supplied with these facts, Lily leaned awhile over the side, giving herself up to a leisurely enjoyment of the spectacle before her. Unclouded sunlight enveloped sea and shore in a bath of purest radiancy. The purpling waters drew a sharp white line of foam at the base of the shore; against its irregular eminences, hotels and villas flashed from the greyish verdure of olive and eucalyptus; and the background of bare and finely-pencilled mountains quivered in a pale intensity of light.

How beautiful it was—and how she loved beauty! She had always felt that her sensibility in this direction made up for certain obtusenesses of feeling of which she was less proud; and during the last three months she had indulged it passionately. The Dorsets' invitation to go abroad

with them had come as an almost miraculous release from crushing
difficulties; and her faculty for renewing herself in new scenes, and casting off problems of conduct as easily as the surroundings in which they
had arisen, made the mere change from one place to another seem, not
merely a postponement, but a solution of her troubles. Moral complications existed for her only in the environment that had produced them;
she did not mean to slight or ignore them, but they lost their reality
when they changed their background. She could not have remained in
New York without repaying the money she owed to Trenor; to acquit
herself of that odious debt she might even have faced a marriage with
Rosedale; but the accident of placing the Atlantic between herself and
her obligations made them dwindle out of sight as if they had been
milestones and she had travelled past them.

Her two months on the Sabrina had been especially calculated to aid
this illusion of distance. She had been plunged into new scenes, and
had found in them a renewal of old hopes and ambitions. The cruise
itself charmed her as a romantic adventure. She was vaguely touched by
the names and scenes amid which she moved and had listened to Ned
Silverton reading Theocritus[1] by moonlight, as the yacht rounded the
Sicilian promontories, with a thrill of the nerves that confirmed her
belief in her intellectual superiority. But the weeks at Cannes and Nice
had really given her more pleasure. The gratification of being welcomed
in high company, and of making her own ascendency felt there, so that
she found herself figuring once more as the "beautiful Miss Bart" in the
interesting journal devoted to recording the least movements of her cosmopolitan companions—all these experiences tended to throw into the
extreme background of memory the prosaic and sordid difficulties from
which she had escaped.

If she was faintly aware of fresh difficulties ahead, she was sure of her
ability to meet them; it was characteristic of her to feel that the only
problems she could not solve were those with which she was familiar.
Meanwhile she could honestly be proud of the skill with which she had
adapted herself to somewhat delicate conditions. She had reason to think
that she had made herself equally necessary to her host and hostess; and
if only she had seen any perfectly irreproachable means of drawing a
financial profit from the situation, there would have been no cloud on
her horizon. The truth was that her funds, as usual, were inconveniently
low; and to neither Dorset nor his wife could this vulgar embarrassment
be safely hinted. Still, the need was not a pressing one; she could worry
along, as she had so often done before, with the hope of some happy
change of fortune to sustain her; and meanwhile life was gay and beautiful and easy, and she was conscious of figuring not unworthily in such
a setting.

She was engaged to breakfast that morning with the Duchess of Beltshire, and at twelve o'clock she asked to be set ashore in the gig. Before

1. A third-century B.C. Greek poet credited with the invention of the pastoral, a poem extolling the
virtues of country life.

this she had sent her maid to enquire if she might see Mrs. Dorset; but
the reply came back that the latter was tired, and trying to sleep. Lily
thought she understood the reason of the rebuff. Her hostess had not
been included in the Duchess's invitation, though she herself had made
the most loyal efforts in that direction. But her grace was impervious to
hints, and invited or omitted as she chose. It was not Lily's fault if Mrs.
Dorset's complicated attitudes did not fall in with the Duchess's easy
gait. The Duchess, who seldom explained herself, had not formulated
her objection beyond saying: "She's rather a bore, you know. The only
one of your friends I like is that little Mr. Bry—*he's* funny—" but Lily
knew enough not to press the point, and was not altogether sorry to be
thus distinguished at her friend's expense. Bertha certainly *had* grown
tiresome since she had taken to poetry and Ned Silverton.

On the whole, it was a relief to break away now and then from the
Sabrina; and the Duchess's little breakfast, organized by Lord Hubert
with all his usual virtuosity, was the pleasanter to Lily for not including
her travelling-companions. Dorset, of late, had grown more than usually morose and incalculable, and Ned Silverton went about with an air
that seemed to challenge the universe. The freedom and lightness of the
ducal intercourse made an agreeable change from these complications,
and Lily was tempted, after luncheon, to adjourn in the wake of her
companions to the hectic atmosphere of the Casino. She did not mean
to play; her diminished pocket-money offered small scope for the adventure; but it amused her to sit on a divan, under the doubtful protection
of the Duchess's back, while the latter hung above her stakes at a neighbouring table.

The rooms were packed with the gazing throng which, in the afternoon hours, trickles heavily between the tables, like the Sunday crowd
in a lion-house. In the stagnant flow of the mass, identities were hardly
distinguishable; but Lily presently saw Mrs. Bry cleaving her determined
way through the doors, and, in the broad wake she left, the light figure
of Mrs. Fisher bobbing after her like a row-boat at the stern of a tug.
Mrs. Bry pressed on, evidently animated by the resolve to reach a certain
point in the rooms; but Mrs. Fisher, as she passed Lily, broke from her
towing-line, and let herself float to the girl's side.

"Lose her?" she echoed the latter's query, with an indifferent glance
at Mrs. Bry's retreating back. "I daresay—it doesn't matter: I *have* lost
her already." And, as Lily exclaimed, she added: "We had an awful row
this morning. You know, of course, that the Duchess chucked her at
dinner last night, and she thinks it was my fault—my want of management. The worst of it is, the message—just a mere word by telephone—
came so late that the dinner had to be paid for; and Bécassin *had* run it
up—it had been so drummed into him that the Duchess was coming!"
Mrs. Fisher indulged in a faint laugh at the remembrance. "Paying for
what she doesn't get rankles so dreadfully with Louisa: I can't make her
see that it's one of the preliminary steps to getting what you haven't paid

for—and as I was the nearest thing to smash, she smashed me to atoms, poor dear!"

Lily murmured her commiseration. Impulses of sympathy came naturally to her, and it was instinctive to proffer her help to Mrs. Fisher.

"If there's anything I can do—if it's only a question of meeting the Duchess! I heard her say she thought Mr. Bry amusing——"

But Mrs. Fisher interposed with a decisive gesture. "My dear, I have my pride: the pride of my trade. *I* couldn't manage the Duchess, and I can't palm off your arts on Louisa Bry as mine. I've taken the final step: I go to Paris tonight with the Sam Gormers. *They're* still in the elementary stage; an Italian Prince is a great deal more than a Prince to them, and they're always on the brink of taking a courier for one. To save them from that is my present mission." She laughed again at the picture. "But before I go I want to make my last will and testament—I want to leave you the Brys."

"Me?" Miss Bart joined in her amusement. "It's charming of you to remember me, dear; but really——"

"You're already so well provided for?" Mrs. Fisher flashed a sharp glance at her. "*Are* you, though, Lily—to the point of rejecting my offer?"

Miss Bart coloured slowly. "What I really meant was, that the Brys wouldn't in the least care to be so disposed of."

Mrs. Fisher continued to probe her embarrassment with an unflinching eye. "What you really meant was that you've snubbed the Brys horribly; and you know that they know it——"

"Carry!"

"Oh, on certain sides Louisa bristles with perceptions. If you'd even managed to have them asked once on the Sabrina—especially when royalties were coming! but it's not too late," she ended earnestly, "it's not too late for either of you."

Lily smiled. "Stay over, and I'll get the Duchess to dine with them."

"I shan't stay over—the Gormers have paid for my *salon-lit*,"[2] said Mrs. Fisher with simplicity. "But get the Duchess to dine with them all the same."

Lily's smile again flowed into a slight laugh: her friend's importunity was beginning to strike her as irrelevant. "I'm sorry I have been negligent about the Brys——" she began.

"Oh, as to the Brys—it's you I'm thinking of," said Mrs. Fisher abruptly. She paused, and then, bending forward, with a lowered voice: "You know we all went on to Nice last night when the Duchess chucked us. It was Louisa's idea—I told her what I thought of it."

Miss Bart assented. "Yes—I caught sight of you on the way back, at the station."

"Well, the man who was in the carriage with you and George Dor-

---

2. A sleeping compartment on the European railways.

set—that horrid little Dabham who does 'Society Notes from the Riviera'—had been dining with us at Nice. And he's telling everybody that
you and Dorset came back alone after midnight."

"Alone—? When he was with us?" Lily laughed, but her laugh faded
into gravity under the prolonged implication of Mrs. Fisher's look. "We
did come back alone—if that's so very dreadful! But whose fault was it?
The Duchess was spending the night at Cimiez with the Crown Princess;
Bertha got bored with the show, and went off early, promising to meet
us at the station. We turned up on time, but she didn't—she didn't turn
up at all!"

Miss Bart made this announcement in the tone of one who presents,
with careless assurance, a complete vindication; but Mrs. Fisher received
it in a manner almost inconsequent. She seemed to have lost sight of
her friend's part in the incident: her inward vision had taken another
slant.

"Bertha never turned up at all? Then how on earth did she get back?"

"Oh, by the next train, I suppose; there were two extra ones for the
fête. At any rate, I know she's safe on the yacht, though I haven't yet
seen her; but you see it was not my fault," Lily summed up.

"Not your fault that Bertha didn't turn up? My poor child, if only you
don't have to pay for it!" Mrs. Fisher rose—she had seen Mrs. Bry surging back in her direction. "There's Louisa, and I must be off—oh, we're
on the best of terms externally; we're lunching together; but at heart it's
me she's lunching on," she explained; and with a last hand-clasp and a
last look, she added: "Remember, I leave her to you; she's hovering now,
ready to take you in."

Lily carried the impression of Mrs. Fisher's leave-taking away with her
from the Casino doors. She had accomplished, before leaving, the first
step toward her reinstatement in Mrs. Bry's good graces. An affable
advance—a vague murmur that they must see more of each other—an
allusive glance to a near future that was felt to include the Duchess as
well as the Sabrina—how easily it was all done, if one possessed the
knack of doing it! She wondered at herself, as she had so often wondered, that, possessing the knack, she did not more consistently exercise
it. But sometimes she was forgetful—and sometimes, could it be that
she was proud? Today, at any rate, she had been vaguely conscious of a
reason for sinking her pride, had in fact even sunk it to the point of
suggesting to Lord Hubert Dacey, whom she ran across on the Casino
steps, that he might really get the Duchess to dine with the Brys, if *she*
undertook to have them asked on the Sabrina. Lord Hubert had promised his help, with the readiness on which she could always count: it was
his only way of ever reminding her that he had once been ready to do
so much more for her. Her path, in short, seemed to smooth itself before
her as she advanced; yet the faint stir of uneasiness persisted. Had it been
produced, she wondered, by her chance meeting with Selden? She thought

not—time and change seemed so completely to have relegated him to his proper distance. The sudden and exquisite reaction from her anxieties had had the effect of throwing the recent past so far back that even Selden, as part of it, retained a certain air of unreality. And he had made it so clear that they were not to meet again; that he had merely dropped down to Nice for a day or two, and had almost his foot on the next steamer. No—that part of the past had merely surged up for a moment on the fleeing surface of events; and now that it was submerged again, the uncertainty, the apprehension persisted.

They grew to sudden acuteness as she caught sight of George Dorset descending the steps of the Hôtel de Paris and making for her across the square. She had meant to drive down to the quay and regain the yacht; but she now had the immediate impression that something more was to happen first.

"Which way are you going? Shall we walk a bit?" he began, putting the second question before the first was answered, and not waiting for a reply to either before he directed her silently toward the comparative seclusion of the lower gardens.

She detected in him at once all the signs of extreme nervous tension. The skin was puffed out under his sunken eyes, and its sallowness had paled to a leaden white against which his irregular eyebrows and long reddish moustache were relieved with a saturnine effect. His appearance, in short, presented an odd mixture of the bedraggled and the ferocious.

He walked beside her in silence, with quick precipitate steps, till they reached the embowered slopes to the east of the Casino; then, pulling up abruptly, he said: "Have you seen Bertha?"

"No—when I left the yacht she was not yet up."

He received this with a laugh like the whirring sound in a disabled clock. "Not yet up? Had she gone to bed? Do you know at what time she came on board? This morning at seven!" he exclaimed.

"At seven?" Lily started. "What happened—an accident to the train?"

He laughed again. "They missed the train—all the trains—they had to drive back."

"Well——?" She hesitated, feeling at once how little even this necessity accounted for the fatal lapse of hours.

"Well, they couldn't get a carriage at once—at that time of night, you know—" the explanatory note made it almost seem as though he were putting the case for his wife—"and when they finally did, it was only a one-horse cab, and the horse was lame!"

"How tiresome! I see," she affirmed, with the more earnestness because she was so nervously conscious that she did not; and after a pause she added: "I'm so sorry—but ought we to have waited?"

"Waited for the one-horse cab? It would scarcely have carried the four of us, do you think?"

She took this in what seemed the only possible way, with a laugh intended to sink the question itself in his humorous treatment of it. "Well, it would have been difficult; we should have had to walk by turns. But it would have been jolly to see the sunrise."

"Yes: the sunrise *was* jolly," he agreed.

"Was it? You saw it, then?"

"I saw it, yes; from the deck. I waited up for them."

"Naturally—I suppose you were worried. Why didn't you call on me to share your vigil?"

He stood still, dragging at his moustache with a lean weak hand. "I don't think you would have cared for its *dénouement*," he said with sudden grimness.

Again she was disconcerted by the abrupt change in his tone, and as in one flash she saw the peril of the moment, and the need of keeping her sense of it out of her eyes.

"*Dénouement*—isn't that too big a word for such a small incident? The worse of it, after all, is the fatigue which Bertha has probably slept off this time."

She clung to the note bravely, though its futility was now plain to her in the glare of his miserable eyes.

"Don't—don't——!" he broke out, with the hurt cry of a child; and while she tried to merge her sympathy, and her resolve to ignore any cause for it, in one ambiguous murmur of deprecation, he dropped down on the bench near which they had paused, and poured out the wretchedness of his soul.

It was a dreadful hour—an hour from which she emerged shrinking and seared, as though her lids had been scorched by its actual glare. It was not that she had never had premonitory glimpses of such an outbreak; but rather because, here and there throughout the three months, the surface of life had shown such ominous cracks and vapours that her fears had always been on the alert for an upheaval. There had been moments when the situation had presented itself under a homelier yet more vivid image—that of a shaky vehicle, dashed by unbroken steeds over a bumping road, while she cowered within, aware that the harness wanted mending, and wondering what would give way first. Well— everything had given way now; and the wonder was that the crazy outfit had held together so long. Her sense of being involved in the crash, instead of merely witnessing it from the road, was intensified by the way in which Dorset, through his furies of denunciation and wild reactions of self-contempt, made her feel the need he had of her, the place she had taken in his life. But for her, what ear would have been open to his cries? And what hand but hers could drag him up again to a footing of sanity and self-respect? All through the stress of the struggle with him, she had been conscious of something faintly maternal in her efforts to guide and uplift him. But for the present, if he clung to her, it was not in order to be dragged up, but to feel some one floundering in the depths with him: he wanted her to suffer with him, not to help him to suffer less.

Happily for both, there was little physical strength to sustain his frenzy. It left him, collapsed and breathing heavily, to an apathy so deep and prolonged that Lily almost feared the passers-by would think it the result of a seizure, and stop to offer their aid. But Monte Carlo is, of all places, the one where the human bond is least close, and odd sights are the least arresting. If a glance or two lingered on the couple, no intrusive sympathy disturbed them; and it was Lily herself who broke the silence by rising from her seat. With the clearing of her vision the sweep of peril had extended, and she saw that the post of danger was no longer at Dorset's side.

"If you won't go back, I must—don't make me leave you!" she urged.

But he remained mutely resistant, and she added: "What are you going to do? You really can't sit here all night."

"I can go to an hotel. I can telegraph my lawyers." He sat up, roused by a new thought. "By Jove, Selden's at Nice—I'll send for Selden!"

Lily, at this, reseated herself with a cry of alarm. "No, no, *no!*" she protested.

He swung round on her distrustfully. "Why not Selden? He's a lawyer, isn't he? One will do as well as another in a case like this."

"As badly as another, you mean. I thought you relied on *me* to help you."

"You do—by being so sweet and patient with me. If it hadn't been for you I'd have ended the thing long ago. But now it's got to end." He rose suddenly, straightening himself with an effort. "You can't want to see me ridiculous."

She looked at him kindly. "That's just it." Then, after a moment's pondering, almost to her own surprise she broke out with a flash of inspiration: "Well, go over and see Mr. Selden. You'll have time to do it before dinner."

"Oh, *dinner——*" he mocked her; but she left him with the smiling rejoinder: "Dinner on board, remember; we'll put it off till nine if you like."

It was past four already; and when a cab had dropped her at the quay, and she stood waiting for the gig to put off for her, she began to wonder what had been happening on the yacht. Of Silverton's whereabouts there had been no mention. Had he returned to the Sabrina? Or could Bertha—the dread alternative sprang on her suddenly—could Bertha, left to herself, have gone ashore to rejoin him? Lily's heart stood still at the thought. All her concern had hitherto been for young Silverton, not only because, in such affairs, the woman's instinct is to side with the man, but because his case made a peculiar appeal to her sympathies. He was so desperately in earnest, poor youth, and his earnestness was of so different a quality from Bertha's, though hers too was desperate enough. The difference was that Bertha was in earnest only about herself, while he was in earnest about her. But now, at the actual crisis, this difference seemed to throw the weight of destitution on Bertha's side, since at least he had her to suffer for, and she had only herself. At any rate, viewed less ideally, all the disadvantages of such a situation were for the woman; and it was to Bertha that Lily's sympathies now went out. She was not fond of Bertha Dorset, but neither was she without a sense of obligation, the heavier for having so little personal liking to sustain it. Bertha had been kind to her, they had lived together, during the last months, on terms of easy friendship, and the sense of friction of which Lily had recently become aware seemed to make it the more urgent that she should work undividedly in her friend's interest.

It was in Bertha's interest, certainly, that she had despatched Dorset to consult with Lawrence Selden. Once the grotesqueness of the situation accepted, she had seen at a glance that it was the safest in which Dorset could find himself. Who but Selden could thus miraculously combine the skill to save Bertha with the obligation of doing so? The consciousness that much skill would be required made Lily rest thankfully in the greatness of the obligation. Since he would *have* to pull Bertha through she could trust him to find a way; and she put the fullness of her trust in the telegram she managed to send him on her way to the quay.

Thus far, then, Lily felt that she had done well; and the conviction strengthened her for the task that remained. She and Bertha had never been on confidential terms, but at such a crisis the barriers of reserve must surely fall: Dorset's wild allusions to the scene of the morning made Lily feel that they were down already, and that any attempt to rebuild them would be beyond Bertha's strength. She pictured the poor creature shivering behind her fallen defences and awaiting with suspense the moment when she could take refuge in the first shelter that offered. If only that shelter had not already offered itself elsewhere! As the gig traversed the short distance between the quay and the yacht, Lily grew more than ever alarmed at the possible consequences of her long absence. What if the wretched Bertha, finding in all the long hours no soul to turn to—but by this time Lily's eager foot was on the side-ladder, and her first step on the Sabrina showed the worst of her apprehensions to be unfounded; for there, in the luxurious shade of the afterdeck, the wretched Bertha, in full command of her usual attenuated elegance, sat dispensing tea to the Duchess of Beltshire and Lord Hubert.

The sight filled Lily with such surprise that she felt that Bertha, at least, must read its meaning in her look, and she was proportionately disconcerted by the blankness of the look returned. But in an instant she saw that Mrs. Dorset had, of necessity, to look blank before the others, and that, to mitigate the effect of her own surprise, she must at once produce some simple reason for it. The long habit of rapid transitions made it easy for her to exclaim to the Duchess: "Why, I thought you'd gone back to the Princess!" and this sufficed for the lady she addressed, if it was hardly enough for Lord Hubert.

At least it opened the way to a lively explanation of how the Duchess was, in fact, going back the next moment, but had first rushed out to the yacht for a word with Mrs. Dorset on the subject of tomorrow's dinner—the dinner with the Brys, to which Lord Hubert had finally insisted on dragging them.

"To save my neck, you know!" he explained, with a glance that appealed to Lily for some recognition of his promptness; and the Duchess added, with her noble candour: "Mr. Bry has promised him a tip, and he says if we go he'll pass it on to us."

This led to some final pleasantries, in which, as it seemed to Lily, Mrs. Dorset bore her part with astounding bravery, and at the close of which Lord Hubert, from half way down the side-ladder, called back, with an air of numbering heads: "And of course we may count on Dorset too?"

"Oh, count on him," his wife assented gaily. She was keeping up well to the last—but as she turned back from waving her adieux over the side, Lily said to herself that the mask must drop and the soul of fear look out.

Mrs. Dorset turned back slowly; perhaps she wanted time to steady her muscles; at any rate, they were still under perfect control when, dropping once more into her seat behind the tea-table, she remarked to Miss Bart with a faint touch of irony: "I suppose I ought to say good morning."

If it was a cue, Lily was ready to take it, though with only the vaguest sense of what was expected of her in return. There was something unnerving in the contemplation of Mrs. Dorset's composure, and she had to force the light tone in which she answered: "I tried to see you this morning, but you were not yet up."

"No—I got to bed late. After we missed you at the station I thought we ought to wait for you till the last train." She spoke very gently, but with just the least tinge of reproach.

"You missed us? You waited for us at the station?" Now indeed Lily was too far adrift in bewilderment to measure the other's words or keep watch on her own. "But I thought you didn't get to the station till after the last train left!"

Mrs. Dorset, examining her between lowered lids, met this with the immediate query: "Who told you that?"

"George—I saw him just now in the gardens."

"Ah, is that George's version? Poor George—he was in no state to remember what I told him. He had one of his worst attacks this morning, and I packed him off to see the doctor. Do you know if he found him?"

Lily, still lost in conjecture, made no reply, and Mrs. Dorset settled herself indolently in her seat. "He'll wait to see him; he was horribly frightened about himself. It's very bad for him to be worried, and whenever anything upsetting happens, it always brings on an attack."

This time Lily felt sure that a cue was being pressed on her; but it was put forth with such startling suddenness, and with so incredible an air of ignoring what it led up to, that she could only falter out doubtfully: "Anything upsetting?"

"Yes—such as having you so conspicuously on his hands in the small hours. You know, my dear, you're rather a big responsibility in such a scandalous place after midnight."

At that—at the complete unexpectedness and the inconceivable audacity of it—Lily could not restrain the tribute of an astonished laugh.

"Well, really—considering it was you who burdened him with the responsibility!"

Mrs. Dorset took this with an exquisite mildness. "By not having the superhuman cleverness to discover you in that frightful rush for the train? Or the imagination to believe that you'd take it without us—you and he all alone—instead of waiting quietly in the station till we *did* manage to meet you?"

Lily's colour rose: it was growing clear to her that Bertha was pursuing an object, following a line she had marked out for herself. Only, with such a doom impending, why waste time in these childish efforts to avert it? The puerility of the attempt disarmed Lily's indignation: did it not prove how horribly the poor creature was frightened?

"No; by our simply all keeping together at Nice," she returned.

"Keeping together? When it was you who seized the first opportunity to rush off with the Duchess and her friends? My dear Lily, you are not a child to be led by the hand!"

"No—nor to be lectured, Bertha, really; if that's what you are doing to me now."

Mrs. Dorset smiled on her reproachfully. "Lecture you—I? Heaven forbid! I was merely trying to give you a friendly hint. But it's usually the other way round, isn't it? I'm expected to take hints, not to give them: I've positively lived on them all these last months."

"Hints—from me to you?" Lily repeated.

"Oh, negative ones merely—what not to be and to do and to see. And I think I've taken them to admiration. Only, my dear, if you'll let me say so, I didn't understand that one of my negative duties was *not* to warn you when you carried your imprudence too far."

A chill of fear passed over Miss Bart: a sense of remembered treachery that was like the gleam of a knife in the dusk. But compassion, in a moment, got the better of her instinctive recoil. What was this outpouring of senseless bitterness but the tracked creature's attempt to cloud the medium through which it was fleeing? It was on Lily's lips to exclaim: "You poor soul, don't double and turn—come straight back to me, and we'll find a way out!" But the words died under the impenetrable insolence of Bertha's smile. Lily sat silent, taking the brunt of it quietly, letting it spend itself on her to the last drop of its accumulated falseness; then, without a word, she rose and went down to her cabin.

III

Miss Bart's telegram caught Lawrence Selden at the door of his hotel; and having read it, he turned back to wait for Dorset. The message necessarily left large gaps for conjecture; but all that he had recently heard and seen made these but too easy to fill in. On the whole he was surprised; for though he had perceived that the situation contained all the elements of an explosion, he had often enough, in the range of his personal experience, seen just such combinations subside into harmlessness. Still, Dorset's spasmodic temper, and his wife's reckless disregard of appearances, gave the situation a peculiar insecurity; and it was less from the sense of any special relation to the case than from a purely professional zeal, that Selden resolved to guide the pair to safety. Whether, in the present instance, safety for either lay in repairing so damaged a tie, it was no business of his to consider: he had only, on general principles, to think of averting a scandal, and his desire to avert it was increased by his fear of its involving Miss Bart. There was nothing specific in this apprehension; he merely wished to spare her the embarrassment of being ever so remotely connected with the public washing of the Dorset linen.

How exhaustive and unpleasant such a process would be, he saw even more vividly after his two hours' talk with poor Dorset. If anything came out at all, it would be such a vast unpacking of accumulated moral rags as left him, after his visitor had gone, with the feeling that he must fling open the windows and have his room swept out. But nothing should come out; and happily for his side of the case, the dirty rags, however pieced together, could not, without considerable difficulty, be turned into a homogeneous grievance. The torn edges did not always fit—there were missing bits, there were disparities of size and colour, all of which it was naturally Selden's business to make the most of in putting them under his client's eye. But to a man in Dorset's mood the completest demonstration could not carry conviction, and Selden saw that for the moment all he could do was to soothe and temporize, to offer sympathy and to counsel prudence. He let Dorset depart charged to the brim with the sense that, till their next meeting, he must maintain a strictly non-committal attitude; that, in short, his share in the game consisted for the present in looking on. Selden knew, however, that he could not long keep such violences in equilibrium; and he promised to meet Dorset, the next morning, at an hotel in Monte Carlo. Meanwhile he counted not a little on the reaction of weakness and self-distrust that, in such natures, follows on every unwonted expenditure of moral force; and his telegraphic reply to Miss Bart consisted simply in the injunction: "Assume that everything is as usual."

On this assumption, in fact, the early part of the following day was lived through. Dorset, as if in obedience to Lily's imperative bidding, had actually returned in time for a late dinner on the yacht. The repast had been the most difficult moment of the day. Dorset was sunk in one of the abysmal silences which so commonly followed on what his wife called his "attacks" that it was easy, before the servants, to refer it to this cause; but Bertha herself seemed, perversely enough, little disposed to make use of this obvious means of protection. She simply left the brunt of the situation on her husband's hands, as if too absorbed in a grievance of her own to suspect that she might be the object of one herself. To

Lily this attitude was the most ominous, because the most perplexing, element in the situation. As she tried to fan the weak flicker of talk, to build up, again and again, the crumbling structure of "appearances," her own attention was perpetually distracted by the question: "What on earth can she be driving at?" There was something positively exasperating in Bertha's attitude of isolated defiance. If only she would have given her friend a hint they might still have worked together successfully; but how could Lily be of use, while she was thus obstinately shut out from participation? To be of use was what she honestly wanted; and not for her own sake but for the Dorsets'. She had not thought of her own situation at all: she was simply engrossed in trying to put a little order in theirs. But the close of the short dreary evening left her with a sense of effort hopelessly wasted. She had not tried to see Dorset alone: she had positively shrunk from a renewal of his confidences. It was Bertha whose confidence she sought, and who should as eagerly have invited her own; and Bertha, as if in the infatuation of self-destruction, was actually pushing away her rescuing hand.

Lily, going to bed early, had left the couple to themselves; and it seemed part of the general mystery in which she moved that more than an hour should elapse before she heard Bertha walk down the silent passage and regain her room. The morrow, rising on an apparent continuance of the same conditions, revealed nothing of what had occurred between the confronted pair. One fact alone outwardly proclaimed the change they were all conspiring to ignore; and that was the non-appearance of Ned Silverton. No one referred to it, and this tacit avoidance of the subject kept it in the immediate foreground of consciousness. But there was another change, perceptible only to Lily; and that was that Dorset now avoided her almost as pointedly as his wife. Perhaps he was repenting his rash outpourings of the previous day; perhaps only trying, in his clumsy way, to conform to Selden's counsel to behave "as usual." Such instructions no more make for easiness of attitude than the photographer's behest to "look natural"; and in a creature as unconscious as poor Dorset of the appearance he habitually presented, the struggle to maintain a pose was sure to result in queer contortions.

It resulted, at any rate, in throwing Lily strangely on her own resources. She had learned, on leaving her room, that Mrs. Dorset was still invisible, and that Dorset had left the yacht early; and feeling too restless to remain alone, she too had herself ferried ashore. Straying toward the Casino, she attached herself to a group of acquaintances from Nice, with whom she lunched, and in whose company she was returning to the rooms when she encountered Selden crossing the square. She could not, at the moment, separate herself definitely from her party, who had hospitably assumed that she would remain with them till they took their departure; but she found time for a momentary pause of enquiry, to which he promptly returned: "I've seen him again—he's just left me."

She waited before him anxiously. "Well? what has happened? What *will* happen?"

"Nothing as yet—and nothing in the future, I think."

"It's over, then? It's settled? You're sure?"

He smiled. "Give me time. I'm not sure—but I'm a good deal surer."
And with that she had to content herself, and hasten on to the expectant
group on the steps.

Selden had in fact given her the utmost measure of his sureness, had
even stretched it a shade to meet the anxiety in her eyes. And now, as
he turned away, strolling down the hill toward the station, that anxiety
remained with him as the visible justification of his own. It was not,
indeed, anything specific that he feared: there had been a literal truth in
his declaration that he did not think anything would happen. What troubled him was that, though Dorset's attitude had perceptibly changed,
the change was not clearly to be accounted for. It had certainly not been
produced by Selden's arguments, or by the action of his own soberer
reason. Five minutes' talk sufficed to show that some alien influence
had been at work, and that it had not so much subdued his resentment
as weakened his will, so that he moved under it in a state of apathy, like
a dangerous lunatic who has been drugged. Temporarily, no doubt,
however exerted, it worked for the general safety: the question was how
long it would last, and by what kind of reaction it was likely to be followed. On these points Selden could gain no light: for he saw that one
effect of the transformation had been to shut him off from free communion with Dorset. The latter, indeed, was still moved by the irresistible desire to discuss his wrong; but, though he revolved about it with
the same forlorn tenacity, Selden was aware that something always
restrained him from full expression. His state was one to produce first
weariness and then impatience in his hearer; and when their talk was
over, Selden began to feel that he had done his utmost, and might jus-
tifiably wash his hands of the sequel.

It was in this mind that he had been making his way back to the
station when Miss Bart crossed his path; but though, after his brief word
with her, he kept mechanically on his course, he was conscious of a
gradual change in his purpose. The change had been produced by the
look in her eyes; and in his eagerness to define the nature of that look,
he dropped into a seat in the gardens, and sat brooding upon the question. It was natural enough, in all conscience, that she should appear
anxious: a young woman placed, in the close intimacy of a yachting-
cruise, between a couple on the verge of disaster, could hardly, aside
from her concern for her friends, be insensible to the awkwardness of
her own position. The worst of it was that, in interpreting Miss Bart's
state of mind, so many alternative readings were possible; and one of
these, in Selden's troubled mind, took the ugly form suggested by Mrs.
Fisher. If the girl was afraid, was she afraid for herself or for her friends?
And to what degree was her dread of a catastrophe intensified by the
sense of being fatally involved in it? The burden of offence lying mani-
festly with Mrs. Dorset, this conjecture seemed on the face of it gratui-
tously unkind; but Selden knew that in the most one-sided matrimonial

quarrel there are generally counter-charges to be brought, and that they are brought with the greater audacity where the original grievance is so emphatic. Mrs. Fisher had not hesitated to suggest the likelihood of Dorset's marrying Miss Bart if "anything happened"; and though Mrs. Fisher's conclusions were notoriously rash, she was shrewd enough in reading the signs from which they were drawn. Dorset had apparently shown marked interest in the girl, and this interest might be used to cruel advantage in his wife's struggle for rehabilitation. Selden knew that Bertha would fight to the last round of powder: the rashness of her conduct was illogically combined with a cold determination to escape its consequences. She could be as unscrupulous in fighting for herself as she was reckless in courting danger, and whatever came to her hand at such moments was likely to be used as a defensive missile. He did not, as yet, see clearly just what course she was likely to take, but his perplexity increased his apprehension, and with it the sense that, before leaving, he must speak again with Miss Bart. Whatever her share in the situation—and he had always honestly tried to resist judging her by her surroundings—however free she might be from any personal connection with it, she would be better out of the way of a possible crash; and since she had appealed to him for help, it was clearly his business to tell her so.

This decision at last brought him to his feet, and carried him back to the gambling rooms, within whose doors he had seen her disappearing; but a prolonged exploration of the crowd failed to put him on her traces. He saw instead, to his surprise, Ned Silverton loitering somewhat ostentatiously about the tables; and the discovery that this actor in the drama was not only hovering in the wings, but actually inviting the exposure of the footlights, though it might have seemed to imply that all peril was over, served rather to deepen Selden's sense of foreboding. Charged with this impression he returned to the square, hoping to see Miss Bart move across it, as every one in Monte Carlo seemed inevitably to do at least a dozen times a day; but here again he waited vainly for a glimpse of her, and the conclusion was slowly forced on him that she had gone back to the Sabrina. It would be difficult to follow her there, and still more difficult, should he do so, to contrive the opportunity for a private word; and he had almost decided on the unsatisfactory alternative of writing, when the ceaseless diorama of the square suddenly unrolled before him the figures of Lord Hubert and Mrs. Bry.

Hailing them at once with his question, he learned from Lord Hubert that Miss Bart had just returned to the Sabrina in Dorset's company; an announcement so evidently disconcerting to him that Mrs. Bry, after a glance from her companion, which seemed to act like the pressure on a spring, brought forth the prompt proposal that he should come and meet his friends at dinner that evening—"At Bécassin's—a little dinner to the Duchess," she flashed out before Lord Hubert had time to remove the pressure.

Selden's sense of the privilege of being included in such company brought him early in the evening to the door of the restaurant, where he paused to scan the ranks of diners approaching down the brightly lit terrace. There, while the Brys hovered within over the last agitating alternatives of the *menu*, he kept watch for the guests from the Sabrina, who at length rose on the horizon in company with the Duchess, Lord and Lady Skiddaw and the Stepneys. From this group it was easy for him to detach Miss Bart on the pretext of a moment's glance into one of the brilliant shops along the terrace, and to say to her, while they lingered together in the white dazzle of a jeweller's window: "I stopped over to see you—to beg of you to leave the yacht."

The eyes she turned on him showed a quick gleam of her former fear. "To leave—? What do you mean? What has happened?"

"Nothing. But if anything should, why be in the way of it?"

The glare from the jeweller's window, deepening the pallour of her face, gave to its delicate lines the sharpness of a tragic mask. "Nothing will, I am sure; but while there's even a doubt left, how can you think I would leave Bertha?"

The words rang out on a note of contempt—was it possibly of contempt for himself? Well, he was willing to risk its renewal to the extent of insisting, with an undeniable throb of added interest: "You have yourself to think of, you know—" to which, with a strange fall of sadness in her voice, she answered, meeting his eyes: "If you knew how little difference that makes!"

"Oh, well, nothing *will* happen," he said, more for his own reassurance than for hers; and "Nothing, nothing, of course!" she valiantly assented, as they turned to overtake their companions.

In the thronged restaurant, taking their places about Mrs. Bry's illuminated board, their confidence seemed to gain support from the familiarity of their surroundings. Here were Dorset and his wife once more presenting their customary faces to the world, she engrossed in establishing her relation with an intensely new gown, he shrinking with dyspeptic dread from the multiplied solicitations of the *menu*. The mere fact that they thus showed themselves together, with the utmost openness the place afforded, seemed to declare beyond a doubt that their differences were composed. How this end had been attained was still matter for wonder, but it was clear that for the moment Miss Bart rested confidently in the result; and Selden tried to achieve the same view by telling himself that her opportunities for observation had been ampler than his own.

Meanwhile, as the dinner advanced through a labyrinth of courses, in which it became clear that Mrs. Bry had occasionally broken away from Lord Hubert's restraining hand, Selden's general watchfulness began to lose itself in a particular study of Miss Bart. It was one of the days when she was so handsome that to be handsome was enough, and all the rest—her grace, her quickness, her social felicities—seemed the overflow of a bounteous nature. But what especially struck him was the way in which she detached herself, by a hundred undefinable shades,

from the persons who most abounded in her own style. It was in just
such company, the fine flower and complete expression of the state she
aspired to, that the differences came out with special poignancy, her
grace cheapening the other women's smartness as her finely-discrimi-
nated silences made their chatter dull. The strain of the last hours had
restored to her face the deeper eloquence which Selden had lately missed
in it, and the bravery of her words to him still fluttered in her voice and
eyes. Yes, she was matchless—it was the one word for her; and he could
give his admiration the freer play because so little personal feeling remained
in it. His real detachment from her had taken place, not at the lurid
moment of disenchantment, but now, in the sober after-light of discrimination, where he saw her definitely divided from him by the crudeness
of a choice which seemed to deny the very differences he felt in her. It
was before him again in its completeness—the choice in which she was
content to rest: in the stupid costliness of the food and the showy dulness
of the talk, in the freedom of speech which never arrived at wit and
freedom of act which never made for romance. The strident setting of
the restaurant, in which their table seemed set apart in a special glare of
publicity, and the presence at it of little Dabham of the"Riviera Notes,"
emphasized the ideals of a world where conspicuousness passed for distinction, and the society column had become the roll of fame.

It was as the immortalizer of such occasions that little Dabham, wedged
in modest watchfulness between two brilliant neighbours, suddenly
became the centre of Selden's scrutiny. How much did he know of what
was going on, and how much, for his purpose, was still worth finding
out? His little eyes were like tentacles thrown out to catch the floating
intimations with which, to Selden, the air at moments seemed thick;
then again it cleared to its normal emptiness, and he could see nothing
in it for the journalist but leisure to note the elegance of the ladies'
gowns. Mrs. Dorset's, in particular, challenged all the wealth of Mr.
Dabham's vocabulary: it had surprises and subtleties worthy of what he
would have called "the literary style." At first, as Selden had noticed, it
had been almost too preoccupying to its wearer; but now she was in full
command of it, and was even producing her effects with unwonted freedom. Was she not, indeed, too free, too fluent, for perfect naturalness?
And was not Dorset, to whom his glance had passed by a natural transition, too jerkily wavering between the same extremes? Dorset indeed
was always jerky; but it seemed to Selden that tonight each vibration
swung him farther from his centre.

The dinner, meanwhile, was moving to its triumphant close, to the
evident satisfaction of Mrs. Bry, who, throned in apopletic majesty between
Lord Skiddaw and Lord Hubert, seemed in spirit to be calling on Mrs.
Fisher to witness her achievement. Short of Mrs. Fisher her audience
might have been called complete; for the restaurant was crowded with
persons mainly gathered there for the purpose of spectatorship, and
accurately posted as to the names and faces of the celebrities they had
come to see. Mrs. Bry, conscious that all her feminine guests came

under that heading, and that each one looked her part to admiration, shone on Lily with all the pent-up gratitude that Mrs. Fisher had failed to deserve. Selden, catching the glance, wondered what part Miss Bart had played in organizing the entertainment. She did, at least, a great deal to adorn it; and as he watched the bright security with which she bore herself, he smiled to think that he should have fancied her in need of help. Never had she appeared more serenely mistress of the situation than when, at the moment of dispersal, detaching herself a little from the group about the table, she turned with a smile and a graceful slant of the shoulders to receive her cloak from Dorset.

The dinner had been protracted over Mr. Bry's exceptional cigars and a bewildering array of liqueurs, and many of the other tables were empty; but a sufficient number of diners still lingered to give relief to the leave-taking of Mrs. Bry's distinguished guests. This ceremony was drawn out and complicated by the fact that it involved, on the part of the Duchess and Lady Skiddaw, definite farewells, and pledges of speedy reunion in Paris, where they were to pause and replenish their wardrobes on the way to England. The quality of Mrs. Bry's hospitality, and of the tips her husband had presumably imparted, lent to the manner of the English ladies a general effusiveness which shed the rosiest light over their hostess's future. In its glow Mrs. Dorset and the Stepneys were also visibly included, and the whole scene had touches of intimacy worth their weight in gold to the watchful pen of Mr. Dabham.

A glance at her watch caused the Duchess to exclaim to her sister that they had just time to dash for their train, and the flurry of this departure over, the Stepneys, who had their motor at the door, offered to convey the Dorsets and Miss Bart to the quay. The offer was accepted, and Mrs. Dorset moved away with her husband in attendance. Miss Bart had lingered for a last word with Lord Hubert, and Stepney, on whom Mr. Bry was pressing a final, and still more expensive, cigar, called out: "Come on, Lily, if you're going back to the yacht."

Lily turned to obey; but as she did so, Mrs. Dorset, who had paused on her way out, moved a few steps back toward the table.

"Miss Bart is not going back to the yacht," she said in a voice of singular distinctiness.

A startled look ran from eye to eye; Mrs. Bry crimsoned to the verge of congestion, Mrs. Stepney slipped nervously behind her husband, and Selden, in the general turmoil of his sensations, was mainly conscious of a longing to grip Dabham by the collar and fling him out into the street.

Dorset, meanwhile, had stepped back to his wife's side. His face was white, and he looked about him with cowed angry eyes. "Bertha!—Miss Bart . . . this is some misunderstanding . . . some mistake . . ."

"Miss Bart remains here," his wife rejoined incisively. "And, I think, George, we had better not detain Mrs. Stepney any longer."

Miss Bart, during this brief exchange of words, remained in admirable erectness, slightly isolated from the embarrassed group about her. She had paled a little under the shock of the insult, but the discomposure of the surrounding faces was not reflected in her own. The faint disdain of her smile seemed to lift her high above her antagonist's reach, and it was not till she had given Mrs. Dorset the full measure of the distance between them that she turned and extended her hand to her hostess.

"I am joining the Duchess tomorrow," she explained, "and it seemed easier for me to remain on shore for the night."

She held firmly to Mrs. Bry's wavering eye while she gave this explanation, but when it was over Selden saw her send a tentative glance from one to another of the women's faces. She read their incredulity in their averted looks, and in the mute wretchedness of the men behind them, and for a miserable half-second he thought she quivered on the brink of failure. Then, turning to him with an easy gesture, and the pale bravery of her recovered smile—"Dear Mr. Selden," she said, "you promised to see me to my cab."

Outside, the sky was gusty and overcast, and as Lily and Selden moved toward the deserted gardens below the restaurant, spurts of warm rain blew fitfully against their faces. The fiction of the cab had been tacitly abandoned; they walked on in silence, her hand on his arm, till the deeper shade of the gardens received them, and pausing beside a bench, he said: "Sit down a moment."

She dropped to the seat without answering, but the electric lamp at the bend of the path shed a gleam on the struggling misery of her face. Selden sat down beside her, waiting for her to speak, fearful lest any word he chose should touch too roughly on her wound, and kept also from free utterance by the wretched doubt which had slowly renewed itself within him. What had brought her to this pass? What weakness had placed her so abominably at her enemy's mercy? And why should Bertha Dorset have turned into an enemy at the very moment when she so obviously needed the support of her sex? Even while his nerves raged at the subjection of husbands to their wives, and at the cruelty of women to their kind, reason obstinately harped on the proverbial relation between smoke and fire. The memory of Mrs. Fisher's hints, and the corroboration of his own impressions, while they deepened his pity also increased his constraint, since, whichever way he sought a free outlet for sympathy, it was blocked by the fear of committing a blunder.

Suddenly it struck him that his silence must seem almost as accusatory as that of the men he had despised for turning from her; but before he could find the fitting word she had cut him short with a question.

"Do you know of a quiet hotel? I can send for my maid in the morning."

"An hotel—*here*—that you can go to alone? It's not possible."

She met this with a pale gleam of her old playfulness. "What *is*, then? It's too wet to sleep in the gardens."

"But there must be some one——"

"Dear Mr. Selden," she said, "you promised to see me to my cab."

"Some one to whom I can go? Of course—any number—but at *this* hour? You see my change of plan was rather sudden——"

"Good God—if you'd listened to me!" he cried, venting his helplessness in a burst of anger.

She still held him off with the gentle mockery of her smile. "But haven't I?" she rejoined. "You advised me to leave the yacht, and I'm leaving it."

He saw then, with a pang of self-reproach, that she meant neither to explain nor to defend herself; that by his miserable silence he had forfeited all chance of helping her, and that the decisive hour was past.

She had risen, and stood before him in a kind of clouded majesty, like some deposed princess moving tranquilly to exile.

"Lily!" he exclaimed, with a note of despairing appeal; but—"Oh, not now," she gently admonished him; and then, in all the sweetness of her recovered composure: "Since I must find shelter somewhere, and since you're so kindly here to help me——"

He gathered himself up at the challenge. "You will do as I tell you? There's but one thing, then; you must go straight to your cousins, the Stepneys."

"Oh—" broke from her with a movement of instinctive resistance; but he insisted: "Come—it's late, and you must appear to have gone there directly."

He had drawn her hand into his arm, but she held him back with a last gesture of protest. "I can't—I can't—not that—you don't know Gwen: you mustn't ask me!"

"I *must* ask you—you must obey me," he persisted, though infected at heart by her own fear.

Her voice sank to a whisper: "And if she refuses?"—but, "Oh, trust me—trust me!" he could only insist in return; and yielding to his touch, she let him lead her back in silence to the edge of the square.

In the cab they continued to remain silent through the brief drive which carried them to the illuminated portals of the Stepneys' hotel. Here he left her outside, in the darkness of the raised hood, while his name was sent up to Stepney, and he paced the showy hall, awaiting the latter's descent. Ten minutes later the two men passed out together between the gold-laced custodians of the threshold; but in the vestibule Stepney drew up with a last flare of reluctance.

"It's understood, then?" he stipulated nervously, with his hand on Selden's arm. "She leaves tomorrow by the early train—and my wife's asleep, and can't be disturbed."

IV

The blinds of Mrs. Peniston's drawing-room were drawn down against the oppressive June sun, and in the sultry twilight the faces of her assembled relatives took on a fitting shadow of bereavement.

They were all there: Van Alstynes, Stepneys and Melsons—even a stray Peniston or two, indicating, by a greater latitude in dress and manner, the fact of remoter relationship and more settled hopes. The Peniston side was, in fact, secure in the knowledge that the bulk of Mr. Peniston's property "went back"; while the direct connection hung suspended on the disposal of his widow's private fortune and on the uncertainty of its extent. Jack Stepney, in his new character as the richest nephew, tacitly took the lead, emphasizing his importance by the deeper gloss of his mourning and the subdued authority of his manner; while his wife's bored attitude and frivolous gown proclaimed the heiress's disregard of the insignificant interests at stake. Old Ned Van Alstyne, seated next to her in a coat that made affliction dapper, twirled his white moustache to conceal the eager twitch of his lips; and Grace Stepney, red-nosed and smelling of crape, whispered emotionally to Mrs. Herbert Melson: "I couldn't *bear* to see the Niagara anywhere else!"

A rustle of weeds and quick turning of heads hailed the opening of the door, and Lily Bart appeared, tall and noble in her black dress, with Gerty Farish at her side. The women's faces, as she paused interrogatively on the threshold, were a study in hesitation. One or two made faint motions of recognition, which might have been subdued either by the solemnity of the scene, or by the doubt as to how far the others meant to go; Mrs. Jack Stepney gave a careless nod, and Grace Stepney, with a sepulchral gesture, indicated a seat at her side. But Lily, ignoring the invitation, as well as Jack Stepney's official attempt to direct her, moved across the room with her smooth free gait, and seated herself in a chair which seemed to have been purposely placed apart from the others.

It was the first time that she had faced her family since her return from Europe, two weeks earlier; but if she perceived any uncertainty in their welcome, it served only to add a tinge of irony to the usual composure of her bearing. The shock of dismay with which, on the dock, she had heard from Gerty Farish of Mrs. Peniston's sudden death, had been mitigated, almost at once, by the irrepressible thought that now, at last, she would be able to pay her debts. She had looked forward with considerable uneasiness to her first encounter with her aunt. Mrs. Peniston had vehemently opposed her niece's departure with the Dorsets, and had marked her continued disapproval by not writing during Lily's absence. The certainty that she had heard of the rupture with the Dorsets made the prospect of the meeting more formidable; and how should Lily have repressed a quick sense of relief at the thought that, instead of undergoing the anticipated ordeal, she had only to enter gracefully on a long-assured inheritance? It had been, in the consecrated phrase, "always understood" that Mrs. Peniston was to provide handsomely for her niece; and in the latter's mind the understanding had long since crystallized into fact.

"She gets everything, of course—I don't see what we're here for," Mrs. Jack Stepney remarked with careless loudness to Ned Van Alstyne; and the latter's deprecating murmur—"Julia was always a just woman"—

might have been interpreted as signifying either acquiescence or doubt.

"Well, it's only about four hundred thousand," Mrs. Stepney rejoined with a yawn; and Grace Stepney, in the silence produced by the lawyer's preliminary cough, was heard to sob out: "They won't find a towel missing—I went over them with her the very day——"

Lily, oppressed by the close atmosphere, and the stifling odour of fresh mourning, felt her attention straying as Mrs. Peniston's lawyer, solemnly erect behind the Buhl table at the end of the room, began to rattle through the preamble of the will.

"It's like being in church," she reflected, wondering vaguely where Gwen Stepney had got such an awful hat. Then she noticed how stout Jack had grown—he would soon be almost as plethoric as Herbert Melson, who sat a few feet off, breathing puffily as he leaned his black-gloved hands on his stick.

"I wonder why rich people always grow fat—I suppose it's because there's nothing to worry them. If I inherit, I shall have to be careful of my figure," she mused, while the lawyer droned on through a labyrinth of legacies. The servants came first, then a few charitable institutions, then several remoter Melsons and Stepneys, who stirred consciously as their names rang out, and then subsided into a state of impassiveness befitting the solemnity of the occasion. Ned Van Alstyne, Jack Stepney, and a cousin or two followed, each coupled with the mention of a few thousands: Lily wondered that Grace Stepney was not among them. Then she heard her own name—"to my niece Lily Bart ten thousand dollars—" and after that the lawyer again lost himself in a coil of unintelligible periods, from which the concluding phrase flashed out with startling distinctness: "and the residue of my estate to my dear cousin and name-sake, Grace Julia Stepney."

There was a subdued gasp of surprise, a rapid turning of heads, and a surging of sable figures toward the corner in which Miss Stepney wailed out her sense of unworthiness through the crumpled ball of a black-edged handkerchief.

Lily stood apart from the general movement, feeling herself for the first time utterly alone. No one looked at her, no one seemed aware of her presence; she was probing the very depths of insignificance. And under her sense of the collective indifference came the acuter pang of hopes deceived. Disinherited—she had been disinherited—and for Grace Stepney! She met Gerty's lamentable eyes, fixed on her in a despairing effort at consolation, and the look brought her to herself. There was something to be done before she left the house: to be done with all the nobility she knew how to put into such gestures. She advanced to the group about Miss Stepney, and holding out her hand said simply: "Dear Grace, I am so glad."

The other ladies had fallen back at her approach, and a space created itself about her. It widened as she turned to go, and no one advanced to fill it up. She paused a moment, glancing about her, calmly taking the measure of her situation. She heard some one ask a question about the date of the will; she caught a fragment of the lawyer's answer—something about a sudden summons, and an "earlier instrument." Then the tide of dispersal began to drift past her; Mrs. Jack Stepney and Mrs. Herbert Melson stood on the doorstep awaiting their motor; a sympathizing group escorted Grace Stepney to the cab it was felt to be fitting she should take, though she lived but a street or two away; and Miss Bart and Gerty found themselves almost alone in the purple drawing-room, which more than ever, in its stuffy dimness, resembled a well-kept family vault, in which the last corpse had just been decently deposited.

In Gerty Farish's sitting-room, whither a hansom had carried the two friends, Lily dropped into a chair with a faint sound of laughter: it struck her as a humorous coincidence that her aunt's legacy should so nearly represent the amount of her debt to Trenor. The need of discharging that debt had reasserted itself with increased urgency since her return to America, and she spoke her first thought in saying to the anxiously hovering Gerty: "I wonder when the legacies will be paid."

But Miss Farish could not pause over the legacies; she broke into a larger indignation. "Oh, Lily, it's unjust; it's cruel—Grace Stepney must *feel* she has no right to all that money!"

"Any one who knew how to please Aunt Julia has a right to her money," Miss Bart rejoined philosophically.

"But she was devoted to you—she led every one to think——" Gerty checked herself in evident embarrassment, and Miss Bart turned to her with a direct look. "Gerty, be honest: this will was made only six weeks ago. She had heard of my break with the Dorsets?"

"Every one heard, of course, that there had been some disagreement—some misunderstanding——"

"Did she hear that Bertha turned me off the yacht?"

"Lily!"

"That was what happened, you know. She said I was trying to marry George Dorset. She did it to make him think she was jealous. Isn't that what she told Gwen Stepney?"

"I don't know—I don't listen to such horrors."

"I *must* listen to them—I must know where I stand." She paused, and again sounded a faint note of derision. "Did you notice the women? They were afraid to snub me while they thought I was going to get the money—afterward they scuttled off as if I had the plague." Gerty remained silent, and she continued: "I stayed on to see what would happen. They took their cue from Gwen Stepney and Lulu Melson—I saw them watching to see what Gwen would do—Gerty, I must know just what is being said of me."

"I tell you I don't listen——"

"One hears such things without listening." She rose and laid her resolute hands on Miss Farish's shoulders. "Gerty, are people going to cut me?"

"Your *friends*, Lily—how can you think it?"

"Who are one's friends at such a time? Who, but you, you poor trust-ful darling? And heaven knows what *you* suspect me of!" She kissed Gerty with a whimsical murmur. "You'd never let it make any differ-ence—but then you're fond of criminals, Gerty! How about the irre-claimable ones, though? For I'm absolutely impenitent, you know."

She drew herself up to the full height of her slender majesty, towering like some dark angel of defiance above the troubled Gerty, who could only falter out: "Lily, Lily—how can you laugh about such things?"

"So as not to weep, perhaps. But no—I'm not of the tearful order. I discovered early that crying makes my nose red, and the knowledge has helped me through several painful episodes." She took a restless turn about the room, and then, reseating herself, lifted the bright mockery of her eyes to Gerty's anxious countenance.

"I shouldn't have minded, you know, if I'd got the money—" and at Miss Farish's protesting "Oh!" she repeated calmly: "Not a straw, my dear; for, in the first place, they wouldn't have quite dared to ignore me; and if they had, it wouldn't have mattered, because I should have been independent of them. But now—!" The irony faded from her eyes, and she bent a clouded face upon her friend.

"How can you talk so, Lily? Of course the money ought to have been yours, but after all that makes no difference. The important thing——" Gerty paused, and then continued firmly: "The important thing is that you should clear yourself—should tell your friends the whole truth."

"The whole truth?" Miss Bart laughed. "What is truth? Where a woman is concerned, it's the story that's easiest to believe. In this case it's a great deal easier to believe Bertha Dorset's story than mine, because she has a big house and an opera box, and it's convenient to be on good terms with her."

Miss Farish still fixed her with an anxious gaze. "But what *is* your story, Lily? I don't believe any one knows it yet."

"My story?—I don't believe I know it myself. You see I never thought of preparing a version in advance as Bertha did—and if I had, I don't think I should take the trouble to use it now."

But Gerty continued with her quiet reasonableness: "I don't want a version prepared in advance—but I want you to tell me exactly what happened from the beginning."

"From the beginning?" Miss Bart gently mimicked her. "Dear Gerty, how little imagination you good people have! Why, the beginning was in my cradle, I suppose—in the way I was brought up, and the things I was taught to care for. Or no—I won't blame anybody for my faults: I'll say it was in my blood, that I got it from some wicked pleasure-loving ancestress, who reacted against the homely virtues of New Amsterdam, and wanted to be back at the court of the Charleses!" And as Miss Farish continued to press her with troubled eyes, she went on impatiently: "You asked me just now for the truth—well, the truth about any girl is that once she's talked about she's done for; and the more she explains her case the worse it looks.—My good Gerty, you don't happen to have a cigarette about you?"

In her stuffy room at the hotel to which she had gone on landing, Lily Bart that evening reviewed her situation. It was the last week in June, and none of her friends were in town. The few relatives who had stayed on, or returned, for the reading of Mrs. Peniston's will, had taken flight again that afternoon to Newport or Long Island; and not one of them had made any proffer of hospitality to Lily. For the first time in her life she found herself utterly alone except for Gerty Farish. Even at the actual moment of her break with the Dorsets she had not had so keen a sense of its consequences, for the Duchess of Beltshire, hearing of the catastrophe from Lord Hubert, had instantly offered her protection, and under her sheltering wing Lily had made an almost triumphant progress to London. There she had been sorely tempted to linger on in a society which asked of her only to amuse and charm it, without enquiring too curiously how she had acquired her gift for doing so: but Selden, before they parted, had pressed on her the urgent need of returning at once to her aunt, and Lord Hubert, when he presently reappeared in London, abounded in the same counsel. Lily did not need to be told that the Duchess's championship was not the best road to social rehabilitation, and as she was besides aware that her noble defender might at any moment drop her in favour of a new *protégée*, she reluctantly decided to return to America. But she had not been ten minutes on her native shore before she realized that she had delayed too long to regain it. The Dorsets, the Stepneys, the Brys—all the actors and witnesses in the miserable drama—had preceded her with their version of the case; and, even had she seen the least chance of gaining a hearing for her own, some obscure disdain and reluctance would have restrained her. She knew it was not by explanations and counter-charges that she could ever hope to recover her lost standing; but even had she felt the least trust in their efficacy, she would still have been held back by the feeling which had kept her from defending herself to Gerty Farish—a feeling that was half pride and half humiliation. For though she knew she had been ruthlessly sacrificed to Bertha Dorset's determination to win back her husband, and though her own relation to Dorset had been that of the merest good-fellowship, yet she had been perfectly aware from the outset that her part in the affair was, as Carry Fisher brutally put it, to distract Dorset's attention from his wife. That was what she was "there for": it was the price she had chosen to pay for three months of luxury and freedom from care. Her habit of resolutely facing the facts, in her rare moments of introspection, did not now allow her to put any false gloss on the situation. She had suffered for the very faithfulness with which she had carried out her part of the tacit compact, but the part was not a handsome one at best, and she saw it now in all the ugliness of failure.

She saw, too, in the same uncompromising light, the train of conse-

quences resulting from that failure; and these became clearer to her with
every day of her weary lingering in town. She stayed on partly for the
comfort of Gerty Farish's nearness, and partly for lack of knowing where
to go. She understood well enough the nature of the task before her.
She must set out to regain, little by little, the position she had lost; and
the first step in the tedious task was to find out, as soon as possible, on
how many of her friends she could count. Her hopes were mainly centered on Mrs. Trenor, who had treasures of easy-going tolerance for
those who were amusing or useful to her, and in the noisy rush of whose
existence the still small voice of detraction was slow to make itself heard.
But Judy, though she must have been apprised of Miss Bart's return, had
not even recognized it by the formal note of condolence which her friend's
bereavement demanded. Any advance on Lily's side might have been
perilous: there was nothing to do but to trust to the happy chance of an
accidental meeting, and Lily knew that, even so late in the season, there
was always a hope of running across her friends in their frequent passages
through town.

To this end she assiduously showed herself at the restaurants they
frequented, where, attended by the troubled Gerty, she lunched luxuriously, as she said, on her expectations.

"My dear Gerty, you wouldn't have me let the head-waiter see that
I've nothing to live on but Aunt Julia's legacy? Think of Grace Stepney's
satisfaction if she came in and found us lunching on cold mutton and
tea! What sweet shall we have today, dear—*Coupe Jacques* or *Pêches á
la Melba?*"

She dropped the *menu* abruptly, with a quick heightening of colour,
and Gerty, following her glance, was aware of the advance, from an
inner room, of a party headed by Mrs. Trenor and Carry Fisher. It was
impossible for these ladies and their companions—among whom Lily
had at once distinguished both Trenor and Rosedale—not to pass, in
going out, the table at which the two girls were seated; and Gerty's sense
of the fact betrayed itself in the helpless trepidation of her manner. Miss
Bart, on the contrary, borne forward on the wave of her buoyant grace,
and neither shrinking from her friends nor appearing to lie in wait for
them, gave the encounter the touch of naturalness which she could
impart to the most strained situations. Such embarrassment as was shown
was on Mrs. Trenor's side, and manifested itself in the mingling of exaggerated warmth with imperceptible reservations. Her loudly affirmed
pleasure at seeing Miss Bart took the form of a nebulous generalization,
which included neither enquiries as to her future nor the expression of
a definite wish to see her again. Lily, well-versed in the language of these
omissions, knew that they were equally intelligible to the other members
of the party: even Rosedale, flushed as he was with the importance of
keeping such company, at once took the temperature of Mrs. Trenor's
cordiality, and reflected it in his off-hand greeting of Miss Bart. Trenor,
red and uncomfortable, had cut short his salutations on the pretext of a

word to say to the head-waiter; and the rest of the group soon melted away in Mrs. Trenor's wake.

It was over in a moment—the waiter, *menu* in hand, still hung on the result of the choice between *Coupe Jacques* and *Pêches á la Melba*—but Miss Bart, in the interval, had taken the measure of her fate. Where Judy Trenor led, all the world would follow; and Lily had the doomed sense of the castaway who has signalled in vain to fleeing sails.

In a flash she remembered Mrs. Trenor's complaints of Carry Fisher's rapacity, and saw that they denoted an unexpected acquaintance with her husband's private affairs. In the large tumultuous disorder of the life at Bellomont, where no one seemed to have time to observe any one else, and private aims and personal interests were swept along unheeded in the rush of collective activities, Lily had fancied herself sheltered from inconvenient scrutiny; but if Judy knew when Mrs. Fisher borrowed money of her husband, was she likely to ignore the same transaction on Lily's part? If she was careless of his affections she was plainly jealous of his pocket; and in that fact Lily read the explanation of her rebuff. The immediate result of these conclusions was the passionate resolve to pay back her debt to Trenor. That obligation discharged, she would have but a thousand dollars of Mrs. Peniston's legacy left, and nothing to live on but her own small income, which was considerably less than Gerty Far-ish's wretched pittance; but this consideration gave way to the imperative claim of her wounded pride. She must be quits with the Trenors first; after that she would take thought for the future.

In her ignorance of legal procrastinations she had supposed that her legacy would be paid over within a few days of the reading of her aunt's will; and after an interval of anxious suspense, she wrote to enquire the cause of the delay. There was another interval before Mrs. Peniston's lawyer, who was also one of the executors, replied to the effect that, some questions having arisen relative to the interpretation of the will, he and his associates might not be in a position to pay the legacies till the close of the twelvemonth legally allotted for their settlement. Bewildered and indignant, Lily resolved to try the effect of a personal appeal; but she returned from her expedition with a sense of the powerlessness of beauty and charm against the unfeeling processes of the law. It seemed intolerable to live on for another year under the weight of her debt; and in her extremity she decided to turn to Miss Stepney, who still lingered in town, immersed in the delectable duty of "going over" her benefactress's effects. It was bitter enough for Lily to ask a favour of Grace Stepney, but the alternative was bitterer still; and one morning she presented herself at Mrs. Peniston's, where Grace, for the facilitation of her pious task, had taken up a provisional abode.

The strangeness of entering as a suppliant the house where she had so long commanded, increased Lily's desire to shorten the ordeal; and when Miss Stepney entered the darkened drawing-room, rustling with the best quality of crape, her visitor went straight to the point: would she be willing to advance the amount of the expected legacy?

Grace, in reply, wept and wondered at the request, bemoaned the inexorableness of the law, and was astonished that Lily had not realized the exact similarity of their positions. Did she think that only the payment of the legacies had been delayed? Why, Miss Stepney herself had not received a penny of her inheritance, and was paying rent—yes, actually!—for the privilege of living in a house that belonged to her. She was sure it was not what poor dear cousin Julia would have wished—she had told the executors so to their faces; but they were inaccessible to reason, and there was nothing to do but to wait. Let Lily take example by her, and be patient—let them both remember how beautifully patient cousin Julia had always been.

Lily made a movement which showed her imperfect assimilation of this example. "But you will have everything, Grace—it would be easy for you to borrow ten times the amount I am asking for."

"Borrow—easy for me to borrow?" Grace Stepney rose up before her in sable wrath. "Do you imagine for a moment that I would raise money on my expectations from cousin Julia, when I know so well her unspeakable horror of every transaction of the sort? Why, Lily, if you must know the truth, it was the idea of your being in debt that brought on her illness—you remember she had a slight attack before you sailed. Oh, I don't know the particulars, of course—I don't *want* to know them—but there were rumours about your affairs that made her most unhappy—no one could be with her without seeing that. I can't help it if you are offended by my telling you this now—if I can do anything to make you realize the folly of your course, and how deeply *she* disapproved of it, I shall feel it is the truest way of making up to you for her loss."

V

It seemed to Lily, as Mrs. Peniston's door closed on her, that she was taking a final leave of her old life. The future stretched before her dull and bare as the deserted length of Fifth Avenue, and opportunities showed as meagerly as the few cabs trailing in quest of fares that did not come. The completeness of the analogy was, however, disturbed as she reached the sidewalk by the rapid approach of a hansom which pulled up at sight of her.

From beneath its luggage-laden top, she caught the wave of a signalling hand; and the next moment Mrs. Fisher, springing to the street, had folded her in a demonstrative embrace.

"My dear, you don't mean to say you're still in town? When I saw you the other day at Sherry's I didn't have time to ask——"

She broke off, and added with a burst of frankness: "The truth is I was *horrid*, Lily, and I've wanted to tell you so ever since."

"Oh——" Miss Bart protested, drawing back from her penitent clasp; but Mrs. Fisher went on with her usual directness: "Look here, Lily don't let's beat about the bush: half the trouble in life is caused by pretending there isn't any. That's not my way, and I can only say I'm thoroughly ashamed of myself for following the other women's lead. But we'll talk of that by and bye—tell me now where you're staying and what your plans are. I don't suppose you're keeping house in there with Grace Stepney, eh?—and it struck me you might be rather at loose ends."

In Lily's present mood there was no resisting the honest friendliness of this appeal, and she said with a smile: " I *am* at loose ends for the moment, but Gerty Farish is still in town, and she's good enough to let me be with her whenever she can spare the time."

Mrs. Fisher made a slight grimace. "H'm—that's a temperate joy. Oh, I know—Gerty's a trump, and worth all the rest of us put together; but *à la longuè*[1] you're used a little higher seasoning, aren't you, dear? And besides, I suppose she'll be off herself before long—the first of August, you say? Well, look here, you can't spend your summer in town; we'll talk of that later too. But meanwhile, what do you say to putting a few things in a trunk and coming down with me to the Sam Gormers' tonight?"

And as Lily stared at the breathless suddenness of the suggestion, she continued with her easy laugh: "You don't know them and they don't know you; but that don't make a rap of difference. They've taken the Van Alstyne place at Roslyn, and I've got *carte blanche* to bring my friends down there—the more the merrier. They do things awfully well, and there's to be rather a jolly party there this week—" she broke off, checked by an undefinable change in Miss Bart's expression. "Oh, I don't mean *your* particular set, you know: rather a different crowd, but very good fun. The fact is, the Gormers have struck out on a line of their own: what they want is to have a good time, and to have it in their own way. They gave the other thing a few months' trial, under my distinguished auspices, and they were really doing extremely well—getting on a good deal faster than the Brys, just because they didn't care as much— but suddenly they decided that the whole business bored them, and that what they wanted was a crowd they could really feel at home with. Rather original of them, don't you think so? Mattie Gormer *has* got aspirations still; women always have; but she's awfully easy-going, and Sam won't be bothered, and they both like to be the most important people in sight, so they've started a sort of continuous performance of their own, a kind of social Coney Island, where everybody is welcome who can make noise enough and doesn't put on airs. *I* think it's awfully good fun myself— some of the artistic set, you know, any pretty actress that's going, and so on. This week, for instance, they have Audrey Anstell, who made such a hit last spring in 'The Winning of Winny'; and Paul Morpeth—he's painting Mattie Gormer—and the Dick Bellingers, and Kate Corby— well, every one you can think of who's jolly and makes a row. Now don't stand there with your nose in the air, my dear—it will be a good deal better than a broiling Sunday in town, and you'll find clever people as

1. In the long-term view.

well as noisy ones—Morpeth who admires Mattie enormously, always brings one or two of his set."

Mrs. Fisher drew Lily toward the hansom with friendly authority. "Jump in now, there's a dear, and we'll drive round to your hotel and have your things packed, and then we'll have tea, and the two maids can meet us at the train."

It was a good deal better than a broiling Sunday in town—of that no doubt remained to Lily as, reclining in the shade of a leafy verandah, she looked seaward across a stretch of greensward picturesquely dotted with groups of ladies in lace raiment and men in tennis flannels. The huge Van Alstyne house and its rambling dependencies were packed to their fullest capacity with the Gormers' week-end guests, who now, in the radiance of the Sunday forenoon, were dispersing themselves over the grounds in quest of the various distractions the place afforded: distractions ranging from tennis-courts to shooting-galleries, from bridge and whiskey within doors to motors and steam-launches without. Lily had the odd sense of having been caught up into the crowd as carelessly as a passenger is gathered in by an express train. The blonde and genial Mrs. Gormer might, indeed, have figured the conductor, calmly assigning seats to the rush of travellers, while Carry Fisher represented the porter pushing their bags into place, giving them their numbers for the dining-car, and warning them when their station was at hand. The train, meanwhile, had scarcely slackened speed—life whizzed on with a deafening rattle and roar, in which one traveller at least found a welcome refuge from the sound of her own thoughts.

The Gormer *milieu* represented a social out-skirt which Lily had always fastidiously avoided; but it struck her, now that she was in it, as only a flamboyant copy of her own world, a caricature approximating the real thing as the "society play" approaches the manners of the drawing-room. The people about her were doing the same things as the Trenors, the Van Osburghs and the Dorsets: the difference lay in a hundred shades of aspect and manner, from the pattern of the men's waistcoats to the inflexion of the women's voices. Everything was pitched in a higher key, and there was more of each thing: more noise, more colour, more champagne, more familiarity—but also greater good-nature, less rivalry, and a fresher capacity for enjoyment.

Miss Bart's arrival had been welcomed with an uncritical friendliness that first irritated her pride and then brought her to a sharp sense of her own situation—of the place in life which, for the moment, she must accept and make the best of. These people knew her story—of that her first long talk with Carry Fisher had left no doubt: she was publicly branded as the heroine of a "queer" episode—but instead of shrinking from her as her own friends had done, they received her without question into the easy promiscuity of their lives. They swallowed her past as easily as they did Miss Anstell's, and with no apparent sense of any difference in the size of the mouthful: all they asked was that she should—

It was a good deal better than a broiling Sunday in town.

in her own way, for they recognized a diversity of gifts—contribute as much to the general amusement as that graceful actress, whose talents, when off the stage, were of the most varied order. Lily felt at once that any tendency to be "stuck-up," to mark a sense of differences and distinctions, would be fatal to her continuance in the Gormer set. To be taken in on such terms—and into such a world!—was hard enough to the lingering pride in her; but she realized, with a pang of self-contempt, that to be excluded from it would, after all, be harder still. For, almost at once, she had felt the insidious charm of slipping back into a life where every material difficulty was smoothed away. The sudden escape from a stifling hotel in a dusty deserted city to the space and luxury of a great country-house fanned by sea breezes, had produced a state of moral lassitude agreeable enough after the nervous tension and physical discomfort of the past weeks. For the moment she must yield to the refreshment her senses craved—after that she would reconsider her situation, and take counsel with her dignity. Her enjoyment of her surroundings was, indeed, tinged by the unpleasant consideration that she was accepting the hospitality and courting the approval of people she had disdained under other conditions. But she was growing less sensitive on such points: a hard glaze of indifference was fast forming over her delicacies and susceptibilities, and each concession to expediency hardened the surface a little more.

On the Monday, when the party disbanded with uproarious adieux, the return to town threw into stronger relief the charms of the life she was leaving. The other guests were dispersing to take up the same existence in a different setting: some at Newport, some at Bar Harbour, some in the elaborate rusticity of an Adirondack camp. Even Gerty Farish, who welcomed Lily's return with tender solicitude, would soon be preparing to join the aunt with whom she spent her summers on Lake George: only Lily herself remained without plan or purpose, stranded in a backwater of the great current of pleasure. But Carry Fisher, who had insisted on transporting her to her own house, where she herself was to perch for a day or two on the way to the Brys' camp, came to the rescue with a new suggestion.

"Look here, Lily—I'll tell you what it is: I want you to take my place with Mattie Gormer this summer. They're taking a party out to Alaska next month in their private car, and Mattie, who is the laziest woman alive, wants me to go with them, and relieve her of the bother of arranging things; but the Brys want me too—oh, yes, we've made it up: didn't I tell you?—and, to put it frankly, though I like the Gormers best, there's more profit for me in the Brys. The fact is, they want to try Newport this summer, and if I can make it a success for them they—well, they'll make it a success for *me*." Mrs. Fisher clasped her hands enthusiastically. "Do you know, Lily, the more I think of my idea the better I like it—quite as much for you as for myself. The Gormers have both taken a tremendous fancy to you, and the trip to Alaska is—well—the very thing I should want for you just at present."

Miss Bart lifted her eyes with a keen glance. "To take me out of my friends' way, you mean?" she said quietly; and Mrs. Fisher responded with a deprecating kiss: "To keep you out of their sight till they realize how much they miss you."

Miss Bart went with the Gormers to Alaska; and the expedition, if it did not produce the effect anticipated by her friend, had at least the negative advantage of removing her from the fiery centre of criticism and discussion. Gerty Farish had opposed the plan with all the energy of her somewhat inarticulate nature. She had even offered to give up her visit to Lake George, and remain in town with Miss Bart, if the latter would renounce her journey; but Lily could disguise her real distaste for this plan under a sufficiently valid reason.

"You dear innocent, don't you see," she protested, "that Carry is quite right, and that I must take up my usual life, and go about among people as much as possible? If my old friends choose to believe lies about me I shall have to make new ones, that's all; and you know beggars mustn't be choosers. Not that I don't like Mattie Gormer—I *do* like her: she's kind and honest and unaffected; and don't you suppose I feel grateful to her for making me welcome at a time when, as you've yourself seen, my own family have unanimously washed their hands of me?"

Gerty shook her head, mutely unconvinced. She felt not only that Lily was cheapening herself by making use of an intimacy she would never have cultivated from choice, but that, in drifting back row to her former manner of life, she was forfeiting her last chance of ever escaping from it. Gerty had but an obscure conception of what Lily's actual experience had been; but its consequences had established a lasting hold on her pity since the memorable night when she had offered up her own secret hope to her friend's extremity. To characters like Gerty's such a sacrifice constitutes a moral claim on the part of the person in whose behalf it has been made. Having once helped Lily, she must continue to help her; and helping her, must believe in her, because faith is the main-spring of such natures. But even if Miss Bart, after her renewed taste of the amenities of life, could have returned to the barrenness of a New York August, mitigated only by poor Gerty's presence her worldly wisdom would have counselled her against such an act of abnegation. She knew that Carry Fisher was right: that an opportune absence might be the first step toward rehabilitation; and that, at any rate, to linger on in town out of season was a fatal admission of defeat.

From the Gormers' tumultuous progress across their native continent, she returned with an altered view of her situation. The renewed habit of luxury—the daily waking to an assured absence of care and presence of material ease—gradually blunted her appreciation of these values, and left her more conscious of the void they could not fill. Mattie Gormer's undiscriminating good-nature, and the slap-dash sociability of her friends, who treated Lily precisely as they treated each other—all these characteristic notes of difference began to wear upon her endurance; and the more she saw to criticize in her companions, the less justification she found for making use of them. The longing to get back to her former surroundings hardened to a fixed idea; but with the strengthening of her purpose came the inevitable perception that, to attain it, she must exact fresh concessions from her pride. These, for the moment, took the unpleasant form of continuing to cling to her hosts after their return from Alaska. Little as she was in the key of their *milieu*, her immense social facility, her long habit of adapting herself to others without suffering her own outline to be blurred, the skilled manipulation of all the polished implements of her craft, had won for her an important place in the Gormer group. If their resonant hilarity could never be hers, she contributed a note of easy elegance more valuable to Mattie Gormer than the louder passages of the band. Sam Gormer and his special cronies stood indeed a little in awe of her; but Mattie's following, headed by Paul Morpeth, made her feel that they prized her for the very qualities they most conspicuously lacked. If Morpeth, whose social indolence was as great as his artistic activity, had abandoned himself to the easy current of the Gormer existence, where the minor exactions of politeness were unknown or ignored, and a man could either break his engagements, or keep them in a painting-jacket and slippers, he still preserved his sense of differences, and his appreciation of graces he had no time to cultivate. During the preparations for the Brys' *tableaux* he had been immensely struck by Lily's plastic possibilities—"not the face: too self-controlled for expression; but the rest of her—gad, what a model she'd make!"—and though his abhorrence of the world in which he had seen her was too great for him to think of seeking her there, he was fully alive to the privilege of having her to look at and listen to while he lounged in Mattie Gormer's dishevelled drawing-room.

Lily had thus formed, in the tumult of her surroundings, a little nucleus of friendly relations which mitigated the crudeness of her course in lingering with the Gormers after their return. Nor was she without pale glimpses of her own world, especially since the breaking-up of the Newport season had set the social current once more toward Long Island. Kate Corby, whose tastes made her as promiscuous as Carry Fisher was rendered by her necessities, occasionally descended on the Gormers, where, after a first stare of surprise, she took Lily's presence almost too much as a matter of course. Mrs. Fisher, too, appearing frequently in the neighbourhood, drove over to impart her experiences and give Lily what she called the latest report from the weather-bureau; and the latter, who had never directly invited her confidence, could yet talk with her more freely than with Gerty Farish, in whose presence it was impossible even to admit the existence of much that Mrs. Fisher conveniently took for granted.

Mrs. Fisher, moreover, had no embarrassing curiosity. She did not wish to probe the inwardness of Lily's situation, but simply to view it from the outside, and draw her conclusions accordingly; and these con-

clusions, at the end of a confidential talk, she summed up to her friend
in the succinct remark: "You must marry as soon as you can."

Lily uttered a faint laugh—for once Mrs. Fisher lacked originality.
"Do you mean, like Gerty Farish, to recommend the unfailing panacea
of 'a good man's love'?"

"No—I don't think either of my candidates would answer to that
description," said Mrs. Fisher after a pause of reflection.

"Either? Are there actually two?'

"Well, perhaps I ought to say one and a half—for the moment."

Miss Bart received this with increasing amusement. "Other things
being equal, I think I should prefer a half-husband: who is he?"

"Don't fly out at me till you hear my reasons—George Dorset."

"Oh——" Lily murmured reproachfully; but Mrs. Fisher pressed on
unrebuffed. "Well, why not? They had a few weeks' honeymoon when
they first got back from Europe, but now things are going badly with
them again. Bertha has been behaving more than ever like a mad-
woman, and George's powers of credulity are very nearly exhausted.
They're at their place here, you know, and I spent last Sunday with
them. It was a ghastly party—no one else but poor Neddy Silverton,
who looks like a galley-slave (they used to talk of my making that poor
boy unhappy!)—and after luncheon George carried me off on a long
walk, and told me the end would have to come soon."

Miss Bart made an incredulous gesture. "As far as that goes, the end
will never come—Bertha will always know how to get him back when
she wants him."

Mrs. Fisher continued to observe her tentatively. "Not if he has any
one else to turn to! Yes—that's just what it comes to: the poor creature
can't stand alone. And I remember him such a good fellow, full of life
and enthusiasm." She paused, and went on, dropping her glance from
Lily's: "He wouldn't stay with her ten minutes if he *knew*—"

"Knew——?" Miss Bart repeated.

"What *you* must, for instance—with the opportunities you've had! If
he had positive proof, I mean——"

Lily interrupted her with a deep blush of displeasure. "Please let us
drop the subject, Carry: it's too odious to me." And to divert her companion's attention she added, with an attempt at lightness: "And your
second candidate? We must not forget him."

Mrs. Fisher echoed her laugh. "I wonder if you'll cry out just as loud
if I say—Sim Rosedale?"

Miss Bart did not cry out: she sat silent, gazing thoughtfully at her
friend. The suggestion, in truth, gave expression to a possibility which,
in the last weeks, had more than once recurred to her; but after a moment
she said carelessly: "Mr. Rosedale wants a wife who can establish him
in the bosom of the Van Osburghs and Trenors."

Mrs. Fisher caught her up eagerly. "And so *you* could—with his money!
Don't you see how beautifully it would work out for you both?"

"I don't see any way of making him see it," Lily returned, with a laugh intended to dismiss the subject.

But in reality it lingered with her long after Mrs. Fisher had taken leave. She had seen very little of Rosedale since her annexation by the Gormers, for he was still steadily bent on penetrating to the inner Paradise from which she was now excluded; but once or twice, when nothing better offered, he had turned up for a Sunday, and on these occasions he had left her in no doubt as to his view of her situation. That he still admired her was, more than ever, offensively evident; for in the Gormer circle, where he expanded as in his native element, there were no puzzling conventions to check the full expression of his approval. But it was in the quality of his admiration that she read his shrewd estimate of her case. He enjoyed letting the Gormers see that he had known "Miss Lily"— she was "Miss Lily" to him now—before they had had the faintest social existence: enjoyed more especially impressing Paul Morpeth with the distance to which their intimacy dated back. But he let it be felt that that intimacy was a mere ripple on the surface of a rushing social current, the kind of relaxation which a man of large interests and manifold preoccupations permits himself in his house of ease.

The necessity of accepting this view of their past relation, and of meeting it in the key of pleasantry prevalent among her new friends, was deeply humiliating to Lily. But she dared less than ever to quarrel with Rosedale. She suspected that her rejection rankled among the most unforgettable of his rebuffs, and the fact that he knew something of her wretched transaction with Trenor, and was sure to put the basest construction on it, seemed to place her hopelessly in his power. Yet at Carry Fisher's suggestion a new hope had stirred in her. Much as she disliked Rosedale, she no longer absolutely despised him. For he was gradually attaining his object in life, and that, to Lily, was always less despicable than to miss it. With the slow unalterable persistency which she had always felt in him, he was making his way through the dense mass of social antagonisms. Already his wealth, and the masterly use he had made of it, were giving him an enviable prominence in the world of affairs, and placing Wall Street under obligations which only Fifth Avenue could repay. In response to these claims, his name began to figure on municipal committees and charitable boards; he appeared at banquets to distinguished strangers, and his candidacy at one of the fashionable clubs was discussed with diminishing opposition. He had figured once or twice at the Trenor dinners, and had learned to speak with just the right note of disdain of the big Van Osburgh crushes; and all he now needed was a wife whose affiliations would shorten the last tedious steps of his ascent. It was with that object that, a year earlier, he had fixed his affections on Miss Bart; but in the interval he had mounted nearer to the goal, while she had lost the power to abbreviate the remaining steps of the way. All this she saw with the clearness of vision that came to her in moments of despondency. It was success that dazzled her—she could distinguish facts plainly enough in the twilight of failure. And the twi-

light, as she now sought to pierce it, was gradually lighted by a faint
spark of reassurance. Under the utilitarian motive of Rosedale's wooing
she had felt, clearly enough, the heat of personal inclination. She would
not have detested him so heartily had she not known that he dared to
admire her. What, then, if the passion persisted, though the other motive
had ceased to sustain it? She had never even tried to please him—he
had been drawn to her in spite of her manifest disdain. What if she now
chose to exert the power which, even in its passive state, he had felt so
strongly? What if she made him marry her for love, now that he had no
other reason for marrying her?

VI

As became persons of their rising consequence, the Gormers were
engaged in building a country-house on Long Island; and it was a part
of Miss Bart's duty to attend her hostess on frequent visits of inspection
to the new estate. There, while Mrs. Gormer plunged into problems of
lighting and sanitation, Lily had leisure to wander, in the bright autumn
air, along the tree-fringed bay to which the land declined. Little as she
was addicted to solitude, there had come to be moments when it seemed
a welcome escape from the empty noises of her life. She was weary of
being swept passively along a current of pleasure and business in which
she had no share; weary of seeing other people pursue amusement and
squander money, while she felt herself of no more account among them
than an expensive toy in the hands of a spoiled child.

It was in this frame of mind that, striking back from the shore one
morning into the windings of an unfamiliar lane, she came suddenly
upon the figure of George Dorset. The Dorset place was in the immediate neighbourhood of the Gormers' newly-acquired estate, and in her
motor-flights thither with Mrs. Gormer, Lily had caught one or two
passing glimpses of the couple; but they moved in so different an orbit
that she had not considered the possibility of a direct encounter.

Dorset, swinging along with bent head, in moody abstraction, did not
see Miss Bart till he was close upon her; but the sight, instead of bringing
him to a halt, as she had half-expected, sent him toward her with an
eagerness which found expression in his opening words.

"Miss Bart!—You'll shake hands, won't you? I've been hoping to meet
you—I should have written to you if I'd dared." His face, with its tossed
red hair and straggling moustache, had a driven uneasy look, as though
life had become an unceasing race between himself and the thoughts at
his heels.

The look drew a word of compassionate greeting from Lily, and he
pressed on, as if encouraged by her tone: "I wanted to apologize—to ask
you to forgive me for the miserable part I played——"

She checked him with a quick gesture. "Don't let us speak of it: I was
very sorry for you," she said, with a tinge of disdain which, as she instantly
perceived, was not lost on him.

He flushed to his haggard eyes, flushed so cruelly that she repented the thrust. "You might well be; you don't know—you must let me explain. I was deceived: abominably deceived——"

"I am still more sorry for you, then," she interposed, without irony; "but you must see that I am not exactly the person with whom the subject can be discussed."

He met this with a look of genuine wonder. "Why not? Isn't it to you, of all people, that I owe an explanation—"

"No explanation is necessary: the situation was perfectly clear to me."

"Ah——" he murmured, his head drooping again, and his irresolute hand switching at the underbrush along the lane. But as Lily made a movement to pass on, he broke out with fresh vehemence: "Miss Bart, for God's sake don't turn from me! We used to be good friends—you were always kind to me—and you don't know how I need a friend now."

The lamentable weakness of the words roused a motion of pity in Lily's breast. She too needed friends—she had tasted the pang of loneliness; and her resentment of Bertha Dorset's cruelty softened her heart to the poor wretch who was after all the chief of Bertha's victims.

"I still wish to be kind; I feel no ill-will toward you," she said. "But you must understand that after what has happened we can't be friends again—we can't see each other."

"Ah, you *are* kind—you're merciful—you always were!" He fixed his miserable gaze on her. "But why can't we be friends—why not, when I've repented in dust and ashes? Isn't it hard that you should condemn me to suffer for the falseness, the treachery of others? I was punished enough at the time—is there to be no respite for me?"

"I should have thought you had found complete respite in the reconciliation which was effected at my expense," Lily began, with renewed impatience; but he broke in imploringly: "Don't put it in that way—when that's been the worst of my punishment. My God! what could I do—wasn't I powerless? You were singled out as a sacrifice: any word I might have said would have been turned against you——"

"I have told you I don't blame you; all I ask you to understand is that, after the use Bertha chose to make of me—after all that her behaviour has since implied—it's impossible that you and I should meet."

He continued to stand before her, in his dogged weakness. "Is it— need it be? Mightn't there be circumstances——?" he checked himself, slashing at the wayside weeds in a wider radius. Then he began again: "Miss Bart, listen—give me a minute. If we're not to meet again, at least let me have a hearing now. You say we can't be friends after—after what has happened. But can't I at least appeal to your pity? Can't I move you if I ask you to think of me as a prisoner—a prisoner you alone can set free?"

Lily's inward start betrayed itself in a quick blush: was it possible that this was really the sense of Carry Fisher's adumbrations?

"I can't see how I can possibly be of any help to you," she murmured, drawing back a little from the mounting excitement of his look.

Her tone seemed to sober him, as it had so often done in his stormiest moments. The stubborn lines of his face relaxed, and he said, with an abrupt drop to docility: "You *would* see, if you'd be as merciful as you used to be: and heaven knows I've never needed it more!"

She paused a moment, moved in spite of herself by this reminder of her influence over him. Her fibres had been softened by suffering, and the sudden glimpse into his mocked and broken life disarmed her contempt for his weakness.

"I am very sorry for you—I would help you willingly; but you must have other friends, other advisers."

"I never had a friend like you," he answered simply. "And bes des—can't you see?—you're the only person"—his voice dropped to a whisper—"the only person who knows."

Again she felt her colour change; again her heart rose in precipitate throbs to meet what she felt was coming.

He lifted his eyes to her entreatingly. "You do see, don't you? You understand? I'm desperate—I'm at the end of my tether. I want to be free, and you can free me. I know you can. You don't want to keep me bound fast in hell, do you? You can't want to take such a vengeance as that. You were always kind—your eyes are kind now. You say you're sorry for me. Well, it rests with you to show it; and heaven knows there's nothing to keep you back. You understand, of course—there wouldn't be a hint of publicity—not a sound or a syllable to connect you with the thing. It would never come to that, you know: all I need is to be able to say definitely: 'I know this—and this—and this'—and the fight would drop, and the way be cleared, and the whole abominable business swept out of sight in a second."

He spoke pantingly, like a tired runner, with breaks of exhaustion between his words; and through the breaks she caught, as through the shifting rents of a fog, great golden vistas of peace and safety. For there was no mistaking the definite intention behind his vague appeal; she could have filled up the blanks without the help of Mrs. Fisher's insinuations. Here was a man who turned to her in the extremity of his loneliness and his humiliation: if she came to him at such a moment he would be hers with all the force of his deluded faith. And the power to make him so lay in her hand—lay there in a completeness he could not even remotely conjecture. Revenge and rehabilitation might be hers at a stroke—there was something dazzling in the completeness of the opportunity.

She stood silent, gazing away from him down the autumnal stretch of the deserted lane. And suddenly fear possessed her—fear of herself, and of the terrible force of the temptation. All her past weaknesses were like so many eager accomplices drawing her toward the path their feet had already smoothed. She turned quickly, and held out her hand to Dorset.

"Goodbye—I'm sorry; there's nothing in the world I can do."

"Nothing? Ah, don't say that," he cried; "say what's true that you abandon me like the others. You, the only creature who could have saved me!"

"Goodbye—goodbye," she repeated hurridly; and as she moved away she heard him cry out on a last note of entreaty: "At least you'll let me see you once more?"

Lily, on regaining the Gormer grounds, struck rapidly across the lawn toward the unfinished house, where she fancied that her hostess might be speculating, not too resignedly, on the cause of her delay; for, like many unpunctual persons, Mrs. Gormer disliked to be kept waiting.

As Miss Bart reached the avenue, however, she saw a smart phaeton with a high-stepping pair disappear behind the shrubbery in the direction of the gate; and on the doorstep stood Mrs. Gormer, with a glow of retrospective pleasure on her open countenance. At sight of Lily the glow deepened to an embarrassed red, and she said with a slight laugh: "Did you see my visitor? Oh, I thought you came back by the avenue. It was Mrs. George Dorset—she said she'd dropped in to make a neighbourly call."

Lily met the announcement with her usual composure, though her experience of Bertha's idiosyncrasies would not have led to include the neighbourly instinct among them; and Mrs. Gormer, relieved to see that she gave no sign of surprise, went on with a deprecating laugh: "Of course what really brought her was curiosity—she made me take her all over the house. But no one could have been nicer—no airs, you know, and so good-natured: I can quite see why people think her so fascinating."

This surprising event, coinciding too completely with her meeting with Dorset to be regarded as contingent upon it, had yet immediately struck Lily with a vague sense of foreboding. It was not in Bertha's habit to be neighbourly, much less to make advances to any one outside the immediate circle of her affinities. She had always consistently ignored the world of outer aspirants, or had recognized its individual members only when prompted by motives of self-interest; and the very capriciousness of her condescensions had, as Lily was aware, given them special value in the eyes of the persons she distinguished. Lily saw this now in Mrs. Gormer's unconcealable complacency, and in the happy irrelevance with which, for the next day or two, she quoted Bertha's opinions and speculated on the origin of her gown. All the secret ambitions which Mrs. Gormer's native indolence, and the attitude of her companions, kept in habitual abeyance, were now germinating afresh in the glow of Bertha's advances; and whatever the cause of the latter, Lily saw that, if they were followed up, they were likely to have a disturbing effect upon her own future.

She had arranged to break the length of her stay with her new friends by one or two visits to other acquaintances as recent; and on her return from this somewhat depressing excursion she was immediately conscious that Mrs. Dorset's influence was still in the air. There had been another exchange of visits, a tea at a country-club, an encounter at a hunt ball; there was even a rumour of an approaching dinner, which Mattie Gormer, with an unnatural effort at discretion, tried to smuggle out of the conversation whenever Miss Bart took part in it.

The latter had already planned to return to town after a farewell Sunday with her friends; and, with Gerty Farish's aid, had discovered a small private hotel where she might establish herself for the winter. The hotel being on the edge of a fashionable neighbourhood, the price of the few square feet she was to occupy was considerably in excess of her means; but she found a justification for her dislike of poorer quarters in the argument that, at this particular juncture, it was of the utmost importance to keep up a show of prosperity. In reality, it was impossible for her, while she had the means to pay her way for a week ahead, to lapse into a form of existence like Gerty Farish's. She had never been so near the brink of insolvency; but she could at least manage to meet her weekly hotel bill, and having settled the heaviest of her previous debts out of the money she had received from Trenor, she had a still fair margin of credit to go upon. The situation, however, was not agreeable enough to lull her to complete unconsciousness of its insecurity. Her rooms, with their cramped outlook down a sallow vista of brick walls and fire-escapes, her lonely meals in the dark restaurant with its surcharged ceiling and haunting smell of coffee—all these material discomforts, which were yet to be accounted as so many privileges soon to be withdrawn, kept constantly before her the disadvantages of her state; and her mind reverted the more insistently to Mrs. Fisher's counsels. Beat about the question as she would, she knew the outcome of it was that she must try to marry Rosedale; and in this conviction she was fortified by an unexpected visit from George Dorset.

She found him, on the first Sunday after her return to town, pacing her narrow sitting-room to the imminent peril of the few knick-knacks with which she had tried to disguise its plush exuberances; but the sight of her seemed to quiet him, and he said meekly that he hadn't come to bother her—that he asked only to be allowed to sit for half an hour and talk of anything she liked. In reality, as she knew, he had but one subject: himself and his wretchedness; and it was the need of her sympathy that had drawn him back. But he began with a pretence of questioning her about herself, and as she replied, she saw that, for the first time, a faint realization of her plight penetrated the dense surface of his self-absorption. Was it possible that her old beast of an aunt had actually cut her off? That she was living alone like this because there was no one else for her to go to, and that she really hadn't more than enough to keep alive on till the wretched little legacy was paid? The fibres of sympathy were nearly atrophied in him, but he was suffering so intensely that he had a faint glimpse of what other sufferings might mean—and, as she perceived, an almost simultaneous perception of the way in which her particular misfortunes might serve him.

When at length she dismissed him, on the pretext that she must dress for dinner, he lingered entreatingly on the threshold to blurt out: "It's been such a comfort—do say you'll let me see you again—" But to this direct appeal it was impossible to give an assent; and she said with friendly decisiveness: "I'm sorry—but you know why I can't."

He coloured to the eyes, pushed the door shut, and stood before her embarrassed but insistent. "I know how you might, if you would—if things were different—and it lies with you to make them so. It's just a word to say, and you put me out of my misery!"

Their eyes met, and for a second she trembled again with the nearness of the temptation. "You're mistaken; I know nothing; I saw nothing," she exclaimed, striving, by sheer force of reiteration, to build a barrier between herself and her peril; and as he turned away, groaning out "You sacrifice us both," she continued to repeat, as if it were a charm: "I know nothing—absolutely nothing."

Lily had seen little of Rosedale since her illuminating talk with Mrs. Fisher, but on the two or three occasions when they had met she was conscious of having distinctly advanced in his favour. There could be no doubt that he admired her as much as ever, and she believed it rested with herself to raise his admiration to the point where it should bear down the lingering counsels of expediency. The task was not an easy one; but neither was it easy, in her long sleepless nights, to face the thought of what George Dorset was so clearly ready to offer. Baseness for baseness, she hated the other least: there were even moments when a marriage with Rosedale seemed the only honourable solution of her difficulties. She did not indeed let her imagination range beyond the day of plighting: after that everything faded into a haze of material well-being, in which the personality of her benefactor remained mercifully vague. She had learned, in her long vigils, that there were certain things not good to think of, certain midnight images that must at any cost be exorcised—and one of these was the image of herself as Rosedale's wife.

Carry Fisher, on the strength, as she frankly owned, of the Brys' Newport success, had taken for the autumn months a small house at Tuxedo; and thither Lily was bound on the Sunday after Dorset's visit. Though it was nearly dinner-time when she arrived, her hostess was still out, and the firelit quiet of the small silent house descended on her spirit with a sense of peace and familiarity. It may be doubted if such an emotion had ever before been evoked by Carry Fisher's surroundings; but, contrasted to the world in which Lily had lately lived, there was an air of repose and stability in the very placing of the furniture, and in the quiet competence of the parlour-maid who led her up to her room. Mrs. Fisher's unconventionality was, after all, a merely superficial divergence from an inherited social creed, while the manners of the Gormer circle represented their first attempt to formulate such a creed for themselves.

It was the first time since her return from Europe that Lily had found herself in a congenial atmosphere, and the stirring of familiar associations had almost prepared her, as she descended the stairs before dinner, to enter upon a group of her old acquaintances. But this expectation was instantly checked by the reflection that the friends who remained loyal were precisely those who would be least willing to expose her to such encounters; and it was hardly with surprise that she found, instead, Mr. Rosedale kneeling domestically on the drawing-room hearth before his hostess's little girl.

Rosedale in the paternal rôle was hardly a figure to soften Lily; yet she could not but notice a quality of homely goodness in his advances to the child. They were not, at any rate, the premeditated and perfunctory endearments of the guest under his hostess's eye, for he and the little girl had the room to themselves; and something in his attitude made him seem a simple and kindly being compared to the small critical creature who endured his homage. Yes, he would be kind—Lily, from the threshold, had time to feel—kind in his gross, unscrupulous, rapacious way, the way of the predatory creature with his mate. She had but a moment in which to consider whether this glimpse of the fireside man mitigated her repugnance, or gave it, rather, a more concrete and intimate form; for at sight of her he was immediately on his feet again, the florid and dominant Rosedale of Mattie Gormer's drawing-room.

It was no surprise to Lily to find that he had been selected as her only fellow-guest. Though she and her hostess had not met since the latter's tentative discussion of her future, Lily knew that the acuteness which enabled Mrs. Fisher to lay a safe and pleasant course through a world of antagonistic forces was not infrequently exercised for the benefit of her friends. It was, in fact, characteristic of Carry that, while she actively gleaned her own stores from the fields of affluence, her real sympathies were on the other side—with the unlucky, the unpopular, the unsuccessful, with all her hungry fellow-toilers in the shorn stubble of success.

Mrs. Fisher's experience guarded her against the mistake of exposing Lily, for the first evening, to the unmitigated impression of Rosedale's personality. Kate Corby and two or three men dropped in to dinner, and Lily, alive to every detail of her friend's method, saw that such opportunities as had been contrived for her were to be deferred till she had, as it were, gained courage to make effectual use of them. She had a sense of acquiescing in this plan with the passiveness of a sufferer resigned to the surgeon's touch; and this feeling of almost lethargic helplessness continued when, after the departure of the guests, Mrs. Fisher followed her upstairs.

"May I come in and smoke a cigarette over your fire? If we talk in my room we shall disturb the child." Mrs. Fisher looked about her with the eye of the solicitous hostess. "I hope you've managed to make yourself comfortable, dear? Isn't it a jolly little house? It's such a blessing to have a few quiet weeks with the baby."

Carry, in her rare moments of prosperity, became so expansively maternal that Miss Bart sometimes wondered whether, if she could ever get time and money enough, she would not end by devoting them both to her daughter.

"It's a well-earned rest: I'll say that for myself," she continued, sinking down with a sigh of content on the pillowed lounge near the fire. "Louisa Bry is a stern task-master: I often used to wish myself back with the Gormers. Talk of love making people jealous and suspicious—it's nothing to social ambition! Louisa used to lie awake at night wondering whether the women who called on us called on *me* because I was with her, or on *her* because she was with me; and she was always laying traps to find out what I thought. Of course I had to disown my oldest friends, rather than let her suspect she owed me the chance of making a single acquaintance—when, all the while, that was what she had me there for, and what she wrote me a handsome cheque for when the season was over!"

Mrs. Fisher was not a woman who talked of herself without cause, and the practice of direct speech, far from precluding in her an occasional resort to circuitous methods, served rather, at crucial moments, the purpose of the juggler's chatter while he shifts the contents of his sleeves. Through the haze of her cigarette smoke she continued to gaze meditatively at Miss Bart, who, having dismissed her maid, sat before the toilet-table shaking out over her shoulders the loosened undulations of her hair.

"Your hair's wonderful, Lily. Thinner—? What does that matter, when it's so light and alive? So many women's worries seem to go straight to their hair—but yours looks as if there had never been an anxious thought under it. I never saw you look better than you did this evening. Mattie Gormer told me that Morpeth wanted to paint you—why don't you let him?"

Miss Bart's immediate answer was to address a critical glance to the reflection of the countenance under discussion. Then she said, with a slight touch of irritation: "I don't care to accept a portrait from Paul Morpeth."

Mrs. Fisher mused. "N—no. And just now, especially—he can do you after you're married." She waited a moment, and then went on: "By the way, I had a visit from Mattie the other day. She turned up here last Sunday—and with Bertha Dorset, of all people in the world!"

She paused again to measure the effect of this announcement on her hearer, but the brush in Miss Bart's lifted hand maintained its unwavering stroke from brow to nape.

"I never was more astonished," Mrs. Fisher pursued. "I don't know two women less predestined to intimacy—from Bertha's standpoint, that is; for of course poor Mattie thinks it natural enough that she should be singled out—I've no doubt the rabbit always thinks it is fascinating the anaconda. Well, you know I've always told you that Mattie secretly longed to bore herself with the really fashionable; and now that the chance has come, I see that she's capable of sacrificing all her old friends to it."

Lily laid aside her brush and turned a penetrating glance upon her friend. "Including *me?*" she suggested.

"Ah, my dear," murmured Mrs. Fisher, rising to push back a log from the hearth.

"That's what Bertha means, isn't it?" Miss Bart went on steadily. "For of course she always means something; and before I left Long Island I saw that she was beginning to lay her toils for Mattie."

Mrs. Fisher signed evasively. "She has her fast now, at any rate. To think of that loud independence of Mattie's being only a subtler form of snobbishness! Bertha can already make her believe anything she pleases—and I'm afraid she's begun, my poor child, by insinuating horrors about you."

Lily flushed under the shadow of her drooping hair. "The world is too vile," she murmured, averting herself from Mrs. Fisher's anxious scrutiny.

"It's not a pretty place; and the only way to keep a footing in it is to fight it on its own terms—and above all, my dear, not alone!" Mrs. Fisher gathered up her floating implications in a resolute grasp. "You've told me so little that I can only guess what has been happening; but in the rush we all live in there's no time to keep on hating any one without a cause, and if Bertha is still nasty enough to want to injure you with the other people it must be because she's still afraid of you. From her standpoint there's only one reason for being afraid of you; and my own idea is that, if you want to punish her, you hold the means in your hand. I believe you can marry George Dorset tomorrow; but if you don't care for that particular form of retaliation, the only thing to save you from Bertha is to marry somebody else."

VII

The light projected on the situation by Mrs. Fisher had the cheerless distinctness of a winter dawn. It outlined the facts with a cold precision unmodified by shade or colour, and refracted, as it were, from the blank walls of the surrounding limitations: she had opened windows from which no sky was ever visible. But the idealist subdued to vulgar necessities must employ vulgar minds to draw the inferences to which he cannot stoop; and it was easier for Lily to let Mrs. Fisher formulate her case than to put it plainly to herself. Once confronted with it, however, she went the full length of its consequences; and these had never been more clearly present to her than when, the next afternoon, she set out for a walk with Rosedale.

It was one of those still November days when the air is haunted with the light of summer, and something in the lines of the landscape, and in the golden haze which bathed them, recalled to Miss Bart the September afternoon when she had climbed the slopes of Bellomont with Selden. The importunate memory was kept before her by its ironic contrast to her present situation, since her walk with Selden had represented an irresistible flight from just such a climax as the present excursion was designed to bring about. But the other memories importuned her also; the recollection of similar situations, as skilfully led up to, but through some malice of fortune, or her own unsteadiness of purpose, always failing of the intended result. Well, her purpose was steady enough now. She saw that the whole weary work of rehabilitation must begin again, and against far greater odds, if Bertha Dorset should succeed in breaking up her friendship with the Gormers; and her longing for shelter and security was intensified by the passionate desire to triumph over Bertha, as only wealth and predominance could triumph over her. As the wife of Rosedale—the Rosedale she felt it in her power to create—she would at least present an invulnerable front to her enemy.

She had to draw upon this thought, as upon some fiery stimulant, to keep up her part in the scene toward which Rosedale was too frankly tending. As she walked beside him, shrinking in every nerve from the way in which his look and tone made free of her, yet telling herself that this momentary endurance of his mood was the price she must pay for her ultimate power over him, she tried to calculate the exact point at which concession must turn to resistance, and the price *he* would have to pay be made equally clear to him. But his dapper self-confidence seemed impenetrable to such hints, and she had a sense of something hard and self-contained behind the superficial warmth of his manner.

They had been seated for some time in the seclusion of a rocky glen above the lake, when she suddenly cut short the culmination of an impassioned period by turning upon him the grave loveliness of her gaze.

"I *do* believe what you say, Mr. Rosedale," she said quietly; "and I am ready to marry you whenever you wish."

Rosedale, reddening to the roots of his glossy hair, received this announcement with a recoil which carried him to his feet, where he halted before her in an attitude of almost comic discomfiture.

"For I suppose that is what you do wish," she continued, in the same quiet tone. "And, though I was unable to consent when you spoke to me this way before, I am ready, now that I know you so much better, to trust my happiness to your hands."

She spoke with the noble directness which she could command on such occasions, and which was like a large steady light thrown across the tortuous darkness of the situation. In its inconvenient brightness Rosedale seemed to waver a moment, as though conscious that every avenue of escape was unpleasantly illuminated.

Then he gave a short laugh, and drew out a gold cigarette-case, in which, with plump jewelled fingers, he groped for a gold-tipped cigarette. Selecting one, he paused to contemplate it a moment before saying: "My dear Miss Lily, I'm sorry if there's been any little misapprehension between us—but you made me feel my suit was so hopeless that I had really no intention of renewing it."

Lily's blood tingled with the grossness of the rebuff; but she checked the first leap of her anger, and said in a tone of gentle dignity: "I have no one but myself to blame if I gave you the impression that my decision was final."

Her word-play was always too quick for him, and this reply held him in puzzled silence while she extended her hand and added, with the faintest inflection of sadness in her voice: "Before we bid each other goodbye, I want at least to thank you for having once thought of me as you did."

The touch of her hand, the moving softness of her look, thrilled a vulnerable fibre in Rosedale. It was her exquisite inaccessibleness, the sense of distance she could convey without a hint of disdain, that made it most difficult for him to give her up.

"Why do you talk of saying goodbye? Ain't we going to be good friends all the same?" he urged, without releasing her hand.

She drew it away quietly. "What is your idea of being good friends?" she returned with a slight smile. "Making love to me without asking me to marry you?"

Rosedale laughed with a recovered sense of ease. "Well, that's about the size of it, I suppose. I can't help making love to you—I don't see how any man could; but I don't mean to ask you to marry me as long as I can keep out of it."

She continued to smile. "I like your frankness; but I am afraid our friendship can hardly continue on those terms."

She turned away, as though to mark that its final term had in fact been reached, and he followed her for a few steps with a baffled sense of her having after all kept the game in her own hands.

"Miss Lily——" he began impulsively; but she walked on without seeming to hear him.

He overtook her in a few quick strides, and laid an entreating hand on her arm. "Miss Lily—don't hurry away like that. You're beastly hard on a fellow; but if you don't mind speaking the truth I don't see why you shouldn't allow me to do the same."

She had paused a moment with raised brows, drawing away instinctively from his touch, though she made no effort to evade his words.

"I was under the impression," she rejoined, "that you had done so without waiting for my permission."

"Well—why shouldn't you hear my reasons for doing it, then? We're neither of us such new hands that a little plain speaking is going to hurt us. I'm all broken up on you: there's nothing new in that. I'm more in love with you than I was this time last year; but I've got to face the fact that the situation is changed."

She continued to confront him with the same air of ironic composure. "You mean to say that I'm not as desirable a match as you thought me?"

"Yes; that's what I do mean," he answered resolutely. "I won't go into what's happened. I don't believe the stories about you—I don't *want* to believe them. But they're there, and my not believing them ain't going to alter the situation."

She flushed to her temples, but the extremity of her need checked the retort on her lip and she continued to face him composedly. "If they are not true," she said, "doesn't *that* alter the situation?"

He met this with a steady gaze of his small stocktaking eyes, which made her feel herself no more than some superfine human merchandise. "I believe it does in novels; but I'm certain it don't in real life. You know that as well as I do: if we're speaking the truth, let's speak the whole truth. Last year I was wild to marry you, and you wouldn't look at me: this year—well, you appear to be willing. Now, what has changed in the interval? Your situation, that's all. Then you thought you could do better; now——"

"You think you can?" broke from her ironically.

"Why, yes, I do: in one way, that is." He stood before her, his hands in his pockets, his chest sturdily expanded under its vivid waistcoat. "It's this way, you see: I've had a pretty steady grind of it these last years, working up my social position. Think it's funny I should say that? Why should I mind saying I want to get into society? A man ain't ashamed to say he wants to own a racing stable or a picture gallery. Well, a taste for society's just another kind of hobby. Perhaps I want to get even with some of the people who cold-shouldered me last year—put it that way if it sounds better. Anyhow, I want to have the run of the best houses; and I'm getting it too, little by little. But I know the quickest way to queer yourself with the right people is to be seen with the wrong ones; and that's the reason I want to avoid mistakes."

Miss Bart continued to stand before him in a silence that might have expressed either mockery or a half-reluctant respect for his candour, and after a moment's pause he went on: "There it is, you see. I'm more in love with you than ever, but if I married you now I'd queer myself for good and all, and everything I've worked for all these years would be wasted."

She received this with a look from which all tinge of resentment had faded. After the tissue of social falsehoods in which she had so long moved it was refreshing to step into the open daylight of an avowed expediency.

"I understand you," she said. "A year ago I should have been of use to you, and now I should be an encumbrance; and I like you for telling me so quite honestly." She extended her hand with a smile.

Again the gesture had a disturbing effect upon Mr. Rosedale's self-command. "By George, you're a dead game sport, you are!" he exclaimed; and as she began once more to move away, he broke out suddenly— "Miss Lily—stop. You know I don't believe those stories—I believe they were all got up by a woman who didn't hesitate to sacrifice you to her own convenience——"

Lily drew away with a movement of quick disdain: it was easier to endure his insolence than his commiseration.

"You are very kind; but I don't think we need discuss the matter farther."

But Rosedale's natural imperviousness to hints made it easy for him to brush such resistance aside. "I don't want to discuss anything; I just want to put a plain case before you," he persisted.

She paused in spite of herself, held by the note of a new purpose in his look and tone; and he went on, keeping his eyes firmly upon her: "The wonder to me is that you've waited so long to get square with that woman, when you've had the power in your hands." She continued silent under the rush of astonishment that his words produced, and he moved a step closer to ask with low-toned directness: "Why don't you use those letters of hers you bought last year?"

Lily stood speechless under the shock of the interrogation. In the words preceding it she had conjectured, at most, an allusion to her supposed influence over George Dorset; nor did the astonishing indelicacy of the reference diminish the likelihood of Rosedale's resorting to it. But now she saw how far short of the mark she had fallen; and the surprise of learning that he had discovered the secret of the letters left her, for the moment, unconscious of the special use to which he was in the act of putting his knowledge.

Her temporary loss of self-possession gave him time to press his point; and he went on quickly, as though to secure completer control of the situation: "You see I know where you stand—I know how completely she's in your power. That sounds like stage-talk, don't it?—but there's a lot of truth in some of those old gags; and I don't suppose you bought those letters simply because you're collecting autographs."

She continued to look at him with a deepening bewilderment: her only clear impression resolved itself into a scared sense of his power.

"You're wondering how I found out about 'em?" he went on, answering her look with a note of conscious pride. "Perhaps you've forgotten that I'm the owner of the Benedick—but never mind about that now. Getting on to things is a mighty useful accomplishment in business, and I've simply extended it to my private affairs. For this is partly my affair, you see—at least, it depends on you to make it so. Let's look me situation straight in the eye. Mrs. Dorset, for reasons we needn't go into, did you a beastly bad turn last spring. Everybody knows what Mrs. Dorset is, and her best friends wouldn't believe her on oath where their own interests were concerned; but as long as they're out of the row it's much easier to follow her lead than to set themselves against it, and you've simply been sacrificed to their laziness and selfishness. Isn't that a pretty fair statement of the case?—Well, some people say you've got the neatest kind of an answer in your hands: that George Dorset would marry you tomorrow, if you'd tell him all you know, and give him the chance to show the lady the door. I daresay he would; but you don't seem to care for that particular form of getting even, and, taking a purely business view of the question, I think you're right. In a deal like that, nobody comes out with perfectly clean hands, and the only way for you to start fresh is to get Bertha Dorset to back you up, instead of trying to fight her."

He paused long enough to draw breath, but not to give her time for the expression of her gathering resistance; and as he pressed on, expounding and elucidating his idea with the directness of the man who has no doubts of his cause, she found the indignation gradually freezing on her lip, found herself held fast in the grasp of his argument by the mere cold strength of its presentation. There was no time now to wonder how he had heard of her obtaining the letters: all her world was dark outside the monstrous glare of his scheme for using them. And it was not, after the first moment, the horror of the idea that held her spellbound, subdued to his will; it was rather its subtle affinity to her own inmost cravings. He would marry her tomorrow if she could regain Bertha Dorset's friendship; and to induce the open resumption of that friendship, and the tacit retractation of all that had caused its withdrawal, she had only to put to the lady the latent menace contained in the packet so miraculously delivered into her hands. Lily saw in a flash the advantage of this course over that which poor Dorset had pressed upon her. The other plan depended for its success on the infliction of an open injury, while this reduced the transaction to a private understanding, of which no third person need have the remotest hint. Put by Rosedale in terms of business-like give-and-take, this understanding took on the harmless air of a mutual accommodation, like a transfer of property or a revision of boundary lines. It certainly simplified life to view it as a perpetual adjustment, a play of party politics, in which every concession had its recognized equivalent: Lily's tired mind was fascinated by this escape from fluctuating ethical estimates into a region of concrete weights and measures.

Rosedale, as she listened, seemed to read in her silence not only a gradual acquiescence in his plan, but a dangerously far-reaching perception of the chances it offered; for as she continued to stand before him without speaking, he broke out, with a quick return upon himself: "You see how simple it is, don't you? Well, don't be carried away by the idea that it's *too* simple. It isn't exactly as if you'd started in with a clean bill of health. Now we're talking let's call things by their right names, and clear the whole business up. You know well enough that Bertha Dorset couldn't have touched you if there hadn't been—well—questions asked before—little points of interrogation, eh? Bound to happen to a good-looking girl with stingy relatives, I suppose; anyhow, they *did* happen, and she found the ground prepared for her. Do you see where I'm coming out? You don't want these little questions cropping up again. It's one thing to get Bertha Dorset into line—but what you want is to keep her there. You can frighten her fast enough—but how are you going to keep her frightened? By showing her that you're as powerful as she is. All the letters in the world won't do that for you as you are now; but with a big backing behind you, you'll keep her just where you want her to be. That's *my* share in the business—that's what I'm offering you. You can't put the thing through without me—don't run away with any idea that you can. In six months you'd be back again among your old worries, or worse ones; and here I am, ready to lift you out of 'em tomorrow if you say so. *Do* you say so, Miss Lily?" he added, moving suddenly nearer.

The words, and the movement which accompanied them, combined to startle Lily out of the state of tranced subservience into which she had insensibly slipped. Light comes in devious ways to the groping consciousness, and it came to her now through the disgusted perception that her would-be accomplice assumed, as a matter of course, the likelihood of her distrusting him and perhaps trying to cheat him of his share of the spoils. This glimpse of his inner mind seemed to present the whole transaction in a new aspect, and she saw that the essential baseness of the act lay in its freedom from risk.

She drew back with a quick gesture of rejection, saying, in a voice that was a surprise to her own ears: "You are mistaken—quite mistaken—both in the facts and in what you infer from them."

Rosedale stared a moment, puzzled by her sudden dash in a direction so different from that toward which she had appeared to be letting him guide her.

"Now what on earth does that mean? I thought we understood each other!" he exclaimed; and to her murmur of "Ah, we do *now*," he retorted with a sudden burst of violence: "I suppose it's because the letters are to *him*, then? Well, I'll be damned if I see what thanks you've got from him!"

VIII

The autumn days declined to winter. Once more the leisure world was in transition between country and town, and Fifth Avenue, still deserted at the week-end, showed from Monday to Friday a broadening stream of carriages between house-fronts gradually restored to consciousness.

The Horse Show, some two weeks earlier, had produced a passing semblance of reanimation, filling the theatres and restaurants with a human display of the same costly and high-stepping kind as circled daily about its ring. In Miss Bart's world the Horse Show, and the public it attracted, had ostensibly come to be classed among the spectacles disdained of the elect; but, as the feudal lord might sally forth to join in the dance on his village green, so society, unofficially and incidentally, still condescended to look in upon the scene. Mrs. Gormer, among the rest, was not above seizing such an occasion for the display of herself and her horses; and Lily was given one or two opportunities of appearing at her friend's side in the most conspicuous box the house afforded. But this lingering semblance of intimacy made her only the more conscious of a change in the relation between Mattie and herself, of a dawning discrimination, a gradually formed social standard, emerging from Mrs. Gormer's chaotic view of life. It was inevitable that Lily herself should constitute the first sacrifice to this new ideal, and she knew that, once the Gormers were established in town, the whole drift of fashionable life would facilitate Mattie's detachment from her. She had, in short, failed to make herself indispensable; or rather, her attempt to do so had been thwarted by an influence stronger than any she could exert. That influence, in its last analysis, was simply the power of money: Bertha Dorset's social credit was based on an impregnable bank-account.

Lily knew that Rosedale had overstated neither the difficulty of her own position nor the completeness of the vindication he offered: once Bertha's match in material resources, her superior gifts would make it easy for her to dominate her adversary. An understanding of what such domination would mean, and of the disadvantages accruing from her rejection of it, was brought home to Lily with increasing clearness during the early weeks of the winter. Hitherto, she had kept up a semblance of movement outside the main flow of the social current; but with the return to town, and the concentrating of scattered activities, the mere fact of not slipping back naturally into her old habits of life marked her as being unmistakably excluded from them. If one were not a part of the season's fixed routine, one swung unsphered in a void of social non-existence. Lily, for all her dissatisfied dreaming, had never really conceived the possibility of revolving about a different centre: it was easy enough to despise the world, but decidedly difficult to find any other habitable region. Her sense of irony never quite deserted her, and she could still note, with self-directed derision, the abnormal value suddenly acquired by the most tiresome and insignificant details of her former life. Its very drudgeries had a charm now that she was involuntarily released from them: card-leaving, note-writing, enforced civilities to the dull and elderly, and the smiling endurance of tedious dinners—how pleasantly such obligations would have filled the emptiness of her days! She did indeed leave cards in plenty; she kept herself, with a smiling and valiant persistence, well in the eye of her world; nor did she suffer any of those gross rebuffs which sometimes produce a wholesome reaction of contempt in their victim. Society did not turn away from her, it simply drifted by, preoccupied and inattentive, letting her feel, to the full measure of her humbled pride, how completely she had been the creature of its favour.

She had rejected Rosedale's suggestion with a promptness of scorn almost surprising to herself: she had not lost her capacity for high flashes of indignation. But she could not breathe long on the heights; there had been nothing in her training to develop any continuity of moral strength: what she craved, and really felt herself entitled to, was a situation in which the noblest attitude should also be the easiest. Hitherto her intermittent impulses of resistance had sufficed to maintain her self-respect. If she slipped she recovered her footing, and it was only afterward that she was aware of having recovered it each time on a slightly lower level. She had rejected Rosedale's offer without conscious effort; her whole being had risen against it; and she did not yet perceive that, by the mere act of listening to him, she had learned to live with ideas which would once have been intolerable to her.

To Gerty Farish, keeping watch over her with a tenderer if less discerning eye than Mrs. Fisher's, the results of the struggle were already distinctly visible. She did not, indeed, know what hostages Lily had already given to expediency; but she saw her passionately and irretrievably pledged to the ruinous policy of "keeping up." Gerty could smile now at her own early dream of her friend's renovation through adversity: she understood clearly enough that Lily was not of those to whom privation teaches the unimportance of what they have lost. But this very fact, to Gerty, made her friend the more piteously in want of aid, the more exposed to the claims of a tenderness she was so little conscious of needing.

Lily, since her return to town, had not often climbed Miss Farish's stairs. There was something irritating to her in the mute interrogation of Gerty's sympathy: she felt the real difficulties of her situation to be incommunicable to any one whose theory of values was so different from her own, and the restrictions of Gerty's life, which had once had the charm of contrast, now reminded her too painfully of the limits to which her own existence was shrinking. When at length, one afternoon, she put into execution the belated resolve to visit her friend, this sense of shrunken opportunities possessed her with unusual intensity. The walk up Fifth Avenue, unfolding before her, in the brilliance of the hard winter sunlight, an interminable procession of fastidiously-equipped carriages—giving her, through the little squares of brougham-windows, peeps of familiar profiles bent above visiting-lists, of hurried hands dispensing notes and cards to attendant footmen—this glimpse of the ever-revolving wheels of the great social machine made Lily more than ever conscious of the steepness and narrowness of Gerty's stairs, and of the cramped blind-alley of life to which they led. Dull stairs destined to be mounted by dull people: how many thousands of insignificant figures were going up and down such stairs all over the world at that very moment—figures as shabby and uninteresting as that of the middle-aged lady in limp black who descended Gerty's flight as Lily climbed to it!

"That was poor Miss Jane Silverton—she came to talk things over with me: she and her sister want to do something to support themselves," Gerty explained, as Lily followed her into the sitting-room.

"To support themselves? Are they so hard up?" Miss Bart asked with a touch of irritation: she had not come to listen to the woes of other people.

"I'm afraid they have nothing left: Ned's debts have swallowed up everything. They had such hopes, you know, when he broke away from Carry Fisher; they thought Bertha Dorset would be such a good influence, because she doesn't care for cards, and—well, she talked quite beautifully to poor Miss Jane about feeling as if Ned were her younger brother, and wanting to carry him off on the yacht, so that he might have a chance to drop cards and racing, and take up his literary work again."

Miss Farish paused with a sigh which reflected the perplexity of her departing visitor. "But that isn't all; it isn't even the worst. It seems that Ned has quarrelled with the Dorsets; or at least Bertha won't allow him to see her, and he is so unhappy about it that he has taken to gambling

again, and going about with all sorts of queer people. And cousin Grace
Van Osburgh accuses him of having had a very bad influence on Bertie,
who left Harvard last spring, and has been a great deal with Ned ever
since. She sent for Miss Jane, and made a dreadful scene; and Jack
Stepney and Herbert Melson, who were there too, told Miss Jane that
Bertie was threatening to marry some dreadful woman to whom Ned
had introduced him, and that they could do nothing with him because
now he's of age he has his own money. You can fancy how poor Miss
Jane felt—she came to me at once, and seemed to think that if I could
get her something to do she could earn enough to pay Ned's debts and
send him away—I'm afraid she has no idea how long it would take her
to pay for one of his evenings at bridge. And he was horribly in debt
when he came back from the cruise—I can't see why he should have
spent so much more money under Bertha's influence than Carry's: can
you?"

Lily met this query with an impatient gesture. "My dear Gerty, I
always understand how people can spend much more money—never
how they can spend any less!"

She loosened her furs and settled herself in Gerty's easy-chair, while
her friend busied herself with the tea-cups.

"But what can they do—the Miss Silvertons? How do they mean to
support themselves?" she asked, conscious that the note of irritation still
persisted in her voice. It was the very last topic she had meant to discuss—it really did not interest her in the least—but she was seized by a
sudden perverse curiosity to know how the two colourless shrinking victims of young Silverton's sentimental experiments meant to cope with
the grim necessity which lurked so close to her own threshold.

"I don't know—I am trying to find something for them. Miss Jane
reads aloud very nicely—but it's so hard to find any one who is willing
to be read to. And Miss Annie paints a little——"

"Oh, I know—apple-blossoms on blotting-paper; just the kind of thing
I shall be doing myself before long!" exclaimed Lily, starting up with a
vehemence of movement that threatened destruction to Miss Farish's
fragile tea-table.

Lily bent over to steady the cups; then she sank back into her seat.
"I'd forgotten there was no room to dash about in—how beautifully one
does have to behave in a small flat! Oh, Gerty, I wasn't meant to be
good," she sighed out incoherently.

Gerty lifted an apprehensive look to her pale face, in which the eyes
shone with a peculiar sleepless lustre.

"You look horribly tired, Lily; take your tea, and let me give you
this cushion to lean against."

Miss Bart accepted the cup of tea, but put back the cushion with an
impatient hand.

"Don't give me that! I don't want to lean back—I shall go to sleep
if I do."

"Well, why not, dear? I'll be as quiet as a mouse," Gerty urged affectionately.

"No—no; don't be quiet; talk to me—keep me awake! I don't sleep at night, and in the afternoon a dreadful drowsiness creeps over me."

"You don't sleep at night? Since when?"

"I don't know—I can't remember." She rose and put the empty cup on the tea-tray. "Another, and stronger, please; if I don't keep awake now I shall see horrors tonight—perfect horrors!"

"But they'll be worse if you drink too much tea."

"No, no—give it to me; and don't preach, please," Lily returned imperiously. Her voice had a dangerous edge, and Gertie noticed that her hand shook as she held it out to receive the second cup.

"But you look so tired: I'm sure you must be ill——"

Miss Bart set down her cup with a start. "Do I look ill? Does my face show it?" She rose and walked quickly toward the little mirror above the writing-table. "What a horrid looking-glass—it's all blotched and discoloured. Any one would look ghastly in it!" She turned back, fixing her plaintive eyes on Gerty. "You stupid dear, why do you say such odious things to me? It's enough to make one ill to be told one looks so! And looking ill means looking ugly." She caught Gerty's wrists, and drew her close to the window. "After all, I'd rather know the truth. Look me straight in the face, Gerty, and tell me: am I perfectly frightful?"

"You're perfectly beautiful now, Lily: your eyes are shining, and your cheeks have grown so pink all of a sudden——"

"Ah, they *were* pale, then—ghastly pale, when I came in? Why don't you tell me frankly that I'm a wreck? My eyes are bright now because I'm so nervous—but in the mornings they look like lead. And I can see the lines coming in my face—the lines of worry and disappointment and failure! Every sleepless night leaves a new one—and how can I sleep, when I have such dreadful things to think about?"

"Dreadful things—what things?" asked Gerty, gently detaching her wrists from her friend's feverish fingers.

"What things? Well, poverty, for one—and I don't know any that's more dreadful." Lily turned away and sank with sudden weariness into the easy-chair near the tea-table. "You asked me just now if I could understand why Ned Silverton spent so much money. Of course I understand—he spends it on living with the rich. You think we live *on* the rich, rather than with them: and so we do, in a sense—but it's a privilege we have to pay for! We eat their dinners, and drink their wine, and smoke their cigarettes, and use their carriages and their opera-boxes and their private cars—yes, but there's a tax to pay on every one of those luxuries. The man pays it by big tips to the servants, by playing cards beyond his means, by flowers and presents—and—and—lots of other things that cost; the girl pays it by tips and cards too—oh, yes, I've had to take up bridge again—and by going to the best dress-makers, and having just the right dress for every occasion, and always keeping herself fresh and exquisite and amusing!"

She leaned back for a moment, closing her eyes, and as she sat there, her pale lips slightly parted, and the lids dropped above her fagged brilliant gaze, Gerty had a startled perception of the change in her face—of the way in which an ashen daylight seemed suddenly to extinguish its artificial brightness. She looked up, and the vision vanished.

"It doesn't sound very amusing, does it? And it isn't—I'm sick to death of it! And yet the thought of giving it all up nearly kills me—it's what keeps me awake at night, and makes me so crazy for your strong tea. For I can't go on in this way much longer, you know—I'm nearly at the end of my tether. And then what can I do—how on earth am I to keep myself alive? I see myself reduced to the fate of that poor Silverton woman— slinking about to employment agencies, and trying to sell painted blotting-pads to Women's Exchanges![1] And there are thousands and thousands of women trying to do the same thing already, and not one of the number who has less idea how to earn a dollar than I have!"

She rose again with a hurried glance at the clock. "It's late, and I must be off—I have an appointment with Carry Fisher. Don't look so worried, you dear thing—don't think too much about the nonsense I've been talking." She was before the mirror again, adjusting her hair with a light hand, drawing down her veil, and giving a dexterous touch to her furs. "Of course, you know, it hasn't come to the employment agencies and the painted blotting-pads yet; but I'm rather hard-up just for the moment, and if I could find something to do—notes to write and visiting-lists to make up, or that kind of thing—it would tide me over till the legacy is paid. And Carry has promised to find somebody who wants a kind of social secretary—you know she makes a specialty of the helpless rich."

Miss Bart had not revealed to Gerty the full extent of her anxiety. She was in fact in urgent and immediate need of money: money to meet the vulgar weekly claims which could neither be deferred nor evaded. To give up her apartment, and shrink to the obscurity of a boardinghouse, or the provisional hospitality of a bed in Gerty Farish's sitting-room, was an expedient which could only postpone the problem confronting her; and it seemed wiser as well as more agreeable to remain where she was and find some means of earning her living. The possibility of having to do this was one which she had never before seriously considered, and the discovery that, as a bread-winner, she was likely to prove as helpless and ineffectual as poor Miss Silverton, was a severe shock to her self-confidence.

Having been accustomed to take herself at the popular valuation, as a person of energy and resource, naturally fitted to dominate any situation

1. Existing in seventy-five cities in the United States, women's exchanges provided outlets for women's work while preserving the anonymity of the worker. Exchanges sold bread, pastry, jams, and needlework to give an income to gentlewomen otherwise facing poverty.

in which she found herself, she vaguely imagined that such gifts would be of value to seekers after social guidance; but there was unfortunately no specific head under which the art of saying and doing the right thing could be offered in the market, and even Mrs. Fisher's resourcefulness failed before the difficulty of discovering a workable vein in the vague wealth of Lily's graces. Mrs. Fisher was full of indirect expedients for enabling her friends to earn a living, and could conscientiously assert that she had put several opportunities of this kind before Lily; but more legitimate methods of bread-winning were as much out of her line as they were beyond the capacity of the sufferers she was generally called upon to assist. Lily's failure to profit by the chances already afforded her might, moreover, have justified the abandonment of farther effort on her behalf; but Mrs. Fisher's inexhaustible good-nature made her an adept at creating artificial demands in response to an actual supply. In the pursuance of this end she at once started on a voyage of discovery in Miss Bart's behalf; and as the result of her explorations she now summoned the latter with the announcement that she had "found something."

Left to herself, Gerty mused distressfully upon her friend's plight, and her own inability to relieve it. It was clear to her that Lily, for the present, had no wish for the kind of help she could give. Miss Farish could see no hope for her friend but in a life completely reorganized and detached from its old associations; whereas all Lily's energies were centred in the determined effort to hold fast to those associations, to keep herself visibly identified with them, as long as the illusion could be maintained. Pitiable as such an attitude seemed to Gerty, she could not judge it as harshly as Selden, for instance, might have done. She had not forgotten the night of emotion when she and Lily had lain in each other's arms, and she had seemed to feel her very heart's blood passing into her friend. The sacrifice she had made had seemed unavailing enough; no trace remained in Lily of the subduing influences of that hour; but Gerty's tenderness, disciplined by long years of contact with obscure and inarticulate suffering, could wait on its object with a silent forbearance which took no account of time. She could not, however, deny herself the solace of taking anxious counsel with Lawrence Selden, with whom, since his return from Europe, she had renewed her old relation of cousinly confidence.

Selden himself had never been aware of any change in their relation. He found Gerty as he had left her, simple, undemanding and devoted, but with a quickened intelligence of the heart which he recognized without seeking to explain it. To Gerty herself it would once have seemed impossible that she should ever again talk freely with him of Lily Bart; but what had passed in the secrecy of her own breast seemed to resolve itself, when the mist of the struggle cleared, into a breaking down of the bounds of self, a deflecting of the wasted personal emotion into the general current of human understanding.

It was not till some two weeks after her visit from Lily that Gerty had the opportunity of communicating her fears to Selden. The latter, having presented himself on a Sunday afternoon, had lingered on through the dowdy animation of his cousin's tea-hour, conscious of something in her voice and eye which solicited a word apart; and as soon as the last visitor was gone Gerty opened her case by asking how lately he had seen Miss Bart.

Selden's perceptible pause gave her time for a slight stir of surprise.

"I haven't seen her at all—I've perpetually missed seeing her since she came back."

This unexpected admission made Gerty pause too; and she was still hesitating on the brink of her subject when he relieved her by adding: "I've wanted to see her—but she seems to have been absorbed by the Gormer set since her return from Europe."

"That's all the more reason: she's been very unhappy."

"Unhappy at being with the Gormers?"

"Oh, I don't defend her intimacy with the Gormers; but that too is at an end now, I think. You know people have been very unkind since Bertha Dorset quarrelled with her."

"Ah——" Selden exclaimed, rising abruptly to walk to the window, where he remained with his eyes on the darkening street while his cousin continued to explain: "Judy Trenor and her own family have deserted her too—and all because Bertha Dorset has said such horrible things. And she is very poor—you know Mrs. Peniston cut her off with a small legacy, after giving her to understand that she was to have everything."

"Yes—I know," Selden assented curtly, turning back into the room, but only to stir about with restless steps in the circumscribed space between door and window. "Yes—she's been abominably treated; but it's unfortunately the precise thing that a man who wants to show his sympathy can't say to her."

His words caused Gerty a slight chill of disappointment. "There would be other ways of showing your sympathy," she suggested.

Selden, with a slight laugh, sat down beside her on the little sofa which projected from the hearth. "What are you thinking of, you incorrigible missionary?" he asked.

Gerty's colour rose, and her blush was for a moment her only answer. Then she made it more explicit by saying: "I am thinking of the fact that you and she used to be great friends—that she used to care immensely for what you thought of her—and that, if she takes your staying away as a sign of what you think now, I can imagine its adding a great deal to her unhappiness."

"My dear child, don't add to it still more—at least to your conception of it—by attributing to her all sorts of susceptibilities of your own." Selden, for his life, could not keep a note of dryness out of his voice; but he met Gerty's look of perplexity by saying more mildly: "But, though you immensely exaggerate the importance of anything I could do for Miss Bart, you can't exaggerate my readiness to do it—if you ask me to."

He laid his hand for a moment on hers, and there passed between them, on the current of the rare contact, one of those exchanges of meaning which fill the hidden reservoirs of affection. Gerty had the feeling that he measured the cost of her request as plainly as she read the significance of his reply; and the sense of all that was suddenly clear between them made her next words easier to find.

"I do ask you, then; I ask you because she once told me that you had been a help to her, and because she needs help now as she has never needed it before. You know how dependent she has always been on ease and luxury—how she has hated what was shabby and ugly and uncomfortable. She can't help it—she was brought up with those ideas, and has never been able to find her way out of them. But now all the things she cared for have been taken from her, and the people who taught her to care for them have abandoned her too; and it seems to me that if some one could reach out a hand and show her the other side—show her how much is left in life and in herself——" Gerty broke off, abashed at the sound of her own eloquence, and impeded by the difficulty of giving precise expression to her vague yearning for her friend's retrieval. "I can't help her myself: she's passed out of my reach," she continued. "I think she's afraid of being a burden to me. When she was last here, two weeks ago, she seemed dreadfully worried about her future: she said Carry Fisher was trying to find something for her to do. A few days later she wrote me that she had taken a position as private secretary, and that I was not to be anxious, for everything was all right, and she would come in and tell me about it when she had time; but she has never come, and I don't like to go to her, because I am afraid of forcing myself on her when I'm not wanted. Once, when we were children, and I had rushed up after a long separation, and thrown my arms about her, she said: 'Please don't kiss me unless I ask you to, Gerty'—and she *did* ask me, a minute later; but since then I've always waited to be asked."

Selden had listened in silence, with the concentrated look which his thin dark face could assume when he wished to guard it against any involuntary change of expression. When his cousin ended, he said with a slight smile: "Since you've learned the wisdom of waiting, I don't see why you urge me to rush in——" but the troubled appeal of her eyes made him add, as he rose to take leave: "Still, I'll do what you wish, and not hold you responsible for my failure."

Selden's avoidance of Miss Bart had not been as unintentional as he had allowed his cousin to think. At first, indeed, while the memory of their last hour at Monte Carlo still held the full heat of his indignation, he had anxiously watched for her return; but she had disappointed him by lingering in England, and when she finally reappeared it happened that business had called him to the West, whence he came back only to learn that she was starting for Alaska with the Gormers. The revelation of this suddenly-established intimacy effectually chilled his desire to see her. If, at a moment when her whole life seemed to be breaking up, she could cheerfully commit its reconstruction to the Gormers, there was no reason why such accidents should ever strike her as irreparable. Every step she took seemed in fact to carry her farther from the region where, once or twice, he and she had met for an illumined moment; and the recognition of this fact, when its first pang had been surmounted, produced in him a sense of negative relief. It was much simpler for him to judge Miss Bart by her habitual conduct than by the rare deviations from it which had thrown her so disturbingly in his way; and every act of hers which made the recurrence of such deviations more unlikely, confirmed the sense of relief with which he returned to the conventional view of her.

But Gerty Farish's words had sufficed to make him see how little this view was really his, and how impossible it was for him to live quietly with the thought of Lily Bart. To hear that she was in need of help—even such vague help as he could offer—was to be at once repossessed by that thought; and by the time he reached the street he had sufficiently convinced himself of the urgency of his cousin's appeal to turn his steps directly toward Lily's hotel.

There his zeal met a check in the unforeseen news that Miss Bart had moved away; but, on his pressing his enquiries, the clerk remembered that she had left an address, for which he presently began to search through his books.

It was certainly strange that she should have taken this step without letting Gerty Farish know of her decision; and Selden waited with a vague sense of uneasiness while the address was sought for. The process lasted long enough for uneasiness to turn to apprehension; but when at length a slip of paper was handed him, and he read on it: "Care of Mrs. Norma Hatch, Emporium Hotel," his apprehension passed into an incredulous stare, and this into the gesture of disgust with which he tore the paper in two, and turned to walk quickly homeward.

IX

When Lily woke on the morning after her translation to the Emporium Hotel, her first feeling was one of purely physical satisfaction. The force of contrast gave an added keenness to the luxury of lying once more in a soft-pillowed bed, and looking across a spacious sunlit room at a breakfast-table set invitingly near the fire. Analysis and introspection might come later; but for the moment she was not even troubled by the excesses of the upholstery or the restless convolutions of the furniture. The sense of being once more lapped and folded in ease, as in some dense mild medium impenetrable to discomfort, effectually stilled the faintest note of criticism.

When, the afternoon before, she had presented herself to the lady to whom Carry Fisher had directed her, she had been conscious of entering a new world. Carry's vague presentment of Mrs. Norma Hatch (whose reversion to her Christian name was explained as the result of her latest divorce), left her under the implication of coming "from the West," with the not unusual extenuation of having brought a great deal of money with her. She was, in short, rich, helpless, unplaced: the very subject for Lily's hand. Mrs. Fisher had not specified the line her friend was to take; she owned herself unacquainted with Mrs. Hatch, whom she "knew about" through Melville Stancy, a lawyer in his leisure moments, and the Falstaff[1] of a certain section of festive club life. Socially, Mr. Stancy might have been said to form a connecting link between the Gormer world and the more dimly-lit region on which Miss Bart now found herself entering. It was, however, only figuratively that the illumination of Mrs. Hatch's world could be described as dim: in actual fact, Lily found her seated in a blaze of electric light, impartially projected from various ornamental excrescences on a vast concavity of pink damask and gilding, from which she rose like Venus from her shell.[2] The analogy was justified by the appearance of the lady, whose large-eyed prettiness had the fixity of something impaled and shown under glass. This did not preclude the immediate discovery that she was some years younger than her visitor, and that under her showiness, her ease, the aggression of her dress and voice, there persisted that ineradicable innocence which, in ladies of her nationality, so curiously coexists with startling extremes of experience.

The environment in which Lily found herself was as strange to her as its inhabitants. She was unacquainted with the world of the fashionable New York hotel—a world over-heated, over-upholstered, and over-fitted with mechanical appliances for the gratification of fantastic requirements, while the comforts of a civilized life were as unattainable as in a desert. Through this atmosphere of torrid splendour moved wan beings as richly upholstered as the furniture, beings without definite pursuits or permanent relations, who drifted on a languid tide of curiosity from restaurant to concert-hall, from palm-garden to music-room, from "art exhibit" to dress-maker's opening. High-stepping horses or elaborately equipped motors waited to carry these ladies into vague metropolitan distances, whence they returned, still more wan from the weight of their sables, to be sucked back into the stifling inertia of the hotel routine. Somewhere behind them, in the background of their lives, there was doubtless a real past, peopled by real human activities: they themselves were probably the product of strong ambitions, persistent energies, diversified contacts with the wholesome roughness of life; yet they had no more real existence than the poet's shades in limbo.[3]

Lily had not been long in this pallid world without discovering that Mrs. Hatch was its most substantial figure. That lady, though still floating in the void, showed faint symptoms of developing an outline; and in

1. A comic character in several of Shakespeare's plays—fat, lecherous, deceitful, and self-indulgent, but also engaging and full of enthusiasm for life.

2. In Roman myth Venus, the goddess of love and beauty, was born from the foam of the sea and first appeared riding a scallop shell, a scene that was depicted by the Florentine Botticelli in his famous painting *The Birth of Venus*, to which Wharton is probably alluding.

3. A reference to the region inhabited by blameless but unbaptized and therefore unsaved spirits in the *Inferno* by the poet Dante Alghieri (1265–1321).

this endeavour she was actively seconded by Mr. Melville Stancy. It was Mr. Stancy, a man of large resounding presence, suggestive of convivial occasions and of a chivalry finding expression in "first-night" boxes[4] and thousand dollar bonbonnières, who had transplanted Mrs. Hatch from the scene of her first development to the higher stage of hotel life in the metropolis. It was he who had selected the horses with which she had taken the blue ribbon at the Show, had introduced her to the photographer whose portraits of her formed the recurring ornament of "Sunday Supplements," and had got together the group which constituted her social world. It was a small group still, with heterogeneous figures suspended in large unpeopled spaces; but Lily did not take long to learn that its regulation was no longer in Mr. Stancy's hands. As often happens, the pupil had outstripped the teacher, and Mrs. Hatch was already aware of heights of elegance as well as depths of luxury beyond the world of the Emporium. This discovery at once produced in her a craving for higher guidance, for the adroit feminine hand which should give the right turn to her correspondence, the right "look" to her hats, the right succession to the items of her *menus*. It was, in short, as the regulator of a germinating social life that Miss Bart's guidance was required; her ostensible duties as secretary being restricted by the fact that Mrs. Hatch, as yet, knew hardly any one to write to.

The daily details of Mrs. Hatch's existence were as strange to Lily as its general tenor. The lady's habits were marked by an Oriental indolence and disorder peculiarly trying to her companion. Mrs. Hatch and her friends seemed to float together outside the bounds of time and space. No definite hours were kept; no fixed obligations existed: night and day flowed into one another in a blur of confused and retarded engagements, so that one had the impression of lunching at the tea-hour, while dinner was often merged in the noisy after-theatre supper which prolonged Mrs. Hatch's vigil till day-light.

Through this jumble of futile activities came and went a strange throng of hangers-on—manicures, beauty-doctors, hair-dressers, teachers of bridge, of French, of "physical development": figures sometimes indistinguishable, by their appearance, or by Mrs. Hatch's relation to them, from the visitors constituting her recognized society. But strangest of all to Lily was the encounter, in this latter group, of several of her acquaintances. She had supposed, and not without relief, that she was passing, for the moment, completely out of her own circle; but she found that Mr. Stancy, one side of whose sprawling existence overlapped the edge of Mrs. Fisher's world, had drawn several of its brightest ornaments into the circle of the Emporium. To find Ned Silverton among the habitual frequenters of Mrs. Hatch's drawing-room was one of Lily's first astonishments; but she soon discovered that he was not Mr. Stancy's most important recruit. It was on little Freddy Van Osburgh, the small slim heir of the Van Osburgh millions, that the attention of Mrs. Hatch's

---

4. Much sought-after theater boxes (small separate areas of the balcony) for the opening nights of operas and plays.

group was centred. Freddy, barely out of college, had risen above the horizon since Lily's eclipse, and she now saw with surprise what an effulgence he shed on the outer twilight of Mrs. Hatch's existence. This, then, was one of the things that young men "went in" for when released from official social routine; this was the kind of "previous engagement" that so frequently caused them to disappoint the hopes of anxious hostesses. Lily had an odd sense of being behind the social tapestry, on the side where the threads were knotted and the loose ends hung. For a moment she found a certain amusement in the show, and in her own share of it: the situation had an ease and unconventionality distinctly refreshing after her experience of the irony of conventions. But these flashes of amusement were but brief reactions from the long disgust of her days. Compared with the vast gilded void of Mrs. Hatch's existence, the life of Lily's former friends seemed packed with ordered activities. Even the most irresponsible pretty woman of her acquaintance had her inherited obligations, her conventional benevolences, her share in the working of the great civic machine; and all hung together in the solidarity of these traditional functions. The performance of specific duties would have simplified Miss Bart's position; but the vague attendance on Mrs. Hatch was not without its perplexities.

It was not her employer who created these perplexities. Mrs. Hatch showed from the first an almost touching desire for Lily's approval. Far from asserting the superiority of wealth, her beautiful eyes seemed to urge the plea of inexperience: she wanted to do what was "nice," to be taught how to be "lovely." The difficulty was to find any point of contact between her ideals and Lily's.

Mrs. Hatch swam in a haze of indeterminate enthusiasms, of aspirations culled from the stage, the newspapers, the fashion-journals, and a gaudy world of sport still more completely beyond her companion's ken. To separate from these confused conceptions those most likely to advance the lady on her way, was Lily's obvious duty; but its performance was hampered by rapidly-growing doubts. Lily was in fact becoming more and more aware of a certain ambiguity in her situation. It was not that she had, in the conventional sense, any doubt of Mrs. Hatch's irreproachableness. The lady's offences were always against taste rather than conduct; her divorce record seemed due to geographical rather than ethical conditions; and her worst laxities were likely to proceed from a wandering and extravagant good-nature. But if Lily did not mind her detaining her manicure for luncheon, or offering the "Beauty-Doctor" a seat in Freddy Van Osburgh's box at the play, she was not equally at ease in regard to some less apparent lapses from convention. Ned Silverton's relation to Stancy seemed, for instance, closer and less clear than any natural affinities would warrant; and both appeared united in the effort to cultivate Freddy Van Osburgh's growing taste for Mrs. Hatch. There was as yet nothing definable in the situation, which might well resolve itself into a huge joke on the part of the other two; but Lily had a vague sense that the subject of their experiment was too young, too rich and too credulous. Her embarrassment was increased by the fact that Freddy seemed to regard her as coöperating with himself in the social development of Mrs. Hatch: a view that suggested, on his part, a permanent interest in the lady's future. There were moments when Lily found an ironic amusement in this aspect of the case. The thought of launching such a missile as Mrs. Hatch at the perfidious bosom of society was not without its charm: Miss Bart had even beguiled her leisure with visions of the fair Norma introduced for the first time to a family banquet at the Van Osburghs'. But the thought of being personally connected with the transaction was less agreeable; and her momentary flashes of amusement were followed by increasing periods of doubt.

The sense of these doubts was uppermost when, late one afternoon, she was surprised by a visit from Lawrence Selden. He found her alone in the wilderness of pink damask, for in Mrs. Hatch's world the tea-hour was not dedicated to social rites, and the lady was in the hands of her masseuse.

Selden's entrance had caused Lily an inward start of embarrassment; but his air of constraint had the effect of restoring her self-possession, and she took at once the tone of surprise and pleasure, wondering frankly that he should have traced her to so unlikely a place, and asking what had inspired him to make the search.

Selden met this with an unusual seriousness: she had never seen him so little master of the situation, so plainly at the mercy of any obstructions she might put in his way. "I wanted to see you," he said; and she could not resist observing in reply that he had kept his wishes under remarkable control. She had in truth felt his long absence as one of the chief bitternesses of the last months: his desertion had wounded sensibilities far below the surface of her pride.

Selden met the challenge with directness. "Why should I have come, unless I thought I could be of use to you? It is my only excuse for imagining you could want me."

This struck her as a clumsy evasion, and the thought gave a flash of keenness to her answer. "Then you have come now because you think you can be of use to me?"

He hesitated again. "Yes: in the modest capacity of a person to talk things over with."

For a clever man it was certainly a stupid beginning; and the idea that his awkwardness was due to the fear of her attaching a personal significance to his visit, chilled her pleasure in seeing him. Even under the most adverse conditions, that pleasure always made itself felt: she might hate him, but she had never been able to wish him out of the room. She was very near hating him now; yet the sound of his voice, the way the light fell on his thin dark hair, the way he sat and moved and wore his clothes—she was conscious that even these trivial things were inwoven with her deepest life. In his presence a sudden stillness came upon her, and the turmoil of her spirit ceased; but an impulse of resistance to this stealing influence now prompted her to say: "It's very good of you to present yourself in that capacity; but what makes you think I have any-thing particular to talk about?"

Though she kept the even tone of light intercourse, the question was framed in a way to remind him that his good offices were unsought; and for a moment Selden was checked by it. The situation between them was one which could have been cleared up only by a sudden explosion of feeling; and their whole training and habit of mind were against the chances of such an explosion. Selden's calmness seemed rather to harden into resistance, and Miss Bart's into a surface of glittering irony, as they faced each other from the opposite corners of one of Mrs. Hatch's ele-phantine sofas. The sofa in question, and the apartment peopled by its monstrous mates, served at length to suggest the turn of Selden's reply.

"Gerty told me that you were acting as Mrs. Hatch's secretary; and I knew she was anxious to hear how you were getting on."

Miss Bart received this explanation without perceptible softening. "Why didn't she look me up herself, then?" she asked.

"Because, as you didn't send her your address, she was afraid of being importunate." Selden continued with a smile: "You see no such scruples restrained me; but then I haven't as much to risk if I incur your displea-sure."

Lily answered his smile. "You haven't incurred it as yet; but I have an idea that you are going to."

"That rests with you, doesn't it? You see my initiative doesn't go beyond putting myself at your disposal."

"But in what capacity? What am I to do with you?" she asked in the same light tone.

Selden again glanced about Mrs. Hatch's drawing-room; then he said, with a decision which he seemed to have gathered from this final inspec-tion: "You are to let me take you away from here."

Lily flushed at the suddenness of the attack; then she stiffened under it and said coldly: "And may I ask where you mean me to go?"

"Back to Gerty in the first place, if you will; the essential thing is that it should be away from here."

The unusual harshness of his tone might have shown her how much the words cost him; but she was in no state to measure his feelings while her own were in a flame of revolt. To neglect her, perhaps even to avoid her, at a time when she had most need of her friends, and then suddenly and unwarrantably to break into her life with this strange assumption of authority, was to rouse in her every instinct of pride and self-defence.

"I am very much obliged to you," she said, "for taking such an interest in my plans; but I am quite contented where I am, and have no inten-tion of leaving."

Selden had risen, and was standing before her in an attitude of uncon-trollable expectancy.

"That simply means that you don't know where you are!" he exclaimed.

Lily rose also, with a quick flash of anger. "If you have come here to say disagreeable things about Mrs. Hatch——"

"It is only with your relation to Mrs. Hatch that I am concerned."

"My relation to Mrs. Hatch is one I have no reason to be ashamed of. She has helped me to earn a living when my old friends were quite resigned to seeing me starve."

"Nonsense! Starvation is not the only alternative. You know you can always find a home with Gerty till you are independent again."

"You show such an intimate acquaintance with my affairs that I suppose you mean—till my aunt's legacy is paid?"

"I do mean that; Gerty told me of it," Selden acknowledged without embarrassment. He was too much in earnest now to feel any false constraint in speaking his mind.

"But Gerty does not happen to know," Miss Bart rejoined, "that I owe every penny of that legacy."

"Good God!" Selden exclaimed, startled out of his composure by the abruptness of the statement.

"Every penny of it, and more too," Lily repeated; "and you now perhaps see why I prefer to remain with Mrs. Hatch rather than take advantage of Gerty's kindness. I have no money left, except my small income, and I must earn something more to keep myself alive."

Selden hesitated a moment; then he rejoined in a quieter tone: "But with your income and Gerty's—since you allow me to go so far into the details of the situation—you and she could surely contrive a life together which would put you beyond the need of having to support yourself. Gerty, I know, is eager to make such an arrangement, and would be quite happy in it——"

"But I should not," Miss Bart interposed. "There are many reasons why it would be neither kind to Gerty nor wise for myself." She paused a moment, and as he seemed to await a farther explanation, added with a quick lift of her head: "You will perhaps excuse me from giving you these reasons."

"I have no claim to know them," Selden answered, ignoring her tone; "no claim to offer any comment or suggestion beyond the one I have already made. And my right to make that is simply the universal right of a man to enlighten a woman when he sees her unconsciously placed in a false position."

Lily smiled. "I suppose," she rejoined, "that by a false position you mean one outside of what we call society; but you must remember that I had been excluded from those sacred precincts long before I met Mrs. Hatch. As far as I can see, there is very little real difference in being inside or out, and I remember your once telling me that it was only those inside who took the difference seriously."

She had not been without intention in making this allusion to their memorable talk at Bellomont, and she waited with an odd tremor of the nerves to see what response it would bring; but the result of the experiment was disappointing. Selden did not allow the allusion to deflect him from his point; he merely said with completer fulness of emphasis: "The question of being inside or out is, as you say, a small one, and it happens to have nothing to do with the case, except in so far as Mrs. Hatch's desire to be inside may put you in the position I call false."

In spite of the moderation of his tone, each word he spoke had the effect of confirming Lily's resistance. The very apprehensions he aroused hardened her against him: she had been on the alert for the note of personal sympathy, for any sign of recovered power over him; and his attitude of sober impartiality, the absence of all response to her appeal, turned her hurt pride to blind resentment of his interference. The conviction that he had been sent by Gerty, and that, whatever straits he conceived her to be in, he would never voluntarily have come to her aid, strengthened her resolve not to admit him a hair's breadth farther into her confidence. However doubtful she might feel her situation to be, she would rather persist in darkness than owe her enlightenment to Selden.

"I don't know," she said, when he had ceased to speak, "why you imagine me to be situated as you describe; but as you have always told me that the sole object of a bringing-up like mine was to teach a girl to get what she wants, why not assume that that is precisely what I am doing?"

The smile with which she summed up her case was like a clear barrier raised against farther confidences: its brightness held him at such a distance that he had a sense of being almost out of hearing as he rejoined: "I am not sure that I have ever called you a successful example of that kind of bringing-up."

Her colour rose a little at the implication, but she steeled herself with a light laugh.

"Ah, wait a little longer—give me a little more time before you decide!" And as he wavered before her, still watching for a break in the impenetrable front she presented: "Don't give me up; I may still do credit to my training!" she affirmed.

X

Look at those spangles, Miss Bart—every one of 'em sewed on crooked."

The tall forewoman, a pinched perpendicular figure, dropped the condemned structure of wire and net on the table at Lily's side, and passed on to the next figure in the line.

There were twenty of them in the work-room, their fagged profiles, under exaggerated hair, bowed in the harsh north light above the utensils of their art; for it was something more than an industry, surely, this creation of ever-varied settings for the face of fortunate womanhood. Their own faces were sallow with the unwholesomeness of hot air and sedentary toil, rather than with any actual signs of want: they were employed in a fashionable millinery establishment, and were fairly well clothed and well paid; but the youngest among them was as dull and colourless as the middle-aged. In the whole work-room there was only one skin beneath which the blood still visibly played; and that now burned

"Look at those spangles, Miss Bart,—every one of 'em sewed on crooked."

with vexation as Miss Bart, under the lash of the forewoman's comment, began to strip the hat-frame of its over-lapping spangles.

To Gerty Farish's hopeful spirit a solution appeared to have been reached when she remembered how beautifully Lily could trim hats. Instances of young lady-milliners establishing themselves under fashionable patronage, and imparting to their "creations" that indefinable touch which the professional hand can never give, had flattered Gerty's visions of the future, and convinced even Lily that her separation from Mrs. Norma Hatch need not reduce her to dependence on her friends.

The parting had occurred a few weeks after Selden's visit, and would have taken place sooner had it not been for the resistance set up in Lily by his ill-starred offer of advice. The sense of being involved in a transaction she would not have cared to examine too closely had soon afterward defined itself in the light of a hint from Mr. Stancy that, if she "saw them through," she would have no reason to be sorry. The implication that such loyalty would meet with a direct reward had hastened her flight, and flung her back, ashamed and penitent, on the broad bosom of Gerty's sympathy. She did not, however, propose to lie there prone, and Gerty's inspiration about the hats at once revived her hopes of profitable activity. Here was, after all, something that her charming listless hands could really do; she had no doubt of their capacity for knotting a ribbon or placing a flower to advantage. And of course only these finishing touches would be expected of her: subordinate fingers, blunt, grey, needle-pricked fingers, would prepare the shapes and stitch the linings, while she presided over the charming little front shop—a shop all white panels, mirrors, and moss-green hangings—where her finished creations, hats, wreaths, aigrettes and the rest, perched on their stands like birds just poising for flight.

But at the very outset of Gerty's campaign this vision of the green-and-white shop had been dispelled. Other young ladies of fashion had been thus "set-up," selling their hats by the mere attraction of a name and the reputed knack of tying a bow; but these privileged beings could command a faith in their powers materially expressed by the readiness to pay their shop-rent and advance a handsome sum for current expenses. Where was Lily to find such support? And even could it have been found, how were the ladies on whose approval she depended to be induced to give her their patronage? Gerty learned that whatever sympathy her friend's case might have excited a few months since had been imperilled, if not lost, by her association with Mrs. Hatch. Once again, Lily had withdrawn from an ambiguous situation in time to save her self-respect, but too late for public vindication. Freddy Van Osburgh was not to marry Mrs. Hatch; he had been rescued at the eleventh hour—some said by the efforts of Gus Trenor and Rosedale—and despatched to Europe with old Ned Van Alstyne; but the risk he had run would always be ascribed to Miss Bart's connivance, and would somehow serve as a summing-up and corroboration of the vague general distrust of her. It was a relief to those who had hung back from her to find themselves thus justified, and they were inclined to insist a little on her connection with the Hatch case in order to show that they had been right.

Gerty's quest, at any rate, brought up against a solid wall of resistance; and even when Carry Fisher, momentarily penitent for her share in the Hatch affair, joined her efforts to Miss Farish's, they met with no better success. Gerty had tried to veil her failure in tender ambiguities; but Carry, always the soul of candour, put the case squarely to her friend.

"I went straight to Judy Trenor; she has fewer prejudices than the others, and besides she's always hated Bertha Dorset. But what *have* you done to her, Lily? At the very first word about giving you a start she flamed out about some money you'd got from Gus; I never knew her so hot before. You know she'll let him do anything but spend money on his friends: the only reason she's decent to me now is that she knows I'm not hard up.—He speculated for you, you say? Well what's the harm? He had no business to lose. He *didn't* lose? Then what on earth—but I never *could* understand you, Lily!"

The end of it was that, after anxious enquiry and much deliberation, Mrs. Fisher and Gerty, for once oddly united in their effort to help their friend, decided on placing her in the work-room of Mme. Regina's renowned millinery establishment. Even this arrangement was not effected without considerable negotiation, for Mme. Regina had a strong prejudice against untrained assistance, and was induced to yield only by the fact that she owed the patronage of Mrs. Bry and Mrs. Gormer to Carry Fisher's influence. She had been willing from the first to employ Lily in the show-room: as a displayer of hats, a fashionable beauty might be a valuable asset. But to this suggestion Miss Bart opposed a negative which Gerty emphatically supported, while Mrs. Fisher, inwardly unconvinced, but resigned to this latest proof of Lily's unreason, agreed that perhaps in the end it would be more useful that she should learn the trade. To Regina's work-room Lily was therefore committed by her friends, and there Mrs. Fisher left her with a sigh of relief, while Gerty's watchfulness continued to hover over her at a distance.

Lily had taken up her work early in January: it was now two months later, and she was still being rebuked for her inability to sew spangles on a hat-frame. As she returned to her work she heard a titter pass down the tables. She knew she was an object of criticism and amusement to the other work-women. They were, of course, aware of her history—the exact situation of every girl in the room was known and freely discussed by all the others—but the knowledge did not produce in them any awkward sense of class distinction: it merely explained why her untutored fingers were still blundering over the rudiments of the trade. Lily had no desire that they should recognize any social difference in her; but she had hoped to be received as their equal, and perhaps before long to show herself their superior by a special deftness of touch, and it was humiliating to find that, after two months of drudgery, she still betrayed her lack of early training. Remote was the day when she might aspire to exercise the talents she felt confident of possessing; only experienced workers were entrusted with the delicate art of shaping and trimming the hat, and the forewoman still held her inexorably to the routine of preparatory work.

She began to rip the spangles from the frame, listening absently to the buzz of talk which rose and fell with the coming and going of Miss Haines's active figure. The air was closer than usual, because Miss Haines, who had a cold, had not allowed a window to be opened even during the noon recess; and Lily's head was so heavy with the weight of a sleepless night that the chatter of her companions had the incoherence of a dream.

"I *told* her he'd never look at her again; and he didn't. I wouldn't have, either—I think she acted real mean to him. He took her to the Arion Ball, and had a hack for her both ways. . . . She's taken ten bottles, and her headaches don't seem no better—but she's written a testimonial to say the first bottle cured her, and she got five dollars and her picture in the paper. . . . Mrs. Trenor's hat? The one with the green Paradise? Here, Miss Haines—it'll be ready right off. . . . That was one of the Trenor girls here yesterday with Mrs. George Dorset. How'd I know? Why, Madam sent for me to alter the flower in that Virot hat— the blue tulle: she's tall and slight, with her hair fuzzed out—a good deal like Mamie Leach, on'y thinner. . . ."

On and on it flowed, a current of meaningless sound, on which, startlingly enough, a familiar name now and then floated to the surface. It was the strangest part of Lily's strange experience, the hearing of these names, the seeing the fragmentary and distorted image of the world she had lived in reflected in the mirror of the working-girls' minds. She had never before suspected the mixture of insatiable curiosity and contemptuous freedom with which she and her kind were discussed in this underworld of toilers who lived on their vanity and self-indulgence. Every girl in Mme. Regina's work-room knew to whom the headgear in her hands was destined, and had her opinion of its future wearer, and a definite knowledge of the latter's place in the social system. That Lily was a star fallen from that sky did not, after the first stir of curiosity had subsided, materially add to their interest in her. She had fallen, she had "gone under," and true to the ideal of the race, they were awed only by success—by the gross tangible image of material achievement. The consciousness of her different point of view merely kept them at a little distance from her, as though she were a foreigner with whom it was an effort to talk.

"Miss Bart, if you can't sew those spangles on more regular I guess you'd better give the hat to Miss Kilroy."

Lily looked down ruefully at her handiwork. The forewoman was right: the sewing on of the spangles was inexcusably bad. What made her so much more clumsy than usual? Was it a growing distaste for her task, or actual physical disability? She felt tired and confused: it was an effort to put her thoughts together. She rose and handed the hat to Miss Kilroy, who took it with a suppressed smile.

"I'm sorry; I'm afraid I am not well," she said to the forewoman.

Miss Haines offered no comment. From the first she had augured ill of Mme. Regina's consenting to include a fashionable apprentice among her workers. In that temple of art no raw beginners were wanted, and Miss Haines would have been more than human had she not taken a certain pleasure in seeing her forebodings confirmed.

"You'd better go back to binding edges," she said drily.

Lily slipped out last among the band of liberated work-women. She did not care to be mingled in their noisy dispersal: once in the street, she always felt an irresistible return to her old standpoint, an instinctive shrinking from all that was unpolished and promiscuous. In the days—how distant they now seemed!—when she had visited the Girls' Club with Gerty Farish, she had felt an enlightened interest in the working-classes; but that was because she looked down on them from above, from the happy altitude of her grace and her beneficence. Now that she was on a level with them, the point of view was less interesting.

She felt a touch on her arm, and met the penitent eye of Miss Kilroy.

"Miss Bart, I guess you can sew those spangles on as well as I can when you're feeling right. Miss Haines didn't act fair to you."

Lily's colour rose at the unexpected advance: it was a long time since real kindness had looked at her from any eyes but Gerty's.

"Oh, thank you: I'm not particularly well, but Miss Haines was right. I *am* clumsy."

"Well, it's mean work for anybody with a headache." Miss Kilroy paused irresolutely. "You ought to go right home and lay down. Ever try orangeine?"

"Thank you." Lily held out her hand. "It's very kind of you—I mean to go home."

She looked gratefully at Miss Kilroy, but neither knew what more to say. Lily was aware that the other was on the point of offering to go home with her, but she wanted to be alone and silent—even kindness, the sort of kindness that Miss Kilroy could give, would have jarred on her just then.

"Thank you," she repeated as she turned away.

She struck westward through the dreary March twilight, toward the street where her boarding-house stood. She had resolutely refused Gerty's offer of hospitality. Something of her mother's fierce shrinking from observation and sympathy was beginning to develop in her, and the promiscuity of small quarters and close intimacy seemed, on the whole, less endurable than the solitude of a hall bedroom[1] in a house where she could come and go unremarked among the other workers. For a while she had been sustained by this desire for privacy and independence; but now, perhaps from increasing physical weariness, the lassitude brought about by hours of unwonted confinement, she was beginning to feel acutely the ugliness and discomfort of her surroundings. The day's task

---

1. The smallest, cheapest room in a boarding house, formed by partitioning off the end of a hallway.

done, she dreaded to return to her narrow room, with its blotched wall-paper and shabby paint; and she hated every step of the walk thither, through the degradation of a New York street in the last stages of decline from fashion to commerce.

But what she dreaded most of all was having to pass the chemist's at the corner of Sixth Avenue. She had meant to take another street: she had usually done so of late. But today her steps were irresistibly drawn toward the flaring plate-glass corner; she tried to take the lower crossing, but a laden dray crowded her back, and she struck across the street obliquely, reaching the sidewalk just opposite the chemist's door.

Over the counter she caught the eye of the clerk who had waited on her before, and slipped the prescription into his hand. There could be no question about the prescription: it was a copy of one of Mrs. Hatch's, obligingly furnished by that lady's chemist. Lily was confident that the clerk would fill it without hesitation; yet the nervous dread of a refusal, or even of an expression of doubt, communicated itself to her restless hands as she affected to examine the bottles of perfume stacked on the glass case before her.

The clerk had read the prescription without comment; but in the act of handing out the bottle he paused.

"You don't want to increase the dose, you know," he remarked.

Lily's heart contracted. What did he mean by looking at her in that way?

"Of course not," she murmured, holding out her hand.

"That's all right: it's a queer-acting drug. A drop or two more, and off you go—the doctors don't know why."

The dread lest he should question her, or keep the bottle back, choked the murmur of acquiescence in her throat; and when at length she emerged safely from the shop she was almost dizzy with the intensity of her relief. The mere touch of the packet thrilled her tired nerves with the delicious promise of a night of sleep, and in the reaction from her momentary fear she felt as if the first fumes of drowsiness were already stealing over her.

In her confusion she stumbled against a man who was hurrying down the last steps of the elevated station. He drew back, and she heard her name uttered with surprise. It was Rosedale, fur-coated, glossy and pros-perous—but why did she seem to see him so far off, and as if through a mist of splintered crystals? Before she could account for the phenome-non she found herself shaking hands with him. They had parted with scorn on her side and anger upon his; but all trace of these emotions seemed to vanish as their hands met, and she was only aware of a con-fused wish that she might continue to hold fast to him.

"Why, what's the matter, Miss Lily? You're not well!" he exclaimed; and she forced her lips into a pallid smile of reassurance.

"I'm a little tired—it's nothing. Stay with me a moment, please," she faltered. That she should be asking this service of Rosedale!

He glanced at the dirty and unpropitious corner on which they stood, with the shriek of the "elevated" and the tumult of trams and waggons contending hideously in their ears.

"We can't stay here; but let me take you somewhere for a cup of tea. The *Longworth* is only a few yards off, and there'll be no one there at this hour."

A cup of tea in quiet, somewhere out of the noise and ugliness, seemed for the moment the one solace she could bear. A few steps brought them to the ladies' door of the hotel he had named, and a moment later he was seated opposite to her, and the waiter had placed the tea-tray between them.

"Not a drop of brandy or whiskey first? You look regularly done up, Miss Lily. Well, take your tea strong, then; and, waiter, get a cushion for the lady's back."

Lily smiled faintly at the injunction to take her tea strong. It was the temptation she was always struggling to resist. Her craving for the keen stimulant was forever conflicting with that other craving for sleep—the midnight craving which only the little phial in her hand could still. But today, at any rate, the tea could hardly be too strong: she counted on it to pour warmth and resolution into her empty veins.

As she leaned back before him, her lids drooping in utter lassitude, though the first warm draught already tinged her face with returning life, Rosedale was seized afresh by the poignant surprise of her beauty. The dark pencilling of fatigue under her eyes, the morbid blue-veined pallour of the temples, brought out the brightness of her hair and lips, as though all her ebbing vitality were centred there. Against the dull chocolate-coloured background of the restaurant, the purity of her head stood out as it had never done in the most brightly-lit ball-room. He looked at her with a startled uncomfortable feeling, as though her beauty were a forgotten enemy that had lain in ambush and now sprang out on him unawares.

To clear the air he tried to take an easy tone with her. "Why, Miss Lily, I haven't seen you for an age. I didn't know what had become of you."

As he spoke, he was checked by an embarrassing sense of the complications to which this might lead. Though he had not seen her he had heard of her; he knew of her connection with Mrs. Hatch, and of the talk resulting from it. Mrs. Hatch's *milieu* was one which he had once assiduously frequented, and now as devoutly shunned.

Lily, to whom the tea had restored her usual clearness of mind, saw what was in his thoughts and said with a slight smile: "You would not be likely to know about me. I have joined the working classes."

He stared in genuine wonder. "You don't mean——? Why, what on earth are you doing?"

"Learning to be a milliner—at least *trying* to learn," she hastily qualified the statement.

Rosedale suppressed a low whistle of surprise. "Come off—you ain't serious, are you?"

"Perfectly serious. I'm obliged to work for my living."

"But I understood—I thought you were with Norma Hatch."

"You heard I had gone to her as her secretary?"

"Something of the kind, I believe." He leaned forward to refill her cup.

Lily guessed the possibilities of embarrassment which the topic held for him, and raising her eyes to his, she said suddenly: "I left her two months ago."

Rosedale continued to fumble awkwardly with the tea-pot, and she felt sure that he had heard what had been said of her. But what was there that Rosedale did not hear?

"Wasn't it a soft berth?" he enquired, with an attempt at lightness.

"Too soft—one might have sunk in too deep." Lily rested one arm on the edge of the table, and sat looking at him more intently than she had ever looked before. An uncontrollable impulse was urging her to put her case to this man, from whose curiosity she had always so fiercely defended herself.

"You know Mrs. Hatch, I think? Well, perhaps you can understand that she might make things too easy for one."

Rosedale looked faintly puzzled, and she remembered that allusiveness was lost on him.

"It was no place for you, anyhow," he agreed, so suffused and immersed in the light of her full gaze that he found himself being drawn into strange depths of intimacy. He who had had to subsist on mere fugitive glances, looks winged in flight and swiftly lost under covert, now found her eyes settling on him with a brooding intensity that fairly dazzled him.

"I left," Lily continued, "lest people should say I was helping Mrs. Hatch to marry Freddy Van Osburgh—who is not in the least too good for her—and as they still continue to say it, I see that I might as well have stayed where I was."

"Oh, Freddy——" Rosedale brushed aside the topic with an air of its unimportance which gave a sense of the immense perspective he had acquired. "Freddy don't count—but I knew *you* weren't mixed up in that. It ain't your style."

Lily coloured slightly: she could not conceal from herself that the words gave her pleasure. She would have liked to sit there, drinking more tea, and continuing to talk of herself to Rosedale. But the old habit of observing the conventions reminded her that it was time to bring their colloquy to an end, and she made a faint motion to push back her chair.

Rosedale stopped her with a protesting gesture. "Wait a minute— don't go yet; sit quiet and rest a little longer. You look thoroughly played out. And you haven't told me——" He broke off, conscious of going farther than he had meant. She saw the struggle and understood it; understood also the nature of the spell to which he yielded as, with his eyes on her face, he began again abruptly: "What on earth did you mean by saying just now that you were learning to be a milliner?"

"Just what I said. I am an apprentice at Regina's."

"Good Lord—*you?* But what for? I knew your aunt had turned you down: Mrs. Fisher told me about it. But I understood you got a legacy from her——"

"I got ten thousand dollars; but the legacy is not to be paid till next summer."

"Well, but—look here: you could *borrow* on it any time you wanted."

She shook her head gravely. "No; for I owe it already."

"Owe it? The whole ten thousand?"

"Every penny." She paused, and then continued abruptly, with her eyes on his face: "I think Gus Trenor spoke to you once about having made some money for me in stocks."

She waited, and Rosedale, congested with embarrassment, muttered that he remembered something of the kind.

"He made about nine thousand dollars," Lily pursued, in the same tone of eager communicativeness. "At the time, I understood that he was speculating with my own money: it was incredibly stupid of me, but I knew nothing of business. Afterward I found out that he had *not* used my money—that what he said he had made for me he had really given me. It was meant in kindness, of course; but it was not the sort of obligation one could remain under. Unfortunately I had spent the money before I discovered my mistake; and so my legacy will have to go to pay it back. That is the reason why I am trying to learn a trade."

She made the statement clearly, deliberately, with pauses between the sentences, so that each should have time to sink deeply into her hearer's mind. She had a passionate desire that some one should know the truth about this transaction, and also that the rumour of her intention to repay the money should reach Judy Trenor's ears. And it had suddenly occurred to her that Rosedale, who had surprised Trenor's confidence, was the fitting person to receive and transmit her version of the facts. She had even felt a momentary exhilaration at the thought of thus relieving herself of her detested secret; but the sensation gradually faded in the telling, and as she ended her pallour was suffused with a deep blush of misery.

Rosedale continued to stare at her in wonder; but the wonder took the turn she had least expected.

"But see here—if that's the case, it cleans you out altogether?"

He put it to her as if she had not grasped the consequences of her act; as if her incorrigible ignorance of business were about to precipitate her into a fresh act of folly.

"Altogether—yes," she calmly agreed.

He sat silent, his thick hands clasped on the table, his little puzzled eyes exploring the recesses of the deserted restaurant.

"See here—that's fine," he exclaimed abruptly.

Lily rose from her seat with a deprecating laugh. "Oh, no—it's merely a bore," she asserted, gathering together the ends of her feather scarf.

Rosedale remained seated, too intent on his thoughts to notice her movement. "Miss Lily, if you want any backing—I like pluck——" broke from him disconnectedly.

"Thank you." She held out her hand. "Your tea has given me a tremendous backing. I feel equal to anything now."

Her gesture seemed to show a definite intention of dismissal, but her companion had tossed a bill to the waiter, and was slipping his short arms into his expensive overcoat.

"Wait a minute—you've got to let me walk home with you," he said.

Lily uttered no protest, and when he had paused to make sure of his change they emerged from the hotel and crossed Sixth Avenue again. As she led the way westward past a long line of areas which, through the distortion of their paintless rails, revealed with increasing candour the *disjecta membra*[2] of bygone dinners, Lily felt that Rosedale was taking contemptuous note of the neighbourhood; and before the doorstep at which she finally paused he looked up with an air of incredulous disgust.

"This isn't the place? Some one told me you were living with Miss Farish."

"No: I am boarding here. I have lived too long on my friends."

He continued to scan the blistered brown stone front, the windows draped with discoloured lace, and the Pompeian decoration of the muddy vestibule; then he looked back at her face and said with a visible effort: "You'll let me come and see you some day?"

She smiled, recognizing the heroism of the offer to the point of being frankly touched by it. "Thank you—I shall be very glad," she made answer, in the first sincere words she had ever spoken to him.

That evening in her own room Miss Bart—who had fled early from the heavy fumes of the basement dinner-table—sat musing upon the impulse which had led her to unbosom herself to Rosedale. Beneath it she discovered an increasing sense of loneliness—a dread of returning to the solitude of her room, while she could be anywhere else, or in any company but her own. Circumstances, of late, had combined to cut her off more and more from her few remaining friends. On Carry Fisher's part the withdrawal was perhaps not quite involuntary. Having made her final effort on Lily's behalf, and landed her safely in Mme. Regina's work-room, Mrs. Fisher seemed disposed to rest from her labours; and Lily, understanding the reason, could not condemn her. Carry had in fact come dangerously near to being involved in the episode of Mrs. Norma Hatch, and it had taken some verbal ingenuity to extricate herself. She frankly owned to having brought Lily and Mrs. Hatch together, but then she did not know Mrs. Hatch—she had expressly warned Lily that she did not know Mrs. Hatch—and besides, she was not Lily's keeper, and really the girl was old enough to take care of herself. Carry did not put her own case so brutally, but she allowed it to be thus put for her by

2. Literally, dismembered limbs; figuratively, garbage.

her latest bosom friend, Mrs. Jack Stepney: Mrs. Stepney, trembling
over the narrowness of her only brother's escape, but eager to vindicate
Mrs. Fisher, at whose house she could count on the "jolly parties" which
had become a necessity to her since marriage had emancipated her from
the Van Osburgh point of view.

Lily understood the situation and could make allowances for it. Carry
had been a good friend to her in difficult days, and perhaps only a friendship like Gerty's could be proof against such an increasing strain. Gerty's
friendship did indeed hold fast; yet Lily was beginning to avoid her also.
For she could not go to Gerty's without risk of meeting Selden; and to
meet him now would be pure pain. It was pain enough even to think of
him, whether she considered him in the distinctness of her waking
thoughts, or felt the obsession of his presence through the blur of her
tormented nights. That was one of the reasons why she had turned again
to Mrs. Hatch's prescription. In the uneasy snatches of her natural dreams
he came to her sometimes in the old guise of fellowship and tenderness;
and she would rise from the sweet delusion mocked and emptied of her
courage. But in the sleep which the phial procured she sank far below
such half-waking visitations, sank into depths of dreamless annihilation
from which she woke each morning with an obliterated past.

Gradually, to be sure, the stress of the old thoughts would return; but
at least they did not importune her waking hour. The drug gave her a
momentary illusion of complete renewal, from which she drew strength
to take up her daily work. The strength was more and more needed as
the perplexities of her future increased. She knew that to Gerty and Mrs.
Fisher she was only passing through a temporary period of probation,
since they believed that the apprenticeship she was serving at Mme.
Regina's would enable her, when Mrs. Peniston's legacy was paid, to
realize the vision of the green-and-white shop with the fuller competence acquired by her preliminary training. But to Lily herself, aware
that the legacy could not be put to such a use, the preliminary training
seemed a wasted effort. She understood clearly enough that, even if she
could ever learn to compete with hands formed from childhood for their
special work, the small pay she received would not be a sufficient addition to her income to compensate her for such drudgery. And the realization of this fact brought her recurringly face to face with the temptation
to use the legacy in establishing her business. Once installed, and in
command of her own work-women, she believed she had sufficient tact
and ability to attract a fashionable *clientèle*; and if the business succeeded she could gradually lay aside money enough to discharge her
debt to Trenor. But the task might take years to accomplish, even if she
continued to stint herself to the utmost; and meanwhile her pride would
be crushed under the weight of an intolerable obligation.

These were her superficial considerations; but under them lurked the
secret dread that the obligation might not always remain intolerable. She
knew she could not count on her continuity of purpose, and what really
frightened her was the thought that she might gradually accommodate

herself to remaining indefinitely in Trenor's debt, as she had accommodated herself to the part allotted her on the Sabrina, and as she had so nearly drifted into acquiescing with Stancy's scheme for the advancement of Mrs. Hatch. Her danger lay, as she knew, in her old incurable dread of discomfort and poverty; in the fear of that mounting tide of dinginess against which her mother had so passionately warned her. And now a new vista of peril opened before her. She understood that Rosedale was ready to lend her money; and the longing to take advantage of his offer began to haunt her insidiously. It was of course impossible to accept a loan from Rosedale; but proximate possibilities hovered temptingly before her. She was quite sure that he would come and see her again, and almost sure that, if he did, she could bring him to the point of offering to marry her on the terms she had previously rejected. Would she still reject them if they were offered? More and more, with every fresh mischance befalling her, did the pursuing furies seem to take the shape of Bertha Dorset; and close at hand, safely locked among her papers, lay the means of ending their pursuit. The temptation, which her scorn of Rosedale had once enabled her to reject, now insistently returned upon her; and how much strength was left her to oppose it?

What little there was must at any rate be husbanded to the utmost; she could not trust herself again to the perils of a sleepless night. Through the long hours of silence the dark spirit of fatigue and loneliness crouched upon her breast, leaving her so drained of bodily strength that her morning thoughts swam in a haze of weakness. The only hope of renewal lay in the little bottle at her bed-side; and how much longer that hope would last she dared not conjecture.

XI

Lily, lingering for a moment on the corner, looked out on the afternoon spectacle of Fifth Avenue.

It was a day late in April, and the sweetness of spring was in the air. It mitigated the ugliness of the long crowded thoroughfare, blurred the gaunt rooflines, threw a mauve veil over the discouraging perspective of the side streets, and gave a touch of poetry to the delicate haze of green that marked the entrance to the Park.

As Lily stood there, she recognized several familiar faces in the passing carriages. The season was over, and its ruling forces had disbanded; but a few still lingered, delaying their departure for Europe, or passing through town on their return from the South. Among them was Mrs. Van Osburgh, swaying majestically in her C-spring barouche, with Mrs. Percy Gryce at her side, and the new heir to the Gryce millions enthroned before them on his nurse's knees. They were succeeded by Mrs. Hatch's electric victoria, in which that lady reclined in the lonely splendour of a spring toilet obviously designed for company; and a moment or two later came Judy Trenor, accompanied by Lady Skiddaw, who had come over for her annual tarpon fishing and a dip into "the street."

This fleeting glimpse of her past served to emphasize the sense of aimlessness with which Lily at length turned toward home. She had nothing to do for the rest of the day, nor for the days to come; for the season was over in millinery as well as in society, and a week earlier Mme. Regina had notified her that her services were no longer required. Mme. Regina always reduced her staff on the first of May, and Miss Bart's attendance had of late been so irregular—she had so often been unwell, and had done so little work when she came—that it was only as a favour that her dismissal had hitherto been deferred.

Lily did not question the justice of the decision. She was conscious of having been forgetful, awkward and slow to learn. It was bitter to acknowledge her inferiority even to herself, but the fact had been brought home to her that as a bread-winner she could never compete with professional ability. Since she had been brought up to be ornamental, she could hardly blame herself for failing to serve any practical purpose; but the discovery put an end to her consoling sense of universal efficiency.

As she turned homeward her thoughts shrank in anticipation from the fact that there would be nothing to get up for the next morning. The luxury of lying late in bed was a pleasure belonging to the life of ease; it had no part in the utilitarian existence of the boarding-house. She liked to leave her room early, and to return to it as late as possible; and she was walking slowly now in order to postpone the detested approach to her doorstep.

But the doorstep, as she drew near it, acquired a sudden interest from the fact that it was occupied—and indeed filled—by the conspicuous figure of Mr. Rosedale, whose presence seemed to take on an added amplitude from the meanness of his surroundings.

The sight stirred Lily with an irresistible sense of triumph. Rosedale, a day or two after their chance meeting, had called to enquire if she had recovered from her indisposition; but since then she had not seen or heard from him, and his absence seemed to betoken a struggle to keep away, to let her pass once more out of his life. If this were the case, his return showed that the struggle had been unsuccessful, for Lily knew he was not the man to waste his time in an ineffectual sentimental dalliance. He was too busy, too practical, and above all too much preoccupied with his own advancement, to indulge in such unprofitable asides.

In the peacock-blue parlour, with its bunches of dried pampas grass, and discoloured steel engravings of sentimental episodes, he looked about him with unconcealed disgust, laying his hat distrustfully on the dusty console adorned with a Rogers statuette.[1]

Lily sat down on one of the plush and rosewood sofas, and he deposited himself in a rocking-chair draped with a starched antimacassar which scraped unpleasantly against the pink fold of skin above his collar.

---

1. A small-scale sculpture on a patriotic or sentimental theme by the American artist John Rogers (1829–1904). Mass-produced and very popular, these pieces represented American middle-class culture in the late nineteenth century; by the early twentieth century, however, they symbolized an old fashioned, shabby-genteel lack of imagination.

"My goodness—you can't go on living here!" he exclaimed.

Lily smiled at his tone. "I am not sure that I can; but I have gone over my expenses very carefully, and I rather think I shall be able to manage it."

"Be able to manage it? That's not what I mean—it's no place for you!"

"It's what I mean; for I have been out of work for the last week."

"Out of work—out of work! What a way for you to talk! The idea of your having to work—it's preposterous." He brought out his sentences in short violent jerks, as though they were forced up from a deep inner crater of indignation. "It's a farce—a crazy farce," he repeated, his eyes fixed on the long vista of the room reflected in the blotched glass between the windows.

Lily continued to meet his expostulations with a smile. "I don't know why I should regard myself as an exception——" she began.

"Because you *are*; that's why; and your being in a place like this is a damnable outrage. I can't talk of it calmly."

She had in truth never seen him so shaken out of his usual glibness; and there was something almost moving to her in his inarticulate struggle with his emotions.

He rose with a start which left the rocking-chair quivering on its beam ends, and placed himself squarely before her.

"Look here, Miss Lily, I'm going to Europe next week: going over to Paris and London for a couple of months—and I can't leave you like this. I can't do it. I know it's none of my business—you've let me understand that often enough; but things are worse with you now than they have been before, and you must see that you've got to accept help from somebody. You spoke to me the other day about some debt to Trenor. I know what you mean—and I respect you for feeling as you do about it."

A blush of surprise rose to Lily's pale face, but before she could interrupt him he had continued eagerly: "Well, I'll lend you the money to pay Trenor; and I won't—I—see here, don't take me up till I've finished. What I mean is, it'll be a plain business arrangement, such as one man would make with another. Now, what have you got to say against that?"

Lily's blush deepened to a glow in which humiliation and gratitude were mingled; and both sentiments revealed themselves in the unexpected gentleness of her reply.

"Only this: that it is exactly what Gus Trenor proposed; and that I can never again be sure of understanding the plainest business arrangement." Then, realizing that this answer contained a germ of injustice, she added, even more kindly: "Not that I don't appreciate your kindness—that I'm not grateful for it. But a business arrangement between us would in any case be impossible, because I shall have no security to give when my debt to Gus Trenor has been paid."

Rosedale received this statement in silence: he seemed to feel the note of finality in her voice, yet to be unable to accept it as closing the question between then.

In the silence Lily had a clear perception of what was passing through his mind. Whatever perplexity he felt as to the inexorableness of her course—however little he penetrated its motive—she saw that it unmistakably tended to strengthen her hold over him. It was as though the sense in her of unexplained scruples and resistances had the same attraction as the delicacy of feature, the fastidiousness of manner, which gave her an external rarity, an air of being impossible to match. As he advanced in social experience this uniqueness had acquired a greater value for him, as though he were a collector who had learned to distinguish minor differences of design and quality in some long-coveted object.

Lily, perceiving all this, understood that he would marry her at once, on the sole condition of a reconciliation with Mrs. Dorset; and the temptation was the less easy to put aside because, little by little, circumstances were breaking down her dislike for Rosedale. The dislike, indeed, still subsisted; but it was penetrated here and there by the perception of mitigating qualities in him: of a certain gross kindliness, a rather helpless fidelity of sentiment, which seemed to be struggling through the hard surface of his material ambitions.

Reading his dismissal in her eyes, he held out his hand with a gesture which conveyed something of this inarticulate conflict.

" 'If you'd only let me, I'd set you up over them all—I'd put you where you could wipe your feet on 'em!' he declared; and it touched her oddly to see that his new passion had not altered his old standard of values."

Lily took no sleeping-drops that night. She lay awake viewing her situation in the crude light which Rosedale's visit had shed on it. In fending off the offer he was so plainly ready to renew, had she not sacrificed to one of those abstract notions of honour that might be called the conventionalities of the moral life? What debt did she owe to a social order which had condemned and banished her without trial? She had never been heard in her own defence; she was innocent of the charge on which she had been found guilty; and the irregularity of her conviction might seem to justify the use of methods as irregular in recovering her lost rights. Bertha Dorset, to save herself, had not scrupled to ruin her by an open falsehood; why should she hesitate to make private use of the facts that chance had put in her way? After all, half the opprobrium of such an act lies in the name attached to it. Call it blackmail and it becomes unthinkable; but explain that it injures no one, and that the rights regained by it were unjustly forfeited, and he must be a formalist indeed who can find no plea in its defence.

The arguments pleading for it with Lily were the old unanswerable ones of the personal situation: the sense of injury, the sense of failure, the passionate craving for a fair chance against the selfish despotism of society. She had learned by experience that she had neither the aptitude nor the moral constancy to remake her life on new lines; to become a worker among workers, and let the world of luxury and pleasure sweep by her unregarded. She could not hold herself much to blame for this ineffectiveness, and she was perhaps less to blame than she believed. Inherited tendencies had combined with early training to make her the highly specialized product she was: an organism as helpless out of its narrow range as the sea-anemone torn from the rock. She had been fashioned to adorn and delight; to what other end does nature round the rose-leaf and paint the humming-bird's breast? And was it her fault that the purely decorative mission is less easily and harmoniously fulfilled among social beings than in the world of nature? That it is apt to be hampered by material necessities or complicated by moral scruples?

These last were the two antagonistic forces which fought out their battle in her breast during the long watches of the night; and when she rose the next morning she hardly knew where the victory lay. She was exhausted by the reaction of a night without sleep, coming after many nights of rest artifically obtained; and in the distorting light of fatigue the future stretched out before her grey, interminable and desolate.

She lay late in bed, refusing the coffee and fried eggs which the friendly Irish servant thrust through her door, and hating the intimate domestic noises of the house and the cries and rumblings of the street. Her week of idleness had brought home to her with exaggerated force these small aggravations of the boarding-house world, and she yearned for that other luxurious world, whose machinery is so carefully concealed that one scene flows into another without perceptible agency.

At length she rose and dressed. Since she had left Mme. Regina's she had spent her days in the streets, partly to escape from the uncongenial promiscuities of the boarding-house, and partly in the hope that physical fatigue would help her to sleep. But once out of the house, she could not decide where to go; for she had avoided Gerty since her dismissal from the milliner's, and she was not sure of a welcome anywhere else.

The morning was in harsh contrast to the previous day. A cold grey sky threatened rain, and a high wind drove the dust in wild spirals up and down the streets. Lily walked up Fifth Avenue toward the Park, hoping to find a sheltered nook where she might sit; but the wind chilled her, and after an hour's wandering under the tossing boughs she yielded to her increasing weariness, and took refuge in a little restaurant in Fifty-ninth Street. She was not hungry, and had meant to go without luncheon; but she was too tired to return home, and the long perspective of white tables showed alluringly through the windows.

The room was full of women and girls, all too much engaged in the rapid absorption of tea and pie to remark her entrance. A hum of shrill voices reverberated against the low ceiling, leaving Lily shut out in a little circle of silence. She felt a sudden pang of profound loneliness. She had lost the sense of time, and it seemed to her as though she had not spoken to any one for days. Her eyes sought the faces about her, craving a responsive glance, some sign of an intuition of her trouble. But the sallow preoccupied women, with their bags and note-books and rolls of music, were all engrossed in their own affairs, and even those who sat by themselves were busy running over proof-sheets or devouring magazines between their hurried gulps of tea. Lily alone was stranded in a great waste of disoccupation.

She drank several cups of the tea which was served with her portion of stewed oysters, and her brain felt clearer and livelier when she emerged once more into the street. She realized now that, as she sat in the restaurant, she had unconsciously arrived at a final decision. The discovery gave her an immediate illusion of activity: it was exhilarating to think that she had actually a reason for hurrying home. To prolong her enjoyment of the sensation she decided to walk; but the distance was so great that she found herself glancing nervously at the clocks on the way. One of the surprises of her unoccupied state was the discovery that time, when it is left to itself and no definite demands are made on it, cannot be trusted to move at any recognized pace. Usually it loiters; but just when one has come to count upon its slowness, it may suddenly break into a wild irrational gallop.

She found, however, on reaching home, that the hour was still early enough for her to sit down and rest a few minutes before putting her plan into execution. The delay did not perceptibly weaken her resolve. She was frightened and yet stimulated by the reserved force of resolution which she felt within herself: she saw it was going to be easier, a great deal easier, than she had imagined.

At five o'clock she rose, unlocked her trunk, and took out a sealed packet which she slipped into the bosom of her dress. Even the contact with the packet did not shake her nerves as she had half-expected it would. She seemed encased in a strong armour of indifference, as though the vigorous exertion of her will had finally benumbed her finer sensibilities.

She dressed herself once more for the street, locked her door and went out. When she emerged on the pavement, the day was still high, but a threat of rain darkened the sky and cold gusts shook the signs projecting from the basement shops along the street. She reached Fifth Avenue and began to walk slowly northward. She was sufficiently familiar with Mrs. Dorset's habits to know that she could always be found at home after five. She might not, indeed, be accessible to visitors, especially to a visitor so unwelcome, and against whom it was quite possible that she had guarded herself by special orders; but Lily had written a note which she meant to send up with her name, and which she thought would secure her admission.

She had allowed herself time to walk to Mrs. Dorset's, thinking that the quick movement through the cold evening air would help to steady her nerves; but she really felt no need of being tranquillized. Her survey of the situation remained calm and unwavering.

As she reached Fiftieth Street the clouds broke abruptly, and a rush of cold rain slanted into her face. She had no umbrella and the moisture quickly penetrated her thin spring dress. She was still half a mile from her destination, and she decided to walk across to Madison Avenue and take the electric car. As she turned into the side street, a vague memory stirred in her. The row of budding trees, the new brick and limestone house-fronts, the Georgian flat-house with flower-boxes on its balconies, were merged together into the setting of a familiar scene. It was down this street that she had walked with Selden, that September day two years

ago; a few yards ahead was the doorway they had entered together. The
recollection loosened a throng of benumbed sensations—longings, regrets,
imaginings, the throbbing brood of the only spring her heart had ever
known. It was strange to find herself passing his house on such an errand.
She seemed suddenly to see her action as he would see it—and the fact
of his own connection with it, the fact that, to attain her end, she must
trade on his name, and profit by a secret of his past, chilled her blood
with shame. What a long way she had travelled since the day of their
first talk together! Even then her feet had been set in the path she was
now following—even then she had resisted the hand he had held out.

All her resentment of his fancied coldness was swept away in this
overwhelming rush of recollection. Twice he had been ready to help
her—to help her by loving her, as he had said—and if, the third time,
he had seemed to fail her, whom but herself could she accuse? . . .
Well, that part of her life was over; she did not know why her thoughts
still clung to it. But the sudden longing to see him remained; it grew to
hunger as she paused on the pavement opposite his door. The street was
dark and empty, swept by the rain. She had a vision of his quiet room,
of the bookshelves, and the fire on the hearth. She looked up and saw a
light in his window; then she crossed the street and entered the house.

XII

The library looked as she had pictured it. The green-shaded lamps
made tranquil circles of light in the gathering dusk, a little fire flickered
on the hearth, and Selden's easy-chair, which stood near it, had been
pushed aside when he rose to admit her.

He had checked his first movement of surprise, and stood silent, waiting for her to speak, while she paused a moment on the threshold, assailed
by a rush of memories.

The scene was unchanged. She recognized the row of shelves from
which he had taken down his La Bruyère, and the worn arm of the chair
he had leaned against while she examined the precious volume. But
then the wide September light had filled the room, making it seem a
part of the outer world: now the shaded lamps and the warm hearth,
detaching it from the gathering darkness of the street, gave it a sweeter
touch of intimacy.

Becoming gradually aware of the surprise under Selden's silence, Lily
turned to him and said simply: "I came to tell you that I was sorry for
the way we parted—for what I said to you that day at Mrs. Hatch's."

The words rose to her lips spontaneously. Even on her way up the
stairs, she had not thought of preparing a pretext for her visit, but she
now felt an intense longing to dispel the cloud of misunderstanding that
hung between them.

Selden returned her look with a smile. "I was sorry too that we should
have parted in that way; but I am not sure I did n't bring it on myself.
Luckily I had foreseen the risk I was taking——"

"So that you really did n't care——?" broke from her with a flash of her old irony.

"So that I was prepared for the consequences," he corrected good-humouredly. "But we'll talk of all this later. Do come and sit by the fire. I can recommend that arm-chair, if you'll let me put a cushion behind you."

While he spoke she had moved slowly to the middle of the room, and paused near his writing-table, where the lamp, striking upward, cast exaggerated shadows on the pallour of her delicately-hollowed face.

"You look tired—do sit down," he repeated gently.

She did not seem to hear the request. "I wanted you to know that I left Mrs. Hatch immediately after I saw you," she said, as though continuing her confession.

"Yes—yes; I know," he assented, with a rising tinge of embarrassment.

"And that I did so because you told me to. Before you came I had already begun to see that it would be impossible to remain with her—for the reasons you gave me; but I would n't admit it—I would n't let you see that I understood what you meant."

"Ah, I might have trusted you to find your own way out—don't overwhelm me with the sense of my officiousness!"

His light tone, in which, had her nerves been steadier, she would have recognized the mere effort to bridge over an awkward moment, jarred on her passionate desire to be understood. In her strange state of extra-lucidity, which gave her the sense of being already at the heart of the situation, it seemed incredible that any one should think it necessary to linger in the conventional outskirts of word-play and evasion.

"It was not that—I was not ungrateful," she insisted. But the power of expression failed her suddenly; she felt a tremor in her throat, and two tears gathered and fell slowly from her eyes.

Selden moved forward and took her hand. "You are very tired. Why won't you sit down and let me make you comfortable?"

He drew her to the arm-chair near the fire, and placed a cushion behind her shoulders.

"And now you must let me make you some tea: you know I always have that amount of hospitality at my command."

She shook her head, and two more tears ran over. But she did not weep easily, and the long habit of self-control reasserted itself, though she was still too tremulous to speak.

"You know I can coax the water to boil in five minutes," Selden continued, speaking as though she were a troubled child.

His words recalled the vision of that other afternoon when they had sat together over his tea-table and talked jestingly of her future. There were moments when that day seemed more remote than any other event in her life; and yet she could always relive it in its minutest detail.

She made a gesture of refusal. "No: I drink too much tea. I would rather sit quiet—I must go in a moment," she added confusedly.

Selden continued to stand near her, leaning against the mantelpiece. The tinge of constraint was beginning to be more distinctly perceptible under the friendly ease of his manner. Her self-absorption had not allowed her to perceive it at first; but now that her consciousness was once more putting forth its eager feelers, she saw that her presence was becoming an embarrassment to him. Such a situation can be saved only by an immediate outrush of feeling; and on Selden's side the determining impulse was still lacking.

The discovery did not disturb Lily as it might once have done. She had passed beyond the phase of well-bred reciprocity, in which every demonstration must be scrupulously proportioned to the emotion it elicits, and generosity of feeling is the only ostentation condemned. But the sense of loneliness returned with redoubled force as she saw herself forever shut out from Selden's inmost self. She had come to him with no definite purpose; the mere longing to see him had directed her; but the secret hope she had carried with her suddenly revealed itself in its death-pang.

"I must go," she repeated, making emotion to rise from her chair. "But I may not see you again for a long time, and I wanted to tell you that I have never forgotten the things you said to me at Bellomont, and that sometimes—sometimes when I seemed farthest from remembering them—they have helped me, and kept me from mistakes; kept me from really becoming what many people have thought me."

Strive as she would to put some order in her thoughts, the words would not come more clearly; yet she felt that she could not leave him without trying to make him understand that she had saved herself whole from the seeming ruin of her life.

A change had come over Selden's face as she spoke. Its guarded look had yielded to an expression still untinged by personal emotion, but full of a gentle understanding.

"I am glad to have you tell me that; but nothing I have said has really made the difference The difference is in yourself—it will always be there. And since it *is* there, it can't really matter to you what people think: you are so sure that your friends will always understand you."

"Ah, don't say that—don't say that what you have told me has made no difference. It seems to shut me out—to leave me all alone with the other people." She had risen and stood before him, once more completely mastered by the inner urgency of the moment. The consciousness of his half-divined reluctance had vanished. Whether he wished it or not, he must see her wholly for once before they parted.

Her voice had gathered strength, and she looked him gravely in the eyes as she continued. "Once—twice—you gave me the chance to escape from my life, and I refused it: refused it because I was a coward. Afterward I saw my mistake—I saw I could never be happy with what had contented me before. But it was too late: you had judged me—I understood. It was too late for happiness—but not too late to be helped by the thought of what I had missed. That is all I have lived on—don't take it from me now! Even in my worst moments it has been like a little light in the darkness. Some women are strong enough to be good by themselves, but I needed the help of your belief in me. Perhaps I might have resisted a great temptation, but the little ones would have pulled me down. And then I remembered—I remembered your saying that such a life could never satisfy me; and I was ashamed to admit to myself that it could. That is what you did for me—that is what I wanted to thank you for. I wanted to tell you that I have always remembered; and that I have tried—tried hard . . ."

She broke off suddenly. Her tears had risen again, and in drawing out her handkerchief her fingers touched the packet in the folds of her dress. A wave of colour suffused her, and the words died on her lips. Then she lifted her eyes to his and went on in an altered voice.

"I have tried hard—but life is difficult, and I am a very useless person. I can hardly be said to have an independent existence. I was just a screw or a cog in the great machine I called life, and when I dropped out of it I found I was of no use anywhere else. What can one do when one finds that one only fits into one hole? One must get back to it or be thrown out into the rubbish heap—and you don't know what it's like in the rubbish heap!"

Her lips wavered into a smile—she had been distracted by the whimsical remembrance of the confidences she had made to him, two years earlier, in that very room. Then she had been planning to marry Percy Gryce—what was it she was planning now?

The blood had risen strongly under Selden's dark skin, but his emotion showed itself only in an added seriousness of manner.

"You have something to tell me—do you mean to marry?" he said abruptly.

Lily's eyes did not falter, but a look of wonder, of puzzled self-interrogation, formed itself slowly in their depths. In the light of his question, she had paused to ask herself if her decision had really been taken when she entered the room.

"You always told me I should have to come to it sooner or later!" she said with a faint smile.

"And you have come to it now?"

"I shall have to come to it—presently. But there is something else I must come to first." She paused again, trying to transmit to her voice the steadiness of her recovered smile. "There is some one I must say goodbye to. Oh, not *you*—we are sure to see each other again—but the Lily Bart you knew. I have kept her with me all this time, but now we are going to part, and I have brought her back to you—I am going to leave her here. When I go out presently she will not go with me. I shall like to think that she has stayed with you—and she'll be no trouble, she'll take up no room."

She went toward him, and put out her hand, still smiling. "Will you let her stay with you?" she asked.

He caught her hand, and she felt in his the vibration of feeling that had not yet risen to his lips. "Lily—can't I help you?" he exclaimed.

She looked at him gently. "Do you remember what you said to me once? That you could help me only by loving me? Well—you did love me for a moment; and it helped me. It has always helped me. But the moment is gone—it was I who let it go. And one must go on living. Goodbye."

She laid her other hand on his, and they looked at each other with a kind of solemnity, as though they stood in the presence of death. Something in truth lay dead between them—the love she had killed in him and could no longer call to life. But something lived between them also, and leaped up in her like an imperishable flame: it was the love his love had kindled, the passion of her soul for his.

In its light everything else dwindled and fell away from her. She understood now that she could not go forth and leave her old self with him: that self must indeed live on in his presence, but it must still continue to be hers.

Selden had retained her hand, and continued to scrutinize her with a strange sense of foreboding. The external aspect of the situation had vanished for him as completely as for her: he felt it only as one of those rare moments which lift the veil from their faces as they pass.

"Lily," he said in a low voice, "you must n't speak in this way. I can't let you go without knowing what you mean to do. Things may change—but they don't pass. You can never go out of my life."

She met his eyes with an illumined look. "No," she said, 'I see that now. Let us always be friends. Then I shall feel safe, whatever happens."

"Whatever happens? What do you mean? What is going to happen?"

She turned away quietly and walked toward the hearth.

"Nothing at present—except that I am very cold, and that before I go you must make up the fire for me."

She knelt on the hearthrug, stretching her hands to the embers. Puzzled by the sudden change in her tone, he mechanically gathered a handful of wood from the basket and tossed it on the fire. As he did so, he noticed how thin her hands looked against the rising light of the flames. He saw too, under the loose lines of her dress, how the curves of her figure had shrunk to angularity; he remembered long afterward how the red play of the flame sharpened the depression of her nostrils, and intensified the blackness of the shadows which struck up from her cheekbones to her eyes. She knelt there for a few moments in silence; a silence which he dared not break. When she rose he fancied that he saw her draw something from her dress and drop it in to the fire; but he hardly noticed the gesture at the time. His faculties seemed tranced, and he was still groping for the word to break the spell.

She went up to him and laid her hands on his shoulders. "Goodbye," she said, and as he bent over her she touched his forehead with her lips.

XIII

The street-lamps were lit, but the rain had ceased, and there was a momentary revival of light in the upper sky.

Lily walked on unconscious of her surroundings. She was still treading the buoyant ether which emanates from the high moments of life. But gradually it shrank away from her and she felt the dull pavement beneath her feet. The sense of weariness returned with accumulated force, and for a moment she felt that she could walk no farther. She had reached the corner of Forty-first Street and Fifth Avenue, and she remembered that in Bryant Park there were seats where she might rest.

That melancholy pleasure-ground was almost deserted when she entered it, and she sank down on an empty bench in the glare of an electric street-lamp. The warmth of the fire had passed out of her veins, and she told herself that she must not sit long in the penetrating dampness which struck up from the wet asphalt. But her willpower seemed to have spent itself in a last great effort, and she was lost in the blank reaction which follows on an unwonted expenditure of energy. And besides, what was there to go home to? Nothing but the silence of her cheerless room—that silence of the night which may be more racking to tired nerves than the most discordant noises: that, and the bottle of chloral by her bed. The thought of the chloral was the only spot of light in the dark prospect: she could feel its lulling influence stealing over her already. But she was troubled by the thought that it was losing its power—she dared not go back to it too soon. Of late the sleep it had brought her had been more broken and less profound; there had been nights when she was perpetually floating up through it to consciousness. What if the effect of the drug should gradually fail, as all narcotics were said to fail? She remembered the chemist's warning against increasing the dose; and she had heard before of the capricious and incalculable action of the drug. Her dread of returning to a sleepless night was so great that she lingered on, hoping that excessive weariness would reinforce the waning power of the chloral.

Night had now closed in, and the roar of traffic in Forty-second Street was dying out. As complete darkness fell on the square the lingering occupants of the benches rose and dispersed; but now and then a stray figure, hurrying homeward, struck across the path where Lily sat, looming black for a moment in the white circle of electric light. One or two of these passers-by slackened their pace to glance curiously at her lonely figure; but she was hardly conscious of their scrutiny.

Suddenly, however, she became aware that one of the passing shadows remained stationary between her line of vision and the gleaming asphalt; and raising her eyes she saw a young woman bending over her.

"Excuse me—are you sick?—Why, it's Miss Bart!" a half-familiar voice exclaimed.

Lily looked up. The speaker was a poorly-dressed young woman with a bundle under her arm. Her face had the air of unwholesome refinement which ill-health and overwork may produce, but its common prettiness was redeemed by the strong and generous curve of the lips.

"You don't remember me," she continued, brightening with the pleasure of recognition, "but I'd know you anywhere, I've thought of you such a lot. I guess my folks all know your name by heart. I was one of the girls at Miss Farish's club—you helped me to go to the country that time I had lung-trouble. My name's Nettie Struther. It was Nettie Crane then—but I daresay you don't remember that either."

Yes: Lily was beginning to remember. The episode of Nettie Crane's timely rescue from disease had been one of the most satisfying incidents of her connection with Gerty's charitable work. She had furnished the girl with the means to go to a sanatorium in the mountains: it struck her now with a peculiar irony that the money she had used had been Gus Trenor's.

She tried to reply, to assure the speaker that she had not forgotten; but her voice failed in the effort, and she felt herself sinking under a great wave of physical weakness. Nettie Struther, with a startled exclamation, sat down and slipped a shabbily-clad arm behind her back.

"Why, Miss Bart, you *are* sick. Just lean on me a little till you feel better."

A faint glow of returning strength seemed to pass into Lily from the pressure of the supporting arm.

"I'm only tired—it is nothing," she found voice to say in a moment; and then, as she met the timid appeal of her companion's eyes, she added involuntarily: "I have been unhappy—in great trouble."

"*You* in trouble? I've always thought of you as being so high up, where everything was just grand. Sometimes, when I felt real mean, and got to wondering why things were so queerly fixed in the world, I used to remember that *you* were having a lovely time, anyhow, and that seemed to show there was a kind of justice somewhere. But you must n't sit here too long—it's fearfully damp. Don't you feel strong enough to walk on a little ways now?" she broke off.

"Yes—yes; I must go home," Lily murmured, rising.

Her eyes rested wonderingly on the thin shabby figure at her side. She had known Nettie Crane as one of the discouraged victims of over-work and anæmic parentage: one of the superfluous fragments of life destined to be swept prematurely into that social refuse-heap of which Lily had so lately expressed her dread. But Nettie Struther's frail envelope was now alive with hope and energy: whatever fate the future reserved for her, she would not be cast into the refuse-heap without a struggle.

"I am very glad to have seen you," Lily continued, summoning a smile to her unsteady lips. "It will by my turn to think of you as happy—and the world will seem a less unjust place to me too."

"Oh, but I can't leave you like this—you're not fit to go home alone. And I can't go with you either!" Nettie Struther wailed with a start of

recollection. "You see, it's my husband's night-shift—he's a motor-man—
and the friend I leave the baby with has to step upstairs to get *her* husband's supper at seven. I did n't tell you I had a baby, did I? She'll be
four months old day after tomorrow, and to look at her you would n't
think I'd ever had a sick day. I'd give anything to show you the baby,
Miss Bart, and we live right down the street here—it's only three blocks
off." She lifted her eyes tentatively to Lily's face, and then added with a
burst of courage: "Why won't you get right into the cars and come home
with me while I get baby's supper? It's real warm in our kitchen, and
you can rest there, and I'll take *you* home as soon as ever she drops off
to sleep."

It *was* warm in the kitchen, which, when Nettie Struther's match had
made a flame leap from the gas-jet above the table, revealed itself to Lily
as extraordinarily small and almost miraculously clean. A fire shone
through the polished flanks of the iron stove, and near it stood a crib in
which a baby was sitting upright, with incipient anxiety struggling for
expression on a countenance still placid with sleep.

Having passionately celebrated her reunion with her offspring, and
excused herself in cryptic language for the lateness of her return, Nettie
restored the baby to the crib and shyly invited Miss Bart to the rocking-
chair near the stove.

"We've got a parlour too," she explained with pardonable pride; "but
I guess it's warmer in here, and I don't want to leave you alone while
I'm getting baby's supper."

On receiving Lily's assurance that she much preferred the friendly
proximity of the kitchen fire, Mrs. Struther proceeded to prepare a bottle
of infantile food, which she tenderly applied to the baby's impatient lips;
and while the ensuing degustation went on, she seated herself with a
beaming countenance beside her visitor.

"You're sure you won't let me warm up a drop of coffee for you, Miss
Bart? There's some of baby's fresh milk left over—well, maybe you'd
rather just sit quiet and rest a little while. It's too lovely having you here.
I've thought of it so often that I can't believe it's really come true. I've
said to George again and again: 'I just wish Miss Bart could see me
now—'and I used to watch for your name in the papers, and we'd talk
over what you were doing, and read the descriptions of the dresses you
wore. I have n't seen your name for a long time, though, and I began to
be afraid you were sick, and it worried me so that George said I'd get
sick myself, fretting about it." Her lips broke into a reminiscent smile.
"Well, I can't afford to be sick again, that's a fact: the last spell nearly
finished me. When you sent me off that time I never thought I'd come
back alive, and I did n't much care if I did. You see I did n't know about
George and the baby then."

She paused to readjust the bottle to the child's bubbling mouth.

"You precious—don't you be in too much of a hurry! Was it mad
with mommer for getting its supper so late? Marry Anto'nette—that's

what we call her: after the French queen in that play at the Garden[1]—I told George the actress reminded me of you, and that made me fancy the name . . . I never thought I'd get married, you know, and I'd never have had the heart to go on working just for myself."

She broke off again, and meeting the encouragement in Lily's eyes, went on, with a flush rising under her anæmic skin: "You see I wasn't only just *sick* that time you sent me off—I was dreadfully unhappy too. I'd known a gentleman where I was employed—I don't know as you remember I did type-writing in a big importing firm—and—well—I thought we were to be married: he'd gone steady with me six months and given me his mother's wedding ring. But I presume he was too stylish for me—he travelled for the firm, and had seen a great deal of society. Work girls are n't looked after the way you are, and they don't always know how to look after themselves. I did not . . . and it pretty near killed me when he went away and left off writing . . . It was then I came down sick—I thought it was the end of everything. I guess it would have been if you had n't sent me off. But when I found I was getting well I began to take heart in spite of myself. And then, when I got back home, George came round and asked me to marry him. At first I thought I could n't, because we'd been brought up together, and I knew he knew about me. But after a while I began to see that that made it easier. I never could have told another man, and I'd never have married without telling, but if George cared for me enough to have me as I was, I did n't see why I should n't begin over again—and I did."

The strength of the victory shone forth from her as she lifted her irradiated face from the child on her knees.

"But, mercy, I did n't mean to go on like this about myself, with you sitting there looking so fagged out. Only it's so lovely having you here, and letting you see just how you've helped me." The baby had sunk back blissfully replete, and Mrs. Struther softly rose to lay the bottle aside. Then she paused before Miss Bart.

"I only wish I could help *you*— but I suppose there's nothing on earth I could do" she murmured wistfully.

Lily, instead of answering, rose with a smile and held out her arms; and the mother, understanding the gesture, laid her child in them.

The baby, feeling herself detached from her habitual anchorage, made an instinctive motion of resistance; but the soothing influences of digestion prevailed, and Lily felt the soft weight sink trustfully against her breast. The child's confidence in its safety thrilled her with a sense of warmth and returning life, and she bent over, wondering at the rosy blur of the little face, the empty clearness of the eyes, the vague tendrilly motions of the folding and unfolding fingers. At first the burden in her arms seemed as light as a pink cloud or a heap of down, but as she

---

1. Marie Antoinette (1755–93) was the wife of Louis XVI and queen of France; she was executed by the Revolutionary Tribunal during the French Revolution. Madison Square Garden was an imposing building in New York City where athletic as well as dramatic spectacles took place.

continued to hold it the weight increased, sinking deeper, and penetrating her with a strange sense of weakness, as though the child entered into her and became a part of herself.

She looked up, and saw Nettie's eyes resting on her with tenderness and exultation.

"Would n't it be too lovely for anything if she could grow up to be just like you? Of course I know she never *could*—but mothers are always dreaming the craziest things for their children."

Lily clasped the child close for a moment and laid her back in her mother's arms.

"Oh, she must not do that—I should be afraid to come and see her too often!" she said with a smile; and then, resisting Mrs. Struther's anxious offer of companionship, and reiterating the promise that of course she would come back soon, and make George's acquaintance, and see the baby in her bath, she passed out of the kitchen and went alone down the tenement stairs.

As she reached the street she realized that she felt stronger and happier: the little episode had done her good. It was the first time she had ever come across the results of her spasmodic benevolence, and the surprised sense of human fellowship took the mortal chill from her heart.

It was not till she entered her own door that she felt the reaction of a deeper loneliness. It was long after seven o'clock, and the light and odours proceeding from the basement made it manifest that the boarding-house dinner had begun. She hastened up to her room, lit the gas, and began to dress. She did not mean to pamper herself any longer, to go without food because her surroundings made it unpalatable. Since it was her fate to live in a boarding-house, she must learn to fall in with the conditions of the life. Nevertheless she was glad that, when she descended to the heat and glare of the dining-room, the repast was nearly over.

In her own room again, she was seized with a sudden fever of activity. For weeks past she had been too listless and indifferent to set her possessions in order, but now she began to examine systematically the contents of her drawers and cupboard. She had a few handsome dresses left—survivals of her last phase of splendour, on the Sabrina and in London—but when she had been obliged to part with her maid she had given the woman a generous share of her cast-off apparel. The remaining dresses, though they had lost their freshness, still kept the long unerring lines, the sweep and amplitude of the great artist's stroke, and as she spread them out on the bed the scenes in which they had been worn rose vividly before her. An association lurked in every fold; each fall of lace and gleam of embroidery was like a letter in the record of her past. She was startled to find how the atmosphere of her old life enveloped her. But, after all, it was the life she had been made for: every dawning tendency in her had been carefully directed toward it, all her interests and activities had been taught to centre around it. She was like some rare flower grown for exhibition, a flower from which every bud had been nipped except the crowning blossom of her beauty.

Last of all, she drew forth from the bottom of her trunk a heap of white drapery which fell shapelessly across her arm. It was the Reynolds dress she had worn in the Bry *tableaux*. It had been impossible for her to give it away, but she had never seen it since that night, and the long flexible folds, as she shook them out, gave forth an odour of violets which came to her like a breath from the flower-edged fountain where she had stood with Lawrence Selden and disowned her fate. She put back the dresses one by one, laying away with each some gleam of light, some note of laughter, some stray waft from the rosy shores of pleasure. She was still in a state of highly-wrought impressionability, and every hint of the past sent a lingering tremor along her nerves.

She had just closed her trunk on the white folds of the Reynolds dress when she heard a tap at her door, and the red fist of the Irish maid-servant thrust in a belated letter. Carrying it to the light, Lily read with surprise the address stamped on the upper corner of the envelope. It was a business communication from the office of her aunt's executors, and she wondered what unexpected development had caused them to break silence before the appointed time.

She opened the envelope and a cheque fluttered to the floor. As she stooped to pick it up the blood rushed to her face. The cheque represented the full amount of Mrs. Peniston's legacy, and the letter accompanying it explained that the executors, having adjusted the business of the estate with less delay than they had expected, had decided to anticipate the date fixed for the payment of the bequests.

Lily sat down beside the desk at the foot of her bed, and spreading out the cheque, read over and over the *ten thousand dollars* written across it in a steely business hand. Ten months earlier the amount it stood for had represented the depths of penury; but her standard of values had changed in the interval, and now visions of wealth lurked in every flourish of the pen. As she continued to gaze at it, she felt the glitter of the visions mounting to her brain, and after a while she lifted the lid of the desk and slipped the magic formula out of sight. It was easier to think without those five figures dancing before her eyes; and she had a great deal of thinking to do before she slept.

She opened her cheque-book, and plunged into such anxious calculations as had prolonged her vigil at Bellomont on the night when she had decided to marry Percy Gryce. Poverty simplifies book-keeping, and her financial situation was easier to ascertain than it had been then; but she had not yet learned the control of money, and during her transient phase of luxury at the Emporium she had slipped back into habits of extravagance which still impaired her slender balance. A careful examination of her cheque-book, and of the unpaid bills in her desk, showed that, when the latter had been settled, she would have barely enough to live on for the next three or four months; and even after that, if she were to continue her present way of living, without earning any additional money, all incidental expenses must be reduced to the vanishing point. She hid her eyes with a shudder, beholding herself at the entrance of that ever-narrowing perspective down which she had seen Miss Silverton's dowdy figure take its despondent way.

It was no longer, however, from the vision of material poverty that she turned with the greatest shrinking. She had a sense of deeper empoverishment—of an inner destitution compared to which outward conditions dwindled into insignificance. It was indeed miserable to be poor—to look forward to a shabby, anxious middle-age, leading by dreary degrees of economy and self-denial to gradual absorption in the dingy communal existence of the boarding-house. But there was something more miserable still—it was the clutch of solitude at her heart, the sense of being swept like a stray uprooted growth down the heedless current of the years. That was the feeling which possessed her now—the feeling of being something rootless and ephemeral, mere spin-drift of the whirling surface of existence, without anything to which the poor little tentacles of self could cling before the awful flood submerged them. And as she looked back she saw that there had never been a time when she had had any real relation to life. Her parents too had been rootless, blown hither and thither on every wind of fashion, without any personal existence to shelter them from its shifting gusts. She herself had grown up without any one spot of earth being dearer to her than another: there was no centre of early pieties, of grave endearing traditions, to which her heart could revert and from which it could draw strength for itself and tenderness for others. In whatever form a slowly-accumulated past lives in the blood—whether in the concrete image of the old house stored with visual memories, or in the conception of the house not built with hands, but made up of inherited passions and loyalties—it has the same power of broadening and deepening the individual existence, of attaching it by mysterious links of kinship to all the mighty sum of human striving.

Such a vision of the solidarity of life had never before come to Lily. She had had a premonition of it in the blind motions of her mating-instinct; but they had been checked by the disintegrating influences of the life about her. All the men and women she knew were like atoms whirling away from each other in some wild centrifugal dance: her first glimpse of the continuity of life had come to her that evening in Nettie Struther's kitchen.

The poor little working-girl who had found strength to gather up the fragments of her life, and build herself a shelter with them, seemed to Lily to have reached the central truth of existence. It was a meagre enough life, on the grim edge of poverty, with scant margin for possibilities of sickness or mischance, but it had the frail audacious permanence of a bird's nest built on the edge of a cliff—a mere wisp of leaves and straw, yet so put together that the lives entrusted to it may hang safely over the abyss.

Yes—but it had taken two to build the nest; the man's faith as well as the woman's courage. Lily remembered Nettie's words: *I knew he knew*

about me. Her husband's faith in her had made her renewal possible—
it is so easy for a woman to become what the man she loves believes her
to be! Well—Selden had twice been ready to stake his faith on Lily Bart;
but the third trial had been too severe for his endurance. The very quality of his love had made it the more impossible to recall to life. If it had
been a simple instinct of the blood, the power of her beauty might have
revived it. But the fact that it struck deeper, that it was inextricably wound
up with inherited habits of thought and feeling, made it as impossible to
restore to growth as a deep-rooted plant torn from its bed. Selden had
given her of his best; but he was as incapable as herself of an uncritical
return to former states of feeling.

There remained to her, as she had told him, the uplifting memory of
his faith in her; but she had not reached the age when a woman can live
on her memories. As she held Nettie Struther's child in her arms the
frozen currents of youth had loosed themselves and run warm in her
veins: the old life-hunger possessed her, and all her being clamoured for
its share of personal happiness. Yes—it was happiness she still wanted,
and the glimpse she had caught of it made everything else of no account.
One by one she had detached herself from the baser possibilities, and
she saw that nothing now remained to her but the emptiness of renunciation.

It was growing late, and an immense weariness once more possessed
her. It was not the stealing sense of sleep, but a vivid wakeful fatigue, a
wan lucidity of mind against which all the possibilities of the future were
shadowed forth gigantically. She was appalled by the intense clearness
of the vision; she seemed to have broken through the merciful veil which
intervenes between intention and action, and to see exactly what she
would do in all the long days to come. There was the cheque in her
desk, for instance—she meant to use it in paying her debt to Trenor; but
she foresaw that when the morning came she would put off doing so,
would slip into gradual tolerance of the debt. The thought terrified her—
she dreaded to fall from the height of her last moment with Lawrence
Selden. But how could she trust herself to keep her footing? She knew
the strength of the opposing impulses—she could feel the countless hands
of habit dragging her back into some fresh compromise with fate. She
felt an intense longing to prolong, to perpetuate, the momentary exaltation of her spirit. If only life could end now—end on this tragic yet
sweet vision of lost possibilities, which gave her a sense of kinship with
all the loving and foregoing in the world!

She reached out suddenly and, drawing the cheque from her writing-
desk, enclosed it in an envelope which she addressed to her bank. She
then wrote out a cheque for Trenor, and placing it, without an accompanying word, in an envelope inscribed with his name, laid the two
letters side by side on her desk. After that she continued to sit at the
table, sorting her papers and writing, till the intense silence of the house
reminded her of the lateness of the hour. In the street the noise of wheels
had ceased, and the rumble of the "elevated" came only at long intervals

through the deep unnatural hush. In the mysterious nocturnal separation from all outward signs of life, she felt herself more strangely confronted with her fate. The sensation made her brain reel, and she tried to shut out consciousness by pressing her hands against her eyes. But the terrible silence and emptiness seemed to symbolize her future—she felt as though the house, the street, the world were all empty, and she alone left sentient in a lifeless universe.

But this was the verge of delirium . . . she had never hung so near the dizzy brink of the unreal. Sleep was what she wanted—she remembered that she had not closed her eyes for two nights. The little bottle was at her bedside, waiting to lay its spell upon her. She rose and undressed hastily, hungering now for the touch of her pillow. She felt so profoundly tired that she thought she must fall asleep at once; but as soon as she had lain down every nerve started once more into separate wakefulness. It was as though a great blaze of electric light had been turned on in her head, and her poor little anguished self shrank and cowered in it, without knowing where to take refuge.

She had not imagined that such a multiplication of wakefulness was possible: her whole past was reënacting itself at a hundred different points of consciousness. Where was the drug that could still this legion of insurgent nerves? The sense of exhaustion would have been sweet compared to this shrill beat of activities; but weariness had dropped from her as though some cruel stimulant had been forced into her veins.

She could bear it—yes, she could bear it; but what strength would be left her the next day? Perspective had disappeared—the next day pressed close upon her, and on its heels came the days that were to follow—they swarmed about her like a shrieking mob. She must shut them out for a few hours; she must take a brief bath of oblivion. She put out her hand, and measured the soothing drops into a glass; but as she did so, she knew they would be powerless against the supernatural lucidity of her brain. She had long since raised the dose to its highest limit, but tonight she felt she must increase it. She knew she took a slight risk in doing so—she remembered the chemist's warning. If sleep came at all, it might be a sleep without waking. But after all that was but one chance in a hundred: the action of the drug was incalculable, and the addition of a few drops to the regular dose would probably do no more than procure for her the rest she so desperately needed. . . .

She did not, in truth, consider the question very closely—the physical craving for sleep was her only sustained sensation. Her mind shrank from the glare of thought as instinctively as eyes contract in a blaze of light—darkness, darkness was what she must have at any cost. She raised herself in bed and swallowed the contents of the glass; then she blew out her candle and lay down.

She lay very still, waiting with a sensuous pleasure for the first effects of the soporific. She knew in advance what form they would take—the gradual cessation of the inner throb, the soft approach of passiveness, as though an invisible hand made magic passes over her in the darkness.

The very slowness and hesitancy of the effect increased its fascination: it was delicious to lean over and look down into the dim abysses of unconsciousness. Tonight the drug seemed to work more slowly than usual: each passionate pulse had to be stilled in turn, and it was long before she felt them dropping into abeyance, like sentinels falling asleep at their posts. But gradually the sense of complete subjugation came over her, and she wondered languidly what had made her feel so uneasy and excited. She saw now that there was nothing to be excited about—she had returned to her normal view of life. Tomorrow would not be so difficult after all: she felt sure that she would have the strength to meet it. She did not quite remember what it was that she had been afraid to meet, but the uncertainty no longer troubled her. She had been unhappy, and now she was happy—she had felt herself alone, and now the sense of loneliness had vanished.

She stirred once, and turned on her side, and as she did so, she suddenly understood why she did not feel herself alone. It was odd—but Nettie Struther's child was lying on her arm: she felt the pressure of its little head against her shoulder. She did not know how it had come there, but she felt no great surprise at the fact, only a gentle penetrating thrill of warmth and pleasure. She settled herself into an easier position, hollowing her arm to pillow the round downy head, and holding her breath lest a sound should disturb the sleeping child.

As she lay there she said to herself that there was something she must tell Selden, some word she had found that should make life clear between them. She tried to repeat the word, which lingered vague and luminous on the far edge of thought—she was afraid of not remembering it when she woke; and if she could only remember it and say it to him, she felt that everything would be well.

Slowly the thought of the word faded, and sleep began to enfold her. She struggled faintly against it, feeling that she ought to keep awake on account of the baby; but even this feeling was gradually lost in an indistinct sense of drowsy peace, through which, of a sudden, a dark flash of loneliness and terror tore its way.

She started up again, cold and trembling with the shock: for a moment she seemed to have lost her hold of the child. But no—she was mistaken—the tender pressure of its body was still close to hers: the recovered warmth flowed through her once more, she yielded to it, sank into it, and slept.

XIV

The next morning rose mild and bright, with a promise of summer in the air. The sunlight slanted joyously down Lily's street, mellowed the blistered house-front, gilded the paintless railings of the door-step, and struck prismatic glories from the panes of her darkened window.

When such a day coincides with the inner mood there is intoxication in its breath; and Selden, hastening along the street through the squalor of its morning confidences, felt himself thrilling with a youthful sense of adventure. He had cut loose from the familiar shores of habit, and launched himself on uncharted seas of emotion; all the old tests and measures were left behind, and his course was to be shaped by new stars.

That course, for the moment, led merely to Miss Bart's boarding-house; but its shabby door-step had suddenly become the threshold of the untried. As he approached he looked up at the triple row of windows, wondering boyishly which one of them was hers. It was nine o'clock, and the house, being tenanted by workers, already showed an awakened front to the street. He remembered afterward having noticed that only one blind was down. He noticed too that there was a pot of pansies on one of the window sills, and at once concluded that the window must be hers: it was inevitable that he should connect her with the one touch of beauty in the dingy scene.

Nine o'clock was an early hour for a visit, but Selden had passed beyond all such conventional observances. He only knew that he must see Lily Bart at once—he had found the word he meant to say to her, and it could not wait another moment to be said. It was strange that it had not come to his lips sooner—that he had let her pass from him the evening before without being able to speak it. But what did that matter, now that a new day had come? It was not a word for twilight, but for the morning.

Selden ran eagerly up the steps and pulled the bell; and even in his state of self-absorption it came as a sharp surprise to him that the door should open so promptly. It was still more of a surprise to see, as he entered that it had been opened by Gerty Farish—and that behind her, in an agitated blur, several other figures ominously loomed.

"Lawrence!" Gerty cried in a strange voice, "how could you get here so quickly?"—and the trembling hand she laid on him seemed instantly to close about his heart.

He noticed the other faces, vague with fear and conjecture—he saw the landlady's imposing bulk sway professionally toward him; but he shrank back, putting up his hand, while his eyes mechanically mounted the steep black walnut stairs, up which he was immediately aware that his cousin was about to lead him.

A voice in the background said that the doctor might be back at any minute—and that nothing, upstairs, was to be disturbed. Someone else exclaimed: "It was the greatest mercy—" then Selden felt that Gerty had taken him gently by the hand, and that they were to be suffered to go up alone.

In silence they mounted the three flights, and walked along the passage to a closed door. Gerty opened the door, and Selden went in after her. Though the blind was down, the irresistible sunlight poured a tempered golden flood into the room, and in its light Selden saw a narrow bed along the wall, and on the bed, with motionless hands, and calm unrecognizing face, the semblance of Lily Bart.

That it was her real self, every pulse in him ardently denied. Her real self had lain warm on his heart but a few hours earlier—what had he to do with this estranged and tranquil face which, for the first time, neither paled nor brightened at his coming?

Gerty, strangely tranquil too, with the conscious self-control of one who has ministered to much pain, stood by the bed, speaking gently, as if transmitting a final message.

"The doctor found a bottle of chloral—she had been sleeping badly for a long time, and she must have taken an over-dose by mistake. . . . There is no doubt of that—no doubt—there will be no question—he has been very kind. I told him that you and I would like to be left alone with her—to go over her things before any one else comes. I know it is what she would have wished."

Selden was hardly conscious of what she said. He stood looking down on the sleeping face which seemed to lie like a delicate impalpable mask over the living lineaments he had known. He felt that the real Lily was still there, close to him, yet invisible and inaccessible; and the tenuity of the barrier between them mocked him with a sense of helplessness. There had never been more than a little impalpable barrier between them—and yet he had suffered it to keep them apart! And now, though it seemed slighter and frailer than ever, it had suddenly hardened to adamant, and he might beat his life out against it in vain.

He had dropped on his knees beside the bed, but a touch from Gerty aroused him. He stood up, and as their eyes met he was struck by the extraordinary light in his cousin's face.

"You understand what the doctor has gone for? He has promised that there shall be no trouble—but of course the formalities must be gone through. And I asked him to give us time to look through her things first——"

He nodded, and she glanced about the small bare room. "It won't take long," she concluded.

"No—it won't take long," he agreed.

She held his hand in hers a moment longer, and then, with a last look at the bed, moved silently toward the door. On the threshold she paused to add: "You will find me downstairs if you want me."

Selden roused himself to detain her. "But why are you going? She would have wished——"

Gerty shook her head with a smile. "No: this is what she would have wished——" and as she spoke a light broke through Selden's stony misery, and he saw deep into the hidden things of love.

The door closed on Gerty, and he stood alone with the motionless sleeper on the bed. His impulse was to return to her side, to fall on his knees, and rest his throbbing head against the peaceful cheek on the pillow. They had never been at peace together, they two; and now he felt himself drawn downward into the strange mysterious depths of her tranquillity.

But he remembered Gerty's warning words—he knew that, though time had ceased in this room, its feet were hastening relentlessly toward the door. Gerty had given him this supreme half-hour, and he must use it as she willed.

He turned and looked about him, sternly compelling himself to regain his consciousness of outward things. There was very little furniture in the room. The shabby chest of drawers was spread with a lace cover, and set out with a few gold-topped boxes and bottles, a rose-coloured pin-cushion, a glass tray strewn with tortoise-shell hairpins—he shrank from the poignant intimacy of these trifles, and from the blank surface of the toilet-mirror above them.

These were the only traces of luxury, of that clinging to the minute observance of personal seemliness, which showed what her other renunciations must have cost. There was no other token of her personality about the room, unless it showed itself in the scrupulous neatness of the scant articles of furniture: a washing-stand, two chairs, a small writing-desk, and the little table near the bed. On this table stood the empty bottle and glass, and from these also he averted his eyes.

The desk was closed, but on its slanting lid lay two letters which he took up. One bore the address of a bank, and as it was stamped and sealed, Selden, after a moment's hesitation, laid it aside. On the other letter he read Gus Trenor's name; and the flap of the envelope was still ungummed.

Temptation leapt on him like the stab of a knife. He staggered under it, steadying himself against the desk. Why had she been writing to Trenor—writing, presumably, just after their parting of the previous evening? The thought unhallowed the memory of that last hour, made a mock of the word he had come to speak, and defiled even the reconciling silence upon which it fell. He felt himself flung back on all the ugly uncertainties from which he thought he had cast loose forever. After all, what did he know of her life? Only as much as she had chosen to show him, and measured by the world's estimate, how little that was! By what right—the letter in his hand seemed to ask—by what right was it he who now passed into her confidence through the gate which death had left unbarred? His heart cried out that it was by right of their last hour together, the hour when she herself had placed the key in his hand. Yes—but what if the letter to Trenor had been written afterward?

He put it from him with sudden loathing, and setting his lips, addressed himself resolutely to what remained of his task. After all, that task would be easier to perform, now that his personal stake in it was annulled.

He raised the lid of the desk, and saw within it a cheque-book and a few packets of bills and letters, arranged with the orderly precision which characterized all her personal habits. He looked through the letters first, because it was the most difficult part of the work. They proved to be few and unimportant, but among them he found, with a strange commotion of the heart, the note he had written the day after the Brys' entertainment.

"When may I come to you?"—his words overwhelmed him with a realization of the cowardice which had driven him from her at the very moment of attainment. Yes—he had always feared his fate, and he was too honest to disown his cowardice now; for had not all his old doubts started to life again at the mere sight of Trenor's name?

He laid the note in his card-case, folding it away carefully, as something made precious by the fact that she had held it so; then, growing once more aware of the lapse of time, he continued his examination of the papers.

To his surprise, he found that all the bills were receipted; there was not an unpaid account among them. He opened the cheque book, and saw that, the very night before, a cheque of ten thousand dollars from Mrs. Peniston's executors had been entered in it. The legacy, then, had been paid sooner than Gerty had led him to expect. But, turning another page or two, he discovered with astonishment that, in spite of this recent accession of funds, the balance had already declined to a few dollars. A rapid glance at the stubs of the last cheques, all of which bore the date of the previous day, showed that between four or five hundred dollars of the legacy had been spent in the settlement of bills, while the remaining thousands were comprehended in one cheque, made out, at the same time, to Charles Augustus Trenor.

Selden laid the book aside, and sank into the chair beside the desk. He leaned his elbows on it, and hid his face in his hands. The bitter waters of life surged high about him, their sterile taste was on his lips. Did the cheque to Trenor explain the mystery or deepen it? At first his mind refused to act—he felt only the taint of such a transaction between a man like Trenor and a girl like Lily Bart. Then, gradually, his troubled vision cleared, old hints and rumours came back to him, and out of the very insinuations he had feared to probe, he constructed an explanation of the mystery. It was true, then, that she had taken money from Trenor; but true also, as the contents of the little desk declared, that the obligation had been intolerable to her, and that at the first opportunity she had freed herself from it, though the act left her face to face with bare unmitigated poverty.

That was all he knew—all he could hope to unravel of the story. The mute lips on the pillow refused him more than this—unless indeed they had told him the rest in the kiss they had left upon his forehead. Yes, he could now read into that farewell all that his heart craved to find there; he could even draw from it courage not to accuse himself for having failed to reach the height of his opportunity.

He saw that all the conditions of life had conspired to keep them apart; since his very detachment from the external influences which swayed her had increased his spiritual fastidiousness, and made it more difficult for him to live and love uncritically. But at least he *had* loved her—had been willing to stake his future on his faith in her—and if the moment had been fated to pass from them before they could seize it, he saw now that, for both, it had been saved whole out of the ruin of their lives.

It was this moment of love, this fleeting victory over themselves, which had kept them from atrophy and extinction; which, in her, had reached out to him in every struggle against the influence of her surroundings, and in him, had kept alive the faith that now drew him penitent and reconciled to her side.

He knelt by the bed and bent over her, draining their last moment to its lees; and in the silence there passed between them the word which made all clear.

BACKGROUNDS AND CONTEXTS

EDITH WHARTON

Selected Letters †

To William Crary Brownell[1]

The Mount
Lenox, Mass.
June 25 [1904]

Dear Mr. Brownell,

I return the reviews[2] with many thanks. I have never before been discouraged by criticism, because when the critics have found fault with me I have usually abounded in their sense, & seen, as I thought, a way of doing better the next time; but the continued cry that I am an echo of Mr. James (whose books of the last ten years I can't read, much as I delight in the man), & the assumption that the people I write about are not "real" because they are not navvies & char-women, makes me feel rather hopeless. I write about what I see, what I happen to be nearest to, which is surely better than doing cowboys de chic. . . . But this is not business. As to yr. letter of June 23, it fills me with compunction. Of course the understanding was that, on our return to Italy, I should get, or take, photos to complete the Backgrounds. But the bad weather in Italy made it impossible for us to go there, on my husband's account, & I should of course have written you that I couldn't get the photos, since they are not of a kind that one can order from a distance.

I am *very* sorry, & make my excuses to you all—Now what shall we do? I have another article, "March in Italy," which is nearly done, & which will make the book of the requisite length, I think—but if you want photos we are at a standstill.

It is more likely that we may go to Italy in the winter, for though my husband is so much better, he seems to be so only because we had no cold weather—still, that will not be decided till his Dr. comes home in September—Meanwhile I must leave it to you to decide whether the book shall be put off on the chance of my being able to get photos on the spot next winter (& also do still another article) or whether you want to give up the pictures—

I might get some photos for Italian Backgrounds (the article) but for Splügen impossible!

†From *The Letters of Edith Wharton*, eds. R. W. B. Lewis & Nancy Lewis (New York: Charles Scribner's Sons, 1988) 91–92, 94–100.

1. The head of Scribner's book publishing depart-ment [Editor].

2. Of *The Descent of Man*, EW's third collection of short stories, published in April 1904.

I am glad Mrs. Brownell is improving at the Pier, & I still hope for a Sunday from you later on—

My hand is all right, thanks—

Yrs Guiltily
       E. Wharton

Wouldn't it have helped "The Descent" to put in the two new stories?

To William Crary Brownell

The Mount
Lenox, Mass.
August 5, 1905

Dear Mr. Brownell,

Even when I sank to the depth of letting the illustrations be put in the book[1]—&, oh, I wish I hadn't now!—I never contemplated a text in the title-page.[2] It was all very well for The Valley, where the verse simply "constated" a fact, but in this case, where it inculcates a moral, I might surely be suspected of plagiarizing from Mrs. Margaret Sangster's beautiful volume, "Five Days with God."[3]

Seriously. I think the title explains itself amply as the tale progresses, & I have taken the liberty of drawing an inexorable blue line through the text.

I am pushing off to the end any reference to what you say about my story—I am so surprised & pleased, & altogether taken aback, that I can't decently compose my countenance about it. I was pleased with bits, myself; but as I go over the proofs the whole thing strikes me as so loosely built, with so many dangling threads, & cul-de-sacs, & long dusty stretches, that I had reached the point of wondering how I had ever dared to try my hand at a long thing— So your seeing a certain amount of architecture in it rejoices me above everything—my theory of what the novel ought to be is so exorbitant, that I am always reminded of Daudet's "Je rêve d'un aigle, j'accouche d'un colibri."—[4]

Well— thanks for taking the trouble to write me what you did, & may Moosehead do you all the good in the world—

Yrs Sincerely E. Wharton

I approve choice of frontpiece

Ms: FL

1. *The House of Mirth*, to be published on October 14, 1905, in a first edition of forty thousand copies.

2. The original epigraph, which EW now deletes, is from Ecclesiastes 7:4: "The heart of the wise is in the house of mourning; but the heart of fools is in the house of mirth."

3. Margaret Sangster (1838–1912) was an extremely popular American poet, one of whose main themes was the proper performance of religious duties.

4. A characteristic reflection by Alphonse Daudet (1840–1897) about his experience as a novelist: "I

To Charles Scribner[1]

The Mount
Lenox, Mass.
November 11, 1905

Dear Mr. Scribner,

It is a very beautiful thought to me that 80,000 people should want to read "The House of Mirth," & if the number should ascend to 100,000 I fear my pleasure would exceed the bounds of decency.

Seriously, I am of course immensely interested & amused by all these "returns," & very grateful to you for sending them to me.—And by the way, I hope you got that photograph I sent you about ten days ago, with my eyes down, *trying to look modest?!* The photographer swore he would send it off punctually, but I have had my doubts, as he hasn't sent me one yet. It was to go direct to Mr. Chapin.

I shall be in town for one day next week—Friday, the 17th—& if by any chance you should want to see me about anything, will you send a line to 23 E. 33rd St?—I am going to see Miss Marbury[2] about dramatizing the H. of M., as I am having so many bids for it.

Thanks again for your letter.

Sincerely Yrs
    Edith Wharton

Ms:FL

To William Roscoe Thayer[1]

The Mount,
Lenox, Mass
November 11 [1905]

Dear Professor Thayer,

By a pleasant coincidence, I was talking of you with Robert Minturn[2] a few weeks ago, saying how much I admired your essay on historical methods in the "Atlantic," & how deeply I was indebted to "The Dawn of Italian Independence" for such light on that intricate & engrossing period as I needed in writing my Italian novel.

Judge then, how pleased & surprised I was to receive your letter the other day, & to learn that I had been able to make ever so slight a return for the great pleasure your admirable book has long given me.

dream of an eagle, and I give birth to a humming-bird."

1. Charles Scribner (1821–1871), Wharton's publisher.

2. Elisabeth Marbury (1856–1933), friend and companion of Elsie de Wolfe and one of the first successful author's agents. Among her clients at this time was the playwright Clyde Fitch.

1. William Roscoe Thayer (1859–1923); Boston writer, biographer, and historian.

2. Minturn, afflicted with chronic ill health, was a linguist and a connoisseur of art; he was a member of a leading New York family and an old friend of EW.

I am particularly & quite inordinately pleased with what you say of my having—to your mind—been able to maintain my readers' interest in a group of persons so intrinsically uninteresting, except as a social manifestation. I knew that my great difficulty lay there, & if you think I have surmounted it, I shall go about with a high head.—But—before we leave the subject—I must protest, & emphatically, against the suggestion that I have "stripped" New York society. New York society is still amply clad, & the little corner of its garment that I lifted was meant to show only that little atrophied organ—the group of idle & dull people—that exists in any big & wealthy social body. If it seems more conspicuous in New York than in an old civilization, it is because the social organization with us is so much smaller & less elaborate—&, if as I believe, it is more harmful in its influence, it is because fewer responsibilities attach to money with us than in other societies.—

Forgive this long discourse—but you see I had to come to the defense of my own town, which, I assure you, has many mansions outside of the little House of Mirth.

I hope when I am next in Boston I may have the pleasure of thanking you in person for your letter, which I value more than anything my book has brought me.

> Sincerely Yrs
>   Edith Wharton

I wish you felt a little more kindly toward poor Lily!

To Edward L. Burlingame[1]

November 23 [1905]

Dear Mr. Burlingame,

There is sweet music in "I told you so," when used as you use it! Thank you very much for writing to remind me of your hopeful prognostications—I have not heard from Mr. Brownell since he wrote, about a month ago, a very kind letter to break to me, with all gentleness, the fact that the H. of M. would probably not go above 40,000.—

I am especially glad to find that you think its large circulation a sign of awakening taste in our fellow-countrymen—at least in 100,000 of them. I was almost afraid that, reversing the experience of Saul the son of Kish, I had gone out to seek a kingdom & found all the asses!![2]

I sent Mr. Scribner only the *serious* letters, but I have a trunkful of funny ones which I will bring to town with me. One lady is so carried away that she writes: "I love, not every word in the book, but every period & comma." I hope she meant to insert an "only" after the "not"—

---

1. The editor of *Scribner's Magazine*, the publication in which *The House of Mirth* initially appeared   as a serial [Editor].
2. The reference is to I Samuel 9.

Well, it's all great fun, & you did it all by accepting the Last Giustiniani[3]—do you remember!

Sincerely Yrs
    Edith Wharton

To Dr. Morgan Dix[1]

The Mount
Lenox, Mass.
December 5 [1905]

Dear Dr. Dix,

You would have to write in a very different strain to keep me even twenty-four hours from answering your letter; & I must begin by telling you how touched I am that you would have found time to send it, & how proud—yes, quite inordinately so!—that you should have thought my novel worthy of such careful reading & close analysis.—

Few things could have pleased me more than the special form which your commendation has taken; for, lightly, as I think of my own equipment, I could not do anything if I did not think seriously of my trade; & the more I have considered it, the more has it seemed to me valuable & interesting only in so far as it is "a criticism of life."—It almost seems to be that bad & good fiction (using the words in their ethical sense) might be defined as the kind which treats of life trivially & superficially, & that which probes deep enough to get at the relation with the eternal laws; & the novelist who has this feeling is so often discouraged by the comments of readers & critics who think a book "unpleasant" because it deals with unpleasant conditions, that it is a high solace & encouragement to come upon the recognition of one's motive. No novel worth anything can be anything but a novel "with a purpose," & if anyone who cared for the moral issue did not see in my work that I care for it, I should have no one to blame but myself—or at least my inadequate means of rendering my effects.

Social conditions as they are just now in our new world, where the sudden possession of money has come without inherited obligations, or any traditional sense of solidarity between the classes, is a vast & absorb-

3. EW's poem "The Last Giustiniani" was her first work to see print. It was accepted by Edward L. Burlingame for publication in the October 1889 issue of *Scribner's*. The twelve-stanza poem is a piece of historical romance set in eighteenth-century Italy and tells of the last member of the Giustiniani family, who was released from his monkish vows in order to marry and perpetuate his race. The same theme was dramatized in *Guy Domville* (1895), by Henry James, who may have read EW's poem.

1. Morgan Dix (1827–1908) was rector of Trinity Church in New York from 1862 onwards. His long letter of December 1, 1905, said in part: "This book places you at the head of the living novelists of our country or of the English-writing authors of our day. It is a terrible but just arraignment of the social misconduct which begins in folly and ends in moral and spiritual death. . . . To me the reading of your book has been like a walking the wards of some infirmary set apart for the treatment of pestilential disease: the same ghastly wrecks of humanity, the same mephitic odours, the same miasma of afflorescent corruption."

ing field for the novelist, & I wish a great master could arise to deal with it—but perhaps I may have a chance to talk of these things with you, for I do not mean to be again in New York without making a very determined effort to see you & Mrs. Dix.

We never stay there long now, because the cold weather is bad for my husband, but we shall be in our house during January, & perhaps we can persuade you & Mrs. Dix to come & dine some night alone so that we may have an unrestrained talk.

I remember with pride your allusion to my little story, "The Reckoning"[2]—& it has always been a great pleasure to me that, in your busy & beneficent life, you have found time to follow with such sympathy what I have tried to do. Believe me, dear Dr. Dix,

Ever sincerely Yrs,
Edith Wharton

Thorstein Veblen

[Conspicuous Leisure and Conspicuous Consumption] †

*   *   *

[T]he term "leisure," as here used, does not connote indolence or quiescence. What it connotes is non-productive consumption of time. Time is consumed non-productively (1) from a sense of the unworthiness of productive work, and (2) as an evidence of pecuniary ability to afford a life of idleness. But the whole of the life of the gentleman of leisure is not spent before the eyes of the spectators who are to be impressed with that spectacle of honorific leisure which in the ideal scheme makes up his life. For some part of the time his life is perforce withdrawn from the public eye, and of this portion which is spent in private the gentleman of leisure should, for the sake of his good name, be able to give a convincing account. He should find some means of putting in evidence the leisure that is not spent in the sight of the spectators. This can be done only indirectly, through the exhibition of some tangible, lasting results of the leisure so spent—in a manner analogous to the familiar exhibition of tangible, lasting products of the labour performed for the gentleman of leisure by handicraftsmen and servants in his employ.

---

2. "The Reckoning" was contained in *The Descent of Man* of 1904. It is the sad tale of an emancipated young woman who, after jettisoning her husband on the principle of being faithful to her own desires, is herself set aside by her second husband on the same doctrine.

† From *The Theory of the Leisure Class: An Economic Study of Institutions* (New York: Macmillan, 1899) 43, 44–45, 75–80, 53–54, 167–72, 179–82.

* * *

As seen from the economic point of view, leisure, considered as an employment, is closely allied in kind with the life of exploit; and the achievements which characterise a life of leisure, and which remain as its decorous criteria, have much in common with the trophies of exploit. But leisure in the narrower sense, as distinct from exploit and from any ostensibly productive employment of effort on objects which are of no intrinsic use, does not commonly leave a material product. The criteria of a past performance of leisure therefore commonly take the form of "immaterial" goods. Such immaterial evidences of past leisure are quasi-scholarly or quasi-artistic accomplishments and a knowledge of processes and incidents which do not conduce directly to the furtherance of human life. So, for instance, in our time there is the knowledge of the dead languages and the occult sciences; of correct spelling; of syntax and prosody; of the various forms of domestic music and other household art; of the latest proprieties of dress, furniture, and equipage; of games, sports, and fancy-bred animals, such as dogs and race-horses. In all these branches of knowledge the initial motive from which their acquisition proceeded at the outset, and through which they first came into vogue, may have been something quite different from the wish to show that one's time had not been spent in industrial employment; but unless these accomplishments had approved themselves as serviceable evidence of an unproductive expenditure of time, they would not have survived and held their place as conventional accomplishments of the leisure class.

* * *

Conspicuous consumption of valuable goods is a means of reputability to the gentleman of leisure. As wealth accumulates on his hands, his own unaided effort will not avail to sufficiently put his opulence in evidence by this method. The aid of friends and competitors is therefore brought in by resorting to the giving of valuable presents and expensive feasts and entertainments. Presents and feasts had probably another origin than that of naïve ostentation, but they acquired their utility for this purpose very early, and they have retained that character to the present; so that their utility in this respect has now long been the substantial ground on which these usages rest. Costly entertainments, such as the potlatch or the ball, are peculiarly adapted to serve this end. The competitor with whom the entertainer wishes to institute a comparison is, by this method, made to serve as a means to the end. He consumes vicariously for his host at the same time that he is a witness to the consumption of that excess of good things which his host is unable to dispose of single-handed, and he is also made to witness his host's facility in etiquette.

In the giving of costly entertainments other motives, of a more genial kind, are of course also present. The custom of festive gatherings probably originated in motives of conviviality and religion; these motives are also present in the later development, but they do not continue to be the sole motives. The latter-day leisure-class festivities and entertainments may continue in some slight degree to serve the religious need and in a higher degree the needs of recreation and conviviality, but they also serve an invidious purpose; and they serve it none the less effectually for having a colourable non-invidious ground in these more avowable motives. But the economic effect of these social amenities is not therefore lessened, either in the vicarious consumption of goods or in the exhibition of difficult and costly achievements in etiquette.

As wealth accumulates, the leisure class develops further in function and structure, and there arises a differentiation within the class. There is a more or less elaborate system of rank and grades. This differentiation is furthered by the inheritance of wealth and the consequent inheritance of gentility. With the inheritance of gentility goes the inheritance of obligatory leisure; and gentility of a sufficient potency to entail a life of leisure may be inherited without the complement of wealth required to maintain a dignified leisure. Gentle blood may be transmitted without goods enough to afford a reputably free consumption at one's ease. Hence results a class of impecunious gentlemen of leisure, incidentally referred to already. These half-caste gentlemen of leisure fall into a system of hierarchial gradations. Those who stand near the higher and the highest grades of the wealthy leisure class, in point of birth, or in point of wealth, or both, outrank the remoter-born and the pecuniarily weaker. These lower grades, especially the impecunious, or marginal, gentlemen of leisure, affiliate themselves by a system of dependence or fealty to the great ones; by so doing they gain an increment of repute, or of the means with which to lead a life of leisure, from their patron. * * *

Throughout this graduated scheme of vicarious leisure and vicarious consumption the rule holds that these offices must be performed in some such manner, or under some such circumstance or insignia, as shall point plainly to the master to whom this leisure or consumption pertains, and to whom therefore the resulting increment of good repute of right inures. The consumption and leisure executed by these persons for their master or patron represents an investment on his part with a view to an increase of good fame.

*   *   *

* * * [T]here is reason to believe that the institution of ownership has begun with the ownership of persons, primarily women. The incentives to acquiring such property have apparently been: (1) a propensity for dominance and coercion; (2) the utility of these persons as evidence of the prowess of their owner; (3) the utility of their services.

Personal service holds a peculiar place in the economic development. During the stage of quasi-peaceable industry, and especially during the earlier development of industry within the limits of this general stage, the utility of their services seems commonly to be the dominant motive to the acquisition of property in persons. Servants are valued for their services. But the dominance of this motive is not due to a decline in the absolute importance of the other two utilities possessed by servants. It is rather that the altered circumstances of life accentuate the utility of servants for this last-named purpose. Women and other slaves are highly valued, both as an evidence of wealth and as a means of accumulating wealth. Together with cattle, if the tribe is a pastoral one, they are the usual form of investment for a profit. To such an extent may female slavery give its character to the economic life under the quasi-peaceable culture that the woman even comes to serve as a unit of value among peoples occupying this cultural stage—as for instance in Homeric times. Where this is the case there need be little question but that the basis of the industrial system is chattel slavery and that the women are commonly slaves. The great, pervading human relation in such a system is that of master and servant. The accepted evidence of wealth is the possession of many women, and presently also of other slaves engaged in attendance on their master's person and in producing goods for him.

* * *

With the disappearance of servitude, the number of vicarious consumers attached to any one gentleman tends, on the whole, to decrease. The like is of course true, and perhaps in a still higher degree, of the number of dependents who perform vicarious leisure for him. In a general way, though not wholly nor consistently, these two groups coincide. The dependent who was first delegated for these duties was the wife, or the chief wife; and, as would be expected, in the later development of the institution, when the number of persons by whom these duties are customarily performed gradually narrows, the wife remains the last. In the higher grades of society a large volume of both these kinds of service is required; and here the wife is of course still assisted in the work by a more or less numerous corps of menials.

* * *

[N]o line of consumption affords a more apt illustration than expenditure on dress. It is especially the rule of the conspicuous waste of goods that finds expression in dress, although the other, related principles of pecuniary repute are also exemplified in the same contrivances. Other methods of putting one's pecuniary standing in evidence serve their end effectually, and other methods are in vogue always and everywhere; but expenditure on dress has this advantage over most other methods, that our apparel is always in evidence and affords an indication of our pecuniary standing to all observers at the first glance. It is also true that admitted expenditure for display is more obviously present, and is, perhaps, more universally practised in the matter of dress than in any other line of consumption. No one finds difficulty in assenting to the commonplace that the greater part of the expenditure incurred by all classes for apparel is incurred for the sake of a respectable appearance rather than for the protection of the person. And probably at no other point is the sense of shabbiness so keenly felt as it is if we fall short of the standard set by social usage in this matter of dress. It is true of dress in even a higher degree than of most other items of consumption, that people will undergo a very considerable degree of privation in the comforts or the necessaries of life in order to afford what is considered a decent amount of wasteful consumption; so that it is by no means an uncommon occurrence, in an inclement climate, for people to go ill clad in order to appear well dressed. And the commercial value of the goods used for clothing in any modern community is made up to a much larger extent of the fashionableness, the reputability of the goods than of the mechanical service which they render in clothing the person of the wearer.

*   *   *

But the function of dress as an evidence of ability to pay does not end with simply showing that the wearer consumes valuable goods in excess of what is required for physical comfort. Simple conspicuous waste of goods is effective and gratifying as far as it goes; it is good *prima facie* evidence of pecuniary success, and consequently *prima facie* evidence of social worth. But dress has subtler and more far-reaching possibilities than this crude, first-hand evidence of wasteful consumption only. If, in addition to showing that the wearer can afford to consume freely and uneconomically, it can also be shown in the same stroke that he or she is not under the necessity of earning a livelihood, the evidence of social worth is enhanced in a very considerable degree. Our dress, therefore, in order to serve its purpose effectually, should not only be expensive, but it should also make plain to all observers that the wearer is not engaged in any kind of productive labour. In the evolutionary process by which our system of dress has been elaborated into its present admirably perfect adaptation to its purpose, this subsidiary line of evidence has received due attention. A detailed examination of what passes in popular apprehension for elegant apparel will show that it is contrived at every point to convey the impression that the wearer does not habitually put forth any useful effort. It goes without saying that no apparel can be considered elegant, or even decent, if it shows the effect of manual labour on the part of the wearer, in the way of soil or wear. The pleasing effect of neat and spotless garments is chiefly, if not altogether, due to their carrying the suggestion of leisure—exemption from personal contact with industrial processes of any kind. Much of the charm that invests the patent-leather shoe, the stainless linen, the lustrous cylindrical hat, and the walking-stick, which so greatly enhance the native dignity of a gentleman, comes of their pointedly suggesting that the wearer cannot when so attired bear a hand in any employment that is directly and immediately of any human use. Elegant dress serves its purpose of elegance not only in that it is expensive, but also because it is the insignia of leisure. It not only shows that the wearer is able to consume a relatively large value, but it argues at the same time that he consumes without producing.

The dress of women goes even farther than that of men in the way of demonstrating the wearer's abstinence from productive employment. It needs no argument to enforce the generalisation that the more elegant styles of feminine bonnets go even farther towards making work impossible than does the man's high hat. The woman's shoe adds the so-called French heel to the evidence of enforced leisure afforded by its polish; because this high heel obviously makes any, even the simplest and most necessary manual work extremely difficult. The like is true even in a higher degree of the skirt and the rest of the drapery which characterises woman's dress. The substantial reason for our tenacious attachment to the skirt is just this: it is expensive and it hampers the wearer at every turn and incapacitates her for all useful exertion. The like is true of the feminine custom of wearing the hair excessively long.

But the woman's apparel not only goes beyond that of the modern man in the degree in which it argues exemption from labour; it also adds a peculiar and highly characteristic feature which differs in kind from anything habitually practised by the men. This feature is the class of contrivances of which the corset is the typical example. The corset is, in economic theory, substantially a mutilation, undergone for the purpose of lowering the subject's vitality and rendering her permanently and obviously unfit for work. It is true, the corset impairs the personal attractions of the wearer, but the loss suffered on that score is offset by the gain in reputability which comes of her visibly increased expensiveness and infirmity. It may broadly be set down that the womanliness of woman's apparel resolves itself, in point of substantial fact, into the more effective hindrance to useful exertion offered by the garments peculiar to women.

*   *   *

[T]he dress of women differs substantially from that of men. In woman's dress there is an obviously greater insistence on such features as testify to the wearer's exemption from or incapacity for all vulgarly productive employment. This characteristic of woman's apparel is of interest, not only as completing the theory of dress, but also as confirming what has already been said of the economic status of women, both in the past and in the present.

As has been seen in the discussion of woman's status under the heads of Vicarious Leisure and Vicarious Consumption, it has in the course of economic development become the office of the woman to consume vicariously for the head of the household; and her apparel is contrived with this object in view. It has come about that obviously productive labour is in a peculiar degree derogatory to respectable women, and therefore special pains should be taken in the construction of women's dress, to impress upon the beholder the fact (often indeed a fiction) that the wearer does not and can not habitually engage in useful work. Propriety requires respectable women to abstain more consistently from useful effort and to make more of a show of leisure than the men of the same social classes. It grates painfully on our nerves to contemplate the necessity of any wellbred woman's earning a livelihood by useful work. It is not "woman's sphere." Her sphere is within the household, which she should "beautify," and of which she should be the "chief ornament." The male head of the household is not currently spoken of as its ornament. This feature taken in conjunction with the other fact that propriety requires more unremitting attention to expensive display in the dress and other paraphernalia of women, goes to enforce the view already implied in what has gone before. By virtue of its descent from a patriarchal past, our social system makes it the woman's function in an especial degree to put in evidence her household's ability to pay. According to the modern civilised scheme of life, the good name of the household to which she belongs should be the special care of the woman; and the system of honorific expenditure and conspicuous leisure by which this good name is chiefly sustained is therefore the woman's sphere. In the ideal scheme, as it tends to realise itself in the life of the higher pecuniary classes, this attention to conspicuous waste of substance and effort should normally be the sole economic function of the woman.

At the stage of economic development at which the women were still in the full sense the property of the men, the performance of conspicuous leisure and consumption came to be part of the services required of them. The women being not their own masters, obvious expenditure and leisure on their part would redound to the credit of their master rather than to their own credit; and therefore the more expensive and the more obviously unproductive the women of the household are, the more creditable and more effective for the purpose of the reputability of the household or its head will their life be. So much so that the women have been required not only to afford evidence of a life of leisure, but even to disable themselves for useful activity.

It is at this point that the dress of men falls short of that of women, and for a sufficient reason. Conspicuous waste and conspicuous leisure are reputable because they are evidence of pecuniary strength; pecuniary strength is reputable or honorific because, in the last analysis, it argues success and superior force; therefore the evidence of waste and leisure put forth by any individual in his own behalf cannot consistently take such a form or be carried to such a pitch as to argue incapacity or marked discomfort on his part; as the exhibition would in that case show not superior force, but inferiority, and so defeat its own purpose. So, then, wherever wasteful expenditure and the show of abstention from effort is normally, or on an average, carried to the extent of showing obvious discomfort or voluntarily induced physical disability, there the immediate inference is that the individual in question does not perform this wasteful expenditure and undergo this disability for her own personal gain in pecuniary repute, but in behalf of some one else to whom she stands in a relation of economic dependence; a relation which in the last analysis must, in economic theory, reduce itself to a relation of servitude.

To apply this generalisation to women's dress, and put the matter in concrete terms: the high heel, the skirt, the impracticable bonnet, the corset, and the general disregard of the wearer's comfort which is an obvious feature of all civilised women's apparel, are so many items of evidence to the effect that in the modern civilised scheme of life the woman is still, in theory, the economic dependent of the man,—that, perhaps in a highly idealised sense, she still is the man's chattel. The homely reason for all this conspicuous leisure and attire on the part of women lies in the fact that they are servants to whom, in the differentiation of economic functions, has been delegated the office of putting in evidence their master's ability to pay.

*   *   *

MRS. BURTON KINGSLAND

[The Duties of a House-Guest] †

It does not require a Solomon to draw up a code of laws for the conduct of a guest. One may say, "It is not a difficult rôle to play," and yet any one who has had the least experience in entertaining knows that one guest may be a kill-joy and another an inspiration.

It begins with the invitation. A ready acceptance is flattering, and a prompt regret an evidence of good breeding and thoughtful consideration. It is a mistaken idea that a tardy regret seems to convey reluctance.

Having accepted an invitation to dine or visit at a friend's house, to quote a well-known society leader, "Nothing but your own funeral should prevent your keeping the engagement."

Punctuality is said to be a royal virtue, and the heads of the nations set an example of the most minute exactitude in that respect as a matter of pure courtesy. Nothing is more trying to the temper of hostess and cook than belated guests, and no one has the right to sacrifice others to his convenience.

We should show ourselves responsive to any effort made to entertain us, be easily amused, and let it be seen that we have come with the expectation of enjoying ourselves. There is an art in being entertained as well as in entertaining. Nothing is so gratifying to a hostess as a happy, animated guest. * * *

Those who second the efforts of their hostess instead of making demands upon her, who help her to entertain her other guests, are those whose presence comes to be considered one of the essentials of a successful social event. * * *

† From *Etiquette for All Occasions* (New York: Doubleday, Page, 1901) 294–305, 410–11.

It is, of course, superfluous to suggest that a guest is bound by every law of courtesy to conform in everything to the habits of the household as far as possible. The most agreeable visitors are those who make no trouble for any one, who find everything pleasant that their hostess arranges for them, who in little unsolicited ways are ready to make themselves useful. The gifts and accomplishments of all should be at the call of their hosts. Every one should be able to make some contribution to the general entertainment, and with cheerful alacrity, but with no shade of ostentation, be ready to comply with the slightest intimation of host and hostess of their desire for assistance.

A guest should never appear thoughtless of or indifferent to the convenience of the rest. Some persons think that because they are visitors, they need be only the recipients of attention. They should fall in readily with any plan proposed for their pleasure, but must not seem dependent for amusement. * * *

If anything unpleasant occur, a guest should see nothing, but maintain a discreet absent-mindedness; and the whole decalogue of good behavior is broken at once if one visitor criticises to another either a fellow guest or a member of the host's family, or discusses any of their affairs or interests unless it be to praise. * * *

[Well-bred guests] endeavor to show themselves at their best when others are invited to meet them, taking pains to second all the efforts of their hostess.

When private theatricals or musicals are given, the hostess, or others who superintend the affair, will always be grateful to those who, putting aside personal preference, enter heartily into the parts assigned them, more anxious to give pleasure than to display their accomplishments. An old proverb says, "Never mention a rope in the family of a man that was hanged." The application is obvious.

It were well to remember, too, that one's ailments are never matter of public interest, and self and its belongings should never form a prominent part in one's conversation. It is optional with a guest whether or not he will attend church with his hosts. No worldly etiquette imposes his presence, but it is usually felt to be more considerate for guests to attend church if provision is made to take them there. * * *

Guests should not allow their hosts to incur needless expense in their behalf. They should in a city pay their own car-fares, cab-hires, and express charges; but if the host will not permit this, it is in better taste to yield the point than to insist upon it. * * *

In case of a protracted visit, where the guest fits into the family life, one needs to observe all the little courtesies even more carefully than if one were to make a briefer stay. Not the least among obligations is the frequent self-effacement, to give the household the opportunity of privacy.

The feeing of servants upon one's departure from a friend's house seems to some to be in questionable taste, but it has become an almost universal custom, and principles must sometimes make concessions to popularity where no question of right and wrong is involved.

In England the omission of the custom would be regarded as an evidence of parsimony or of ignorance, and it must be confessed that, human nature being what it is, work is done with better grace and with less care to the hosts when self-interest supplies a spur.

It is sometimes a matter of embarrassment to know just how much one ought to give. It is a pretty safe rule that if a woman has spent a few days or a week at a friend's house, a dollar may be given to the housemaid who has cared for her room, and if she has given personal service, brushing gowns, bringing the breakfast-tray, etc.—a dollar and a half at least and two dollars at most will be sufficient. Sometimes the maid of the hostess performs these services for the guest, in which case a dollar should be given her and one to the housemaid. Any *extra* service should be recognized by an additional half-dollar. A single woman rarely tips the butler, but she should "remember" the coachman who drives her to the station. Fifty cents or a dollar may be given him, according to his service during her visit. * * *

One should endeavor, in timing one's departure, to make as little trouble as possible for one's host, whose convenience may be better considered in the choice of one train than another. Should it be necessary to take an early train, it is considerate for a woman guest to urge her hostess not to rise earlier than her habit is, but to let her say good-bye the night before, and trust to the good offices of some trusty servant to see her off. A man visitor would take this for granted, and bid his hostess and her family farewell before retiring for the night.

When taking leave of one's hosts, adieux should be said to each member of the family, and farewell messages sent to any who may not be present.

There is a suggestion that ought not to be required, and yet is of such importance that it were best, perhaps, not to omit its mention. It is that a guest should hold sacred anything that he or she may have learned of the family life, or of the peculiarities of any member of a household where hospitality has been accepted. A person visiting at different houses cannot be too careful to avoid repeating anything that may reflect in the slightest degree upon his entertainers, or satisfy the ignoble curiosity of one at the expense of another.

Such social traitors there have been, but their popularity is usually short-lived, every one rightly judging that nothing secures his immunity from like treatment, where no honorable reticence can be counted upon.

*   *   *

Yacht Etiquette

A man opulent enough to have his own yacht, needs little tutoring how to make it a pleasure to his friends for a few hours' sail or for days on end. Where unmarried men and women compose a party, a chaperon is a necessity.

A "gig" or launch conveys the guests to the yacht from the shore, and the host stands at the gangway to greet them as they arrive and to assist them on deck. After which he has only to follow the rules which govern social functions on land.

The attention due the chaperon—whom he places at his right hand at table—and the pleasure of his guests will thereafter be his agreeable duty. Special care and attention will of course be shown to any one affected by the motion.

The proper entertainments for a yacht in harbor are luncheons, dinners, dances, and short cruises, the preparations for which need not be elaborate.

* * *

C. LOTHROP HIGGINS

[Vocations for the Trained Woman: Millinery] †

Millinery as an occupation offers to the young woman who has had a college training a field of activity where constant demands are being made for that ability which has already proved to be of great use to the business woman as well as to the professional.

There is plenty of room for good brain work in the millinery business. The demand to-day is for those who can not only perform the work planned and assigned to them, but plan work for others and direct them in it. To be a millinery designer or a so-called first-class trimmer requires much more than the ability to put right colors together, or to evolve a stylish hat. One must, in addition, have had the training in which quick thought and action are called upon at all times, for under her direction the makers, copyists, and apprentices are guided in every part of their work. On the accuracy of her orders, as given to them, depend largely the successes or failures in their work, and to bring out the best results from each individual is almost entirely a question of her temperament. The responsibilities of the trimmer, therefore, do not end with her own work. She requires great capacity and ability along many lines. In her work, originality counts for much; also artistic conceptions, a trained eye for form and color as well as accuracy in lines and angles. But in addition there must be ability to impart to others and to direct and guide them. All these are the elements which combine to make a first-class trimmer.

Trimmers and designers are, as a rule, people of temperament and natural artistic ability. Add to these qualifications a well-developed mind,

† From *Vocations for the Trained Woman: Opportunities Other Than Teaching*, ed. Agnes F. Perkins, A.M. (Boston: Women's Educational and Industrial Union, 1910) 113–15.

and the result is a work-woman to whom any establishment is willing to pay just tribute in a financial way. The demand for such women is always in excess of the supply. A good trimmer, even in the smaller cities, commands a salary of $20 or even more a week. In our larger cities $25 and upwards, and to some even $35 and more, is paid. Those who devote themselves exclusively to designing of course demand still larger salaries, and are hard to find at any price. * * *

So far, apprenticeship has been the general means of training. Girls have begun in the workroom, usually as a result of circumstances not from special aptitude, and have been advanced step by step as ability or demand necessitated. To-day trade schools and domestic arts departments are rising on all sides, designed to save the long period of apprenticeship. As yet, however, the practical milliner has had too little experience with graduates of these schools to tell whether such training can be substituted for that gained by actual experience in the workroom.

The dark side of the millinery business lies in the short seasons. People leave the city earlier every year, and return later. The work, therefore, that should take months in accomplishment, must be crowded into a few short weeks. The ability of quick workers is in great demand, and yet you will learn in any millinery establishment that a very small proportion of those employed in its workroom are first-class workers.

In more than twenty years of business experience I have found the best results brought about by those women who have had the advantages of a good education. Better system, better perception of the needs and the individuality of the customer, characterize their effort, while their interest in the work has raised the standard in the millinery business both in the Old World and in the New.

The salesroom of an exclusive millinery house offers to a woman with tact, patience, and adaptability to circumstances and customers, an established position, where the cultured, college-bred woman has an opportunity to exercise in many ways the results of her training. A saleswoman with artistic inclinations and a pleasing address, who is interested in her business relations, may in a few seasons build up a personal following of customers, not only reflecting her good judgment but adding materially to her value and to that of the house employing her. A first-class saleswoman is not easily found, and she demands a salary ranging from $15 to $30 a week.

* * *

MRS. JOHN VAN VORST
and MARIE VAN VORST

[The Experience of a Lady as a Factory Girl]†

*   *   *

As I draw nearer the factory I move with a stream of fellow workers pouring toward the glass cage of the timekeeper. He greets me and starts me on my upward journey with a wish that I shall not get discouraged, a reminder that the earnest worker always makes a way for herself.

"What will you do about your name?" "What will you do with your hair and your hands?" "How can you deceive people?" These are some of the questions I had been asked by my friends.

Before any one had cared or needed to know my name it was morning of the second day, and my assumed name seemed by that time the only one I had ever had. As to hair and hands, a half-day's work suffices for their undoing. And my disguise is so successful I have deceived not only others but myself. I have become with desperate reality a factory girl, alone, inexperienced, friendless. I am making $4.20 a week and spending $3 of this for board alone, and I dread not being strong enough to keep my job. I climb endless stairs, am given a white cap and an apron, and my life as a factory girl begins. I become part of the ceaseless, unrelenting mechanism kept in motion by the poor.

The factory I have chosen has been built contemporaneously with reforms and sanitary inspection. There are clean, well-aired rooms, hot and cold water with which to wash, places to put one's hat and coat, an obligatory uniform for regular employees, hygienic and moral advantages of all kinds, ample space for work without crowding.

Side by side in rows of tens or twenties we stand before our tables waiting for the seven o'clock whistle to blow. In their white caps and blue frocks and aprons, the girls in my department, like any unfamiliar class, all look alike. My first task is an easy one; anybody could do it. On the stroke of seven my fingers fly. I place a lid of paper in a tin jar-top, over it a cork; this I press down with both hands, tossing the cover, when done, into a pan. In spite of myself I hurry; I cannot work fast enough—I outdo my companions. How can they be so slow? I have finished three dozen while they are doing two. Every nerve, every muscle is offering some of its energy. Over in one corner the machinery for sealing the jars groans and roars; the mingled sounds of filling, washing, wiping, packing, comes to my eager ears as an accompaniment for the simple work assigned to me. One hour passes, two, three hours; I fit ten, twenty, fifty dozen caps, and still my energy keeps up.

† From *The Woman Who Toils, Being the Experience of Two Ladies as Factory Girls* (New York: Doubleday, Page, 1903) 22–27.

The forewoman is a pretty girl of twenty. Her restless eyes, her metal-
lic voice are the messengers who would know all. I am afraid of her. I
long to please her. I am sure she must be saying *"How well the new girl
works."*

Conversation is possible among those whose work has become
mechanical. Twice I am sent to the storeroom for more caps. In these
brief moments my companions volunteer a word of themselves.

"I was out to a ball last night," the youngest one says. "I stayed so late
I didn't feel a bit like getting up this morning."

"That's nothing," another retorts. "There's hardly an evening we don't
have company at the house, music or somethin'; I never get enough
rest."

And on my second trip the pale creature with me says:

"I'm in deep mourning. My mother died last Friday week. It's awful
lonely without her. Seems as though I'd never get over missing her. I
miss her *dreadful*. Perhaps by and by I'll get used to it."

"Oh, no, you won't," the answer comes from a girl with short skirts.
"You'll never get used to it. My ma's been dead eight years next month
and I dreamt about her all last night. I can't get her out o' me mind."

Born into dirt and ugliness, disfigured by effort, they have the same
heritage as we: joys and sorrows, grief and laughter. With them as with
us gaiety is up to its old tricks, tempting from graver rivals, making duty
an alien. Grief is doing her ugly work: hollowing round cheeks, black-
ening bright eyes, putting her weight of leaden loneliness in hearts here-
tofore light with youth.

When I have fitted 110 dozen tin caps the forewoman comes and
changes my job. She tells me to haul and load up some heavy crates
with pickle jars. I am wheeling these back and forth when the twelve
o'clock whistle blows. Up to that time the room has been one big dynamo,
each girl a part of it. With the first moan of the noon signal the dynamo
comes to life. It is hungry; it has friends and favourites—news to tell.
We herd down to a big dining-room and take our places, five hundred
of us in all. The newspaper bundles are unfolded. The ménu varies
little: bread and jam, cake and pickles, occasionally a sausage, a bit of
cheese or a piece of stringy cold meat. In ten minutes the repast is over.
The dynamo has been fed; there are twenty minutes of leisure spent in
dancing, singing, resting, and conversing chiefly about young men and
"sociables."

At 12:30 sharp the whistle draws back the life it has given. I return to
my job. My shoulders are beginning to ache. My hands are stiff, my
thumbs almost blistered. The enthusiasm I had felt is giving way to a
numbing weariness. I look at my companions now in amazement. How
can they keep on so steadily, so swiftly? Cases are emptied and refilled;
bottles are labeled, stamped and rolled away; jars are washed, wiped and
loaded, and still there are more cases, more jars, more bottles. Oh! the
monotony of it, the never-ending supply of work to be begun and finished, begun and finished, begun and finished! Now and then some one

cuts a finger or runs a splinter under the flesh; once the mustard machine broke—and still the work goes on, on, on! New girls like myself, who had worked briskly in the morning, are beginning to loiter. Out of the washing-tins hands come up red and swollen, only to be plunged again into hot dirty water. Would the whistle never blow? Once I pause an instant, my head dazed and weary, my ears strained to bursting with the deafening noise. Quickly a voice whispers in my ear:

"You'd better not stand there doin' nothin'. If *she* catches you she'll give it to you."

On! on! bundle of pains! For you this is one day's work in a thousand of peace and beauty. For those about you this is the whole of daylight, this is the winter dawn and twilight, this is the glorious summer noon, this is all day, this is every day, this is *life*. Rest is only a bit of a dream, snatched when the sleeper's aching body lets her close her eyes for a moment in oblivion.

Out beyond the chimney tops the snowfields and the river turn from gray to pink, and still the work goes on. Each crate I lift grows heavier, each bottle weighs an added pound. Now and then some one lends a helping hand.

"Tired, ain't you? This is your first day, ain't it?"

The acid smell of vinegar and mustard penetrates everywhere. My ankles cry out pity. Oh! to sit down an instant!

"Tidy up the table," some one tells me; "we're soon goin' home."

Home! I think of the stifling fumes of fried food, the dim haze in the kitchen where my supper waits me; the children, the band of drifting workers, the shrill, complaining voice of the hired mother. This is home.

I sweep and set to rights, limping, lurching along. At last the whistle blows! In a swarm we report; we put on our things and get away into the cool night air. I have stood ten hours; I have fitted 1,300 corks; I have hauled and loaded 4,000 jars of pickles. My pay is seventy cents.

*   *   *

MARY CADWALADER JONES

[Working Girls' Clubs]†

A Working Girls' Society or Club, as defined officially in their own reports, is "an organization formed among busy girls and young women, to secure by co-operation means of self-support, opportunities for social intercourse, and the development of higher and nobler aims."

It is now ten years since the first was started, and at a convention held in New York in 1890, the clubs of New York, Brooklyn, Boston, and

---

† From "Woman's Opportunities in Town and Country," *The Woman's Book* 2 (New York: Charles Scribner's Sons, 1894) 201–210. Mary Cadwalader Jones was Edith Wharton's sister-in-law, and the book in which this essay appeared was published by the same firm that published *The House of Mirth* eleven years later. It is very likely that Wharton knew of this essay and read it.

Philadelphia were represented, and papers were read by many girls and women who had been interested in them from the beginning. One of these, by Miss Iselin, now Mrs. Henderson, has valuable suggestions as to the best way of setting to work to get one up, and may be quoted:

"You must bear in mind that the members of a Working Girls' Club are to be chiefly working women and girls who come home too tired, after a long day in the shop or factory, to make any great exertion, even with pleasure as the result. Therefore, start the club in the neighborhood from which you expect to draw members. * * * [I]n all the cases the greatest assistance in this matter can be had by consulting with members of other clubs, if there are others in the place, or, if there are none, with the prospective members; for I take it for granted that no one will be foolish enough to try to start a society in any place without first having some personal acquaintance with working women and girls, either in club life or in the many other ways in which such personal relations are possible. * * *

"After having talked matters over with those seven or eight [interested working girls], as well as with the wage-earners who have promised you their aid, hire a floor or two floors, sub-letting one to a woman, who in return for reduced rent keeps your rooms clean and gives you the use of her kitchen for cooking classes. In some cases it is best to take the whole house, sub-letting the rooms that are not needed; in this way you have the control of the house, which is very important; but, of course, you run the risk of having the rooms vacant on your hands. Furnish the club-rooms simply, cocoa matting on the floors, plenty of strong camp-chairs, deal tables covered with bright cloths, colored prints and photographs on the walls, two lamps and such ornaments as you can collect, and you will have as pretty and cheerful club-rooms as anyone can desire. Of course, a piano is indispensable. Furnishing and your first month's rent will cost from two hundred and seventy-five to three hundred and twenty-five dollars—it ought not to cost more, and if anything is given it will naturally cost less. This money must be given or obtained in some way by outsiders. It does not seem possible for club members to raise it, unless the amount is borrowed on easy terms and the future club members pay it back by fairs or entertainments; but there are few, I fancy, who are brave enough to start with so heavy a load on their backs. * * *

"Now for a few words as to the running expenses of a club and the possibility of meeting them out of the membership dues. I believe the rents are higher in the city of New York than anywhere else in this country, so if it is possible to make a club entirely self-supporting in New York, it would be easier in other cities, and still easier in villages. The usual club dues are from twenty to twenty-five cents a month, so that a club with a regular paying membership of two hundred, which in my opinion is quite large enough, would have at the former rate an income of forty dollars per month, and at the latter fifty dollars. In small places the membership will hardly reach two hundred, but the expenses will also be smaller. I think it can be proved that the monthly expenses of a club are about as follows: Rent, $25; coal, $4; gas, $3; cleaning, $4; piano, $4; total $40. When the rent is higher I should suggest that the dues be twenty-five cents a month, which gives an extra ten dollars. Of course this does not leave any margin for extra expenses, but these should and could be met by especial efforts on the part of club members in the way of small entertainments. I know that in many cases it has been found difficult, nay impossible, to make clubs self-supporting, but that it ought to be the aim, almost the highest aim, of every club, I must maintain; until this is accomplished Working Girls' Societies will not, in my opinion, have reached their greatest usefulness. A Working Girls' Club which is nothing but a charitable society is a contradiction in terms. I do not mean by this to disparage the many excellent charitable societies started for the benefit of working girls, but I do mean that, with our avowed principles and aims, we are not strictly honest unless we strain every nerve in the direction of making our clubs self-supporting."

*   *   *

Miss Florence Bayard Lockwood contributed the following useful hints regarding the literary element in club life: "Almost the first act of a new club is to get together a few books as a nucleus, and sometimes these books are bought from a fund set apart for the purpose. But very often the club has not the money, and the first books are given. It may not be out of place here to suggest to anyone who is going to give books to a club library, that old or second-hand interesting books are always most acceptable, but that schoolbooks or books whose pages the original owners themselves have never been tempted to turn, are not the best material for the mind of a tired working girl. It is a curious fact how willing people are to send books to a club library which they themselves would never dream of reading.

"In the New York club libraries at present, the proportion of fiction averages two-thirds; one-third of the members averaging two books a month. Averages, however, are rather deceitful things, as in one club the proportion of members taking out books rises to over one-half the membership, while in another it sinks to an eighth. In all the clubs the different books are taken out by the same members, who may be said to form the reading public of the clubs. I give here the books most in demand, as a suggestion to anyone buying new books for their library: Dickens heads the list, then Scott and the Schönberg-Cotta series; 'Ben Hur;' 'Queechy,' by Miss Warner; Grace Aguilar's works; George Eliot; Mrs. A. D. Whitney; Mrs. Wister's translations from the German; 'John Halifax;' the Elsie series; E. P. Roe; 'Little Lord Fauntleroy;' Thackeray, Miss Alcott. In one club there has been a constant demand for 'Looking Backward,' and there is always a demand for short stories.

*   *   *

A recent article in *Scribner's Magazine*, written by Mrs. Davidge, who, as Miss Clara Potter, was an earnest worker in the clubs from the start, states that they have now more than two thousand members in the city of New York alone, and that in 1893 the sum of $5,156.25 was paid out in dues from the pockets of working-girls. * * * [I]f paid teachers are employed for extra classes an additional fee is charged, and only those join who wish to pay it. Physical culture and singing have proved to be the most popular of these classes, but instruction has also been given, sometimes by volunteers, in dress-making, cooking, millinery, first aid to the injured, etc., each class having the use of the club-room on a certain evening in the week, leaving it free for general attendance on social occasions, business meetings, and the nights on which practical talks are held under the management of the women of leisure who are interested in the club. Sometimes a course is chosen, such as "Famous Women," "Talks on Hygiene," and the like, or general subjects are discussed, as "What is Wealth?" or, "When women take men's places and cut down wages, what is the effect upon the home?" As Mrs. Davidge justly says, "The success of a series of such talks naturally depends largely upon the leader and on her ability to impart information clearly, and in an interesting manner. It is also important to draw as many girls as possible into the discussion that follows the 'talk,' to evoke the opinion of 'modest members and to hold the attention of all.'

"It is difficult to imagine anything better for a girl who has everything she wants at home, than to be brought into friendly contact with other girls who are obliged to face the hard side of life, but it is not altogether easy to establish such a relation, because we Americans are proverbially independent, sensitive, and intolerant of the least approach to anything like condescension." Three years ago Miss Lockwood sent to *Scribner's Magazine* an Open Letter upon this subject, which is so true and suggestive that it should be read by anyone who is interested in the question of how far one class can help another. She wrote:

"It is personality, I think, which is the weightiest factor, and which makes success or failure. Good as the general work may be, intelligent as are the lines upon which it is carried on, faithful as are the workers, it is the personal force which, in nine cases out of ten, fits the keystone in the arch, binds the girls together, and makes the club a success; and one may add, it is the giving of that personal force which so often breaks down the worker in the end. It is this, and not the literal amount of time and labor and wisdom given, although they too must play their part— this personal element which in theory is so ignored.

"The clubs need workers, need ladies to help carry on and extend the work; there is room now for any number of women: ten, twenty, or a hundred can have their hands filled with work, if they will come forward and stretch them out to us and help us try to make life happier and more full of meaning, and freer from temptation, for the girls and women who have to work for their living in our great stores and factories. Not to raise up those who fall—that task is for others—but to help the weak-hearted and the strong-hearted to bear more joyfully the burden of life and difficulties and temptations which would daunt the bravest and the strongest.

"We want the best you can give us; we want women who come to the work *con amore*, not merely to do the orthodox modicum demanded now by society from all unmarried or childless women—and we don't want only the women who have nothing else to do. * * * [W]e need the best you can give us, and that it is not only to the women who can devote their energies exclusively to the work, but also to the society belle, the clever writer, the crack lawn-tennis player, and the happy daughter, that we turn.

"The working girls want more than classes and club-rooms—they want inspiration and sympathy; often an individual inspiration and sympathy to fit their individual needs. The best that we can give them is our best morally and mentally, the results of our most earnest prayer and practice, of our clearest and hardest thinking. The influence on the worker is perhaps one of the best results of the work—although it may not be an ostensible end in view—for one cannot with honesty, nor indeed with any comfort to oneself, lead a life outside the club wilfully inconsistent with the light in which one appears to the girls; for, never mind how little we desire to be looked upon as examples, we are looked upon as such even by the girls with whom we have least personal contact, and we are apt to find that their belief in us, and constant reference to us, is a pretty sharp reminder of our own shortcomings, even in such minor matters as untidy bureau drawers and buttonless boots—not to speak of the graver questions of living which are continually raised, and whose solution is complicated by the real differences of position and education.

"There are two kindred questions about which there has been and still is much controversy, and, I think, many serious mistakes made: First, in underestimating the intelligence of the girls, particularly in practical matters, in which it is apt to be far greater than our own; and secondly, in belittling our advantages in order to conciliate their prejudices. In many cases these prejudices do not exist, and even when they do the differences in our position and education are sure to come to the front sooner or later, and by frankly recognizing them in the beginning as an advantage, we prevent their being regarded later on as a barrier. The girls are sure to end by knowing that we keep servants, wear evening dresses, and go to the opera; and by plainly speaking of these things when necessary (the necessity will be rare) as comforts won for us by our husbands' or our fathers' intelligence and labor, we make the distinction in our way of living more one of degree than one of kind. When once recognized, the truth will make our relations with the girls of more value than when it existed on an ignorant or mistaken foundation.

"The very leisure and knowledge we are able to put at their disposal comes from this difference of conditions, and it is shirking our responsibility as women of a leisure class when we attempt to pretend that our conditions of life are the same as theirs. The newspapers in this country are successful in giving the working classes a false idea of the occupations and pleasures of the 'upper classes.' They represent them in all their most sensational and regrettable moments, and but little record is made of the majority of well-to-do and educated people with whom plain living and high thinking have not come to be a dead letter. In our most natural and laudable efforts not to patronize the girls, we are apt to forget that we are foregoing the natural advantages of our birthrights in attempting to appear to them as anomalous women from nowhere, instead of ladies whose life and education in perhaps wealthy homes, has inspired us with the desire to share what we consider our real advantages with our less fortunate sisters.

"It is a great pleasure, this club work—work which any woman with a warm heart will find repaying. Much has been said, but it would be difficult to say enough, of the gratitude and responsiveness of the girls to any effort made in their behalf. No one who has not had the experience can realize the pleasure and stimulus of being looked up to and followed, however undeservedly, by a clubful of hard-working girls. The labor is great, but the rewards are infinitely greater, and there are not many of us, I fancy, who would not tell you that they had gained vastly more than they had given."

CHARLES DANA GIBSON

[Marrying for Money]†

The Latest Nobleman. "Girls, girls, don't press his grace. He can only take one of you, and with him it is purely a matter of business."

†From Fairfax Downey, *Portrait of an Era as Drawn by C. D. Gibson* (New York: Charles Scribner's Sons, 1936) 112–13, 120, 139, 283.

Two Blind Women.

The Merry-Go-Round.

A Castle in the Air. These young girls who marry old millionaires should stop dreaming.

CHARLOTTE PERKINS GILMAN

[Women and Economics]†

* * * We are the only animal species in which the female depends on the male for food, the only animal species in which the sex-relation is also an economic relation. With us an entire sex lives in a relation of economic dependence upon the other sex, and the economic relation is combined with the sex-relation. The economic status of the human female is relative to the sex-relation.

It is commonly assumed that this condition also obtains among other animals, but such is not the case. There are many birds among which, during the nesting season, the male helps the female feed the young, and partially feeds her; and, with certain of the higher carnivora, the male helps the female feed the young, and partially feeds her. In no case does she depend on him absolutely, even during this season, save in that of the hornbill, where the female, sitting on her nest in a hollow tree, is walled in with clay by the male, so that only her beak projects; and then he feeds her while the eggs are developing. But even the female hornbill does not expect to be fed at any other time. The female bee and ant are economically dependent, but not on the male. The workers are females, too, specialized to economic functions solely. And with the carnivora, if the young are to lose one parent, it might far better be the father: the mother is quite competent to take care of them herself. With many species, as in the case of the common cat, she not only feeds herself and her young, but has to defend the young against the male as well. In no case is the female throughout her life supported by the male.

In the human species the condition is permanent and general, though there are exceptions, and though the present century is witnessing the beginnings of a great change in this respect. We have not been accustomed to face this fact beyond our loose generalization that it was "natural," and that other animals did so, too.

To many this view will not seem clear at first; and the case of working peasant women or females of savage tribes, and the general household industry of women, will be instanced against it. Some careful and honest discrimination is needed to make plain to ourselves the essential facts of the relation, even in these cases. The horse, in his free natural condition, is economically independent. He gets his living by his own exertions, irrespective of any other creature. The horse, in his present condition of slavery, is economically dependent. He gets his living at the hands of his master; and his exertions, though strenuous, bear no direct relation

---

† From *Women and Economics: A Study of the Economic Relation Between Men and Women as a Factor in Social Evolution* (Boston: Small, Maynard, 1900) 5–9, 63–64, 86–93.

to his living. In fact, the horses who are the best fed and cared for and the horses who are the hardest worked are quite different animals. The horse works, it is true; but what he gets to eat depends on the power and will of his master. His living comes through another. He is economically dependent. So with the hard-worked savage or peasant women. Their labor is the property of another: they work under another will; and what they receive depends not on their labor, but on the power and will of another. They are economically dependent. This is true of the human female both individually and collectively.

In studying the economic position of the sexes collectively, the difference is most marked. As a social animal, the economic status of man rests on the combined and exchanged services of vast numbers of progressively specialized individuals. The economic progress of the race, its maintenance at any period, its continued advance, involve the collective activities of all the trades, crafts, arts, manufactures, inventions, discoveries, and all the civil and military institutions that go to maintain them. The economic status of any race at any time, with its involved effect on all the constituent individuals, depends on their world-wide labors and their free exchange. Economic progress, however, is almost exclusively masculine. Such economic processes as women have been allowed to exercise are of the earliest and most primitive kind. Were men to perform no economic services save such as are still performed by women, our racial status in economics would be reduced to most painful limitations.

To take from any community its male workers would paralyze it economically to a far greater degree than to remove its female workers. The labor now performed by the women could be performed by the men, requiring only the setting back of many advanced workers into earlier forms of industry; but the labor now performed by the men could not be performed by the women without generations of effort and adaptation. Men can cook, clean, and sew as well as women; but the making and managing of the great engines of modern industry, the threading of earth and sea in our vast systems of transportion, the handling of our elaborate machinery of trade, commerce, government,—these things could not be done so well by women in their present degree of economic development.

This is not owing to lack of the essential human faculties necessary to such achievements, nor to any inherent disability of sex, but to the present condition of woman, forbidding the development of this degree of economic ability. The male human being is thousands of years in advance of the female in economic status. Speaking collectively, men produce and distribute wealth; and women receive it at their hands. As men hunt, fish, keep cattle, or raise corn, so do women eat game fish, beef, or corn. As men go down to the sea in ships, and bring coffee and spices and silks and gems from far away, so do women partake of the coffee and spices and silks and gems the men bring.

The economic status of the human race in any nation, at any time, is governed mainly by the activities of the male: the female obtains her share in the racial advance only through him.

* * *

With the growth of civilization, we have gradually crystallized into law the visible necessity for feeding the helpless female; and even old women are maintained by their male relatives with a comfortable assurance. But to this day—save, indeed, for the increasing army of women wage-earners, who are changing the face of the world by their steady advance toward economic independence—the personal profit of women bears but too close a relation to their power to win and hold the other sex. From the odalisque with the most bracelets to the débutante with the most bouquets, the relation still holds good,—woman's economic profit comes through the power of sex-attraction.

When we confront this fact boldly and plainly in the open market of vice, we are sick with horror. When we see the same economic relation made permanent, established by law, sanctioned and sanctified by religion, covered with flowers and incense and all accumulated sentiment, we think it innocent, lovely, and right. The transient trade we think evil. The bargain for life we think good. But the biological effect remains the same. In both cases the female gets her food from the male by virtue of her sex-relationship to him. In both cases, perhaps even more in marrriage because of its perfect acceptance of the situation, the female of genus homo, still living under natural law, is inexorably modified to sex in an increasing degree.

* * *

Another instance of so grossly unjust, so palpable, so general an evil that it has occasionally aroused some protest even from our dull consciousness is this: the enforced attitude of the woman toward marriage. To the young girl, as has been previously stated, marriage is the one road to fortune, to life. She is born highly specialized as a female: she is carefully educated and trained to realize in all ways her sex-limitations and her sex-advantages. What she has to gain even as a child is largely gained by feminine tricks and charms. Her reading, both in history and fiction, treats of the same position for women; and romance and poetry give it absolute predominance. Pictorial art, music, the drama, society, everything, tells her that she is *she*, and that all depends on whom she marries. Where young boys plan for what they will achieve and attain, young girls plan for whom they will achieve and attain. Little Ellie and her swan's nest among the reeds is a familiar illustration. It is the lover on the red roan steed she planned for. It is Lancelot riding through the sheaves that called the Lady from her loom at Shalott: "he" is the coming world.

With such a prospect as this before her; with an organization specially developed to this end; with an education adding every weight of precept and example, of wisdom and virtue, to the natural instincts; with a social environment the whole machinery of which is planned to give the girl a chance to see and to be seen, to provide her with "opportunities"; and with all the pressure of personal advantage and self-interest added to the sex-instinct,—what one would logically expect is a society full of desperate and eager husband-hunters, regarded with popular approval.

Not at all! Marriage is the woman's proper sphere, her divinely ordered place, her natural end. It is what she is born for, what she is trained for, what she is exhibited for. It is, moreover, her means of honorable livelihood and advancement. *But*—she must not even look as if she wanted it! She must not turn her hand over to get it. She must sit passive as the seasons go by, and her "chances" lessen with each year. Think of the strain on a highly sensitive nervous organism to have so much hang on one thing, to see the possibility of attaining it grow less and less yearly, and to be forbidden to take any step toward securing it! This she must bear with dignity and grace to the end.

To what end? To the end that, if she does not succeed in being chosen, she becomes a thing of mild popular contempt, a human being with no further place in life save as an attachée, a dependant upon more fortunate relatives, an old maid. The open derision and scorn with which unmarried women used to be treated is lessening each year in proportion to their advance in economic independence. But it is not very long since the popular proverb, "Old maids lead apes in hell," was in common use; since unwelcome lovers urged their suit with the awful argument that they might be the last askers; since the hapless lady in the wood prayed for a husband, and, when the owl answered, "Who? who?" cried, "Anybody, good Lord!" There is still a pleasant ditty afloat as to the "Three Old Maids of Lynn," who did not marry when they could, and could not when they would.

The cruel and absurd injustice of blaming the girl for not getting what she is allowed no effort to obtain seems unaccountable; but it becomes clear when viewed in connection with the sexuo-economic relation. Although marriage is a means of livelihood, it is not honest employment where one can offer one's labor without shame, but a relation where the support is given outright, and enforced by law in return for the functional service of the woman, the "duties of wife and mother." Therefore no honorable woman can ask for it. It is not only that the natural feminine instinct is to retire, as that of the male is to advance, but that, because marriage means support, a woman must not ask a man to support her. It is economic beggary as well as a false attitude from a sex point of view.

Observe the ingenious cruelty of the arrangement. It is just as humanly natural for a woman as for a man to want wealth. But, when her wealth is made to come through the same channels as her love, she is forbidden to ask for it by her own sex-nature and by business honor. Hence the millions of mismade marriages with "anybody, good Lord!" Hence the million broken hearts which must let all life pass, unable to make any attempt to stop it. Hence the many "maiden aunts," elderly sisters and daughters, unattached women everywhere, who are a burden on their male relatives and society at large. This is changing for the better, to be sure, but changing only through the advance of economic independence for women. A "bachelor maid" is a very different thing from "an old maid."

This, then, is the reason for the Andromeda position of the possibly-to-be-married young woman, and for the ridicule and reproach meted out to her. Since women are viewed wholly as creatures of sex even by one another, and since everything is done to add to their young powers of sex-attraction; since they are marriageable solely on this ground, unless, indeed, "a fortune" has been added to their charms,—failure to marry is held a clear proof of failure to attract, a lack of sex-value. And, since they have no other value, save in a low order of domestic service, they are quite naturally despised. What else is the creature good for, failing in the functions for which it was created? The scorn of male and female alike falls on this sexless thing: she is a human failure.

It is not strange, therefore, though just as pitiful,—this long chapter of patient, voiceless, dreary misery in the lives of women; and it is not strange, either, to see the marked and steady change in opinion that follows the development of other faculties in woman besides those of sex. Now that she is a person as well as a female, filling economic relation to society, she is welcomed and accepted as a human creature, and need not marry the wrong man for her bread and butter. So sharp is the reaction from this unlovely yoke that there is a limited field of life to-day wherein women choose not to marry, preferring what they call "their independence,"—a new-born, hard-won, dear-bought independence. That any living woman should prefer it to home and husband, to love and motherhood, throws a fierce light on what women must have suffered for lack of freedom before.

This tendency need not be feared, however. It is merely a reaction, and a most natural one. It will pass as naturally, as more and more women become independent, when marriage is not the price of liberty. The fear exhibited that women generally, once fully independent, will not marry, is proof of how well it has been known that only dependence forced them to marriage as it was. There will be needed neither bribe nor punishment to force women to true marriage with independence.

Along this line it is most interesting to mark the constant struggle between natural instinct and natural law, and social habit and social law, through all our upward course. Beginning with the natural functions and instincts of sex, holding her great position as selecter of the best among competing males, woman's beautiful work is to improve the race by right marriage. The feeling by which this is accomplished, growing finer as we become more civilized, develops into that wide, deep, true, and lasting love which is the highest good to individual human beings. Following its current, we have always reverenced and admired "true love"; and our romances, from the earliest times, abound in praise of the princess who marries the page or prisoner, venerating the selective power in woman, choosing "the right man" for his own sake. Directly against this runs the counter-current, resulting in the marriage of con- venience, a thing which the true inner heart of the world has always hated. Young Lockinvar is not an eternal hero for nothing. The person- ified type of a great social truth is sure of a long life. The poor young hero, handsome, brave, good, but beset with difficulties, stands ever against the wealth and power of the bad man. The woman is pulled hither and thither between them, and the poor hero wins in the end. That he is heaped with honor and riches, after all, merely signifies our recognition that he is the higher good. This is better than a sun-myth. It is a race-myth, and true as truth.

So we have it among us in life to-day, endlessly elaborated and weak- ened by profuse detail, as is the nature of that life, but there yet. The girl who marries the rich old man or the titled profligate is condemned by the popular voice; and the girl who marries the poor young man, and helps him live his best, is still approved by the same great arbiter. And yet why should we blame the woman for pursuing her vocation? Since marriage is her only way to get money, why should she not try to get money in that way? Why cast the weight of all self-interest on the "prac- tical" plane so solidly against the sex-interest of the individual and of the race? The mercenary marriage is a perfectly natural consequence of the economic dependence of women.

* * *

OLIVE SCHREINER

[Sex-Parasitism]†

* * * Again and again in the history of the past, when among human creatures a certain stage of material civilisation has been reached, a curi- ous tendency has manifested itself for the human female to become more or less parasitic; social conditions tend to rob her of all forms of active, conscious, social labour, and to reduce her, like the field-tick, to the passive exercise of her sex functions alone. And the result of this parasitism has invariably been the decay in vitality and intelligence of the female, followed after a longer or shorter period by that of her male descendants and her entire society.

Nevertheless, in the history of the past the dangers of the sex-parasit- ism have never threatened more than a small section of the females of the human race, those exclusively of some comparatively small domi- nant race or class; the mass of women beneath them being still com- pelled to assume many forms of strenuous activity. It is at the present day, and under the peculiar conditions of our modern civilisation, that

†From *Woman and Labour* (London: T. Fisher Unwin, 1911) 78–82.

for the first time sex-parasitism has become a danger, more or less remote, to the mass of civilised women, perhaps ultimately to all.

In the very early stages of human growth, the sexual parasitism and degeneration of the female formed no possible source of social danger. Where the conditions of life rendered it inevitable that all the labour of a community should be performed by the members of that community for themselves, without the assistance of slaves or machinery, the tendency has always been rather to throw an excessive amount of social labour on the female. Under no conditions, at no time, in no place, in the history of the world have the males of any period, of any nation, or of any class, shown the slightest inclination to allow their own females to become inactive or parasitic, so long as the actual muscular labour of feeding and clothing them would in that case have devolved upon *themselves!*

The parasitism of the human female becomes a possibility only when a point in civilisation is reached (such as that which was attained in the ancient civilisations of Greece, Rome, Persia, Assyria, India, and such as to-day exists in many of the civilisations of the East, such as those of China and Turkey), when, owing to the extensive employment of the labour of slaves, or of subject races or classes, the dominant race or class has become so liberally supplied with the material goods of life, that mere physical toil on the part of its own female members has become unnecessary. It is when this point has been reached, and never before, that the symptoms of female parasitism have in the past almost invariably tended to manifest themselves, and have become a social danger. The males of the dominant class have almost always contrived to absorb to themselves the new intellectual occupations, which the absence of necessity for the old forms of physical toil made possible in their societies; and the females of the dominant class or race, for whose muscular labours there was now also no longer any need, not succeeding in grasping or attaining to these new forms of labour, have sunk into a state in which, performing no species of active social duty, they have existed through the passive performance of sexual functions alone, with how much or how little of discontent will now never be known, since no literary record has been made by the woman of the past, of her desires or sorrows. Then, in place of the active labouring woman, upholding society by her toil, has come the effete wife, concubine, or prostitute, clad in fine raiment, the work of others' fingers; fed on luxurious viands, the result of others' toil, waited on and tended by the labour of others. The need for her physical labour having gone, and mental industry not having taken its place, she bedecked and scented her person, or had it bedecked and scented for her, she lay upon her sofa, or drove or was carried out in her vehicle, and, loaded with jewels, she sought by dissipations and amusements to fill up the inordinate blank left by the lack of productive activity. And as the hand whitened the frame softened, till, at last, the very duties of motherhood, which were all the constitution of her life left her, became distasteful, and, from the instant when her infant came damp from her womb, it passed into the hands of others, to be tended and reared by them; and from youth to age her offspring often owed nothing to her personal toil. In many cases so complete was her enervation, that at last the very joy of giving life, the glory and beatitude of a virile womanhood, became distasteful; and she sought to evade it, not because of its interference with more imperious duties to those already born of her, or to her society, but because her existence of inactivity had robbed her of all joy in strenuous exertion and endurance in any form. Finely clad, tenderly housed, life became for her merely the gratification of her own physical and sexual appetites, and the appetites of the male, through the stimulation of which she could maintain herself. And, whether as kept wife, kept mistress, or prostitute, she contributed nothing to the active and sustaining labours of her society. She had attained to the full development of that type which, whether in modern Paris or New York or London, or in ancient Greece, Assyria, or Rome, is essentially one in its features, its nature, and its results. She was the "fine lady," the human female parasite—the most deadly microbe which can make its appearance on the surface of any social organism.[1]

* * *

LORINE PRUETTE, PH.D.

[The Waste of Women in America] †

The figures of the United States Census show from 1880 to 1920 a progressive increase in the number of women gainfully employed, from more than two millions in 1880 to eight and a half millions today. In spite of this increase, of the total number of women in this country today who are over ten years of age, one in five, or only 21.1 per cent are gainfully employed. A casual glance at these figures must make us wonder what that other eighty per cent are doing. Do the young girls in school, the mothers with small children, and the old and infirm make up that eighty per cent? Even if we add to these three classes all the active housewives, themselves unpaid, but taking the place of a paid servant, we have not yet reached the total, we have not explained away the apparent wastefulness expressed in the figures that show practically eighty per cent of America's womanhood as outside the ranks of the gainfully employed.

Society still tolerates much waste; it can apparently still afford to. It

1. The relation of female parasitism generally, to the peculiar phenomenon of prostitution, is fundamental. Prostitution can never be adequately dealt with, either from the moral or the scientific standpoint, unless its relation to the general phenomenon of female parasitism be fully recognised. It is the failure to do this which leaves so painful a sense of abortion on the mind, after listening to most modern utterances on the question, whether made from the emotional platform of the moral reformer, or the intellectual platform of the would-be scientist. We are left with a feeling that the matter has been handled but not dealt with: that the knife has not reached the core.

† From *Women and Leisure: A Study of Social Waste* (New York: E. P. Dutton, 1924) 8–9.

has never yet learned to lead a truly economic life. Its factories still continue in great part to produce non-essentials. The voice of him who enjoins conservation is still that of "one crying in the wilderness." The economist may continue to draw his picture of the piled up wealth of the world, one gigantic heap from which countless tiny ants are busily carrying away each his little bit; he may declare that what is drawn away for one purpose may not also be taken away for another, that what goes into producing *de luxe* automobiles may not also make shoes for children; his picture is not looked upon and his words pass away.

Wastage is everywhere about us, wastage in raw materials, in mechanical processes, in man power,—how then can we look for conservation of woman power? Will woman, as civilization becomes more and more complex, as the world's treasures are more and more exploited, become increasingly the displayer, all her energies devoted to creating out of herself nothing but the material symbol of some man's power to make money, in all the social gradations adopting so far as possible the "theory of the leisure class"?

We may now be living in the "pleasure" stage, having gained such control over nature as to put us beyond the "pain" stage. But that control is vested in one thing only, in surplus: surplus of food, surplus of knowledge, of inventions, of energy. If the non-producers come to over-shadow the producers we begin to eat into that surplus. If we keep our women in general upon a half-time job we cut down potential production one-fourth. As the population of the world increases more intensive effort becomes necessary to keep up that surplus upon which depends man's control of nature. Beyond a certain point an acre of ground does not yield a larger crop, beyond a fixed although unknown limit more food cannot be obtained. Too much pleasure economy may be expected to return us to a pain economy.

*   *   *

JOHN HIGHAM

Ideological Anti-Semitism in the Gilded Age†

[F]rom 1870 to 1900 * * * the exceptionally fortunate position which American Jews had secured in the eighteenth and early nineteenth centuries was seriously weakened. During those years two types of anti-Semitism became visible. The first is social anti-Semitism: a pattern of discrimination. The second is political or ideological anti-Semitism: a power-hungry agitation addressed to the entire body politic, which blames the major ills of society on the Jews. * * *

To begin to understand the attitudes involved in either social or ideological anti-Semitism, it is necessary first of all to guard against the cate-

† From *Send These to Me: Immigrants in Urban America* by John Higham (2nd ed., The Johns Hopkins University Press), reprinted by permission of the author, copyright 1984.

gorizing tendency that distinguishes too sharply between anti-Semites and philo-Semites. * * * Stated positively, this premise simply means that most people waver between conflicting attitudes and seldom enjoy an undivided state of mind. * * *

In the case of the Jew, especially diverse and conflicting attitudes have always existed side by side in American minds. The Jewish stereotype took two entirely different forms, one religious and the other economic; and in either case attractive elements mingled with unlovely ones. Seen in religious terms, the Jew was a portentous figure, at once the glorious agent of divine purpose and the deserving victim of His vengeance. In this orthodox Christian view, the Jews were God's Chosen People, miraculously preserved and sustained; yet they were also an unfaithful people who suffered justly for their betrayal. * * *

A similar duality complicated the economic stereotype of Jews: they represented both the capitalist virtues and the capitalist vices. On the favorable side, the Jew commonly symbolized an admirable keenness and resourcefulness in trade. In this sense his economic energy seemed very American.[1] In another mood, however, keenness might mean cunning; enterprise might shade into avarice. Along with encomiums on the Jew as a progressive economic force—a model of commercial energy and integrity—went frequent references to conniving Shylocks. The earliest published plays containing Jewish characters (1794, 1823) portrayed Shylock types, and by the 1840's the verb "to Jew," meaning to cheat by sharp practice, was becoming a more or less common ingredient of American slang.[2] In the early nineteenth century the bright side of these judgments outshone the tarnished. Later, in an increasingly secularized society, the whole religious image declined, and the unattractive elements in the economic stereotype grew more pronounced. The latent conflict between favorable and unfavorable attitudes came more clearly into the open.

In the late nineteenth century a remarkably friendly attitude toward Jews still prevailed widely. Protestant ministers and Reform rabbis frequently exchanged pulpits. Rising Jewish capitalists joined in general community affairs and built lavish homes in the most exclusive neighborhoods.[3] The traditional American image of the Jew as a constructive economic force—a model of commercial enterprise, energy, and integrity—still provided material for popular orators and storytellers.[4] On the other hand, a distrust that expressed itself in the negative side of the

1. Rudolf Glanz, "Jew and Yankee: A Historic Comparison," *Jewish Social Studies*, VI (1944), 3–30.
2. Stephen Bloore, "The Jew in American Dramatic Literature (1794–1930)," *Publication of the American Jewish Historical Society*, XL (1951), 345–60; Mixford M. Mathews, ed., *A Dictionary of Americanisms on Historical Principles*, 2 vols. (Chicago, 1951), I, 905; "Present State of the Jewish People in Learning and Culture," *North American Review*, LXXXIII (1856), 368.

3. *Public Opinion*, III (August 27, 1887), 423; Stuart E. Rosenberg, *The Jewish Community in Rochester, 1843–1925* (New York, 1954), 105–6.
4. Hezekiah Butterworth, *In Old New England: The Romance of a Colonial Fireside* (New York, 1895), 46–78; New York *Herald*, September 15, 1891; Zebulon B. Vance, *The Scattered Nation* (New York, 1904). For background see Selig Adler, "Zebulon B. Vance and the 'Scattered Nation,' " *Journal of Southern History*, VII (August, 1941), 357–77.

economic stereotype steadily gained ground during the post-Civil War decades. Since this distrust clashed with the prevailing temper of American culture, anti-Semitic attitudes were often covert and usually blurred by a lingering respect. Many Americans were both pro- and anti-Jewish at the same time.

* * *

In this connection it should be observed that the unusual ambition and competitive drive for which the Jews are widely admired were not unmixed blessings in the late nineteenth century. These incentives propelled them upward in American society with amazing rapidity. Jewish wealth became conspicuous; Jewish power was an easy inference. In the innocence of their pride Jewish spokesmen publicized with glowing words the economic success some of their people enjoyed. One asserted in a popular magazine, for example, that the Jews controlled the finances of San Francisco. Another alleged that on Jewish holidays the business of the exchanges almost ceased.[5]

Meanwhile, the fame of the European Rothschild family vividly stimulated the imagination of a public avid for news of the very rich. During the Gilded Age the Rothschild name suggested, in the words of a contemporary biographer, "visions of untold wealth and unrivalled power, which appear so startling and amazing as to be more appropriate to romance than real life." The New York *Tribune* took for granted its readers' awareness of the "immense influence wielded by the Jewish princes of finance upon the Western Governments of Europe."[6] Unfortunately, the Rothschilds, who specialized in government loans, became involved in one of the most unpopular financial transactions the United States Treasury ever undertook. When President Cleveland's efforts to save the gold standard culminated in 1895 in a secretly negotiated contract to buy gold in Europe, three names appeared on the contract: J. P. Morgan and Company, August Belmont and Company, and N. M. Rothschild and Sons. By singling out the Rothschilds as the key figures in the transaction, silverites found all the evidence they needed of how the Jewish money power profited from American distress.[7]

At the very time the Rothschilds were exercising the American imagination and German Jews in considerable numbers were climbing the social ladder, the arrival of a mass immigration from eastern Europe further complicated the whole Jewish problem. Most native Americans thrown into contact with the impoverished, unkempt throngs from the

5. Gustav Adolph Danziger, "The Jew in San Francisco: The Last Half Century," *Overland Monthly*, XXV (April, 1895), 382; Henry Hanaw, *Jew Hating and Jew Baiting: An Essay* (Nashville, 1894), 8; Isaac Markens, *The Hebrews in America* (New York, 1888), passim.

6. John Reeves, *The Rothschilds: The Financial Rulers of Nations* (Chicago, 1887), 1. See also Joel Benton, "The Rothschilds," *Munsey's Magazine*, VII (April, 1892), 37–40; New York *Tribune*, Sep-

tember 19, 1891, p. 6, and constant references by Populist publications, such as *National Economist* (Washington), October 8, 1892, p. 6.

7. "Issue and Sale of Bonds," *House Reports*, 53 Cong., 3 Sess., No. 1824, p. 3; James A. Barnes, *John G. Carlisle: Financial Statesman* (New York, 1931), 390–91, 397; *Review of Reviews*, XI (March, 1895), 261; *Jewish Messenger*, LXXVIII (July 12, 1895), 4.

ghettos of eastern Europe viewed them with distaste.[8] Many German-American Jews, appalled at the outlandish looks and ways of the new-comers, feared that their own reputation was suffering from the popular habit of judging all Jews as alike. As early as 1872 a popular magazine article by a German-American Jew begged the public not to judge all Jews by the "ignorant . . . bigoted, and vicious" Poles and Russians who clustered around Chatham Street and East Broadway.[9] Although such statements were obviously drenched in prejudice, one cannot dismiss them as wholly without foundation. Certainly the new immigration accentuated the aura of foreignness that still clung to American images of the Jew. Moreover, this mass migration involved the Jews promi-nently in the multiple ethnic conflicts that arose along with the increas-ing volume and diversity of the whole immigrant influx.

Whatever may be the exact weight of these various factors in shaping feeling about the Jews, the role that the victim plays in any ethnic fric-tion explains only part of the hostility he meets. An appreciation of the ambiguity of ethnic stereotypes and of the objective dimension in group conflict may prevent simplification or sentimentality; but these approaches may leave the controlling factors in the larger social context entirely unexplored. Here a third rule of procedure suggests itself. To identify the critical elements in a conflict situation requires a consistently com-parative approach. In other words, the status of American Jewry in a given era needs to be related to the experience of other American ethnic groups in the same period, to the Jewish experience in other periods of American history, and to the concurrent fate of Jews in other countries.

At the lowest and most immediate level of comparison, it is evident that many immigrant groups underwent attack in late-nineteenth-cen-tury America, though in varying ways and degrees.[1] Here it is sufficient to say that the Jews met neither as much hostility nor as much tolerance as certain other minorities. Although rapid social advancement appar-ently exposed and sensitized many Jews to more social discrimination than other European groups felt, in other respects they fared somewhat better. They did not fall victim to as much violence as did the Italians, and there was no organized anti-Semitic movement comparable to the anti-Catholic American Protective Association. Still, the Jews did con-stitute one of the prominent ethnic targets in the 1880's and 1890's. Certainly they did not share the relative exemption from nativist attack that the Scandinavians, for example, enjoyed. Comparisons of this kind indicate that the Jew experienced neither the unusual disadvantage which the New Deal interpretation implied nor the warm acceptance some-

8. John Higham, *Strangers in the Land: Patterns of American Nativism, 1860–1925* (New Bruns-wick, 1955), 66–67. See also *Allgemeine Zeitung des Judenthums* (Berlin), LV (October 9, 1891), appendix, p. 4.

9. W. M. Rosenblatt, "The Jews: What They Are Coming To," *Galaxy*, XIII (January, 1872), 47–48; *23rd Annual Convention of District Grand Lodge No. 6, I.O.B.B.*, 1891, appendix, p. 19. See also Zosa Szajkowski, "The Attitude of Amer-ican Jews to East European Jewish Immigration (1881–1893)," *Publication of the American Jewish Historical Society*, XL (March, 1951), 222–32.

1. Higham, *Strangers in the Land*, 26–27, 66–67, 92–94.

times suggested by the neoliberal view.[2] Moreover, such comparisons call attention to a fact of utmost significance—that anti-Semitism formed an integral part of a larger, more complex upswing of antiforeign feeling.

But perhaps a broader comparison in point of time and space may help to explain the link between anti-Semitism and the other ethnic tensions that arose along with it in late-nineteenth-century America. A general look backward across the whole development of political anti-Semitism in the United States and western Europe during the last hundred years discloses three periods of special intensity. On both sides of the Atlantic ideological agitation against Jews rose and fell more or less simultaneously. It reached a first crest in the late 1880's and 1890's, a second in the years immediately after the First World War, and a third in the 1930's. The first period saw the emergence of Adolf Stoecker in Germany, Édouard Drumont in France, and a movement against Jewish immigration in England. The second, from 1919 to 1923, brought the international circulation of the notorious *Protocols*, an outbreak of anti-Semitic journalism in England, the emergence of the National Socialist part in Germany and the assassination of Walter Rathenau and, in America, the crusades of Henry Ford and the Ku Klux Klan. The climax, here and in Germany, came in the thirties. In the intervals between these periods two breathing spells occurred. Anti-Semitism made no significant advances in America or western Europe in the early years of the twentieth century; and again in the mid-twenties the agitation declined.[3] The vast difference of intensity between America and some European countries should not obscure a common rhythm.

If, then, ideological anti-Semitism has ebbed and flowed on an international level, one cannot find the decisive forces that activated it by a merely internal examination of American traditions, circumstances, or habits of mind. Interpretation must pivot upon general developments in western civilization—developments that repeatedly inflamed or dampened anti-Semitism on both sides of the Atlantic at roughly the same time.

Here the economic interpretation—if broadly construed and stripped of the polemical character it had in New Deal historiography—offers a still valid insight. Certainly the cyclical rhythm of political anti-Semitism has depended upon factors that were partly economic. Each of the periods of anti-Semitic agitation was one of depression in both America and western Europe. Yet not of depression alone. In each case, economic distress functioned as one element in a complex of social and economic dislocations within the western nations. The years from 1873

---

2. Handlin, "American Views of the Jew," 326–29, compares the Jewish stereotype with other ethnic stereotypes but asserts that *none* of them reflected a deprecatory attitude. The truth would seem to be rather that *all* of them involved unflattering elements, but in different degrees. The further contention that Jews accepted the comic caricature of themselves (though in fact many Jews indignantly rejected it) points to a fact of minority psychology,

not to the absence of hostility.

3. The downswing in the early twentieth century is treated in Hannah Arendt, *The Origins of Totalitarianism* (New York, 1951), 50–53, and Paul W. Massing, *Rehearsal for Destruction: A Study of Political Anti-Semitism in Imperial Germany* (New York, 1949), 113–48. On the 1920's see Sachar, *Sufferance Is the Badge*, 23–33, 256–57, 322, 351–53.

to 1896 unleashed severe class conflicts and a general unrest that revived during the postwar disorganization after 1918 and reached a culmination in the 1930's. There was good cause to believe that the whole social system was somehow being undermined. The tensions relaxed in the early twentieth century as the achievements of imperialism and social democracy made themselves felt. Again, in the mid-1920's a growing stability revived confidence in the existing social order.

But social and economic frustrations did not stir up ethnic frictions automatically. The recurrent pattern of social and economic strain was accompanied by a persistent ideological disturbance. Each of the crisis periods produced a powerful display of nationalism, and it was the blindly cohesive energy of nationalism that channeled internal discontents into agitation against foreign influences. Consequently anti-Semitism in the modern world has reached maximum intensity as an integral component of movements aimed at defending the nation from various perils originating beyond its frontiers.

With these considerations in mind, the ethnic scene in America in the late nineteenth century becomes more intelligible. It was a time of mass strikes, widening social chasms, unstable prices, and a degree of economic hardship unfamiliar in earlier American history. On the same scene a strong upsurge of nationalism expressed itself in jingoist outbursts against England and other countries, proliferation of patriotic societies, a powerful tariff agitation, and the birth of a movement for immigration restriction that increased by leaps and bounds. In broad outline, both the social situation and the nationalist response paralleled the contemporary experience of western Europe. In such a likely context for anti-Semitism, the Jews of America were fortunate to have suffered as little as they did. The relative mildness of American, as compared to European, anti-Semitism must be attributed not only to the more tolerant traditions of the United States but also to the presence within the country of a great variety of ethnic targets. Since the fire of American nationalists was scattered among many adversaries, no one minority group bore the brunt of the attack. Hatred of Catholics, of Chinese, of the new immigration as a whole, and above all a diffuse nativist hostility to the whole immigrant influx overshadowed specifically anti-Jewish agitation. Nevertheless, a good deal of distinctively anti-Semitic sentiment also emerged. Significantly, it was strongest in those sectors of the population where a particularly explosive combination of social discontent and nationalistic aggression prevailed.

Three groups in late-nineteenth-century America harbored anti-Jewish feelings that went beyond mere social discrimination: some of the agrarian radicals caught up in the Populist movement; certain patrician intellectuals in the East, such as Henry and Brooks Adams and Henry Cabot Lodge; and many of the poorest classes in urban centers. Different as they were, each of these groups found itself at a special disadvantage in the turmoil of an industrial age—the poor because it exploited them, the patricians because it displaced them. Thus Henry Adams, whose anti-Semitism lacked the democratic restraints that qualified the thinking of the Populists, agreed with them in identifying the Jew with the menace of plutocracy. To judge from his published letters, it was only in the late 1880's, after a sense of the powerlessness of his own aristocratic class had settled upon him, that Adams began to see the Jew as the supreme expression of a commercial, bourgeois society. The depression of the nineties put matters in a still worse light for both of the Adams brothers. The economic collapse indicated to them the approach of a general social catastrophe, and the Jew loomed as both the symbol of a materialistic society and an agent of its destruction. In "a society of Jews and brokers," Henry Adams wrote in 1893, "I have no place." He looked forward to a complete smash-up. "Then, perhaps, men of our kind might have some chance of being honorably killed in battle."[4] It is worth adding that the Adamses were not the only upper-class intellectuals who felt this way. The same patrician pessimism underlay the anti-Semitic outbursts in Vance Thompson's elegantly bohemian magazine, M'lle New York.[5]

Beside a common resentment against a business culture, the patrician and the plebeian anti-Semite shared a similar kind of belligerent nationalism. Both had a touch of the jingo spirit and longed for a militant assertion of American power. There is evidence that jingoism arose mostly from the underdog elements in American society—notably from the urban lower classes who read the yellow press and from the southern and western Democrats and Populists who chafed under the stodgy respectability of Cleveland and McKinley.[6] Nevertheless, some of the most ardent jingoes belonged to the patrician elite, and they were capable of talking much like the mob about the need for reviving patriotism and about the pernicious influence of the "international Jew" over the American government. Henry Adams might not always concur with Brooks's avid pursuit of war and empire, but they agreed that America would somehow have to strike off the chains of Europe if it would free itself from Shylock's grasp.[7]

[T]he Jews also suffered directly at the hands of their fellow immigrants. In the urban slums of the late nineteenth century "Jew-baiting" became a daily occurrence.

Beginning, apparently, in the 1880's, the Jewish peddlers who swarmed through the poorer districts of the large cities were continually taunted, stoned, and otherwise manhandled by street gangs. Beard-pulling was one of the commonest forms of bedevilment,[8] but more serious assaults

4. Worthington C. Ford, ed., *Letters of Henry Adams*, 2 vols. (Boston, 1938), I, 388–89; II, 33–35, 98, 111; Thornton Andersen, *Brooks Adams: Constructive Conservative* (Ithaca, 1951), 60. Barbara M. Solomon, *Ancestors and Immigrants: A Changing New England Tradition* (Cambridge, Mass., 1956), 32–42, works out more carefully and extensively the same general point that has been made here about Henry Adams.

5. *M'lle New York*, I (November–December, 1895), n.p., and II (November, 1898), 2. See also

Henry James, *The American Scene* (New York, 1907), 131, 138–39.

6. Richard Hofstadter, "Manifest Destiny and the Philippines," in Daniel Aaron, ed., *America in Crisis* (New York, 1952), 177–82.

7. Harold Dean Cater, ed., *Henry Adams and His Friends: A Collection of Unpublished Letters* (Boston, 1947), 391; Anderson, *Brooks Adams*, 73. See also *M'lle New York*, I (September, 1895), 2.

8. Louis Wirth, *The Ghetto* (Chicago, 1928), 180–81; *American Hebrew*, LXV (May 19, 1899), 71.

became increasingly frequent in the 1890's. Irish and German rowdies seem to have caused most of the trouble. In 1899 a united protest from fourteen Jewish societies in Brooklyn declared: "No Jew here can go on the street without exposing himself to the danger of being pitilessly beaten."[9] Appeals for police protection were generally futile. At the end of the century, therefore, eastern European Jews in Chicago, Brooklyn, Worcester, and Holyoke formed protective associations designed to prosecute offenders and arouse officials.[1]

The climactic incident occurred on New York's Lower East Side in 1902. The occasion was a solemn event in the history of the New York ghetto: the mass funeral of the leading figure in the Orthodox community, Rabbi Jacob Joseph. Thousands of mourners took part in the vast, formless procession that followed the coffin from synagogue to synagogue en route to the grave in Brooklyn. To reach the Grand Street ferry, the procession had to pass through the Irish district near the East River. The Irish resented the constant encroachment of the teeming Jewish colony upon their own shrinking domain,[2] and Jewish funeral parties had often been molested on the same route before. As the wailing throng surged past a big factory where many of the local Irish worked, the employees pelted the crowd with iron nuts and bolts. A riot ensued as the Jews threw back the missiles and tried to break into the building. Order was almost restored when the arrival of two hundred police reserves made matters much worse.[3] The New York police force was predominantly Irish and had a reputation for brutal treatment of East Side Jews. Political rivalry had recently inflamed bad feelings; the Jews had rebelled en masse against Tammany Hall in the mayoralty election of 1901, in which police corruption was the main issue.[4] Accordingly, the police hurled themselves upon what remained of the funeral procession with abusive language and flailing clubs. All told, about two hundred were injured, mostly Jews, with most of the injuries brought on by the police.

* * *

9. *Die Welt* (Vienna), III (June 2, 1899), 8. Cf. the troubles that a Jewish storekeeper's daughter had in a Welsh mining town in Iowa in the 1890's. Edna Ferber, *A Peculiar Treasure* (New York, 1939), 40–42, 50.

1. *American Hebrew*, LXV (July 14 and August 18, 1899), 307, 482; New York *Tribune*, June 29, 1899, p. 11; *Die Welt*, III (March 24, 1899), 10; (August 11, 1899), 13.

2. Philip Cowen, *Memories of an American Jew* (New York, 1932), 289. On the ethnic geography of the East Side see *Reports of the Industrial Commission*, 19 vols. (Washington, D.C., 1901), XV, p. xlvi and maps facing p. 470.

3. Testimony given to the Mayor's investigating committee is summarized in *American Hebrew*, LXI (August 15–22, 1902), 355–56, 384, and the official report appears on pp. 497–98. See also New York *Tribune*, July 31, 1902, pp. 1, 3; New York *World*, July 31, 1902, pp. 1–2, and August 2, 1902, p. 4.

4. *American Hebrew*, LXI (August 15, 1902), 355–56; Charles Bernheimer, ed., *The Russian Jew in the United States* (Philadelphia, 1905), 257. The overwhelmingly Gaelic complexion of the New York police force is evident from the random lists of names in *Report of the Police Department of the City of New York*, 1900, pp. 48–56.

Tableau Vivant of "The Dying Gladiator"†

The Dying Gladiator.

†From Jack W. McCullough, *Living Pictures on the New York Stage* (Ann Arbor: UMI Research Press, 1981) 96.

CRITICISM

Contemporary Reviews

THE INDEPENDENT

Mrs. Wharton's Latest Novel †

Mrs. Wharton's new novel is a story of society life, its refined feroci-ties, its sensual extravagances, its delicate immoralities and, above all, the tragedies which underlie its outward appearance of mirth and pros-perity. Society, indeed, is the coming field in fiction for the author who knows how to reap his literary wheat from the tares that are sowed there. And we ought not to complain: These books are missionary efforts of a sensational kind, made in behalf of what is the most corrupt class of people in the world, if we are to take seriously the representations of writers like Mrs. Wharton and Robert Grant.

But there is one curious thing about the dogma upon which these stories are founded. It is that old-fashioned one, "the soul that sinneth it shall die." Now ministers have been obliged to abandon the rigors of this doctrine in the pulpit, or, at least, to emphasize it less; but these novelists dramatize it with all the terrors of their imagination, and they demonstrate it by the life of every character in the story. Thus the men and women in this novel who go about showing their ghastly mirth give the impression of being "hair hung and breeze shaken," as the old preachers would say, over the ancient lake of fire and brimstone. This same class of writers find their ethics by what may be called the dredging process. Formerly we all got our morals and golden texts from the lives of saints and from the Holy Scriptures, whether we were writing or actually living them. But now it is the fashion to get them out of the cesspools of vice. The author who can portray the most sins in the best style is the most popular literary preacher now.

And, according to this standard, Mrs. Wharton should stand very high. She has selected a situation in that circle of society where conditions make for the destruction rather than the development of honor and vir-tue. The heroine, a capable, well poised woman, is inmeshed in it. And this is the tragedy—that a creature so morally sane should be subjected to a process sure to prove disintegrating. Her acting, her subterfuges, her pitiful treacheries are simply the threads of a common web which entan-

† From *The Independent* (July 10, 1905): 113.

gles with her every person in her set. She is surrounded by men and women whose esthetic sensibilities are so highly developed that they have become emasculated. Their pleasures are self-indulgences founded upon some social form of almost every vice. Meanwhile beauty is her own spirit's art of expression, just as religion might be a nun's. The need of money, the petty intrigues and delicately veiled temptations which follow, sully conscience and damage self-respect, even if they do not betray the woman to her moral death. And the whole picture is the more distressing than if the victim were a man, because the destroying of a woman means the passing of a finer spiritual nature. The thing must be accomplished with a frightful delicacy which is not so essential in the destruction of a man's character.

We all have the diathesis of iniquity in us, to be sure; but the question is how far right are these authors who prove that the development of the disease depends upon environment? And since it is such an excusing doctrine, it will be easy to inculcate. Then what will be the effect when these people accept it and resign themselves to being the inane creatures of circumstances? If Mrs. Wharton could write a story dramatizing a means of escape for her victims she would do a better business. As it is we would not be convinced even if the heroine marries for love instead of money. That depends upon the author's conception of what the sequel should be in order to make a good story. We know that in real life the woman could not hold out against such terrible odds. The trouble is our literary exponents have a spell cast over their imaginations. Their eyes are holden. And never since the old days in Greece, when men accepted fate with pagan cheerfulness, has fatalism been so emphasized as it is now, particularly in fiction. The difference is that we lack the pagan cheerfulness.

Some writers have a permanent literary style, others have merely a fleeting fashion of expression, which is not founded upon art and which is meant to appeal to the passing fancy of the public mind. Now some years ago, when Mrs. Wharton's stories first began to attract attention, it was claimed that she had that rare thing, distinction in literary style. And she still has a fine manner, but it is like the fine gowns of her heroines, a fashion of the times for interpreting decadent symptoms in human nature. What she says will not last, because it is simply the fashionable drawing of ephemerel types and still more ephemeral sentiments.

E. E. HALE, JR.

Mrs. Wharton's "The House of Mirth" †

*   *   *

Some time since it was said by a master of a very different kind of fiction that "it is one thing to remark and to dissect, with the most cutting logic, the complications of the human spirit; it is quite another to give them body and blood." Observation, analysis, logic: these processes, probably, Mrs. Wharton has employed rather more than Stevenson would have done. But whatever Mrs. Wharton may have done herself, these intellectual operations are not obvious in her book. "In anything fit to be called by the name of reading," continues the same authority, "the process should be absorbing and voluptuous; we should gloat over a book, be rapt clean out of ourselves, and rise from the perusal, our mind filled with the busiest kaleidoscopic dance of images, incapable of sleep or of continuous thought." That is a very exact description of a mental state that many will probably experience on reading *The House of Mirth*. It is not observation, analysis, logic; it is real humanity, if not the whole of it, and that is something likely to hold our interest and absorb our attention. After perhaps a slight repulsion at first, one is attracted to the unhappy butterfly, and follows her flutterings with a growing feeling, to which the last few pages come with a suave and necessary relief.

And after that, what then? one may ask. Suppose you are voluptuously absorbed, that your mind sees stars, that you cannot sleep? Is that all one can say? Is there no moral teaching? No problem? No message? No criticism of life? There is not, very fortunately, any one of these things. There is nothing that needs to be discussed or talked about, or answered. There is simply the impression of poignant tragedy, the pity and awe with which one becomes silent.

MARY MOSS

[Review of *The House of Mirth*] †

In *The House of Mirth* * * * Miss Bart's actions not only surprise you, but you are even ready to dispute Mrs. Wharton's knowledge of what her heroine really did do. Lily is a very complete study of the siren of a girl, too poor to keep up with the set in which she moves, who is unfortunately too radically snobbish to cut free from it. Her hold upon this

† From *The Bookman* 22 (1905): 366.   † From *Atlantic Monthly* 97 (1906): 52–53.

society lies in beauty, elegance, adaptability, and willingness to amuse superfluous husbands (here again woman is the aggressor). Yet under this pliability, she is victim to a self-indulgence so boundless that, at last resort, it amounts to a fair imitation of principle. To be consistent, with her utterly sordid ideals, Lily should promptly knock herself down to the highest bidder. Yet at the very moment when the dull, eligible suitor has finally come to terms, Miss Bart must always see the sweetness of frisking off with a detrimental. She is too fastidious for the life she is leading, but unfit for any other available one. As a point of probability, would not Lily either have early succumbed or managed her way to better things? But when you find yourself discussing the truth of a novel, you are really paying it high tribute. Moreover, such inconsistencies are perhaps likely in a person whose conduct is guided entirely by taste, without a shadow of conviction. Lily is no more deliberately venal than she is deliberately decent. Certain surroundings and a comforting sense of being "in things" are necessary to her existence. A balloon may not scheme to get gas; it merely collapses without. On the whole, I believe that Mrs. Wharton knows the truth about Lily. She was as incapable of meanness as of any other form of economy. She only wanted a pretty gown, fresh flowers, a roll of dollars in her pocket for bridge, a pleasant companion, and all doors hospitably open to her. Simple, rational needs! That her income, though ample for a plainer life, was quite unequal to the pace of her friends naturally plunged her into trouble. As for the society in which poor Lily moves, Mrs. Wharton has no colors too black, no acid too biting, for its unredeemed odiousness and vulgarity. She shows its sensuality to be mere passionless curiosity; she displays its cautious balancing of affairs so that reputations are preserved, not lost, in the divorce courts; her people, with regard to the quality commonly known as virtue, resembling rich defaulters who are lucky enough through a technicality to miss a term in jail. The whole is brilliantly well conceived, brilliantly executed. Facets of light glitter before your eyes at the mere thought of it. No cheap sacrifice is made to the buying public's supposed craving for sweet pretty endings. There is but one lack. Read it with approval, with enjoyment. Put it down and go your way refreshed by a novel that held your attention unflaggingly to the end. That is exactly the crux! * * * For all its brilliancy, *The House of Mirth* has a certain shallowness; it is thin. At best, Lily can only inspire interest and curiosity. You see, you understand, and you ratify, but unfortunately, you do not greatly care.

MARY K. FORD

[Excerpt from "Two Studies in Luxury"] †

*   *   *

No one can follow the fortunes of Lily Bart without realizing the deteriorating effect of a luxurious life upon the moral fibre of human beings; and the utterances of President Roosevelt upon the merits of a life of endeavor gain new force from Mrs. Wharton's brilliant social satire. Lily recognizes the best in people, and so far appreciates it that she refrains from many acts that others of her set consider permissible; but her standards are constantly being lowered, and she is continually skirting the edge of shady transactions so that finally, when by no fault of her own she finds herself in a very unpleasant predicament, she has really herself to thank for it. Her moral fibre has been so undermined by her self-indulgent way of life that she has neither the courage nor the decision to grasp the best when it is within reach. Even Selden, the nearest approach to a hero that the book contains, is infected by this same fatal vacillation, and only realizes when too late what he and Lily might have been to each other. * * * "The House of Mirth" contains nothing sadder than the glimpse we get of Lily's early home, her extravagant mother, her overworked father—a home of which her own miserable death is the legitimate outcome.

And what a lesson the book teaches! It is not for nothing that Mrs. Wharton has taken her title from the Book of Ecclesiastes, that cry of satiety that has come down the ages to us with its burden of "Vanity of vanities! all is vanity!"—a cry even more significant now than when it was uttered nearly three thousand years ago by the wisdom-sated monarch who in these words summed up his experience of life.

THE NATION

[Review of *The House of Mirth*] †

*   *   *

Occasionally Mrs. Wharton's clear, severe vision wavers. She intimates that her Lily Bart is superior to her world, that she chafes in chains, and has intermittent attacks of soft and even sanctifying emotions. Mrs. Wharton is weakest when she is merciful. Miss Bart does seem to throw up her game at a critical moment and to let coveted prizes slip through her fingers; but such misfortunes strike us as unforeseen

† From *The Critic* 48 (1906): 249–50.   † From *The Nation* (London) 31 (1905): 447–48.

results of her folly or of an unexpected checkmate. There is no evidence of instinctive recoil from an intention recognized as ignoble. Even her final rejection of the monstrous conditions on fulfilment of which Mr. Rosedale has expressed a willingness to marry her, fails to establish any moral worth.

Blackmail is a resort of the infamous. A decent girl, one not necessarily clever or kind or well-bred, would have sent Mrs. Dorset's compromising letters back to her as soon as they fell into her hands. It is by the temptations that Miss Bart permitted to visit her that her character finally fails to commend itself for sympathetic judgment or compassion. "Dingy" is her favorite appellation for those who do not live in splendor on their own or other people's incomes. She had a mortal horror of dinginess, external dinginess, but lived and moved delightedly among souls of a dinginess incomparable, beyond furbishing. The poor girl's inward eye was a feeble organ not susceptible of cultivation.

A hasty mental comparison between Miss Bart and famous heroines of society fiction, both English and French, suggests many points of resemblance, though in one respect she stands alone in dreary isolation. She has not a particle of genuine, fundamental, good human feeling, and has very little bad. Her assumed tender emotion for the cautious, not to say canny, Mr. Selden (a cold prig), never convinces any one, not even him. She cherishes no affectionate sentiments towards the mother who did her poor best for her, the aunt who supported her, the rich women who dressed her, or the poor friend who adored her. In no society could such a being exist except in that where the dismal and (to the reader) often tedious drama of her life goes on. The denizens of her 'House of Mirth' are revolting. They eat and drink, expensively and often, but are never merry. They never think, and their talk is as the crackling of thorns. They break the seventh commandment without the excuse of passion, apparently playing with adultery and divorce (as they seem to play bridge for high stakes and drive motor-cars) in order to assert privilege, to earn the absurd epithet, "smart." They have no ideas, no intellectual interests, neither wit nor humor nor tact nor grace.

If this is American society, the American House of Mirth, it is utterly unsuitable for conversion into literature. Literature demands all that such society has not—ideas, intellectual interests, sentiment, passion, humor, wit, tact, and grace; it can get along perfectly well without money, which is the only desire or possession of such society, its only claim for recognition even by the newspapers. A feeling for fair play obliges us to protest Mrs. Wharton's picture as a prejudiced one, yet it is not consciously unveracious. Though depressing, it is not wholly unprofitable. A perusal of Miss Bart's melancholy history will hardly incite those who are in society to pause and examine themselves, but it may cause those who are outside the ring to praise God for that he has been pleased to make them "dingy."

THE SATURDAY REVIEW

[Review of *The House of Mirth*] †

Somewhat aweary though we are of the chronicles and exposures of what is vulgarly called "smart society" Miss Wharton's book, dealing as it does with these distasteful subjects, is still a noteworthy achievement. It is indeed a biting criticism of modern civilisation with its luxury worship and mean conventions. It is an appeal for our nobler illusions. The heroine of the novel, Lily Bart, is a masterly study of the modern American woman with her coldly corrupt nature and unhealthy charm. In her characterisation of Lily Bart the author exhibits an unerring instinct. She endows her with life and vitality and the reader follows every step in her chequered career with growing interest and excitement. Young, beautiful and fascinating, full of the joy of life, Lily Bart has been brought up among a "fast" set of people where every whim is gratified regardless of cost. The expense of keeping up the pace is too much for her scanty means and she finds herself at last deep in debt. Although innocent of intention of actual wrong she turns for assistance to a married man, the husband of one of her friends who promises to multiply her income by some mysterious investments on the Stock Exchange. She has a very rude awakening when she at last discovers that the wonderful "dividends" she has been obtaining have come out of his pocket, and that his interest in her affairs is by no means disinterested. Her discovery comes too late, after the man has hopelessly compromised her in the eyes of the world. Her friends and relatives "cut her" and she is left practically alone in the world except for one kind ugly woman friend who of course sticks to her through good report and ill—in the way ugly women have. It must not be supposed that Miss Wharton represents Lily Bart as a model of injured innocence. Quite the contrary. She is a thorough woman of the world, spoilt and selfish and yet withal intensely loveable. It is the striking art of Miss Wharton as a writer that keeps the reader's sympathy from first to last. She can evoke the emotions of pity, horror and love. In Lily Bart she has created a character that will haunt the imagination of the reader and live in his memory. The book is one of the few novels which can claim to rank as literature.

† From *The Saturday Review* (London) 101 (1906): 209–10.

Modern Critical Views

MILLICENT BELL

[Wharton as Businesswoman: Publishing *The House of Mirth*] †

A novelist, surely, is just someone who writes novels. In this competence he is unlike other men, but not necessarily in the rest of his character. In particular, he need not be more inept in the practical management of his life than a specialist in another line. This would be too obvious to state were it not for the fact that the ancient legend persists that creative artists of any kind must be either saints or fools, persons inadequate in everything except the practice of a unique gift. The fact seems to be that a successful novelist is more likely to be a person of well-developed practicality. He has had to learn along the way that books are not only expressions of the spirit, but also end-products in a complex manufacturing process, objects of cost and price in the book-trade.

Yet one cannot help some surprise in finding this true of Edith Wharton. Was she not, to begin with, a "lady" out of a time and world when the word meant absolute indifference to business? Even the men of her class were, as she describes them in many of her stories, too proud and too ignorant of the methods of money-making to apply their intelligence to augmenting an inherited wealth. If they had any artistic talent at all, they were content to remain genteel dabblers; art seemed to them to be one of those higher activities which by its very nature should fail to pay. Mrs. Wharton, on the other hand, deserved the name of a professional in every sense. She trained herself to work assiduously at her craft, to be tirelessly self-critical, to measure her work by an absolute standard. And at the same time she developed an effective grasp of the commercial values that govern a literary career. She was never sentimental about the meaning of success or fame; she believed they should and could be made to reward the artist materially.

Her emergence as artist and literary merchandizer is visible in a nearly-continuous series of letters which she exchanged with representatives of her publishers, Charles Scribner's Sons, for over thirty years. The exis-

† From "Lady Into Author: Edith Wharton and the House of Scribner," *American Quarterly* 9 (1957): 295–96, 298–300.

tence of such a record is a piece of extraordinary fortune. Writers seldom remain with a single house for so long and more seldom still do letters survive to preserve the fugitive episodes that once meant so much to the actors.

*   *   *

Already upon the publication of her first book of fiction she had shown a capacity for gauging her weight and bringing it to bear. She did not gain a position of effective bargaining power, however, until 1905 when *The House of Mirth* achieved its popular success. The conception of this work had itself represented a new stage of growth for the author. She was already forty-two years old; she had written one historical novel which had achieved a certain limited distinction; chiefly she was known for her unemphatic short stories in the manner of Henry James. The novel she now launched in the pages of *Scribner's* was to overturn completely the general view of her, for it was planned as a full-scale study of contemporary life, a realistic, even sensational, presentation of the hidden world of the very rich. Writing it, moreover, she learned for the first time the value of consistent application. Edward Burlingame,[1] issuing one of those fortuitous challenges that often determined the careers of artists, had forced her to the achievement. She recalled afterwards how "amid the distractions of a busy and hospitable life, full of friends and travel, reading and gardening," she had dawdled over her first chapters until one day Burlingame asked her if she could furnish a serial to take the place of one that had unexpectedly been withdrawn from the magazine. It would have to be ready in four or five months. Meeting this exigent assignment bent her, she later declared, to the discipline of daily writing, turning her "from a drifting amateur into a professional."[2]

Her professionalism meant also that she would be able to take herself seriously as a seller of goods. Although her confidence in her artistic powers was still uncertain (it had needed strong persuasion from Brownell[3] to convince her that the book showed "a certain amount of architecture" [8/5/05]), she understood the meaning of popular acceptance. "After the Enormous Sales of 'The House of Mirth' which I predict for next November you will see my prices leap up!" she wrote, not altogether in jest, when the serial was only three months old (3/26/05). And when serious negotiations were started for her next book, she elaborated: "As to the terms, it seems to me that the incipient popularity of 'The House of Mirth' might permit me to name [an advance of] $8,000 . . . and perhaps you would think it reasonable, if the sale of the volume exceeded 10,000 to raise the royalties to 20%" (5/19/05). Her expectations were more than confirmed, as we shall see in a moment. And in her next

---

1. The editor of *Scribner's Magazine*, the publication in which *The House of Mirth* initially appeared as a serial [Editor].
2. Edith Wharton, *A Backward Glance* (New York:

D. Appleton-Century, 1934), pp. 207–208.
3. The head of Scribner's book publishing department [Editor].

contract, her royalty, never greater previously than fifteen per cent, was increased to twenty per cent, as she had proposed.

The House of Mirth was a resounding success. After 30,000 copies had been sold in the first three weeks of publication, Brownell was moved to caution her against extravagant hopes: "It is not a love story, you know, after all; and if it sells as few books that are have done, shall we not have to revise our ideas of the dear public?" (10/26/05). But the curve refused to flatten. By the end of the month 60,000 copies had been ordered from the publisher (10/30/05) and ten days later 80,000 orders prompted Charles Scribner to declare to Mrs. Wharton: "I do not remember that we have ever published any book the sale of which has been so rapid" (11/10/05). In another ten days sales reached the 100,000 mark (11/20/05). The success of *The House of Mirth* continued, and for the next four months it was listed as the nation's top best-seller. In the fall of 1905 she was already at work upon her next novel, *The Fruit of the Tree*, and when Scribner announced that the 100,000th copy of *The House of Mirth* had been sold, she outlined to him her plans for the new work—and reminded him about the royalty increase she expected. There is a bit of jocular menace in her description of her new hero: ". . . he is going to be a *very* strong man; so strong that I believe he will break all records. Perhaps in consideration of his strength you will think it not unreasonable to start with a 20% royalty? If you were to refuse, he is so violent that I don't know whether I can answer for the consequences!" (11/22/05).

*   *   *

LOUIS AUCHINCLOSS

[*The House of Mirth* and Old and New New York] †

*   *   *

The House of Mirth (1905) marks [Edith Wharton's] coming of age as a novelist. At last, and simultaneously, she had discovered both her medium and her subject matter. The first was the novel of manners and the latter the assault upon the old Knickerbocker society in which she had grown up of the new millionaires, the "invaders" as she called them, who had been so fabulously enriched by the business growth following the Civil War. New money had poured into New York in the 1880's and 1890's and turned the Joneses' quite old Fifth Avenue into a dizzy parade of derivative façades from Azay-le-Rideau to the Porch of the Maidens.[1] The Van Rensselaers and Rhinelanders might purse their lips at the ostentation of the Vanderbilts, but in a dollar world the biggest bank balance was bound to win out. A Livingston would marry a Mills,

---

† From *Pioneers and Caretakers: A Study of Nine American Women Novelists* (New York: Dell, 1965) 25–29.

1. Azay-le-Rideau is a town in western France containing a famous Renaissance chateau; the Porch of the Maidens is a classical Greek structure [*Editor*].

as in an earlier day a Schermerhorn had married an Astor. For what, really, did that older world have that was so special? It was all very well for James to describe the Newport of his childhood, surviving into this gilded age, as a little bare white open hand suddenly crammed with gold, but the fingers of that little hand closed firmly enough over the proffered bullion. The sober brown stucco of Upjohn's country villas concealed a materialism as rampant as any flaunted by the marble halls of Richard Morris Hunt.[2] Mrs. Wharton saw clearly enough that the invaders and defenders were bound ultimately to bury their hatchet in a noisy, stamping dance, but she saw also the rich possibilities for satire in the contrasts afforded by the battle line in its last stages and the pathos of the individuals who were fated to be trampled under the feet of those boisterous truce makers.

Lily Bart, the heroine of *The House of Mirth*, stems from both worlds. Her father is related to the Penistons and the Stepneys, but is driven by her mother, a more ordinary creature, to make a fortune which, not being of invader blood, he is bound to lose. Lily, orphaned, is loosed on the social seas with only her beauty and charm for sails and no rudder but a ladylike disdain for shabby compromises and a vague sense that there must be somewhere a better life than the one into which she has drifted. Her rich friends, who use her as a social secretary to write notes and as a blind to shield them from importunate and suspicious husbands, cannot understand the squeamishness which keeps her, at the critical moment, from extracting a proposal from the rich bachelor whom she has not been too squeamish to pursue. Her respectable relatives, on the other hand, of an older society, cannot understand her smoking or gambling or being seen, however briefly, in the company of married men. Lily falls between two stools. She cannot bring herself to marry the vulgar Mr. Rosedale for all his millions, or the obscure Lawrence Selden, for all their affinity. She postpones decisions and hopes for the best and in the meanwhile seeks to distract herself. But we know from the start that she is doomed. She has only her loveliness, and what is that in a world that puts its store in coin and hypocrisy? The other characters, of both new and old New York, seem strangely and vindictively united in a constant readiness to humiliate her: Grace Stepney to tell tales on her, Mrs. Peniston to disinherit her, Bertha Dorset to abandon her in a foreign port, Gus Trenor to try to seduce her, his wife to say he has. We watch with agonized apprehension as Lily turns and doubles back, as she keeps miraculously rehabilitating herself, each time on a slightly lower level. For no matter how hard she struggles, without money she is unarmed in that arena. And in the end when she finally compromises and is willing to marry Rosedale, it is too late. He will not have

2. Richard Upjohn (1802–78), an American architect best known for designing churches in the Gothic style (e.g., Trinity Church in New York City), created Kingscote in Newport, Rhode Island (1839), a summer house in the Gothic style. Richard Morris Hunt (1827–95), widely recognized as the leading American architect of the nineteenth century, designed a number of summer homes in Newport, including the sumptuous Gilded Age palaces of the Vanderbilts: Marble House and The Breakers [Editor].

her, and she falls to the job at the milliner's and the ultimate overdose of sleeping tablets. But we finish the book with the conviction that in the whole brawling, terrible city Lily is the one and only lady.

Of course, in sober afterthought it is incredible that supposed ladies and gentlemen should behave quite so despicably, that George Dorset should stand by so basely when his wife evicts Lily from the yacht, that Jack Stepney should be so grudging, that nobody should raise a finger to help Lily except Selden, who takes her to a hotel in a cab. But as one reads it, it is altogether convincing. The hunted creature is at bay; it is the whole brute world against, not the principles of Lily Bart, or even the good taste of Lily Bart, but simply, in the last analysis, against the beauty of Lily Bart. Lily's beauty is the light in which each of her different groups would like to shine, but when they find that it illuminates their ugliness they want to put it out. It is a beauty, however, that is indestructible, even in poverty, even in death, a beauty that the Trenors and Dorsets, with all their taste and money and ingenuity, can never hope to duplicate, a beauty that is the haunting symbol of what society might be—and isn't.

Lily's physical appearance gives a centripetal pull to a story that might otherwise ramble. When we first see her, through Selden's eyes in Grand Central Station, she is beginning to lose her purity of tint after eleven years of late hours and dancing, yet everything about her is still "vigorous and exquisite, at once strong and fine." Not until he sees her in her last great social triumph, as Reynolds' Mrs. Lloyd in a *tableau vivant* at the Brys', with poised foot and lifted arm, all "soaring grace," is the full poetry of her loveliness revealed to him. Then he sees her as divested of the trivialities of her world and catching "a note of that eternal harmony of which her beauty was a part."

As adversity deepens, he notices a subtle change in her appearance. It has lost the transparency through which fluctuations of the spirit were sometimes tragically visible and has fused into a hard, brilliant substance. Later, at the reading of Mrs. Peniston's disinheriting will, we see her "tall and noble in her black dress." Rosedale meets her in the street, drooping with lassitude, and is struck by the way the dark penciling of fatigue under her eyes and the morbid, blue-veined pallor of her temples bring out the brightness of her hair and lips. He sees her beauty as a "forgotten enemy" that has lain in ambush to spring out on him unawares. And Selden, watching her for the last time kneeling on the hearthrug, will remember long afterward "how the red play of the flame sharpened the depression of her nostrils, and intensified the blackness of the shadows which stuck up from her cheekbones to her eyes." A few hours later he is to see her on her narrow bed, "with motionless hands and calm, unrecognizing face, the semblance of Lily Bart."

The different levels of society in *The House of Mirth* are explored with a precision comparable to that of Proust, whom Mrs. Wharton was later so greatly to admire. We follow Lily's gradual descent from "Bellomont" on the Hudson and the other great country houses of a world where the old and new societies had begun to merge, to the little court of the Gormers, who, although rich enough to be ultimately accepted, are still at the stage of having to fill their house with hangers-on, to the bogus intellectual world of Carry Fisher who pretends to like interesting people while she earns her living helping climbers up the social ladder, to the final drop into the gilded hotel of the demimondaine Norma Hatch. Lily learns that money is the common denominator of all these worlds and that the differences between them consist only in the degrees of scent with which its odor is from time to time concealed. Van Wyck Brooks accused Mrs. Wharton of knowing nothing of the American West, and perhaps she did not, but she had a firsthand knowledge of where the profits of the frontier had gone. Lily Bart, weary on foot, watching the carriages and motors of her former friends ply up and down Fifth Avenue, Mrs. Van Osburgh's C-spring barouche, Mrs. Hatch's electric victoria, is seeing the natural successors of the covered wagon.

I do not suppose that Mrs. Wharton intended Lawrence Selden to constitute the last and greatest of Lily's trials, but so he strikes me. He is a well-born, leisurely bachelor lawyer, with means just adequate for a life of elegant solitude, who spends his evenings, when not leafing through the pages of his first editions, dining out in a society that he loves to ridicule. Lily knows that he is a neutral in the battle of life and death in which she is so desperately engaged, and she asks only that he hold her hand briefly in moments of crisis or brush her lips with a light kiss. He does, in the end, decide to marry her, but as she has been too late for Rosedale, so is he too late for her, and he can only kneel by her bed and give to her lifeless lips the last of his airy kisses. Mrs. Wharton's attitude toward Selden's type of man is enigmatic. He may be a villain in "The Dilettante," or he may at least pose as a hero in The House of Mirth. She is careful in the latter to point out for his sake, whenever he condemns Lily Bart, that appearances have been against her. Perhaps she conceived him as an abused lover in the Shakespearean sense, as an Othello or a Posthumus.[3] But Othello and Posthumus are quick to believe the worst because of the very violence of their passions. An eye as dry as Selden's should be slower to be deceived. I incline to the theory that Mrs. Wharton really intended us to accept this plaster-cast figure for a hero, but that she had a low opinion of heroes in general. When Lily suddenly retorts to Selden that he spends a great deal of his time in a society that he professes to despise, it is as if the author had suddenly slipped into the book to express a contempt that the reader is not meant to share.***

*   *   *

---

3. Heroes in the tragedy Othello and the late comedy Cymbeline [Editor].

CYNTHIA GRIFFIN WOLFF

Lily Bart and the Beautiful Death †

In *"The House of Mirth* Revisited" Diana Trilling observes the parallel between Lily Bart's decline and "the inevitable defeat of art in a crass materialistic society."[1] Trilling does not develop all of the implications of this statement, though she goes on to remark that "Lily herself possesses the quality of a fine work of art" and that "her own ambitions are those of art."[2] Certainly "new New York's" reduction of all values—emotional, ethical, artistic—to questions of portable property was a consistent object of Wharton's scorn and satire; yet at least insofar as the problem of art is concerned, Lily's role in *The House of Mirth* is a more complex one than Trilling's observation can describe. Within the world of the novel, both Lily and her friends perceive her confusedly: she is an uncertain blend of art and nature with a "streak of sylvan freedom in her nature that lent such savour to her artificiality."[3] Often neither she nor her closest observers can distinguish between the merely spontaneous and the studiedly affecting (the careless lack of definition in her "suicide" is of a piece with the rest of her behavior). Indeed, it is not too much to say that this consistent confusion between the ideal and the real as it is manifested by all the characters in the novel—and the resultant depersonalization of the chrysalid character that is Lily's only inheritance—leads directly to the heart of the tragedy.

Before we begin a detailed examination of the effect on Lily Bart of the confusion that attends her attempts at self-definition, we must digress to examine the notions of visual art and artistic expression that pervade *The House of Mirth*. (It is important throughout the course of this discussion to be clear that we are not examining *Wharton's own* notions of art, but the artistic environment that surrounds Lily Bart.) During this period newly wealthy Americans went to Europe and bought "old masters"—not for their beauty but for the instant evidence they gave of culture and limitless success. Wharton gives us repeated testimony to the effect that art acquired by such people and in such a manner remained essentially external to the lives of its owners. Nevertheless, "new New York" was not without its aesthetic self-images, for there was a veritable explosion of lesser art in America at this time; and this art was specifically designed to capture the spirit of America (the ideal Republic) and its people—particularly, as it happens, its women.

One of the most widely visible art forms developed during this period

---

† Reprinted with permission from *American Literature*, Vol. 46, No. 1. Copyright 1974 by Duke University Press.

1. Diana Trilling, *"The House of Mirth* Revisited," in *Edith Wharton*, ed. Irving Howe (Englewood Cliffs, N.J., 1963), p. 109.
2. Ibid., pp. 109–110.
3. Edith Wharton, *The House of Mirth* (New York, 1905), p. 19. All further quotations from *The House of Mirth* are identified in the text by page number.

was the mural. The first extensive use of murals appeared at the Chicago exhibition in 1893; and the tone set there was to be repeated uncounted times, in post offices and public libraries—on any wall suitable for general enlightenment and delight. The tone of such murals is remarkably consistent: they represent in all their manifestations the virtues of a democratic, industrial society; and they embody this panoply of virtues in the figures of chaste women and girls, "an extraordinary number of sexless females, draped in white or the national colors or some other appropriate tinted garments and variously labeled 'Justice,' 'America,' 'The Law,' 'Alma Mater,' 'The Future,' 'The Triumph of Manhattan,' or 'The Ballet.' "[4] The deliberate idealizing of the colossal women who adorned the walls of public buildings could hardly be mistaken for realistic representation; these are women used as symbols, mere visual embodiments of virtue. Yet the possible inference is not without significance: "Our women are pure"—so the public lesson could be read— "indeed, they are effortless monuments of purity." Whatever exigencies the men of America had found necessary in preserving the order of things (and in amassing corporate and national wealth), their women are portrayed symbolically as rising above aberration, relentlessly and uncomplicatedly pure. Small wonder that "for this America the gilded goddess of Daniel Chester French was an appropriate symbol, bearing in one hand the liberty cap and in the other a globe on which an eagle perched."[5]

The clear use of woman as *symbol* of virtue becomes somewhat ambiguous when we examine the portrait art of the period. Here, too, it is the woman (not her successful husband) who is the artist's most frequent subject; and late nineteenth- early twentieth-century portraiture offers now more beguilingly realistic representation of the same virtues that had been splashed across the walls of public buildings. Occasionally the same artists worked in both media; for example, John Singer Sargent, the premier portrait painter of the day, was widely applauded for his murals as well. Here in the area of portraiture, the artist's attitude toward his subject is difficult to define. The techniques suggest a quest for genuine representation, and contemporary criticism indicates that the portrait artist was regarded as one who could render the depths and psychological complexity of his subjects. Thus in an introduction to a 1903 collection of the works of Sargent, the popular poet Alice Meynell imputes a special quality of perception to him.[6]

It is certainly open to question whether such men as Sargent or Abbott Thayer were actually motivated by an attempt to render the various com-

4. Howard Mumford Jones, *The Age of Energy* (New York, 1970), p. 251.
5. Oliver W. Larkin, *Art and Life in America* (New York, 1949), p. 322.
6. "[Criticism] has even granted to the portrait painter, as master of one of the intelligent arts, the praise due to a master of the intellectual arts, calling him psychologist. . . . One may hesitate to name Mr. Sargent, as he has been named, a psychologist. . . . He proves himself rather to be observant and vigilant, nay simple, as a great artist must be. How many and various qualities, mental and physical, meet to prepare that direct and single contemplation of the world might give us matter for surmise; for contemplation there is—something more than observation; and something more than perception—insight." Alice Meynell, *The Work of John S. Sargent* (New York, 1903), introduction.

plex levels of "the *real* woman." Wharton gives a skeptical view of the
society portraitist in *Custom of the Country*: "All [new society] asked of
a portrait was that the costume should be sufficiently 'life-like,' and the
face not too much so; and a long experience in idealizing flesh and
realizing dress-fabrics had enabled Mr. Popple to meet both demands.
'Hang it,' Peter Van Degen pronounced, standing before the easel in an
attitude of inspired interpretation, 'the great thing in a man's portrait is
to catch the likeness—we all know that; but with a woman's it's different—a woman's picture has got to be pleasing. Who wants it about if it
isn't?' "[7] A damning indictment of both artist and patron, for what the
society of new New York wants is, in the long run, deception; and it is,
apparently, deception that the artist was willing (consciously or not) to
provide—the pleasing illusion that the *idealized* rendering of the women
who were painted was in fact *realistic* representation. Modern criticism
of such portrait art tends to support Wharton's indictment.

> Sargent's brush-stroke impressionism was undeniably masterly, and
> Thayer's competent enough; Gibson's drawing style was a brilliant
> graphic counterpart to it. St. Gaudens, Ward, and French, all paid
> nominal service to Realism of concept and texture. But in every
> case, this modernism was specious and superficial; all these men
> were incorrigible idealizers. . . . Though [Sargent] used the tech-
> niques of his chronological contemporaries Manet and Renoir, he
> was the spiritual contemporary of Reynolds and Gainsborough.
> Reynolds would have thoroughly approved the subtle idealization
> of a portrait [like that of the Wyndham Sisters] which equated three
> upper-class women with the Three Fates on the classic Parthenon;
> he would have regarded it as a fine example of his "grand manner,"
> a fulfillment of the artist's duty to make the world a nobler place
> than it is. Reynolds, however, would never have tried or wanted to
> think of it as "realistic," as Sargent and his contemporaries were
> wont to do.[8]

Thus "neo-classical" portraiture and mural work fostered a public
delusion about the nature of women—an untruth at once so palatable
and so generally insisted upon that its lofty expectations concerning the
feminine nature could not easily be dismissed, either by women themselves or by the men who "worshipped" them. What is more, this confusion between the real and the ideal, reiterated throughout American
neo-classical art, found substantial reinforcement in the Art Nouveau
movement of the same period. Here as in portraiture and murals "it is
the woman who is featured, almost to the total exclusion of the male."[9]
The emphasis is different: woman's capacity to be decorative is her chief
attraction. "In spite of, or perhaps because of, woman's increasing pub-

7. Edith Wharton, *The Custom of the Country*
(New York, 1941), p. 195.
8. Alan Gowans, "Painting and Sculpture," in *The
Arts in America: Nineteenth Century*, Wendell D.
Garrett, Paul F. Norton, Alan Gowans and Joseph

T. Butler (New York, 1969), pp. 263, 261.
9. Jan Thompson, "The Role of Women in the
Iconography of Art Nouveau," *Art Journal*, XXXI,
no. 2 (Winter, 1971–72), 158.

lic role, she was even more zealously patronized as a fragile, helpless object, used in a decorative and literal sense to adorn the household: a man's wealth and position were judged by the style in which he kept his wife."[1]

These two modes of art, flourishing at the same historical period though apparently widely different, share a number of attitudes toward women. The rarefied virtue of the neo-classical woman is greatly diminished in the woman of Art Nouveau; but it finds expression in flowing, sentimentalized visual renderings.[2] Here her purity is identified with the repeated floral motif: and of these masses of flowers, none were more consistently used than the lilies adapted from Japanese art themes—Easter lilies, tiger lilies, water lilies, liquescent calla lilies, fluttering clusters of lily-of-the-valley—they droop and spring from page after page, painting after painting. The Junoesque impressiveness of mural art is absent from Art Nouveau, which depicts its women as tall but willowy, attenuated forms surmounted by a halo of bright, abundant hair. Visual renderings of the woman as source of inspiration portray her as though she had grown naturally in her floral surroundings, a being literally incorporated into a world of nature which is—ironically and perversely—flat and unnatural. The confusion between art and nature is sustained.

But the spiritual may descend to the sensational: there is a latent sexuality in the Art Nouveau woman. Her layers of clinging drapery and the fullness of her hair often offer a promise, if not more, of concealed passion. Loïe Fuller, an internationally famous dancer of the period, made extensive use of transparent veiling and colored lights in her performances, and she named her dances after the prevalent Art Nouveau imagery: the Lily Dance, the Fire Dance, and the Butterfly Dance.[3] In the Art Nouveau illustrations of popular advertisement, the sexuality of the woman is more directly, less tastefully, expressed. The High Art Nouveau and the style of the grotesque make the final explicit statement.

It was perhaps the case in this period that one could not enter a significant public building without discovering militant visions of feminine virtue on the walls; however, Art Nouveau penetrated not only public art, but the more private recesses of American culture. Book decoration, pictures and end papers, decorative lettering, chapter headings, all tended to bow to the influence of Art Nouveau. Architectural fittings, the appointments throughout a home, clothing in its multiple mysteries of fabric and underpinning and shoes and hats and accessories—these were all affected by the sinuous line of the New Art. Everywhere Art Nouveau might be cited as synonymous with decorative elegance; and everywhere

1. Ibid., 159.
2. Sargent's portrait of the Wyndham Sisters (cited above as an example of the neoclassical impulse) demonstrates the extent to which these two schools of art interacted. Sargent's portrait was painted in 1899 at the height of the Art Nouveau movement. The figures are elongated with the central figure extended and languid in the most fashionable manner. The ruffling of the dress fabric is sugges-

tive almost of sea foam, and the attenuated fingers of the central figure trail off the right side of the canvas, framed by what appear to be massive groups of flowers, only the edges of which are seen in the picture. The whole, while clearly imitative of Reynolds or Gainsborough, captures the slender, decorative quality of the Art Nouveau woman as well.
3. See Thompson, 163–164.

this influence was felt there was an implicit image of the woman as ultimate exquisite.

These two schools of art—widely different but often overlapping—agreed in one respect: both viewed woman as an essentially "artistic" creation, worthy of representation and innately disposed to "appropriate" behavior. The effect on actual women was direct; it was revealed in their clothing, in the manner in which they wore their hair, in the numerous accoutrements of private life. The varied nuances of this particular notion of femininity would have been familiar to all of Wharton's audience; its atmosphere pervades the world of *The House of Mirth*, creating the distinctive climate in which Lily Bart spends the lingering summer of her youth. For many real women, perhaps for most, the effect of this artistic definition of the feminine might have been superficial. Any woman who was subject to strong alternative influences and any woman who had significant real life roles to play might reflect the aesthetic attitude toward women and women's virtue in little more than a fashionable attitude. But other women, women like Lily who had nothing more to offer than a superb capacity to render themselves agreeable, might be lured by the seductive confusion between representation and reality. Should this confusion occur, the woman would view herself not as a person but as an object—to be admired, to be sustained in her beauty. The men around her would have significance principally as connoisseurs or collectors. It is this exquisite, empty image of self that has contaminated Lily's life; it is, ultimately, this confusion between the ideal and the real that leads to her final tragedy.

It is not altogether easy to trace the origins of Lily's failure. Lily's past is conjured in memories of a mother who had "died of a deep distrust. She hated dinginess, and it was her fate to be dingy" (p. 55). The agonies felt by Lily's mother when she is called upon to confront poverty spring from a relatively vulgar desire for display. "Mrs. Bart was famous for the unlimited effect she produced on limited means; and to the lady and her acquaintances there was something heroic in living as though one were much richer than one's bankbook denoted" (p. 46). Thus Lily's mother cares for artistry principally as an indication of the family's monetary status. She is entirely familiar with the rate of exchange in the world in which she lives, and she nurtures and indulges Lily's beauty—first as the visible sign of the family's station (Lily had, typically, a "dazzling debut") and finally as its one remaining asset. Lily is trained to become a decorative object.

Lily's own ability to assess the various forms of currency in her society is a good deal less fully developed. Her mother had been "a wonderful manager," a woman with the cold-blooded capacity to limit her private delicacies in pursuit of public display. Lily, on the other hand, has been pampered and spoiled: she is childishly, sublimely insensitive to the facts that inform her mother's management and "she knew very little of the value of money" (p. 49). She sees money almost as a natural resource that is supplied by a "neutral tinted" father who "filled an intermediate space between the butler and the man who came to wind the clocks" (p. 45). She has been encouraged in the expansive development of her taste at the expense of practical knowledge. The family's concerted effort in the production and sustaining of Lily's aesthetic nature has endowed her with a limitless responsiveness to beauty—in herself and elsewhere; but her rarefied sensitivity has left her absolutely dependent upon finding an environment that will support such refinement. She is not merely self-indulgent. She genuinely needs the quick succession of fashionable clothes, the "dressing-case of the most complicated elegance" (p. 178), the "few frivolous touches, in the shape of a lace-decked toilet table and a little painted desk surmounted by photographs" (p. 176); these examples of the New Art are the necessary accessories to her personality. "No; she was not made for mean and shabby surroundings, for the squalid compromises of poverty. Her whole being dilated in an atmosphere of luxury; it was the background she required, the only climate she could breathe in" (pp. 39–40). Lily's mother wanted artistic effects because they suggested wealth, success. Lily needs wealth because it is the only atmosphere in which her exquisite femininity can thrive. As she finally realizes, "she had been brought up to be ornamental, [and] she could hardly blame herself for failing to serve any practical purpose" (p. 480).

Lily could not have become the finished masterpiece she is without a good deal of innate talent: thus in the creation of the *tableaux vivants* "her vivid plastic sense, hitherto nurtured on no higher food than dressmaking and upholstery, found eager expression in the disposal of draperies, the study of attitudes, the shifting of lights and shadow" (p. 211). Here the Art Nouveau insistence upon woman as the ultimate artistic elegance is made clear (though for reasons we shall discuss later, Lily chooses the "classical" work of Reynolds to emulate). The contemporary reader might well have been reminded of Loïe Fuller's somewhat more sensational use of drapery and lighting in her public displays (Ned Van Alstyne obviously reacts to Lily's nudity and the purely physical suggestiveness of her pose). This fascination with sweeping, clinging drapery, the addiction to personal accessories of every sort, the pitiful longing to "re-do" Aunt Penniston's house are all assertions of Lily's beautiful, limited "self."[4]

One of Lily's genuine virtues is that she never fully loses her naiveté, never completely corrupts the artistic finish of her nature. Yet she is, from the very beginning of the novel, portrayed as conscious of the distortions created by a society that offers such flattering limitations of the woman's role. " 'A girl must [marry to get out of dingy routine], a man may if he chooses.' She surveyed [Selden] critically. 'Your coat's a little shabby, but who cares? It doesn't keep people from asking you to dine. If I were shabby no one would have me: a woman is asked out as much

---

4. Interestingly, the influence of Art Nouveau in the rendering of Lily Bart may be seen in the illustrations by A. B. Wenzell that appeared both in the serialized form in *Scribner's Magazine* and in the 1905 hard-cover edition. Lily is, not surprisingly, tall, willowy and elongated, with clouds of hair massed about her face. Her garments are clinging and trailing, and she is often portrayed almost dissolving into a background of flowers.

for her clothes as for herself. The clothes are the background, the frame, if you like: they don't make success, but they are a part of it. Who wants a dingy woman? We are expected to be pretty and well-dressed till we drop—and if we can't keep it up alone, we have to go into partnership' " (pp. 17–18). Her beauty—even more, her general aesthetic aura—is not only her fortune in this newly capitalistic society; it is the only thing about her that makes her interesting or valuable to others. The man who marries her will select her as the final prize in his collection; Lily knows this fact, and her "skill in enhancing [her beauty], the care she took of it, the use she made of it, seemed to give it a kind of permanence. . . . She knew that Mr. Gryce was of the small chary type most inaccessible to impulses and emotions. . . . But Lily had known the species before: she was aware that such a guarded nature must find one huge outlet of egoism, and she determined to be to him what his Americana had hitherto been: the one possession in which he took sufficient pride to spend money on it. She knew that this generosity to self is one of the forms of meanness, and she resolved so to identify herself with her husband's vanity that to gratify her wishes would be to him the most exquisite form of self-indulgence."

Lily never does learn her mother's capacity for management, and in the transactional portions of her life she suffers a failure of will, a revulsion, perhaps, from the final human compromise. The everyday habit of self-adornment indicates that Lily has internalized the New Art's notion of woman; but the merely decorative is in the end not entirely sufficient for Lily. Even when she was very young, "there was in Lily a vein of sentiment . . . which gave an idealizing touch to her most prosaic purposes. She liked to think of her beauty as a power for good, as giving her the opportunity to attain a position where she should make her influence felt in the vague diffusion of refinement and good taste" (p. 54). But this pining after moral significance brings with it no capacity to make choices, draw difficult distinctions, or bear hardship; it is, like much else in her nature, diffuse and indolent. She is genuinely puzzled by the difficulties (when they come to her attention, as they rarely do) of the moral life conscientiously lived. "She could not breathe long on the heights; there had been nothing in her training to develop any continuity of moral strength: what she craved, and really felt herself entitled to, was a situation in which the noblest attitude should also be the easiest" (p. 422). She would be like the Wood Nymph of the Art Nouveau, her evocative purity casually, "naturally," placed in a bower of flowers—or like the unwaveringly chaste women of the neo-classical school, poised to preside majestically over significant public events. In other words, virtue and nobility should be effortless companions to her artistically rendered self.

Most often, Lily handles her moral queasiness by choosing not to know the full implications of her plight. She permits the pleasing aesthetic *appearance* that she can give a situation to substitute for its reality. "She was always scrupulous about keeping up appearances to herself.

Her personal fastidiousness had a moral equivalent, and when she made a tour of inspection in her own mind there were certain closed doors she did not open" (p. 131). When an acceptable interpretation cannot be found, Lily characteristically removes herself to a different, more spiritually consoling atmosphere. After all, "moral complications existed for her only in the environment that had produced them; she did not mean to slight or ignore them, but they lost their reality when they changed their background" (p. 314). This need to avoid serious moral reflection is, of course, a principal cause of her social downfall. She must accept Gus Trenor's "tip" as a fraternal gesture; she is not prepared to sort out the moral and financial problems that would be revealed by a frank appraisal. She must perceive Bertha Dorset's invitation as springing first from mere friendship and then from deep wells of human need; the option of recognizing Bertha's malicious and immoral use of her raises problems that she has not the stamina to resolve. She must linger lazily in her secretary/companion role to Mrs. Hatch until all the world believes in her actual duplicity; she has not the discipline to refuse (nor, ironically, the sustained habit of calculation to partake in that lady's social rise). In the end when Lily tries to review her relationship to Bertha and Selden dispassionately, she cannot overcome the deficiencies of a life devoted to evasion: "What debt did she owe to a social order which had condemned and banished her without trial? She had never been heard in her own defense; she was innocent of the charge on which she had been found guilty; and the irregularity of her conviction might seem to justify the use of methods as irregular in recovering her lost rights" (p. 486). But she cannot think her way through these complexities (the possibility of going directly to Selden does not occur as an option, for reasons that we shall discuss later); she has not been bred to offer anything more than the *appearance* of moral righteousness: "Was it her fault that the purely decorative mission is less easily and harmoniously fulfilled among social beings than in the world of nature? That it is apt to be hampered by materialistic necessities or complicated by moral scruples?" (p. 487).

When her habits of moral evasion fail her as Lily meets one reversal after another, she does not put her aesthetic-moral talents to a real examination of the problem; instead she reverts to a more energetic summoning of the Grand Manner, an infusion of her being with the *appearance* of spiritual command which never corresponds to the fact of increasing inner desolation. When Bertha dismisses her and Selden offers support of sorts, Lily rises and stands "before him in a kind of clouded majesty, like some deposed princess moving tranquilly to exile" (p. 353). When Gerty Farish makes similar gestures of sympathy and help, "she drew herself up to the full height of her slender majesty, towering like some dark angel of defiance above the troubled Gerty" (p. 362). This behavior represents a literal translation of the confusion in Lily's early training that had led her to believe that "the noblest attitude should also be the easiest." If one supposes attitude to signify not a habit of mind but merely an artistic pose, a semblance, then Lily can continue for a while to satisfy the "moral" demands of her deeply aesthetic nature.

It is a nature that needs, in all its manifestations, the reassurance of a perceptive audience. In the passages cited just above, Lily gains some measure of deceptive confidence by convincing the onlookers of the consonance between appearance and reality. This manner of relating to others is relatively consistent throughout the novel. Indeed, it is an indispensable clue to understanding the role that Selden plays.

Selden's artistic training has been as thorough as Lily's, though it has a strong neo-classical bias: "in a different way, he was, as much as Lily, the victim of his environment' (p. 245). His tastes incline him to appreciate instructive art; and while he is susceptible to the decorative (as both his initial reactions to Lily and the history of his affair with Bertha Dorset suggest), the full depth of his aesthetic passion has a moralistic character. "It had been Selden's fate to have a charming mother: her graceful portrait, all smiles and Cashmere, still emitted a faded scent of the undefinable quality. . . . His views of womankind in especial were tinged by the remembrance of the one woman who had given him his sense of 'values'" (pp. 245–246). Selden has learned, from the example of his parents' elegant poverty, a moral finickiness that is every bit as divorced from reality as Lily's. Selden's parents have both refused to compromise the pursuit of absolute quality in their material lives, but they adopt a pious, self-congratulatory attitude toward what they perceive as their habit of "restraint." They are self-deceived; they suffer from the sin of pride. "Neither one of the couple cared for money, but their disdain of it took the form of always spending a little more than was prudent. . . . Selden senior had an eye for a picture, his wife an understanding of old lace; and both were so conscious of restraint and discrimination in buying that they never quite knew how it was that the bills mounted up" (p. 245).

The son grows up believing that life fully led must necessarily satisfy both his own moral habit of self-righteous other-worldliness and the indulgence of his keenest sensitivities; and the fact that these two appetites might be mutually contradictory is a problem that Selden has no capacity to confront. Given the attitudes of the society of which he is a part, it is not surprising that Selden chooses instead to project these ambivalences into his notions of femininity. "Life shorn of either feeling appeared to him a diminished thing; and no where was the blending of the two ingredients so essential as in the character of a pretty woman" (p. 246).

He has been trained as a connoisseur, well equipped to appreciate the nuances of Lily's display; but he necessarily carries his own artistic-moral complications into their relationship. Lily must be beautiful, but her beauty must have an uplifting quality; she must be beautiful, all the while appearing to be above material concerns. (Even inherited wealth would not solve Lily's predicament thus defined, for Lily could seem

genuinely above material concerns only if she ignored or rejected whatever wealth she might have—and ignoring the uses of money, as even
Lily knows, would diminish her capacity for the very decorative display
that Selden so admires.) Until his entanglement with Lily Bart, Selden
had handled this essential contradiction in his own nature and in his
expectations about the nature of women by a series of "voluntary exclusions" (p. 244). Quite wisely, "he had meant to keep free from permanent ties. . . . There had been a germ of truth in his declaration to Gerty
Farish that he had never wanted to marry a 'nice' girl: the adjective
connoting, in his cousin's vocabulary, certain utilitarian qualities which
are apt to preclude the luxury of charm" (pp. 244–245). Selden would
have Miss Bart be a Lily of the Field in very truth, enacting her parable
of beauty effortlessly. Little wonder that in judging her "he had always
made use of the 'argument from design' " (p. 6). And yet . . . this "streak
of sylvan freedom" is not central; it only lends interest, for Selden, to
her "artificiality." The Lily unadorned would, after all, fail to sustain
his interest.

The novel opens with a meeting between Selden and Lily, establishing the terms of their relationship and alerting the reader to Wharton's
structuring of the process of Lily's decline.[5] The narrator begins in Selden's mind, presents Lily only as *he* sees her, and shows him to have the
lingering, appraising, inventorial mind of the experienced collector: he
is fascinated with her surface appearance, misses no detail of her exquisite finish. He thinks, automatically one must suppose, in the categories
of the connoisseur. He remarks the chiaroscuro effect of "her vivid head,
relieved against the dull tints of the crowd," takes in the details of her
clothing and "the purity of tint, that she was beginning to lose after
eleven years of late hours and indefatigable dancing" (p. 4). As they walk
up Madison Avenue the inspection continues with Selden "taking a luxurious pleasure in her nearness: in the modeling of her little ear, the
crisp upward wave of her hair . . . and the thick planting of her straight
black lashes" (pp. 6–7).

Selden's reactions to this surfeit of decorative art reveal, even here,
his inbred moral-aesthetic ambiguities. There is first the self-indulgence
of his appreciation of her, then the startled, guilty awareness of the monetary implications of even such indulgence as this, then disapproval—
but not of his own indulgence, rather disapproval projected onto Lily—
and finally the longing to see such beauty allied in some indefinable way
with the lofty virtue that his nature craves:

5. Edith Wharton was insistent upon the impor-
tance of this first chapter—see "The Criticism of
Fiction," in *TLS*, May 14, 1914 and *A Backward
Glance* (New York, 1934), p. 208. Walter B.
Rideout has noted her emphasis—see "Edith
Wharton's *The House of Mirth*, 1905," in *Twelve
Original Essays on Great American Novels*, ed.
Charles Shapiro (Detroit, 1958)—but Rideout
seems to view the chapter as having three major
parts, the scene in Grand Central, the visit to Selden's apartment and the encounter with Rosedale. Since the first and third of these take up
together only four pages out of a total of 22 in the
chapter, it seems more sensible to see the chapter
in its establishing the nature of Lily's relationship
to Selden; in truth, almost the entire chapter is
devoted to the explication of that relationship.

Everything about her was at once vigorous and exquisite, at once strong and fine. He had a confused sense that she must have cost a great deal to make, that a great many dull and ugly people must, in some mysterious way, have been sacrificed to produce her. He was aware that the qualities distinguishing her from the herd of her sex were chiefly external: as though a fine glaze of beauty and fastidiousness had been applied to vulgar clay. Yet the analogy left him unsatisfied, for a coarse texture will not take a high finish; and was it not possible that the material was fine, but that circumstance had fashioned it into a futile shape? (p. 7)

Selden's musings might almost pass for social criticism were it not for the fact that the "futile shape" he seems to deplore is a shape he obviously and extensively admires and that his admiration is part of the continuing "circumstance" that fashions it. There is satire, of course; but it inheres in the narrator's use of irony—an irony which places Selden as part of the *uninformed* audience.

His assessment of Lily is gradually revealed to deal almost entirely with externals: he is willing at every point to accept the appearance for reality. Thus, while people have indeed "been sacrificed" to "produce" Lily, the reader learns (though Selden never fully does) that the principal sacrifice has been Lily herself. While he imputes "far-reaching intentions" to her "simplest acts" (p. 3), we discover that Lily is capable only of short-term schemes, one of which—the learning-up of Americana for Percy Gryce—is hatched here under Selden's unsuspecting eye. When Lily does essay direct frankness, attempting to move beyond the superficialities of their emotional relationship, Selden responds with a nervous evasion into inconsequential flirtation, though "he felt a slight shiver down his spine as he ventured this" (p. 12)—even this pseudo-intimacy. Their "frankness" leads to nothing more than an inventory of Lily's chances for marriage and a continuation of Selden's "appreciation" of Lily, now that he has settled her at a safe emotional distance. Selden is thoroughly encapsulated in his own preoccupations, needs, and prejudices. The ambiguities that grow out of his early experiences make him reluctant to permit serious emotional ties; his stance as connoisseur gives a socially acceptable definition to this reluctance, and the pervasive judgmental quality of his manner generally precludes sympathetic response. She is for him here merely an object for appraising examination. Lily, by contrast, is all too able to see the world (herself in particular) through *his* eyes—to identify with his values and his artistic standards. She is, as even this first exchange suggests, willing to try to meet him on some common emotional ground. Yet if she is to meet him at all, it must be on his terms, for his values are settled.

Selden's thorough capacity for sensuous aesthetic enjoyment is revealed in this first scene; the other half of his oddly-assorted nature, the moralistically righteous side, is revealed in their second intimate encounter. He draws her on to talk about her schemes, her failure to find "success";

and then he turns on her "worldliness" to outline his own image of success. " 'My idea of success,' he said, 'is personal freedom. . . . [Freedom] from everything—from money, from poverty, from ease and anxiety, from all the material accidents. To keep a kind of republic of the spirit—that's what I call success' " (p. 108). Lily is attracted to this Utopian vision; her moral fastidiousness is offended by the necessity of maintaining herself as a "collectable." Yet she cannot help questioning the genuine workability of Selden's system. " 'The only way not to think about money is to have a great deal of it' " (p. 110), she sensibly replies. Selden, flushed with the purity of his vision, discounts real world problems. " 'You might as well say that the only way not to think about air is to have enough to breathe. That is true enough in a sense; but your lungs are thinking about the air, if you are not. And so it is with your rich people—they may not be thinking of money, but they're breathing it all the while; take them into another element and see how they squirm and gasp!' " (pp. 110–111). Lily's wry observation that he seems to spend a lot of time " 'in the element you disapprove of' " (p. 111) elicits only the evasion that he is an "amphibious" creature.

Wharton offers clear satire here—not in Selden's remarks, but in the illogical self-deception of his narrowly virtuous position. Like Gryce, Selden will accept Lily only if she can identify herself with his "vanity." Gryce's vanity is of a simple order: he collects Americana; he would add her to that collection. Selden's is more complex—and more seductive. He luxuriates in her studied decorative quality: he would have her retain that quality (not become "nice," to use Gerty Farish's term), but he would have her absolutely reject the material world that sustains it. What is more, as his subsequent behavior reveals, he would have her do this without sympathetic support from him. He is to remain aloof, judgmental.

His attitude of sustained condemnation wears away at Lily's confidence. " 'You despise my ambitions—you think them unworthy of me!' . . . 'Well, isn't that a tribute? I think them quite worthy of most of the people who live by them.' . . . 'Why do you do this to me? . . Why do you make the things I have chosen seem hateful to me if you have nothing to give me instead?' " (pp. 113–114). Lily's words move Selden to a declaration, and her answering tears almost, but not entirely break his stance of ironic detachment.

At this point the lovers seem united in some higher sphere: "The soft isolation of the falling day enveloped them: they seemed lifted into a finer air. All the exquisite influences of the hour trembled in their veins" (pp. 116–117). However, Wharton is quick to alert us to the fact that it is only in this other-world that they can be united. In order to be morally worthy of Selden's collection, Lily must not waver in her disdain for the things of this world: as little as a fleeting hesitation will betray sufficient flaw. And that hesitation comes almost immediately when the sound of a motor car intrudes the real world upon them. Lily falters, remembering the excuse she has made to the other guests, remembering particularly her evasions with Percy Gryce; her remembrance is sufficient to return Selden's somewhat softened manner to an attitude of contempt.

> "I had no idea it was so late. We shall not be back till after dark," she said, almost impatiently.
>
> Selden was looking at her with surprise: it took him a moment to regain his usual view of her; then he said, with an uncontrollable note of dryness: "That was not one of our party; the motor was going the other way." (p. 118)

Lily's weakness is everywhere evident: in the crudest terms, she wants to copper her bets. However, given the flimsiness of Selden's lofty moral system and—even more significant—given his incapacity to cast off his own cold disdain and guide her through her moments of uncertainty, Lily's hesitation is at least understandable. Later (pp. 517–518), Lily is to review this moment and place the blame for its failure very heavily on herself; but the reader, who can view the entire House of Mirth more clearly and critically than Lily, sees the contributing effect of Selden's attitude.

There are other kinds of men—men who can love sympathetically, who can tolerate weakness in the beloved—but these men exist outside the House of Mirth. For all his vulgar preoccupation with money, Mr. Rosedale is revealed as having traces of compassion, elements of sympathy which are being systematically eradicated by his "successful" social climbing. Nettie, disgraced and reclaimed, who gives Lily "her first glimpse of the continuity of life" (p. 516), suggests an alternative, too, in the husband who has "faith," who can "know" the deepest failures of his wife and not recoil. But within the House of Mirth there is no alternative; and both Lily and Selden are too thoroughly acclimated to live elsewhere.

Wharton's satire of "a frivolous society" whose "tragic implication lies in its power of debasing people and ideals"[6] is structured on a series of such intimate confrontations between Selden and Lily. Ironically, given Selden's self-consciously moral definition of his own role, he is changed very little by his contact with Lily's tragedy. He is always the connoisseur, always willing to evade complicity; and at the very end of the novel as at the beginning, we return to view Lily through his judging and imperceptive eyes. He still regards her as a moral-aesthetic object—the episode with her has proved uplifting, "he could even draw from it courage not to accuse himself for having failed to reach the height of his opportunity" (p. 532)—and he still has no knowledge of or sympathy with her pain. By contrast Lily does gain insight, though not the capacity to free herself. She recognizes that "the very quality of [Selden's] love had made it the more impossible to recall to life" (p. 517). Yet Lily has been formed to accept a definition of femininity of which men like Selden are the supreme evaluators. The first two confrontations outline the conflicting demands she must satisfy, and the scenes with Selden that follow detail her desperate and finally fatal efforts to satisfy them. Lily comes closest to Selden's expectations for her in the third encounter, the evening of the *tableaux vivants*.

Her choice of costume reveals her increased understanding of Selden's visionary demands of her; and though she toys with a presentation that would emphasize the purely decorative, she settles finally on a perfect union of the sensual and the morally significant: she presents herself in the classical guise of Reynolds's "Mrs. Lloyd."

> Her pale draperies, and the background of foliage against which she stood, served only to relieve the long dryad-like curves that swept upward from her poised foot to her lifted arm. The noble buoyancy of her attitude, its suggestive grace, revealed the touch of poetry in her beauty that Selden always felt in her presence. (p. 217).

Wharton means the reader to understand this as an illusionary image of Lily; it touches, is intended to touch, "the vision-building faculty in Selden" (p. 216). It is doubly an artifice, being a recreation of a portrait which is, itself, an idealized and exalted rendering of reality. It reveals nothing of Lily's suffering—nothing, even, of the artistic effort that has been expended in producing it. It is the instantiation of ideal beauty as employed by the artist to elevate the life of the beholder; this being and only such a being as this could inhabit Selden's "republic of the spirit." And in it Selden fancies that he sees before him for the first time "the real Lily Bart" (p. 217). Selden has made an error that captures the essence of his society's demands for the "best" women: he has mistaken the ideal for the real.

Lily savors her success, prolonging the illusion in her interview after the display (an interview which is held, appropriately enough, in the false summer of a conservatory). "The magic place was deserted. . . . Selden and Lily stood still, accepting the unreality of the scene as a part of their own dream-like sensations" (p. 221). Yet the attempt to move from this level to more mundane reality fails: Selden can "love" Lily, on his own terms; but he cannot "help" her surmount the inconsistencies of her nature (see p. 222).

Selden's inability to have a loving faith in Lily's capacity for redemption is underlined by his reaction to seeing her emerge from Gus Trenor's house later that evening. As in the second confrontation, the moment of "perfect union" is destroyed by a hint (not a confirmation) of weakness. Selden moves from a totality of adoration to a totality of disdain; and though Lily is, ironically, not guilty of the transgression he imputes to her, his capacity for understanding and his tolerance for imperfection are so slight that he is rendered incapable of knowing her true situation. (The same mistake almost occurs at the end of the novel when Selden, going through Lily's papers, finds the note to Trenor. Only the accident of its being open saves Lily's reputation, for even in this moment Selden is willing to condemn her.) Hereafter, the relationship between Selden and Lily is but a chronicle of her destruction. She saves face in Italy by an adoption of "the Grand Manner"; and Selden characteristically accepts this fiction. She rises to her one act of genuine heroism in the destruction of his letters, but by this time "her presence was becoming an embarrassment to him" (p. 496); and when he confronts her lifeless body, he has lost forever the opportunity to discover that she has sacrificed herself to preserve his reputation and his memory of her. A significant measure of the final insufficiency of Selden's view of Lily is the startling fact that he *never does* know that she possessed Bertha's letters to him, never does know that she destroyed them when she might have saved herself by using them.

Wharton herself saw the tragedy of the novel as centering in the character of Lily,[7] and a modern reader can trace rather explicitly the ways in which Lily has been destroyed. Constrained by the monetary and emotional impoverishment of her life, Lily has adopted her society's images of women narrowly and literally: she has long practiced the art of making herself an exquisite decorative object, and under Selden's eye she comes to think of herself as a moral object as well. Yet the crucial term here is "object." She learns to evoke approval and appreciation in others by a subtle and ingenious series of graceful postures. It is an art she has practiced so well and for so long that she can no longer conceive of herself as anything but those postures; she can formulate no other desire than the desire to be seen to advantage. "There were moments when she longed blindly for anything different, anything strange, remote and untried; but the utmost reach of her imagination did not go beyond picturing her usual life in a new setting. She could not figure herself as anywhere but in a drawing-room, diffusing elegance as a flower sheds perfume" (p. 161).

Repeatedly throughout the novel, Wharton gives evidence that Lily's special skill in the representation of herself lies in an uncanny ability to experience herself as others must see her (and thus to anticipate their reactions and control them). On the train when she looks ahead to the possible meeting with Gryce, Lily "arranged herself in her corner with the instinctive feeling for effect which never forsook her" (p. 26). The ceremony of the tea she shares with him is a model of manipulation. Her every mood, motion, public attitude (except for those few impulses for which she pays so dearly) is a deliberate piece of acting. She knows, always, when she is being observed; and she automatically plays to her audience. She has learned so thoroughly to experience herself as an object that is being observed by others—not directly as an integrated human being—that her sense of "self" is confirmed only when she elicits reactions from others; and when she is alone (and she increasingly fears loneliness), her inner emptiness becomes terrifying, unbearable. R. D. Laing's description of the schizoid personality illuminates Lily's problem:

7. Ibid.

The need to be perceived is not, of course, purely a visual affair. It extends to the general need to have one's presence endorsed or confirmed by the other, the need for one's total existence to be recognized; the need, in fact, to be loved. Thus those people who cannot sustain from within themselves the sense of their own identity . . . have no inner conviction that they are alive, may feel that they are real live persons only when they are experienced as such by another. . . . "I am the person that other people know and recognize me to be."[8]

The symptoms of this depersonalization are found everywhere throughout the novel.

For example, Lily's capacity to feel emotion has almost atrophied. Does she love Selden? It is a question she raises almost academically, for she "had no definite experience by which to test the quality of her feelings" (p. 103). Certainly she wants to be loved *by* him, for that would confirm her own sense of worth, of lovability. She has no real capacity for generosity; "the other-regarding sentiments had not been cultivated in Lily" (p. 179). She derives pleasure in giving money to Gerty Farish's charities; but her pleasure is in Gerty's admiration of her act, her "surprise and gratitude. . . . And Lily parted from her with a sense of self-esteem which she naturally mistook for the fruits of altruism" (p. 180). Selden observes, rather cruelly, "that even her weeping was an art" (p. 115); but his judgment of her in this respect is probably correct. She can see herself only as a reflection—in others' judgments of her or literally in the series of mirror images that stalk her through the novel. Whenever she wants to know how she feels, she looks into a mirror to find out. When the mirror returns a reassuring message, life seems good to Lily. "Mrs. Bry's admiration was a mirror in which Lily's self-complacency recovered its lost outline. The sense of being of importance among the insignificant was enough to restore to Miss Bart the gratifying consciousness of power." But when her reverses are not put right by an appreciative audience, her sense of deformity (and unbearable self-loathing) find expression in descriptions of the mirrored "self" that comes almost self-consciously from the school of Dorian Gray. Thus after her encounter with Trenor, she tries to explain her sense of shame to Gerty Farish: "Can you imagine looking into your glass some morning and seeing a disfigurement—some hideous change that has come to you while you slept? Well, I seem to myself like that—I can't bear to see myself in my own thoughts—I hate ugliness, you know" (p. 265). And when Selden reacts to her lapse with Trenor by leaving to go abroad, her response is characteristic and immediate. "She rose, and walking across the floor stood gazing at herself for a long time in the brightly-lit mirror above the mantelpiece. The lines in her face came out terribly—she looked old;

8. R. D. Laing, *The Divided Self* (Great Britain, 1971), p. 119. The whole of the chapter entitled "Self-consciousness" is of great help in understanding Lily's flawed ability to perceive herself.

and when a girl looks old to herself, how does she look to other people?" (p. 289).

Given the entirely dependent nature of Lily's sense of self, we can understand Selden's importance to her: his critical stance adds a moral dimension to her life; for although she has repeatedly succeeded in confirming her effect as a merely decorative object, she has found this success insufficient. Thus intimacy between Lily and Selden involves her adopting his point of view, submitting to his judgments. And his judgment is generally harsh. "That was the secret of his way of readjusting her vision. Lily, turning her eyes from him, found herself scanning her little world through his retina: it was as though the pink lamps had been shut off and the dusty daylight let in" (p. 87). Yet, as we have seen, his own moral-aesthetic code is deeply flawed. It is a code that even he can follow only by a series of suppressed hypocrisies: he is as much a parasite on the society of the House of Mirth as Lily is—she timidly points this fact out, but has not the internal stamina and coherence to pursue her point (pp. 109–115); his affair with Bertha Dorset scarcely justifies the chaste horror he manifests at the possibility that Lily's conduct has been less than absolutely perfect. In submerging her ethical view into his, Lily has accepted impossible standards.

There is, however, an even more seriously destructive element in Selden's system as applied to Lily: all her life she has been an *object* of decorative pleasure, has allowed the reactions of others to be the only mirror in which she can see her "real" self. A genuinely liberating moral system would reject this process of dehumanization; by contrast, Selden's moral system merely continues it. He is willing to judge her worthy if and only if she can become a flawless, absolutely constant embodiment of virtue. When Lily accepts these unattainable ideals as her "realities," accepts Selden's rarefied distillations of femininity as the definition of the self that she must reaffirm in all her daily actions, she is merely continuing on a somewhat loftier plane the lifelong habit of seeing herself as an object to be judged by others. In her relationship to Selden "she longed to be to him something more than a piece of sentient prettiness, a passing diversion to his eye and brain" (p. 152), but she fails (as anyone must) to satisfy the needs of his moral-aesthetic nature. She evokes little more than ironic, detached disapproval. And since she has accepted the notion that his reactions are the only "mirror" in which her "real" self can be reflected, her perception of that self becomes one of increasing disgust and self-loathing. Each episode of gentle admonition on his part is a blow to Lily's self-esteem. "She looked at him helplessly, like a hurt or frightened child: this real self of hers, which he had the faculty of drawing out of the depths, was so little accustomed to go alone" (p. 152). Little wonder that she does not think of loving him; that act would require an independent identity. Instead her needs are expressed in terms that plead for his reassuring response: "it seemed to her that it was for him only she cared to be beautiful" (p. 220).

The artificial quality of Lily's one great success—her impersonation of Reynolds's portrait—indicates the impossibility of sustaining Selden's idealized image on any but an other-worldly level. Thus afterwards she sighs, " 'Ah, love me, love me—but don't tell me so!' " (p. 222).

Lily's acceptance of Selden's demands on her as aesthetic-moral object renders her even less able than before to return to the moral lassitude of an easier environment. "The renewed habit of luxury—the daily waking to an assured absence of care and presence of material ease—gradually blunted her appreciation of these values, and left her more conscious of the void they could not fill" (p. 381). When Selden visits her at Mrs. Hatch's apartment, Lily is conscious of her emotional need for an expression of feeling on his part (p. 449); but when he proffers only cold, cruel judgment, she is incapable of resisting her revulsion from the "real self" that his criticism seems once more to have uncovered. The narrator repeatedly suggests that "the situation between them was one which could have been cleared up only by a sudden explosion of feeling" (p. 449). But the habits of a lifetime cannot be dismissed. Selden has been formed as connoisseur, Lily as collectable; "their whole training and habit of mind were against the chances of such an explosion" (p. 449). Lily must persist to the end with the only roles she understands, and her final preoccupation becomes the reclamation of "self" in Selden's eyes— at no matter what cost.[9] The significance of her death becomes clearer when we define her dilemma in this way. We can never know whether it was a conscious act; so many of her finer gestures seem acts of care- lessness, of thoughtless inattention. Yet the effect of her death is redemptive: it recaptures and fixes forever Selden's esteem for her; it apotheosizes her triumphant *tableau vivant*.

It is not insignificant, then, that her first act upon returning to her room for the last time is the resurrection of the Reynolds dress nor that she should end her life by a final surrender to her fate as aesthetic object. "All her interest and activities had been taught to center around it. She was like some rare flower grown for exhibition, a flower from which every bud had been nipped except the crowning blossom of her beauty. . . . There had never been a time when she had any real relation to life. . . . There was no centre of early pieties, of grave endearing traditions, to which her heart could revert and from which it could draw strength for itself and tenderness for others" (pp. 512–513, 516). She has destroyed Selden's letters; she has paid her debt to Trenor. But these impulsive gestures are not integrated into a sustaining moral vision of herself. Given the limitations of Lily's nature, only Selden's continued faith in her

9. An interesting example of Lily's inability to conceive of herself in any other way than as the object of aesthetic attention can be found in the dreamlike sequence with Nettie and her baby. Though the scene is described in rather general terms, Lily does seem to respond to the baby, per- haps because its rosy helplessness seems a replica of her own state (her death-dreams would confirm this view). Still there is, momentarily, an emo- tional response to another human being, a response that is freed from the anxiety of eliciting the "cor- rect" reaction. Yet at the most intimate point in that moment, Lily reverts to type: the instinct to define herself as the admired artistic object is too deeply ingrained. "At first the burden in her arms seemed as light as a pink cloud or a heap of down, but as she continued to hold it the weight increased, sinking deeper, and penetrating her with a strange sense of weakness, as though the child entered into her and became a part of herself. *She looked up, and saw Nettie's eyes resting on her with tenderness and exultation*" (italics added).

could support such a vision; "the uplifting memory of his faith" (p. 518) cannot. "She felt an intense longing to prolong, to perpetuate, the momentary exaltation of her spirit. If only life could end now" (p. 519). And when Selden confronts her lifeless body, Lily has been irretrievably transformed into an object; her "self" has finally been transfixed, rendered suitably free from weakness and flaw. It is ironic that confronted with this extreme he should feel "that the real Lily was still there, close to him" (pp. 526–527); the "real" Lily—the *only* Lily he can tolerate—is the beautiful idealized memory he carries of her, the most superb piece in his collection.

Selden is satisfied with this resolution to the problem of Lily Bart. He reassures himself that "at least he *had* loved her" (p. 532). The structure of the novel demands more discrimination from the reader: Nettie and the husband "whose faith in her had made her renewal possible" (p. 517) live in the House of Mourning,[1] a place where the moral-aesthetic "vanities" of men like Selden have been relinquished for the saving acceptance of suffering and human limitation. Far from being Wharton's spokesman, Selden is the final object of her sweeping social satire.

Once we reject Selden, reject the lapses into bathetic sentimentality that so aptly render his final moments with Lily, we must revaluate the peculiarly American literary tradition of which this last episode in the novel is a part. For whatever reason, this situation—the death of a beautiful woman as seen through the eyes of her lover—became a set piece in American literature. For example, in a novel like *Daisy Miller* the death of a realistically rendered (and possibly deeply troubled) young woman is described principally in terms of the aesthetic-moral effect it has upon a highly sensitized, lover-like man. She becomes, primarily, the object of his idealistic artistic sensibilities. Until Wharton wrote *The House of Mirth*, no one had troubled to detail what it would be like to be the women thus exalted and objectified. Blake Nevius makes the obvious comparison between the two novels: "Like Winterbourne in *Daisy Miller*, [Selden] is betrayed by his aloofness, his hesitations, his careful discriminations. He is the least attractive ambassador of his 'republic of the spirit,' and Mrs. Wharton knows this as well as her readers."[2] Selden surely does share Winterbourne's inadequacies; but Wharton surpasses James specifically in her ability to reveal the psychological distortions, the self-alienation, that a woman suffers when she accepts the status of idealized object. We see the inner desolation to which Lily is reduced; we know very little of a reliable sort about Daisy, for Daisy's martyrdom (or her canonization) has precipitately robbed her of complexity, perhaps of her full share of humanity.

If (as we must) we condemn Selden for savoring the resonances of

---

1. The passage from Ecclesiastes is relevant: Chapter 7, verses 3–4.
   Sorrow is better than laughter,
      for by sadness of countenance the
      heart is made better.

The heart of the wise is in the house of mourning;
but the heart of fools is in the house of mirth.

2. Blake Nevius, *Edith Wharton: A Study of Her Fiction* (Berkeley and Los Angeles, 1961), p. 59.

Lily's death, we might want to reconsider the moral status of any narrator or any reader who would reduce human suffering to an artistically
satisfying (albeit morally uplifting) experience. We have seen the extent
to which Wharton weaves the confusions of contemporary visual art into
her portrait of that "frivolous society" she would have us scorn; the last
scene of the novel, Lily's own Beautiful Death, encourages us to look
for distortions in the art of fiction as well. Henry James says admiringly
of Sargent's work that he "handles [the delicate feminine elements] with
a special feeling for them, and they borrow a kind of noble intensity
from his brush."[3] Wharton's own portrait of a lady must lead us to wonder how well any real or realistically conceived woman could tolerate
the compliment of being thus ennobled.

R. W. B. LEWIS

[*The House of Mirth* Biographically] †

The House of Mirth was published on October 14, 1905, in a first
edition of forty thousand copies. When, late in the previous March,
Edith noted in her diary that the novel was done, she commented that
she had begun work on it "about Sept. 1903." This was accurate in the
sense that only then did she finally determine the theme of her story: a
theme, in her telling of it, that emerged as much from literary and dramatic meditation as from private reminiscing. As early as 1900, in fact,
she had been mulling over the subject—fashionable society in New York
and perhaps in Newport—and had hit upon several of her characters'
names. But though New York society was something she knew inti-
mately, she also knew it to be a futile and insubstantial affair. The problem, as she recalled telling herself, "was how to extract from such a
subject the typical human significance which is the story-teller's reason
for telling one story rather than another. . . . The answer was that a
frivolous society can acquire dramatic significance only through what its
frivolity destroys."

The answer, she declared in summary, was to be the sensitive and
vital heroine Lily Bart: and the story would be Lily's slow destruction by
a grossly indifferent society. Lily Bart, though distantly perceived and
named in 1900, was not truly born until the end of the summer of 1903.

Work on the novel was delayed nearly a year by Teddy's collapses and
the enforced departure for Europe and by other literary obligations. It
was Edward Burlingame,[1] apparently, who drew Edith back to it in August

---

3. Henry James, "John S. Sargent," in *The Painter's Eye*, ed. John L. Sweeney (Cambridge, Ma.,
1956), p. 226. James originally published this essay
in *Harper's Magazine*, Oct., 1887. It was later
reprinted with emendation in *Picture and Text* in
1893. This quotation is taken from the 1893 version.

† Pages 150–156 form *Edith Wharton: A Biography* by R. W. B. Lewis. Copyright © 1975 by Harper & Row, Publishers, Inc. Reprinted by
permission of the publisher.
1. The editor of *Scribner's Magazine*, where *The
House of Mirth* first appeared as a serial [*Editor*].

1904, by begging her to have the novel ready to begin serialization in *Scribner's* the following January, since another story due to start then had fallen through. Edith worked harder and more steadily than she ever had in her life. It was this experience, she would contend, that finally taught her "this discipline of the daily task" and transformed her once and for all "from a drifting amateur into a professional"—though an outsider might suppose that the author of nine books in eight years had long since acquired that discipline and become a professional. After a period of "black despair," the novel began to go with a rush; by early October, Edith could tell Brownell[2] that she was "fatuously pleased" with it. She managed to have enough of the narrative in shape by the time requested, and *The House of Mirth* ran through eleven issues from January to November 1905.

As the time for book publication approached, Mrs. Wharton flooded Brownell with her customary queries and suggestions, but they were all made with a kind of lordly good humor. Only when she saw the wrapper on the first copies did she rebel. It declared that "for the first time the veil has been lifted from New York society" and further words to that garish effect. "I thought that, in the House of Scribner, the House of Mirth was safe from all such Harperesque methods of *réclame*," she wrote spiritedly. "[Please] do all you can to stop the spread of that pestilent paragraph, and to efface it from the paper cover of future printings. I am sick at the recollection of it!" The paragraph was removed at once.

Ten days after publication Brownell notified Edith Wharton gravely that "so far we have not sold many over 30,000, but perhaps that will satisfy your expectations for the first fortnight." He warned her, more seriously, that the sales would probably slacken off, especially since the story had little love interest, though others at Scribners were talking about "high figures." The figures did indeed continue to climb. Edith observed in her diary that 20,000 more copies were being printed by October 30, and 20,000 more on November 11; by this time Brownell had assured her that the novel was having "the most rapid sale of any book every published by Scribner." One hundred thousand copies were in print as of November 20, and 140,000 by the end of the year. Over the first two months of 1906, Edith could several times record that *The House of Mirth* was still the best-selling novel across the country, as it continued to rival or surpass such other current successes as *The Garden of Allah*, *The Clansman* and Upton Sinclair's *The Jungle*.

For the serial rights, she had been paid an outright fee of $5,000. The contract for the book itself (studied and witnessed by Walter Berry)[3] granted her a royalty of fifteen percent of the list price of $1.50, and by the end of 1905 she had been paid $7,500 against accrued royalties of more than $30,000. Altogether, in the course of that year, Edith Wharton's literary earnings amounted to more than $20,000 (including $2,200 for several short stories, a $1,500 advance on a novella, $1,800 from *Italian Villas*,

---

2. The head of the book publishing department of the publishing firm of Scribner's *[Editor]*.

3. A lawyer and one of Wharton's closest personal friends *[Editor]*.

and another advance of £250 from Macmillan, the English publisher of
The House of Mirth). It is next to impossible to translate the meaning of
income from one period to another with any accuracy; but given the
absence of income tax in the United States of 1905 and the rate of infla-
tion in our own time, one should probably multiply the figure of $20,000
by eight or nine to get some sense of its dollar value today. Edith Wharton's annual expenses, it may be added, were almost always identical
with her income.

Edith received a deluge of letters, many from total strangers. One
woman said that when she read the final installment, she was so overcome that she telegraphed a friend "Lily Bart is dead." Another reader
enclosed a two-cent stamp and begged Mrs. Wharton to write and say
whether it might not have been possible to allow Lily Bart to live and
marry Lawrence Selden. Still another woman, Edith Wharton told Burlingame, wrote: " 'I love, not every word in the book, but every period
and comma.' I hope she meant to insert an 'only' after the 'not . . .
Well, it's all great fun, and you did it all by accepting 'The Last Giustiniani.'[4] Do you remember?"

She was especially gratified, as before, by letters from fellow practi-
tioners of fiction. Charles Eliot Norton huffed a little and laid it down
that no woman not spotlessly virtuous (which ruled out Lily Bart) could
be the heroine of a truly serious novel. But from Queen's Acre, Howard
Sturgis wrote pages of exclamatory and discriminating praise:

> How good! How good! It is to *my* mind the best thing you have
> done, so sustained, so closely woven, so inevitable, so living! I am
> lost in admiration. . . . Except, perhaps, for our beloved Henry, I
> think you are head and shoulders above any other writer of fiction
> of the present day in English (poor dear George Meredith no longer
> counts as "of the present day"). You will be overwhelmed with
> congratulations, of course, but I am not going to make any pretty
> minauderies [coquettish airs] about your not caring for my humble
> opinion. On this one subject (and possibly embroidery) I know what
> I'm talking about.

Hamlin Garland, the author of *Main-Travelled Roads*, wrote appre-
ciatively, as did R. W. Gilder of the *Century*. From his retreat in New
Jersey, Owen Wister sent congratulations and called the book "*un ouv-
rage parfaitement distingué*," adding: "You have set the world discussing. Whenever I emerge from my isolation they're hard at it agreeing
and disagreeing."

The eighty-two-year-old Thomas Wentworth Higginson, whose literary acquaintanceship went back to his baffled espousal of Emily Dick-
inson decades before, said that *The House of Mirth* seemed to him "to
stand at the head of all American fiction, save Hawthorne alone." S.
Weir Mitchell ceremoniously took his hat off "to the writer of *The House*

---

4. A short story by Wharton [*Editor*].

of Mirth, cruelly descriptive name." From Knightsbridge in London, the novelist Mary Cholmondeley found herself "quite unable to put into words" her delight and admiration: "I would give anything to see as deep into life as you do, to know what you know about it, to write as you write about it."

Literate New Yorkers recognized at once that *The House of Mirth* was the first American novel to give an accurate, if also devastating, portrait of their society (Howells and Stephen Crane having attacked society at lower levels). Winthrop Chanler[5] sat up late on an October evening in his upstate New York home, sipping coffee and brandy and reading the novel. He paused to write his wife: "It is a very remarkable book. New York Society as it really is, as one really knows it, has never been written about before. The satire is so right, so deep, and so true to life. One knows all the people without being able to name one of them. Save I think Walter Berry is the hero." Chanler, who had thought that the women in Edith Wharton's earlier stories had sinned rather with their minds than their bodies, was enchanted with Lily Bart. Daisy Chanler surely passed on at least the gist of this, omitting "Winty's" later verdict that the second part of the novel drooped at times.

A long letter from Henry James was more ambiguous. He had spoken to Edith's sister-in-law, in a curiously low-keyed way, about "Mrs. Wharton's pleasantly palpable hit. I much admire the book myself," he said, "though I find it two books and too confused." To Edith herself he described *The House of Mirth* as "altogether a superior thing," instantly modifying that remark by saying that "it is better written than composed," and that Lawrence Selden, the chief male figure, "is too *absent*." But the old master put his finger unerringly on the novel's major achievement. He was, he said, thinking of writing a lecture about "the deadly difficulties" of the novel of manners in America. "When I do that I shall work in a tribute to the great success and the large portrayal of your Lily B. She is very big and true—and very difficult to have *kept* big and true."

There is no evidence that Edith Wharton was put out by James's strictures. She respected him too much; and she had, besides, reached the point where praise as such held relatively little interest for her. Sara Norton[6] was not alone in feeling that what most impressed her about Edith Wharton was "her fine indifference to praise, her conscious sense that her performance, judged by the standards *she* held, was but a slight affair." It might indeed be said that the only illusion she had about her work was the illusion that it was not as good as it actually was.

Her high standards, professional dedication, and general lack of vanity were reflected in a letter to Brownell, after Brownell had read the novel for the first time, in proof. "There can't be two opinions," Brownell insisted. "The way in which the study of *moeurs* melts into a novel of

5. Winthrop and especially his wife Daisy Chanler were close friends of Wharton *[Editor]*.
6. Daughter of the distinguished man of letters

Charles Eliot Norton and a close, lifelong friend with whom Wharton often corresponded *[Editor]*.

character—ah, well, it's the whole shooting-match. It must seem nice and easy to have done an incontestably big thing." How could she possibly develop any further as an artist? "Would it not have been cannier to postpone perfection till you could use it as the cap-sheaf of your oeuvre?" And he had special praise for the way in which the beautiful texture of the novel's substance could be seen "interpenetrating the sapient grand construction."

It was the latter phrase that did most for Edith's morale.

> I was pleased with bits myself; but as I go over the proofs the whole thing strikes me as so loosely built, with so many dangling threads, and cul-de-sacs, and long dusty stretches, that I had reached the point of wondering how I had ever dared to try my hand at a long thing. So your seeing a certain amount of architecture in it rejoices me above everything.—My theory of what the novel ought to be is so exorbitant that I am always reminded of Daudet's *"Je rêve d'un aigle, j'accouche d'un colibri"* ["I dream of an eagle, I give birth to a hummingbird"].

For all its huge commercial success, *The House of Mirth* did not earn uniform approval in the press. Edith was attacked for having provided a warning about modern American society rather than a hope; for not having shown a means of escape for society's victims; for having chosen a subject which was "utterly unsuitable for conversion into literature, which demands ideals and humor"; for not having introduced finer specimens of humanity, and for not exposing enough good in the characters she did present. Such was a large portion of the atmosphere in the American literary marketplace circa 1905.

Even so, the unfavorable commentary had the air of being made knowingly in a lost cause. What permeates the reviews of *The House of Mirth* is the sense, as of a settled fact, that Edith Wharton was one of the two or three most serious and accomplished writers of fiction on the American scene and that the new novel was undeniably her most important work to date. The hostile sought to pick flaws in what was taken for granted to be a novel of distinction. Amid the favorable, the issue was whether *The House of Mirth* could be adjudged a masterpiece or whether it fell just short of that final accolade. It may be added that enlightened critical opinion remains today at that same stage of uncertainty.

The House of Mirth, as its very title suggests, was Edith Wharton's first full-scale survey of the *comédie humaine*, American style. It is set in a time contemporary with its composition, and it covers the last seventeen months in the life of Lily Bart, a beautiful and fashionable but also penniless and imprudent young woman in her late twenties. The action moves between various segments of New York society and an American gathering on the French Riviera, and it is spurred by Lily's extraordinary capacity to get herself, at least half innocently, into situations of a doubtful, even of a scandalous, nature. In Edith Wharton's brilliant characterization of her heroine, Lily Bart possesses a stronger moral *consciousness* than most of her associates, but a wholly insufficient moral *constancy*. With her several special and immensely attractive qualities, she is all too much a product of the environment indicated by the title—a phrase taken from Ecclesiastes; "The heart of fools is in the house of mirth."

The nature and status of women in that society are suggested by the other two titles Edith Wharton originally contemplated. The first was "A Moment's Ornament": women were regarded as ornamental, beautiful objects to be collected and displayed; they were expected to strike elegant attitudes and poses; and their career was a fleeting one. But women were also required to appear flowerlike, gentle, fragile, innocent, lovely; the second title was "The Year of the Rose." Lily Bart was an exceptional flower, but only to a degree. At the end, refusing a gambit which would have restored her social and financial fortunes, she takes an overdose of a sleeping potion and dies.

"Lily" was the name given Edith Jones by the Rutherford children in the Newport days, and Lily Bart undoubtedly incorporates some of Edith Wharton's features. She is endearing, proud, sensitive, and exasperating by turns. Through Lily Bart, moreover, Edith Wharton conveyed her sense of herself as essentially unfitted for the only American society she knew, and as gravely misunderstood by that society. By the same token, if she pointed to no means of escape for Lily, it was because she was aware of none—or any viable alternative life to the one she depicted.

Lawrence Selden, the attractive and seemingly astute lawyer who is drawn to Lily in the opening phases of the narrative, is the one human being who might have supplied such an alternative. He has a vision, about which he is given to holding forth, of what he calls "the republic of the spirit," where the keynote is freedom and where only two or three are encouraged to gather together. But although this betimes was also one of Edith Wharton's ideal images, Selden himself, as she told Sara Norton, was "a negative hero," a sterile and subtly fraudulent figure whose ideas were not much to be trusted.

Selden was also an emblem of masculinity in Edith's world. Fond as she was of her Walter Berrys, her Egerton Winthrops, her Eliot Gregorys—and Selden has a little of each—she knew they had insufficient blood in their veins and could provide little of what an intelligent and ardent woman might crave.

There were, of course, enormous differences in the outward and material circumstances of Edith Wharton and Lily Bart; a reviewer might well be skeptical about the mistress of The Mount[7] coming truly to grips with the downward spiral of Lily's life. Yet behind the trappings of Lenox and Park Avenue was a soul that was familiar with pain, with the feeling of entrapment, with psychological and physical deprivation. The crucial difference between the author and her heroine was Edith Wharton's unshakable belief in the possibilities of life. In the spring after the pub-

---

7. The house in the Berkshire Mountains in Lenox, Massachusetts, which Wharton built early in the twentieth century [*Editor*].

lication of *The House of Mirth*, Edith wrote Sally Norton about a mutual friend who was gravely, perhaps critically, ill, but whose zest was undiminished.

> And how I understand that love of living, of being in this wonderful, astounding world even if one can look at it only through the prison bars of illness and suffering! *Plus je vois*, the more I am thrilled by the spectacle.

Nothing that Edith Wharton said in these years more aptly formulated her consciousness of her relation to the world she lived in.

✳ ✳ ✳

ELIZABETH AMMONS

[Edith Wharton's Hard-Working Lily: *The House of Mirth* and the Marriage Market] †

Economic novels were popular in the United States at the turn of the century. In 1902 Frank Norris's *The Pit* took the Chicago Commodities Exchange for its subject. In 1904 Ellen Glasgow's *The Deliverance* examined the Reconstruction's redistribution of land and status in the rural South. In 1906 Upton Sinclair's *The Jungle* brought to light corruption and exploitation in the meat-packing industry. In keeping with the trend Wharton wrote novels attacking the commerce of marriage. Even the title of *The House of Mirth* suggests, among other things, a mercantile firm.

The book inaugurates Wharton's career as an important social critic. In *The House of Mirth* she leaves far behind the sentimentality of *The Touchstone* (1900) and *Sanctuary* (1903) and analyzes the purpose and price of marriage for women in the American leisure class, which is to say the class envied (no matter how unrealistically) by most of the nation. The novel stakes out fully and for the first time Wharton's essential criticism of marriage as a patriarchal institution designed to aggrandize men at the expense of women.

It may be surprising to learn that Wharton herself was comparatively happy when she wrote *The House of Mirth*. Since the turn of the century, when she first started planning the novel, she had her new home in Lenox, Massachusetts, "The Mount," to enjoy and entertain friends in, and although Teddy's health was beginning to show alarming signs of deterioration, her marriage seems to have eased for the time being into a tolerable routine of housekeeping and travel, some of it shared. When she set to work in earnest on the novel in 1903, she had behind her three volumes of short stories, a book on interior design, *The Decoration of Houses* (with Ogden Codman, Jr.), and three novels. The years

† Reprinted by permission of the University of Georgia Press, from *Edith Wharton's Argument with America* by Elizabeth Ammons, © 1980 the University of Georgia Press.

between 1903 and 1907 saw her go on to publish another volume of short stories, the best-seller *The House of Mirth*, the novella *Madame de Treymes*, and the potential muckraker *The Fruit of the Tree*. She had built a circle of friends which ranged from well-known personalities like Henry James to less famous people like her longtime correspondent and friend, Sara Norton; she had a publisher glad to distribute her work; she had a public eager to read it. It was the first period of sustained confidence in Edith Wharton's life as a writer, and she took for her subject the most popular, and in some ways the most controversial, issue of the day, the marriage question.

She could almost certainly be assured of an audience. The Woman Movement by the turn of the century, in addition to having yielded some socially and politically influential organizations and symbols—the National American Woman's Suffrage Association, the National Federation of Women's Clubs, the Woman's Building at the Chicago World's Fair, the Gibson Girl in the pages of *Life*—was stimulating a new literature in America. In the imaginative realm, fiction about the New Woman burgeoned: emphatically modern heroines such as Hamlin Garland's Rose of *Rose of Dutcher's Cooly* (1895) or Gertrude Atherton's Patience of *Patience Sparhawk and Her Times* (1895), or even Harold Frederic's glamorous Celia in *The Damnation of Theron Ware* (an 1896 best-seller), who illustrates her author's ambivalence on the subject, are typical of the first run of fictive New Women. After this wave of exuberance, however, came a second generation of heroines toward the turn of the century who were less magnificent than the Roses, Patiences, and Celias who continued, by the way, to populate American novels until the 1920s. The second generation were the Carrie Meebers and Edna Pontelliers and Lily Barts, troubled and troubling young women who were not always loved by their American readers (Dreiser's and Chopin's novels were not well received, and even Wharton, though *The House of Mirth* sold well, found her heroine attacked on moral grounds). Likewise there developed in discursive literature, after the first rush of lavish enthusiasm in the popular press, a serious feminist scholarship that challenged naive complacency and self-congratulation. This literature thrived in America between the end of the nineteenth century and the end of the First World War, and it consistently focused on two issues: marriage and work.[1]

The pioneers were Charlotte Perkins Gilman and Thorstein Veblen,[2] both of whom studied the economics of marriage for women and both of whose work helps set the stage for Wharton's treatment of the subject. Although Gilman's confidence in progress clashes with Edith Wharton's

1. The body of feminist scholarship at the turn of the century is large. For my discussion here I've chosen to rely primarily on a representative selection including: Charlotte Perkins Gilman's *Women and Economics* (1898) and *The Man-Made World, Our Androcentric Culture* (1911), Thorstein Veblen's *The Theory of the Leisure Class* (1899), Hildegarde Hawthorne's *Women and Other Women* (1908), Emily James Putnam's *The Lady: Studies in Certain Significant Phases in Her History* (1910), Anna Garlin Spencer's *Woman's Share in Social Culture* (1912), Mary Roberts Coolidge's *Why Women Are So* (1912), Olive Schreiner's *Woman and Labour* (a best-seller in America in 1912, though Schreiner was South African). This list is only a sampling of feminist argument well known at the time Edith Wharton was writing.

2. See pp. 288–293 and 264–271 in this volume.

pessimism, her anatomy of the connection between marriage and femininity has much in common with Wharton's (as Gilman's own grim story about marriage in 1892, "The Yellow Wallpaper," brilliantly attests). In her groundbreaking *Women and Economics: A Study of the Economic Relation between Men and Women as a Factor in Social Evolution,* published in 1898, Gilman analyzes the economics of marriage and shows that the human female's lifelong dependence on the male is neither natural—females of other species gather their own food—nor healthy. The human system breeds excessive "sex-distinction" which makes women, like milch-cows artificially kept lactating, focus their entire identity on gender, to the point that even hands and feet—prehensile and locomotive appendages—become secondary sex characteristics: soft, dainty, and so forth. The cause of the problem is not biology but the social fact that the human female, merely to subsist, has had to develop exaggerated femininity; her "economic profit comes through the power of sex-attraction."[3] Not that woman is supported in return for her labor in the home as wife and mother: "The women who do the most work get the least money, and the women who have the most money do the least work."[4] Rather, a wife, like a horse, as Gilman puts it, labors in partnership with man but lacks autonomy; she is fed and cared for according to her keeper's pleasure and principles. Pleasing a man therefore becomes woman's job in life, which means that the married woman, viewed economically, differs very little from the prostitute; both exchange sexual service for support. It is a concept that Edith Wharton's Gus Trenor, in *The House of Mirth,* understands only too well.

One year after *Women and Economics* appeared, Thorstein Veblen published *The Theory of the Leisure Class: An Economic Study of Institutions* (1899). Convinced that the leisure class serves as the ideal to which all classes aspire in any given culture—an assumption Edith Wharton obviously shared—Veblen analyzes the leisure-class wife's role and differs from Gilman in arguing that, though wives are dependent economically on men, they do fulfill a significant function in the marital economy: that of conspicuous consumer for the male. They display his wealth, and therefore power, by spending his money while leading lives of leisure, "thereby putting in evidence his ability to sustain large pecuniary damage without impairing his superior opulence."[5]

Thus, according to Veblen, the leisure-class wife (and all her imitators) has a definite job to perform, and "it is an occupation of an ostensibly laborious kind. It takes the form, in large measure, of painstaking attention to the service of the master," which means deferring, like the rest of his servants, to his wishes and wearing his livery.[6] Like his footman, the gentleman's wife wears clothing that shows she does not need

3. Charlotte Perkins Gilman, *Women and Economics: A Study of the Economic Relation between Men and Women as a Factor in Social Evolution* (Boston: Small, Maynard and Co., 1898; rpt. Harper, 1966), p. 63.

4. Ibid., pp. 14–15.

5. Thorstein Veblen, *The Theory of the Leisure Class: An Economic Study of Institutions* (New York and London: Macmillan, 1899; rpt. Viking, 1965), p. 108.

6. Ibid., p. 101.

to engage in sweated labor. Indeed, her huge hats, high heels, voluminous skirts, excessively long hair, and corseted midriff all render her unfit for exertion and label her some man's costly possession. She is human chattel with an ornamental function, the prized domestic trophy whose leisure, dependence, and expenditure evidence her husband's financial prowess. For Veblen, and for Wharton, the lady of the leisure class is not an individual to be envied. She is a symbol to be studied, a totem of patriarchal power.

Edith Wharton took the title for her novel from the Bible: "The heart of the wise is in the house of mourning; The heart of fools is in the house of mirth."[7] After experimenting with a couple of names for her heroine—Rose, Julia Hurst (an unsympathetic name that brings to mind costly gems and the powerful Hearst syndicate that Wharton despised), she settled on Lily Bart, a name that calls up another passage from the Bible, this one from the Sermon on the Mount: "And why are you anxious about clothing? Consider the lilies of the field, how they grow; they neither toil nor spin; yet I tell you, even Solomon in all his glory was not arrayed like one of these" (Matt. 6:28; Luke 12:27). The allusion is cynical. Lilies may not spin but they certainly toil, and toil constantly (albeit invisibly, just like Wharton's Lily—in fact the appearance of carefreeness is one of the things that makes both flowers and beautiful women valuable); or they die. Moreover, there are even lilies of the field that toil and toil constantly and still die, killed by drought, flood, frost—any number of external disasters. Wharton's is one of those lilies. She works hard to survive but nevertheless dies prematurely, or more accurately is killed, blotted out. To use Lily's own image, she is thrown out "on the rubbish heap."[8] This happens to her for one reason: she refuses to marry, an action that not only makes her useless to the society Wharton portrays, but also, and for the reasons Gilman and Veblen outline, threatening.

When the novel opens, Lily Bart, at twenty-nine, needs a husband. She has already netted but then let drift away several lucrative proposals of marriage, and she does not have much time left. With no immediate family and no inheritance to fall back on, her only dowry is her beauty and style, and both require enormous upkeep—gowns and accessories from Paris and large sums of cash to wager at fashionable bridge tables. Lily manages because her wealthy friends replenish her wardrobe and purse to keep her among their ranks. "Brought up to be ornamental" (p. 480), she is valuable to them as a symbol, the Veblenesque female whose conspicuous leisure and freedom from sweated labor display her class's superiority to ordinary economic exigencies. Her friend Lawrence Selden, also a blueblood, begins to suspect early in the novel "that she must have cost a great deal to make, that a great many dull and ugly people must, in some mysterious way, have been sacrificed to produce her,"

7. Eccles. 7:4.
8. Edith Wharton, *The House of Mirth* (New York: Charles Scribner's Sons, 1905), p. 498. Further references are to this edition.

and he wonders: "Was it not possible that the material was fine, but that circumstance had fashioned it into a futile shape?" (p. 7).

Lawrence Selden may think that Lily has been fashioned into a futile shape (which is slightly comical coming from him, a dilettante of sorts), but he is wrong. Part of the point of *The House of Mirth*, which charts Lily's expulsion from the leisure class—her two-year descent from favor among the wealthy to death in the hall-bedroom of a shabby working-class boardinghouse—is to dramatize how perfectly trained she is for the important job society expects her to serve as some rich man's wife.

From the first page of the novel Lily Bart is hard at work using the skills of her trade—charm, sex appeal, solicitude—to entertain and give pleasure to other people. Her assignment is to practice the social arts, which consist of dressing well, serving tea properly, receiving and making visits, being a helpful and engaging houseguest, and playing bridge. These chores create a busy work-schedule for the leisure-class young woman; and it *is* work in Wharton's opinion, however degrading. One need only consider Lily's meeting on the train with Percy Gryce, a dull young bachelor worth millions, to appreciate the talent and training that go into her job of drawing him out. Wharton tells us that Lily "felt the pride of a skillful operator" (p. 30). "She had the art of giving self-confidence to the embarrassed" (p. 27). "She questioned him intelligently, she heard him submissively. . . . He grew eloquent under her receptive gaze" (p. 31). Lily beautifully illustrates Veblen's observation that "the servant or wife should not only perform certain offices and show a servile disposition, but it is quite as imperative that they show an acquired facility in the tactics of subservience."[9] Again, in her encounter later with George Dorset, the wealthy husband of a friend who wiles away her time by having affairs with other men, among them Selden, we are told that "Lily's arts . . . are especially adapted to soothe an uneasy egoism" (p. 206). Lily is excellent at her job. Not only has she mastered the social arts, but she knows how to use them to soothe and flatter the egoism of other people, particularly men, in order to gain her own ends without appearing direct or threatening. On the surface she perfectly embodies society's ideal of the female as decorative, subservient, dependent, and submissive; the upper-class norm of the lady as a nonassertive, docile member of society.

But only on the surface. In fact Lily has merely learned to suppress and camouflage her own impulses and ambitions. Even though she acquits herself of the social arts in which she has been so carefully bred, she transgresses other moral and social regulations with which society expects compliance. She visits Selden alone in his apartment; she gets deeply into debt; she borrows money from a married man, Gus Trenor, and is seen leaving his town house late at night; she spends time alone with another married man, Dorset, and becomes the object of rumors; she takes a job as a private secretary to the flashy, nouveau-riche Mrs. Hatch.

9. Veblen, *The Theory of the Leisure Class*, p. 60.

Her behavior is nonconformist, as are her real ambitions. She has "fits of angry rebellion against fate, when she longed to drop out of the race and make an independent life for herself" (p. 61). The seal on her stationery, with its flying ship and the motto *"Beyond!,"* images her true aspiration: she wants to escape—she wants to govern her own course in life. Her problem is that she is equipped for no life except the one she leads.

The job she has been trained for is highly specialized and her skills, if she does not choose to use them as some rich man's wife, are not transferable (or at least not in any way compatible with her pride: she has the opportunity to make money as a human mannequin modeling hats in a millinery shop, but refuses the job; it is simply a vulgar variant on what she is trying to escape). All her training and hard work wasted, Lily realizes late in the novel that she is "no more than some superfine human merchandise," and admits: "I can hardly be said to have an independent existence. I was just a screw or a cog in the great machine I called life, and when I dropped out of it I found I was of no use anywhere else" (pp. 412, 498). Lily is absolutely correct. She has utility only so long as she remains in good standing within the class that produced her.

Her utility within that class is clearly spelled out by Wharton. Men go out into the commercial world to accumulate goods and money, but unless the rich man also accumulates a woman, all his money and property and power do not extend beyond the narrow mercantile world into the social realm, into the society at large. Therefore for a rich man, ownership of a woman is not a luxury, but a necessity. She is his means of disseminating Wall Street power beyond the limited masculine world of Wall Street. Hence the economics of being a woman in Lily's world amount to working as a wife, and working hard, to translate financial power into social power by displaying a particular man's wealth for him. Put simply, the man makes money on Wall Street which he then brings to Fifth Avenue for a woman to turn into social power to aggrandize him (and by association herself).

Simon Rosedale, a Jew, is in the novel precisely because he was not born into the system Wharton describes and therefore he has had to figure out how the "machine," to use Lily's term for it, works. When the novel opens he has already mastered the principles involved. He has accumulated his money on Wall Street and is busy deciding what woman to buy to give him the most prestige and power on Fifth Avenue. He proposes to Lily, frankly characterizing marriage as a smart business deal for both of them ("a plain business statement of the consequences" is how he phrases it), and tells her: "If I want a thing I'm willing to pay: I don't go up to the counter, and then wonder if the article's worth the price. I wouldn't be satisfied to entertain like the Welly Brys; I'd want something that would look more easy and natural, more as if I took it in my stride. And it takes just two things to do that, Miss Bart: money, and the right woman to spend it" (pp. 285, 283). Specifically, he tells Lily,

"I want my wife to make all the other women feel small. I'd never grudge a dollar that was spent on that" (p. 284).

There is only one problem with this system. The most important cog in the machine is a human being; and what if the woman, Lily Bart, does not want to barter herself in marriage? What if she values personal freedom over security and does not want to spend her life owned and ruled by a man any more than she wants to spend it dependent on the charity of her old-fashioned aunt, Mrs. Peniston?

The answer to that question, toward which all of book 1 of *The House of Mirth* is structured, is primitive and brutal: Gus Trenor, who feels he has already bought Lily (he has lent her a large sum of money), tries to collect by attempting to rape her. The first book of Wharton's novel shows Lily's deviancy, her refusal to become the wife of Dilworth Gryce, Selden, or Rosedale, and ends in a sexual confrontation in which the head of the entire economic and social system, its most powerful august patriarch—a man Wharton even names Augustus—literally tries to force Lily into submission. He lures her to his town house late at night under the pretense that his wife is there, but Lily arrives to find that Judy Trenor is not even in town. Only Gus awaits her. He leads her to the darkened back parlor, where nothing but the fireplace gives off light, then tells her they are alone. She is terrified and begins to feel sick as he "pushed a chair between herself and the door. He threw himself in it, and leaned back, looking up at her. 'I'll tell you what I want: I want to know just where you and I stand. Hang it, the man who pays for the dinner is generally allowed to have a seat at the table' " (p. 233). If the mercantile language is the same as Rosedale's, the intent is not. "He rose, squaring his shoulders aggressively, and stepped toward her with a reddening brow. . . . He laughed again. 'Oh, I'm not asking for payment in kind. But there's such a thing as fair play—and interest on one's money—' " (p. 235). He touches her and his "face darkened to rage; her recoil of abhorrence had called out the primitive man" (p. 236). Trenor stops short of his purpose only because Lily is able to mask her terror and he therefore loses his nerve. Were she to show some sign of "weakness"—that is, cry out or weep, Gus would, Wharton leads us to believe, have sprung.

The encounter between Gus and Lily stands at the center of *The House of Mirth* structurally and thematically. It is a violent, ugly scene and probably the most important episode in the book. In its perfect coalescence of predatory economics and sexual politics, the scene explains why Lily, who works very hard to line up prospective husbands, finally lets them all get away from her: she does not want to be owned by any man.

Marriage with Percy Gryce, for example, she foresees as a "game" and knows that if she plays her game well she can become "the one possession in which he took sufficient pride to spend money on it" (p. 78). But by the time Lily envisions marriage with Rosedale, she has lost enthusiasm for manipulating the role of the ornamental, supportive wife. She imagines he will be "kind in his gross, unscrupulous, rapacious way, the way of the predatory creature with his mate" (p. 402); and the very thought evokes an image of "acquiescing in this plan with the passiveness of a sufferer resigned to the surgeon's touch" (p. 403). This image of terrible helplessness reveals a lot about Lily's attitude toward marriage. She refuses to marry Gryce, Dorset, and Rosedale because she loves none of them. But behind her refusals lies a repugnance toward a relationship in which a woman is powerless.

The same reason explains Lily's nervous rejection of Selden. She gives as her reason his relative poverty: life with him would be an extension of the parasitical existence she hopes to escape. He could not afford to provide the things she requires, so it would be foolish to marry him. More significant, however, are Selden's Pygmalion impulses—his desire, like George Darrow and Ralph Marvell after him, characters in *The Reef* and *The Custom of the Country*, to rescue (which means change) the woman he loves. Selden finds his beloved too beautiful for the coarse world; he wants to save her; he wants to "lift Lily to a freer vision of life" (p. 257). As in the Pygmalion story, the key scene is one in which the female appears as a human statue. In Wharton's version, Selden gazes on Lily's frozen beauty as Reynolds's Mrs. Lloyd in a tableau vivant and, yielding to the "vision-making influences as completely as a child to the spell of a fairy-tale" (p. 215), decides to renew his proposal of marriage. Wharton's choice of the painting by Reynolds comments on Selden's romantic impulse, for Mrs. Lloyd, wearing a diaphanous gown, is a graceful yet voluptuous woman captured in the act of inscribing the surname Lloyd on a tree. Obviously this portrait/tableau appeals to Selden's aesthetic sense and at the same time to his sensuality, but also and perhaps more importantly to his vanity—the real motive of Pygmalion, a storybook hero who also fell in love with a statue he envisioned bringing to a higher order of existence. No doubt Selden, the product of his upbringing and environment just as Lily is, would like to remodel his beloved in the image of his mother.

> Unfortunately, he found no way as agreeable as that practised at home; and his views of womankind in especial were tinged by the remembrance of the one woman who had given him his sense of "values." It was from her [his mother] that he inherited his detachment from the sumptuary side of life: the stoic's carelessness of material things, combined with the Epicurean's pleasure in them. Life shorn of either feeling appeared to him a diminished thing; and nowhere was the blending of the two ingredients so essential as in the character of a pretty woman. (p. 246)

This may describe an admirable image of womanhood, but it is one that Lily Bart in no way embodies. Marriage to Selden, though the two do love each other in some ways, clearly would involve what Lily fears from any prospective husband: proprietorship.

Because marriage is the vocation expected of all young women in her class, Lily's refusal to marry inevitably leads to ostracism. She is abandoned by the affluent, and she finds herself completely unable to support herself; her attempt to learn a trade, millinery, ends in dismissal; she cannot master the manual skills involved. She finds herself out on the street, like Ann Eliza Bunner, indigent. Persuaded of her own uselessness and insignificance by loneliness and poverty—the results of failure in the outer work-world—Lily decides that she must try to get back to social acceptance in the leisure class. She therefore determines to marry Rosedale and with that decision, even though the marriage never comes to pass, we see that Lily has been forced, finally, to give up all ambition for independence; the social system has triumphed. Her spirit has been crushed.

The structure of *The House of Mirth* mirrors that gradual, undramatic debilitation of Lily's spirit. Whereas, as R. W. B. Lewis has pointed out, book 1 is conventionally structured by Lily's behavior, book 2 is much more sprawling and chaotic.[1] It is so for a reason. Book 1 is tightly controlled by Lily's actions, actions that defy society's dictum that young women must marry, and therefore actions that lead relentlessly to the sexual violence of the scene between Lily and Gus Trenor at the center of Wharton's novel. The looser structure of book 2 follows the downward gyre of Lily Bart's life from the Dorsets' companion, to the Gormers' social secretary, to Mrs. Hatch's private secretary, to common labor in a millinery workshop, to death in a cheap boardinghouse. Thematically this spiral emphasizes Lily's deteriorating control over her own life. Because she refuses to marry even though she is getting older and poorer, she must accept a series of increasingly despised positions and therefore becomes increasingly ostracized and helpless. The result is her unfocused spin away from potential self-determination to complete subjugation to external control, first from people and eventually from abstract forces such as poverty and anxiety. Book 2 grows chaotic, it disintegrates structurally, to show Lily's life "on the rubbish heap" (p. 498).

The House of Mirth is the first in a series of Wharton novels to examine the dilemma of the young American woman whose objective in life is independence but whose one option is marriage. As Selden remarks in the novel's opening scene, "Isn't marriage your vocation? Isn't it what you're all brought up for?" (p. 13). The modern world may be in its twentieth century, Wharton seems to say, but the issues of marriage and work for women are still far from solved; Lily, for all her new yearnings, has no new ideas or alternatives. (She answers Selden's question, "I suppose so. What else is there?" [p. 13].) This particular heroine is, of course, the product of a very special, conservative class, which does explain her extreme inability to survive (most of Wharton's subsequent heroines will at least not die). Still her life is instructive. She sits in Selden's flat in that first scene in the novel and says, "How delicious to have a place like this all to one's self! What a miserable thing it is to be

---

1. R. W. B. Lewis, "Introduction," *The House of Mirth* (Boston: Houghton Mifflin, 1963), p. xviii.

a woman" (p. 9). Why it is a miserable thing to be a woman is the
subject of *The House of Mirth*, and Lily's story does not exist in isolation.
It has significance for every woman in the novel: from the richest, Mrs.
Charles Augustus Trenor, to the poorest, Mrs. Haffen.

Wharton has Lily's struggle touch and reflect on the lives of a hierar-
chy of women whose fortunes, true to Charlotte Perkins Gilman's generalization, descend the harder they work: from the leisure-class wife or
daughter (Judy Trenor, Bertha Dorset, and Evie Van Osburgh), to the
parvenu (Mrs. Welly Bry and Norma Hatch), to the social conservation-
ist (Mrs. Peniston), to the social parasite (Grace Stepney), to the social
manager (Carry Fisher), to a social worker (Gerty Farish), to an industrial forewoman (Miss Haines), to an office-girl (Nettie Struther), to a
manual laborer (Miss Kilroy), to a charwoman (Mrs. Haffen). All of
these women have one thing in common: dependence on Wall Street.
Without the rich man's money and favor no woman in *The House of
Mirth* could function, and the system is designed to keep women in
divisive and relentless competition for that money and favor. The feud
that fans out between Bertha Dorset and Lily Bart illustrates the point.
When Bertha thinks Lily is trying to steal Selden, she retaliates by stealing Percy Gryce and giving him to Evie Van Osburgh. Meanwhile,
Bertha's love letters to Selden are stolen by his cleaning woman, Mrs.
Haffen, who sells them to Lily, who buys them with money Gus Trenor
gave to her instead of to Carry Fisher, the usual beneficiary of his super-
fluity. Later, to camouflage another love affair and thereby preserve her
lucrative marriage, Bertha libels Lily; that loss of reputation, on top of
Grace Stepney's disparaging revelations, results in Mrs. Peniston's cutting Lily out of her will, which bequeaths the fortune of the late *Mr.*
Peniston.

This labyrinth of exploitation and theft justifies Selden's dismay "at
the cruelty of women to their kind" (p. 352), a cruelty that is not natural
in Wharton's opinion. Relationships between women in this novel, as
in the ones to follow, are frequently hostile. Forbidden to aggress on
each other directly, or aggress on men at all, women prey on each other—
stealing reputations, opportunities, male admirers—all to parlay or retain
status and financial security in a world arranged by men to keep women
supplicant and therefore subordinate. That women by nature feel no
necessity to harm each other, indeed often quite the opposite, Wharton
suggests in a number of instances involving Lily and, significantly, other
women who know what it means to have to depend on oneself for one's
livelihood. Carry Fisher helps Lily find employment among the second-
echelon wealthy after she has been "cut" by the elite. Miss Kilroy, a
fellow "work-woman" in the millinery sewing-room where Lily tries to
get a new start, commiserates with Lily and cheers her with some friendly
words. Nettie Struther, whom Lily met on visits to Gerty Farish's Working Girls' Club and helped out financially (ironically with Gus Trenor's
money), takes Lily home with her when she finds her former benefactress sitting like a derelict on a park bench. Most loyal is Lily's cousin,

Gerty. By no accident Lily runs to her and sleeps in her arms on the night she escapes Gus Trenor's assault. Gerty is at times silly and at times jealous, but she is also sisterly: she extends the same unfailing emotional support to Lily that she has for the downtrodden women she ministers to in her social work. At the beginning of *The House of Mirth* Selden escorts resplendent Lily "past sallow-faced girls in preposterous hats, and flat-chested women struggling with paper bundles and palm-leaf fans. Was it possible that she belonged to the same race?" (p. 6). Wharton answers that question in the end, yes.

Even though we never see it, Gerty's Girls' Club, where Lily meets Nettie Struther, serves as an important symbol in *The House of Mirth*. For her contemporary audience Wharton did not need to do more than refer to the club; its purpose and character would have been well known. For example, as early as 1894 her sister-in-law, Mary Cadwalader Jones, talks about Working Girls' Clubs in her chapter on "Women's Opportunities in Town and Country" in Scribner's *Woman's Book*.[2] She explains that, happily, the days of Lady Bountiful-type philanthropy are past; in its stead is a new type of social work, free of condescension and done by women organized to act as part of a group. Typical would be settlement work, work with Girls' Friendly Societies or Y W C A 's, work with kindergartens and day nurseries, or work with Working Girls' Clubs. The clubs were places where overworked, underpaid shop-girls, typists, stenographers, and other young female laborers could congregate, make friends, and share grievances. They were, in effect, safe harbors for young women employees without friends or family in the city.

The point of alluding to Working Girls' Clubs in *The House of Mirth* is ironic. While Lily labors to survive among the extremely wealthy, some of the money that Gus Trenor tried to buy her with goes, via Gerty, to other young women laborers who are equally exploited, her "sisters" in the world of mercantile and menial labor. Wharton thus establishes in the background of Lily's drama a connection between her problem and that of lower-class women. They are bound together, as Lily's life in the millinery workshop and her statement "I have joined the working classes" (p. 468) finally show quite literally, by the common bond of economic struggle. Five years after *The House of Mirth*, in *The Lady: Studies of Certain Significant Phases of Her History* (1910), the scholar Emily Putnam observed that the leisure-class woman's "prestige is created by the existence of great numbers of less happy competitors who present to her the same hopeless problem as the stoker on the liner presents to the saloon-passenger. If the traveller is imaginative, the stoker is a burden on his mind. But after all, how are saloon-passengers to exist if the stoker does not? Similarly the lady reasons about her sisters five decks below."[3] Wharton constructs *The House of Mirth* to show the existence of these decks *and* the passageway between them. It is no acci-

2. See pp. 278–283 in this volume.
3. Emily James Putnam, *The Lady: Studies in Certain Significant Phases in Her History* (New York: G. P. Putnam's Sons, 1910; rpt. University of Chicago Press, 1969), xxxii.

dent that the last woman we know Lily sees before she dies is Nettie, and the first person to discover her death is Gerty.

The depth of Lily's tragedy becomes fully apparent shortly before her death when she sits in Nettie Struther's tenement kitchen while the young woman prepares supper and feeds the baby. "Such a vision of the solidarity of life had never before come to Lily. . . . All the men and women she knew were like atoms whirling away from each other in some wild centrifugal dance: her first glimpse of the continuity of life had come to her that evening in Nettie Struther's kitchen" (p. 516). Lily envies Nettie's maternal happiness, but even more so the relationship between a man and a woman that created her home: "it had taken two to build the nest; the man's faith as well as the woman's courage" (p. 517). Lily's image of marriage has been so necessarily class-defined in terms of conspicuous consumption that she never saw its potential to secure a bond of faith and courage between a man and woman in order to bring them into the continuity of life through parenthood. *The House of Mirth* does not idealize motherhood per se. It uses an image of motherhood to reinforce its criticism of American marriage, especially in the leisure class, which is so obsessed with producing ornamental wives that the companionate potential of the institution is missed.

Lily's final action in *The House of Mirth* shows the leisure class's complete (and appropriately absentee) victory over her desire for autonomy. She dies by her own hand but not by her conscious will: it is not really suicide. "She did not, in truth, consider the question very closely—the physical craving for sleep was her only sustained sensation" (p. 521). Ironically, Lily craves in the end the docility society has all along expected of her. She increases the dosage of sleeping medicine to achieve "the gradual cessation of the inner throb, the soft approach of passiveness . . . the sense of complete subjugation" (pp. 521–22). On a symbolic level, she is murdered by her culture; and its ghastly triumph is to make her its agent, its last enforcer of a literal and permanent passivity on Lily Bart.

That depressing victory is mitigated somewhat by Wharton's important final image of Lily. She dies totally passive, hallucinating that she cradles in her arms the infant girl-child of another woman. Literally a self-embrace, the poignance of which recalls the night she spent in Gerty's arms at the end of book 1, this image does not really imply unfulfilled motherhood; Lily has no illusion that the baby is hers. Rather, the book ends with Lily's imagining the warmth of Nettie Struther's infant flowing through her drugged, passive, dying body. Half-asleep, she "started up again, cold and trembling with the shock: for a moment she seemed to have lost her hold of the child. But no—she was mistaken—the tender pressure of its body was still close to hers: the recovered warmth flowed through her once more, she yielded to it, sank into it, and slept" (p. 523). In the arms of the ornamental, leisure-class Lily lies the working-class infant female, whose vitality succors the dying woman. In that union of the leisure and working classes lies a new hope—the New

Woman that Wharton would bring to mature life in her next novel, *The Fruit of the Tree* (1907).

* * *

ELAINE SHOWALTER

The Death of the Lady (Novelist): Wharton's *House of Mirth*†

The lady is almost the only picturesque survival in a social order which tends less and less to tolerate the exceptional. Her history is distinct from that of woman though sometimes advancing by means of it, as a railway may help itself from one point to another by leasing an independent line. At all striking periods of social development her status has its significance. In the age-long war between men and women, she is a hostage in the enemy's camp. Her fortunes do not rise and fall with those of women but with those of men.
— Emily James Putnam, *The Lady* (1910)

Perfection is terrible, it cannot have children.
— Sylvia Plath, "The Munich Mannequins"

At the beginning of Edith Wharton's first great novel, *The House of Mirth* (1905), the heroine, Lily Bart, is twenty-nine, the dazzlingly well-preserved veteran of eleven years in the New York marriage market. By the end of the novel, she is past thirty and dead of an overdose of chloral. Like Edna Pontellier, Kate Chopin's heroine in *The Awakening* (1899), who celebrates her twenty-ninth birthday by taking a lover, Lily Bart belongs to a genre we might call "the novel of the woman of thirty," a genre that emerged appropriately enough in American women's literature at the turn of the century. These novels pose the problem of female maturation in narrative terms: What can happen to the heroine as she grows up? What plots, transformations, and endings are imaginable for her? Is she capable of change at all? As the nineteenth-century feminist activist and novelist Elizabeth Oakes Smith noted in her diary, "How few women have any history after the age of thirty!"[1]

Telling the history of women past thirty was part of the challenge Wharton faced as a writer looking to the twentieth century. The threshold of thirty established for women by nineteenth-century conventions of "girlhood" and marriageability continued in the twentieth century as a psychological observation about the formation of feminine identity. While Wharton's ideas about personality were shaped by Darwinian rather than by Freudian determinants, she shared Freud's pessimism about the difficulties of change for women. In his essay "Femininity," for example, Freud lamented the way that women's psyches and personalities became

†©1985 by the Regents of the University of California. Reprinted from *Representations*, Vol. 9, Winter, 1985, pp. 133–49, by permission.

1. Joy Wittenburg, "Excerpts from the Diary of Elizabeth Oakes Smith," *Signs* 9 (1984), 537. The diary covers the year 1861.

fixed by the time they were thirty. While a thirty-year-old man "strikes us as a youthful, somewhat unformed individual, whom we expect to make powerful use of the possibilities for development opened up to him by analysis," Freud wrote, a woman of thirty "often frightens us by her psychical rigidity and unchangeability. Her libido has taken up fixed positions and seems incapable of exchanging them for others."[2] From Wharton's perspective Lily Bart is locked into fixed positions that are social and economic as well as products of the libido. Her inability to exchange these positions for others constitutes an impasse in the age as well as the individual.

Wharton situates Lily Bart's crisis of adulthood in the contexts of a larger historical shift. We meet her first in Grand Central Station, "in the act of transition between one and another of the country houses that disputed her presence at the close of the Newport season," and indeed *The House of Mirth* is a pivotal text in the historical transition from one house of American women's fiction to another, from the homosocial women's culture and literature of the nineteenth century to the heterosexual fiction of modernism.[3] Like Edna Pontellier, Lily is stranded between two worlds of female experience: the intense female friendships and mother-daughter bonds characteristic of nineteenth-century American women's culture, which Carroll Smith-Rosenberg has called "the female world of love and ritual," and the dissolution of these single-sex relationships in the interests of more intimate friendships between women and men that was part of the gender crisis of the turn of the century.[4] Between 1880 and 1910, patterns of gender behavior and relationship were being redefined. As early as the 1880s, relationships between mothers and daughters became strained as daughters pressed for education, work, mobility, sexual autonomy, and power outside the female sphere. Heroines sought friendship from male classmates and companions as well as within their single-sex communities.[5]

These historical and social changes in women's roles had effects on

2. Sigmund Freud, "Femininity," in *The Complete Edition of the Psychological Works of Sigmund Freud* (London, 1964) 22: 112–35.
3. *The House of Mirth* (New York, 1905), 3. All further references to this work will be included parenthetically in the text.
4. Carroll Smith-Rosenberg's influential essay, "The Female World of Love and Ritual: Relations Between Women in Nineteenth-Century America," appeared in the first issue of the feminist journal *Signs*, 1 (1975), 1–30. Along with Nancy F. Cott's *The Bonds of Womanhood: 'Woman's Sphere' in New England, 1780–1835* (New Haven, 1977), Smith-Rosenberg's work defined a woman's culture of intimate emotional relationships, social conventions, and female rituals, "supported and paralleled by severe social restrictions on intimacy between young men and women" (9).
5. The breakdown in women's culture at the turn of the century has been the subject of extensive recent study by feminist social historians. In a symposium on the problem of "women's culture,"

Carroll Smith-Rosenberg noted that by the 1870s and 1880s, "as role options expanded for daughters . . . mothers and other older women frequently acted to thwart their daughters' new role aspirations." The period 1890 to 1920, she argues, "saw a concerted male attack upon the legitimacy of this world of female identification and solidarity, an attack abetted by economic and demographic changes which undermined female institutional structures." See "Politics and Culture in Women's History: A Symposium," *Feminist Studies* 6 (1980), 59, 63. Other important work on this period of gender crisis includes Nancy Sahli, "Smashing: Women's Relationships before the Fall," *Chrysalis* 8 (1979): 17–27; Lillian Faderman, *Surpassing the Love of Men: Romantic Friendships and Love between Women from the Renaissance to the Present* (New York, 1981); and Martha Vicinus, "Sexuality and Power: A Review of Current Work on the History of Sexuality," *Feminist Studies* 8 (1982), 133–56.

women's writing as well. Pre–Civil War American women's fiction, variously described as "woman's fiction," "literary domesticity," or "the sentimental novel," celebrated female solidarity and revised patriarchal institutions, especially Christianity, in feminist and matriarchal terms.[6] Its plots were characterized by warmth, intense sisterly feeling, and a sacramental view of motherhood. As these "bonds of womanhood," in Nancy Cott's term, were being dissolved by cultural pressures toward heterosexual relationships, women's plots changed as well. In 1851, for example, Susan Warner's best-selling novel *The Wide, Wide World* tearfully recounted the history of a girl painfully separated from her mother.[7] But in 1882, in Warner's artistically superior but less-celebrated *Diana*, we are given an astringent and startling modern analysis of the psychological warfare between mother and daughter and the mother's fierce efforts to thwart her daughter's romance. As women's culture came under attack, so too its survivors clung desperately to the past, seeing men as the interlopers in their idyllic community. While some women writers of this generation championed the New Woman, others of the older generation grieved for the passing of the "lost Paradise" of women's culture. In their fiction, male invaders are met with hostility, and the struggle between female generations is sometimes murderous. By the century's end, as Josephine Donovan explains, "the woman-centered, matriarchal world of the Victorians is in its last throes. The preindustrial values of that world, female identified and ecologically holistic, are going down to defeat before the imperialism of masculine technology and patriarchal institutions."[8]

The writers and feminist thinkers of Wharton's transitional generation, Elizabeth Ammons has noted, wrote "about troubled and troubling young women who were not always loved by their American readers." This literature, Ammons points out, "consistently focused on two issues: marriage and work."[9] Seeing marriage as a form of work, a woman's job, it also raises the question of work and especially of creativity. The fiction of this transitional phase in women's history and women's writing is characterized by unhappy endings, as novelists struggled with the problem of going beyond the allowable limits and breaking through the available histories and stories for women.

Unlike some other heroines of the fiction of this transitional phase, Lily Bart is neither the educated, socially conscious, rebellious New

---

6. See Nina Baym, *Woman's Fiction: A Guide to Novels by and about Women in America, 1820–1870* (Ithaca, 1978); Mary Kelley, *Private Women, Public Stage: Literary Domesticity in Nineteenth-Century America* (New York, 1984); and Ann Douglas, *The Feminization of American Culture* (New York, 1977).

7. For two different feminist accounts of *The Wide, Wide World* see Baym, *Woman's Fiction*, 143–50, and Jane Tompkins, "The Other American Renaissance," in *The American Renaissance Reconsidered: Selected Papers from the English Institute, 1982–83*, ed. Walter Benn Michaels and

Donald Pease (Baltimore, 1984).

8. Josephine Donovan, *New England Local Color Literature: A Woman's Tradition* (New York, 1983), 119.

9. Elizabeth Ammons, *Edith Wharton's Argument with America* (Athens, Ga , 1980), 27. [See pp. 345–357 in this volume—*Editor.*] Ammons sees this literature as influenced by such contemporary studies of the economics of marriage as Charlotte Perkins Gilman's *Women and Economics* (1898) and Thorstein Veblen's *The Theory of the Leisure Class* (1899).

Woman, nor the androgynous artist who finds meaning for her life in solitude and creativity, nor the old woman fiercely clinging to the past whom we so often see as the heroine of the post–Civil War local colorists.[1] Her skills and morality are those of the Perfect Lady. In every crisis she rises magnificently to the occasion, as we see when Bertha insults her, her aunt disinherits her, Rosedale rejects her. Lawrence Selden, the would-be New Man to whom she turns for friendship and faith, criticizes Lily for being " 'perfect' to everyone"; but he demands an even further moral perfection that she can finally only satisfy by dying. Lily's uniqueness, the emphasis Wharton gives to her lonely pursuit of ladylike manners in the midst of vulgarity, boorishness, and malice, makes us feel that she is somehow the *last* lady in New York, what Louis Auchincloss calls the "lone and solitary" survivor of a bygone age.[2]

I would argue, however, that Wharton refuses to sentimentalize Lily's position but rather, through associating it with her own limitations as the Perfect Lady Novelist, makes us aware of the cramped possibilities of the lady whose creative roles are defined and controlled by men. Lily's plight has a parallel in Wharton's career as the elegant scribe of upper-class New York society, the novelist of manners and decor. Cynthia Griffin Wolff calls *The House of Mirth* Wharton's "first Kunstlerroman," and in important ways, I would agree; Wharton's *House of Mirth* is also a fictional house of birth for the woman artist. Wolff points out that *The House of Mirth* is both a critique of the artistic representation of women— the transformation of women into beautiful objects of male aesthetic appreciation—and a satiric analysis of the artistic traditions that "had evolved no conventions designed to render a woman as the maker of beauty, no language of feminine growth and mastery." In her powerful analysis of Lily Bart's disintegration, Wharton "could turn her fury upon a world which had enjoined women to spend their artistic inclinations entirely upon a display of self. Not the woman as productive artist, but the woman as self-creating artistic object—that is the significance of the brilliant and complex characterization of Lily Bart."[3] In deciding that a Lily cannot survive, that the lady must die to make way for the modern woman who will work, love, and give birth, Wharton was also signaling her own rebirth as the artist who would describe the sensual worlds of *The Reef, Summer,* and *The Age of Innocence* and who would create the language of feminine growth and mastery in her own work.

We are repeatedly reminded of the absence of this language in the world of *The House of Mirth* by Lily's ladylike self-silencing, her inability to rise above the "word-play and evasion" (494) that restrict her con-

---

1. For discussions of these other transitional heroines of women's fiction, see Grace Stewart, *A New Mythos: The Novel of the Artist as Heroine, 1877–1977* (Montreal, 1981), and Ann Douglas, "The Literature of Impoverishment: The Women Local Colorists in America, 1865–1914," *Women's Studies* 1 (1972), 3–45.

2. "Edith Wharton and Her New Yorks," in *Edith Wharton: A Collection of Critical Essays,* ed. Irving Howe (Englewood Cliffs, N.J., 1962), 36.
3. *A Feast of Words: The Triumph of Edith Wharton* (New York, 1977), 11. [See pp. 320–339 in this volume—*Editor.*]

versations with Selden and to tell her own story. Lily's inability to speak for herself is a muteness that Wharton associated with her own social background, a decorum of self-restraint she had to overcome in order to become a novelist. In one sense, Lily's search for a suitable husband is an effort to be "spoken for," to be suitably articulated and defined in the social arena. Instead, she has the opposite fate; she is "spoken of" by men, and as Lily herself observes, "The truth about any girl is that once she's talked about, she's done for, and the more she explains her case the worse it looks" (364). To become the object of male discourse is almost as bad as to become the victim of male lust; "It was horrible of a young girl to let herself be talked about," Mrs. Peniston reflects in agitation. "However unfounded the charges against her, she must be to blame for their having been made" (205).

Whenever Lily defies routine, the male scandalmongers are there to recycle her for their own profit. After the *tableaux vivants*, her performance and her relationship with Gus Trenor are so racily described in *Town Talk* that Jack Stepney is perturbed, although the elderly rake Ned Van Alstyne, "stroking his mustache to hide the smile behind it," comments that he had "heard the stories before" (254). When Bertha Dorset announces that Lily is not returning to the yacht, the scene is witnessed by Dabham, the society columnist of "Riviera Notes," whose "little eyes," Selden fears, "were like tentacles thrown out to catch the floating intimations with which . . . the air at moments seemed thick" (347). These men can rewrite the story of Lily's life, as they can also enjoy the spectacle of her beauty and suffering.

Although Lily has a "passionate desire" to tell the truth about herself to Selden, she can only hint, can only speak in parables he is totally unable to comprehend. Even the body language of her tears, her emaciation, and her renunciatory gestures are lost on him. On her deathbed, as she is drifting into unconsciousness, Lily is still struggling with the effort to speak: "She said to herself that there was something she must tell Selden, some word she had found that should make life clear between them. She tried to repeat the word, which lingered vague and luminous on the far edge of thought. . . . If she could only remember it and say it to him, she felt that everything would be well" (522). Yet she dies with this word of self-definition on her lips, not the bride of a loving communication, but rather the still unravished bride of quietness. After her death, Selden kneels and bends over her dead body on the bed, like Dracula or little Dabham, "draining their last moment to its lees" (as he has earlier led Gerty on, "draining her inmost thoughts"), "and in the silence there passed between them the word which made all clear" (533). This word, Susan Gubar argues, "is Lily's dead body; for she is now converted completely into a script for his edification, a text not unlike the letters and checks she has left behind to vindicate her life. . . . Lily's history, then, illustrates the terrors not of the word made flesh, but of the flesh made word. In this respect, she illuminates the problems

Wharton must have faced in her own efforts to create rather than be created."[4]

Among the issues the novel raises is the question of writing itself, both in terms of female creativity and in terms of a relationship to literary traditions. Whereas mid-nineteenth-century American women writers, unlike their English and European counterparts, had explicitly and in their writing styles rejected a male literary tradition that seemed totally alien to their culture, Wharton's generation of women writers, who defined themselves as artists, were working out their relationship to both the male and female literary heritage. *The House of Mirth* revises both male and female precursors, as Wharton explores not only the changing worlds of women, but also the transformed and equally limiting worlds of men. In a number of striking respects, *The House of Mirth* goes back to adapt the characteristic plot of mid-nineteenth-century "woman's fiction" and to render it ironic by situating it in the post-matriarchal city of sexual commerce. This plot, as Nina Baym has established, concerned "a young girl who is deprived of the supports she had rightly or wrongly depended on to sustain her throughout life and is faced with the necessity of winning her own way in the world." Despite hardships and trials, the heroine overcomes all obstacles through her "intelligence, will, resourcefulness, and courage." Although she marries, as an indication that her progress toward female maturity has been completed, marriage is not really the goal of this heroine's ordeal, and men are less important to her emotional life than women.[5]

Lily Bart's story alludes to but subverts these sentimental conventions of nineteenth-century women's literature, conventions that dozens of female bestsellers had made familiar. Lily has certainly been deprived of the financial and emotional supports she has been raised to expect and has been even more seriously deprived of the environment for the skills in which she has been trained. First of all, Wharton puts the question of youth itself into question. At twenty-nine, Lily sees eligible "girlhood" slipping into spinsterdom and faces the impending destruction of her beauty by the physical encroachments of adulthood—not simply the aging process, but also anxiety, sexuality, and serious work. Secondly, in contrast to the emotionally intense relationships between mothers, daughters, sisters, and friends in most nineteenth-century women's writing, women's relationships in *The House of Mirth* are distant, formal, competitive, even hostile. Selden deplores "the cruelty of women to their kind" (352). Lily feels no loving ties to the women around her; in her moment of crisis "she had no heart to lean on" (240). Her mother is dead and unmourned; "Her relation with her aunt was as superficial as that of chance lodgers who pass on the stairs" (240). Her treatment of her cousin Grace Stepney is insensitive and distant, and Grace is bitterly jealous of her success. Lily sees and treats other women as her allies, rivals, or inferiors in the social competition; she is no different from the

4. Susan Gubar, "The 'Blank Page' and Female   Elizabeth Abel (Chicago, 1982), 81.
Creativity," in *Writing and Sexual Difference*, ed.   5. See Baym, *Woman's Fiction*, 11–12, 23, 39.

"best friends" she describes to Selden as those women who "use me or abuse me; but . . . don't care a straw what happens to me" (13).

Whereas childbirth and maternity are the emotional and spiritual centers of the nineteenth-century female world, in *The House of Mirth* they have been banished to the margins. Childbirth seems to be one of the dingier attributes of the working class; the Perfect Lady cannot mar her body or betray her sexuality in giving birth. There are scarcely any children occupying the Fifth Avenue mansions and country cottages of Lily's friends. (Judy and Gus Trenor have two teenaged daughters, briefly glimpsed, but not in their mother's company. Judy refers to them only once as having to be sent out of the room because of a guest's spicy stories.)

And whereas the heroine of women's fiction triumphs in every crisis, confounds her enemies and wins over curmudgeons and reforms rakes, Lily is continually defeated. The aunt who should come to her rescue disinherits her; Bertha Dorset, the woman friend who should shelter her, throws her out in order to protect her own reputation; the man who should have faith in her cannot trust her long enough to overcome his own emotional fastidiousness. With stark fatalism rather than with the optimism of woman's fiction Wharton takes Lily from the heights to her death. As Edmund Wilson first noted in his 1937 essay "Justice to Edith Wharton," Wharton "was much haunted by the myth of the Eumenides: and she had developed her own deadly version of the working of the Aeschylean necessity. . . . She was as pessimistic as Hardy or Maupassant."[6] Indeed, Lily's relentless fall suggests the motto of Hardy's *Tess of the D'Urbervilles:* "The Woman Pays." Despite being poor, in debt, disinherited, an outsider in a world of financiers and market manipulators, speculators and collectors, Lily is the one who must pay again and again for each moment of inattention, self-indulgence, or rebellion. "Why must a girl pay so dearly for her least escape from routine?" she thinks after her ill-timed meeting with Rosedale outside Selden's apartment. But while Tess pays with her life for a real fall, Lily pays only for the appearance of one, for her inability to explain or defend herself.

In other respects, many details of the novel allude to an American female literary tradition. As Cynthia Griffin Wolff has shown, the name "Lily" referred to a central motif of art nouveau: the representation of female purity as lilies adapted from Japanese art themes, "Easter lilies, tiger lilies, water lilies, liquescent calla lilies, fluttering clusters of lily-of-the-valley."[7] It was also a name with a special history in nineteenth-century women's writing. Amelia Bloomer's temperance and women's rights journal of the 1850s was called *The Lily*, to represent, as the first issue announced, "sweetness and purity."[8] In women's local-color fiction, "Lily" was a recurring name for sexually attractive and adventurous

6. Edmund Wilson, "Justice to Edith Wharton," in *Edith Wharton: A Collection of Critical Essays,* 20.

7. See Wolff, *A Feast of Words,* 114–15. Wolff also notes that Wharton herself was called "Lily"

as a girl (110).

8. On *The Lily,* see D. C. Bloomer, *Life and Writings of Amelia Bloomer* (Boston, 1895), 41–43.

younger women, as opposed to women of the older generation more
bound to sisterly and communal relationships. In Mary Wilkins Freeman's most famous story, "A New England Nun," Lily Dyer is the
blooming girl to whom the cloistered Louisa Ellis thankfully yields her
red-faced suitor. In Freeman's later "Old Woman Magoun," "Lily" represents the feminine spirit of the new century, a sexuality terrifying to
the old women who guard the female sanctuaries of the past. In this
stark and terrifying story, Old Woman Magoun has managed to keep her
pretty fourteen-year-old granddaughter, Lily, a child within a strictly
female community; but when it becomes clear that she will lose the
orphaned girl both to adolescence and to the predatory sexuality of the
male world, the grandmother poisons her.[9]

Furthermore, Wharton's pairing of Lily Bart with her nemesis, Bertha
Dorset, echoes the pairing of Berthas and Lilys in an earlier feminist
text: Elizabeth Oakes Smith's *Bertha and Lily* (1854). Oakes Smith's
novel describes the relationship of a mother (Bertha) and her illegitimate
daughter (Lily). While the erring Bertha's life has been painful and limited, Lily's future is presented as radiantly hopeful: "She will be an artist,
an orator, a ruler . . . just as her faculties impel." Lily seems to represent the possibilities of the creative buried self Oakes Smith felt in her
own stifled career.[1]

Constance Cary Harrison's *The Anglomaniacs* (1890), a successful novel
of the *fin de siècle* set in the same upper-class New York milieu as *The
House of Mirth*, also has a heroine named Lily, a young heiress who is
pressured to marry a titled Englishman she does not love in order to
satisfy her mother's social ambitions. Like Lily Bart, Lily Floyd-Curtis
has the graceful figure of a "wood-nymph," socializes with a sensitive
bachelor friend who lives "in the Benedick with his violincello," and
attends a charity ball where the dinner table is set to represent a Veronese
painting and she herself is dressed as a Venetian princess.[2]

Wharton is ironically aware of the way that Lily Bart becomes the
object of male myths and fantasies, like that of the wood nymph, that
must be revised from the woman's perspective. Selden insists on seeing
her as a "captured dryad subdued to the conventions of the drawing-
room," yet the image of the dryad is as much one of these drawing-room
conventions as that of the woman of fashion. Indeed, Lily, as Wharton
tells us, "had no real intimacy with nature, but she had a passion for the
appropriate" (19, 101). For her role in the *tableaux vivants*, Lily chooses
to represent the figure of Sir Joshua Reynolds's *Mrs. Lloyd*, in a draped
gown that revealed "long dryad-like curves that swept upwards from her

9. Mary Wilkins Freeman repeatedly used the
name "Lily" for the younger woman in a genera-
tional transition from women's culture to New
Womanhood; see also Lily Almy and Aunt Fidelia
in "A Patient Waiter." The best recent collection
of Freeman's work is *Selected Stories of Mary Wilkins Freeman*, ed. Marjorie Pryse (New York, 1983).

1. I am indebted for these details to Katy Birck-
mayer, "A Critical Introduction to *Bertha and Lily*,"
unpublished paper, Rutgers University, 1984.
2. *The Anglomaniacs* (New York, 1977) was
reprinted with a short introduction by Elizabeth
Hardwick in her series of neglected American
women's writing.

poised foot to her lifted arm" (217). Selden is enraptured by her performance, finding the authentic Lily in the scene; but it is rather the carefully constructed Lily of his desire that he sees. The "streak of sylvan freedom" he perceives in her is rather what he would make of her, and we are reminded that Ezra Pound at this same period was imposing the title "Dryad" on the equally plastic H. D.[3]

The myth of Tarpeia was another case of differing male and female interpretations. Simon Rosedale tells it in garbled form to Lily when he comes to propose to her: "There was a girl in some history book who wanted gold shields or something, and the fellows threw 'em at her, and she was crushed under 'em; they killed her" (284). Tarpeia, the Roman who betrayed her city to the Sabines by opening the Capitoline citadel in exchange for gold bracelets and was crushed by the shields of the invading Sabine army, was also the subject of Louise Guiney's well-known poem of the 1890s that dramatized the paradox of a woman's being condemned by her society for the mercenary and narcissistic values it has encouraged.[4]

Wharton's major revision of a male text, as those critics not obsessed with her alleged apprenticeship to Henry James have noted, was with relation to Oscar Wilde's *Picture of Dorian Gray* (1890). Lily's picture is in one sense her mirror, but it is more fully her realization of the ways in which her society has deformed her. In contrast to Dorian Gray's portrait, Lily's monster in the mirror is not one whose perfect complexion has been marred by lines of worry, shame, or guilt, but rather a woman with a "hard, brilliant" surface (191). In the aftershock of her encounter with Gus Trenor in his empty house, Lily recognizes "two selves in her, the one she had always known, and a new abhorrent being to which it found itself chained" (238). As she tells Gerty, this self seems like a "disfigurement," a "hideous change" that has come to her while she slept; a moral ugliness that she cannot bear to contemplate (265).

Some feminist critics have argued that this "stranger" in Lily, this second and abhorrent self, is the female personality produced by a patriarchal society and a capitalist economy. As Elizabeth Ammons notes, "the system is designed to keep women in divisive and relentless competition" for the money and favor controlled by men. "Forbidden to aggress on each other directly, or aggress on men at all, women prey on each other—stealing reputations, opportunities, male admirers—all to parlay or retain status and financial security in a world arranged by men to keep women suppliant and therefore subordinate." Women employ, exploit, and cheat each other as cold-bloodedly as their Wall Street hus-

3. On H. D. as "Dryad" and on her fashionable "Greekness," see Barbara Guest, *Herself Defined: The Poet H. D. and Her World* (New York, 1984), 33ff.
4. See Sheila A. Tully, "Heroic Failures and the Literary Career of Louise Imogen Guiney," *American Transcendental Quarterly* no. 47–48 (Summer–Fall 1980), 178. Cheryl Walker calls Guiney

"the most interesting of the turn-of-the-century [women] poets"; she sees a commentary on the ambitions and passions of the New Woman in the final words of Guiney's "Tarpeia": "O you that aspire!/Tarpeia the traitor had fill of her woman's desire." See *The Nightingale's Burden: Women Poets and American Culture before 1900* (Bloomington, Ind., 1982), 130–33.

bands carry out deals, but "by nature" women "feel no necessity to harm each other." [5]

Yet the nature of both men and women is in question in the novel rather than given. It is often overlooked that Wharton develops a full cast of male characters in *The House of Mirth*, whose dilemmas parallel those of the women. As historians now recognize, the period 1880–1920 redefined gender identity for American men as well as for American women. Among the characteristics of progressivism and of the masculinity crisis was the increased specialization of men as workers marginal to the family and culture: "According to the capitalistic ethos, men were expected to promote industry and commerce, which they did in abundance, often spending long hours at the office, the plant, or in the fields and forests. With their energies spent, they came home too weary and worn to devote much time and interest to family or friends." [6]

Wharton's critique of the marriage system is not limited to the economic dependency of women but also extends to consider the loneliness, dehumanization, and anxiety of men. Lily's father, a shadowy figure in the prehistory of the novel, establishes the theme of the marginal man. This "neutral-tinted father, who filled an intermediate space between the butler and the man who came to wind the clocks," is a dim and pathetic fixture of Lily's scant childhood memories (45). "Effaced and silent," patient and stooping, he is an exhausted witness to the stresses his society places on men. Even on vacation at Newport or Southampton, "it seemed to tire him to rest, and he would sit for hours staring at the sea-line from a quiet corner of the verandah, while the clatter of his wife's existence went on unheeded a few feet off" (45–46). Mr. Bart does not so much die as get discarded; to his wife, once he had lost his fortune "he had become extinct," and she sits at his deathbed "with the provisional air of a traveller who waits for a belated train to start" (51). Unable to love her father, to feel more for him than a frightened pity, or to mourn him, Lily nonetheless comes to identify with him in her own trial, recalling his sleepless nights in the midst of her own and feeling suddenly "how he must have suffered, lying alone with his thoughts" (266).

The story of Mr. Bart, who in his enigmatic solitude and marginality here strongly resembles Mr. Bartleby, lingers in our consciousness as we read *The House of Mirth*, coloring our impression of even the crudest male characters. If Gus Trenor is beefy and stupid, he is nonetheless repeatedly used by the women in the book, and there is some justice in the words, if not the tone, of his complaint to Lily: "I didn't begin this business—kept out of the way, and left the track clear for the other chaps, till you rummaged me out and set to work to make an ass of me—and an easy job you had of it, too" (234). To Lily, we have seen earlier, Trenor is merely "a coarse dull man . . . a mere supernumerary in the

5. Ammons, *Edith Wharton's Argument with America*, 39.
6. Joe L. Dubbert, "Progressivism and the Mas-culinity Crisis," in *The American Man*, ed. Elizabeth H. Pleck and Joseph H. Pleck (Englewood Cliffs, N.J., 1980), 307.

costly show for which his money paid; surely, to a clever girl, it would be easy to hold him by his vanity, and so keep the obligation on his side" (137). Lily repays her financial debt to Trenor, but never her human one.

If women in this system harm each other, they also do an extraordinary amount of harm to men. It's hard not to feel a sympathy for shy Percy Gryce when Lily sets out to appeal to his vanity and thus to make an ass of *him*: "She resolved so to identify herself with her husband's vanity that to gratify her wishes would be to him the most exquisite form of self-indulgence" (78). Despite the loss to Lily, we must feel that Gryce is better off with even the "youngest, dumpiest, dullest" of the Van Osburgh daughters (146).

Edmund Wilson described the typical masculine figure in Edith Wharton's fiction between 1905 and 1920 as "a man set apart from his neighbours by education, intellect, and feeling, but lacking the force or the courage either to impose himself or to get away."[7] Selden is obviously such a figure, a man who seems initially to be much freer than Lily but who is revealed to be even more inflexible. His failed effort to define himself as the New Man parallels Lily's futile effort to become a New Woman; "In a different way," as Wharton points out, "he was, as much as Lily, the victim of his environment" (245). Selden's limitations are perhaps those of the New Man in every period of gender crisis. Cautious about making a commitment, successful and energetic in his law practice, fond of travel, taking enormous pleasure in his Manhattan apartment with its "pleasantly faded Turkey rug," its carefully chosen collectibles, and its opportunities for intimate entertaining, Selden lacks only jogging shoes and a copy of *The Color Purple* on his coffee table to fit into the culture of the 1980s.

Real change, Wharton shows us in the novel, must come from outside the dominant class-structures. Thus the figure of Simon Rosedale, the Jewish financier making it big on Wall Street, takes on increasing importance as the novel develops. He plays one of the main roles in the triangle with Lily and Selden, and while Selden asserts too late that he has faith in Lily, Rosedale demonstrates his faith by coming to see her in her dingy exile and by offering her money to start again. Rosedale's style is certainly not that of the Perfect Gentleman, and even to the last Lily's ladyhood cannot quite accept him: "Little by little, circumstances were breaking down her dislike for Rosedale. The dislike, indeed, still subsisted; but it was penetrated here and there by the perception of mitigating qualities in him: of a certain gross kindliness, a rather helpless fidelity of sentiment, which seemed to be struggling through the surface of his material ambitions" (485). In order to break out of the social cage, Lily must make compromises with elegance, compromises that ultimately are beyond her scope. But Rosedale, the only man in the novel who likes children (we see him through Lily's eyes "kneeling domesti-

7. Wilson, "Justice to Edith Wharton," 26–27.

cally on the drawing room hearth" with Carry Fisher's little girl [401]), offers the hope of continuity, rootedness, and relatedness that Lily finally comes to see as the central meaning of life.

Lily's changing perceptions of Rosedale are a parallel to the most radical theme in the novel; her growing awareness and finally her merger with a community of working women. With each step downward, each removal to a smaller room, Lily's life becomes more enmeshed with this community, and she sees it in more positive terms. We see her first as an exceptional figure, silhouetted against a backdrop of anonymous female drones in Grand Central Station, "sallow-faced girls in preposterous hats and flat-chested women struggling with paper bundles and palm-leaf fans" (5). For the observant Selden, the contrast to "the herd" only brings out Lily's high gloss: "The dinginess, the crudity of this average section of womanhood made him feel how specialized she was" (6).

The crudest of these women is the charwoman, Mrs. Haffen, whose appearance frames the first part of the novel as that of the typist Nettie Struther frames the end. Leaving Selden's apartment, Lily encounters this woman scrubbing the stairs, stout, with "clenched red fists . . . a broad, sallow face, slightly pitted with smallpox, and the straw-coloured hair through which her scalp shone unpleasantly" (20). In her hardness, ugliness, poverty, and age, Mrs. Haffen is the monstrous specter of everything Lily most dreads, the very heart of dinginess. Trying to make money out of Bertha Dorset's love letters, she also embodies the moral corruption Lily has come to fear in herself, the willingness to sacrifice all sense of value to the need to survive.

Lily's gradual and painful realization that her status as a lady does not exempt her from the sufferings of womanhood is conveyed through her perceptions of her own body as its exquisite ornamentality begins to decline. Her luxuriant hair begins to thin, as Carry Fisher notices (404); her radiant complexion too will become "dull and colourless" in the millinery workshop (455). In the beginning, she is one of the lilies of the field, who neither toils nor spins, nor, certainly, scrubs; her hands are not the "clenched red fists" of anger, labor, rebellion, but art objects "polished as a bit of old ivory" (10). Yet in her confrontation with Gus Trenor, Lily is suddenly aware that these lovely hands are also "helpless" and "useless" (237). Lily has had fantasies of her hands as creative and artistic, dreaming of a fashionable shop in which "subordinate fingers, blunt, grey, needlepricked fingers" would do all the hard work, while her delicate fingers added the distinctive finishing touch (456–57). In reality, she learns, her "untutored fingers" are blundering and clumsy; like the hands of the working women, her hands too have "been formed from childhood for their special work," the work of decoration and display, and they can never compete in the workaday world (477). When Selden sees her for the last time in his apartment, noting "how thin her hands looked" against the fire, it is as if they are fading and disappearing, vestigial appendages useless to her solitary existence (501).

At the center of Lily's awakening to her kinship with other women is

Gerty Farish's Working Girls' Club. Gerty works with a charitable association trying "to provide comfortable lodgings, with a reading-room and
other modest distractions, where young women of the class employed in
down-town offices might find a home when out of work, or in need of a
rest" (179).[8] Visiting this club as Lady Bountiful, Lily nonetheless makes
the first imaginative identification between herself and the working girls,
"young girls, like herself, some perhaps pretty, some not without a trace
of her finer sensibilities. She pictured herself leading such a life as theirs—
a life in which achievement seemed as squalid as failure—and the vision
made her shudder sympathetically" (179).

Yet when she "joins the working classes," Lily also sees "the fragmentary and distorted image of the world she had lived in, reflected in the
mirror of the working-girls' minds" (461). They idealize the society women
whose hats they trim. Lily Bart herself has become a kind of romantic
heroine for Nettie Struther, the working girl she meets in Bryant Park
on her return from Selden's apartment. Nettie has followed Lily's social
career in the newspapers, reading about her dresses, thinking of her as
"being so high up, where everything was just grand" (505). She has
named her baby daughter "Marry Ant'nette" because an actress playing
the queen reminded her of Lily. Their encounter is the strongest moment
of female kinship in the novel, as Lily also sees herself mirrored in Nettie
and her baby, and recognizes that Nettie's achievement is far beyond
any she has previously conceived for herself.

Nettie is a typist who has had an unhappy affair with a man from a
higher social class, a man who promised to marry her but deserted her.
(Margaret McDowell, one of Wharton's critics, leaps to the false conclusion that Nettie has been a prostitute.)[9] Although Nettie felt that her life
was over, she was given the chance to begin again by a man who had
known her from childhood, knew that she had been seduced, and loved
her enough to marry her anyway. There is even an ambiguity about the
paternity of the child; Nettie may have been pregnant when George
married her. This testament of male faith and female courage stands in
sharp contrast to Selden's caution and Lily's despair.

The scene between the two women is unique in *The House of Mirth*
for its intimacy and openness (Lily too tells Nettie that she is unhappy
and in trouble), for its setting in the warm kitchen (the ritual center of
much nineteenth-century woman's fiction), for the presence of the baby,
and for its acknowledgment of physical needs. In holding Nettie's baby,
the untouchable Lily gives in at last to her longing for touch. Folding

8. Elizabeth Ammons points out that Wharton's
contemporary readers would have been familiar with
the institution of the Working Girls' Club; Wharton's sister-in-law Mary Cadwallader Jones had even
written about these clubs in *The Woman's Book*
(1894). See *Edith Wharton's Argument with
America*, 40–41. A book published the same year
as *The House of Mirth*, Dorothy Richardson's *The
Long Day: The Story of a New York Working Girl*
(1905: reprinted in *Women at Work*, ed. William

O'Neill [Chicago, 1972], 3–303), discusses the
relationships between factory girls and the leisured
ladies who offered them charity and also became
the subjects of their fantasies. According to Richardson, working girls even adopted the names of
society heroines from the newspapers and from
romantic novels.

9. Margaret McDowell, *Edith Wharton* (Boston,
1976), 44–45.

the baby, she is also being held, expressing her own hunger for physical bonding: "As she continued to hold it the weight increased, sinking deeper, and penetrating her with a strange sense of weakness, as though the child entered into her and became a part of herself" (510).

Some feminist critics, however, have tended to see the images of the mother and child in this scene, and in Lily's deathbed hallucination of holding the infant, as sentimental and regressive. Patricia M. Spacks, for example, criticizes Lily's "escapist fantasy of motherhood."[1] Cynthia Griffin Wolff maintains that the scene with Nettie "gives poignant evidence of Lily's inability to conceive of herself in any other way than as the object of aesthetic attention," that she is once again self-consciously arranging herself in a *tableau vivant* for Nettie's admiration. Wolff also argues that in her death Lily is relinquishing her "difficult pretenses to adulthood." Thus in Wolff's view the extraordinary passage in which Lily, as she is succumbing to the drug, feels "Nettie Struther's child . . . lying on her arm . . . felt the pressure of its little head against her shoulder" is a sign of Lily's own retreat into the safety of infantilization.[2]

It seems to me, however, that this hallucination speaks rather for Lily's awakened sense of loving solidarity and community, for the vision she has had of Nettie's life as representing "the central truth of existence" (517). That Nettie should be the last person to see Lily alive and that Gerty should be the first to discover her death suggests that Lily's death is an acknowledgment of their greater strength. Doing justice to Lily Bart requires that we see how far she has come even in her death. Unlike the infantilized Edna Pontellier, who never awakens to the dimensions of her social world, who never sees how the labor of the mulatto and black women around her makes her narcissistic existence possible, Lily is a genuinely awakened woman, who fully recognizes her own position in the community of women workers. Whereas Edna's awakening is early, easy, incomplete, and brings a warm liquid sense of satisfaction, Lily's enlightenment is gradual and agonizing: "It was as though a great blaze of electric light had been turned on in her head. . . . She had not imagined that such a multiplication of wakefulness was possible; her whole past was re-enacting itself at a hundred different points of consciousness" (520). Although her awakening proves unendurable, she really tries to overcome rejection, failure, and the knowledge of her own shortcomings. *The House of Mirth* ends not only with a death, but with the vision of a new world of female solidarity, a world in which women like Gerty Farish and Nettie Struther will struggle hopefully and courageously. Lily dies—the lady dies—so that these women may live and grow. As Elizabeth Ammons observes, "In the arms of the ornamental, leisure-class Lily lies the working-class infant female, whose vitality succors the dying woman. In that union of the leisure and working classes

1. Patricia Meyer Spacks, *The Female Imagination* (New York, 1975), 241.
2. Wolff, *A Feast of Words*, 130–31. Wolff maintains that Lily's feelings are primarily narcissistic,

whereas I read the conclusion of the novel as a demonstration of her reawakened emotional capacities.

lies a new hope—the New Woman that Wharton would bring to mature life in her next novel."[3]

For Edith Wharton as novelist, then, *The House of Mirth* also marked a transition to a new kind of fiction. Like Lily Bart, Wharton had retreated from touch, from community, from awakenings to her own sexuality and anger. While the standard pattern for nineteenth-century American women writers was a strong allegiance to the maternal line and the female community, Wharton belonged to the more troubled and more gifted countertradition of women writers who were torn between the literary world of their fathers and the wordless sensual world of their mothers. These two lines of inheritance are generally represented in the literary history of American women writers by the spatial images of the father's library and the mother's garden. Like Margaret Fuller, Edith Wharton felt that "the kingdom of her father's library" was the intellectual center of her development. But unlike Fuller, she did not have the childhood alternative of her mother's garden—a space of sensuality, warmth, and openness. Instead Lucretia Wharton was a chilly woman who censored her daughter's reading, denied her writing paper (as a child Wharton was "driven to begging for the wrappings of the parcels delivered at the house"), withheld physical affection, and met her literary efforts with "icy disapproval."[4]

Nonetheless in her literary memoir, *A Backward Glance*, Wharton called her writing a "secret garden," echoing the title of Frances Hodgson Burnett's popular novel for girls.[5] The connection with maternal space (in Burnett's novel it is the dead mother's garden, lost and overgrown) may have come from her sense of writing as a forbidden joy. From childhood Wharton was possessed with what she called the "ecstasy" of "making up," almost a form of illicit sexual indulgence: "The call came regularly and imperiously and . . . I would struggle against it conscientiously."[6]

The House of Mirth marks the point at which Wharton found herself able to give in to her creative jouissance, to assert her creative power as a woman artist, and to merge the male and female sides of her lineage into a mature fiction that could deal seriously with the sexual relationships of men and women in a modern society. Writing *The House of Mirth* had important professional, literary, and psychological consequences for Wharton's career, and it is clear that she herself thought of it as a turning point in her life as a writer. In her autobiography, Wharton described the process of writing *The House of Mirth* as a serial for *Scribner's Magazine* as one that taught her the work of writing, that transformed her "from a drifting amateur into a professional." Because she had agreed to complete the book within five months, Wharton was

3. Ammons, *Edith Wharton's Argument with America*, 43.
4. See Wolff, *A Feast of Words*, 31, 46–47.
5. Edith Wharton, *A Backward Glance* (New York, 1962), chap. 9. Marilyn French, who notes the reference to Burnett, argues that Wharton's writing always remained secretive and in some sense illegitimate. "Introduction," *The House of Mirth* (New York, 1981), xii.
6. Wharton, *A Backward Glance*, 35.

forced to exchange the leisurely rhythms of the lady novelist's routine, with its manifold "distractions of a busy and hospitable life, full of friends and travel, reading and gardening" for the "discipline of the daily task." The necessity for "systematic daily effort" also redefined and excused the pleasures of "making up" as part of her process of gaining "mastery over my tools."[7]

Under the pressures of the deadline, Wharton also made tough choices about her narrative, choices that reflected her own transition to a more serious artistic professionalism, craftsmanship, and control. In choosing to have Lily die, Wharton was judging and rejecting the infantile aspects of her own self, the part that lacked confidence as a working writer, that longed for the escapism of the lady's world and feared the sexual consequences of creating rather than becoming art. Secondly, Wharton mastered her emotional conflicts as material for art, learning through the process that anger and other strong emotions, including sexual desire, could be safely expressed.[8] The death of the lady is thus also the death of the lady novelist, the dutiful daughter who struggles to subdue her most powerful imaginative impulses. If Lily Bart, unable to change, gives way to the presence of a new generation of women, Edith Wharton survives the crisis of maturation at the turn of the century and becomes one of our American precursors of a literary history of female mastery and growth.

---

7. Ibid., 207–9.
8. See Wolff, A *Feast of Words*, 134–38. Wolff calls *The House of Mirth* a "momentous novel."

Edith Wharton: A Chronology

1862   Edith Newbold Jones born, January 24, in New York City.

1878   Makes her debut in society; her collection of poetry, *Verses*, is privately published; a poem appears in the *Atlantic Monthly*.

1882   Her father, George Frederic Jones, dies.

1885   Marries Edward ("Teddy") Wharton on April 29.

1890   Short story, "Mrs. Manstey's View," published in *Scribner's*.

1897   *The Decoration of Houses*, written with Ogden Codman, is published.

1899   First collection of short stories, *The Greater Inclination*, published.

1900   *The Touchstone*, a short novel, published.

1901   Her mother, Lucretia Rhinelander Jones, dies; second collection of short stories, *Crucial Instances*, issued.

1902   *The Valley of Decision*, Wharton's first long novel, published; Wharton and her husband move into the house she designed in western Massachusetts, The Mount.

1903   *Sanctuary*, a short novel, published.

1904   Third volume of short stories, *The Descent of Man*, published.

1905   *The House of Mirth* published.

1907   *The Fruit of the Tree*, a novel, published.

1908   Love affair with Morton Fullerton, which will last about two years, begins; *A Motor-Flight through France*, a book of travel writing, published.

1909   *Artemis to Actaeon*, a collection of poems, published.

1911   *Ethan Frome*, a short novel, published.

1912   *The Reef*, a novel, published.

1913   Divorce from Teddy Wharton; *The Custom of the Country*, a novel, published.

1914   Permanently residing in France, Wharton becomes actively involved in war relief work.

1915   *Fighting France*, pro-French propaganda essays, published.

1916   *The Book of the Homeless*, edited by Wharton and designed to raise money for war-relief work, published; *Xingu and Other Stories* appears.

1917   *Summer*, short novel, published.

1918   *The Marne* published.

1919   *French Ways and Their Meanings*, essays, published.

1920   *The Age of Innocence*, novel, appears; *In Morocco*, travel essays, published.

1921   Awarded the Pulitzer Prize for *The Age of Innocence*.

1922   *The Glimpses of the Moon*, novel, published.

1923   Receives honorary degree from Yale University; last visit to the United States; *A Son at the Front*, a war novel, appears.

1924   *Old New York*, a collection of four novellas, published.

1925   *The Mother's Recompense*, a novel, published; *The Writing of Fiction*, a collection of theoretical pieces, issued.

1927   *Twilight Sleep*, a novel, published.

1928   Teddy Wharton dies; *The Children*, a novel, published.

1929   The novel *Hudson River Bracketed* appears.

1930   *Certain People*, short stories, brought out.

1932   Sequel to *Hudson River Bracketed*, *The Gods Arrive*, published.

1934   *A Backward Glance*, memoirs, published; at work on *The Buccaneers*, novel left unfinished at her death.

1937   Dies on August 11; buried in the Cimetiere des Gonards in Versailles, France.

Selected Bibliography

For scholarship on Wharton in general and on *The House of Mirth* in particular before 1974, see Marlene Springer, *Edith Wharton and Kate Chopin: A Reference Guide* (Boston: G. K. Hall, 1976).

The authoritative biography is R. W. B. Lewis, *Edith Wharton: A Biography* (New York: Harper and Row, 1975). In addition to an excerpt from that biography, other scholarship on Wharton and *The House of Mirth* represented in full or in part in this volume includes: Millicent Bell, "Lady Into Author: Edith Wharton and the House of Scribner," *American Quarterly* 9 (1957): 295–315; Louis Auchincloss, *Pioneers and Caretakers: A Study of Nine American Women Novelists* (New York: Dell, 1965); Cynthia Griffin Wolff, "Lily Bart and the Beautiful Death," *American Literature* 46 (1974): 16–40; Elizabeth Ammons, *Edith Wharton's Argument with America* (Athens: U of Georgia P, 1980); Elaine Showalter, "The Death of the Lady (Novelist): Wharton's *House of Mirth*," *Representations* 9 (1985): 133–49.

Other recent essays and books of particular interest and importance are: Judith Fetterley, " 'The Temptation to Be a Beautiful Object': Double Standard and Double Bind in *The House of Mirth*," *Studies in American Fiction* 5 (1977): 199–211; Cynthia Griffin Wolff, *A Feast of Words: The Triumph of Edith Wharton* (New York: Oxford UP, 1977); Joan Lidoff, "Another Sleeping Beauty: Narcissism in *The House of Mirth*," *American Quarterly* 32 (1980): 519–39; Wai-Chee Dimock, "Debasing Exchange: Edith Wharton's *The House of Mirth*," *PMLA* 100 (1985): 783–92; Judith Fryer, *Felicitous Space: The Imaginative Structures of Edith Wharton and Willa Cather* (Durham: U of North Carolina P, 1986); Elizabeth Ammons, "New Literary History: Edith Wharton and Jessie Redmon Fauset," *College Literature* 14 (1987): 207–18. R. W. B. Lewis and Nancy Lewis, eds., *The Letters of Edith Wharton* (New York: Charles Scribner's Sons, 1988); Josephine Donovan, *After the Fall* (University Park: Penn State UP, 1989).